the ultimate book of

Spells

THE ULTIMATE BOOK of SPELLS

A complete guide to using magic to improve your life and the world around you

Pamela J. Ball

Capella

This edition published in 2007 by Arcturus Publishing Limited
26/27 Bickels Yard, 151–153 Bermondsey Street,
London SE1 3HA

In Canada published for Indigo Books
468 King St W,
Suite 500,
Toronto,
Ontario M5V 1L8

Picture credits: Arcturus Publishing Ltd; *Pictorial Key to the Tarot*,
A.E. Waite, Dover Publications 103, 104, 105, 106, 107, 108

ISBN: 978-1-84193-577-5

Printed in China

Contents

Introduction

The desire to change and improve that which we have has been around for many thousands of years, if not since man first walked the earth. Magic and spell working have always been a part of that, and indeed still are today. Anyone who practises any form of magic, including spell working, needs to be grounded. This means having both feet firmly planted in reality and also having a basic knowledge of what magic is and is not, what spells can and can't do and what - with practice - you can do with the tools, information and knowledge you have. This book sets out to give you that information in as succinct a manner as possible.

THE FIRST SECTION tells how magic and folklore are intertwined and have been since antiquity, whilst the second defines magic and its different types, spells, and the various components and tools necessary for magical working. A basic knowledge of astrology is tremendously helpful in knowing when to perform magic and when to cast spells, as well as how to understand people, and the next section gives information on astrology, particularly Western, including the Sun signs, planets and houses.

We then introduce and explain the importance of divination and spiritual development in magical working. Divination was originally an attempt to discover what the gods intended for mankind, not just a way of reading the future. The methods we have included are far-ranging and cross many cultures. from the Ogham Alphabet in Norse culture to the Tarot with its roots in Egyptian magic, taking in such things as scrying, palmistry and phrenology along the way.

Next we come to Mysticism and Magic which delves into the myriad spiritual beliefs that allow us to practise magic. Again spanning many, many years you learn a little about the thinking behind magic, among other things how the Jewish Kabbalah has given rise to many magical principles, how and why alchemy developed into the sciences and what part shamanism plays in our understanding of spell making today.

Spell making is such an individual craft that nobody can or indeed should be so bold as to try to tell others what to do. However, in some areas it is useful to receive guidance and we next cover how to prepare yourself and your working area (sacred space). Following this are the best times and correspondences for spell working, particularly astrological and colour. Finally in this section, we advise on the best ways for constructing your spell and rituals also showing you how to record your methods and results.

Before we show you how to use your dreams to achieve and/or enhance your magical results there is the spells compendium to give you a taste of what it all means. Although there are many spells and techniques sprinkled liberally throughout the book, in the compendium they are laid out in categories, these being Friendship, Love and Relationships; Health, Healing and Wellbeing; Money, Luck and Career and Protection. Some spells do not fit easily into these categories, so there is also a section called Potpourri which will help to widen your perspective still further.

Each spell has an introductory paragraph with information as to what type of spell it is, the best time to carry it out and which discipline it comes from (if known). We then tell you what you will need: candles, incense, special tools or objects, then give you the method to use. Some spells require incantations, some invocations and others simple actions to make them work, and this is laid out for you. Lastly we tell you what to expect; results can be unpredictable, and sometimes conspicuous by their absence.

If a spell doesn't work for you in the way that we have suggested, it might be that your intended result does not fit into the overall scheme of things. Do try it again on another occasion and use your intuition to decide what might be changed or adjusted to suit your personality. Have confidence in yourself and never be afraid to experiment.

Popular acceptance of magical powers and spell making will always be mixed. Some people will accept unquestioningly, others will search for alternative causes and others still will remain concerned by the manifestation of such powers. For some people these powers are part of everyday life and it is for each individual to decide whether or not they wish to develop and use them.

It now merely remains for us to wish you health, wealth and happiness and the hope that you enjoy your spell work and its results!

Folklore

The majority of people who are new to spell working will acknowledge that for them common sense backed up by practical action is normally more productive than theoretical or mystical thinking. In magical working, as in everyday life, when we have to handle a wide range of circumstances, common sense in dealing with them will normally produce the best results.

However, when we are confronted with the unusual or difficult, or are faced by extreme anxiety, even the most practical-minded among us will theorize in order to make sense of what is happening. We have not moved such a long way since those times, in the distant past, when our ancestors and people around the world routinely believed that if the crops failed then the gods must be angry. Practices carried out then are still with us in the form of many of the festivals and feasts, which still have relevance in the societies where they began. Some of you may choose not to use the spells in this section, but they do offer a return to basics and give fascinating insights into how our ancestors dealt with everyday challenges.

Festivals and Feasts

FOLKLORISTS BELIEVE THAT the first festivals arose because of the anxieties of early peoples who did not understand the forces of nature and wished to placate them. The people noted the times and seasons when food was plentiful or not and reacted accordingly. Harvest and thanksgiving festivals, for instance, are a relic from the times when agriculture was the primary livelihood for the majority. Festivals also provided an opportunity for the elders to pass on knowledge and the meaning of tribal lore to younger generations and give them the opportunity to let off steam in an acceptable yet controlled way.

General agreement exists that the most ancient festivals and feasts were associated with planting and harvest times or with honouring the dead. These have come down to us in modern times as celebrations with some religious overtones. Harvest festivals are still carried out in many Christian churches and celebrate the fullness of the harvest. Among the most attractive are the harvest-home festivals in Britain where, in the autumn, parish churches are decorated with flowers, fruits and vegetables. Harvest suppers where a community join together to celebrate the bountiful harvest have their beginnings in the pagan beliefs of the three harvest sabbats (Lughnasadh, Mabon and Samhain) belonging to the Wheel of the Year. You will find techniques for celebrating these in the section on the Sabbats on pages 196-204.

The meeting of pagan and Christian

Ways of dealing with problems within the community, which used a blend of Christian and pagan rituals, was partly a product of the interaction between Christianity and paganism. Pagan belief demanded rituals that appeased their gods while Christian thought required that there was a focus on only one God. This meant that such rituals belonging to the Wheel of the Year had to be accommodated into a more acceptable framework. The local clergy therefore became agents of this assimilation process. The mixing of liturgical, medical and folklore medicine was a whole medley of ideas as to how nature functioned.

The line between these ideas was very unclear – rite blended into medical practice or was mixed with apparently magical, and certainly ceremonial, pre-Christian practices. This coming together is evident in a charm ritual for blessing the land, the Aecerbot ritual, which was performed yearly and is still retained centuries later on Plough Monday (usually the first Monday after Epiphany – 6 January).

Originally an Anglo-Saxon fertility ritual, it was gradually Christianized. In this agricultural – or field – remedy for witchcraft, four pieces of turf were taken from the four corners of the land, along with other agricultural products such as fruit, honey, herbs and milk as well as holy water. Certain words (such as 'grow' and 'increase') were said in Latin over these goods. The individual turfs were then anointed and blessed along with the fruits of the farmer's labour, taken to church and placed carefully under the altar. The priest then said four masses over the altar.

The turf was placed back in the ground before sunset, along with four crosses marked with the name of the Apostles. Similar words and prayers to those above were said, including a specially written prayer calling on God, the earth and heavens to help in bringing forth the power of the earth for a successful crop. The ritual was closed by the owner of the field turning around three times while reciting Christian prayers. There followed a similar ritual for blessing the plough using herbs and other sacred items. The strong similarities to the rites calling upon Mother Earth and the Sun God in pre-Christian rituals are quite marked.

Historic customs are often perpetuated in seasonal festivals. One example is Homstrom (celebrated on the first Sunday in February), which is an old Swiss festival exulting in the end of winter with the burning of straw people as symbols of the end of Old Man Winter or the Old God. A similar sort of festival has recently been revived in Scotland round Lammas-tide. Following the success of the 1970s film *The Wicker Man*, which highlighted an ancient pagan festival, today this gathering has been given new meaning as an alternative music festival. The ceremonial burnings commemorate the sacrifices which our ancestors needed in order to feel that they had done what was necessary to achieve a plentiful harvest.

A similar celebration takes place at Queensferry on the east coast of Scotland in August, when the Burryman parades through the town and finishes his day covered with burrs (sticky balls of seeds), possibly representing all the irritations which the townspeople wish to get rid of before the winter.

If you want to celebrate in the same way you might like to make a corn dolly in the shape of a man.

Making a Corn Dolly

YOU WILL NEED

Two small handfuls of corn stalks
Green and yellow wool or cotton
Trailing greenery (ivy or grape vine are ideal)
Appropriately coloured ribbons for the ritual
(e.g. red or orange for Lammas)

METHOD

✤ Take one handful of corn stalks.

✤ Just below the top, bind the stalks with the yellow cotton, tying securely.

✤ 3–5 cm underneath, bind the stalks again; this forms the head of the doll.

✤ Carefully divide the bound bundle into four strands. (The outer two will form the arms, the middle ones the body.)

✤ Gently bend the stalks which represent the arms and bind carefully with the yellow cotton.

✤ Bind the two middle pieces together, criss-crossing the cotton to create a body approximately 10–15 cm (4 in) long.

✤ Use the green cotton to bind the two middle lower sections to represent legs.

✤ Ask for a blessing from an agricultural god.

✤ You might say:

God of plenty, bless now this image of your fertility.

✤ Decorate with the ribbons and trailing greenery.

To represent a feminine deity, leave the bottom section free so that it looks like a skirt. The representation of the male god can also be used at the time of Mabon – the Autumn Equinox – or at Saturnalia in December.

Here is a simple technique for your own use, which commemorates the Burryman and shows you how to make use of a corn dolly. Ideally at Homstrom you would be getting rid of an old dolly, simply by burning it. Lammas would be the time to make a new one for you to keep over the winter.

Winter's End

YOU WILL NEED

White candle
Corn dolly
Fireproof receptacle
Either the sticky burrs from a cleavers plant (which has a cleansing effect) or several pieces of paper on which you have written your irritations

METHOD

✤ Light the candle.

✤ Cup the corn dolly in your hands and review the previous year, particularly winter.

✤ Attach as many of the sticky burrs as you can to the corn dolly, making each one represent something that has irritated you.

✤ Alternatively, tuck the pieces of paper into the corn dolly.

✤ Carefully set the dolly alight and place it in the receptacle.

✤ As the dolly burns say these words or similar:

Begone dull and nasty times
Welcome moments fine
I greet the new times with joy and laughter

✤ When the corn dolly has burnt out, bury the ashes as an offering to the earth or dispose of them in running water.

Nature-based religions gave way to the Christian in other ways as well. For example, the four-leaved clover has long been associated with the sun, good fortune and luck. To pagans it also represented the Goddess form, the quaternity – the fourfold aspects of deity.

In Ireland, St Patrick is thought to have used the trefoil (three-leaved clover) to demonstrate the principle of the Holy Trinity – Father, Son and Holy Spirit – to his followers. He would have used material that was readily available to him rather than the rarer and more magical four-leaved plant, and would thus have signified the move away from intrinsic magical knowledge associated with Mother Earth. Incidentally, the clover plant is thought to give the wearer the ability to see the fairy form.

SHAPE SHIFTING

Spells designed to bring about a difference in bodily appearance in order to dissolve mischievous enchantments by the fairy folk or frequenters of the lower world were legion in most cultures. In Celtic lore for instance, during the process of dissolving the enchantment, having cast a magic circle, the rescuer had to keep repeating the name of the enchanted person to remind them of who they truly were.

Traditionally the enchanted one would go through several metamorphoses or shape shifts in the following order: esk, adder, lion and finally a bolt of red-hot iron. Then returning to human form, they were left completely naked. They had to be covered by a cloak – thus rendered invisible – and washed in milk and then hot water.

If we accept the idea of the evolution of the soul, the stage of heating iron until it is red hot represents the process of transmutation from animal to human. The final purification in milk (which in Irish mythology is a healing substance) and water restores the victim to his normal self – he is reborn.

In many cultures iron is regarded as a tool of purification. It was, and still is, dreaded by the darker powers and many amulets and charms fashioned from the substance were used to avert evil. Iron pins or brooches were stuck in headgear, a piece of iron was often sown into the clothes of children and horseshoes were often used to protect the homes and byres (cowsheds).

Women in childbirth were also said to be protected with iron (see the iron protection incense on p 57), sometimes by a row of nails and at other times by a scythe or pitchfork. This was so that mother and baby were protected from evil spirits, particularly from the night demons who were said to steal babies. Up until quite recently in Scotland in some areas, it was considered highly unwise to leave a baby alone at all, lest it be stolen away by the faeries.

THE EVIL EYE

The evil eye is an ancient, widespread and deeply held belief in more than one third of the world's cultures, but is particularly strongly feared even today in countries of Mediterranean origin, and also in Celtic countries. Different cultures have different ways of dealing with this nuisance.

In Greece, it is thought that it doesn't take much to get the *matiasma,* or the evil eye. If anyone so much as admires your shoes, even from a distance, this envy can put a spell on you. Anyone with blue eyes is particularly suspected of being able to cast the evil eye.

It is believed that mothers have a particular ability to remove it if their son is afflicted. Though the knowledge is passed from mother to daughter, a woman will not always learn the prayers necessary to do this until she becomes a mother herself. At that time she is prayed for herself thus, since she is considered vulnerable:

…and with bright, shining Angels enfold and cherish her, guarding her round about against every attack of invisible spirits; yea, Lord, from sickness and infirmity, from jealousy and envy, and from the evil eye.

A mother can diagnose and then remove an attack of the evil eye in the following way.

Diagnosis of the Evil Eye

YOU WILL NEED ─────────────
Olive oil
Bowl of water

METHOD ─────────────
❖ Drip three drops of olive oil on the surface of the water.
❖ Watch what happens.
❖ If the drops remain distinct there is no evil eye.
❖ If they run together there is.
❖ Dispose of the oil and water safely.
❖ There are many ways of removing the evil eye.

Following is just one:

Removal of the Evil Eye

YOU WILL NEED ───────────
Lemon
Iron nails

METHOD ───────────
❖ Drive the nails with some force into the lemon.
❖ Visualize the evil eye being pierced.
❖ Keep the lemon for three days, by which time it should begin to rot.
❖ If it does not, repeat the procedure.

Here you have externalized the difficulty, checked that the spell worked and repeated the procedure if not. You could then repeat the diagnostic procedure to ensure that you are clear.

The Greek Orthodox Church does forbid people to go to 'readers' or other individuals for use of magical rituals to overcome the evil eye. It is stated quite categorically that such people take advantage of the weakness of superstitious people and destroy them spiritually and financially by playing upon their imagination. However, *Vaskania* – which is another word for the evil eye – is recognized simply as a phenomenon that was accepted by primitive people as fact. It is the jealousy and envy of some people for things they do not possess, such as beauty, youth or courage. Though the Church rejected *Vaskania* as contradicting the concept of divine providence, the prayers of the Church to avert the evil eye are an implicit acceptance of its existence.

In Scotland it seems that the evil eye was more often associated with women and therefore inevitably with the crone, or wise woman, than with men. Anyone with a squint or eyes of different colour could be accused of possessing the evil eye and of using it to cause harm or illness. A charmed burrach or cow fetter could be used to protect animals. Other preventative measures could also be taken, some using plants and trees – such as rowan and juniper – and others using horseshoes and iron stakes. This next technique explains one of the most-loved pieces of Scottish jewellery.

Antler Charm

YOU WILL NEED ───────────
Piece of deer's antler
Hair from a black mare's tail
Silver tip for the antler
Cairngorm stone (a type of smoky quartz)

METHOD ───────────
❖ Wind the horsehair around one end of the antler at least nine times.
❖ Fix the silver tip to the antler. This ensures that there is a balance of male and female energy, which repels the evil eye.
❖ If you wish to make your own jewellery, the gemstone adds additional protection, particularly from fairies
❖ If you wish, you can then consecrate your creation.
❖ It is said that if the antler breaks you have been attacked and you should bury the broken pieces in the earth.

This charm demonstrates how much arcane knowledge can be lost, without people appreciating the real reasons for certain actions. In other cultures the shark's tooth is equally protective.

While the owner of the evil eye did not necessarily need to be a witch, the curse did require the services of a magical person to remove it. In Scotland such arcane knowledge was, and in some cases still is, passed from father to daughter and mother to son. The word *orth* was used for an ordinary spell but a ceremonial magical spell among the Gaelic Celts was signified by the word *bricht*. It is interesting that this word also means 'bright' in dialect – perhaps such a ceremony required an exceptionally bright moonlit night.

Protections and Purifications

There are many folkloric remedies for the evil eye, ranging from painting an eye on the prow of a boat in the Mediterranean, supposedly to outstare the sorcerer, to passing a plate filled with burning coals three times round the head of the victim in India. Iron is always a good specific against the curse of the evil eye, as also are mirrors or glass beads, which dazzle.

By and large it is the idea of envious glances that is the basis of the superstitions and customs surrounding the evil eye. In Turkey, many parents keep new babies out of public view for forty days, lest their beauty invite a jealous glance. In Jewish and Kabbalistic lore, the evil eye is known as *ayin harah* and what follows is a variation of a charming technique to protect a new baby from *ayin harah*.

To Protect a Newborn Baby

This spell uses crystals and symbolism. The blue stone is reputed to bring about harmony in relationships and to help its wearer to be true to themselves, and to be able to openly state their opinion. The blue bead or stone used here should preferably of lapis lazuli, which is considered a stone of truth and friendship.

YOU WILL NEED —————————————————

Blue bead or small stone with a hole
Copal or cedar incense
White candle
Bowls of salt and water
Safety pin

METHOD —————————————————

❖ Light the candle and the incense.
❖ Pass the bead and then the pin through the candle flame, the smoke, the salt and the water.
❖ Repeat the following as many times as you feel necessary:

Great Mother, I ask protection for [name]
That he/she may not come to harm
From forces of evil on this or any other plane.

❖ Put the bead on the safety pin and say:

Through this gift I thee implore
Keep him/her safe for evermore.

❖ Now pass the bead and safety pin three times through the incense smoke, being aware of the available power to protect the new arrival.
❖ Traditionally, the gift is then pinned safely to the baby's shawl.
❖ Let the candle burn out.

Since a newborn baby is still so close to its Creator, only the best and highest vibrational incenses and materials are used. Copal incense is one of the purest and most sacred that there is. It is believed to help open the soul and can stimulate imagination, intuition and creativity. Cedar is used to carry prayers to the Creator. It is used to bridge the gap between heaven and earth and is often associated with breaking misuse of power or powerful forces that may be having a negative influence.

There are, in fact, several customs associated with birth and the surrounding period which have survived without people today necessarily appreciating their magical significance. In Celtic lore, the 'toadstone' protected the newborn from evil spirits and the Virgin Mary nut, actually the seed of the plant *Entada scandens*, counteracted birth pains. The shell of a sea urchin, known as the 'cock's knee stone' – but also representative of the Virgin – has also always been considered to bring good fortune.

Birth and death were, in the minds of people whose lives depended on the cycles of the seasons, very closely connected. This led to a perhaps greater understanding of the two great events in life than we have today. 'Primitive' societies accepted that there would be loss and deprivation through disease around these times and the people would use anything that they considered powerful to help them.

Magical stones were often used as protection against disease, which was generally believed to have been brought by demons and evil spirits. It was said that healing stones could impart their qualities to water and this ability can still be seen today when healers use crystals, or elixirs infused from crystals, in their healing. In both Scotland and Ireland there are many tales of the existence of such stones.

Many plants and herbs were also regarded as specifics against bad spirits. For example, rowan or mountain ash, even today, is often to be found close to isolated cottages or near standing stones as a form of protection. The berries were thought to be the food of the gods. St John's Wort was often carried as a charm against witches and fairies – in the Isle of Man it is said that a fairy horse will rise from the earth and carry you about all night if you tread on the plant.

Incenses are a natural outcome of this use and today we are fortunate to have relatively easy access, particularly via the internet, to the ingredients which are necessary to allow us to use ancient knowledge. Throughout the book there are various recipes for incenses which can be used specifically for protection or as a quick solution to the various problems which can be met on a day-to-day basis. As people become more sophisticated, but equally more aware, problems such as the evil eye do not seem to be particularly relevant, yet jealousy and envy can be a huge cause for concern, both nationally and globally.

Geomancy

THE WORD GEOMANCY (from the Latin *geo*, 'Earth', *mancy* 'prophecy') had a different meaning in ancient times from that it has today and we shall deal with that aspect first. It was a method of divination used to interpret markings on the ground or how handfuls of dirt landed when you tossed them, and was therefore the reading of patterns or signs. Geomancy seems to have appeared as a word in the language used by the common people in 1362, and was one of the most popular forms of divination throughout the Middle Ages. It was apparently suggested to the Pope of the time that it should be integrated into Catholic teachings.

In this form geomancy was – and indeed still is – a practice which involved marking sixteen lines of dashes either in sand or soil with a wand, or, as practised nowadays, on a sheet of paper with a pencil. This is similar to other divinatory methods. The English version of geomancy involved grouping the marks on the ground into 'constellations' with names like Via and Puer, which could then be interpreted.

Once used by commoners and rulers alike, it was probably the basis for the Oraculum said to have been used by Napoleon Bonaparte. This was also known as the Sibylline Leaves, and consisted of a set of instructions, which show the user how to reduce their question to a set of asterisks laid out in various patterns. The answer is divined from these patterns.

Today there are those who have redefined geomancy and taken it away from divination to a point where human consciousness meets, understands and appreciates the energies of the earth. By understanding the interaction between humankind and the earth on which we live, it enables us to live harmoniously with Gaia (Mother Nature) as a complex entity involving the earth's biosphere, atmosphere, oceans and soil.

Geomancy is actually the practice of identifying the subtle energies of the earth that directly affect our health and well-being. It involves pinpointing those energies that are disruptive to our lives and balancing them. It encompasses, as knowledge spreads, the art of the proper placement of both public and spiritual structures, places where we pray, work, play and live. Now, geomancers can find and shape spaces in harmony with both the physical and the spiritual environment of a place. We can do this through Western knowledge of Sacred Geometry or through the Chinese art of Feng Shui (literally meaning 'wind and water').

Feng Shui

ONE OF THE most important adjustments that we can make as we begin to work consistently with magic is to the environment in which we live and to our own personal space. As we reach an internal peace we create tranquillity around us, but equally our environment must nurture us. For the practitioner this means understanding both our living space and our own subtle aura – or energy field – created by our own vitality.

Scientific discoveries that were made during the 20th century mean that we are becoming more and more aware of the constantly shifting fields of energy through which we move in our daily lives. Today we call them electromagnetic fields and talk of 'adjusting the flow'. This concept of energy fields is by no means new, however, because the fact that there was subtle movement between the two polarities of yin and yang (negative and positive) was recognized as far back as 5,000 years ago in the

I Ching (The Book of Changes), which we shall study in more depth later.

The art of Feng Shui gives an understanding of these energies and movements, both tangible and intangible; it is the art of correct placement. Good Feng Shui practitioners will understand the processes of transformation, both internal and external, which can take place when we are in tune with our environment and will do their best to balance the external energies in a way that is appropriate for the task in hand, whether that is creating a harmonious home, a productive working space or a healing vibration.

To understand the theory of Feng Shui we must first redefine our understanding of divination. Divination – in this case using the *I Ching* and the hexagrams as a tool – means being able to ascertain the most likely course of events should we be able to adjust any or all of the energies when we are out of balance. It consists of working with the flow of essential energy and making very subtle adjustments when necessary, so that we approach the ideal or the divine as closely as possible.

Feng Shui can have an effect on every aspect of our lives. The way it is applied can be either beneficial or detrimental (or both) to the way we live and to the surrounding environment. It is by no means a game or fad, but it is a way to live in harmony with nature, as it is understood in the Tao, so that the energy surrounding us works for us rather than against us.

In the West, Feng Shui is not yet accepted as a science, since its principles cannot yet be proved by science – although it does require mathematical calculation. Neither a religion, a philosophy nor a belief system, it puts into practice tools and techniques that enable us to be as perfect as we can and remain so.

A system that has stood the test of time naturally changes to keep pace with knowledge, and it is unfortunate that the superstitious 'silly' side of the wealth of information available to practitioners of Feng Shui has received so much publicity in recent times. The judicious placing and use of mirrors, wind-chimes of a certain type of material, or crystals hung in windows do all enhance the available energy, but only when carried out according to strict laws of correspondence.

The main Feng Shui schools

Over the centuries many different schools of Feng Shui have developed. The basic principles are broadly the same, though each school has a slightly different focus. There are three main schools in existence today:

Form School

This school focuses on the features of the surrounding landscape and the correct use of the positioning of buildings – and, in former times, burial sites – to gain protection from inauspicious winds *(feng)* and provide adequate water to sustain life *(shui),* though the latter's energy can be unpredictable.

A site or building, by tradition, needs the protective or energizing force of particular animals. (The Chinese believe that four celestial animals guard the four directions: the dragon to the east, the red bird or phoenix to the south, the tiger to the west and the tortoise, enlaced by a snake, to the north.) If landforms or other natural features surrounding the site can be seen as such symbols, then the location is extremely fortunate. The building is protected and/or energized according to its position. The art of the practitioner is to minimize or deflect bad energy *(sha)* and bring beneficial energy *(chi)* to the establishment.

Compass School

This style of Feng Shui uses the eight major trigrams of the *I Ching* (see pages 135-143 for a full explanation) and relates them to the eight principal points of the Compass. These are laid out to form the eight-sided figure called the *Pa Kua,* which is used to interpret the favourable and unfavourable locations, not just for buildings as a whole but also house floor plans and room layouts. The Feng Shui practitioner will advise on the correct placement of objects within each 'mansion' and will often advise on colour. The Compass school may also use the Flying Star system, which takes into account the astrological significances (calculated according to the Chinese system) of the time at which the house was built.

The Chinese compass works in the reverse to the Western way of thinking, with the South at the top of the diagram. Just as with Western

THE PA KUA (OR BA GUA)
The Eight Mansions Theory

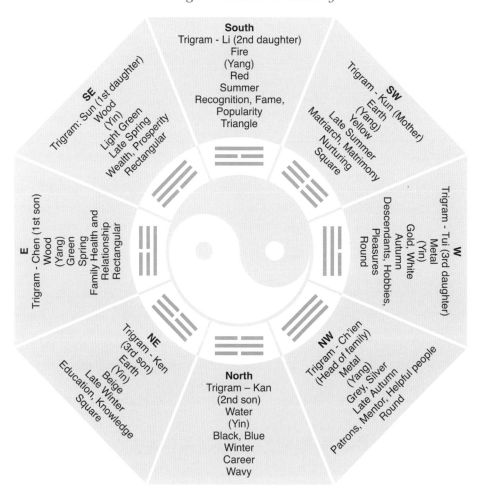

astrology and magical systems, in Chinese thought, each direction is focused on certain important areas of life or significances. Each compass point and trigram has its own 'Mansion' within which are held the energies of that direction, to be drawn on or mitigated at will by the able practitioner.

Above are the significances of each of the eight trigrams. These are, in order, Family Position, Element, Polarity, Colour, Season, Area of Life (most important) and, finally, the Shape which enhances the energy of that section.

Black Hat Sect School

This is a more modern version of Feng Shui which has its roots not only in traditional Feng Shui but also in Tibetan Buddhism and Taoism. In this school, the *Pa Kua* (often called the Ba Gua) is used, but it is based on the direction of the front door of the building, rather than the

compass points. The house or room is divided into eight sectors, similar to the Eight Mansions, each one having a bearing on an aspect of life that might need enhancing.

Shown opposite is a *Pa Kua* calculated for a house that has recently been purchased. Using Chinese astrological calculations, a 'fit' must be found between the occupants' life energy and the energy of the house. There are four helpful areas (Longevity, Prosperity, Health and Excellent) and four unhelpful areas (Death, Disaster, Irritation and Spooks – also known as the 'Six Curses'). The diagram has been drawn in accordance with the Western method of having south at the bottom of the diagram.

The energy of this house is very much in accord with the birth date of one of the occupants, yet there are certain problems associated with it in that, for instance, the kitchen is in the 'Death' area. This means that

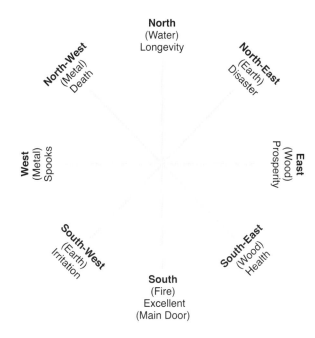

North
(Water)
Longevity

North-West
(Metal)
Death

North-East
(Earth)
Disaster

West
(Metal)
Spooks

East
(Wood)
Prosperity

South-West
(Earth)
Irritation

South-East
(Wood)
Health

South
(Fire)
Excellent
(Main Door)

construct a perfect picture, calculated as 1:1.618034, an 'irrational' number. This concept is still valid today.

To the architect, that same ratio – this time called a Golden Section – is used to calculate a standard proportion for width in relation to height, as used in facades of buildings, in window sizing, in first storey to second storey proportion and at times in the dimensions of paintings and picture frames – in fact, wherever a pleasing proportion is desired.

For the botanist or zoologist this same proportion is seen in nature in the spiral of flower and leaf growth or in the symmetry of a shell. Here we have the best arrangement so that each leaf gets the maximum exposure to light, casting the least shadow on the others. This also provides to falling rain, so the rain is directed back along the leaf and down the stem to the roots. For flowers or petals, it displays them to insects to attract them for pollination. In fact, nature has developed a way of working in an optimum fashion, and so too can we, if we so choose.

either the kitchen must be moved, which is not immediately practical, or certain changes must be made within the area to minimize risk. There is a toilet in the house within the 'Spooks' area, but with a little thought this can be used to keep the area clear – one simply remembers to, quite literally, 'flush away' the negativity.

Presenting Feng Shui in such a simplistic fashion in no way honours the art as it should be. It is much too complex a subject for that, and true practitioners will study for many years to perfect their skill and reach the state of Perfect Man. Feng Shui is one of the ways of the philosophy known as Tao, which assists us to remain in harmony with ourselves and the environment.

We can learn to use geomancy, Sacred Geometry, Feng Shui and indeed even old-style medieval geomancy, to learn and understand the currents within the earth and to divine how best to live in peace and harmony with the rest of the world.

There has always been something magical about mathematics, and indeed, the ancients thought that it showed Divine intention. Platonic solids, which still fascinate today, were used to prove various theories and to form 'perfect' shapes. The magical art of manifestation pays homage to this in many ways. The dodecahedron (a twelve-sided shape) is potentially the most beautiful, but at the same time most unstable, solid – surely a magical figure.

Sacred Geometry

SACRED GEOMETRY MEANS different things to different people. The artists of the Renaissance period discovered the Golden Mean – a ratio which helped them to

Man's efforts to understand the inexplicable have led him down many highways and byways. Perhaps the most fruitful initially for the spell worker or magical practitioner nowadays is to understand magical principles.

Principles and Components

Ancient beliefs and practices are the mainstay of magic. Modern-day spells often have their roots in ancient rituals and today's rituals arise from knowledge of age-old spells.

While we might make an attempt at defining ancient beliefs as applied to the modern day, no definition of magic has ever found universal acceptance, and countless attempts to separate it from religion on the one hand and science on the other, have never been truly successful. What one group of people may label magic, another would label religion, and another science. By choosing only one of these classifications for magic, we close our minds to all the other possibilities that are available to us.

Defining Magic

IT IS SOMETIMES best not to attempt any definition of ancient magic and magical belief. However, in any discussion of magic and its practitioners we must take account of a period in which the magical traditions of several different cultures coalesced and merged into a type of international and even multicultural magical practice, with its own rituals, symbols and words of power. This occurred in the Mediterranean basin and the Near East from the 1st to the 7th centuries AD and is the basis of most of the early, more intellectually based, systems of magic.

Magic and its understanding is, in some ways, a result of the human desire for control, and in this period there was a need to control the natural environment, the social world and the outcome of those forces not fully understand. This underlying desire for control comes to the surface most often in times of change, as we have seen repeatedly over the last fifteen centuries. During this time the techniques may have been modified but the goals have remained the same. The basic laws of magic, of control, still apply today just as they have always done.

Curiosity, exploration and secrecy

One of most interesting characters from early times was Abraham Abulafia (1240–95), who made available much arcane knowledge, which ultimately formed the basis of Kabbalah. Believing in the divine nature of the Hebrew alphabet, he held that God cannot be described or conceptualized using everyday symbols. He therefore used abstract letter combinations and permutations (tzeruf) in intense meditations lasting for hours to reach ecstatic states.

These were spells in the real sense of the word since they literally 'spelt out' the keys to altered states of consciousness – failure to carry through the keys correctly could have a far-reaching effect on the careless practitioner, resulting in madness and other states of illusion. Again, these beliefs have been brought through to the modern day and used to great effect. Controlled use of altered states of consciousness, backed up by empirical evidence, is still one of the most potent tools a magical practitioner or spell worker can have.

The Renaissance period in Europe saw the coming to prominence of many secret societies and scholar-magicians. Because of the burgeoning natural curiosity encouraged by Renaissance principles, a new importance was placed on the actual controlling of the forces of nature. The basis of magic working had previously been seen as harnessing the power of spirits and demons. Now, additionally, the human mind was a factor to be considered and magical working was geared to gaining power, not only over external forces but also over internal states. Much good work was done in understanding the interaction between the spiritual realm and the physical, and how changes can be brought about within the latter. Both Kabbalah and alchemy, one of whose objectives was to transform baser metals into gold, became very popular, as we have seen.

By the 17th century, folk magic and witchcraft were being used side by side, often with little differentiation between them. Most people were alternately fascinated and frightened by energies that offered control of nature coupled with opportunities for enormous wealth. Even King James 1 had fallen foul of Scottish witches, in that they had tried to control his behaviour during his time as King of Scotland. As a result he did his best to control pagan belief in his kingdoms.

Across the known world, witchcraft then became more widely identified with demonic or satanic entities opposed to God and therefore wholly evil. A heretic was defined as a traitor – an offence punishable by death – and the persecution of those who did not conform to the so-called religious thought of the day became relentless. This caused the practice of witchcraft to go underground not just in terms of secrecy but in actuality, for example in the use of caves and secret places, such as Wookey Hole in Somerset, England.

The practice of magic survived however and by the 19th century there is evidence that many secret societies, each surrounded by its own unique mysteries, still survived. Often they were formed by highly creative people who were searching for new and different ways of self-expression. Many of the beliefs of these societies were based on the old traditions, though some differed widely from those of the old alchemists. Rituals and invocations were developed which were supposedly based on the ancient rites, often with a very strong bias towards melodrama. Secret societies have also survived into the present day, though not always with full awareness of the fact that their rituals are based on magical practice.

Modern magic

Today there is a rich heritage of magical practices and beliefs on which we can call to satisfy our need for control over our own lives. Where conventional religion no longer offers an outlet for our sense of belonging, we can turn to magical rituals and spell making to honour our origins. We can make use of the knowledge and practices that have been handed down to us and have survived, often in the face of adversity. The principles that form the basis of magical practice still operate today, as do the various belief systems associated with them.

Many of these belief systems take their names from the Greek word *theo*, meaning god. One can be polytheistic (belief in many gods) yet see all things as being part of one great mystery, or monotheistic (belief in one god) yet recognize that for others there may be many gods. Again one might be atheistic (with no belief in god), with simply a belief in one's own power.

In the working of magical spells no one can tell you what to believe – you must make your own decisions. The words 'paganism' and 'pagan' come from the Latin *paganus*, meaning 'rustic' or 'belonging to the country'. Largely, ancient paganism was pantheistic (believing in all gods) but today the word has come to mean someone who does not recognize the God of the main religions of the world, such as Christianity or Judaism. We are much closer to a belief in the power of nature and for those who seek to use magic and spell making in their daily lives, there is the need for love and respect for all living things. How we express that will be mirrored in our spell making.

What is a Spell?

IN ANCIENT PAGAN communities the elders, or wise ones, had, by their very experience, an awareness of custom and a firm grasp of what had previously worked when trying to gain control over Mother Nature and other powers they did not fully understand. They had access to certain knowledge (and therefore power) that was not readily available to the ordinary individual.

The ancients recognized that words spoken in a certain way, according to custom, seemed to have more of an effect than those spoken on the spur of the moment. As a consequence, their words would have more power, yet the same words spoken by the uninitiated or those who did not understand, did not seem to have the same result.

There are three important aspects when reciting a spell. The first is that words spoken with intensity and passion do have a power all of their own. The next is that the speaker also has a power and an energy which, with practice, he or she may learn to use effectively. The third component, the forces and powers belonging to that which is 'beyond the human being' also have a tremendous power and are called upon, used or directed for a specific purpose. The use of all three of these aspects gives a very powerful spell indeed.

There are several kinds of spell, each of which requires a different approach.

Love spells

Many people's first thought in this context is of love spells – ways of making another person find them sexually attractive and desirable. In theory, love spells should be unconditional and this type should be entirely unselfish and free from self-interest. However, most of the time they obviously cannot be so, unless they are performed by a third party, someone outside the longed-for relationship who is totally dispassionate.

To try to influence someone else directly may well go against the ethics of many practitioners and magicians, though such spells do tend to be the stock-in-trade of many Eastern practitioners. Anyone who wishes to experiment with love spells needs to be aware that such spells come under the category of bidding spells and therefore must be used carefully. Love spells are often accompanied by gifts or love philtres, which are also meant to have an effect on the recipient.

Bidding spells

These are spells where the spell maker commands a particular thing to happen, but without the co-operation of those involved. Trying to make someone do something which they do not want to do, or which goes against their natural inclination, obviously requires a great deal of power and energy and can possibly misfire, causing the originator of the spell a good deal of difficulty.

For this reason, it is wise to preface such spells with words to signify that the outcome will only be in accord with the greater good – that is, that in the overall scheme of things no one will be harmed in any way whatsoever. This ensures that the intent behind the spell is of the purest and that there is not any maliciousness within the practitioner. It means that an able and responsible practitioner must choose their words carefully, even when they are not casting a spell.

One type of bidding spell that is allowable is when a curse or 'hex' is being removed. A hex is a spell that ill-wishes someone and in many cases binds the recipient in some way. A curse is a spell with a much more generalized effect. To remove such a negative spell, it is usual to turn it around and send the malign energy back to the person who summoned it in the first place. You simply command the energy to return from whence it came.

Blessings

These might be counted either as prayers or spells and need a passionate concentration on bringing, for instance, peace of mind or healing to the recipient. They hold no danger for the practitioner but are sometimes more difficult to appreciate since they tend to be more general than other types of magical work. They may be thought of in terms of a positive energy from beyond the practitioner, being channelled towards a specific purpose.

Saying grace before a meal is a form of blessing preceded by an offer of praise and a prayer of thankfulness, an acknowledgement of a gift. The food is enhanced by the act and the blessing is given by drawing on the power vested in the knowledgeable expert. Thus one practitioner may call on the nature gods whereas another might call on the power of Jesus Christ.

Healing spells and charms

Within this type of spell it is wise to go beyond the presenting symptoms and to ask for healing on all levels of existence – physical, mental and spiritual – because the practitioner may not have the knowledge or correct information to enable him to diagnose a condition correctly. The natural energies and specific vibrations are enhanced by invocations, incantations and blessings wherever appropriate.

Frequently, objects such as crystals are charged with energy and power to focus healing or other energies in a quite specific way, often to remind the patient's body of its own ability to heal itself.

Invocations

These call on what is believed to be the ultimate source of power, which differs from spell to spell. Quite literally, they call up that power and ask for permission to use this influence for a stated purpose. Meddling with this power and calling up negative forces is extremely unwise and very foolish.

Spells for selfish personal power or to gain power over others will often backfire on the unwary and may cause damage to the individual who casts them. Invocations of positive forces can do no harm, except that the results can sometimes be highly disconcerting due to the sheer energy created, although the eventual outcome may be good.

Incantations

This type of spell prepares the magical worker and his helpers for further work by heightening their awareness. It does not set out to call up the powers, but appeals to gods, goddesses, powers of nature and so on for help.

Chanting, prayer and hymns are in many ways incantations, particularly when the intent is stated with some passion. An incantation is often very beautiful and rhythmic. Music has always been an efficient way of heightening awareness and altering states of consciousness.

THE ELEMENTS

In most systems of magical working you will find mentioned the four (or sometimes five) Elements, often in conjunction with their directions or, as they are known in magic, quarters of the universe or cardinal points. Together and separately they are extremely powerful sources of energy and can give a tremendous boost to your spell making. Each Element also comes under the protection of one of the Archangels (see pages 249-251).

The four Elements are energies, and manifestations of energy, that make up the entire universe. They also influence our personalities and therefore what we do. Magical working calls to each elemental kingdom and its ruler to protect each cardinal point and its properties. Each Element has an intrinsic power and is known for having certain qualities, natures, moods and magical purposes. Each also has positive and negative traits.

Earth, Air, Fire and Water are the four Elements and you may well find that you work best using one of them in particular. People drawn to candle magic, for instance, are using mainly the Element of Fire, while those who work with incense are using Air with a fair smattering of Earth in the herbs and resins.

The fifth Element is that of spirit, which is the 'binding principle' behind everything. Sometimes known as aether, it is, on the whole, intangible, yet is that which makes everything happen. You are both its representative and its channel, so in using the other Elements in magical working you have a responsibility to act wisely and well.

Earth

Traditionally the direction of this Element is north and the colour normally associated with Earth is green. It is represented on the altar usually by salt or sand. Crystals, because they are totally natural substances, can also be used.

When invoking Earth and the powers of the north, you are looking for recovery and healing and perhaps trying to find answers to questions. These powers deal with gaining knowledge, blessing, creating and shielding. When working within a magical circle, this is the first corner or quarter on which you call for protection.

The principal nature spirits of the Earth are called gnomes. They are said to live underground and guard the earth's treasures. Other groups within the earth's nature spirits ruled by the god Pan are brownies, dryads, Earth spirits, elves and satyrs.

Air

The direction of this Element is east and the colour usually associated with it is yellow. Incense is often used to represent Air, since the movement of the air can be seen in the incense smoke.

When you are looking for inspiration, need new ideas or perhaps to break free from the past or undesired situations, you would use this Element. The quality associated with it is that of thinking or the use of the intellect. When working in a magical circle, Air is the second quarter on which you call for protection.

The sylphs are the Air spirits; their Element has the most subtle energy of the four. They are said to live on the tops of mountains and are volatile and changeable. They are usually perceived with wings and look like cherubs or fairies. One of their tasks is said to be to help humans receive inspiration.

Fire

Fire is the Element of the south and is usually represented by a candle or a cauldron with a fire inside. Its colour is red and its associations are to do with power, determination and passionate energy.

You would call upon this Element for protection from evil forces, cleansing and creativity. The quality associated with Fire is 'doing' and it is a male principle. It is the third quarter or cardinal point on which you call for protection when working in a magical circle.

Without salamanders, the spirit of Fire, it is said that physical fire cannot exist. They have been seen as sparks or small balls of light, but most often they are perceived as being lizard-like in shape and about 30 cm or more in length. They are considered the strongest and most powerful of all the Elementals. As nature spirits they are greatly affected by the way that mankind thinks. Out of control, salamanders can be considered dangerous.

Water

Water is the Element of the west and is represented by a bowl of water or a goblet of wine or fruit juice. Its colour is blue and, because it represents the giving of life, it is associated with the Elements of sea, rain, snow and rivers.

When you need cleansing, revitalizing, the removal of curses or hexes or change of any sort, you will call upon Water. It is to do with emotions, right through from the most basic passions to the most elevated forms of belief. It is predominantly feminine. It is the fourth and final quarter that you invoke in any magical circle.

The undines are the Elemental beings connected with Water and are beautiful and very graceful. The nymph is frequently found in a fountain and the mythical mermaid belongs to the ocean. Some undines inhabit waterfalls, others live in rivers and lakes. Smaller undines are often seen as winged beings that people have mistakenly called fairies.

Spirit

When you feel you are sufficiently adept at using the other Elements, you may begin to use spirit – the fifth Element. This has no special space but is everywhere. It should never ever be used negatively because, particularly when you are weak and tired, it can rebound on you.

You may well find that you instinctively link strongly with the life force as spirit, in which case you are probably succeeding in bringing all the Elements together within yourself. There is no particular colour associated with spirit – perception is all-important. If you choose to represent spirit on the altar, you may do so however you wish. You are free to use your intuition and you must have a very strong awareness of your reason for choosing that particular symbol.

Different Types of Magic

Elemental

IN THIS PARTICULAR type of magic the Elements of Fire, Earth, Air and Water are given their own directional focus to create added power and give extra energy to your spells. You will no doubt find that you tend to favour one particular direction but you should be able to use all of them.

Colour

Perhaps the simplest form of magic is that which involves colour. This method of working is also used in conjunction with various other forms of magic. Colour can enhance, alter and completely change moods and emotions and therefore can be used to represent our chosen goal. At its simplest it can be used alone and in dressing an altar. (See pages 239-240 for some colour correspondences.)

Herbal

Herbal magic is often used alongside many other forms of magic. Used as talismans and amulets – for example in a pouch or bag – herbs become protective; the oil from herbs can also be used in candle magic. There are many different types of herbs available for use in this way. Each herb has its own specific use, but frequently is used along with many other herbs and oils to produce a desired result.

Candle

In candle magic, man discovered the ability to control light and this is one of the oldest forms of magic as well as one of the most simple. Using candles to symbolize ourselves and our beliefs means that we have access to a power beyond ourselves. Candle magic also forms an effective back-up for most other forms of magical working.

Crystal

Every stone or gem has its own attribute which can be used in magic. Crystals are used extensively in healing because of the vibrational impact they can have. Because of this, they lend themselves to the enhancement of any spell making or magical working. Even ordinary stones have their own power and can be used as repositories for all sorts of energies and powers.

Knot

Knot magic works partly with the principle of binding, which is a type of bidding spell, and also with that of weaving, which was traditionally a female intuitive occupation. It utilizes ribbon, rope, string, yarn, or anything that can be knotted or plaited to signify our aspiration. It is a type of representational magic, and is used in conjunction with many of the other forms. The techniques of colour, form and use of energies are all used in its practice.

Representational

Representational magic involves using an object that represents something or someone for whom you are working the spell. It helps in concentrating the energy and visualizing the desire and the end result. Representational objects should never be used for negative purposes.

Symbolic

In this system different symbols, rather than objects, are used to represent various ideas, people or goals. These symbols can be personal to you, or such things as Tarot cards, runes, Hebrew letters or numerology. You will often use symbolic magic in your magical workings and will soon develop your own preferred symbols.

Talismans, amulets and charms

These devices use all the other forms of magic in their formation, but principally representational and symbolic magic. They are 'charged' (given power) magically and usually are worn or carried on the person for protection or good luck. Many are worn around the neck, perhaps as jewellery, or carried in a pouch and incorporate crystals, herbs or other magical objects. There are many types of each of these objects and you will gradually learn to differentiate between them.

Working Magically

WHEN PERFORMING YOUR spells and magical workings, you will find that you need to understand why you use certain tools in specific ways. Before learning how to set up your altar (see page 230), here is a list of the most commonly used tools.

Altar Objects

This is a general term for the objects that you place on your altar – candleholders, flower vases, crystals and so forth – which do not necessarily have a specific magical use of their own; they are present to create an ambience. You should remember to dedicate them to the purpose in hand by presenting them to your chosen deity – you may find it helpful to consult the Deities and the Worship section on pages 205-224 which has a comprehensive selection for your information.

Athame

By tradition, the athame is a ceremonial knife used especially in the performing of spells. It is not intended for cutting herbs and so on: its role is ceremonial, for example indicating the quarters or directions. Ideally it should be of the best and purest metal available. Its handle is usually black and sometimes carved with magical designs and symbols. Many experienced magical practitioners consider that the most powerful athame is one which has been inherited.

Besom

A besom is a different name for a broom, and is particularly associated with the easily recognizable so-called 'witch's broom' of old. It is a particularly personal tool, and is often made specially for the practitioner, with twigs from the tree of her choice. It is usually kept specifically to be used in the sacred space or circle – this time for cleansing – and is also used both symbolically and spiritually.

Boline

The boline is a knife traditionally used in cutting plants, herbs, wands and other objects for spells and other magical workings. It is akin to the gardener's pruning knife as a useful, practical tool. It often has a white handle and a curved blade. It is consecrated because this is a way of honouring its purpose.

Burine

A burine is a sharp-pointed instrument used for inscribing candles and other magical objects with symbols, words and pictures in order to make spells more effective. In many ways, it is more effective than either the boline or the athame and is seen much more as an instrument which pierces a surface rather than cuts it.

Candles

Candles are such an integral part of a spell-maker's work that they have become a whole branch of magic all their own. They represent the Element of Fire, but also light. Various colours bring different things to magical workings and they are an important part of any ritual (see pages 29-30).

Cauldron

Because cauldrons were easily disguised as cooking utensils in olden days, most people today tend to think of them as a large cast-iron pot. There has lately been a return to original materials and nowadays they can be made of almost anything. They are often of a size that can be stood on the altar, or in the sacred space. They are used mainly as containers for herbs, candles and other magical objects.

Chalice

Used as a ceremonial drinking vessel, the chalice is sometimes made from precious metal, although it can also be made from glass. An elegant object, the chalice will usually be beautifully decorated with elaborate designs – which may have magical significance – or jewels and gemstones.

Charcoal

Charcoal is a component of incense and oil burning. Nowadays, the best charcoal is usually found in compressed small discs of about 3 cm (1 inch). These give a burning time of approximately 45 minutes.

Compass

While this may seem a somewhat unusual tool, many spells, rituals and techniques require that you honour or face certain directions or compass points in their performance. It is also necessary to know the correct alignment in Feng Shui. Much the easiest way to work out the directions is by using a compass. It does not need to be particularly decorative, ornate or expensive, merely one with which you are happy to work.

Incense and Oil Burner

The choice of this tool must be a personal matter. An incense burner should give plenty of room to allow the aromas and smoke to disperse properly. Traditional material such as brass or clay may be used. The best shape is slightly flat rather than too concave. Oil burners should be of a sufficient size to allow a long enough time to complete your spell. Burners which allow you to float the oil on water, which then evaporates, are probably the safest.

Paper

During spells you will often need to write your wishes or aims down and it is good to have some paper ready prepared. Parchment type is best, but heavier good quality is perfectly acceptable. You consecrate it by holding it for a short period in the smoke from your favourite incense.

Pen and Ink

Traditionally, quill pens were used for writing spells and incantations, but if you can't find a quill then use the best pen you can afford. Try to keep it especially for magical work and consecrate it by passing it carefully over the top of a candle or through incense. Also buy a good-quality ink and, if not already formulated for magical purposes, consecrate that in the same way. Neither pen nor ink should be used for other purposes.

Pentacle

The pentacle is a shallow dish, which is usually inscribed with a pentagram – a five-pointed star.

It is used as a 'power point' for consecrating other objects such as water or wine in a chalice, amulets and tools.

Pestle and Mortar

The pestle and mortar are so symbolic of the union of God and Goddess that they deserve a special mention within the use of magical tools. Mainly used to prepare herbal mixtures and incenses, they can also become part of your altar furniture when consecrated.

Scrying Tools

Scrying is the practice of using certain channelling tools, which should be consecrated before use – such as crystals, mirrors, coloured water, runes and so forth – to try to gain an insight into external events. Any object can be used for scrying, though usually they are reflective, and they employ the arts of concentration and contemplation.

Staff

The staff is used very frequently by practitioners today, particularly if they are of the Druidic persuasion. Longer than the wand, it has the same attributes and uses. A staff is deliberately fashioned for the practitioner from wood taken from sacred trees, such as oak, hawthorn and hazelnut.

Travelling Tools

Just as most modern-day priests will carry small versions of their consecrated tools with them, in case they are needed, so every magical practitioner can do the same. In some ways the latter are more fortunate, particularly if they work within the nature traditions, as they can often use objects that are readily to hand and dedicate them on the spot.

Making and Dedicating Travelling Tools

You will find information on page 230 on developing a sacred space, and should you choose to work with an athame, wand or chalice, you can use representations that are quite clearly associated with the idea behind the magic. You might wish to carry such things with you for use on your travels, which means that you can set up an altar anywhere, both out of doors and inside, according to your own beliefs. You might also use the material roll as your altar cloth.

YOU WILL NEED

Material such as linen, velvet or felt to make your travelling roll
Broad elastic or material to hold your tools in place
Needle or small paper knife to represent an athame
Small piece of wooden dowelling or a straight twig to represent a wand
Very small tumbler or oyster shell as a chalice
Coin or dog tag with a pentagram etched on it
Suitable lucky charms or cake decorations as representations of your deities
Birthday cake candles
Four small containers, e.g. phials or empty spice jars, for your chosen incense or herbs, salt, water and anointing oil
Matches
Crystals or tumbled stones as cardinal point markers (green, yellow, red and blue stones work well)

METHOD

❖ Make yourself a travelling roll from the material so you can keep your tools together safely. This is similar to the type of carrier in which a carpenter keeps his tools. The elastic will keep them securely in place.

❖ You can also include anything else that you feel is important to your rituals.

❖ Dedicate your objects with an appropriate form of words. You might say:

O Great Mother,
As I travel over your forests, fields and watery ways,
Bless and empower this pouch with its symbols of your power.

Verdant God,
Have me use them wisely and well,
So that together we manifest your authority.
May it always be with me
So that, wherever I am, so also are both of you.

These travelling tools are now dedicated for use anywhere, at any time and under any conditions. Often they can be used unobtrusively without anyone needing to know what you are doing.

Wand

The wand should be no longer than the forearm and is often made from sacred wood (see pages 80-86). Since the wand is a very personal object, it should be chosen carefully and equally carefully attuned to your own energies. It cannot be used magically until it has been consecrated.

Obviously, you will not need to use all of your tools all of the time and you should develop for yourself some way of storing them, so that they retain their potency. You can do this by perhaps keeping them on your altar or in your sacred space. Use a specially dedicated box or other container or, if you know they are not likely to be interfered with, simply wrapped in black silk or velvet. Treat your tools with respect and they will serve you well.

Components of Magical Working

JUST AS A RECIPE contains ingredients, so there are certain components that are needed in magical workings, in order to enhance the power and energy that is created. To the uninitiated some of these may seem strange, yet if we remember that much magic initially had to be performed with only what was immediately and easily available to the practitioner, the use of such items makes a great deal of sense. Candles, crystals, herbs and so on thus become an important part of modern-day spell working.

CANDLES

Candles should be chosen carefully with regard to type, and colour, depending on the purpose of the spell. It is often better to use your intuition when choosing the type of candle, although for ease of reference, below is a list of the principal types. There are other types available, but these are the most suitable for magical working.

Table

The most readily available candle, they are ideal for many of the spells in this book. They usually burn for six to eight hours and need to be properly seated in suitable candlesticks. All colours can be used, but they should not be dipped, except in exceptional circumstances, and should be of the best quality possible. It is sensible to keep a ready supply at hand.

Pillar

This is a free-standing candle. It is usually in the form of a simple pillar, although it can sometimes be made in other shapes which can be used as part of the spell, for example heart shapes for love spells. This type of candle is best burned on a flat holder since it usually takes some time to burn out.

Taper

These candles are tall and thin and need a particularly stable candle-holder. They are either made in a mould, or by the traditional method of dipping a length of wick into hot molten white or coloured wax. For magical purposes they should be coloured all the way through. They can often be used when a quick result is required. Because they are quite fragile, you need to be careful not to break them when anointing them.

Tea lights

These small candles are excellent for use when a candle must be left to burn out, but are less easy to anoint with essential oils. Poured in small metal pots like small votives, they are normally used in oil burners or specially-made tea-light holders. Depending on their size, they usually burn for approximately four hours.

Votive

This type of candle is specially designed as an offering, to carry prayers to whichever deity you honour. As the wax melts, the holder, which is made of glass, can become hot so some care must be taken when using them. They are designed to be long-burning, usually between one and seven days.

Choosing your candles

There are several things you need to remember when choosing a candle:

1. Choose your candle type as above.
2. Candles used for magic should always be virgin (unused) at the start of the working, unless you have deliberately cleared them of past influences. Using candles that have been previously lit can have a detrimental effect on your spell. They may have picked up influences from previous use.
3. Charge your candle before using it. This can be done by anointing it with oils associated with the magic you intend on performing, or by simply touching it and filling it with your own energy (see below)
4. The oils used in the anointing of your candle should, where possible, always be natural fragrances. While charging the candle, smooth from top to bottom when drawing energy toward you, bottom to top when sending energy outwards. Particularly when anointing candles for altar use, anoint from the middle to the top and from the middle to the bottom to signify the union of spiritual and physical realms (see below).
5. If you enjoy craftwork, it is a very good idea to make your own candles for magical use. It is a whole art in itself – you infuse your candles with your own energy and thus increase the magical potency of the candle many times over. It is relatively easy to make your own candles: simply heat the wax until it is liquid and pour into a mould which is threaded with a wick. The wax should now be left to cool, after which the mould can be removed. Oils and colours can be added for extra potency.

Dressing and charging candles

Dressing (anointing) and charging candles are perhaps candle magic in its simplest form. Dressing a candle performs two functions. By anointing it with oil you ensure that it burns safely and you also have the opportunity to infuse it with the required vibration for your working. Charging a candle ensures you fix the intent of your magical working and also dedicates the candle to the appropriate purpose.

Dressing Candles

Any oil can be used for dressing a candle but initially it is best to use either your favourite essential oil, such as frankincense, or perhaps an oil infused with a suitable herb appropriate to the task in hand. (A comprehensive list of oils suitable for various purposes is given on pages 75-80.)

There are various ways to dress a candle but what is important is the direction in which you anoint it. If you remember that working from the top down draws in power from spiritual sources, and working from the bottom up draws in energy from the earth, it is very easy to work correctly for your purpose. Never rub the candle with a back and forth movement, as you will end up with a confusion of energies – not to say a sputtering candle.

YOU WILL NEED ───────────────
Candle
Oil

METHOD ───────────────────
❖ Sit quietly and, holding the candle, think carefully about your intent. If you have learned to meditate, then enter a meditative state and allow the energies to build up within you.
❖ To bring something to you, rub oil on the candle in a downward motion from the top to the middle and then from the bottom to the middle.
❖ To send something away from you, you rub the oil from the middle of the candle out to the ends.
❖ Continue with either movement until you have a sense that you have done enough. If you have any oil left on your hands either rub your hands together until the oil is absorbed or dab the remaining oil from your fingers onto the centre of your forehead, which is the

Third Eye and the seat of vision. Then say the following or something similar:

I cleanse and consecrate this candle
(in the name of your chosen deity of you choose to use one).
May it burn with strength in the service of the Greater Good.

Your candle is now ready for use.

Charging Candles

This is a quick, uncomplicated method of more fully charging a candle. This method can be used without having to set up your altar completely. It can equally be used to charge your altar candles.

YOU WILL NEED ──────────────

A candle or candles of the appropriate colour (if preferred, mark them with appropriate symbols)
A candle holder
Matches rather than a lighter

METHOD ──────────────

✤ Hold the candle in your 'power hand' (the hand you consider you give out energy with).
✤ Open the other hand and turn that palm towards the sky.
✤ Breathe deeply and visualize your goal.
✤ Now perceive whatever you think of as Universal Energy flowing through the palm that is turned skyward, filling your body.
✤ Visualise that Universal Energy mixing within you with the energy of your intention.
✤ Now allow that mixed energy to flow into the candle.
✤ Be conscious of the energy as it builds up.
✤ Feel the energy streaming into the candle.
✤ Fill it from bottom to top as though the candle were an empty vessel.
✤ If you are comfortable with doing so, speak your intention out loud.
✤ As you place the candle in its holder, stabilize the thought within the candle so that it will be converted into pure clear intent.
✤ Strike a match above the candle
✤ Draw down the flame toward the candle, lighting the wick.

✤ Extinguish the match flame, but do not blow it out in case you blow out the candle.
✤ Stay with the candle for a few moments visualizing your intention, feeling its energy moving into the universe.
✤ Leave the area and let the candle burn right down as it does its work.

Candle colour and the symbols inscribed on them create additional power. As you become more proficient, you will find yourself using certain colours and symbols more often. Try not to be too rigid, and always be open to widening your focus.

Candle colours

Many different colours are used in candle magic and below are listed the most common ones, along with their key associations and purposes. You may not wish to use black candles because of their association with the darker side of magic. If so, dark grey is a good substitute. White can be used as a substitute if your chosen colour is not available.

White
• The Goddess
• Higher Self
• Purity
• Peace
• Virginity

Black
• Binding
• Shape shifting
• Protection
• Repels negativity

Brown
• Special favours
• To influence friendships
• Healing earth energies

Orange
• General success
• Property deals
• Legal matters
• Justice
• Selling

Purple
• Third eye
• Psychic ability
• Hidden knowledge
• To influence people in high places
• Spiritual power

Blue
• The Element of Water
• Wisdom
• Protection
• Calm
• Good fortune
• Opening communication
• Spiritual inspiration

Pink
• Affection
• Romance
• Caring
• Nurturing
• Care for the planet earth

Green

- The Element of Earth
- Physical healing
- Monetary success
- Mother Earth
- Tree and plant magic
- Growth
- Personal goals

Red

- The Element of Fire
- Passion
- Strength
- Fast action
- Career goals
- Lust
- Driving force
- Survival

Silver

- The Moon Goddess
- Astral energy
- Female energy
- Telepathy
- Clairvoyance
- Intuition
- Dreams

Copper

- Professional growth
- Business productivity
- Career manoeuvres
- Passion
- Money goals

Gold

- The Sun God
- Promote winning
- Male power
- Happiness

Yellow

- The Element of Air
- Intelligence
- The Sun
- Memory
- Imagination supported by logic
- Accelerating learning
- Clearing mental blocks

Signs from candle-burning

Not every magical practitioner takes heed of the manner in which spell-casting or ritual candles burn; there is often a great deal to be learnt from understanding a little bit more about how to interpret the way a candle burns. In voodoo and Afro-Caribbean magic, for instance, spiritual workers who 'set lights', as it is called, for clients will automatically take notice of such details and incorporate their findings in any further work.

It is worth remembering that some candles are simply poorly made and will burn badly no matter what you do with them. If the wick is the wrong size, for instance, the candle may be no use for magical work. It is nice to make one's own candles, although there is quite an art to it and the novice may end up feeling rather frustrated, if the intention behind the candle is not quite right.

External factors can also play a huge part in how candles burn. The way the candle is placed in the holder, the temperature in the surrounding area, an open window causing a draught, and other such things can all make a difference. Equally, the candle can be affected by your own mood and really until you have learned how to meditate using a candle flame you need not worry too much to begin with. All that having been said, here are some of the things to watch for when burning candles.

The candle gives a clean, even burn This might be called a successful burn and suggests the spell will most likely achieve the right result. If a glass-encased candle burns and leaves no marks on the glass that is best. If a free-standing candle leaves little or no residue, this is by far the best result.

The flame flares, dips, gutters, repeatedly Check first for draughts and then decide intuitively whether there is a pattern to the flaring and guttering. If you are performing the spell with someone in mind, you may feel the recipient of your spell is trying to block your efforts. Sit quietly for a while until you feel you have grasped the significance of the pattern, which may be because the spell itself is not right for the time. In this case simply be prepared to try again another time.

A free-standing candle runs and melts a lot while burning This gives you an opportunity to observe the flow of wax for signs. Quickly melting wax shows there is a good deal of positivity available. If one side burns quicker than the other, a balance can sometimes be achieved by turning the candle round and it is useful to note how many times you do this, since this can indicate the number of adjustments the person may have to make to ensure success. Other people prefer to let nature take its course and to watch the wax run for signs, without interfering in its movements.

A free-standing candle burns down to a puddle of wax or sets in runs down the side of the candle When this happens, most workers will examine the shape of the wax for a sign. For instance, a heart-shaped wax puddle is a good sign if you are burning a red candle for a love spell. You may see something of importance there, for the shape of the run may suggest an outcome regarding the matter at hand. Wax puddles come in all kinds of shapes; most candle-workers look for symbols in the wax, or sometimes use numerology or other divination techniques similar to teacup reading, to discover meaning.

A glass-encased candle burns clean to begin with but 'dirty' with a great deal of smoke later This indicates that things will go well to begin with, but there are other conditions that have not yet revealed themselves and will need to be resolved. Someone may be working against the required outcome, so the correct timing and correspondences of further spells are crucial. Information on timings and correspondences can be found on pages 233-239.

A free-standing candle lets out a lot of smoke but burns clean at the end Difficult conditions need to be dealt with first of all but eventually conditions improve.

There is a dirty, black burn (especially one that deposits soot on a glass-encased candle) This means things are not going to go well – the spell may not work, the blessing may fail, the person is in deeper stress or trouble than you first thought. There is a great deal of negativity around. Sometimes it is good to change the focus of the candle and ask that it be used to burn off the negativity, which will enable you to get a handle on the situation.

The candle goes out before completely burning This can mean that the spell you are using is not the most appropriate one and you need to use stronger means than you first employed. It can also mean that someone is actively working against you. In this case it is wise to go back to the beginning and start your whole spell over again.

The candle tips over and flames up into a potential fire hazard Provided that you know you have placed the candles properly, this indicates there is danger about for you and your client. You should clear your sacred space and cleanse it by whatever means you prefer. It is probably wise to wait a while before retrying the spell and remember to take a ritual bath (see page 227) before you do.

The candle burns too quickly Generally a fast burn is good, but an overly fast burn means that although the work will go well, its effect will not last long. Again you might wait before retrying the spell, though sometimes a fast result is required. You should use your own judgement.

Disposal of candle wax

In European-American traditions, many people bury candle wax and other remains after a spell is cast. Burial toward the appropriate quarter of the compass is considered a thoughtful way to go about this. Some neo-pagans dispose of ritual or spell remains in a bonfire or fireplace.

If the intention of the spell is positive or involves matters around your own home, like blessing, love-drawing, money-drawing, or home protection, it is perfectly acceptable to wrap the materials in a cloth or paper packet and bury them.

If you are removing hexes or opposing negativity, you would burn the packet, bury it, flush it into a stream or allow it to blow away on the four winds as far away from your own home as possible. Many people follow tradition and throw the packet over the left shoulder (into the face of the Devil) and walk away without looking back. If the intention of the spell is not centred on matters close to home, or if you do not have a suitable garden, you can wrap the materials in a cloth or paper packet and throw them in running water over your left shoulder and walk away. Alternatively, you can take the materials to a crossroads – any place where two roads cross – and throw the packet into the centre of the crossroads over your left shoulder and walk away.

CRYSTALS

There are many crystals that can be used in magical workings and as you become more practised in spell making, and more interested in their various attributes, you will discover for yourself that certain crystals resonate for you more than others. These are perhaps the ones that you will put in your talisman bag, or use in your healing rituals.

Crystals are such an fundamental part of spell working, with so many levels of awareness inherent in them, that it is well worth taking the time to learn as much as you can about them, in order that you can use them in whatever way is appropriate for you. You might, for instance, like to place a large crystal of, say, rock quartz on your altar as representative of the Earth Element and all its power and goodness. On the other hand, you may wish to wear a 'charged' crystal (a crystal that has had extra energy added to it) to protect you.

Using techniques for 'finding' crystals and being open to them 'finding' you, are the best ways of obtaining the crystals you need. Because our lives are so busy, many of us will come into contact with crystals only as gifts or in a commercial environment. You may acquire them by various methods, for example buying them, receiving them as gifts, or very occasionally unearthing them.

One relatively common way of 'finding' the best crystal for you is by using the 'first recognition' method.

• Stand in front of a group of crystals.
• Close your eyes.
• Open your eyes quickly and pick up the first crystal you see or the one that attracts you in any way.
• When holding a particular crystal or running your hand over it, you may find that your hands tingle or you have some other physical reaction. This usually means it is for you.
• At other times you may feel drawn to a particular crystal without knowing why. The crystal may not necessarily be for you, and could be for somebody else or a purpose not yet specified.

If you are choosing a crystal for a specific purpose (meditation, healing, and so forth), hold that purpose in mind as you choose. Usually you will sense an energy 'reaction' from a particular crystal, perhaps in the form of a tingling sensation, heat or a flash of light.

A Meditation on Jade

In Chinese thought, jade is very highly regarded, since it is said to embody the five cardinal virtues: charity, modesty, courage, justice and wisdom. For this reason, it can be used as an aid to meditation and a tool for self-development. At its simplest you might use a piece of jade simply to consider these virtues in a somewhat objective fashion, to enhance your understanding. A slightly more complex way of working with its deeper meaning is given below.

YOU WILL NEED
A piece of jade, preferably polished
Paper
Pen

METHOD
❖ Sit quietly and contemplate your piece of jade.
❖ Bring to mind each of the cardinal virtues in turn, deciding what part each plays in your life.
❖ Write down those aspects that you consider might need further consideration.
❖ For the next five days consider a single virtue each day in meditation, remembering to write down your insights or conclusions so that they may be considered at a later date.
❖ As you do this, be conscious that the jade is gradually becoming infused with your awareness and therefore becoming a powerful tool.
❖ When you feel ready to move onto the next stage of development, be aware that the Chinese also believe that the nine qualities of jade reflect the best attributes of humanity:
Its smoothness suggests benevolence.
Its polish, knowledge.
Its firmness, righteousness.
Its harmlessness, virtuous action.
Its spotlessness, purity.
Its imperishability, endurance.
Visible flaws, ingenuousness
Its tactile quality, morality.
Its sound on being struck, music.
❖ In the same way as above, contemplate each of the stone's features and its corresponding attributes and resolve to develop more of these within your life.

Your piece of jade can now be carried as an aide memoire to help you focus on those qualities which you feel you need to develop. The fact that you have spent quite a long time in drawing the inherent knowledge from the stone means that you can now have easy access to that knowledge when you are not able to do a full meditation.

Cleansing a crystal

When you acquire a new crystal you should first of all cleanse it and then dedicate the crystal for the purpose intended. This can be done simply by holding the crystal while consciously thinking that it will be used only for good, or during a meditation. You could also call upon your deities, if you wish, using your own ritual.

There are many different ways of cleansing crystals. Below are several of the more practical approaches.

- Take the crystal to the sea, clean it thoroughly in the sea water, and allow the water to wash over it for several minutes. The crystal should then be left in the sun or in moonlight, whichever pleases you most, where it can 'energize'.
- If you cannot use sea water, soak the crystal in salt water for anything from one to seven days – you will know instinctively how long is needed. Use the proportions of approximately three tablespoons of salt to a cup of water (the water must fully cover the stones), put the salt water in a glass container with the crystals and leave in a sunny or moonlit place.
- Bury the crystal in commercial sea salt for at least seven and up to 24 hours (overnight is good), then rinse it with pure water and 'energize' it in the sun as before. *Note:* Salt or abrasive substances may impair the surface of your crystal; this will not affect the properties of the crystal, but is aesthetically not very pleasing.
- If you have a sacred space out in the open, bury the crystals for 24 hours, and as you bury them ask that they may be cleansed ready for your work. Don't forget to mark the spot where they are buried – it is very easy to lose them!

- Smudge the crystal thoroughly with, for example, a sage smudge stick (see page 51) or favourite incense. That is, allow the crystal to be engulfed in the smoke until such times as it feels clear. Suspend smaller crystals in the smoke or burn incense underneath larger stones. The incense section, beginning on page 53, gives numerous examples
- Put the crystal in the middle of a large group of crystals or on top of another mineral (one which is a specific energizer, such as copper for the qualities of Venus) for 12 to 24 hours.
- Clean the crystal in flowing spring, lake, river or tap water and then energize it by leaving it in the sun. It is important to think of the crystal being cleansed by the movement of the water.

Programming a crystal

Crystals are prepared for programming by charging them. Programming a crystal aligns the energy of the crystal to the intent. Using a carefully thought-out affirmation and directing this to the centre of the crystal is sufficient to programme it. Below are three of the most common ways of programming.

- Place the crystal on a large crystal cluster dedicated to the specific purpose for which it is required.
- Place the crystal in the centre of a circle of other crystals whose ends are pointing towards the centre and the new crystal.
- Put the crystal in sun and/or moonlight, stating the specific intent connected with the crystal. Many people believe that the days relating to the summer and winter solstices, the Full and the New Moon, and the vernal and autumnal equinox are more heavily charged than other days.

Magical crystals and stones

To get you started in your use of crystals and gemstones, there is a list below of those that you are most likely to use in your workings. To make it easy, they are categorized according to their planetary influence. The correspondences here are for the seven planets used by the Ancients before the transpersonal planets of Uranus, Neptune and Pluto were discovered. This astrological classification has the idea of crystals being captured light or energy, and the knowledge that the power of the planets can be harnessed by this method, is a powerful aid in spell making.

The Sun

The Sun is generally associated with strength, determination, vitality and self-expression. It also relates to the arts, banking, corporate bodies, fame, fatherhood, government office, health, honour and esteem, influence, leadership, nobility, organization, public acclaim, rulership and teaching.

Aventurine promotes health, vigour and cheerfulness; it promises emotional moral support in new commercial undertakings; gets rid of doubt, diminishes anxiety and eases bodily aches and pains; strengthens resolve against hardship.

Citrine is linked with boldness, courage, mastery; it promises victory over sporting, business or romantic rivalry; wards off infections and any unwanted attention; prevents accident or injury, especially on journeys.

Diamond heightens awareness, encourages enterprise and strengthens resolve; it brings personal progression and acclaim; affords relief from mental or emotional stress, confounds enmity and protects from physical dangers.

Heliodor gives the advantage to speculators, gamblers and sportsmen; promotes prosperity and happiness; prevents deception and disillusionment; lifts depression and helps the body recover and recuperate.

Topaz bestows courage, determination, desire, confidence and judgment; promises health and joy and prosperity; improves physical fitness and raises the spirits; overcomes envy and malice.

Tourmaline brightens up the imagination and sharpens the intellect; promotes harmony and brings financial reward; defends the home from theft; improves vision, relieves tension and lifts depression.

Zircon energizes the body and will; heightens awareness and sharpens the intellect; brings rich rewards; overcomes obstacles or opposition; strengthens the constitution; safeguards travellers and property.

The Moon

The Moon generally rules over domesticity, emotional responses, fluidity, inspiration, instinct and sensitivity. It also rules over feeling and rhythm. It relates to antiques, commitment, inevitability, introspection, isolation, karma, maturity, mining, morality, property management, social welfare and tenacity.

Chalcedony attracts public favour, recognition and financial reward; increases popularity, enthusiasm and fitness; dispels gloom, despondency, envy or anger; affords protection to travellers and helps nursing mothers.

Feldspar (also felspar) strengthens bonds of affection and promotes marital happiness; it is associated with fertility; mitigates quarrels and poor situations; protects from sunstrokes, headaches and nosebleeds.

Flint expands consciousness and prompts prophetic dreams; improves memory and heightens intellectual capacity. It also helps ward off physical danger, dispels melancholy and aids union between children and parents.

Gypsum signifies hope and youthfulness, and benefits children and adults wanting to 'go it alone'. It reduces swellings and aids digestion; averts the envy of others; and brings peace of mind.

Labradorite brings prophetic visions and expands consciousness; promotes harmonious relationships; dispels anxiety, enmity and strife; gives relief from nervous disorders.

Magnesite clarifies vision, both literally and figuratively; improves profitability and wins admiration and respect; provides freedom from adversity; aids digestion and releases emotional stress.

Moonstone affords vitality and fertility; awards success to artistic and creative efforts and new commercial projects; heals relationship rifts; protects crops; aids digestion and concentration.

Morganite induces love, devotion and friendship; promises career advancement or improved financial viability; reconciles difference of opinion and dispels anger; offers safety to travellers in any dimension.

Pearl rewards charitable deeds and selfless actions with love and respect; promotes harmony and understanding; protects those travelling over water; eases muscular tension and lifts depression.

Pumice is linked with purity, vision, truth and development. It helps sociability and personal gain; bestows success on long-term ventures; guards against illusion and delusion; brings comfort to a troubled mind or spirit.

Rock crystal represents purity, hope and chastity; expands conscious awareness and prophetic visions; brings trust and harmony; dispels bad dreams, delusion and illusion; safeguards the very young and astral travellers from harm.

Mercury

Mercury rules communication, healing, hyper-activity, the intellect, shrewdness and versatility. It relates to accountancy, curiosity, impressionism, invention, land or air travel, language, learning, mathematics, the media, public speaking, publishing of all types, vehicles and wit.

Agate promotes good health and fortune; increases physical stamina and brings benefits through wills or legacies; repels anger, mistrust and enmity; affords protection against rumour and gossip.

Chrysoprase brings joy to the wearer; sharpens the intellect, opens up new areas and rewards initiative; gets rid of envy, jealousy and complacency; dispels anxiety, lifts depression and helps insomnia.

Onyx looks after business shrewdness; vitalizes the imagination and increases stamina; dispels nightmares and eases tension; brings emotional and mental relief.

Sardonyx inspires love, romance and vitality; helps confidence and fitness; ensures a result in contractual difficulties; wards off infectious disease; improves vision; heals fragile relationships.

Serpentine attracts respect and admiration; sharpens the intellect; rewards innovation and creativity; offers the wearer protection from hostility, jealousy or rivalry; improves the effect of medicine.

Tiger's eye defeats the opponent and ensures victory in any competitive situation; commands love and loyalty; offers protection from treachery and deception; strengthens the body's immune system.

Venus

Venus correlates to harmony, growth and development as well as love and marriage. It also extends to aesthetics, the affections, dance and music, fashion, femininity, materialism, personal finances, pleasure, relationships, sexuality and union.

Almandine is linked with achievement, improvement, self-confidence and determination. It enhances psychic ability; makes clear existing problems or difficulties; overcomes rivalry and obstacles in the form of human behaviour.

Aquamarine encourages hope, and promotes youthfulness and physical fitness. It is a powerful token of love and friendship; eases digestive or nervous disorders and mental distress; renews confidence and energy; relaxes fear.

Azurite commands social success and friendship as well as constancy in love; improves vision, both physically and psychically; protects from deceit and disillusion; affords help to those faced with generative difficulties.

Beryl represents hope, friendship, and domestic harmony; sharpens the intellect and favours new commercial projects; clarifies and resolves problems; reduces susceptibility to deception or disillusionment.

Cat's eye encourages success in speculative ventures or competitive sport; strengthens ties of love or affection; protects the home from danger; brings relief to those with respiratory problems.

Coral helps vitality, good humour and harmonious relationships; expands horizons and helps encourage development; prevents damage to crops and property; protects travellers, mariners and small children.

Emerald favours love and lovers, promising constancy and fidelity; inspires confidence and emotional fulfilment; strongly protective, especially against deceit or delusions; ensures safety of travellers and expectant mothers.

Jade promotes good health and good situations; favours artistic and musical endeavours; dulls pain and helps soundness of sleep; also improves a poor memory; and is strongly protective.

Lapis lazuli inspires confidence, courage and friendship. It helps the wearer to succeed, anywhere; averts danger and preserves travellers and expectant mothers from harm; eases circulation problems.

Malachite wins favourable judgements in law-suits or actions; enhances social standing and increases prosperity; lifts depression, induces sound sleep and serenity; affords protection against infection.

Opal signifies fidelity and friendship; highlights psychic and prophetic talents; stimulates memory and intellect; and improves vision, digestion and resistance to stress. It also safeguards property against theft.

Rose quartz enhances psychic awareness and creative talents; sharpens intellect; preserves the home and family; heals rifts; brings peace of mind and understanding.

Turquoise inspires health, wealth and happiness; affords a successful conclusion to any constructive enterprise; counteracts negative influences; wards off harmful psychic or physical harm.

Mars

Mars symbolizes competition and confrontation, determination, focus and masculinity. It is also related to an adventurous spirit, the armed forces, courage, engineering, the fire service, forcefulness, male sexuality, metalwork, speed of reactions and sports.

Bauxite enlivens the personality and strengthens the will to succeed; it encourages wise investment and fruitful speculation; lifts flagging spirits and speeds recovery from illness; negates strife and reconciles parted lovers.

Bloodstone promotes eloquence, trust, loyalty, and devotion; boosts courage, vitality and the ability to earn money; heals discord; relieves digestive orders or stress and strengthens recuperative powers.

Carbuncle increases energy, determination and confidence; boosts income and social standing; maintains physical fitness and fights infection; reconciles differences between friends.

Haematite promotes successful legal action and official contracts; increases sexual drive and fitness; helps overcome nervousness and irritability; improves circulation.

Jasper helps in psychic development; inspires confidence, friendship and loyalty; defends home and family; inhibits unwanted pregnancy.

Magnetite prompts respect of others, loyalty and devotion; increases stamina and virility; promises success and happiness; brings relief from stressful situations; helps speed recovery from illness or depression.

Ruby highlights vitality and virility, bringing pleasure and prosperity; it is good for property development; protects crops and offers security to descendants; dispels strife and dissent.

Jupiter

Jupiter covers charity, majesty, mental and physical searching, might and wisdom. It also covers friendships, good judgement, knowledge and understanding, legal matters, philosophy, theosophy, travelling abroad and any other long journeys.

Alexandrite refreshes the body and mind, and brings hidden talents to the fore. It is strongly protective especially against deceit or treachery; it awards relief from imaginary fears or phobias.

Blue John attracts honours, wealth, prestige and social success; improves business and personal relationships; guards the wearer against injury or accident while travelling; mitigates the envy of others.

Calomine favours visionary and human undertakings; affords success to joint ventures, especially overseas; deflates skin and fever irritation; dispels parental anxiety and helps with uneasy consciences.

Carnelian helps with peace, pleasure and prosperity; brings joy to those going on a long journey or moving house; offers protection to travellers, speakers and expectant mothers; assuages strife, anger and disappointment.

Obsidian encourages boldness, determination and vigour; overwhelms opposition and promotes personal achievement; is strongly protective against psychic attack, accident or injury; and strengthens weakened spirits or tiredness of the body.

Sapphire affords good health, strength and efficiency; heightens perception and rewards commercial and social efforts; is strongly protective against antagonism and malice; effects reconciliation between lovers.

Spinel enhances speculative powers and creativity. It rewards efforts made towards financial prosperity and social prestige; guards against psychic attack, mental stress and emotional blackmail; ensures safety for travellers.

Enhancing Communication

Here is a simple way to use one of the stones ruled by Jupiter in a particularly modern way, at the same time also appealing to the gods of communication. This is an example of combining several energies for one purpose.

The crystal carnelian can be used when you want – or need – to be heard. It is also an excellent stone to wear or carry when you need to speak in public for it strengthens the voice, provides self-confidence and confers eloquence on the speaker. It is used to counteract doubt and negative thoughts and is employed in this spell for that purpose.

YOU WILL NEED ————————————

A small piece of carnelian
An incense such as benzoin which is sacred to Mercury, Roman god of communication

METHOD ————————————————

✤ The night before you are due to speak light your incense.
✤ Hold the carnelian in the smoke of the incense.
✤ Say:

> *Mercury, Ogmios, Heracles*
> *Gods of eloquence and right speech*
> *Help me tomorrow to say the right thing*
> *To make myself heard.*

✤ Sleep with the carnelian under your pillow, as one of its properties is to prevent nightmares.
✤ The next day either have the piece of carnelian discreetly in front of you where you can see it or in your pocket where you can easily reach it.

✤ When stuck for words or in difficulty, either touch the stone or mentally make a link with it which will enable you to overcome the blockage.

Simply having something else to focus on in such a situation is good anyway, but having appealed to the gods, you draw on the very source of communication and on the qualities of the crystal. Remember to thank the gods – who are from three different cultures – afterwards. You may need their help again.

Saturn

Saturn signifies concentration, conversation, destiny, experience and perseverance. It relates to agriculture, antiques, career status, economy, karma, isolation, tenacity, maturity, mining, morality and social welfare.

Alabaster brings success in litigation, official and contractual disputes, and wins respect, recognition and reward. It heals rifts; offers protection against loss of status; and inhibits disease.

Alunite attracts good fortune, health and happiness; helps understanding and domestic harmony; speeds recovery from illness; protects home and property against physical and psychic danger.

Borax inspires confidence, perseverance and determination; it helps to make bad situations good; overcomes fear and hesitation and self doubt; improves circulation and offers relief from migraine, indigestion and/or gout.

Garnet helps with devotion, humour and loyalty; increases drive and determination and physical fitness; wards off thunder and lightning and protects travellers from injury or contagious disease.

Granite wins friendship and fortune; helps with confidence, particularly in the area of examination sitting or employment; eases depression; resolves conflict and helps find practical solutions to current problems.

Jet strengthens determination and focus; affords success to those heading into business; eases childbirth and dispels fever; offers protection against gossip and harmful actions.

Marble improves financial position and status in the community; commands respect and admiration; relieves headaches, and stress; preserves home and property from fire, flood and storms.

Meerschaum benefits philanthropic ventures and investment; favours those working in big organizations; clarifies problems and provides practical solutions; relieves anxiety, depression and nervousness.

Scheelite highlights diplomacy, business acumen and self-assurance; promises commercial and domestic happiness; alleviates strife and envy; is handy for nervous disorders and nursing mothers.

Sulphur highlights clear expression and physical fitness; rewards professional acumen with public acclaim; is powerful against malice; purifies the blood and relieves menstrual tension.

Crystals can have many uses and the spell below uses their power to enhance a healing technique. When you eventually know your planetary correspondences well, you can use the above crystals for many purposes.

A Crystal Healing Spell

This spell is used in this instance to charge (energize) water for healing. You can drink the water or juice, or use the former in your bath. By using planetary significances you can see how many aspects of your magical working might be enhanced.

YOU WILL NEED

A crystal appropriate for your needs (in this case it would be for healing, although if you use the crystal for another purpose, you would obviously choose an appropriate crystal for that use)
A glass of water or fruit juice

METHOD

❖ Place the crystal in the glass of water or juice overnight, or for 24 hours if you want a balance of solar and lunar energies

❖ After removing the crystal, drink the water or juice and visualize its energy flowing through you.

❖ You can use the crystal again for the same purpose.

❖ Repeat whenever you feel necessary.

❖ If you choose to use the water in your bath, you may like to dedicate the bath for its specific purpose by simply saying:

I dedicate this bath to the healing of [state difficulty]

❖ Since in this case the crystal has been used in liquid, you may need to recharge it, in which case bury it in earth in a safe place until you need it again.

This technique uses the power of the crystal, but in returning it to the earth you are acknowledging the power of Mother Earth, as well as the Elements.

One way of using crystals is to keep an assortment of small ones in a special talisman bag. The simplest method of use is to shake the bag, and while focusing on the question to be asked, take out the first two or three that you touch. See if the answer comes spontaneously to mind, before you consult the lists above or below for correspondences.

You can also cast your crystals into a specially drawn circle, the first crystal drawn being the crystal of Self, the second the crystal of others and the third being the crystal of happiness to come. Boards on to which crystals are thrown are available from specialist shops and have proved useful for many people. More complex questions can be answered and guidance for the future gained by using crystals with any suitable Tarot spread.

The associations of some of the more common crystals are as follows:

Agate	Success in worldly matters
Amethyst	Shifts in consciousness and life changes
Black agate	Prosperity and courage
Red agate	Longevity and good health
Aventurine	Growth and expansion
Blue lace agate	A need for healing
Citrine	Wisdom in celestial matters
Diamond	Permanence
Emerald	Fertility

Jade	Immortality and perfection
Red jasper	Worldly affairs
Lapis lazuli	Favoured by the divine
Clear quartz	Self-healing and love
Ruby	Passion and power
Sapphire	Chastity and truth
Snowflake obsidian	Closure of a challenging time
Tiger's eye	The need to look beneath the surface
White quartz	Change of a profound nature
Unakite	Integration and composure

Enhancing your magic

Crystals and stones are gifts from nature and as mentioned above can also be used to enhance your rituals and magic. They can become sacred, magical tools in their own right. When consecrating a circle, creating your sacred space or making a shrine, you may like to search out stones which can represent the Elements, so here are a few suggestions:

Air

When looking for stones to represent Air, you need to think of crystal-clear stones or yellowish-tinged ones. A quartz crystal point can often be picked up quite cheaply and, of course, it does not matter if it is flawed because, with a little imagination, these flaws can often look like clouds. Quartz pebbles are often found on the seashore, weathered by the water.

Fire

Stones to represent Fire should be red or orange or sometimes black. Any stone which has the feeling of passion or fiery emotion will do very well – carnelian or red jasper work particularly well. Volcanic rocks, or other very hard ones, often signify Fire since they are the outcome of fire from the earth.

Water

Blue or blue-green stones are good if you wish to represent Water and if you are near the sea you might find a piece of salt or sand-blasted glass, which is ideal. Although glass is man-made, nature has done its work. White or greyish pebble stones actually found in water are also very useful, while a piece of stone with seaweed attached is also good. Some agates are very pretty and can echo wave patterns.

Earth

The colours for Earth are green and brown, and many of the stones associated with Earth are green as well. All stones are the product of Earth so almost any stone will do, particularly if you have got to know it as suggested above. Use it wisely and it will always repay you. Remember that you do not need polished stones for this – the more natural they are the better.

Spirit

Most clear crystals can be used to represent the fifth Element of aether, or Spirit, as can the purple-hued ones. Amethyst is particularly good, as it is both a transmitter and a receiver of psychic and spiritual energy. Mostly, those stones which are capable of representing spirit will 'speak' to you and if you choose more than one you will have to use your intuition so that you choose the right one for your purpose.

Preparing a crystal circle

If you wish to use stones and crystals when laying out your circle or sacred space, you can use a mixture of both. You might mark each quarter with a large stone, particularly if you are outside, and then place other appropriate stones on top. Even if you use candles to mark the four quarters of the circle, you could surround or circle each candle with any or all of the following gems, either rough or polished:

North:	moss agate, emerald, jet, olivine, salt, black tourmaline
East:	imperial topaz, citrine, mica, pumice
South:	amber, obsidian, rhodochrosite, ruby, lava, garnet
West:	aquamarine, chalcedony, jade, lapis lazuli, moonstone, sugilite

Over time, gather a number of appropriate stones together. Beginning and ending in the

Principles and Components

north, lay out 7, 9, 21 or 40 stones of any size to define your circle. (These are magical numbers and will enhance the power, so always bear in mind the purpose of your circle.) If you normally use ribbon or cord to mark out your circle, your stones can be placed either inside the cord or ribbon or in place of it.

If the magical working to be conducted within the circle is sending the power outwards, place any crystal with definite points facing outward. If the magic is of a protective nature, place them with points facing inward.

Use your good sense when constructing your circle. If it is outdoors, somewhere you use often and think of as your sacred space, you may wish to leave the larger stones in position and carry the smaller gems with you. This way, no matter where you are, you can mark out a circle with the small stones and have available the power and energy of the larger space available to you.

The subtle energies of crystals

Crystals have their own inherent energy, which means that it is very simple to use them as protective or energizing objects. This in ancient times would have made them amulets (see the Antler Charm spell on page 12). However, if you are going to use stones and crystals magically, you have to use some kind of technique to 'wake them up' so that you can use their more subtle energies successfully. It could be said they need to be reminded of their power.

There are many ways of awakening – reactivating – crystals, perhaps sounding prayer or other bells or wind chimes near to the crystal. This aligns the energy of the crystal structure so it can be efficiently directed.

The Breastplate of Judgement spoken of in the Bible uses this principle of subtle energies. It was said to have four rows of three gems set in gold. Different versions are given in different bibles. The New International Version, for instance, states that the gems are ruby, topaz, beryl, turquoise, sapphire, emerald, jacinth, agate, amethyst, chrysolite, onyx and jasper. Initially, the gems were said to represent the twelve tribes of Israel but they now signify various aspects of personality and may be worn to enhance your magic.

Many precious and semi-precious stones were used by the ancient Egyptians in their magic-making. The best known were amethyst (for its spiritual qualities) carnelian (which symbolized energy, dynamism and power) and the most highly prized of Egyptian semi-precious stones, lapis lazuli, representing the all-embracing night sky. The red and green forms of jasper were thought to give very positive energies, while sard – a reddish-brown version of chalcedony (silicon dioxide) – was used to fashion scarab amulets. Feldspar was another stone considered to be extremely precious and was used in jewellery connected with fertility. Serpentine, dark green (almost black) and easily carved, was used to fashion heart amulets. Turquoise was also used symbolically to denote vegetation and new life.

The body is an extremely sensitive instrument and in some senses the magical practitioner uses it as simply another tool in their workings. Traditionally, the main nerve ganglions (groups of nerve fibres) in the physical body have their counterpart within the more subtle energy field, which is our spiritual self. When working magically you have a responsibility to keep your aura (subtle body) as clear and as healthy as possible. One of the ways in which you can do this is to use crystals to help with that internal balance. When you know you are under pressure or are going to be doing a particular type of spell, it is very easy to pop a particular crystal into your charm or amulet bag in order to enhance the energy.

You can see that sacred spaces and other places where you choose to work magically can be enhanced in many ways. Crystals are only one way of doing so, and using herbs, once you know enough about them, is another. Remember the principle that using both will enhance the power four-fold.

HERBS

Most magical practices make use of herbs in various ways, usually in rituals and other magical workings. Often they are used as incense, when they are crushed and powdered, or as oils. Their properties mean that they create a type of force field that intensifies the vibration needed. Additionally, when the practitioner calls upon the power of the gods and spirits, the herbs become even more effective.

In ancient times, the duality between positive and negative, active and passive and, by association, masculine and feminine was important in understanding the type of energy that a plant had. In magical terms, plants are categorized as masculine or feminine in order to reflect that division. It was felt that each plant was looked after or ruled by the gods and goddesses and, because the planets represented the deities through their association with astrology, each plant could be recognized through that rulership.

Each plant's energies also belonged to one of the Elements. The four Elements (Earth, Air, Fire and Water) are the building blocks of the universe and are found in all things in varying amounts. The ruling Element in anything is the most important part in its make-up. Herbs and plants in their simplicity can be allocated to a single Element. Each deity has its own particular qualities, so where a plant is dedicated to that deity, those attributes are recognized. You can see that the more knowledge you have of these things, in some ways the more complex your working becomes. In fact, having the knowledge actually makes your spell working easier, because it enables you to be completely specific.

When man chose to remember and make use of these very subtle energies, he found that his magical workings were enhanced. He called upon the 'powers' from several different viewpoints which, when combined, meant that he was making use of a very holistic energy. It might be said that man was calling upon the salesman, the sales director and the managing director of energy.

From our perspective, we can rely on the knowledge of the ancients to help us also make the right connections. We, perhaps more than ever, need to make contact with the subtle spiritual energy levels. To put it another way: through the plant we make a connection with its spirit and so therefore with the greater spiritual realms that stand behind the whole of existence. To expand further, masculine herbs are those with strong fiery vibrations, feminine herbs are softer in their effect, quiet and subtle.

You can see from this that, when using herbs and plants, you need to think very carefully about your ritual or spell.

Simply having particular herbs in your sacred space or having them about your person is sufficient to begin the process of enhancing the area or your personal vibration. You can use them in incense and dedicate them to the appropriate Elements and deities. Many of the herbs mentioned can be obtained from a good herbalist, though for those of you who are truly interested it would be worth while creating a small herb garden or growing them on your windowsill.

The uses of herbs

Protection

Such herbs guard against physical and psychic attacks, injury, accidents and such things as wicked spirits. They usually offer protection in a general sort of way.

Love

The vibration of these herbs is such that they can help you to meet new people, to overcome shyness and let others know that you are open to new relationships. They put out a particular vibration so that those who are interested will answer the call. The safest way to use them is to accept that several people may be attracted to you and you will then be able to make an informed choice.

Fidelity

Some herbs and plants can by tradition be used to ensure fidelity. You do have to have a firm belief that you have a right to another's devotion before imposing your will on them. Using a spell for fidelity amounts to a binding spell and you must make allowances for the person's own integrity. It should always be remembered that it is unwise, and sometimes unhelpful, to both parties to hold anyone in a relationship against their will.

Healing

Many herbs have healing properties, which can help from both a physical and a magical viewpoint. A practitioner working from both points of view can be of tremendous help in managing illness. However, always remember to advise anyone you work with in this way to seek qualified medical assistance. Never allow yourself to be drawn into being a substitute for medical help.

Health

Not only the smell of herbs and plants but also their vibration can help to prevent illness and restore good health. So, if you are prone to illness, carry health herbs with you and make sure they are always as fresh as possible.

Luck

Luck is the knack of being in the right place at the right time and being able to act on instinct. Luck herbs help you create your own good fortune. Once you have such a foundation, you can build upon it.

Money

It is sometimes easier to visualize the outcome of having money – that is, what you are going to spend the money on – than visualizing actual money coming to you. Certain herbs create an environment in which things can happen. They enable the creation of the means to fulfil your needs – perhaps a gift, a pay rise or some such thing.

There are two listings given in this section. The first acts as a kind of quick reference point for you and is divided into uses. The second goes into more detail, giving the gender of the plant, which planet it is ruled by and its Element. This second list is particularly useful because, as you become more knowledgeable, you will want to be more specific in your choices.

Attracting men: Jasmine, juniper (dried berries worn as a charm), lavender, lemon verbena, lovage, orris root, patchouli
Attracting women: Henbane, holly, juniper (dried berries worn as a charm), lemon verbena, lovage, orris root, patchouli
Banishing: Hyssop, lilac, St John's Wort
Cleansing: Cinnamon, clove, lovage (powdered root), pine, thyme (in baths), vervain (of sacred spaces)
Courage: Basil, garlic, mullein, nettle, St John's Wort, thyme, wormwood, yarrow
Exorcism: Angelica, basil, birch, frankincense, juniper, garlic, St John's Wort
Fertility: Acorns, geranium, hawthorn, mandrake, orange (dried and powdered peel), pine, poppy, sage, sunflower (seeds)
Friendship: Lemon, rose, passionflower
Good fortune: Ash (leaves), heather, nutmeg, rose, vetivert
Happiness: Anise, catnip, lily of the valley, marjoram, saffron
Harmony: Hyacinth, heliotrope, lilac, meadowsweet
Healing: Aloe, ash, camomile, cinnamon, comfrey, eucalyptus, fennel, garlic, hops, marjoram, mint, nettle, pine, rosemary, saffron, sage, sandalwood, thyme, yarrow
Hex-breaking: Chilli pepper, galangal, vertivert
Love: Apple, Balm of Gilead, basil, caraway, catnip, coriander, cowslip, dill, gardenia, ginger, ginseng, honeysuckle, jasmine, lavender, linden, marigold, marjoram, meadowsweet, mistletoe, myrtle, rose, rosemary, valerian, vervain, violet (mixed with lavender), yarrow
Luck: Apple, ash (leaves), hazel, holly (for newly-weds), ivy (for newly-weds), mint, rose, rowan, vervain, violet (flowers)
Lust: Cinnamon, lemongrass, nettle, rosemary, violet
Meditation: Camomile, elecampane, frankincense, vervain
Mental powers: Caraway, lily of the valley, rosemary, vanilla, walnut
Money: Camomile, cinnamon, clove, comfrey, fennel, ginger, mint, poppy, vervain
Peace: Aloe, camomile, gardenia, lavender, myrtle, violet
Power: Carnation, cinnamon, ginger, rosemary, rowan
Prosperity: Acorn, almond, ash, basil, benzoin, honeysuckle
Note: There are so many herbs suitable for the next three categories and the choice is such a personal one that only a few suggestions are included. Your own further research will very much enhance your magical workings.
Protection: Aloe, angelica (root), anise, Balm of Gilead, basil, bay laurel, black pepper,

caraway, camomile, dill (for children), dragon's blood, fennel, garlic, hawthorn, holly, hyssop, lavender, mandrake, meadowsweet, mistletoe, mugwort, nettle, periwinkle, rose, rosemary, rowan, sage, St John's Wort, sandalwood, vervain, witch hazel, wormwood

Psychic powers: Ash (leaves), bay laurel, bay leaves, cinnamon, cowslip, elecampane, eyebright, hyssop, lavender, marigold, mugwort, nutmeg, rose, thyme, wormwood, yarrow

Purification: Anise, betony, cinquefoil, dragon's blood, frankincense, hyssop, lavender, lemon, oak leaves, pine, rosemary, rue, sandalwood, thyme, valerian, vervain

Success: Cinnamon, ginger, lemon balm, rowan

Sleep: Catnip, hops, lavender, thyme, valerian, vervain

Spirituality: Cinnamon, clover, frankincense, myrrh, sandalwood

Wisdom: Peach (fruit), sage, sunflower

The A–Z of Magical Plants

Aloe is feminine and ruled by the Moon. Its Element is Water. Its magical properties are protection, success and peace. Aloe has always been known for its healing qualities, for treating wounds and maintaining healthy skin. It helps to combat a variety of bacteria that commonly cause infections in skin wounds.

Amaranth (cockscomb) is feminine and ruled by Saturn. Its Element is Fire. When used magically, it is said to repair a broken heart, so therefore would be useful in certain love spells and rituals. Formerly it was reputed to bestow invisibility.

Angelica is a masculine plant ruled by Venus. Its Element is Fire. It is particularly useful when dealing with protection and exorcism; the root can be carried as an amulet with the dried leaves being burnt during exorcism rituals.

Anise is masculine and ruled by the Moon or Jupiter. Its Element is Air. Its magical properties are useful in protection and purification spells. It brings awareness and joy.

Apple is feminine and ruled by Venus. Its Element is Water. It is used most effectively in the making of magical wands, in love spells and good luck charms.

Ash is masculine and ruled by the Sun. Its Element is Water. Its uses are protective and it is often chosen as a material for making brooms for cleansing and wands for healing. If the leaves are put underneath a pillow, they will help to induce intuitive dreams. The leaves also bring luck and good fortune when carried in a pocket or bag worn around the neck.

Balm of Gilead is feminine and ruled by Saturn. Its Element is Water. The buds are carried to ease a broken heart and can be added to love and protection charms and spells.

Basil, one of the most masculine of plants, is ruled by Mars and has Fire as its Element. It is protective, good for love and is said to promote wealth and business success. It is also useful for healing relationships and for assuring genuineness in a partner.

Basil for Business

Many Hindu families keep a tulsi or Holy Basil plant in a specially-built structure, which has images of deities installed on all four sides, with an alcove for a small earthenware oil lamp. Here basil is used very simply to enhance business matters. Just how widely it is used throughout the world is shown by the use of the second technique, which is said to ensure that you will always be prosperous. This latter technique owes a great deal to voodoo and the technique of floor washing.

YOU WILL NEED ───────────────

Basil seeds and plant
Pots containing compost
Small oil lamp

METHOD ──────────────────

❖ Place the pot and plants where they can be safely left.
❖ Carefully nurture the seeds to maturity.
❖ Whenever practical, light the oil lamp and keep it burning. This action honours the goddess Tulsi who fell in love with Krishna and calls upon her beneficence.

Note: Mature leaves can be used for this next technique. The resulting decoction is said to attract clients and prevent theft.

YOU WILL NEED

Glass jar or metal container
Handful of basil leaves
One pint of boiling water

METHOD

✤ Shred the basil leaves into the container.
✤ Pour the boiling water over the leaves.
✤ Allow to steep for four days.
✤ Strain out the leaves and reserve the remaining liquid.
✤ Sprinkle the liquid over the thresholds and windowsills of the business premises and anywhere else the public is likely to go.

You may also choose to work according to feng shui principles (see the Pa Kua diagram on page 16) and place the plants in the prosperity area. The nurturing of the seeds obviously has significant symbolism in the growing of the business, so it is good to have plants in various stages of development. As you can see, this spell uses information gained from several cultures, showing how universal herbal magic can truly be.

Bay laurel is a masculine plant ruled by the Sun and the Element of Fire. It promotes wisdom and is also a protector, bringing to the fore the ability to develop psychic powers. It forces out negative energy.

Benzoin is a masculine plant that the Sun rules, along with the Element of Air. A good purifier and preservative, it is used widely in purification incenses.

Betony is masculine and is ruled by Jupiter and the Element of Fire. Its magical properties are protection and purification. It can be added to incense for this purpose or stuffed in a pillow to prevent nightmares.

Caraway is a masculine plant ruled by the planet of Mercury. Its Element is Air. Its magical properties are protection and passion. When added to love sachets and charms, it attracts a lover in the more physical aspect.

Carnation is masculine and is ruled by the Sun. Its Element is Fire. Traditionally, it was worn by witches for protection during times of persecution. It adds energy and power when used as an incense during a ritual.

Catnip is feminine and is ruled by Venus. Its Element is Water. Its magical properties are connected with cat magic, familiars, joy, friendship and love. As an incense it may be used to consecrate magical tools.

Camomile is masculine, and is ruled by the Sun or Venus. Its Element is Water. Its magical properties show that it is good as a meditation incense, for centring and creating an atmosphere of peace. Sprinkle it in your home for protection, healing and money. Plant camomile in your garden to be the guardian of the land, and you will have certain success. It is an excellent calming herb.

Celandine is masculine and is ruled by the Sun. Its Element is Fire. When worn as an amulet it helps the wearer to escape unfair imprisonment and entrapment. It alleviates depression.

Cinquefoil is masculine and is ruled by Jupiter. Its Element is Earth. Hang it around your doors and windows to protect you from evil. It is used in spells and charms for prosperity, purification and protection.

Cinnamon is masculine and is ruled by the Sun. Its Element is Fire. Its magical properties are used to help in spiritual quests, augmenting power, love, success, psychic work, healing and cleansing. It is used in incense for healing, clairvoyance and high spiritual vibrations; it is also reputed to be a male aphrodisiac. Use it in prosperity charms. It is an excellent aromatic and makes a good anointing oil for any magical working.

Clove is masculine and is ruled by the Sun. Its Element is Fire. Wear it in an amulet or charm to dispel negativity and bind those who speak ill of you. Cloves strung on a red thread can be worn as a protective charm. It helps with money matters, visions, cleansing and purification.

Clover is masculine and is ruled by Mercury; it is also associated with the Triple Goddess. Its Element is Air. Use it in rituals for beauty, youth, healing injuries, and helping alleviate mental difficulties. A four-leaved clover is said to enable one to see fairies and is considered a general good-luck charm.

Comfrey is a feminine plant and is ruled by Saturn. Its Element is Water. It is useful for travel, casting spells for money and healing. It also honours the Crone aspect of the Goddess.

Coriander is masculine and is ruled by Mars and

the Element Fire. It is a protector of the home and is useful in the promotion of peace. It encourages longevity and is helpful in love spells.

Cowslip is feminine, ruled by Venus with its Element Water. Said to bring luck in love, it also induces contact with departed loved ones during dreams. A woman who washes her face with milk infused with cowslip will draw her beloved closer to her.

Cypress is masculine and is ruled by Saturn and its Element Earth. It is connected with death. Often used to consecrate ritual tools, cypress also has preservative qualities.

Daisy is feminine and is ruled by Venus and the Element Water. If you decorate your house with it on Midsummer's Eve, it will bring happiness into the home. Daisies are also worn at Midsummer for luck and blessings. Long ago, young maidens would weave daisy chains and wear them in their hair to attract their beloved.

Dandelion is masculine plant and is ruled by Jupiter and the Element Air. It is useful for divination and communication.

Dill is masculine and is ruled by Mercury. Its Element is Fire. It is useful in love charms. Dill may also be hung in children's rooms to protect them against evil spirits and bad dreams.

Dragon's blood is masculine, and is ruled by Mars with the Element Fire. A type of palm, it is widely included in love, protection and purification spells, usually in the form of a resin. It is carried for good luck; a piece of the plant kept under the bed is said to cure impotency. Dragon's blood increases the potency of other incense.

Elder is a feminine plant ruled by Venus and the Element Air. Its branches are widely used for magical wands and it is considered bad luck to burn elder wood. Leaves hung around the doors and windows are said to ward off evil.

Elecampane is a masculine plant ruled by Mercury and the Element Earth. It is a good aid in meditation and for requesting the presence of spirits.

Eucalyptus is feminine and is ruled by the Moon and the Element Air. It is used in healing rituals and in charms and amulets. If the leaves are put around a blue candle and burnt, this is good for increasing healing energies.

Eyebright is masculine and is ruled by the Sun. Its Element is Air. This plant is said to induce clairvoyant visions and dreams if you anoint the eyelids daily with an infusion of leaves.

Fennel is masculine and is ruled by Mercury. Its Element is Fire. Including the seeds in money charms is said to bring prosperity and ward off evil spirits. The plant itself is used for purification and protection.

Fern is feminine and is ruled by the planet Saturn and the Element Earth. This plant is a powerful protector and if grown near your home will ward off negativity.

Frankincense is a masculine herb under the rulership of the Sun and therefore the Element of Fire. A purifier of ritual spaces, it is probably the most powerful aid to meditation there is.

Gardenia is feminine and is ruled by the Moon with its Element Water. Used extensively in Moon incenses, it attracts good spirits to rituals and enhances the love vibration.

Garlic is a masculine herb ruled by the planet Mars and consequently the Element of Fire. It protects and is a useful healer and promoter of courage.

Ginger is a masculine herb ruled by Mars and Fire. It encourages power and success, especially in love and financial dealings. It is also a good base for spells because it enhances the vibration.

Ginseng is masculine, ruled by the Sun with the Element of Fire. It aids love and lust and is useful in enhancing beauty. It is also a good reliever of stress.

Hawthorn is masculine, ruled by Mars and the Element of Fire. It is used in protective sachets. It can enforce celibacy and chastity and is said to promote happiness in marriage or other relationships.

Hazel is masculine and ruled by the Sun and the Element of Air. It is a very good wood for magical wands and is the only wood that should be used for divining. It also promotes good luck, particularly when it is bound by red and gold thread.

Heartsease is feminine, ruled by Saturn and the Element of Water. It is actually a wild pansy and demonstrates its power by its name. If you can find any then it can be used iwith other herbs to ease the pain of a broken relationship.

Herbal Heartsease

Broken relationships are extremely painful and the hurt often needs to be dealt with very quickly. This spell, using three different techniques, helps to keep things under control until you can look forward in a positive fashion.

Cleansing bath

YOU WILL NEED

Handful of either heartsease, or/and jasmine, roses, hibiscus and honeysuckle flowers
Essential oils in any of these perfumes
Rose quartz

METHOD

✤ Add the herbs to the bath along with the essential oils.
✤ Place the rose quartz in the bath.
✤ Soak in the bath for at least ten minutes allowing the hurt to be dissolved.
✤ Remove the rose quartz.
✤ Take the plug half out, so the water begins to drain away.
✤ As it does so, replace with fresh water to signify new energy coming into your life.
✤ Carry the rose quartz with you or keep it under your pillow.

Healing sachet

YOU WILL NEED

Two 10 cm squares of red or white material
Needle with pink thread
Herbs as above
Small piece of rose or clear quartz
Small quantity of dried beans for banishment

METHOD

✤ Make a sachet by sewing together three sides of the material with the pink thread
✤ Fill the sachet with the herbs, quartz and beans, then sew up the final side.
✤ As you do so, know that the pain will pass.
✤ Hang the sachet in a prominent position so that you can feel its healing vibration.

Healing face wash

YOU WILL NEED

Herbs as above

Boiling water
Heatproof bowl (clear glass if possible)
Glass bottle

METHOD

✤ Infuse the herbs by pouring boiling water over them into the bowl and allowing the resultant liquid to cool.
✤ If you wish, allow it to stand overnight in moonlight to absorb the power the Moon gives us.
✤ Decant the liquid into a clean bottle and use as a face wash on cotton wool or tissue.
✤ As you do so, remind yourself that you are lovable and will heal from this hurt.

At one and the same time, these techniques are gentle in their action and also offer support on an emotional level. Working in three ways, they allow body, mind and spirit to be relaxed and at peace.

Holly is masculine and is ruled by Mars and its Element of Fire. When planted around the home it protects against evil. Holly water is said to protect babies, and when thrown at wild animals it calms them down. The leaves and berries can be carried as an amulet by a man to heighten his masculinity and virility, enabling him to attract a lover.

Honeysuckle is feminine and is ruled by Jupiter and its Element Earth. Planted outside the home it brings good luck. It is also used in prosperity spells and love charms, and to heighten psychic ability.

Hops, a masculine plant ruled by Mars and the Element of Water, is best used in healing and for aiding sleep.

Hyssop is masculine. Its ruler is Jupiter and its Element of Fire. The plant was widely used during the Middle Ages for purification, cleansing and consecration rituals. Use it in purification baths, and for protective and banishing spells. Hyssop works best in the form of an essential oil in incense.

Ivy is a masculine plant, ruled by Saturn and its Element Water. It protects the houses it grows on from evil and harm. In the old traditions, ivy and holly were given to newly-weds as good-luck charms.

Jasmine is feminine and is ruled by Jupiter and

the Element Earth. It attracts men and has been used throughout history by women for this purpose.

Juniper is a masculine plant, ruled by the Sun and its Element Fire. It gives protection against accidents, harm and theft. Once they have been dried and worn as a charm, the berries are used to attract lovers. Juniper also breaks hexes and curses.

Lavender is a masculine plant ruled by Mercury and the Element of Air. It is one of the most useful herbs and can be used for healing, promoting good wishes and sleep; it can also be used to attract men.

Lemon balm is feminine and is ruled by the Moon or Neptune. Its Element is Water. It is a strong aphrodisiac, promotes fertility but is also an anti-depressant that is especially useful at the end of a relationship.

Lemon verbena is feminine, ruled by Venus and the Element Air. It is used in love charms to promote youth, beauty and attractiveness to the opposite sex. Wear it around your neck or place it under a pillow to prevent bad dreams. It helps to heal wounds.

Lilac is a feminine plant that is ruled by the planet Venus. Its Element is Air. It is a good protector that also banishes evil and can be used for exorcism rituals.

Linden is feminine, ruled by Jupiter and its Element Water. It is said to be the tree of immortality and is associated with conjugal love or attraction and longevity. It is supposed to help in preventing intoxication.

Lovage is masculine, ruled by the Sun. Its Element is Water. The dried and powdered root should be added to cleansing and purification baths to release negativity. Carry it to attract love and the attention of the opposite sex. Also carry it when meeting new people.

Mandrake is a masculine plant ruled by Mercury and the Element Earth. It is very useful in incense for increasing the sex drive (both male and female) and is best used prior to the Full Moon.

Marigold is masculine and ruled by the Sun. Its Element is Fire. Prophecy, legal matters, the psyche, seeing magical creatures, love, divination dreams, business or legal affairs and renewing personal energy are all assisted by marigold. It is good for finding someone who has done you wrong. It is sometimes added to love sachets. It should be gathered at noon.

Marjoram is masculine and is ruled by Mercury with the Element Air. It protects against evil and aids love and healing; it is also helpful for those who are grieving.

Meadowsweet is feminine, its planet is Jupiter and it is ruled by Water. It is a sacred herb of the Druids and gives protection against evil influences; it also promotes love, balance and harmony. Place meadowsweet on your altar when making love charms and conducting love spells to increase their potency. It can be worn at Lammas to join with the Goddess.

Mint (spearmint and peppermint) is a masculine plant that is ruled by Mercury or Venus and has the Element Air. It promotes healing, the ability to gain money and is useful for successful travel. Known to be a digestive, it also calms the emotions.

Mugwort is a feminine plant that is ruled by Venus and the Element of Air. It is probably the most widely used herb by witches and promotes psychic ability and gives prophetic dreams. It is very good for astral projection.

Mullein is a masculine plant, ruled by Saturn and has the Element of Fire. This is used for courage and protection from wild animals and also from evil spirits. It is also used for cleansing and purifying ritual tools and altars and the cleansing of psychic places and sacred spaces before and after working. It guards against nightmares and can be substituted for graveyard dust.

Myrrh is a feminine plant that is ruled by the Moon or Jupiter and Water. It is purifying and protective and is especially useful when used with frankincense.

Myrtle is feminine, ruled by Venus, and its Element is Water. Myrtle was sacred to the Greek goddess Venus and has been used in love charms and spells throughout history. It should be grown indoors for good luck. Carry or wear myrtle leaves to attract love; charms made of the wood have special magical properties. Wear fresh myrtle leaves while making love charms, potions or during rituals for love and include it in them. Myrtle tea drunk every three days maintains youthfulness.

Nettle is a masculine plant ruled by Mars and its Element is Fire. It is a guard against danger and promotes courage.

Nutmeg is feminine, ruled by Jupiter, and its Element is Air. It helps to develop clairvoyance and psychic powers. When used with green candles it aids prosperity. It is also said to help teething.

Oak is masculine and is ruled by the Sun and the Element of Fire. It is often used by witches and used in power wands. It also protects against evil spirits and can also be used to promote a better sex life.

Orange is a feminine plant ruled by Jupiter and the Element of Water. It can be used as a love charm, while in the Orient it is used for good luck.

Orris root is a feminine plant, is ruled by Venus and has the Element of Water. The powder is used as a love-drawing herb and to increase sexual appeal. Used in charms, amulets, sachets, incenses and baths it will also protect you. Hung on a cord it can act as a pendulum.

Parsley is a masculine herb that is ruled by Mercury and Air. It wards off evil and is a useful aid to those who drink too much. Parsley may be used in purification baths and as a way to stop misfortune.

Patchouli is a feminine plant which is ruled by Saturn. Its Element is Earth. This plant is aphrodisiac and an attractant of lovers for either sex. It is sometimes used in fertility talismans and can be substituted for graveyard dust. Use it with green candles to ensure prosperity. Sprinkle it on money to spread your wealth.

Pennyroyal is a masculine plant ruled by Mars; its Element is Fire. It is used for protection, and, because it prevents weariness during long journeys, it is often carried on ships. Pennyroyal is also an insect deterrent. It should be avoided while pregnant.

Pepper (black) is a masculine plant which is ruled by Mars with its Element of Fire; it can be used in protective charms against the evil eye. Mixed with salt it dispels evil, which may be why it is used on food.

Pimpernel is a masculine plant which is ruled by Mercury and has the Element of Air. You should wear it to keep people from deceiving you. It wards off illness and stops accidents. The juice is used to purify and empower ritual weapons.

Pine is masculine and ruled by Mars; it has the Element of Air. It aids you to focus and if burnt it will help to cleanse the atmosphere where it is burnt. Its sawdust is often used as a base for incense, particularly in those associated with money.

Poppy is feminine, ruled by the Moon, and has the Element of Water. It is said that you can eat poppy seeds as a fertility charm; they can also be used in love sachets. Also carry the seeds or dried seed-pod as a prosperity charm.

Rose is a feminine plant that is ruled by Venus and the Element of Water. It is perhaps the most widely used plant in love and good-luck workings. Roses are also added to 'fast luck' mixtures designed to make things happen quickly. It is also a good calmer when situations become difficult.

Rosemary is a masculine plant that is ruled by the Sun and the Element of Fire. It improves memory and sleep; it is an excellent purifier. It should be used to cleanse your hands before performing magic or rituals. Hang it in doorways to prevent thieves entering.

Rowan is a masculine plant which is ruled by the Sun and the Element of Fire. Rowan wood is used for divining rods and wands; its leaves and bark are used in divination rituals. It is also used for protection, good luck and healing. When two twigs are tied together to form a cross it is a protective device.

Rue is masculine, ruled by the Sun and the Element of Fire. Protective when hung at a door, it can break hexes by sending the negativity back from whence it came. It is good for clarity of mind, clearing the mind of emotional clutter and purification of ritual spaces and tools.

Saffron is masculine, ruled by the Sun and the Element of Fire. It was used in rituals to honour the Goddess of the Moon, Ashtoreth. It dispels melancholy and restores sexual prowess in men. It is used to cleanse the hands in healing processes and is also used in prosperity incenses.

Sage is masculine, ruled by either Jupiter or Venus and the Element of Air. It promotes financial gain and good wishes; it is also a good healer and protector.

St John's Wort is a masculine plant that is ruled by the Sun and the Element of Fire. This protects against bad dreams and encourages the willpower to do something difficult.

Sandalwood is feminine, ruled by the Moon, and its Element is Air. It has high spiritual vibrations so should be mixed with frankincense and burned at the time of the Full Moon. Anything visualized at this time is said to come true. It also clears negativity, so is good for purification, protection and healing workings.

Sunflower is masculine and is ruled by the Sun and the Element of Fire. It is extremely useful, for the seeds aid fertility while the plant allows you to discover the truth, if you sleep with it under your bed. It is said to guard the garden against marauders and pests.

Thyme is a feminine herb that is ruled by the planet Venus and the Element of Water. It is a good guardian against negative energy and an extremely good cleanser if combined with marjoram. It helps to develop psychic powers and is said to make women irresistible.

Valerian is feminine and is ruled by Venus and the Element of Water. One of the best sleep enhancers available, it also promotes love and rids your house of evil. It is said to protect against lightning.

Vanilla is feminine, ruled by Venus, and its Element is Water. The bean is used in a love charms, while the oil is worn as an aphrodisiac. Mix it with sugar to make love infusions.

Vervain is feminine and is ruled by Venus with the Element of Earth. Good for the ritual cleansing of sacred space, magical cleansing baths and purification incenses, it should be hung over the bed to prevent nightmares. Vervain is also excellent for use in prosperity charms and spells as it brings good luck and inspiration. It should be picked before sunrise. While it is said to control sexual urges (supposedly for seven years), it is also used in love and protection charms, presumably to ensure fidelity.

Violet is feminine, ruled by Venus, and its Element is Water. It brings changes in luck or fortune. Mix with lavender for a powerful love charm. A violet and lavender compress will help in eliminating headaches. The flowers are carried as a good-luck charm. The scent will soothe, clear the mind and relax the wearer.

Walnut is masculine, ruled by the Sun, and the Element is Fire. Carry the nut as a charm to promote fertility and strengthen the heart. It attracts lightning.

Willow is feminine and ruled by the Moon. The Element is Water. Willow wands can be used for healing and are at their strongest when used at the New Moon. Willow guards against evil and this is where the expression 'knock on wood' comes from.

Witch hazel is masculine, ruled by the Sun, with the Element of Fire. The wood is used to make divining rods. Witch hazel gives protection and promotes chastity, healing the heart. It cools all the passions.

Wormwood is masculine, ruled by Mars, with the Element of Air. Wormwood is poisonous but is sometimes burned in smudge sticks to gain protection from wandering spirits. It is said that it enables the dead to be released from this plane so they may find peace. It is also used in divinatory and clairvoyance incenses, initiation rites and tests of courage. Mixed with sandalwood, it summons spirits.

Yarrow is feminine and ruled by Venus. Its Element is Water. There is evidence that yarrow was often a component in incense used for incantations. It is a powerful incense additive for divination and love spells, too. It exorcises evil, dispelling negativity, yet also enhances psychic ability and divination. Yarrow tea drunk prior to divination will enhance powers of perception; a touch of peppermint enhances the action of this brew and always helps it to work better. The plant is also used in courage, love and marriage charms.

Yarrow Spell

It is said that yarrow enhances a telepathic link between lovers, loving friends and members of your immediate family. It is also very good if you use it as a sort of psychic telephone line between members of a development circle (several people working together for one another's development) or a healing circle.

YOU WILL NEED ───────────

Mercury incense
Pieces of yarrow stalk preferably from a single stalk (If not then at least from the same plant)

METHOD

+ Light the incense.
+ Consecrate the stalks by passing them three times through the incense.
+ Say:

I dedicate these stalks for the purpose of
communication between us.
May they be used wisely and well.

+ Now distribute them to the people with whom you wish to be in contact.
+ If doing this as part of a group ritual then spend a few moments making a mental link with each person in the group.
+ When you need to be in contact, need help or wish to draw on the power of the group, hold your piece of stalk in your left hand and call on the other person or persons.

Herbs and incenses had a far greater meaning in times gone by, and now that we are able to grow so many more herbs in pots, and obtain the raw ingredients from specialist shops, we can revert to the old ideas and use many of the powers and correspondences our forebears knew so well. Yarrow is often seen as a weed, but in fact has many magical uses.

Yucca is masculine, and ruled by Mars. Its Element is Fire. Yucca is said to help with shape-shifting. If a strand of a leaf is tied around one's head and then an animal is visualized the wearer becomes (takes on the qualities of) that animal. Yucca is used to purify the body before performing magic. To get rid of illness, bathe at least twice using suds from the boiled plant juices. A cross formed from yucca leaves is said to protect the hearth, the centre of the home.

Practical Uses for Herbs

Herbs have always had extremely practical uses in addition to magical properties. Traditionally, women who had learned their craft as witches had also learned about the healing properties of the herbs they used. This aspect of a witch's abilities falls into the category of folk medicine, but it also entailed the women linking in with an ancient tradition by which a deity was assigned to each herb.

Sometimes witches earned a reputation for being able to achieve miracles, but when something went wrong they would be blamed for it or accused of putting the evil eye on people they did not like. Notwithstanding that they had done their best with the resources they had, these women were both revered and feared. Often the women would add other strange ingredients to their lotions and potions. In Scotland as late as 1865 there is gruesome evidence that the ashes from a human skull were much sought after as an ingredient in a cure for epilepsy. In this particular case, the powder was required to be added to a mixture administered to a girl suffering from fits.

Today many ingredients, similar to those used by our ancestors, are available to us for healing purposes. Unlike the healers of old, we can avail ourselves of scientific information to ensure that we use specific herbs appropriately. Below are some recipes that have proved their worth. Often it is the synergy (combined influence) of the herbs that makes them so effective. Just as essential oils derived from plants can be combined, so also can the herbs themselves in order to achieve a particular end.

Acid Indigestion Warm a cup of milk and steep four eucalyptus leaves in it. Drink this to ease discomfort.

Athlete's Foot Besides keeping your feet dry and powdered with orris root, try a vinegar rinse of one cup of water and one teaspoon of cider vinegar to which one tablespoon of thyme and red clover have been added. Soak for 15 minutes daily.

Bee/Wasp Stings A drop of myrrh juice on the sting will help draw out the poison.

Bruises Take 600 ml (1 pint) of almond oil and 450 g (1 lb) each of Balm of Gilead and St John's Wort, which you should bruise by pounding in a pestle and mortar. Warm together over a low flame. When the oil has taken all the colour out of the buds, cool and strain the liquid. Then apply as needed to the bruised area.

Burns A poultice made from wheat flour, molasses and baking soda will relieve a burn and often hasten the healing process.

Chancre Sore Sorrel (approximately a handful) soaked in warm water until soft, then strained and drunk as a tea, will help clear them up.

Chapped Skin To 25 g (1 oz) of melted wax add 110 g (4 oz) of glycerine and 4–5 drops of oil of roses or rejuvenating oil. Warm until well mixed and apply as needed.

Coughs In 1.7 litres (3 pints) of boiling water, place a large quantity of peppermint leaves, 150 ml (5 fl oz) of rum, 85 ml (3 fl oz) of lemon juice, 25 g (1 oz) of cinnamon bark and 25 g (1 oz) of comfrey root. Blend well, then allow to cool and strain. Add 225 g (8 oz) of sugar and 50 ml (2 fl oz) of honey. Bring the mixture to a rolling boil. Cool and store in an air-tight container.

Dandruff Mix together one measure each of violet leaves, peppermint, nettle, red clover, witch hazel and rosemary. Before shampooing, warm a quarter measure of the dried herbs in two measures of water and use as a rinse.

Eye Rinse In 300 ml (8 fl oz) of water, warm 25 g (1 oz) of elderflowers and a half teaspoon of salt. Strain and use as needed to refresh eyes or relieve itching.

Fever Infuse the peel of two oranges and one lemon in whisky. Take two teaspoons after each meal.

Heartburn Add two teaspoons each of cinnamon, lavender flowers, baking soda, peppermint leaves and half a teaspoon ground ginger to 125 ml (4 fl oz) of water and allow to steep. Strain and drink warm after meals.

Itching Blood root pulverized and steeped in apple vinegar until well incorporated then added to lotions made from aloe, coconut oil, and/or cocoa butter will ease itching.

Sleeplessness Equal quantities of the stalks and leaves of valerian, catnip and peppermint made into a tea will ensure better sleep.

Sore Throat Tea made from sage leaves and mixed with honey and lemon will ease a sore throat.

Stomach Ache A tea of equal quantities of mint, strawberry leaf, catnip and blackberry mixed with one tablespoon of brandy should ease the stomach.

An alternative is ground brown rice steeped in warm water for 15 minutes. Add sugar and nutmeg to taste. Add to boiled milk and drink.

Toothache Mix oils of peppermint and clove. (You can then mix this with a teaspoon of rum, if liked.) Apply directly to the tooth.

Urticaria Infuse 600 g (21 oz) of black alder bark in 1.1 litres (2 pints) of water and 225 ml (7 fl oz) olive oil. Wash the affected area frequently. An easy alternative is a poultice of clay mud.

Wound Infections Add two sliced onions and 50 g each of beeswax, honey and elder leaves to 275 g of petroleum jelly. Warm over a low flame for about 30 minutes. Strain and apply to the wound with a clean dressing.

Smudge Sticks

Anyone who works with herbs knows that they can work on very subtle levels, particularly the spiritual. 'Smudging' is traditionally a Native American spiritual practice, which is used to clear an atmosphere of spiritual contamination and negativity. Smudge sticks are long bundles of sweet-smelling plant substance, which are wound tightly then lit at one end until they catch fire. It is then blown out so it continues to glow as it releases the smoke.

The Native Americans would use plants such as sage, cedar, sweet grass or wormwood. A plant called prairie lavender is also used in some places as a smudge stick, although it is not the same type of lavender we know in Europe.

Cedar Some so-called cedars are actually members of the juniper family. Many types of cedar needles are used for smudge sticks.

Sage There are many different types of sage – *Salvia apiana* and *Salvia columbarne* are two of the best-known. Most grow very tall and have long lives. (Sage brush is not a part of the sage family – it belongs to the wormwood clan, although this too is used for smudging.)

Sweet grass Sometimes called vanilla grass, this is a tall green grass that turns yellow when dried. The aroma of sweet grass is more pungent when the plant is dried.

Wormwood In Native American culture *Artemisia spinescens* is occasionally used for smudge sticks. Artemesias, sometimes called sage, belong to the wormwood family; they have no connection to the sage we know in Europe.

There are now many good commercial types of smudge stick available, but you may like to make your own. The leaves and soft stalks are the parts of the plants used.

Making a Smudge Stick or Herb Bundle

The first thing to remember when you are making your own smudge sticks is that, as with any spiritual intent, be sure to wash and cleanse yourself – deliberately getting rid of any negative energy in the process – before you begin. There are also a few other guidelines you'll need to follow.

- Before picking the plant matter, honour the plant and ask its permission to take a branch or stem for your spiritual intent. Respect the plant and let it continue to give of its life.
- When picking stems, make sure they are long enough to be bound together.
- Use any of the herbs mentioned above or use pine or cypress, if your location allows. You do not have to use plants and herbs that are in your immediate vicinity – though, if you have grown the plants yourself, this will give you tremendous satisfaction.
- If you want to, add essential oils, but use them sparingly and try to choose one that will enhance the purpose of, or add an extra quality to, your bundle.

YOU WILL NEED

Selection of leaves and stems
Elastic band
Thick cotton twine
Small bowl

METHOD

❖ Arrange a small handful of leaves and stems fairly symmetrically into a bundle – don't use too many.
❖ Put the stems in the elastic band to keep the pieces together while you tie the bundle, removing it when you have finished.
❖ Take a long piece of thick cotton twine and place the bundle top (the thicker end) in the middle of it.
❖ Using the two ends of the twine, bind the bundle together tightly in a criss-cross fashion, starting at the top and finishing at the bottom part of the stems. (Take your time over this – the more secure you make the bundle the better it will burn. Some leaves or twigs may protrude, so you need a receptacle to catch falling ashes.)
❖ Bind the end of your bundle securely with the twine and perhaps make a dedication to your purpose.
❖ You will now have a cone-shaped bundle. Let it dry out thoroughly before burning it, because it won't burn properly if it is at all damp.
❖ To use the herb bundle, light the thicker top end and then blow out the flame out so it smoulders. Some bits may drop out of the bundle so remember to have a bowl or receptacle handy to catch them.

Smudge sticks are moved to where the fragrant smoke is needed. In rituals, you would use the cardinal points. Walk around slowly, wafting the smoke into the corners of the room as you do so. (You may have to keep blowing on the lit end to keep it burning.) As you blow, remember that you are using the principle of Air. You can also direct the smoke with either of your hands, the small branch of a plant, or even a special crystal or stone. Amber can also be used – especially appropriate as it is a resin from a plant. This action should get rid of any negative vibrations at the same time as energizing the protective frequencies.

If you want to smudge a friend (or yourself), waft the smoke all around the body, starting at the head and gradually moving down to the feet. Move in a clockwise direction because this creates positivity. You can direct the smoke with your hand or a feather or whatever feels good for you. A seashell is a good idea since it represents the Goddess. You can also chant or sing at this time. Whatever you do, do it with a pure mind and spirit. When you have finished, keep the bundle safe until it has extinguished itself and then open a window to clear the space.

Decorative bundles

If you don't intend to burn the bundle then there are many other possibilities open to you. Bundles can be bound with colour, feeling and meaning. Oils will add energy and aroma. You can use spices, fruits, fragrant wood, minerals, crystals, resins or flowers like rose, marigold or lavender. Depending on how you plan to display the bundle, you can use pretty much anything that has meaning and fragrance.

INCENSE

As well as making use of herbs as plants, decorations and for healing, their most important use in magic was – and still is – in incense. Incense symbolizes the Element Air and the spiritual realms and has been part of ritual use by magical workers and priests alike for thousands of years. Granular incense, with its basis of resins and gums, is nowadays usually preferred for magical workings or ritual worship. It has a magic all of its own. For this reason a good incense burner will be one of your most important tools. You should choose this carefully, and not just for its aesthetic sense, because it is vital that the incense is allowed to burn properly.

Since time immemorial, people have burned sweet-smelling woods, herbs and resins to perfume, cleanse and clarify the atmosphere in which they exist. During outdoor rituals special woods and herbs with magical qualities would be thrown onto bonfires or into altar cauldrons. In the home, open-hearth fires could be used to give off perfumed smoke which sweetened or freshened the air. The word 'perfume' means 'through smoke'.

Initially, resins and gums were used most successfully, so in areas where resinous trees grew, incenses were used to honour the gods. Egypt became especially renowned for its high standard of blending and the use of ritual incense. There was a particular class of incense – which is still available today – called Khyphi. It required magical techniques and the finest ingredients for its manufacture.

❊ Kyphi Incense ❊

1 part myrrh resin
1 part frankincense resin
1 part gum arabic
1 part Balm of Gilead buds
1 part cassia or cinnamon
Few drops of lotus oil
Few drops of musk oil

Nowadays incense is most often encountered in the form of joss sticks, which were introduced to the West in the 1960s by travellers to India who brought them back with them. For short rituals these work very well, though they are not to everyone's taste. Dhoop, or incense cones, as they are known, are another way of using the same material.

The best method of using incense is to burn the granular type on a charcoal disc. By this method the charcoal disc is lit and placed in a fireproof receptacle. The incense is then piled onto the concave surface and allowed to do its work. After use, the charcoal discs remain very hot. You should dispose of them very carefully, dousing them with water and ensuring they are no longer 'alive' and thus potentially harmful. You might like to bury what remains of the incense as an offering to the earth.

Making and using incenses

Many of the herbs already discussed are suitable for incense, if you wish to make your own. You should choose your correspondences carefully, according to your spell or ritual, and may like to make incense in tune with the cycles of life and planetary correspondences. You will soon find out through experimentation what works for you. You can also use essential oils as part of your incense-making, if you so wish.

The use of incense in magical workings can be quite a personal act of worship; the various blends can sometimes either appeal to your senses or smell absolutely foul, often depending on your mood. For this reason, a number of blends from numerous sources are given here. Experiment until you settle on your own particular favourites and then work from there.

There does need to be some clarification of the lists of ingredients, however. A 'part' indicates one measure or a proportion, which may be a teaspoon, a cup and so forth. Fractions indicate portions of a part. Personal experience shows that making small quantities is best as the incense then stays fresher and is often more cost-effective. If you plan on making quantities of several types of incense, collect a number of individual portion jars in which jams and honeys are packed. Such an amount is ideal for your immediate use.

Unless otherwise specified, use dried herbs, flowers, roots and resins, since these are often both easier to get hold of than fresh and are packed in suitable quantities and compositions for incense-making. The more unusual herbs, oils and resins can usually be obtained from any good herbalist or New Age shop, and there are now also several suppliers who supply by mail order and will often blend their own mixtures.

Although incense has been used since time immemorial in religious rites and rituals, often in the hope that changes of awareness can be achieved, modern law is very specific in its classification of mind-altering substances. Therefore, do not intentionally use them for this purpose, but rather as representatives of the Air Element in your rituals. In true magic it is the intent that is the important aspect, so the extensive list given here is divided under broad headings of appropriate purposes. The general method of preparation remains the same.

Initial purchase of the various ingredients is quite expensive, so if you work with other people you may wish to share the cost in some way. Start off with the first ingredient, grind it small and then add each subsequent ingredient in small quantities until it smells and feels right.

Incense Preparation

This is an accepted way of making incense, but you do need to be patient. The art of blending is highly skilled and your own experiments will show you the best methods for you. If you know your correspondences, you can call on the various deities to help you in your task, or just simply bear in mind the ultimate purpose of your incense. Most oils and binders such as the gums are added last.

YOU WILL NEED

Pestle and mortar
(Your pestle and mortar can be of any material, though one that does not pick up the perfumes of the ingredients is obviously best. If you do not have a pestle and mortar, a chopping board and rolling pin will suffice, though it is messier this way.)
  Set of measuring spoons
  Large bowl in which to blend your mixture thoroughly
  Your chosen herbs, resins, oils etc.
  Small containers with lids
  Labels
  Charcoal blocks for burning the incense

METHOD

❖ Make sure that you grind each quantity of the herbs and resins as small as possible.
❖ When each ingredient is ground, place it in your large bowl, reserving a small quantity in the right proportions of each ingredient with which to do a test run.
❖ Mix in each ingredient thoroughly as you add it to the bowl. Mixing by hand is probably most successful, since this allows you to introduce your own personal vibration. You could also use a wand of sacred wood reserved specifically for the purpose if you wish.
❖ As you mix, say:

May this herb [resin/oil] enhance the power
Of this offering for the spirits of Air

❖ Add any oil last and make sure that this is thoroughly mixed in and not left in one place in the mixture.
❖ When all ingredients are combined, spend some time thinking about your purpose and gently mixing and remixing your incense.
❖ Remember that if you are making incense for a particular purpose, the herbs and resins used should correspond to that purpose, therefore your incense may not necessarily smell as pleasant as you would like.
❖ If wished, ask for a blessing or consecration for the incense, as follows:

May this the work of my two hands
Be blessed for the purpose of [state purpose]

❖ Now test your sample by lighting a charcoal block, placing the incense on it then burning it carefully in a safe place.

Your incense is now ready, though it is best not to use it for at least 24 hours to enable the perfumes and qualities to blend properly. Many incenses blend, change and strengthen when stored correctly and incense often improves with keeping, so your sample may not smell the same as your stored incense. If it is to your liking and you feel it is suitable for your purpose, fill the containers, secure them tightly and label them clearly. They should be stored in a cool, dark place.

Incense Blends
Banishing, Exorcism and Purification

All the following incenses work on the principle that certain energies need to be banished in order for the practitioner to work effectively. The creation of peace, purification of the area and, of course, exorcism of unwanted spirits all come under this heading. Do think very carefully about what you wish to achieve before deciding which incense is right for your purpose. Suggestions are given here or the purpose is clearly indicated in the title.

It is always possible to make substitutions in the ingredients. They can all be mixed and matched ad infinitum, though you may have to experiment with the quantities until the incense 'feels' right (or until it smells right).

Banishing and Exorcism

Banishing Incense

1 part bay leaves
2 parts cinnamon
1 part rose petals
2 parts myrrh resin
pinch of salt

Clearing Incense

1 part frankincense resin
1 part copal resin
1 part myrrh resin
1/2 part sandalwood

Burn this with the windows open.

Exorcism Incense

3 parts frankincense resin
1 part rosemary
1 part bay leaves
1 part avens
1 part mugwort
1 part St John's Wort
1 part angelica
1 part basil

Burn this incense with the windows open to drive out very heavy spiritual negativity from your surroundings.

Ending Negativity Incense

1 part marjoram
1 part thyme
1/2 part oregano
1/4 part bay leaves
1/4 part cloves

Jinx-removing Incense

2 parts clove
1 part deerstongue
Few drops of rose geranium oil

This incense can be used when you think someone is against you.

Uncrossing Incense

2 parts lavender
1 part rose
2 parts bay
1 part verbena

Use this incense when you feel you or your home has been 'cursed' or you are under attack.

Purification

Purification Incense 1

2 parts sandalwood
1 part cinnamon
2 parts bay
1 part vervain
pinch of salt

Burn this incense with the windows open to clear a disturbed home after an argument, for instance.

Purification Incense 2

2 parts sandalwood
1 part cinnamon

Leave the windows open to clear an atmosphere quickly.

❊ Purification Incense 3 ❊

3 parts frankincense resin
2 parts dragon's blood resin
1 part myrrh resin
1 part sandalwood
1 part wood betony
$\frac{1}{2}$ part dill seed
Few drops of rose geranium oil

This is good for clearing your new home of old energies.

❊ Domestic Tranquillity Incense ❊

$\frac{3}{4}$ part sage
$\frac{1}{4}$ part rue
$\frac{1}{2}$ part ground ivy
Few drops of bayberry oil
$\frac{1}{4}$ part bayberry
$1\frac{1}{4}$ parts linden (lime)

❊ Hearth and Home Incense ❊

2 parts dragon's blood resin
$\frac{1}{2}$ part juniper
$\frac{1}{2}$ part sassafrass
$\frac{1}{2}$ part orange flowers
2 parts myrrh resin
$\frac{1}{2}$ part rose petals

This incense should be burnt when you wish to create a safe, warm, loving home.

❊ ❊ ❊

Protection

There are many ways of protecting both yourself and your own space by the use of incense. If you simply wish to protect against the intrusion of negative energies, it is probably best to use those incenses that are based mainly on the resinous substances. This is for two reasons. First, most resins are relatively slow-burning, high-vibrational energy substances, so their effect is long-lasting; secondly, you have more opportunity when grinding them to introduce specific intents into the incense. Perhaps, for instance, you might wish to protect yourself against the jealousy of a former lover or against financial loss. Using substances which have a high vibration helps to build a 'wall' of protection, which means that neither the bad thought nor the subtle energies activated on a more spiritual level can harm you.

Some of the incenses below are specifically to protect against not just negativity on a purely physical plane, but also malign energy deliberately directed at you and your loved ones. Incense such as the ones for psychic protection will give you the security you need to know that you can combat such gross intrusion.

Other incenses mean that you can react quickly to outside influences should you need to do so. There are many alternatives in this, as in other sections, so that you can decide for yourself which ones work best for you. A lot will depend on what is local to you, and so far as protection incenses are concerned, the sensitivities can change depending on the environment surrounding the individual. Where the incense is for a specific purpose, that information is given.

Once again, it is always possible when making these incenses to substitute the ingredients. They can all be mixed and matched ad infinitum, though you may have to experiment with the quantities until they 'feel' right (or until they smell right).

❊ Peace and Protection Incense ❊

4 parts lavender
3 parts thyme
2 parts vervain
3 parts basil
1 part frankincense resin
Pinch of rue
Pinch of benzoin resin
Few drops of bergamot oil
Few drops of jasmine oil

This can be used in both peace and protection spells and rituals.

❊ Protection Incense 1 ❊

$\frac{1}{2}$ part bay leaves
$\frac{1}{2}$ part cloves
$\frac{3}{4}$ part oregano
$\frac{3}{4}$ part sandalwood

Protection Incense 2

4 parts verbena
1 part galangal root (ground)
1 part peppermint
1 part cinnamon
$\frac{1}{2}$ part rue

Protection Incense 3

$\frac{1}{4}$ part basil
$\frac{1}{2}$ part cinnamon
$\frac{1}{2}$ part rosemary
$1\frac{1}{2}$ parts thyme
$\frac{1}{2}$ part sage
$\frac{1}{2}$ part star anise

Total Protection Incense

2 parts frankincense resin
1 part dragon's blood resin
$\frac{1}{2}$ part wood betony

This incense creates quite a high vibration and protects on all levels of existence.

Iron Protection Incense

$\frac{1}{4}$ part iron filings
1 part galangal root (powdered)
Few drops of citronella oil

This incense uses the ancient idea that iron will change a negative vibration.

New Orleans Protection Incense

2 parts myrrh resin
$\frac{1}{2}$ part bay leaves
1 part cloves
1 part cinnamon

This is an incense often used in Hoodoo work.

Sandalwood Protection Incense

3 parts sandalwood
2 parts juniper
1 part vetivert

Pennyroyal Protection Incense

2 parts verbena or vetivert
1 part galangal
1 part pennyroyal
$\frac{1}{4}$ part rue
$\frac{1}{2}$ part cinnamon

Rosemary Protection Incense

2 parts rosemary
$\frac{1}{2}$ part orris root (ground)
1 part basil
1 part frankincense resin

10 Herb Protection Incense

2 parts frankincense resin
2 parts myrrh resin
1 part juniper berries
$\frac{1}{2}$ part rosemary
$\frac{1}{4}$ part avens
$\frac{1}{4}$ part mugwort
$\frac{1}{4}$ part yarrow
$\frac{1}{4}$ part St John's Wort
$\frac{1}{2}$ part angelica
1 part basil

5 Resins Protection Incense

2 parts frankincense resin
1 part copal resin
1 part myrrh resin
$\frac{1}{2}$ part dragon's blood resin
$\frac{1}{2}$ part gum arabic

Home Protection Incense

$\frac{1}{2}$ part frankincense resin
$\frac{3}{4}$ part sage
$\frac{1}{2}$ part basil
$\frac{1}{2}$ part mistletoe
$\frac{1}{4}$ part garlic (mix of dried and ground)
$\frac{3}{4}$ part rosemary
$\frac{1}{4}$ part rue
1 part sandalwood
$\frac{1}{2}$ part myrrh resin
$\frac{1}{2}$ part orris root
$\frac{1}{2}$ part yarrow

Note: The next two incenses can be used if you wish to protect your surroundings against theft and burglary.

❋ Prevent Theft Incense ❋

1 part ground ivy
$1/2$ part juniper
$1^1/2$ parts rosemary

❋ Stop Theft Incense ❋

$1/2$ part dogwood
$1/4$ part caraway
$1/2$ part rosemary
$1/4$ part tarragon
1 part willow
Few drops honeysuckle oil

Note: The next four incenses deal specifically with protection on a psychic level, while the two following deal with the effects of an unwanted spiritual visitation. They could be considered to belong to the banishing and exorcism categories.

❋ Psychic Protection Incense 1 ❋

$1/2$ part elder
1 part cinquefoil
$1/2$ part bay leaves
$1/8$ part valerian

❋ Psychic Protection Incense 2 ❋

$1/4$ part broom
$1/2$ part agrimony
$1/2$ part basil
$1/4$ part cranesbill
1 part vetivert
$1/2$ part oregano

❋ Psychic Protection Incense 3 ❋

$1/4$ part frankincense resin
$1/2$ part oregano
$1/4$ part lovage
$1/2$ part cloves
$1/4$ part ginger root (ground)
$1/2$ part sandalwood
$1/4$ part star anise

❋ Psychic Protection Incense 4 ❋

$1/2$ part benzoin resin
$1/4$ part dragon's blood resin
$1/2$ part frankincense resin
$1/4$ part camphor gum
$1/2$ part cassia
$1/4$ part patchouli
2 parts sandalwood

Each ingredient in this incense is a resin.

Note: These next two incenses help to keep your home clear of spirit interference unless you have specifically asked for spirit to be present.

❋ Spirits Depart Incense ❋

2 parts fennel seed
2 parts dill seed
$1/2$ part rue

❋ Spirit Portal Incense ❋

$1/2$ part cinnamon
$1/2$ part lavender
pinch of wormwood

Note: The next five protection incenses all have as their main ingredients resins, particularly frankincense. If you dislike the perfume of frankincense, experiment with the proportions of your other resins.

❋ Protection Incense 1 ❋

4 parts frankincense resin
3 parts myrrh resin
2 parts juniper berries
1 part rosemary
$1/2$ part avens
$1/2$ part mugwort
$1/2$ part yarrow
$1/2$ part St. John's Wort
$1/2$ part angelica
$1/2$ part basil

This incense is so all-enveloping that it will protect against almost everything.

❊ Protection Incense 2 ❊

2 parts frankincense resin
1 part dragon's blood powder or resin
½ part betony

This incense is particularly potent when attempting to visualize the source of your problem.

❊ Protection Incense 3 ❊

2 parts frankincense resin
1 part sandalwood
½ part rosemary

❊ Protection Incense 4 ❊

1 part frankincense resin
1 part myrrh resin
½ part clove

❊ Protection Incense 5 ❊

2 parts frankincense resin
1 part copal resin
1 part dragon's blood powder or resin

* * *

Lust, Love and Relationships

The idea of trying to influence someone else directly goes against the ethics of many practitioners and magicians. One must be very careful because incense prepared with the intention of trying to make someone do that which they do not want to, or which goes against their natural inclination, can possibly misfire and cause the originator of such a spell a good deal of difficulty.

Love incense really should only be used with the intent that the occurrence will only be in accordance with the Greater Good, whether it be the beginning or the ending. That is, that you are helping something to happen, not forcing it. Apart from that, many of these incenses have a beautiful perfume and can help to create a loving, supportive atmosphere.

It is always possible when preparing incense to make substitutions in the ingredients. They can all be mixed and matched ad infinitum, though you may have to experiment with the quantities until they 'feel' right (or until they smell right).

There are many different aspects to relationships. In this section the individual titles of each recipe are self-explanatory.

❊ Loving Friends Incense ❊

½ part acacia
1 part rosemary
¼ part elder
½ part frankincense resin
1 part dogwood

❊ Attract a Lover Incense ❊

1 part lovage
½ part orris root (ground)
1 part lemon verbena
¼ part patchouli
Few drops of lemon verbena oil

❊ Attract Love Incense ❊

½ part cloves
1 part rose
¼ part saw palmetto
½ part juniper
Few drops of musk oil
Few drops of rose oil
½ part red sandalwood

❊ Draw and Strengthen Love Incense ❊

2 parts sandalwood
½ part basil
½ part bergamot
Few drops of rose oil
Few drops of lavender oil

❊ Love Incense 1 ❊

1 part orris root (ground)
Few drops musk oil
1 part sandalwood
1 part violet
Few drops of gardenia oil

❋ Love Incense 2 ❋

2 parts dragon's blood resin
1 part orris root (ground)
$\frac{1}{2}$ part cinnamon
$\frac{1}{2}$ part rose petals
Few drops of musk oil
Few drops of patchouli oil

❋ Love Incense 3 ❋

1 part patchouli
Few drops of musk oil
Few drops of civet oil
Few drops of ambergris oil

This incense makes the opposite sex more aware of you.

❋ Love Incense 4 ❋

1 part violets
1 part rose petals
$\frac{1}{2}$ part olive leaves

❋ Love Incense 5 ❋

2 parts sandalwood
2 parts benzoin resin
1 part rosebuds
Few drops of patchouli oil
Few drops of rose oil

❋ Love Incense 6 ❋

2 parts sandalwood
$\frac{1}{2}$ part basil
$\frac{1}{2}$ part bergamot
Few drops of rose oil
Few drops of lavender oil

Burn this incense to attract love, to strengthen the love you have and also to expand your ability to give and receive love.

❋ Increase Love Incense ❋

$\frac{1}{2}$ part benzoin
$\frac{1}{4}$ part jasmine
1 part rose
$\frac{1}{4}$ part patchouli
$\frac{1}{2}$ part musk root
$\frac{1}{2}$ part sandalwood
Few drops of musk oil
Few drops of civet oil
Few drops of rose oil
Few drops of jasmine oil

This incense can be used in love rituals when you wish to strengthen the bonds between you.

Note: The next three incenses are all thought to have an effect on the libido.

❋ Fiery Passion Incense ❋

$\frac{3}{4}$ part yohimbe
$\frac{1}{2}$ part cinnamon
$\frac{1}{4}$ part ginger root
$2\frac{1}{2}$ parts damiana
Few drops of ambergris oil

❋ Passion Incense ❋

$\frac{1}{2}$ part cranesbill
$1\frac{1}{4}$ parts cascara
$\frac{1}{2}$ part savory
Few drops of civet oil
$\frac{1}{2}$ part musk root

❋ Physical Love Incense ❋

$\frac{3}{4}$ part damiana
$\frac{1}{2}$ part yohimbe
$\frac{1}{2}$ part musk root
$\frac{3}{4}$ part cascara
Few drops of bergamot oil
Few drops of ambergris oil

Fidelity Incense

¹⁄₄ part basil
¹⁄₄ part dragon's blood resin
1 part red sandalwood
¹⁄₂ part rosemary
1 part dogwood
Few drops of honeysuckle oil

Marital Bliss Incense

1 part vanilla bean (ground)
2 parts wintergreen
1 part khus khus
1 part narcissus
Few drops of wintergreen oil

Burn this incense at night, just before you go to bed.

Virility Incense

¹⁄₂ part holly
¹⁄₄ part patchouli
¹⁄₂ part savory
¹⁄₂ part mandrake
Few drops of civet oil
¹⁄₄ part dragon's blood resin
¹⁄₂ part oak
¹⁄₄ part musk root
Few drops of musk oil

Conceive a Child Incense

¹⁄₂ part mistletoe
1 part mandrake
1¹⁄₂ parts motherwort
Few drops of strawberry oil

Fertility Incense 1

³⁄₄ part allspice
¹⁄₂ part fennel
³⁄₄ part star anise
1 part sandalwood

Fertility Incense 2

¹⁄₂ part basil
¹⁄₂ part dragon's blood resin
¹⁄₄ part holly
1 part pine
¹⁄₄ part juniper berries

Note: The following five incenses should be used carefully because it is not wise to try to influence someone against their will. Your choice of words when performing the ritual is important.

Stay at Home Incense

¹⁄₂ part clove
¹⁄₂ part allspice
¹⁄₂ part deerstongue
1 part mullein
1 part sage

Break Off an Affair Incense

¹⁄₄ part camphor
1 part slippery elm
1¹⁄₂ parts pennyroyal

Divorce Incense

¹⁄₂ part frankincense resin
¹⁄₂ part rue
¹⁄₂ part allspice
¹⁄₄ part marjoram
³⁄₄ part pennyroyal
¹⁄₂ part yarrow
¹⁄₈ part camphor resin
¹⁄₂ part sandalwood

End an Affair Incense

¹⁄₄ part menthol
1¹⁄₂ parts willow
1¹⁄₂ parts lavender

☀ Love Breaker Incense ☀

¹/₂ part vetivert
1 part patchouli
1 part lemongrass
¹/₂ part mullein

This incense can be used to aid the smooth break-up of a relationship.

☀ Release and Ending Incense ☀

¹/₂ part bay
¹/₂ part lemon balm
¹/₄ part yarrow
¹/₂ part pennyroyal
1 part willow
Few drops of lemon balm oil
Few drops of peppermint oil

* * *

Business, Money, Prosperity and Success

After love incense, incense that can be used to bring about success in business affairs and finance are the ones that intrigue people most. On the quiet, many business people who use incense would concede that they have received assistance, but they would hate to admit it publicly. These incenses are especially appropriate for those who value secrecy, because they can be used without fuss to create circumstances where the desired effect becomes inevitable.

Using these incenses might be considered by some to be employing thaumaturgy – magic that is designed to have an effect specifically on the mundane world. Wherever possible, keep your intent as altruistic and as clearly in mind as you can when using incense. The 'higher' the intent, the more likely it is to happen because it can be said to be in accord with the Greater Good. It is suggested that any prosperity, money or success you receive as a consequence is tithed; that is, a portion is dedicated to good causes – in old-style belief, 10 per cent.

It is always possible when preparing incense to make substitutions in the ingredients. They can all be mixed and matched ad infinitum, though you may have to experiment with the quantities until they 'feel' right (or until they smell right).

■ Business

These first ten incenses are burnt when you wish to increase your personal portfolio and business acumen. Burning the confidence incenses, for instance, will help you to gain confidence, but only if you have something to build on in the first place.

☀ Business Incense ☀

2 parts benzoin resin
1 part cinnamon
1 part basil

☀ Confidence Incense 1 ☀

1 part rosemary
¹/₄ part garlic
¹/₂ part camomile
1 part musk root

☀ Confidence Incense 2 ☀

1 part St John's Wort
1 part thyme
¹/₂ part oak
¹/₄ part sweet woodruff

☀ Recognition Incense ☀

2 parts benzoin resin
1 part rue
1 part sandalwood

This incense can be used when you feel your efforts should be recognized and rewarded.

Note: These next three incenses should be used when you require a little extra 'oomph' to carry you along a chosen path.

☀ Determination Incense 1 ☀

¹/₂ part althea
¹/₂ part camomile
1 part thyme
¹/₄ part garlic

❋ Determination Incense 2 ❋

1 part rosemary
1 part willow
1 part musk root
Few drops of musk oil

❋ Determination Incense 3 ❋

½ part allspice
1¼ parts St John's Wort
½ part southernwood
¾ part willow

Note: These following two incenses can be used to encourage the flow of money towards you.

❋ Financial Gain Incense 1 ❋

1 part lovage
1 part bay
¼ part cinnamon
½ part meadowsweet

❋ Financial Gain Incense 2 ❋

½ part star anise
¼ part poppy seed
½ part mistletoe
½ part juniper
1 part cherry

❋ Financial Increase Incense ❋

¼ part cucumber
¾ part allspice
1 part sunflower
¼ part saw palmetto
½ part marigold

This incense can be used when you are deliberately wishing to increase what you already have; that is, make a profit, rather than simply gain money.

Note: These following two incenses may be used when additional information or insight is needed either in specific circumstances or on a day-to-day basis. They are good incenses to burn in a training situation.

❋ Gain Knowledge and Wisdom Incense 1 ❋

¼ part angelica
¼ part vervain
1 part sage
½ part Solomon's Seal

❋ Knowledge and Wisdom Incense 2 ❋

1 part Solomon's Seal
¼ part benzoin resin
½ part vervain
½ part cloves
½ part bay

❋ Money Incense 1 ❋

1 part basil
1 part cinquefoil
½ part hyssop
½ part galangal

❋ Money Incense 2 ❋

1¼ parts lavender
¼ part camomile
¼ part comfrey
1 part red clover
¼ part acacia

❋ More Money Incense ❋

¾ part cinnamon
½ part dragon's blood resin
1¼ parts cascara

Note: These next five incenses are good for accruing more than your immediate needs. The last two enable you to call in, and give, favours when necessary.

❊ Prosperity Incense ❊

1 part frankincense resin
½ part cinnamon
¼ part nutmeg
½ part balm

❊ Wealth Incense ❊

1 part nutmeg
½ – 1 part pepperwort
1 pinch saffron

❊ Increased Wealth Incense ❊

2 parts frankincense resin
1 part cinnamon
1 part nutmeg
½ part clove
½ part ginger
½ part mace

❊ Riches and Favours Incense 1 ❊

2 parts benzoin resin
½ part clove
½ part pepperwort

❊ Riches and Favours Incense 2 ❊

2 parts benzoin resin
1 part wood aloe
½ part peppermint
½ part clove

Note: These next three incenses are used to pull success towards you, whatever you may perceive that to be.

❊ Success Incense 1 ❊

½ part basil
½ part bay
1 part cedar
½ part oak

❊ Success Incense 2 ❊

¼ part mistletoe
½ part marigold
½ part sunflower
¼ part onion
1 part sandalwood

❊ Success Incense 3 ❊

¼ part frankincense resin
½ part sweet woodruff
1½ parts vetivert
¼ part angelica
1 part sandalwood

Note: This following incense can be used when you wish to build on success you have already had.

❊ Greater Success Incense ❊

1½ parts sandalwood
½ part sarsaparilla
½ part motherwort
½ part quassia
Few drops of jasmine oil

■ *Luck*

These next four incenses are all designed to bring good fortune. Your intent is very important when you use a first-rate luck incense. The incenses open the way to winning, rather than actually winning for you.

❊ Good Luck in Life Incense ❊

½ part musk root
1½ part rose
½ parts red clover
½ part galangal root
Few drops of rose oil

❊ Good Luck Incense ❊

½ part dragon's blood resin
½ part mistletoe
1 part cascara
1 part linden

Improve Luck Incense

1 part rosemary
½ part dragon's blood resin
½ part musk root
½ part sandalwood
Few drops of rose oil
Few drops of musk oil

Games of Chance Incense

½ part dragon's blood resin
2 parts gum mastic resin
1 part frankincense resin

This incense could be used, for example, when you wish to try your luck and place a bet.

* * *

Physical and Emotional Health and Healing

Any incense used for the purpose of health and healing should only be used as an adjunct to other methods. If you are prepared to use incense in this way, you will probably have an awareness of alternative healing methods anyway, but they cannot – and should never – be used as substitutes for proper medical advice.

Many of the herbs given here are those which have been used for centuries to alleviate certain conditions, but bearing in mind modern laws and thought, you must make your own decisions as to their effective use. Seek the help of your herbalist or medical practitioner as to the nature of the ingredients and what form they should take (root, powder, and so forth).

It is always possible when preparing incense to make substitutions in the ingredients. They can all be mixed and matched ad infinitum, though you may have to experiment with the quantities until they 'feel' right (or until they smell right).

Physical Health

Cold-healing Incense

1¼ parts pine
½ part cedar
⅛ part camphor
⅛ part menthol
½ part spruce
Few drops of pine oil

Resins have always had their part to play in incense. This particular incense will help ease the symptoms of a cold – you can see from its ingredients it is as much medicinal as magical.

Healing Incense 1

2 parts myrrh resin
1 part cinnamon
1 pinch saffron

Healing Incense 2

1 part rose
1 part eucalyptus
1 part pine
1 pinch saffron

Healing Incense 3

1 part rosemary
1 part juniper

When used in oil form – that is, on a tissue placed on a radiator or in a burner – this incense is easily used in a hospital environment.

Regain Health Incense

3 parts myrrh resin
2 parts nutmeg
1 part cedar
1 part clove
½ part balm
½ part poppy seeds
Few drops of pine oil
Few drops of sweet almond oil

This incense acts as a good 'pick-me-up'.

Emotional Health

All of these incenses help to alter the state of mind and increase the ability to think positively.

✳ Courage Incense ✳

2 parts dragon's blood powder or resin
1 part frankincense resin
1 part rose geranium
1/4 part tonka beans
Few drops of musk oil

✳ Ease Emotional Pain Incense ✳

3 parts bay
3/4 part allspice
1/4 part dragon's blood powder
3/4 part frankincense resin or gum arabic

✳ End Negativity and Give Hope Incense 1 ✳

1 part thyme
1/2 part rue
1/2 part sweet woodruff
1/2 part cloves

✳ End Negativity and Give Hope Incense 2 ✳

1 part dittany
1/2 part camomile
1/4 part patchouli

✳ Happiness Incense 1 ✳

1/2 part myrrh resin
1/4 part marjoram
1 part dittany
3/4 part sandalwood
3/4 part oregano
Few drops of spearmint oil

✳ Happiness Incense 2 ✳

1 part oregano
1 part rosemary
1 part marigold

✳ 'Poor Me' Incense ✳

1/2 part cloves
1/4 part juniper
2 parts willow
1/8 part menthol
Few drops of eucalyptus oil
Few drops of wintergreen oil

This incense can be used for when you feel the whole world is against you.

✳ Tranquillity Incense ✳

1 part sage
1 1/2 parts rose
1/4 part benzoin resin
1/2 part meadowsweet
Few drops of rose oil

This incense induces a sense of tranquillity which allows you to rebalance and recharge your batteries.

Note: These next two incenses give strength and integrity in a chosen task.

✳ Strength Incense 1 ✳

1/2 part dragon's blood powder or resin
1/2 part musk root
1 1/2 parts vetivert
1/2 part cinquefoil
Few drops of musk oil
Few drops of Ambergris oil

✳ Strength Incense 2 ✳

1/2 part cinnamon
1/4 part dragon's blood powder or resin
1/4 part frankincense resin
1/2 part musk root
1/4 part patchouli
1 part vetivert
1/4 part yarrow
Few drops of musk oil

⁂ Study Incense ⁂

2 parts gum mastic
1 part rosemary

Burn this incense to strengthen the conscious mind for study, to develop concentration and to improve your memory.

* * *

Psychic Powers, Divination and Prophetic Dreams

Remembering that the use of mind-altering substances should be very carefully considered, this section sets about indicating substances that alter your sensitive vibrational rate. Each one of us consists of at least a physical body, an astral body and a spiritual aspect. These subtle energies can be successfully adjusted to connect us with other subtle vibrations – it is a little like logging on to a computer and connecting with a particular programme.

The incenses below help us to do this and enable us to work without interference from other less manageable energies. They put us in touch with those inner powers that we use to penetrate other dimensions and help us to develop them without disquiet. Their specific purpose is, by and large, stated in the name of the incense.

It is always possible when preparing incense to make substitutions in the ingredients. They can all be mixed and matched ad infinitum, though you may have to experiment with the quantities until they 'feel' right (or until they smell right).

■ Divination

The following six incenses can be used as part of divinatory rituals.

⁂ Divination Incense 1 ⁂

1 part St John's Wort
³/₄ part wormwood
³/₄ part bay
¹/₂ part frankincense resin

⁂ Divination Incense 2 ⁂

³/₄ part cinquefoil
¹/₈ part valerian
¹/₂ part deerstongue
¹/₂ part frankincense resin
1 part sandalwood

⁂ Divination Incense 3 ⁂

¹/₂ part cinnamon
¹/₂ part chickweed
1 part thyme
1 part sandalwood

⁂ Divination Incense 4 ⁂

1 part yarrow
1 part St John's Wort
¹/₄ part frankincense resin
¹/₂ part bay

⁂ Divination Incense 5 ⁂

1 part lavender
1 part rose
¹/₂ part star anise
¹/₂ part sandalwood

⁂ Divination Incense 6 ⁂

2 parts sandalwood
1 part orange peel
¹/₂ part mace
¹/₂ part cinnamon

■ Psychic Powers

These next four incenses are particularly good for enhancing the psychic powers during magical rituals.

⁂ Psychic Power Incense ⁂

1 part frankincense resin
¹/₄ part bistort

⁂ Psychic Incense 1 ⁂

2 parts sandalwood
1 part gum arabic

❊ Psychic Incense 2 ❊

2 parts sandalwood
1 part gum acacia (or arabic)

❊ Psychic Incense 3 ❊

1 part frankincense resin
1 part sandalwood
1 part cinnamon
1 part nutmeg
Few drops of orange oil
Few drops of clove oil

■ *Past Lives*

These next two incenses can be used when you wish to find out about past lives.

❊ Recall Past Lives Incense ❊

1½ parts sandalwood
½ part water lily
½ part holly
½ part frankincense resin
Few drops of lilac oil

❊ Remember Past Lives Incense ❊

1 part sandalwood
½ part cinnamon
½ part myrrh resin
Few drops of myrrh oil
Few drops of cinnamon oil
Few drops of cucumber oil

■ *Spirit Presence*

These next three incenses are good when you wish to invite positive energies to be present during magical rituals.

❊ Spirit Incense 1 ❊

1 part sandalwood
1 part lavender

Burn on your altar or in your sacred space.

❊ Spirit Incense 2 ❊

2 parts sandalwood
1 part willow bark

This incense is a good one to use (particularly outdoors) when performing rituals during the waxing Moon.

❊ Open Eyes To Spirit World ❊

1 part gum mastic
1 part amaranth
1 part yarrow

■ *Visions*

The next five incenses can all be used as part of rituals where you wish to make a connection with other realms.

❊ Psychic Vision Incense ❊

3 parts frankincense resin
1 part bay
½ part damiana

❊ Second Sight Incense ❊

1 part parsley
½ part hemp seeds
½ part frankincense resin

❊ Sight Incense ❊

2 parts gum mastic
2 parts juniper
1 part sandalwood
1 part cinnamon
1 part calamus
Few drops of patchouli oil
Few drops of ambergris oil

❊ Vision Incense ❊

3 parts cinquefoil
3 Parts chicory root
1 part clove

⁕ Gypsy Sight Incense ⁕

1 part mugwort
¹/₂ part clove
¹/₂ part cinquefoil

Gypsies in particular use this incense when they wish to strengthen their psychic visions.

Celestial Influences

This section is probably for those of you who have chosen to travel a little further on your voyage of discovery. The incenses again are used to make a link or to enhance a specific purpose. It will depend on your own personal belief whether, for instance, you wish to use a specific incense to link with planetary energy or to use a specific incense at the times of the various Sabbats and Moon phases. Planetary influences and correspondences are explained more fully in the Spells Preparation section.

Accepted use has meant that certain woods and herbs are associated with days of the week, seasons of the year and lunar cycles. What follows is an easy-to-consult listing to enable you to get the best out of your rituals. There is nothing to stop you from mixing and matching as you so wish. You may find certain aromas more pleasurable than others.

Days of the Week

The incenses and oils below may be used alone or combined for your daily rituals for maximum effect. They have been recommended according to the planetary ruler of the days of the week.

The Seasons

The following fragrances, either as plants or – where appropriate – essential oils, can be used to welcome each new season in your personal rituals.

Spring: All sweet scents, particularly daffodil, jasmine and rose.

Summer: All spicy scents, particularly carnation, clove and ginger.

Autumn: All earthly scents, particularly oak moss, patchouli and vetiver.

Winter: All resinous and woody scents, particularly frankincense, pine and rosemary.

The following seven incenses are suitable for the various seasons and can be used either to honour the turning of the year or the ideas inherent in seasonal worship.

⁕ Spring Incense ⁕

¹/₄ part primrose
1 part cherry
1 part rose
¹/₂ part sandalwood
Few drops of lilac oil
Few drops of rose oil
Few drops of strawberry oil

⁕ Summer Incense 1 ⁕

1¹/₂ parts lavender
1 part St John's Wort
¹/₂ part mistletoe

Day of the Week	Planetary Influence	Aroma
Monday	Moon	Jasmine, lemon, sandalwood, Stephanotis
Tuesday	Mars	Basil, coriander, ginger, nasturtium
Wednesday	Mercury	Benzoin, cary sage, eucalyptus, lavender
Thursday	Jupiter	Clove, lemon balm, melissa, oakmoss, star anise
Friday	Venus	Cardamon, palma rosa, rose, yarrow
Saturday	Saturn	Cypress, mimosa, myrrh, patchouli
Sunday	Sun	Cedar, frankincense, neroli, rosemary

❋ Summer Incense 2 ❋

1 part cedar
¹⁄₂ part juniper
1 part sandalwood

❋ Autumn Incense ❋

¹⁄₄ part oak
¹⁄₂ part pine
¹⁄₄ part frankincense resin
¹⁄₄ cinnamon
¹⁄₄ part cloves
¹⁄₂ part rosemary
¹⁄₄ part sage
¹⁄₂ part pomegranate

❋ Winter Incense ❋

1¹⁄₄ parts lavender
¹⁄₂ part cloves
¹⁄₂ part cinnamon
¹⁄₄ part benzoin resin
¹⁄₄ part patchouli
¹⁄₄ part mistletoe
¹⁄₄ part orris root
Few drops of bergamot oil

❋ Winter Incense 2 ❋

¹⁄₂ part mistletoe
¹⁄₄ part holly
¹⁄₂ part bay
¹⁄₂ part oak
1 part pine
¹⁄₂ part cedar
Few drops of pine oil
Few drops of cedar oil

◼ *The Lunar Cycle*

Incense and perfumes can be utilized during the phases of the Moon to put you in touch with lunar energy.

Sandalwood is particularly appropriate for the first quarter when the Moon's waxing enhances spirituality.
Jasmine has the full-blown energies of the Full Moon.
Lemon, which is more ethereal, is symbolic of

the lessening of the Moon's influence as it wanes in the last quarter.
Camphor signifies the similarly cold New Moon.

◼ *The Elements*

Tradition dictates that you honour the four 'directions' and their appropriate Elements. The following four incenses are suitable for honouring the four directions or cardinal points before moving onto the ritual proper. You can then use any of the other incenses for their appropriate purpose.

❋ Air Incense ❋

2 parts benzoin resin
1 part gum mastic
¹⁄₂ part lavender
¹⁄₄ part wormwood
1 pinch mistletoe

❋ Earth Incense ❋

1 part pine
1 part thyme
Few drops patchouli oil

❋ Fire Incense ❋

2 parts frankincense resin
1 part dragon's blood resin
1 part red sandalwood
1 pinch saffron

❋ Water Incense ❋

2 parts benzoin resin
1 part myrrh resin
1 part sandalwood
Few drops of lotus oil

◼ *Planetary*

These incenses can be used when you wish to call particularly on the power of the planets in your rituals. Incenses suitable for use with Neptune, Uranus and Pluto are not included, as here you might like to use your own intuition. You will find the significances of the planets in the astrological section on pages 93-94.

☀ Sun Incense 1 ☀

*3 parts frankincense resin
2 parts myrrh resin
1 part wood aloe
½ part Balm of Gilead
½ part bay
½ part carnation
Few drops of ambergris oil
Few drops of musk oil
Few drops of olive oil*

Burn this incense to draw on the influences of the Sun and for spells involving promotions, friendships, healing, energy and magical power.

☀ Sun Incense 2 ☀

*3 parts frankincense resin
2 parts sandalwood
1 part bay
1 pinch saffron
Few drops of orange oil*

☀ Sun Incense 3 ☀

*3 parts frankincense resin
2 parts galangal root
2 parts bay
¼ part mistletoe
Few drops of red wine
Few drops of honey*

☀ Egyptian Solar Incense ☀

*3 parts frankincense resin
1 part clove
½ part red sandalwood
½ part sandalwood
¼ part orange flowers
3 pinches of orris root*

☀ Moon Incense 1 ☀

*2 parts juniper
1 part calamus
½ part orris root
¼ part camphor
Few drops of lotus oil*

☀ Moon Incense 2 ☀

*4 parts sandalwood
2 parts wood aloe
1 part eucalyptus
1 part crushed cucumber seeds
1 part mugwort
½ part ranuculus blossoms
1 part selenetrope (you can substitute gardenia or
jasmine if you cannot find selenetrope easily)
Few drops of ambergris oil*

☀ Moon Incense 3 ☀

*2 parts juniper berries
1 part orris root
1 part calamus
Few drops of spirits of camphor or camphor
tincture or ¼ part genuine camphor
Few drops of lotus bouquet oil*

☀ Moon Incense 4 ☀

*2 parts myrrh resin
2 parts gardenia petals
1 part rose petals
1 part lemon peel
½ part camphor
Few drops of jasmine oil*

☀ Moonfire Incense 5 ☀

*1 part rose
1 part orris root
1 part bay
1 part juniper
1 part dragon's blood powder or resin
½ part potassium nitrate (saltpetre)*

Burn this incense when you wish to call on the power of the Moon while performing divination and love rituals. The potassium nitrate (saltpetre) is included to make the incense sparkle and glow. Do not add too much though, and add it gradually – it will explode.

Earth Incense

2 parts pine
1 part patchouli
1 part cypress
1 pinch salt

Mercury Incense 1

2 parts benzoin resin
1 part mace
½ part marjoram
Few drops of lavender oil

Burn this incense to invoke Mercury's powers and qualities when performing rituals for such things as intelligence, travel and divination.

Mercury Incense 2

2 parts sandalwood
1 part mace
1 part marjoram
1 part mint or a few drops of mint oil

Venus Incense 1

2 parts sandalwood
1 part benzoin resin
1 part rose petals
Few drops of rose oil
Few drops of patchouli oil

A Venus Ritual for Beauty

The goddess Venus is the goddess of beauty and the planet Venus – the brightest object in the sky other than the Sun and the Moon – is known as both the Morning and the Evening Star, thus this spell is best performed either in the morning or in the evening or both. Venus' mirror was said to have a handle, which is why her symbol is the shape it is.

YOU WILL NEED
White candle
Mirror, preferably with handle
If using a round mirror, inscribe
it with this symbol on the back

Venus incense
Silver or glass bowl
Rosewater
Cotton wool

METHOD

❖ Light the candle and the incense.
❖ Put the rosewater in the bowl.
❖ Take the mirror in your left hand and, catching the reflection of the candle in the mirror, project the light all the way round your sacred space. (If you are good at this you might do this three times in all but it is not necessary.)
❖ As you do so, ask the goddess of love to bless your space and grace it with her presence.
❖ Replace the mirror face up in a position where you can see to use it.
❖ Hold the bowl up in your hands and ask the goddess to consecrate the contents.
❖ Dampen the cotton wool with the rosewater and gently wipe your face with it.
❖ As you look in the mirror, ask the goddess now to bless you.
❖ You might use words such as these:

Goddess of Beauty, Goddess of Love
As I perform this age-old ritual, help me now
Make me beautiful, not to rival you
But always to honour and praise you.

❖ Replace the bowl on the altar and sit quietly, allowing the feeling of beauty to flow through you.
❖ When finished, dispose of everything carefully and use the mirror as part of your beauty routine.

In effect what you have done here is to use the mirror first to project Venus' light and secondly as a tool to beautify yourself. This shows how everyday objects can easily become magical tools in everyday routines.

Venus Incense 2

3 parts wood aloe
1 part red rose petals
Few drops of olive oil
Few drops of musk oil
Few drops of ambergris oil

You may find it easier to mix the oils together first. Burn this for help from Venus in spells for love, healing and rituals involving women and beauty.

Mars Incense 1

2 parts galangal root
1 part coriander
1 part cloves
1/2 part basil
Pinch of black pepper

Mars Incense 2

2 parts dragon's blood powder or resin
1 part cardamom
1 part clove
1 part Grains of Paradise

This is a good incense to use if you need the assertive qualities of Mars.

Mars Incense 3

4 parts benzoin resin
1 part pine needles or resin
Scant pinch of black pepper

Burn this incense to utilize the powers and attributes of Mars or during spells involving lust, competition of any sort and anything to do with the masculine.

Jupiter Incense

1 part clove
1 part nutmeg
1 part cinnamon
1/2 part balm
1/2 part lemon peel

Remember that Jupiter is the planet and god of expansion, so you need to be very specific in your intent when calling upon Jupiter.

Saturn Incense 1

2 parts sandalwood resin
2 parts myrrh resin
1 part Dittany of Crete
Few drops of cypress oil
Few drops of patchouli oil

This is the recommended Saturn incense formula. Remember that Saturn does put blocks in the way, but then also encourages from behind.

Saturn Incense 2

2 parts cypress
1 part myrrh resin
1 part dittany
Few drops of patchouli oil

Ceremonial and Consecrational

Here we have put together some of the older types of incense. Some are suitable for consecrating your altar, your tools, your circle and other artefacts, while others will help strengthen the magic in the ritual itself.

Altar Incense

1 part frankincense resin
1/2 part myrrh resin
1/4 part cinnamon

❊ Consecration Incense ❊

1 part mace
½ part frankincense resin
1 part benzoin resin
1 part gum arabic

This incense can be used for consecrating your sacred space as well as any tools you may need.

❊ Ceremonial Magic Incense ❊

1 part frankincense resin
½ part gum mastic
¼ part sandalwood

❊ Ritual Magic Incense ❊

2 parts frankincense resin
1 part wood aloe
Few drops of musk oil
Few drops of ambergris oil

❊ Circle Incense ❊

2 parts frankincense resin
1 part myrrh resin
1 part benzoin resin
½ part sandalwood
¼ part cinnamon
½ part rose
½ part bay
¼ part vervain
¼ part rosemary

❊ Sacred Space Incense ❊

½ part bay
½ part camphor
½ part lavender
½ part broom
½ part linden
½ part ground ivy

❊ Crystal Purification Incense ❊

2 parts frankincense resin
2 parts copal resin
1 part sandalwood
1 part rosemary

This incense is used when consecrating your crystals so that they work magically for you. It 'wipes' all other vibration and aligns the crystal with your purpose.

❊ Offertory Incense ❊

2 parts frankincense resin
1 part myrrh resin
1 part cinnamon
½ part rose petals
½ part vervain

Burn this incense while honouring the goddesses and gods and also as an offering during rituals.

❊ Talisman and Amulet Consecration Incense ❊

2 parts frankincense resin
1 part cypress
1 part tobacco
1/2 part ash

❊ Talisman Consecration ❊

2 parts frankincense resin
1 part cypress
1 part ash leaves
1 part tobacco
1 pinch valerian
1 pinch alum
1 pinch of asafoetida powder (smells horrible)

❊ Temple Incense ❊

3 parts frankincense resin
2 parts myrrh resin
Few drops of lavender oil
Few drops of sandalwood oil

Burn this incense in your sacred space or grove. You can also use this as a general magical incense or to consecrate your shrine.

❋ Universal Incense ❋

3 parts frankincense resin
2 parts benzoin resin
1 part myrrh resin
1 part sandalwood
1 part rosemary

Burn this incense for all positive magical purposes. If used for negative magical goals, it will cancel out the spell or ritual.

The use of incense becomes such a part of everyday life that you will often find yourself feeling quite bereft when you are not within your own personally enhanced environment. Given below is a way of being able to enhance your environment wherever you are.

Incense Cones

These cones are useful if you are travelling and do not have access to your normal sources of supply. You could, of course, pop them into your travelling tools roll (see page 26). However, grinding charcoal is extremely messy and it tends to fly everywhere. Try wrapping a few briquettes of barbeque charcoal in several layers of newspaper or old cloth and giving it some hefty thumps with a hammer. Think of Thor, whose symbol is a hammer, while you are doing it.

YOU WILL NEED ───────────────

6 parts ground charcoal
1 part ground benzoin
2 parts ground sandalwood
1 part ground orris root
Pestle and mortar
Bowl
6 drops essential oil (use the oil from of one of the ingredients in your chosen incense)
2–4 parts incense according to any of the given recipes above
10 per cent by weight of potassium nitrate
gum tragacanth or gum arabic

METHOD ──────────────────

❖ Mix the first four ingredients in the pestle until well blended.

❖ Add the essential oil and mix again.
❖ You will need to create a fine powdered mixture with a fine texture so use a good mortar!
❖ Add 2–4 parts of your chosen incense mixture, grinding and empowering it thoroughly.
❖ Place all these ingredients in the bowl and combine them well with your hands, thinking all the time of your intended purpose.
❖ Weigh and add 10 per cent potassium nitrate (which is a white powder). Mix until thoroughly blended. Never add more than 10 per cent, otherwise it will explode.
❖ Add the tragacanth glue or gum arabic. Do this a teaspoon at a time, mixing with your hands in a large bowl until all ingredients are dampened and the mixture is stiff and doughlike.
❖ Shape the mixture into small cones and let it dry slowly for 2–7 days either in the sun, a slow oven or an airing cupboard.

OILS

At various points in the book, you will read of the many oils that can be utilized as adjuncts to the various types of magic. They are an easy way of using plants in magical workings, particularly when space is at a premium.

Below are some oils that should be part of every magical practitioner's way of working. For your reference their Latin names are also given. All of them are simple to acquire and even though the initial expense may seem to be prohibitive, if they are stored according to directions, they will last for some time. (If you want to delve further into the art of using essential oils, there are many good reference books available.)

Cinnamon (*Cinnamomum zeylanicum*), with its warm vibration, brings into our hearts love from higher realms, if only we allow it. The warm glow of cinnamon exudes right through space and time, transforming sadness into happiness. Cinnamon was used in China in 2700BC, and was known to the Egyptians by 1500BC.

Clary sage (*Salvia sclarea*) has benefits for both the physical and mental aspects of mankind, teaching us to be content with what we have. It brings prosperity of the spirit, and the realization that most problems arise in our imagination. This herb lifts the spirit and links with eternal wisdom.

Frankincense *(Boswellia carterii)* holds some of the wisdom of the universe, both spiritual and meditative. Able to cleanse the most negative of influences, it operates as a spiritual prop in a wide range of circumstances. It works far beyond the auric field, affecting the very subtle realms of energy and adapting the spiritual state. Frankincense is sometimes called olibanum.

Geranium *(Pelargonium graveolens)* resonates with Mother Earth and all that is feminine. It typifies the archetypal energy of Goddess culture. Its energy is transformational and as such it must always be used with respect. It comforts, opens our hearts and heals pain.

Jasmine *(Jasminum officinale)* provides us with our personal sanctuary and allows us access to a greater understanding of the spirit. It is said that jasmine brings the angelic kingdom within our reach, thus allowing us to be the best we can. It gives understanding and acceptance of the true meaning of spirituality.

Lavender *(Lavendula augustifolia)* is caring and nurturing. By allowing the heavenly energies close to the physical, it brings about healing and thus signifies the protective love of Mother Earth. Gentle and relaxing, it changes the perception to enable one to make progress. Lavender will not allow negative emotion to remain present within the aura for long.

Myrrh *(Commiphora myrrha)* signifies the pathway of the soul, allowing us to let go when the time is right. Wounds of body, mind and spirit are healed by myrrh and it brings realization that we no longer need to carry our burdens, releasing them from deep within. When combined with other oils, it enhances – and is enhanced by – them.

Neroli *(Citrus aurantium)* is one of the most precious essential oils, its vibration being one of the highest. It is pure spirit and is loving and peaceful. It brings self-recognition and respite because it allows development of a new perspective, allowing us to cast off the bonds of old ways of relating and to develop unconditional love. In magical working it allows one to be a pure channel.

Nutmeg *(Myristica fragrans)* helps us to reconnect with the higher realms of spirit and to experience again a sense of spiritual wonderment. When the spirit is affected by disappointment, spiritual pain and displacement, nutmeg works to bring hopes, dreams and prayers back into focus. At one time, nutmeg was given to people who were thought to be possessed by spirits.

Rose absolut *(Rosa centifolia)* In India the 'Great Mother' was known as the 'Holy Rose' and this personification reveals just how profound the effects of this perfume are when used magically. Said to be the perfume of the guardians or messengers who guide us in times of need, it is a soul fragrance which allows us to access the divine mysteries. It is associated with the true needs of the human heart.

Rosemary *(Rosmarinus officinalis)* reminds us of our purpose and of our own spiritual journey. It opens the human spirit to understanding and wisdom, and encourages confidence and clarity of purpose. It cleanses the aura and enables us to assist others in their search for spirituality.

Sandalwood *(Santalum album)* acts as a bridge between heaven and earth and allows us to make contact with divine beings. It enables us to be calm enough to hear the music of the spheres and beings us into balance with the cosmos. It clarifies our strength of conviction.

Ylang ylang *(Cananga odorata)* gives a new appreciation of the sensual side of our being. It balances the spirit so that we can be open to pleasures of the physical realm while still appreciating spiritual passions. It brings a sense of completion to the tasks that belong to the physical realm. Used magically, it achieves a balanced manifestation.

Ritual Bathing

One way in which essential oils can be used is in preparation for ritual and spell making. Magical practitioners know that ritual bathing is an intrinsic part of any working and that they should come to their work as pure and unsullied as possible. Purification baths are not about personal cleanliness, but are part of acknowledging that the power and energy will flow more freely through a cleansed 'vessel'. On pages 227-228 there is a method for a ritual bath, as well as a way of preparing bath salts.

Essential oils have within them all four of the Elements, a fact that many people like to acknowledge. They are products of the Earth, having been distilled they flow (Water), they will burn (Fire) and they release perfume (Air). When the water and salt – which also has a cleansing effect – of a ritual bath are combined, we have a perfect vehicle for cleansing our subtle energies.

Below are some ideas for you to try as blends for use in your ritual bath. The particular blends do have different effects, depending on the individual, so experiment until you find the one that suits you best. Make sure the oils are well blended.

※ Ritual Bath Oil Blends ※

Neroli 3 drops
Orange 1 drop
Petitgrain 2 drops

Myrtle 3 drops
Clary sage 1 drop
Lemon 1 drop

Rosemary 2 drops
Eucalyptus 1 drop
Lavender 3 drops

Chamomile 3 drops
Mandarin 3 drops

Frankincense 4 drops
Lemon 2 drops

Rose 3 drops
Neroli 3 drops

▧ *Essential oil blends*

Essential oils can be used in spells to generate a higher vibration. The following blends can be used for anointing candles and for blessing objects as well as for personal use. Ideally, when you combine oils, they should be well shaken together and left for at least an hour so that the synergy begins to work. Synergy takes place when the subtle vibrations of the oils blend to create a further vibration, therefore enhancing their energy.

One of the main interests of many readers is relationship and security. Below are some oil blends that deal with this area of life; most of these recipes have been attributed to the Romanies.

If you are intending on using essential oils as massage oils, remember to use a carrier oil such as almond or grapeseed. Neat essential oils should, as a rule, never be used directly on the skin or ingested.

※ Romance Magnet Oil ※

2 drops ylang ylang oil
2 drops sandalwood oil
2 drops clary sage oil

To attract love, rub romance magnet oil onto a pink candle and then burn it for three hours a day, every day, until the person makes an advance. The candle should be snuffed rather than blown out.

※ Lover's Oil ※

5 drops rosewood oil
5 drops rosemary oil
3 drops tangerine oil
3 drops lemon oil

Lover's oil may be used to enhance a relationship in all sorts of ways. Consecrate a candle with lover's oil and light it half an hour before your date arrives.

※ Marriage Oil ※

2 drops frankincense oil
3 drops cypress oil
2 drops sandalwood oil

This combination of oils is used to reinforce a marriage relationship, whether the union is good or not. It may also be used to help steer a relationship towards marriage or further commitment. Simply burn a pink or lilac-coloured candle anointed with marriage oil when you and your partner are together.

❋ Desire Oil ❋

3 drops lavender oil
3 drops orange oil
1 drop lemon oil

Desire oil is meant to entice another person to want you. If someone already does, but needs a little pushing, a red, orange, pink, blue, or white candle should be anointed and lit when the two of you are together. If you love someone and they are showing no response, speak their name as you light a candle blessed with desire oil.

Allow the candles to burn for two hours before you snuff them out.

Repeat, until the person reacts.

❋ Dream Potion ❋

10 drops jasmine oil
10 drops nutmeg oil
3 drops clary sage

This oil can be used to enhance the atmosphere of the bedroom before sleep. It is best burnt in an aromatherapy lamp rather being used as a body oil.

❋ To Strengthen an Existing Relationship ❋

10 drops rose oil
10 drops sandalwood oil
5 drops lavender oil

This oil can be used as a perfume or to scent the atmosphere. The following two recipes can be used in the same way.

Note: The skin reacts in different ways to perfume and it has been found that men and women prefer different aromas. These next two oils take both these facts into account.

❋ To Draw Love Towards You ❋

10 drops rose oil
5 drops jasmine oil
5 drops ylang ylang

This blend is for use if you are female.

❋ To Draw Love Towards You ❋

5 drops rose oil
15 drops sandalwood
2 drops vetiver
10 drops patchouli

This blend is for use if you are male.

Aphrodisiac Oils

Use the following two potent mixtures as a perfume or added to 50 ml (2 fl oz) of unscented massage oil (such as grapeseed or almond oil) and have fun!

10 drops ylang ylang
2 drops cinnamon
5 drops sweet orange
3 drops jasmine oil

10 drops patchouli
10 drops sandalwood
10 drops ylang ylang

Oils for Ritual Work

The following oil blends can all be used in ritual work.

❋ Sacred Space Blend ❋

20 drops juniper berry oil
10 drops frankincense oil
10 drops sandalwood oil
5 drops rosemary oil
2 drops nutmeg oil

This is a good blend to use when you need to create a sacred space or magical circle. Burnt in an aromatherapy lamp it clears and enhances the atmosphere.

❋ Prosperity Blend ❋

Equal parts of patchouli and basil oil

This combination creates the right vibration for prosperity of all sorts (not necessarily financial).

⚘ Altar Oil Blend ⚘

4 parts frankincense
3 parts myrrh
1 part galangal
1 part vervain
1 part lavender

This blend is one that can be used to anoint your altar, if you use one, or to diffuse around your sacred space at regular intervals, before you undertake any ritual, to purify and empower the space.

⚘ Goddess Oil Blend ⚘

10 drops neroli oil
5 drops nutmeg oil
10 drops sandalwood oil
10 drops jasmine oil

When you invoke the Goddess, this oil is wonderful for allowing your vibration to meet with hers at any time of the year.

⚘ Protection Blend ⚘

10 drops juniper oil
5 drops vetiver oil
5 drops basil oil
2 drops clove oil

Should you feel that you are in need of protection, this oil can be burnt in an aromatherapy burner or sprinkled on a tissue and placed on a warm radiator.

Using Essential Oils in the Auric Field

As they begin working magically, almost all practitioners will find that they become more sensitive to the vibrations of the ordinary, everyday world. A crowded train, for instance, when you are bombarded by the various vibrations of your fellow travellers, can be very difficult to handle. This difficulty arises because your own particular 'force field', called the aura – which you carry with you always – begins to vibrate at a different level than the one to which you are accustomed and do not notice on an everyday level.

If you begin to do a great deal of magical work, you must learn to protect yourself, perhaps from onslaughts of negativity or subtle vibrations over which others have no control. Always remember that you have at your disposal the means for control and it should become a regular part of your routine to enhance your own aura and to protect that of others. Essential oils can help you to do this.

Methods of Using Oils for Protective Purposes

Method 1 Put just one drop of your chosen pure essential oil in the centre of your palm and rub your hands together. In this instance the oil is used neat. Holding your hands about 10 cm (4 in) away from your body, smooth around the outside of this space, starting from the top of your head down to your feet and then back up again. Make sure you have covered every part that you can reach of this very subtle body. This is also known as protecting your aura.

Method 2 Use your chosen oils in a spray or diffuser, spraying around your body and over the top of your head again, ensuring that you cover the whole area. Prepare your oils in advance, combining them as necessary. Leave them for a week in a quiet, dark place away from electrical equipment. On the eighth day use a new fragrance sprayer, preferably a glass bottle, add about 25 ml (1 fl oz) of the purest water available and the essential oils and shake the sprayer vigorously. This can also be used to protect your sacred space or immediate environment.

Energizing Oils

The following are energizing oils and will give a real lift to your power (the proportions used can be to your own personal preference):

Basil, Coriander, Eucalyptus, Fir, Lemon, Peppermint, Spruce

Harmonizing Oils

The oils in this next group are used for establishing harmony, both in person who uses them and in the atmosphere:

Clary sage, Fennel, Geranium, Ginger, Juniper, Lavender, Mandarin, Orange, Petitgrain

Following is a selection of recipes based on all these oils:

Cleansing blend

Pine 4 drops
Lemon 3 drops
Basil 3 drops
Fir needle 5 drops
Spruce 5 drops

This blend cleanses the aura, as suggested above, and gives an idea of the correct proportions to use.

Aura harmonization

Geranium 4 drops
Juniper 2 drops
Orange 6 drops
Fennel 1 drop
Petitgrain 6 drops

This blend is particularly useful when you wish to cleanse and harmonize your aura.

Connecting with the Essential

The oils below help you to make a connection with your spiritual self, the essential you:

Frankincense, Rose, Neroli, Linden blossom
Jasmine

Linking blend

Galbanum 1 drop
Frankincense 4 drops
Jasmine 2 drops
Neroli 7 drops
Rose 7 drops

THE MAGIC OF NATURE AND TREES

Having looked at the components of spells and magical workings, it is now time to turn our attention to magical woods and trees. Natural objects, such as trees, are such an integral part of magic that any practitioner worth their salt has to have a fairly extensive knowledge of their meanings and properties.

We can gain a clear picture of the role of trees in the sacred life of the people of ancient Europe by looking at the myths and stories dealing with mystical states of consciousness. The following quote, from the ancient Scandinavian Poetic Edda, refers to the archetypal journey into shamanic knowledge undertaken by the god Odin. The story is that, in order to acquire eternal wisdom, Odin hung for nine days upside down on the Tree of Knowledge:

I know that I hung on the windswept tree.
The wisest know not from whence
Spring the roots of that ancient tree.

To the peoples of the old world, the trees around them provided building materials and weaponry and also fuel for heat and cooking. Many woods, however, also provided a powerful spiritual presence. Those believed to be sacred shared certain traits, though different cultures accorded their trees varying significances. The great oak, the mystical yew and so many others, are reminders of the power that trees have on our lives – the power of the tree's spirit could grant that tree a central place in the folklore and mythology of a culture. Even today we find that certain trees capture our imagination and our thoughts. Once we accept that trees are living things, filled with the essence and energy of the Elementals and of Mother Earth, we sense power, which is often visible to those who have taken the trouble to see.

The lore that surrounds particular trees or woods often reflects the power the old ones sensed and drew from their presence, and this can be seen in the combination of oak, ash and thorn. All three trees are counted as sacred in the Druidic tradition and are part of the Celtic Tree Calendar (as is elder). They are often called the 'Fairy Triad' because groves that include all three of them are truly magical places where it is said you can spot fairies.

Traditionally, if you take wood from a tree for magical purposes, make sure you ask the tree for permission to do so and leave a gift in its place.

The trees listed below are those which were – and indeed still are – considered to have magical properties.

Alder

This tree was sacred to the Druids. To this day, some water diviners still use its forked branches, traditionally called 'wishing rods'. It is still considered a crime to cut down a sacred alder tree and the culprit is considered to be the cause of any trouble in the community.

The alder is associated with courage and represents the evolving spirit. It commemorates Bran, who was a mighty warrior of ancient Britain. In one battle, Bran fights the Ash King on behalf of the Alder King. Though he loses the battle, he is still recognized as a great warrior.

Alder wood is used in dairy vessels and to make whistles, as the pith is easily pushed out of the green shoots. Several of these shoots can be bound together and trimmed to the desired length for producing various notes – this whistle can be used to entice Air Elementals. The old superstition of 'whistling up the wind' began with this custom.

Apple

This is another tree sacred to the Druids. There are several magical uses for the apple. An apple-wood wand is the appropriate one to use if you want to make shamanic journeys, since the apple is used as a calling sign to the Otherworld. The wand will help you physically, mentally and spiritually connect to the apple tree. You might also use apple cider in any spells calling for blood or wine.

Apple indicates choice, and is useful for love and healing magic. When choices are offered, the biggest test is to select only one and not to waste energy in vacillation.

Ash

Since ancient times, some have believed that the first man was created from the branches and flesh of the ash tree. Druid wands were often made of ash, for they were good for healing and general and solar magic, on account of the wood's straight grain. It is said that you should put fresh ash leaves under your pillow to stimulate psychic dreams.

One mythological belief focuses on when Christianity was brought to Northern Europe. The Scandinavian gods of the north were obviously affected by this new belief of Christianity and transformed themselves into witches. The ash became their favourite tree, since it contained a good deal of knowledge. In Celtic mythology the ash is known as the tree of enchantment, because the Celts believed that they came from the Great Deep or the undersea land of Tethys.

Birch

Known as Lady of the Woods, paper birch and white birch, the birch tree, being symbolic of fertility and new birth, is closely associated with the waxing phase of the Moon. Girls would often give their lovers a twig of birch as a sign of encouragement to indicate that they no longer wished to be maidens. The 'besom wedding' was, for a long time, considered legal and jumping the broomstick – usually made of birch – is still part of pagan ceremony. In Norse mythology, the birch is dedicated to Thor. Emotionally, the birch is all about being nurtured and cared for; spiritually we are cleansed and made ready for the future.

The following love charm uses, in birch, the recognition of the change from maiden to mother and is an indication to the universe that you are ready to take on the responsibility of partnership.

A Love Charm

YOU WILL NEED

Strips of birch bark gathered at the New Moon
Red ink and pen
Love Incense 6 (on page 60)

METHOD

❖ Write on the birch strip
  Bring me true love
❖ Burn the strip along with the incense and say:

> *Goddess of love, God of desire,*
> *Bring to me sweet passion's fire.*

❖ Alternatively, cast the bark into a stream or other flowing water, saying:

> *Message of love, I set you free,*
> *to capture a love and return to me.*

Blackthorn

Blackthorn is a winter tree with a black bark and truly nasty thorns, which are sometimes used negatively in poppet magic. The thorny hedges symbolize the idea that you may discover new opportunities or direction if you are prepared to deal with a chaotic situation first. Blackthorn indicates outside influences that must be obeyed and may well appear when a negative challenge is presented. This tree teaches its lessons well and will help to create a psychic barrier to protect you against similar situations arising in the future. The white flowers are seen even before the leaves in the spring. The wood is used for the shillelagh, a protective staff.

Broom

Also known as Scotch broom or Irish broom, it can be substituted for furze (gorse) at the time of the spring equinox. Sweep your outside ritual areas with it to purify and protect them; burning the blooms and shoots is said to calm the wind. Broom multiplies profusely if there is a need for its protective powers. The Irish called it the 'physician's power' because of its diuretic properties.

Cedar

Also known as the tree of life, arbor vitae and yellow cedar, this tree grows to a great height and has a very imposing spread. The wood is reddish-white, fragrant, and close-grained, particularly in older trees. Size made a tree important, but this is only part of the reason that it was much revered by the Ancients. The oil that it produces is highly preservative and the tree's longevity is part of its sacredness.

To draw Earth energy and ground yourself, place the palms of your hands against the ends of the leaves. It is often used in incenses to honour the gods.

Elder

Also known as ellhorn, elderberry and lady elder, this is a tree the Druids used to regulate their communities and to bless. Elder wands can be used to drive out evil spirits or thought forms. Music played on panpipes or flutes of elder has the same power as the wand. As a protection against evil (and later against witchcraft), its twigs were carried, while its branches were hung in the doorways of houses and cowsheds and buried in graves. Ancient folklore states that you put your baby at risk if its crib is made from elder wood; you run the risk of the fairies coming to take your baby away. In German-Scandinavian folklore the Hydermolder is a particularly malign nature spirit associated with elder.

Elderflowers have many magical uses. You can keep some on your altar to use with any spell which calls on the energy of the fairies or nature spirits. They are particularly useful when performing rituals for prosperity, healing, binding, banishing and protection.

Elder is sacred to the White Lady and midsummer solstice, and it is said that standing under an elder tree at midsummer will help you see the fairies. The elder is also the Old Crone aspect of the Triple Goddess, and her protection and blessing is powerful.

A Blessing

METHOD

❖ Scatter elder leaves and berries to the four directions, and over the object or person to be blessed.

❖ Say:

> *Goddess of Wisdom, Goddess of Mystery,*
> *Third of the Threefold,*
> *Bless now this [person/object]*
> *As transformation comes to pass.*

At Samhain (31 October), the last of the elderberries are picked with solemn ceremony. The wine made from these berries was considered to be the last sacred gift of the Earth Goddess.

Elm

A slightly fibrous, tan-coloured wood with a slight sheen, elm wood is valued for its resistance to splitting. The inner bark was used for cordage and chair caning. Elm is often associated with Mother and Earth Goddesses, and was said to be the abode of fairies. Elm adds stability and grounding to a spell. Once known as 'elven', its nature spirit is the elf. When carried by humans elm will ensure a new love.

Fir

Fir is a very tall slender tree that grows in mountainous regions on the upper slopes. Its cones respond to varying weather conditions by opening and closing. Symbolically, fir indicates high perspectives with a clear vision of what is beyond and yet to come.

Fir is known as the birth tree; its silver needles are burned at childbirth to bless and protect the mother and baby, and to clear the environment. According to Scandinavian folklore, the spirit or Genii of the Forest is traditionally depicted as holding an uprooted fir tree.

It is believed that the fir tree has strong connections with the owner of the land where it stands. Should a fir tree ever be struck by lightning, begin to wither or be touched, it is said that death is present, and the owner will die.

Hawthorn

Also known as May tree, white thorn, haegthorn and quickthorn, this is one of the most wild, enchanted and sacred of trees. It can live to a great age, becoming gnarled in the process. Hawthorn is traditionally used to make psychic shields for the innocent and vulnerable, particularly children – often at puberty when the youngster may be particularly sensitive.

The hawthorn tree is associated with the sacred as well as with inauspicious events. Because the hawthorn guarded the celestial fire, to destroy a hawthorn was to incur the wrath of the gods. Wands made of this wood are of great power. The blossoms are highly erotic to men. Hawthorn can be used for protection, love and marriage spells. You can make a charm ball, which incorporates these, at first light at Samhain.

Charm Ball

The charm ball that you make represents your new self with all its dreams and aspirations. Each year, as you replace it with a new one, it then becomes a representation of the troubles and difficulties of the previous year. It is similar to the Sun Wheel used during the Sabbat

performed at Litha. You burn the old one on a bonfire of straw, ash twigs and acorns (see ash and oak above and below).

YOU WILL NEED

Hawthorn twigs
White ribbon

METHOD

* As you fashion and weave the ball by bending and interlocking the twigs, visualize what you want for you and yours, and how you wish the coming year to be.
* Finish it off by tying it with the white ribbon.
* Hang it in a window or doorway.

Hazel

The hazel tree has long been magical and is used to gain knowledge, wisdom and poetic inspiration and the art of communication. It is said that it was the nine magical hazelnuts that gave the Salmon of Knowledge its wisdom. Wands made of this wood symbolize white magic and healing, while forked sticks are traditionally used to find water or buried treasure.

If you are in need of magical protection, string hazelnuts on a cord and hang them up in your home or sacred space and carry them with you when out and about. When you are working with nature, a circle drawn around you with a hazel twig will enhance the energy.

Holly

A white wood with an almost invisible grain, holly is similar in appearance to ivory. Associated with death and rebirth, holly may be used in spells to do with sleep or rest, and to ease death's transition. This symbolism is evident in both pagan and Christian lore, and holly is important at Yuletide. In Celtic mythology, holly is the evergreen twin of the oak. It is called a kerm-oak. The oak rules the light part of the year, while holly rules the dark part.

Holly suggests directed balance and the courage to fight if the cause is just. A symbol of luck and good fortune, a bag of its leaves and berries carried by a man is said to increase his ability to attract women.

Ivy

Ivy is evergreen and represents the ever-present aspects of the human psyche. Traditionally regarded as the harbinger of death, ivy is associated by the Celts with their lunar goddess Arianrhod and her ritual, which marks the opening of the portal to the Otherworld, but is also a symbol of hope for better things to come.

Ivy was worn as a crown at the winter feast of Saturnalia. It is associated primarily with fidelity and is a symbol of married love and loyalty and stable relationships. Houses with ivy growing on them are reputedly safe from psychic attack. Ivy represents all that is mysterious and mystical.

Juniper

An evergreen coniferous tree, which has prickly leaves and dark purple berries, juniper is used in numerous incenses. Berries were used with thyme in Druid and Grove incenses for visions and manifestation, the smoke being helpful to the working. Also used for protection and purification, juniper can be grown by the door where it discourages thieves. A small bunch of twigs or a few berries in a pouch can also be hung in the rafters of a building or over the lintel of the doorway, as a longer-term protection against accidents and also to attract love.

Mistletoe

Also known as birdlime, all-heal and Golden Bough, mistletoe is probably the most well-known and sacred plant of the Druids. It rules the winter solstice, when bunches of mistletoe can be hung around the home as a protective device. It is extremely poisonous and should only be used homoeopathically under the strict supervision of a qualified practitioner. It is used magically to combat despair, to bring beautiful dreams, to unlock the secrets of immortality and to protect the bearer from werewolves.

The wood can be used for wands and ritual items, or such items can be placed in a mistletoe infusion to strengthen their power.

Oak

Oak is such an all-purpose tree, providing food, shelter and spiritual regeneration, that it is considered sacred by just about every culture that has encountered it. The oak was the 'King of Trees' and Druids and Priestesses 'listened' to the tree and its inhabitants to acquire wisdom. Acorns gathered at night hold the greatest fertility powers and oak galls, also known as Serpent Eggs, are sometimes used in magical charms.

The oak has the propensity to help you to find new understanding. This brings strength and courage in adversity. The oak tree nourishes our faith in ourselves and enables us to aim for what we most desire. Wands made from an oak which has been struck by lightning are considered to be particularly powerful; first since lightning does not strike twice in the same place and secondly, because the wand is empowered by the blast of energy. When you burn oak leaves, the smoke purifies the atmosphere lending strength, success and stability to your magic.

Pine

The pine tree is an evergreen and is known for its ability to cleanse the personal environment. It is one of the seven chieftain trees of the Irish. There are numerous ways it can be used. To purify and sanctify an outdoor ritual area, brush the ground with a branch of pine wood; for the home or indoors, mix the dried needles with equal parts of juniper and cedar and burn (this leaves quite an exceptional odour). The cones and nuts can be carried as a fertility charm, while a cleansing and stimulating bath can be prepared by placing a few handfuls of pine needles in a loose-woven bag. To make things easier you could, of course, use a few drops of the essential oil in running water.

Pine is very efficacious when used with other herbs and incenses to accumulate wealth, as shown in the incense below.

❋ Wealth Incense ❋

2 parts pine needles or resin
1 part cinnamon
1 part galangal root
Few drops of patchouli oil

Rowan

Also known as mountain ash, witchwood, sorb apple and quickbeam, the rowan has long been known as an aid and protection against enchantment by beguiling. Sacred to the Druids and the Goddess Brigit, it is a very magical tree, which is used for wands and amulets. A forked rowan branch can help find water; wands of rowan wood are for knowledge, locating metal and general divination. Indeed, this is the wood to use for making any magical tool that has anything to do with divining, invocation and communication with the spirit realms. The rowan has the ability, perhaps more than any other tree, to help us increase our psychic abilities. It has a beneficial energy, which will increase our abilities to receive visions and insights.

In the past it was valued as a protection against enchantment, witches, unwanted influences and evil spirits. Sprigs of rowan were placed over doorways and fixed to cattle sheds to protect the animals from harm. Speer posts – magically protective house timbers inscribed with runes and magically charged patterns – were traditionally made of rowan wood. Rowan bushes were often grown near stone circles as protective devices.

Rowan will help you to discriminate between what will do you harm and good, and help you deal with anything which threatens you.

Willow

Also known as white willow, Tree of Enchantment and witches aspirin, and one of the seven sacred trees of the Irish, the willow is a Moon tree sacred to the Goddess. There are legends and myths of willows being able to move around, to use their branches like arms and to communicate through their whispering leaves. One of the nature spirits, called a hamadryad, often makes its home in a willow tree and the willow is thought to give an understanding of the feminine principle.

It is said that priests, priestesses and all types of artisans sat among these trees to gain eloquence, inspiration, skills and prophecies. The willow will always enhance inspired leaps of the imagination, as it is known as a tree of dreaming and enchantment. It is recommended for use when seeking to assimilate the teachings of a wise woman, or master or any oral tradition. Willow wands are used for any ritual associated with the Moon and as a protection on deep journeys into the underworld and the unconscious, since the willow tree has always been associated with death.

In Celtic mythology it is associated with the creation myth of two scarlet sea serpent eggs which contained the Sun and the Earth. These eggs were hidden in the boughs of the willow tree until they hatched, thus bringing forth earthly life.

Yew

A smooth, gold-coloured wood with a wavy grain, the yew is an ancient tree species that has survived since before the Ice Age and, as such, has been revered and used by humankind throughout the ages. Because of its longevity and the way it regenerates itself by growing new trunks from within, it has come to represent everlasting life, immortality, renewal, regeneration, rebirth and transformation.

Many churches and churchyards once stood in a circle of yews representing the passage from life to death, a belief based on old Druidic custom. The yew is sacred to Hecate (the Crone aspect of the Triple Goddess) and therefore the ancient wisdom of the feminine, and is also a symbol of the old magic.

Considered to be the most potent tree for protection against evil, magically it is a means of connecting to your ancestors, bringing dreams and Otherworld journeys. This is one of its most valuable attributes, for it provides us with the opportunity to face death, to progress further than fear and to establish communication through visions with what lies beyond. These all bring about an understanding and clear insight. It is thought by many to be the original 'World Tree' (Yggdrasil) of Scandinavian mythology.

Ask the Trees

Sometimes, when we are troubled or need the answer to a query, it is good to call upon the powers of the trees in one of the following ways.

YOU WILL NEED
A fallen twig or piece of bark
A burin, used only for working with plant life

METHOD

❖ Carve a representation of the problem, or a word to represent it, on the twig or bark.

❖ Hold the twig up to the sun and ask your question either out loud or quietly to yourself.

❖ Now sit quietly and listen to the rustle of the trees.

❖ As you do so you may find the answer to your question forms in your mind.

❖ If not, do not worry, just trust that the answer will come to you in due course.

❖ Bury the twig in the ground where you have been. (This has a two-fold purpose: you are returning the plant matter where it belongs and also leaving the problem behind.)

Second method

YOU WILL NEED

Pieces of paper cut in the shape of leaves
A coloured marker pen appropriate to the problem
(e.g. yellow for emotional, red for health)
Several handfuls of dead leaves

METHOD

❖ Write the various aspects of your problem on the paper leaves with the marker pen.

❖ Sit in a comfortable position with the paper leaves and dried leaves in front of you.

❖ 'Stir' the paper leaves into the dried leaves thinking of your problem all the while.

❖ Say these words or similar:

Spirits of the woods and dells
Help that in this forest dwells
Take my problem far from me
And from this trouble set me free

❖ Now ensuring that the paper leaves are well covered, thank the Dryads (see overleaf) and walk away.

Utilizing trees' energies

In the section on divination, you will see how it is possible to use the living energy of wood in the Runes and Ogham Staves. Here you'll find out how it is possible to make use of the qualities and energies of trees in ways that are truly magical. Each time you perform any spell or ritual, you are putting yourself in tune with the energies that surround you. Always bear in mind that any adjustment that happens in performing magic – or any ritual for that matter – is on the inner planes initially. This adjustment is far more subtle than whatever happens on an outer level – what occurs there is as a result of the changes you make internally.

Becoming aware of what is happening on both levels will give you a much better understanding of everything around you and how the various interactions take place. Hopefully, you will not feel that you have to have power over these interactions, but will approach everything that you do in a spirit of co-operation. Ultimately, as you become more proficient at making your own personal adjustments, you may even achieve a strong sense of collaboration – that you are very much part of a greater whole. Your own consciousness will become sensitive to the subtle energies available to you, and there will be more evidence that you are living in harmony with all aspects of Nature.

Finding your place

Should you wish to work outside, you will become much more conscious of other energies in operation. Working with the power of nature, you will become aware that each plant, animal, rock, and other entity has a particular vibration or resonance. For magic of this type to work properly, you need to be in tune with these particular resonances. These vibrations are capable of uniting in a sort of composite energy that expresses the spirit or power of a particular natural area.

They are not the Elementals, which tend to be a much more raw untutored energy and therefore more difficult to control. Nature Spirits can be extremely powerful allies, possess real natural intelligence and are psychically powerful. You should be able to sense nature spirits and to determine if they are receptive to a planned ritual. They may well actively participate in magical workings, and often will channel tremendous amounts of power into the magic being performed. You will soon get used to the idea that they are there because they want to be, and that this is nature channelling her power into the magic in her own way. Never try to command Nature Spirits

– rather invite their participation – and you may be surprised at the results.

To Sense the Natural Spirit of a Place

When entering an area of woodland or to find a site for a ritual, find a place first of all which feels right. It is not possible to describe that feeling, you will simply 'know' that it feels good. Then do the following, either individually or, if in a group, as a guided meditation.

❖ Feel the Air all around you, relax and put yourself in tune with it.

❖ Breathe deeply and allow your inner spirit to respond to the subtle energies. At this point you may experience a heightening of perception.

❖ Picture, if you can, a glow around your solar plexus. As you breathe, begin to feel the glow expand, purifying your body and energizing you. Then allow it to reach beyond you to fill your aura – your energy field.

❖ Feel yourself glowing, balanced, purified and full of power, becoming at one with the energies around you.

❖ Seek out and make a connection with your inner or higher self, and begin to feel your intuition operating more fully.

Now become aware of the Elements around you and experience yourself as each of these in turn. You will find that you will adopt your own order. Feel yourself as:

❖ Earth, noting how your physical body belongs to, but is separate from, Mother Earth.

❖ Fire, the light of the sun, warm, alive, energizing, allowing life and channelling the power to communicate with nature.

❖ Air, full of life, movement and intelligence, touching everything with which it comes into contact.

❖ Water, life-giving, refreshing, cleansing, emotional and intuitive, a part of every living thing.

❖ Finally accept yourself as a blend of all of these Elements.

Now, concentrating on yourself as this completely whole being:

❖ Experience the glow you worked with previously as love or power.

❖ Expand the light and love beyond your own immediate boundaries to the surrounding area and feel yourself as part of it.

❖ Ask permission of the place to use it for your ritual or spell, and invite the Nature Spirits to join you.

Realistically, you may feel nothing at all, in which case you may assume that you can continue. Any unease means that you should stop, while if the area goes still and seems to be waiting, you may continue.

❖ Communicate why you have come, either by thought or words spoken aloud. Invite the spirits to join in sharing with you and the work you intend to do.

❖ Visualize the energy you are channelling, extending as far as it can go, merging with the energies that belong to the rest of the cosmos.

❖ Feel the power of the earth flowing up through your feet and body.

❖ Feel the power from the sky and channel this power outwards, combining it with the power of the earth, if you can. This can happen together or separately and is used for communicating with Nature.

❖ See the energy expanding and merging with the other energies around.

❖ Now become even more aware:

❖ Close your eyes; sit on the earth if you can, and sense your deep connection with it while allowing more light, love and energy to flow through you.

❖ Invite receptive spirits to join you and to make themselves known. Be alert to signals that may vary from inner feelings to physical senses or perceptions. The experience is yours and unique to you.

❖ If you are part of a group, someone might start playing a drum at a rate of about one beat per second or playing a flute or similar instrument; you should listen to the rhythm and let it take you deeper.

❖ Let the rhythm and the connections you have made awaken the part of you that most naturally communicates with other life forms.

❖ Confirm that you work with natural forces, that you are one who knows, understands and communicates with Nature.

✤ Let this part of yourself become part of your consciousness. Let it awaken your inner senses and allow yourself to receive as well as give out information.

When you feel ready, slowly open your eyes and look around, while remaining aware of the energy flowing both from and to you. You may sense light or a powerful energy coming from certain areas that have responded to your awareness. It is difficult to say what to expect, but you may test your perception by requesting a different signal for positive and negative responses; the light might become brighter or dimmer, for instance. You may get other signals, such as a feeling of power or love returning from a certain direction. Perhaps the type of response will be unexpected; simply follow your intuition.

You are now ready to begin with your chosen ritual. Do not be too surprised, however, if it no longer seems necessary. The stating of the intent is often enough to have it taken care of by the Nature Spirits, and your energy is better used elsewhere. Do not be disappointed, just acknowledge the help you have had and promise to return another time. Simply use your intuition, for the more you use the particular spot the more powerful it can become.

NATURE SPIRITS

Dryads are the principal Nature Spirits, mainly of forests and trees, and were known in all the Celtic countries. The Celts believed them to be spirits who dwelt in trees, and were very careful to pay them respect. The Druids considered themselves to be inspired by Dryads, particularly by those that lived in oak trees. The Greeks and Romans believed that flocks and fields were protected by them and that they could give the gift of prophecy. Nymphs and Dryads were companions of the god Pan, particularly in his aspect of Nature god. You can also make them your companions, either in your own garden or your special place.

Calling the Dryads

As you become more proficient, you may find you can actually see, as well as sense, nature spirits. Each category of Dryad has a particular magical significance and tends to work with only one aspect of nature, though they will also take responsibility for what surrounds their own particular domain. Thus some will work with groves, valleys and trees, but will protect the source of water that helps to nurture their charges, such as grottoes, streams and lakes.

YOU WILL NEED
Birthday cake candles of different colours
Ice cream sticks or nutshells such as walnuts
Water in a natural pool, pond or bowl

METHOD
✤ Use different coloured candles to attract different 'families' of Dryad.
✤ Fix the candles into the half shells or onto the slivers of wood with hot wax. (This can be very fiddly, but be patient. Use half candles if this is easier.)
✤ Light each candle with a blessing and float your boats on the surface of the water.
✤ Send loving thoughts to the Nature Spirits and ask them to join you.
✤ You might use an invocation such as:

Awake you spirits of the forest green
Join me now
Let yourselves be seen

✤ Now sit quietly and just listen.
✤ Shortly you will sense the presence of the Dryads; often there are strange rustlings in the trees or vegetation. You may feel them as they brush past or play around you.
✤ Initially you will probably not be able to differentiate between them, but as time goes on you will sense subtle differences.
✤ Half close your eyes and see if you can glimpse them. Don't be too disappointed if nothing happens immediately, just accept that you will be aware of them eventually.
✤ Now, invite them to play with you by saying:

Come, Dryads all, come join with me
Explore earth, sky, sand and sea
Show me, guide me, take my hands
Together thus, we see new lands
New vistas, new horizons and knowledge of old
Come together, in power enfold

❖ When they are comfortable with you, and you with them, thank them for coming and leave the area tidy.

❖ You can leave the candles to burn out if it is safe to do so.

While it may seem strange to be invoking spirits of Earth or greenery, a little thought will show you that all living things are interconnected and this is simply one way of making such a connection.

You can see from the information in this chapter that spells and magical working can be as simple or as complex as one wishes to make them. It will depend on your own personal preference – and indeed the intention of the spell – as to what you will wish to use and what you will wish to do. We are extremely lucky in this day and age to have many choices available to us and many disciplines, tried and tested through long experience, of which to make use.

It was formerly thought that the spell maker should stick to only one discipline and become proficient at that, being initiated only into their own craft. As knowledge expands however and we realize that there are similarities in the magics that can be produced, it can do no harm to make the effort to understand other people's ways of working and to incorporate these into our own practice.

Folk magic arose from the need to understand the cycle of the year with all its idiosyncrasies. The Kabbalah, which is explored in the Mysticism and Magic section, is a source of information unparalleled in magical work and arises from a mystical tradition, which has its roots in Jewish thought. If the former is one end of the spectrum and the latter the other, we have a whole range of experience with which to work.

Knowledge of astrology is, in many ways, the mid-point of this spectrum and reveals information that would otherwise be hidden.

Astrology

Very early agricultural societies, such as
Chinese, Babylonian and Egyptian, linked the
regular movements of the Sun, planets and stars
to the seasons, the rains and the growth cycles
of their crops. Indeed, the principles on which
modern astrology is based in the West were laid
down around 4,000 years ago in Babylon,
present-day south-eastern Iraq. Intriguingly, as
far back as 1500BC the Chinese sages who
recorded and pondered the frequency of natural
events such as floods, droughts and
earthquakes demonstrating the cyclical nature
of the universe, were thought to have
divinatory powers – to be in contact with
the Divine.

Astrological Power

IN ESSENCE, ASTROLOGY is the study of how the Sun, the Moon, and other planets and stars are related to life on earth. It has long been believed that these heavenly bodies form patterns that reveal a person's character or future. (The analytical psychologist C.G Jung stated that one cannot give an astrological assessment of both at the same time.) In addition to its influence on individuals, astrology has been, and still is, applied over wider areas. For centuries, comets, eclipses of the Sun and Moon and other unusual astronomical events have been taken as portents of war and calamities.

THE DEVELOPMENT OF ASTROLOGY

To Babylonian astrologers, the movements of the heavenly bodies were linked to a complex mythology, which, somewhat modified, became the basis of astrological interpretations in the West. With the development of mathematics, they were able to prepare refined astrological observations and calendars, much more sophisticated than anything available to the ancient Egyptians and their contemporaries in other parts of the world.

Astrology in China, however, is actually a form of philosophical guidance rather than astrology in the western sense of the word; it is much concerned with the whole person, whereas the astrology that has come to us in the West is concerned with mapping out events that may or may not happen in the future.

Being aware of the psychology of the ordinary people, the Chinese sages, who were wise and ambitious men, evolved a social system that came eventually to be codified by philosophers such as Confucius and Lao-tze. They believed that if the known universe was influenced by recognizable cycles, then, by extension, so too was the nature of man. In a perfect world, the philosophers decreed, everyone would live for sixty years, which were divided by the five Elements – Wood, Fire, Earth, Metal and Water – resulting in twelve earthly branches, which would then evolve into twelve years each of which was eventually assigned an animal.

Chinese astrology is thus based on years consisting of twelve months running in cycles of twelve years. Each twelve-month period is named after an animal which rules for a year before bowing to the next in the cycle. In the beginning these twelve cycles were simply referred to as the Twelve Branches.

The Twelve Chinese Animals

The twelve Chinese astrological animals are the Rat, the Ox, the Tiger, the Rabbit, the Dragon, the Snake, the Horse, the Sheep (sometimes the Goat or occasionally the Ram), the Monkey, the Rooster, the Dog and the Pig. The Dragon is the only mythological beast in the menagerie and although it is a frightening beast to westerners, to the Chinese it is seen as a something of a benefactor. Each of the animals has a well-defined nature (not necessarily the same to the Chinese as it is to westerners) and people born in the year of a particular animal are thought to possesses those qualities, sometimes in a yin (–, passive) and sometimes in a yang (+, more assertive) way.

Because the Chinese calendar is a combination of lunar and solar activity, the starting and finishing dates of each year vary. The Chinese New Year starts on the first day of the first moon, usually at the end of January or beginning of February. The Chinese also add an extra month every seven years over a nineteen-year cycle to regulate the calculations. Thus, someone born in 1995 by the western calendar may be a Dog if he was born between 1 January and 31 January that year, or a Pig if born on or after that date.

If you wish to research further, there are many sites on the internet which give information on the dates for, and qualities of, the animals.

Activating and Animating your Astrological Animal

This spell derives from the ancient traditions of Chinese magic. In the same way as a totem animal can be brought closer, we can activate and animate the qualities of the celestial animals as we progress on our magical journey.

YOU WILL NEED

An image of your astrological animal
Needle or rose thorn
Your little finger

METHOD

❖ Prick your little finger with the needle or thorn.

❖ Rub the resulting drop of blood over the image's eyes.

❖ Place the image where you can see it easily as you go about your daily tasks.

❖ At the end of each day, look back on the day and decide how well you have incorporated your animal's qualities in your life.

❖ Resolve to do better each day until you feel you have succeeded in your task.

You may well find that you are drawn to people – or indeed people are drawn to you – with the qualities you are requesting. It is helpful to accept that this is a powerful way to learn to understand people.

The Babylonians' astronomical and astrological studies were preserved and later developed by the Greeks and the Arabs and astrology was popular in the Europe of the Roman Empire. Not surprisingly, therefore, early astrology was strongly linked with astronomy and religion.

The link with astronomy persisted until the time of Tycho Brahe and Johannes Kepler in the 16th century. With the advent of more accurate scientific instruments, the science of astronomy and the intuitive art of astrology began to separate. It is only with the advent of highly accurate computers in this day and age that the two begin to converge in a way they have not done hitherto.

Other civilizations had, in the meantime, also developed their own methods of astrology. When the Spanish conquistadors overcame Mexico and Guatemala in the early 16th century, among the writings they found were several intricately detailed astronomical treatises dating from a thousand years before. These had been drawn up by the Mayans, who developed astrological systems capable of foretelling the changes that we are going through today. In common with eastern methods, there is an uncanny accuracy in all astrological systems.

Zodiacal astrology

There are two main methods of astrological calculation in use around the world today. In the first, a chart is drawn up according to the date, place and time of birth of the person whose horoscope is being cast. This method can also be used to calculate the best moment for significant events, such as a wedding or a business inauguration. These calculations are obviously important in the art of spell making and various astrological and planetary correspondences are given throughout the book. In the second method, the chart is cast for a precise moment when a question can be asked by the subject and answered by the horoscope.

For ease of calculation, the zodiac – or picture of the sky – is divided into twelve parts called signs. Originally developed by the ancient Egyptians and refined by the Babylonians, Greeks and Romans, the names for the plant signs and constellations (groups of stars) are those we still use today. Each of the signs has certain characteristics, which are largely determined by the planet which rules that part of the zodiac and the constellation therein. Astrologers believe that the planets have an effect on a person's character, moderated by the planets' proximity to the constellations.

Some of these names refer back to the beliefs of the Babylonians. For example, the heaviest rainfall, considered to be the giver of life and good harvest, occurred in Babylon when the Sun was in a certain constellation. As a result, astrologers called that constellation Aquarius, the water bearer, a name that western astrology still uses today, though more in the sense of life-giver. Other constellations are called after animals who had particular significance: Cancer the Crab, Leo the Lion and so on. A complete list is given below.

Astrologers originally placed the Earth at the centre of things, and for the purposes of calculation still do today. Around the Earth revolve the planets, which for astrological purposes include the Sun and the Moon. (Until 1757, when William Herschel announced the discovery of Uranus, astrologers knew of just seven planets beyond Earth– the Sun, Moon,

Venus, Mercury, Mars, Saturn and Jupiter.) Each planet creates an energy that affects a person in its own particular way.

Just to complicate matters, astrologers divide the Earth's surface into twelve houses, each of which presents certain characteristics of an individual's life. Detailed information is given below.

The Birth Chart

To draw up an accurate birth chart the astrologer needs to know the exact time (Greenwich Mean Time), date and place of birth. An astrologer nowadays will have a set of Ephemeris tables, or preferably, for accuracy's sake, access to a computer software program, which shows the position of the planets within each constellation for as far back as needs be.

Each of the twelve signs is associated with definite aspects of character – temperament, physiology and other attributes. In establishing the relative positions of the heavenly bodies in their charts, astrologers can give a fair assessment of the future for the subject and advise them of paths to follow or actions or decisions to make.

More general horoscopes can be cast for all those born under a particular sign for any period – day, week, month and year – and these are the horoscopes that most of us read in our morning papers or glossy magazines. Newspapers began publishing them in the UK in the 1930s and it wasn't long before they spread to other countries.

Interest in astrology has increased since then and today, with many more people seeking to live their lives more in tune with the natural rhythms and cycles of nature, with their minds more open to new horizons, astrology is more widely followed than ever before.

Astrologers divide the circle of the elliptic (the path of the Earth round the Sun) into twelve equal sections of 30 degrees each. The first starts at the point where the Earth's equator, projected into space, crosses the plane of the elliptical on 21 March – the vernal or spring equinox. This is the first day of Aries, the first sign of the Zodiac. Each of the sections is allocated one of the Zodiac signs.

Sun sign	From – To
Aries, the Ram	21 March – 20 April
Taurus, the Bull	21 April – 21 May
Gemini, the Twins	22 May – 21 June
Cancer, the Crab	22 June – 23 July
Leo, the Lion	24 July – 23 August
Virgo, the Virgin	24 August – 23 September
Libra, the Scales	24 September – 23 October
Scorpio, the Scorpion	24 October – 22 November
Sagittarius, the Archer	23 November – 21 December
Capricorn, the Goat	22 December – 20 January
Aquarius, the Water Bearer	21 January – 19 February
Pisces, the Fish	20 February – 20 March

(These are the generally accepted dates: occasionally they may differ by a day.)

It is not possible in the confines of a book such as this to detail every aspect of the horoscope and what each one means. The variations are too many and too detailed to allow that. But thanks to modern technology, having a personal birth chart drawn up is no longer the preserve of the rich and royal as it was in times gone by. There are several excellent web sites from where, for a fee, a personal chart can be obtained. All the enquiring reader has to do is refer to a decent search engine, key in the appropriate words and a range of options will appear.

The Planets

The Ancients, believing that the Earth was at the centre of things, thought there were five planets. When it was realized that the Earth was a planet, astrologers disregarded this, and decided to keep our planet at the centre.

However, following the discovery of Uranus

by William Herschel in 1781, of Neptune by Johanne Galle in 1846 and of Pluto by Clyde Tombaugh in 1930, both astrologers and astronomers were forced to reconsider. It is probably no coincidence that these planets are considered to affect global matters more closely than they do individual concerns.

The planets and gods, for the Ancients, seemed to be interchangeable. Below we show the qualities of each of the planets and the effect they may have on our lives. The list is in the right order from an astrological perspective. Throughout the rest of the book there are other references to the planets and their various correspondences, so that you can use their energies constructively.

The Sun tells of our basic nature and qualities and of how we express ourselves. It shows our basic needs, the life force within us. The Sun also highlights the power of the individual to meet the challenges of everyday life.

The Moon and our emotional nature go hand in hand. It influences the type of nurturing we need from our mothers to make us complete, well-rounded people. It is also influences how we relate to others.

Mercury, the messenger of the gods, is said to tell us about our intellects and the way in which we express our ideas. It is also connected to our siblings and our relationships with them.

Venus, named in honour of the goddess of love, is said to be concerned with our relationships and the choices we make in life, both personal and material. It influences the decisions we make, especially when it comes to deciding the things and people we value.

Mars, named after the god of war, is the planet most concerned with the way we assert ourselves and what it is that drives us. It powers our activities and energies.

Saturn, the Roman deity who devoured all but three of his children, controls our ambitions, the way we accept (or don't accept) our responsibilities and the structure of our lives. In indicating our ability to order our talents, it forces us to take stock of our assets and liabilities.

Jupiter, the supreme god in the Roman pantheon, tells us of our need for expansion, abundance and wisdom. It is concerned with

what we believe in and the philosophies that colour our lives. Being an expansive planet, it is also linked with excess.

Neptune, the Roman god of the sea, demonstrates our need to be at one with the rest of humanity. It shows us how to be compassionate and complete, but it encourages a grey area between fantasy and reality and makes it difficult for us to distinguish between the two.

Uranus, the personification of the Greek heaven, loves the original and unconventional, whether it be astonishing invention or wilful rebellion.

Pluto, the Roman ruler of the infernal regions, is the planet that tells us transformation is possible, pointing us in the direction in which we can experience regeneration and showing how we can achieve it.

The Houses

Everything in astrology has its own particular significance, especially the position of the planets in the various houses. By knowing the associations that each planet has, and marrying these with the aspects of our lives with which the houses are connected, astrologers can tell us much about ourselves. For example, knowing that Jupiter is connected with wisdom, and the fifth house with self-expression, children, identity, security and play, someone with Jupiter in the fifth house might be seen to have an ability to help children to express themselves creatively.

House	Concerns
First	Self-absorption, personal projection and appearance.
Second	Values, self-worth, finances and assets, and security.
Third	Travel, local network, siblings and communications.
Fourth	Foundations, family, ancestors and home atmosphere.
Fifth	Self-expression, children, identity, security and play.
Sixth	Service, working environment, health and integration.

Seventh	Partnership, dealings with others and adversaries.
Eighth	Others' resources, inheritance, secret powers and death.
Ninth	Long-distance travel, higher education and the law.
Tenth	Ambitions, authorities, goals and professional expression.
Eleventh	Social affinities, groups, friendships and political visions.
Twelfth	Withdrawal, isolation, the divine and inner worlds.

The Elements

The four Elements – Fire, Earth, Air and Water – all play their part in astrology, each influencing in turn, in specific ways, three of the zodiac signs.

Fire is associated with creativity, with vitality, enthusiasm, excitement, passion, energy, exhibitionism and having the ability to entertain.

Earth is the material Element, concerned as it is with routine, the law, savings, tradition, building and legacy.

Air is the Element of the intellect, of ideas, the thought process, explanations, gregariousness and discussion.

Water is all about the emotions – about love and anger, sentiment and sympathy, caring and tenderness.

Sun signs

Aries

With Fire its Element and Mars its ruler, people born under Aries are often lean and muscular, with a liking for competitive sports or games. They have a strong sense of their own individuality, and the idea of living a life of obscurity doesn't appeal to them whatsoever. Extrovert to a fault and outspoken when pushed, they can often find themselves in trouble!

Busy, restless and impatient, they are enthusiastic about all of their new ventures, regarding everything as an adventure, though when their enthusiasm wanes they will leave others to pick up the pieces. They are idealists, and can set their own standards and live by them, regardless of opinion or who they might hurt.

Quick-tempered, argumentative and undiplomatic, they loathe anyone interfering in their affairs – even if most of the decisions they make are on impulse – are completely incapable of telling a lie or – largely – apologizing when they are wrong.

Often considered to be the baby of the Zodiac, they partner other Fire signs well, though there may be competition as to who comes first. Because they themselves are freedom-lovers they appreciate that need, but are often unable to give others that luxury. The coolness of the Aquarian is good for them and Scorpio will keep them on their toes

Taurus

Ruled by Venus and influenced by Earth, Taureans are often physically attractive, with large eyes and a steady gaze.

Affectionate and charming, they are instinctive creatures, though they do not give their trust easily. Given time, they often come to major decisions without knowing how they have done so.

Stubborn to a fault rather than patient, they will worry at a problem until they have come to a conclusion that suits their nature. They dislike risks, needing a basic security, but are also luxury-loving creatures and this can sometimes cause them conflict. Their career will sometimes reflect this conflict, often being in the public sector or financial field, providing basic necessities plus a margin for impulsive spending.

In relationships, they are slow to commit but usually loyal to their chosen partner and expect fidelity in return. They can be possessive in love and do need a conscientious and ambitious partner. Capricorn and Virgo are therefore good for them, whereas the Fire signs may cause them some difficulty.

Gemini

Ruled by Mercury and under the influence of Air, Geminis are forever being accused of being two-faced and superficial, but more accurately are versatile and adaptable. Immaculate and often youthful in appearance, they work hard to keep themselves in good shape.

Socially, Geminians are flexible creatures, taking all kinds of lifestyles in their stride. Tolerance, a liberal attitude and a degree of restlessness allow them to go further afield in their social adventurism than perhaps others might care to experience, though they do have to guard against sheer foolhardiness. Highly perceptive, there is a tendency for Geminis to make the assumption that they are right, but in fact it is usually because they are one step ahead anyway. Broadcasting, journalism or a literary career are ideal for word-loving Geminis, and they will often prefer to work freelance.

They need to be in partnership – though this may not simply be romantically – and are constantly looking for a soulmate. Being romantically involved with a Gemini is an exciting, stimulating affair – not necessarily a long-term attachment, but a breathtaking one all the same.

Cancer

Ruled by the Moon with the Element of Water, Cancerians are home-lovers and home-makers. A real haven where they can get away from it all, they will use their home to advantage to plan their next moves, plot revenge, deal with their own moodiness or simply protect loved ones.

Often crab-like in their movements, with long arms and legs, they can glide around, hardly seeming to touch the ground, having camouflaged themselves as they approach. At work they can be very ambitious – even ruthless – in getting to where they want to be. They can easily form alliances for the sake of convenience, and just as easily break them. One thing which never changes is their tenacity and commitment to their goals. Natural career choices are the caring professions.

In relationships they can be over-protective, forming emotionally satisfying ones with other Water signs, but also with more earthy individuals. If their lover is unfaithful, that's the one time they act out of character and seek immediate revenge. Although they may not seem so, they are usually somewhat sensitive souls and can take umbrage quite quickly They are good at giving the impression they think is expected of them.

Leo

Ruled by the Sun and a Fire sign to boot, all Leos love to be the centre of attention and they flourish on admiration. They thrive on challenges and will rise to them with all the energy, enthusiasm and vitality at their disposal. In contrast, when they perceive there is no need for activity they can appear incredibly lazy.

Slender and athletic of body, and with a fine mane of (often wild) hair, Leos frequently look like lions. They guard their personal dignity and self-esteem fiercely, hate to suffer embarrassment and don't tolerate fools lightly. Their love of colour and parade draws them to such things as the theatre. The flamboyant display of big emotions by larger-than-life characters, and the flowery language that often accompanies such performances, all cater to their admiration of the grand parade.

Leos are full of ideas and have the confidence to translate them into action. Impetuosity and impatience, however, sometimes lead them to take unnecessary risks. It would bring them greater respect if they were to sit down and think things through a bit more often. However, it bores them to sit around and theorize for too long.

Whoever Leo decides to settle down with – often other Fire signs or passionate individuals – must be willing to be subservient on occasions and also to tolerate their partner flirting, often outrageously, in their presence if they are feeling in need of attention. They must also always be one hundred per cent loyal.

Virgo

Virgo's planet is Mercury, the messenger of the gods, its Element Earth. Virgoans are extremely good at watching the purse strings and ensuring that all the little details are taken care of. Having the patience, love of routine and interest to nurture these details – frequently overlooked by others – means that whatever project they begin has its roots firmly planted in the ground.

Liking to live as naturally as possible, Virgos tend to be careful about how they eat and what exercise they take. Often conservationist in their nature, they care deeply about the planet on which they live and dislike waste and unnecessary profligacy. Highly critical of others, they hate to admit that they themselves can make mistakes.

Shyness and nervousness can make Virgos appear to be withdrawn and sometimes isolated, which makes it difficult for people to get to know them. They are such good organizers that their real talents are often harnessed on behalf of others and their careers are frequently supportive – administrators, accountants and the like.

Relationships do not need to be overtly passionate, though they do feel things very deeply. Relationships with those signs which can offer them a basic security are the most fulfilling.

Libra

With Venus as the sign's ruling planet, Librans are often thought to be the most beautiful of all the signs in the Zodiac. With a graceful, elegant frame, a creamy, clear complexion, glowing, velvety hair, and fine bone structure and teeth, they have an endless supply of energy, both mental and physical. Librans do have a reputation for balance, but can often be extreme in their behaviour. They hate arguments and are often the first to pour oil on troubled water. Much preferring harmony, they seek this through, for instance, a love of poetry – the harmonious balance of words – or through a love of art, often of the Oriental kind where everything is undisturbed and tranquil. Many Librans are fascinated by politics and may well take it up as a career. Design is also a field that attracts them.

Librans often need to be coaxed out of their shell before they will declare themselves, though whether they are partnered or not, they do like to flirt with the opposite sex. With Air as Libra's Element, Gemini is just the sign to help Libra to achieve the balance that is so important in their lives. As Aquarians share with Libra a tendency to call a spade a spade and a dislike of anything false or imitative, the two signs can be well matched romantically.

Scorpio

With Pluto, the planet that reveals our ability to effect transformation, as its ruling body, it is no surprise to learn that Scorpios can change at the drop of a hat – polite and charming one minute, rude and aggressive the next. They like things to run according to plan. Sometimes though their single-mindedness can become too rigid, and they need to walk a fine line between being purposeful and obsessive. The complexion of a typical Scorpio is often sallow, and in other ways they can seem to be very average – except for their eyes, which seem to have the ability to see right into the depths!

Scorpio's Element is Water, which results in a highly volatile set of emotions. Feelings can swell from small ripples into absolute tidal waves, which is fine, so long as they don't become dammed up inside. Frustration will eventually spill over and innocent people may then suffer. A moody Scorpio tends to hurt itself as much as others.

Money means a great deal to Scorpios, and a life of poverty would be too much to ask. Scorpios love the challenges of big business and jobs in which their negotiating skills can be best used, but they also like to feel that they are in control. This trait can also be seen in relationships, for they do like to feel that they are the dominant partner, whatever the other's sign.

Sagittarius

Jupiter is the sign of the archer's ruling planet, and one linked with excess. Fire is Sagittarius's Element, and for many of them life is an exciting game, full of gambles and opportunities, which often work out. Sagittarians are often tall and athletic, with an ability to take anything they do further than most other people. The visionaries of the Zodiac, they often do not see obstacles until they come up against them, and hate to be constrained in any way. They have a highly developed sense of morality and principle, and instinctively respond to humanitarian issues, having a passionate belief in freedom on all levels, physical, mental and spiritual.

The Sagittarian love of independence makes it hard for other signs who set their hearts on a permanent relationship. They must be prepared to understand when Sagittarius tries to make a bid for freedom, just to prove they can. Other Fire signs can often allow such freedom, as can Gemini, provided some kind of agreement is reached first. On the career front, Sagittarians need that same freedom of expression, so often choose to work freelance in occupations where they can use their imagination and their intellectual ability.

Capricorn

Capricornians' Element is Earth and their ruler is Saturn, so life is one associated with routine and tradition. Their cool manner and controlled emotional disposition earn them the respect of many, as people see in them evidence of the maturity they themselves so often need. Sometimes quite small in stature, they nevertheless have the stamina to get to the top of their own particular mountain and to stay there when they do. Their dark, piercing eyes often appear to be questioning other people's motives, but in fact they are assessing the pros and cons of their own position in order to make the right moves. Highly moral in everything they do, they have a great deal to teach others if

they can overcome their own shyness. Patience is their watchword but revenge their downfall, for unfortunately they can bear grudges for a very long time.

Capricorns are steadfast and loyal and they expect the same in return. They do not give up easily, even if a relationship is not working well, so they need a partner who will give them the support they need, whatever form that may be. They often need someone to steer them away from being gloomy, so Fire signs can be good.

Aquarius

Uranus being a modern planet and the ruler of this sign suggests that Aquarians have to be 'in the know'. Their Element is Air, so they are largely humanitarian, dispensers of love and knowledge. Often accused of being detached and uninterested in emotional and intimate matters, they give the wealth of their hearts and minds away freely, sometimes without being asked. They have done what they do best – communicated the gifts of their spirit for the benefit of society at large. They tend to view institutions not just as impersonal labyrinths serving only those who 'belong', but as potential beacons for the masses.

Often tall, with a high forehead, typical Aquarians tend to have excellent bone structure, and touches of the unusual in the way they present themselves. Their eccentric behaviour often finds them the centre of gossip, and their sharp wit can be both their defence mechanism and their weapon.

In relationships, boredom is the enemy. Once this happens, they will be anxious to move off into new areas of experience, sometimes not even bothering to look back, sometimes even expecting the co-operation of everyone around them. Anyone with a good intellect will keep them intrigued, however, since they are ever curious. Aquarians often look to the sciences as a career for the same reason. They also make good actors and writers, enjoying independent research.

Pisces

Neptune, the sign's ruling planet, tends to blur reality and fantasy, so it is no surprise that Pisceans are the daydreamers of the Zodiac, though with Water as its ruler they equally have the ability to go with the flow without getting stressed. Pisceans do get distressed by indecision, their own or other people's, and can put their peers in the position of having to make decisions for them. Picking up strangers as they wander along the path of life, they have the propensity both to care for the underdog, and themselves be victimized.

Pisceans are often especially happy people – laughing and smiling more than most other signs, especially when they are trying to impress the opposite sex. They hate being alone and really need their friends to give them the affection they crave. They can however be highly strung and prone to extravagant displays of emotion and temper.

When they fall in love, their partner has to learn to treat them with kid gloves. They don't mind being dominated, as long as they can see the fairness of it, and it suits them to put their partner first. They appreciate having money but more for what it can do, rather than what it can buy, so caring Cancer or selfish Scorpio can both be good for them. Pisceans do not make the best bosses in the world, but they do make excellent carers, and so many of them find nursing an attractive proposition.

The above 'snapshots' of the Sun signs of Western astrology do no more than skim the surface of the subject. Since so many other factors must be taken into account when using the information, Sun signs allow us to understand what people will accept and what will upset them, according to their own personal beliefs. For instance, Scorpios will be much more interested in why a person thinks the way they do, whereas a Gemini will be more interested in how.

Many people will go no further than simply understanding themselves through their Sun signs. However, in order really to put ourselves in touch with the full range of our spiritual abilities, we do need to delve a little deeper and develop our magical powers. One of the first things that we need to do is to put ourselves in touch with the Divine (the true meaning of divination). Eastern disciplines such as yoga, which are self-exploratory, can sometimes give us a more efficient start than the more logical western ways.

Magic and Divination

Divination and spell working have been inextricably linked since time immemorial, and today many people develop their own ways of working, which are often based on older methods. It is frequently helpful to be able to clarify or enhance your results using more than one method, although it is an old tradition that the gods (or powers that be) do not like to be questioned continually. The pendulum, for instance, may not function efficiently after a time of protracted use and must be left to rest.

When dealing with esoteric matters, it is always wise to treat whatever method you are using with respect and integrity. Developing spiritually is an integral and necessary part of spell working.

Spiritual Development

YOGA TEACHES US that the siddhis, or powers, will only evolve properly as part of our overall spiritual development, and among these is the power to be a spell worker and magical person. There are many types of psychic skills. Often the people who develop these skills prefer to be known as sensitives rather than psychics. The most common psychic skills are clairaudience (receiving information by hearing), clairsentience (by sensing), and clairvoyance (by seeing). People may develop gifts in healing, or psychic surgery (operation on the physical body to remove such things as diseased organs and tumours).

As well as these better-known skills there are others such as psychokinesis (the movement of objects), psychic photography (without the use of a camera, an image is imprinted on photographic paper) and psychic portraiture (the ability to draw the sitter's spirit guides and loved ones). These are all developments that take place in keeping with the sensitive's personality, and are often modified or disappear as the individual understands his or her own psyche and reaches for further spiritual enlightenment.

Many sensitives, channellers (known of old as 'mediums') and magical workers fear psychic attack, although correct spiritual development and good practice will make such an occurrence unlikely. The belief is that as the aura, or subtle body as it is sometimes known, is an extremely sensitive instrument, it can be influenced by negative thoughts and misplaced emotion in much the same way that a physical body can be injured.

At certain stages of development this is indeed true, but if you believe in the principle of personal responsibility, there would have to be a certain degree of collusion on the part of the recipient of such an attack. This is why in the initial stages of learning, the magical practitioner will come across many protection spells and techniques and will learn how to cast a circle of protection for themselves.

A simple way of dealing with a situation where you feel you are under attack is to use visualization, such as mirroring the ill-will away from oneself. There follows one such technique.

Ring of Protection

In this method of working you place a protective shield around yourself or your home, so that no harm can come to you, it or the people therein.

YOU WILL NEED ———————————
The power of your own mind

METHOD ———————————
❖ Visualize a ring of light surrounding your property.
❖ Ask your guardians or favourite deities (see pages 205-224) to protect you, your home and its occupants for as long as necessary.
❖ Reinforce the circle of light whenever you think about it or in the case of your home, whenever you go away.

It really is that simple and means that you trust your own abilities.

Incidentally, when under any kind of attack one may always mentally ask for Divine justice in the knowledge that 'what goes around, must come around' in due course. Often inaction is as effective as action. This enables us to rest easy, recognizing that we cannot always know what the result will be, yet secure in the knowledge that justice will prevail.

Divination

DIVINATION WAS INITIALLY an attempt to discover what the divine intent was – that is, what the gods intended for mankind, and therefore for each individual. It was recognized that certain patterns and symbols meant different things and, as with the principle 'as above, so below', that the gods' intent could be mirrored or pictured in everyday life.

Hence, symbols were seen in the way that candles burn, or in the way that tea leaves formed patterns, or even in the way that the entrails of slaughtered animals fell. Such things could be studied and the patterns could be interpreted successfully. Those people capable of interpreting the simple symbols would tend to develop their psychic abilities, and would be able to make intuitive interpretations.

The patterns seen in the palms of the hands or in the way that cards fell were gradually discovered to have a common meaning, and from these observations a body of knowledge was developed. This, combined with intuitive interpretation, led to the development of other methods of divination, which could more properly be called sciences. This was particularly so when mathematical calculation became involved, as in numerology and astrology. The *I Ching,* for instance, with its 64 hexagrams (six-line figures), is as complex in its permutations as many of today's modern computer programs.

Today the method of divination in spell working usually depends on whether the diviner has a scientific or artistic nature. This section covers the most widely used methods and tools, along with some of the more widely accepted meanings of the latter's symbols. As you become progressively more proficient in the various psychic skills, you will find that you develop your own library of meanings. At that point you are becoming more truly a weaver of spells.

The Tarot

THE HISTORY OF both Tarot and playing cards is lost in the mists of time. Some claim that the Tarot cards were first used in ancient Egypt, others that they were the invention of the ancient Chinese. As India has also been put forward as the place whence they originated, the truth is that no one can say for certain who first used pieces of card with images inscribed on them in order to tell a story or divine the future. Tarot is said to mean 'truth'.

There is a belief that their use was spread by the Romanies or Knights Templar (or both) as they wandered throughout Europe. Certainly in the Middle Ages there are cards known to have been in existence that were used, if not for divination, then certainly to trace the development of man – and probably the known world through various stages of development – as he undertook a spiritual journey of discovery.

Modern Tarot

It was the magus Eliphas Levi in the 19th century who brought the Tarot back into prominence after it had largely fallen into disuse. He called it 'the universal key of magical works' and felt it was a true philosophical machine, a veritable oracle and above all 'the key of all ancient religious dogmas'. In fact, he provided no evidence to support his beliefs, but such was his intuition and enthusiasm that he carried all before him, and convinced others that because he said it was so, it was so.

He had a profound effect on those who followed him and people today still interpret the cards according to his strictures. It was he who made available to the ordinary man the connection between Tarot and the Kabbalah (an influential type of Jewish mysticism, which we look at in the Mysticism and Magic section) and gave explanations of that figure we now call the Tree of Life.

More than anything, Eliphas Levi helped to change the way that the people of his time viewed magic. Rather than the folkloric aspects of magic which had been prevalent until then, he showed that magic could be a carefully thought-out system of belief that supported and sustained people, allowed for creativity and gave, in effect, a course of instruction, which led to development of the spirit.

As is the case with so much in the occult arts, he could offer no real proof that what he said was right, though in fact he was simply following in the footsteps of those who had gone before him. However, it would take a great deal to disprove his findings.

There were various occultists who picked up on Levi's information, most notably Oswald Wirth, who was probably the first to design cards which showed the significance of the Hebrew letters in the Major Arcana. The Order of the Golden Dawn in the 1930s also did a great deal to further the cause of Tarot, giving it a particularly Masonic flavour. Interestingly, if one studies the Tarot to any great depth, there is still a sense that one is entering a body of knowledge hidden from the uninitiated.

Finally, it was the hippie culture of the 1960s and 1970s that brought the Tarot back into popular use and gave us the universal appeal that it has nowadays. Today, with over three hundred different designs to choose from, it might seem rather difficult for the beginner to decide which one to select. There was once a belief that you should be given your first pack of Tarot cards, but since it is an intuitive tool, it is quite in order to choose your own, though you may wish to use money that has been given as a gift. Any good occult shop will allow you time to handle a number of packs, and you should use your intuition to select one which pleases you.

THE TAROT PACK

The Tarot pack comprises 78 cards. Of prime importance are those of the Major Arcana, numbered 0 to XXI (21), which are variously supposed to depict the soul's journey through life, man's psychological states, where the Holy Grail is hidden and so on. There are then 56 cards of the Minor Arcana, divided into the four suits. Popular belief had it that originally the suits of the Minor Arcana represented the different strata of society – Cups were the clergy, Wands the peasants, Pentacles the tradesmen and Swords the aristocracy.

Each card has its own meaning, influenced by the way the cards present themselves and the way in which they are laid out, but it is the diviner's intuition that is perhaps the most important element of any reading. Purists will prefer to use the older-style packs, though an interesting exercise, once you have familiarized yourself with the basic meanings, is to develop your own pack. It is this that has given such diversity to packs developed over the last fifty years.

Many card readers keep their cards in a specially consecrated box or silk bag or pouch. Some insist that the pack is shuffled in a certain way and that it is given and received with the left hand only, or the right. There are no hard and fast rules. If it is right for you, then that is the right way for you to do it.

The Major Arcana

Names do sometimes vary from pack to pack, depending on which school of thought the artist and author belonged to, but the numbers are a constant. The cards are known as the Major Arcana because they are concerned with deep, more spiritual and perhaps magical issues; these 22 cards represent the innermost qualities of the questioner's psyche and personality.

0. The Fool

This card usually depicts a traveller ignoring the small animal below that seems to be attacking him. Over one shoulder is a stick from which hangs a bag. He carries a walking staff to help him on his way. This card is the only un-numbered one and shows a character without rules or definitions, without an agenda in the world.

In divination the Fool suggests lack of thought, carelessness, which can lead to degradation. Reversed, the image can depict a sense of chaos. The Fool travels light and lack of thought can also come from innocence, a carelessness from not being weighed down with worldly concerns.

Associations: The path of life, the way forward. New ventures, stepping into the unknown. In magic, he is used to depict the freedom of spirit necessary in the adept.

I. The Magician

This is depicted as a man standing, left arm holding a wand raised to the heavens, right arm lowered towards the earth beneath him. In front of the figure is a table on which, among other things, are the symbols of the Minor Arcana. His hat is shaped like the symbol for infinity.

This is man, upright, being part of heaven and earth; capable of infinite possibilities and of shaping the world; of making things manifest. This is generally positive and creative, but can suggest trickery and manipulation.

In divination he represents the enquirer (if it

is a man), and when reversed suggests that he is at odds with the world. If the enquirer is a woman, this card suggests a change of position. **Associations:** Logos; the Trickster or Mountebank; Hermes/Mercury; Adam, the first man. In magical workings, you might appeal through this card to Hermes or use it to signify the beginning of a project by placing it on your altar.

II. The High Priestess

This shows a seated woman holding an open book; behind her is a veil. She is sometimes shown wearing the three-tiered papal crown. The book suggests the book of wisdom, while the veil suggests that which is hidden.

In divination this card can represent the female enquirer. The card represents mysticism, hidden or secret knowledge and occult science. Reversed, it suggests unhappy consequences as a result of occult science.

The High Priestess is the card of unconscious intuition and knowledge, the veil of the soul, wisdom and clairvoyance, with a suggestion of morality.

Associations: Isis, keeper of hidden mysteries, of the secrets of life, death and resurrection; the female pope. In magical terms she may represent Sophia as the principal of wisdom.

III. The Empress

This shows a woman seated face-on, wings coming from behind her back. She wears a crown and holds in one hand a sceptre with a globe and cross (the alchemical symbol of antimony, the state of near perfection) and in the other a shield depicting an eagle (symbol of royalty and the spirit).

In divination she represents woman, mother and domestic happiness; the female life-giving force. Reversed, she suggests infidelity, inconstant love leading to stagnation and sterility.

She is the feminine ruler, life-giver, counsellor, open to all, practical and decisive.
Associations: Demeter; Hera; aspects of Isis.

IV. The Emperor

A man is seen in profile, crowned and seated, usually on a throne, one leg crossed over the other. In his right hand he holds the sceptre, crowned with globe and cross, as does the Empress, and in front of him is the shield with the image of the eagle.

In divination this represents man in his positive aspects: will-power, authority, strength and courage. Reversed, it shows the softer aspect: benevolence, clemency and pity.

He is the embodiment of masculine power and authority in worldly matters, coupled with intelligence and sensibility, though with the danger of abusing power and becoming tyrannical. (The ideal archetypal father/husband in the proverbial 2.4 family with the Empress as wife.)

Associations: Zeus/Jupiter; demiurge (creator of the world) of Platonic philosophy; in harmony with the Great Bear.

V. The Hierophant

A man is seated between two pillars, holding an ornate staff in his left hand, right hand raised in midair (to bless or to emphasize). Before him kneel two smaller figures.

In divination he represents wisdom, intelligence, asceticism and inspiration. Reversed, he suggests craftiness and guile.

He is the teacher. Like the High Priestess, he knows the mysteries, but is the conscious ward of self-knowledge and spiritual power, the marriage or union of earthly and heavenly principles. His danger is fanaticism, intolerance and bigotry.

Associations: The Pope; Christ; Logos.

VI. The Lovers

In the centre stands a young man between two women, one with her hand on his shoulder, the other with a hand on his heart. Above, framed by the Sun, Cupid/Eros hovers with an arrow ready to fire.

In divination this card represents love, youthful indecision, hesitation and instability.

Reversed, it suggests broken romance, inconstancy and heartache.

It is the card of choices, and of temptation. It implies inexperience, a putting to the test of learnt ideas, but it gives no indication of who or what to choose. It represents dilemma.
Associations: Gemini, Mercury.

VII. The Chariot

This portrays a man facing head-on, riding in a canopied chariot drawn by two horses. The man wears a crown and breastplate and carries a sceptre; on either shoulder is a mask, one taken to represent Urim and the other Thummim (Jewish oracular devices). The horses are often shown pulling in slightly different directions.

This card symbolizes triumph, success and victory. Reversed, it suggests discouragement, quarrels or defeat. The chariot and horses suggest a harnessing and controlling of forces, the triumph and advancement of spiritual nature over physical nature. Following the Lovers, this card suggests the successful balancing of alternatives, and progression, though there is always the danger of overriding ambition or headlong haste.
Associations: Apollo's chariot in its heavenly orbit, Buddha's chariot drawn by a white ox.

VIII. Justice

Justice is portrayed as a woman face-on, sometimes seated between two columns, holding in one hand a sword and in the other a set of scales. She represents impartiality, balanced judgement, integrity and arbitration, but when reversed suggests bad judgement or legal trouble.

While the scales represent balance and order, the sword represents the power to enforce fairness, judgement and discipline. There is always the danger that the latter could be misused and lead to constraint or intolerance with the scales uneven.
Associations: Athena; Anubis weighing the souls of the dead.

IX. The Hermit

This shows an old man, wearing a cloak and walking with a staff. He carries a lantern before him, lighting the way.

The card suggests the need for prudence and wisdom, and perhaps watchfulness and caution against hidden enemies. Reversed, it suggests excessive caution or timidity.

The lantern is a symbol of truth and wisdom. The fact that the old man is walking and the lantern is shaded by his cloak suggests the need to search for such wisdom, yet he carries his own light and thus indicates that the wisdom or truth is his own. The hermit is an isolated character with none of the trappings of worldly acquisition. His isolation may derive from loneliness, fear, poverty or despondency.
Associations: The notion of the hermit or pilgrim is common to all religions. The card corresponds to the Hebrew letter *teth*, which is the ideogram of a serpent swallowing its own tail, representing unending wisdom; the hermit's staff is reminiscent of the rod of Aaron.

X. The Wheel of Fortune

This shows a wheel rotated on its own axis by an unmanned handle. On the rim of the wheel are three creatures, part animal, part human. The one at the top, resting on a platform, is sometimes likened to the Sphinx. The other two cling to the rim of the wheel, the one on the right facing upwards and the one on the left facing downwards.

This card illustrates that good and bad luck are equally possible; that fortune is always changing, so if the card is in upright it is favourable, but if reversed it suggests unlucky influences. The card of chance, it shows the cyclical nature of the universe, and the inevitability of change.
Associations: The Tibetan Wheel of Life, the Zodiac. Some regard the symbolism of this card as deriving from the Egyptians, associating the ascending and descending figures with Horus and Set and thus the eternal balancing of good and evil.

XI. Strength

A young woman (sometimes an androgynous figure) wearing a crowned hat shaped in the

symbol of infinity stands holding open the mouth of a lion or beast.

This card represents strength and courage, and promises success to those who can direct their natural gifts and willpower. Reversed, it means fruitless striving and dissipated energy.

The beast is subdued by gentleness and intelligence and this implies the channelling of brutish instinct and strength through inner spiritual strength. In that sense the card represents both forms of power and can, badly placed, suggest fury and despotism.

Associations: The lion in most cultures is associated both with primitive strength and with majesty and justice.

XII. The Hanged Man

A man is suspended upside down, hanging by one leg, the other crossed behind him. The pole from which he hangs is supported on either side by two trees; the sap 'bleeds' where the branches have been cut. In some images his hands are tied behind his back, but he never appears tortured.

In divination this card represents self-denial and sacrifice and perhaps trials or vicissitudes. When the card is reversed, this sacrifice may be unnecessary or does not fit into a 'normal' pattern.

The sacrifice of the man is voluntary and suggests a deliberate suspension of the material world, lack of concern for the physical.

Associations: Christ; martyrs in general. In the Tree of Life it is the Path between Gevurah (strength) and Hod (glory).

XIII. Death

A skeleton, smiling grimly, wields a scythe, scattering limbs, hands, heads, and leaves.

As the leaves among the scattered limbs imply, death is a part of life and regeneration and this card suggests change rather than literal death, an end of one part of life and therefore also the beginning of another. It is a form of transition, possibly liberation and transformation, which may not be bad, though it may engender fear. The card can also suggest inflexibility, a reluctance to change.

Associations: The 'Grim Reaper'; all endings, whether catastrophic or not.

XIV. Temperance

A young woman, with wings coming from her back, stands on the earth, pouring water from one jug to another.

This card represents vitality, life, fruitfulness and balance, restraint. It can foretell a beneficial partnership. Reversed, it loses the restraint and the vitality can become restlessness and dissolution.

Water has always been associated with the source, life, creation and ablution, new life. The flowing of life suggests harmony, communication and equilibrium, but equally it suggests the possibility of stagnation and apathy if the card is badly placed.

Associations: The cups can be associated with the chalice, the Holy Grail; water is source, regeneration and also emotion.

XV. The Devil

A naked figure with bat-like wings, and horns coming from his head, hovers or stands above a circle. His feet are cloven and he holds a staff or sceptre in his hand. Tied to that by ropes from their necks, stand two naked figures, also with horns, tails and pointed ears.

This forebodes temptation, and implies weakness, lack of protection and possibly illness. Reversed, it suggests the temptation is from a malign source and is difficult to resist.

The two chained figures represent enslavement to physical, instinctual desires. However, base instincts are animal and therefore neither good nor bad. The magnetism of such instincts has power and potential, which can be positive. It is the card of passion or perversion.

Associations: Pan; Baphomet, the creator of evil; Lucifer, Angel of Light becomes Angel of darkness.

XVI. The Tower

This usually depicts a tower, its top blown off by lightning or flame. It is surrounded by circles (coins) falling from the ruin and shows two people, upside down, falling out of the building. Sometimes the flame is a green ear of corn bursting out from the top of the tower.

In divination this portends a sudden calamity, change or loss of structure. Reversed, it bodes lesser ills. If placed near the suit of pentacles, it can suggest an unexpected legacy.

This is the card of 'hubris' or 'pride-before-a-fall'; the destruction of man's constructs, the breaking down of established order. However, out of the destruction of the old a new world can begin, hence the ear of corn in some depictions. The two figures falling represent the complete reversal of previously held belief.

Associations: The Tower of Babel, and man's aspiration to reach God; sudden revelation; the blinding flash of inspiration.

XVII. The Star

This card shows a naked woman, pouring water from two jugs into the river at which she kneels. Above her are eight stars, each with eight points and beyond her, amid the hills in the distance, is a bird on a tree.

This is the card of hope. Water is poured into the land, symbolizing the regeneration of the source of life. Reversed, this card suggests difficulties, loss and lack of hope.

Reminiscent of the Temperance card, the stars suggest a flow of life on a large scale, not simply a balance of nature. It is the first card to portray the cosmos. The woman's nudity implies a oneness with the world around her.

Associations: Isis and the rejuvenation of the

Nile; Eve in paradise; stars as gods; Both the Qu'ran and Hindu idea of bird as soul; the river of life.

XVIII. The Moon

In the centre of the card is a Moon radiating over a flowing river. On either side of the river is a tower before which a dog is baying. In the river is a crayfish. The Moon is the only card that does not contain a person.

Traditionally, in divination the Moon suggests deception, obscurity and concealed dangers. Reversed, it suggests the enquirer will come to grief through his own duplicity.

The Moon waxes and wanes, controls tides and cycles and is associated with the mysterious feminine. The river suggests emotion, the unconscious, the deep, while the dogs suggest the mediators between the physical and psychic worlds; the crayfish devours the corrupt and regenerates the river. So while the Moon suggests obscurity, it is also the door between the unconscious, inspiration and prophecy.

Associations: The River Styx and the dog that guards it; Hecate, Isis, Artemis.

XIX. The Sun

Two half-naked people play in front of a wall, the Sun above them radiating a golden glow.

This is a happy card, signifying peace, contentment and possibly a happy marriage. Even when reversed, it still bodes well.

The Sun is a source of light and power that enables growth and embodies a joy of life. As the Moon represents the unconscious self so the Sun is the vital, energetic self. However, the figures are contained within a wall, and this suggests not only the self but happiness on an earthly plane.

Associations: Apollo; Ra; Atum, the creator, Osiris; all peoples have worshipped the Sun in some form. The two figures are sometimes associated with Castor and Pollux.

XX. Judgement

In this card an angelic figure blows a trumpet, calling the figures below to account.

This is the card of the Day of Judgement. On an earthly plane we must be our own judge, and be able to give good accounts of who we are and what we have been. Our past deeds must be looked at and justified in the light of our present knowledge before we move on. This does not mean the ending of the world, but the ending of the world as we know it.

In divination it represents a judgement of what has gone before – that we must take account of past performance before deciding on a future course of action.

Associations: The Resurrection; eternal life; the Angel of Doom.

XXI. *The World*

In this card a figure stands barefoot, with only one foot connected to the earth, within an enclosing wreath (sometimes the ourobos, the symbol of infinity). The figure represented is either female or hermaphrodite. Surrounding it are the symbols for the four seasons, the four Elements, or, according to some interpretations, the Bull, the Lion, the Man and the Eagle.

From a divinatory point of view, this card represents ultimate success and a well-regulated life.

In spiritual terms it suggests a completion. The trials and tribulations of the journey have been overcome, and the individual is now able to take his position in the cosmic dance. He has attained a state of unity and is within the world but not of it.

Associations: Creation; completion; the cosmic egg; achievement.

The Minor Arcana

Whereas the cards in the Major Arcana reflect the big issues in life, those in the Minor Arcana show humdrum, day-to-day events and how these affect you. These are the things that occupy most of our lives, and although they often seem insignificant, it is frequently our reaction to them that sets off major changes.

Levi pointed out that the ten numerical cards of each suit corresponded to the ten Sephiroth (centres of divine energy) in the Kabbalah; the four suits corresponded to the four Elements,

thus Coins (later called Pentacles) are Earth, Cups are Water, Sceptres (later called Wands) are Air, and Swords are Fire.

Indeed it is because of this, on a more mundane level, that the four suits all have their own interpretations and correspondences:

Pentacles Money, stability and material matters.
Cups Love, happiness, harmony, sensitivity, fertility and unity.
Wands Work, creativity, reputation, fame, enterprise and efficiency.
Swords Ideas and communications, hostility, struggle, bitterness and malice.

A Tarot reading that includes the Minor Arcana can reveal many things, including – perhaps most importantly – whether your life has become entrenched in a pattern, in which case the cards can help you change repetitive cycles and broaden your outlook. The Minor Arcana reflect not just life's experiences but also the manner in which you externalize them.

Each of the cards in the pack has its own meanings – one for when it is drawn properly and one when it is reversed. A reversed Minor Arcana card turns its upright meaning negative, though many readers consider that it also represents the potential for its upright meaning. The suits, too, have their own correspondences, which are significant, when many cards of the same suit turn up in a spread. Broadly, the numbered cards from one to ten all have specific meanings, their final interpretation tempered by the suit to which they belong. These basic meanings are shown below.

Aces are the seeds or beginning of things. They represent unity and the creative principle.
Twos represent duality, opposites but also partnership. There is often ambivalence inherent in this number. It is a manifestation of an essential diversity or polarity.
Threes signify birth, life and death, the Holy Trinity and any aspect where things become visible or manifest. The triangle is often used in magical workings to signify a spiritual presence in the physical world.

Fours are solid, tangible and stable structures, uniting physical and spiritual principles in one coherent whole. The number four unites the four Elements and calls for obedience.

Fives indicate power, domination and victory, and sometimes a tension between useful and constructive enterprises and wanton acts of destruction. They are always active and forceful.

Sixes signify hesitation, difficulties that can be smoothed over and oppositions which can be moulded for good. However, they can also suggest changes for the worse and an internal revolt.

Sevens are the organization of universal energy, the perfect dynamic and magical manifestation. There may be conflict but change is usually for the better. This is the Holy or cosmic number, which initiates vast transformation.

Eights can suggest suffering and the working through of one's destiny. Also, they are the union of the physical and spiritual realms and therefore the number of transcendence. Inevitably there is fear attached to this process, but that can be overcome.

Nines are the number of initiation, of endings and beginnings. Signifying passivity, they suggest acceptance, not of the status quo but of that which must happen. They forecast the return to Unity.

Tens reassure us that nothing is permanent, but that there is always hope and positive change. A continual process of regeneration takes place and there is promise of a new phase of existence.

To demonstrate how to make sense of a card in a spread, here are a few examples:

- The seven of Pentacles might be read as a change for the better in material circumstances, the best use of material resources.
- The four of Wands suggests a new stability in an enterprise connected with work or in one's home environment. There is no stasis, but there is potential movement.
- The six of Cups indicates that there is some hesitation and difficulty on the emotional front which can eventually be overcome.

The more accomplished one becomes, the easier it is to read the numbered cards. Their meanings often become clearer in the light of the cards of the Major Arcana or when the court cards are introduced.

The court cards

There are 16 court cards in the Tarot pack, each suit having a King, a Queen, a knight and a page, or sometimes a page and a princess. Often seen as people in the enquirer's environment, they can also be read as qualities required within a situation.

Kings are mature males, authority figures who embody power and paternalism, achievement and responsibility. If a King appears in a spread and is not recognized, he can sometimes represent the enquirer's own more assertive, driven side. Reversed, Kings can be seen as inflexible and perhaps a domineering aspect.

Queens are generally maternal figures and, like the Kings, figures of authority with inherent fertility and wisdom. When a Queen is unrecognized, she can stand for the enquirer's own intuitive nurturing side in relationships, motives and intentions. Reversed she shows a tendency to be possessive about the qualities of her suit, and sometimes destructive.

Knights are young people who are on the verge but who have not achieved full maturity. Their qualities are usually somewhat untutored, and may represent an uncharacteristic quality that is slowly developing in the enquirer. Immaturity and an inherent selfishness are indicated by a reversed knight.

Pages or princesses refer to children or young teenagers of either sex, the child within and undeveloped potential. They can also suggest spontaneity, according to the suit. Reversed, they indicate a childish attitude.

When using the court cards for divination, you take the meaning of the card and the meaning of the suit and combine the two. Thus, the King of Pentacles might represent a banker, while the Knight of Cups might represent an idealistic seeker of truth.

The Tarot is a complex system of divination, its meanings subtle but deep. On a superficial level it is just another form of 'fortune-telling', but the cards have a deeper significance, offering insights into the forces that are at work in both your life and within the innermost self. The Major Arcana, when laid out like a clock-face, depicts man's spiritual journey and how he learns about himself. When the Minor Arcana is then shuffled and laid out beneath these cards you can gain a fairly clear idea of the problems and difficulties there are with each of these phases of existence.

In this book, which is, after all, about spell making, this brief description of the Tarot is intended to give you a sense of how to use divination in its purest form – that is, approaching the divine. The way of working with Tarot described below will allow you to do just this.

Tarot Meditation

Meditating on the cards in this way gives you a depth of understanding and perception that it is probably not possible to achieve in any other way. This can be done with each card so that your overall understanding becomes quite phenomenal. Ideally you should do the meditation before you go to sleep and then sleep with the card under your pillow to enhance your dreams. You will find a slightly enhanced method of understanding archetypal images through dreams in the Magical Dreaming section on page 343.

YOU WILL NEED

The Major Arcana of your chosen pack
A quiet place free from interruptions

METHOD

✦ Form a circle of the cards in order, placing the Fool in the middle. (This is both your starting and your finishing point.)
✦ Study this card carefully with all its imagery and recognize that this represents you as you set out upon your journey of discovery.
✦ Visualize yourself as the Fool and sense what you think his personality is like.
✦ Next look carefully at the other images in the card and try to sense what relevance they have to the main figure.
✦ How for instance would you use them; how would there be an interaction between them?

✦ If you are able to, try to 'be' each image in turn in a similar way to the IFE technique on page 342, but do not be too disappointed if this is difficult to begin with; with practice it gets easier.
✦ Now return to the main figure and sense yourself within the landscape of the card.
✦ See everything very clearly with a fresh sense of wonder.
✦ At this point, like Alice Through The Looking Glass, you may well have transcended reality, that you are actually experiencing the card and are not merely an observer.
✦ Spend a few moments in this state before returning to your own reality and re-orientating yourself in the everyday.

Having learnt how to experience the imagery of this card, you can then continue to learn about all of the other Major Arcana. Initially, choose a card at random out of the twenty-two and work with it in the same way as you have done with the Fool.

Ultimately you will wish to work with each of the cards in turn, recognizing how they fit together into a coherent journey. Do not be in a hurry to undertake this process. Study of the Tarot can be a lifelong experience, rewarding and instructive. Indeed, having completed one circuit of the cards, you can begin again, taking as a starting place the next image in sequence. Always return to the Fool as his spirituality expands in line with your enhanced knowledge.

Reading the cards

Before the cards are laid out, they must be shuffled. While doing so, focus your mind on the matter in hand. The enquirer then cuts the pack into three separate piles. These represent physical, emotional and spiritual conditions. You as the reader then observe how the pack is reassembled, accepting that whichever pile is placed on top is the most important aspect to be considered. That is, the question is either a material, emotional or spiritual one and you can concentrate most fully on that aspect.

The enquirer then chooses the cards according to the preferred method; they can be chosen straight off the top of the pack or chosen at random. Another way is to fan the cards out after they have been shuffled and to draw out the number of cards required at random, turning the cards over as they are read.

It is possible to do a simple reading for yourself using just the court cards. Shuffle them and lay them face down in a fan shape. Select four cards at random and place them in a pile. Dealing from the top, place a card, face down, nearest to you. Placing the second card directly above the first, repeat the process, until you have four cards in a vertical line. Now, read the cards in the order in which you laid them out.

The first card, the one nearest you, is who you are now. The second card, the one above, is who or what will help you. The third card tells who or what will oppose you. The fourth is who you will become.

Spreads

There are many ways of creating what is called a spread. The simplest is the Three Spread – the first card represents the past and is placed at the left of the surface. The second card (the present) is placed to the right of the first and the third (the future) to the right of the second. They are then read in that order.

The Clock spread

This is a very easy way to lay out the cards, and if wished, can help to pinpoint the right time to take action. The reader should establish from the enquirer what time frame they want to use. Thus a three-month reading would mean that each position reads for one week; for a six-month period each card signifies two weeks; whereas for a year, each position would stand for one month.

The cards are laid out with one card in the centre to enable the reader to divine the attitude of the enquirer, then twelve cards are laid around the perimeter of a circle clockwise, starting at one o'clock and finishing at twelve. To enhance the reading, up to six more cards from the total pack are laid at each position until the pack is used up. Those cards are then interpreted to help give guidance in the light of the original card.

You should allow your intuition to tell you how many cards to lay at each position, so do not worry if some of the original cards seem to need fewer cards and less interpretation than others.

The Horoscope spread

The Horoscope spread is based on the twelve houses of the Zodiac. Imagining a clock face, the first card is laid at nine o'clock, the second at eight o'clock and so on with the twelfth card at 10 o'clock. This spread is often used to focus on potential, character, relationships and career. The areas each card covers are as follows:

First	Personality
Second	Personal values and monetary matters
Third	Communications and short journeys
Fourth	Home and family
Fifth	Romance, creativity and children
Sixth	Vocation and health
Seventh	Relationships
Eighth	Shared resources
Ninth	Long journeys and matters philosophical
Tenth	Career goals and aspirations
Eleventh	Friends and hopes
Twelfth	Unconscious mind and hidden limitations

THE HOROSCOPE SPREAD

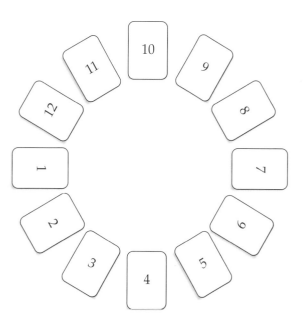

The Celtic Cross

The Celtic Cross is one of the most widely used spreads, being the most general and non-specific of layouts, showing the history behind the question, current influences, hurdles that have to be cleared, social factors and the likely outcome. This layout is usually taken to be more of a short-term one, so answers to questions are valid for no more than three months, past or future. There is a certain amount of leeway allowed in the positioning of the cards, since it becomes such a personal tool, and the information below is therefore only one of many possible explanations.

The first card is positioned vertically in the centre, the second next to it, the third horizontally along the bottom of the first. The fourth card is to the left of these three and the fifth to the right. The sixth card is positioned below the central three, the seventh above. Cards eight, nine and ten and eleven lie in a vertical line to the extreme right of the fifth, the eighth at the bottom of the column, the eleventh at the top. The aspects the cards cover are:

First – the significator
This describes the nature of the enquirer and their present circumstances.

Second – the influences
This gives the atmosphere, personalities or emotions that have a bearing on the question.

Third – the difficulties
This outlines the history, events and problems that have led to the question being asked and also any blocks to progress.

Fourth – the recent past
This tells of something that has just happened that has a direct influence on the question.

Fifth – the present
This shows the current hopes, fears and emotional state of the enquirer.

Sixth – underlying feelings
This is how the future may be affected by the enquirer.

Seventh – attitude
This defines future influences that may affect the situation.

Eighth – other's perspectives
This specifies the feeling of those close to the questioner about what is being asked.

Ninth – pros and cons
This gives a cool, detached analysis of the question.

Tenth – Action
This demonstrates any further action which needs to be taken.

Eleventh – The outcome
This rounds off the whole reading and allows the reader to be sure that the enquirer is in possession of what they need to know.

You may like to have more than one set of Tarot cards available for use, perhaps one which reads for more spiritual questions, which you use with the intention of approaching the divine, and one for more mundane matters.

If you carry out a number of spells or rituals you may find it convenient to use the Tarot to answer ethical or moral questions which might otherwise worry you. The Tarot cards used in this way become such an extension of your personality that you can trust them implicitly to give you a true picture of your own motivations, obstacles and spiritual strictures.

Generally, Tarot cards can be used to give more spiritually orientated readings. While many readers would not wish to use ordinary playing cards in the same way, many people can be considerably worried by the esoteric significances and are happier to consult the playing cards in the same way as purists would use the Tarot.

Playing Cards

ORDINARY PLAYING CARDS are derived from the Minor Arcana and court cards of the Tarot. The first cards to arrive in Britain came from France five hundred years ago, probably from the city of Rouen, and the design of the cards today is still based on a pattern used all those years ago. The court cards still show figures wearing clothes that date back to the 14th century. According to legend these costumes derive from the pack designed by Odette, the mistress of Charles VI of France, having been given a pack by Romanies who brought them from the East.

The suitmarks – spades, hearts, diamonds and clubs – are also French, although they have been given English names. Since they were introduced to Britain, what we now call 'the English pattern' has spread to the USA and other English-speaking countries. In other parts of the world, playing cards have developed differently. France uses cards that deviate slightly from the English pattern, although the four suits remain the same; Italy, Spain, Germany and Switzerland have packs that are all quite different. Clubs become acorns in Germany and Switzerland and swords in Italy and Spain. Diamonds are bells in Germany and Switzerland and coins in Italy and Spain. Spades are flowers in Switzerland, leaves in Germany and batons in Spain and Italy. Hearts are shields in the Swiss pack, hearts in the German one and cups in the other two.

What is constant is that in these and all other countries where cards are played, they can be used to divine the future – and, being descended from the Tarot, probably always have been.

Reading the cards

As with the Tarot, the cards may be read for you or for anyone else and can be used to answer a simple question or to give a more in-depth reading. Tradition has it that cards that are to be used for divinatory purposes should not be consulted on any other occasion and should be wrapped in black silk when not in use. Some people also believe that if the cards are kept on a high shelf, this raises what the cards say to a level that is above worldliness.

If the reading is for someone else, shuffle the pack first and then give it to the enquirer (some say left hand to left hand, but as usual let instinct be your guide) to be shuffled or mixed again.

The pack is now cut three times by the enquirer, and the cards spread out face down, either in an overlapping row or a circle. (The reason for using the left hand is that it is believed to have symbolic access to the right side of the brain, the side that controls intuition.) The cards to be read are then selected at random, and put in the spread.

The Mystical Seven spread reinforces the magical powers of the circle with the six-pointed star known as Solomon's Seal, believed by medieval alchemists to be especially powerful. After the cards have been shuffled or mixed, seven cards are selected from the complete pack. Imagining a clock face, and beginning at twelve o'clock, the first six cards are laid, still face down, on the six points of the Seal (two, four, six, eight and ten o'clock working clockwise). The seventh card is placed face up in the centre and represents the immediate conditions around the enquirer.

The first six cards are now turned over, in the order in which they were placed in the spread. Take an overall view of these cards. Does any one suit predominate? Is one notable by its absence? This can be as significant as the cards themselves. An abundance of clubs, for example, may indicate that career matters are to the fore. Similarly if the same card from each suit appears, this will also be significant. Four of the same number indicates a heightened result; three indicate that different forces are acting in harmony; and two of the same number can foretell conflicts of interest, reconciliation or maybe a new connection, depending on the suits.

With practice, many spreads used in Tarot readings can also be used when divining the future from ordinary cards.

The meaning of the cards

Because, in many cases, the position of the cards can change their significance, their individual and relative meanings can often be widely different. What follows can only be general. However, experience shows that even with general meanings, the information can be surprisingly accurate. As in most practices to do with cards, the Ace is highest in value and importance.

Clubs

Clubs are linked with ambitions and achieving them successfully, with career matters, health, business partnerships, communication and expansion. The suit also has strong connections with older, mature people.

The Ace signifies a new beginning, perhaps a

new perspective on old, restrictive problems. There may be illness, either for the enquirer or someone in their immediate family.

The King represents a successful, ambitious person, if somewhat impatient and insensitive. He can be innovative and a brilliant communicator, but also uncompromising. He offers help in difficult situations.

The Queen is a good organizer. Energetic and tactful, she can sometimes run out of energy when overstretched. She can be trusted to do her best, and is a good ally.

The Jack is impetuous and inclined to give up easily, particularly if he gets confused. If his energy can be focused properly he does get things done, but may require help along the way.

The ten forecasts the realization of long-term goals and the learning of new skills. Personal happiness is assured, sometimes from a legacy, though an old friend may disappear from view.

The nine suggests too much responsibility, leading to self-doubt and loss of confidence. Delegation of non-essential matters would help, though a friend's advice may not prove useful. In a woman's reading, the card can suggest widowhood.

The eight presages sudden opportunities, but warns against speculation. You may strike out on your own or receive an interesting proposition which should be carefully considered.

The seven offers success and satisfaction, though not at the expense of personal principles. Legal advice should be taken when necessary, particularly over the achievement of a long-term goal.

The six indicates a period of tranquillity which can be used to work towards bringing in new contacts or to take a welcome break. Niggling health issues will improve, making you feel more energetic than previously.

The five almost inevitably represents minor problems, caused perhaps through tiredness and carelessness. You need to stand your ground and recognize that everything has not yet come out into the open.

The four instructs you to move on, having first won the trust of others, then establishing clear lines of communication. Previous responsibilities and promises may need reassessing in the light of new knowledge.

The three suggests expansion in many different directions. Travel may be important, extra commitments or new opportunities offered. Sometimes, this card forecasts multiple marriages.

The two advises that you need to achieve a balance between work and health. There may be disappointment of some sort, and a business relationship may have to be reassessed.

Diamonds

Diamonds refer to practical matters – money, property in general and the home, animals and children. The suit reflects qualities of patience.

The Ace augurs new ventures of a practical or financial nature. It promises a flood of prosperity and perhaps a change of home. However, the surge in prosperity lessens, particularly if the card is followed by a spade.

The King is a reliable man, patient and affectionate, who does his best to have your life run smoothly. Given to deeds rather than words, the King promises a great deal of travel.

The Queen is practical and organized, good at solving problems and making everyone feel at home. Loyal to a fault, she is sometimes not to be trusted, and often represents a long-term relationship rather than an actual person.

The Jack is a youthful, practical person showing common sense and a supportive, helpful attitude. The responsible way he handles money might make him seem wise beyond his years.

The ten radiates success, either with new ventures or financial or domestic commitments. Ensure that you are in control of the situation if money changes hands.

The nine counsels independent thought and action, expanding horizons and putting personal interests first. Risk-taking through new business interests is in order, provided firm foundations are in place.

The eight announces an unexpected change in domestic and financial arrangements, possibly through the discovery of a new skill, possibly as a result of a short journey. Restlessness should be channelled into making tangible improvements to your life.

The seven brings changes, and harmony at home and in financial matters, often in the form of a new job. It favours long-term plans and dreams, provided you trust your intuition. Children or animals may bring fresh contentment.

The six stresses that you should avoid making too many commitments, either legal or financial, and should pay attention to the small print. Think carefully before you act and be sure of your ground. Family matters may be of concern, and a gift is possible.

The five may put temporary financial or practical obstacles in your path. Stay focused, accept help, adjust your conduct and plans when necessary, and all will be well. You may lose something of value.

The four puts limits on monetary and practical matters and you should consider the risks involved in what you do. There may be difficult decisions to be made concerning the home or the family, especially children.

The three suggests that there is stability in the conditions around you. Extra commitments or responsibilities may seem something of a burden now, but are important in the long term. Disappointments can be handled now. This card can also foretell a birth.

The two says that a new venture will turn out to be built on firm foundations. Increased prosperity is on the cards, too, as well as the prospect of a change of address.

Hearts

This suit is linked with love and emotions, relationships and intuitions, young people who have left their teenage years behind but have not reached forty and people, regardless of age, who are in love.

The Ace signifies that you are on the brink of a new friendship that could blossom into romance. If a sudden burst of intuition, particularly regarding people, has just occurred or is experienced in the near future, this card says to trust it. It may be time to move on.

The King indicates a charismatic, older, probably altruistic man, who has the ability to make others feel special. He can be a tender, open-hearted romantic, but he can put his personal emotions on the sidelines if he deems it necessary.

The Queen is a caring, nurturing person who can be almost too empathetic, losing herself in service to others. An older woman who is established in a long-term relationship, she has a tendency to sentimentality, which can mean that those she cares for never reach full emotional independence.

The Jack is sentimental and loves being in love. The card indicates sometimes a young person, but equally an older, emotionally vulnerable, incurable romantic. He can also stand for a best friend.

The ten indicates that emotional happiness and fulfilment comes through others. It suggests someone who gives emotionally and who gets tremendous satisfaction from caring. It is a card of happy relationships, and lifts the tone of other surrounding cards.

The nine, sometimes known as the wish card, is one of self-confidence, happiness and emotional independence. A new venture will bring a rise in esteem and a boost to the finances.

The **eight** warns that one relationship is about to enter a new phase. You should beware of jealousy and of emotional blackmail which could be destructive and should be brought to an end. The eight also signifies a holiday or break with a loved one.

The **seven** tells you to trust your instincts and intuition, to listen to what your dreams are saying. You are in tune spiritually with those close to you and friends and colleagues are co-operating. There is a warning to be on your guard, since a one-time friend may be fickle and false.

The **six** presages a time of harmony in friendship and love. Good friends bring a positive influence to bear on your life and rifts, particularly with older people, can be healed. A child's endeavours will pay dividends.

The **five** suggests that it is better to see a relationship for what it is, lest misunderstandings and jealousy, albeit unfounded, cloud the horizon. Passion and honesty together bring truth. This is not an either/or situation.

The **four** suggests some sort of emotional choice has to be made, especially if there are any doubts about the strength of another's commitment. Creatively, restlessness and dissatisfaction with the emotional side of our lives can spur us on.

The **three** highlights rivalry that love or even simple friendship can encourage, if that love is not unconditional. There is the potential for stress as you balance your own needs, so try to remain objective in your assessments.

The **two** indicates that a love match is about to be made that could lead to marriage. With care, friendships will deepen, long-standing quarrels mend, bridges be built and two seemingly unconnected aspects of life will come together in a totally unexpected way.

Spades

Perhaps the most challenging of the four suits, spades are associated with older people and with ageing in general. The suit is connected to the didactic, formal and traditional, to coping with challenges, especially those that can be seen as limiting in some way and to justice.

The **Ace** traditionally forecasts doom and gloom and sometimes death. Often however, a difficult time, perhaps involving some sort of sadness, comes to an end and a new day with fresh challenges dawns. The card also predicts an appreciation of a new form of learning.

The **King** is a harsh, disapproving and pedantic perfectionist, who has a vast store of knowledge which makes him impatient of the mistakes other people make. Rather than being seen as vulnerable, he chooses to prefer his own company to that of others. A legal matter concerning a dark man may affect you.

The **Queen,** often known as the Queen of Sorrows, is a critical, disapproving, mature woman. Possessive of her family and friends, she will defend them tooth and nail, for loyalty is her cardinal virtue. Be warned not to trust such a woman, even if appearances suggest that you should.

The **Jack** is young, or immature, with a malicious tongue and a sarcastic wit, which those at whom it is not directed often find clever and very funny. This however often hides deep hurt.

The **ten** is the card of disappointment, albeit transitory, for there are good times just around the corner. An aspect of life has run its course and a new beginning is in order. Financial worries come to the fore, sparked off by a third party.

The **nine** says that no obstacle is insurmountable if you are confident and remember that victory has to be fought for, not thought about. You have more knowledge than you realize, so there is no need to fear failure.

The **eight** indicates change, if you can cut your ties with yesterday and view the future with confidence. Expressing your fears lets you see that the future has many possibilities, thanks to new contacts and previously unexplored avenues. The eight can also herald a time when frustration will turn to anger and anger to tears. You can learn to use this anger positively, rather than letting it beat you.

The seven says that if logic fails and expert opinion is against you, your intuition can stand you in good stead. Make the most of any advantages you have over others, even if in doing so, there could be conflict: remember you have right on your side.

The six signifies unexpected help from authority, giving unexpected calm after an unsettling time. Self-doubt may have dominated thinking and actions, giving rise to angry words. Where a relationship has been going through a bad patch, matters take a turn for the better.

The five tells you to marshal your facts and be prepared to use them if you are to avoid the spiteful actions and dishonest dealings of others. Disillusionment means that you keep your own counsel, in order to see plans through to successful completion.

The four says that inner fears based on past disappointments, perhaps betrayal, may put limitations and obstacles in the way of your ambitions. Losses may seem unfair and life's injustices may hurt, but you should continue to move forward.

The three advises that if reason is brought to bear, rivalry and malice can be swept to one side. Challenges should be accepted and obstacles overcome even if doing so costs time and effort. Trifling matters gain considerable significance in the future.

The two indicates that a choice between unappealing alternatives may have to be made. Logic is called for, especially if the choice concerns conflict between two acquaintances or perhaps two distinct aspects of life. Beware lest there's an unfortunate accident, or a period of separation from a loved one.

Crystal Gazing

CRYSTAL GAZING HAS its roots in prehistory, when the tribe member who was credited with the gift of seeing, peered into a reflective surface to discern what lay round the corner. It was not necessarily a crystal: a stretch of calm, still water served the purpose just as well.

In slightly more modern times, Nostradamus, the renowned seer whose prophesies continue to unfold many centuries after his death, would sit alone at night, gazing into a bowl of water held in a brass tripod and lit by a candle. In the mirror-like surface he saw his visions, many of which are still relevant today. His English contemporary, Dr John Dee, whose divinatory talents were recognized by Queen Elizabeth I, used a shiny black obsidian mirror to help in his prophesying.

Traditionally, the ball used for crystal gazing should be a gift from someone with the talent, but nowadays they are easily available from specialist shops in a variety of crystals – clear or smoky quartz, beryl, and obsidian are the most popular – and glass. Glass ones should be examined particularly closely for any blemishes or bubbles that could be distracting, though a good reader will allow these imperfections to help in their readings. A deep blue or yellowish beryl is particularly favourable to the production of symbolic visions, with clear colourless quartz often yielding the best results. Some clairvoyants prefer an ovoid or egg-shaped mass of glass or crystal instead of a sphere.

Why visions may be seen in crystals has baffled scientists for many years, and no conclusive explanation is available. Perhaps the best one comes from a teacher of psychology, who suggested that the crystal heightened awareness by making the nerve endings fire in a different way from normal.

Purchasing and preparing your crystal ball

If you are buying a crystal ball yourself (preferably with money given to you) be relaxed and receptive as possible. Handle several crystal balls, which are usually about 10 cm in diameter. How do they fit in your hand? Are they perfectly plain spheres or do they have angles and planes within them? Most people find that when they go to buy their crystal ball, they keep returning to one, no matter how many they look at and handle. If this happens, that is the ball to buy, for that is the one that will work best for you.

To prepare the ball for divinatory work, wash it in a mild solution of vinegar and water, then polish it with a soft cloth. When it is not being used, the ball should be wrapped in a dark cloth, preferably silk or velvet. Keep it out of direct sunlight, which affects sensitivity. Some gazers unwrap their crystal ball and put it in a moonlit place during a Full Moon, which enhances the crystal's power.

Crystals do pick up vibrations when handled by other people, so a ball should not be handled by anyone other than the reader without permission. If someone else is to handle it, the hands must be cupped around it, and after use, the ball may either be washed in vinegar or water or held under running water while visualizing it surrounded with bright, shining light. Many practitioners feel it is enough for they themselves to 'clear' or clean the ball by holding it. That done, the ball should be wrapped until it is to be used again.

Using your Crystal Ball

Not everybody finds the crystal ball to be the best divinatory tool for them, so do not worry if occasionally what you 'see' seems to be fantastical or negative. You should practise often in order to feel secure in your use of your crystal. If your readings seem to be consistently negatively focused, then perhaps the best advice would be to choose another form of divination. Do remember that you will, with patience, develop your own way of working.

YOU WILL NEED ───────────────

Purification incense or smudge stick
Dark-coloured cloth (preferably velvet)
Crystal ball
Votive candle

METHOD ───────────────

❖ Clear the crystal ball by holding in the lit incense or smudge stick smoke. (Another way of clearing is to hold the crystal ball in running water for a short while.)

❖ Darken the room around you and light the candle. Put the crystal ball safely on the dark cloth to minimize reflections.

❖ Place the lit candle so that there is enough illumination for you to see into your ball clearly (often slightly to the left of the crystal ball). Experiment with the best position for you – you may find, for instance, that the candle is best behind you.

❖ Ensure that you are sitting comfortably. Clear your mind of everyday thoughts and make sure you have made a good connection with both spiritual and earth energies. (You can do this by mentally reaching upwards to spiritual energy and downwards to the centre of the earth, uniting the two.)

❖ Hold the crystal ball in both hands. While rotating it gently, think of the purpose you have in mind. Using your own form of words, if you wish to, call upon your favourite deities (see pages 205-224) or guide for help in achieving your aim.

❖ Focus initially on a spot slightly in front of or behind your crystal ball. Gradually you will find your eyes drawn to a particular spot within the ball itself. Concentrate on that spot and allow your mind to relax so that it can take in new impressions. You may experience yourself as 'entering' the crystal or becoming aware of a different dimension.

Because you are concentrating, your body will probably become somewhat tense. If this should happen, simply breathe out for longer than you are breathing in and allow yourself to relax. As you do this, you will find that your awareness and sense of self changes. You may find yourself becoming apparently larger or smaller. This is not unusual and allows you to transcend the dimensional barriers we all experience in everyday life.

❖ If you find your eyes closing, allow them to do so. If you find yourself moving involuntarily or becoming aware of certain energies, do not become concerned as this also is perfectly natural in changing awareness. This state is known as automatism.

✤ Either out loud or silently, state the question to which you require an answer. If you have no specific question, then just ask for guidance.

✤ You will now find that impressions come and go and that you can, with some clarity, be aware of the answers you seek. Let these impressions flow until such times as you instinctively 'know' that there is no more information.

✤ Now begin to become aware once more of your experience of the crystal. You may find yourself floating inside it, aware of its boundaries. This experience is totally individual and cannot be quantified.

✤ Gradually become aware of the feeling of the crystal in your hands and the sense of your own body as it returns to normal. Finally, become aware of the room you are in. Adjust your breathing and open your eyes.

✤ Sit quietly for a few moments assimilating the experience. Make sure you have fully returned to everyday consciousness. If you called on the deities, thank them for the experience, then either cover your crystal ball with the velvet cloth or put it back where it is kept.

It takes time and concentration to use the crystal ball successfully. Learning to concentrate properly is a talent that has many other applications, so it is well worth the effort and time.

Your first attempt should last no longer than ten minutes, gradually increasing the time of each session, at first to fifteen minutes, then twenty and so on, but no session should ever last longer than one hour. Time each session with a watch or clock positioned so that you can see its face, but will not be distracted by its ticking.

The presence of another person can be distracting at first. With experience comes the ability to answer the questions of others, as their energies become part of the ambience.

Gazers often find that small, glittering points of light appear in the mist before it clears, and what has been described as an ocean of blue space forms, within which visions appear. These visions are sometimes symbolic, the meaning of

the symbols often being similar to those seen in tea-leaf reading or other symbology known to the reader, or for some they may be more scenic in nature. Visions that appear in the background lie further ahead than those that are to the front, which denote the present of the immediate future.

When images come, no effort should be made to keep them there: they should be allowed to come and go, ebbing and flowing like the tide, with no attempt being made to control them.

Scrying

SCRYING TOOLS ARE used in a similar way to the crystal ball in the development of clairvoyance – seeing the past and the future and understanding the present. Scrying requires concentration and so you need an object to focus your mind. Before you use any tool for scrying, you may like to prepare your own incense for use while you work. Unfortunately, the scrying incense is not very pleasant-smelling, but it does do its job very well. Use it in very small amounts.

❋ Scrying Incense ❋

1 part mugwort
1 part wormwood

Instructions for preparing the incense are on page 54.

Simple tools such as a black bowl or cauldron are very effective for scrying. According to folklore, people used what they had available, and so their tools were often ordinary household objects such as bowls and mirrors. For scrying you should choose a new bowl, not old, used kitchen utensils, since these may have vibrations, scratches or other marks which will affect your reading.

Scrying Bowl

You may wish to make your own bowl, in which case you can decorate the outside of it with symbols in keeping with your own beliefs.

The bowl should be made and/or consecrated during the fourth quarter or Waning Moon. Information on the Moon's quarters can be found in many newspapers or on the internet.

YOU WILL NEED

A simple bowl whose shape you like, preferably with a dark inner surface (if it lacks this, paint the inside with non-toxic paint or use a similar mixture to the one given in Magic Mirror below)
Water or divining liquid
Votive candle

METHOD

❖ First prepare your divining liquid (see below).
❖ Put the scrying bowl safely on a firm surface. Fill the scrying bowl with the liquid to about 2.5 cm (1 inch) from the top.
❖ Place the lit candle so that you can see into the bowl. (Experiment with the best position for you.)
❖ Now use your scrying bowl in the same way as you would do for the crystal ball.

You do not have to use specially prepared liquid for scrying, but it may please you to do so. When you have prepared your own liquid, you have personalized your scrying bowl and therefore the resulting perceptions should be easier to understand.

Divining Liquid

This should be made during the third quarter of the Moon to give time for the liquid to infuse sufficiently for use during the fourth quarter. The herbs used can be entirely of your own choice, but do include those which are known to help clairvoyance such as jasmine, rose petals and hyssop.

YOU WILL NEED

Dried herbs
Sea salt
A large clear bottle or jar
Water
Small bowl (not your scrying bowl)

METHOD

❖ In the small bowl, mix the herbs together.

Add one part herb mixture to four parts water. Stir in 3 teaspoons of sea salt.
❖ Pour the mixture into the jar, cover and place in a sunny spot.
❖ Keep an eye on the distillation process. If the amount of liquid diminishes, you can add enough water to sustain the original level. Leave it as undisturbed as possible so both the Moon and Sun energy will blend with the herbs and water until needed.

During the time of the fourth quarter, strain the herbs and store the liquid, which will look rather like tea, in a lidded container until you wish to use it.

A magic mirror is another tool that can be used in the same way as your crystal ball or scrying bowl. Some practitioners will simplify the procedure by merely spraying black enamel paint on the back of a sheet of thick glass. Others may choose to use a double-sided round mirror, with the thought that the magnifying side enhances any working they do. Remember to consecrate your mirror before you use it. You might like to use the divining liquid above to wash your mirror as part of that process.

Magic Mirror

To make a magic mirror you should prepare it as the Full Moon wanes. Ideally you should leave it for one whole cycle of the Moon before using it for scrying, turning back negativity or any other magical purpose.

YOU WILL NEED

20 x 25 cm (8 x 10 inch) photo frame with a removable back and removable glass
Black high-gloss paint (not aerosol spray)
Dried and powdered psychic-enhancing herbs such as hyssop, dragon's blood, orris root, anise seed and any variety of dried moss
Disposable mixing container
Paintbrush

METHOD

❖ Mix the paint and herbs together until you have a thick, tar-like substance.
❖ While mixing, visualize the light of the Moon entering the paint and say:

By the Moon's darkest light,
Perception of the night,
Become part of my skills,
And thus banish all ills.

❖ Paint one side of the glass with the paint-herb mixture using long, straight strokes. Cover the surface completely, leaving no gaps.

❖ When dry, reassemble the frame with the painted side down so that the flat unpainted side shows through the frame.

❖ Leave your mirror outside in moonlight for as long as you can; otherwise keep it covered by a dark cloth.

Your mirror can also be used to reflect negativity back to where it belongs. If you do use it for this purpose, you should cleanse it and reconsecrate it for the purposes of scrying.

Dowsing

DOWSING WITH EITHER a cleft stick or a pendulum can be used to sense the negative or positive energies in a house or piece of land. Geopathic stress – energy trapped due to old watercourses, drainage pipes, archaeological features or other difficulties, such as ancient graves – can be pinpointed and steps taken to neutralize or enhance the energy. The art of feng shui and the placement of crystals, wind chimes, mirrors, small shrines and other statues can all be used to achieve this.

Dowsing using a divining rod is also called rhabdomancy, divining, water witching, or doodlebugging. By tradition a cleft stick of a living material, such as hazel wood, is used, However, most woods will suffice, and you can even make your own rods from wire, such as an old coathanger. Almost anything can be searched for by this method, including water, underground caves, lost jewellery and ley lines (energy lines within the earth).

The cleft stick, which is thought to have been the origin of the magician's wand, is held lightly in both hands and the ground (or map, if done at a distance) is quartered – divided into sections – until the stick dips in a recognizable way. With experience, the dowser will be able to pinpoint what he is looking for with astonishing accuracy.

The origin of the art of dowsing is not clear, but the earliest sign of its use is found in a grave inscription in Brittany dating from 4,500 to 5,000 years ago. Even today, although its efficacy has been proved many times, no one knows exactly how it works. However, bearing in mind that brain activity is electrical, there may be some interaction between the electro-magnetic fields of the dowser, the rod and the object being dowsed for. Experiments have shown that 'sensitives' are more able to pick up these subtle vibrations from people if there is excitement, suggesting that dowsing and telepathy share basic principles.

Dowsing may also be performed with a pendulum, in which case the method is slightly different. Initially, until more experience is gained, the question put by the dowser has to be in a form answerable by a simple 'yes' or 'no'. How the pendulum swings depends on the energy levels within the questioner. For some people a clockwise swing denotes 'yes' and an anti-clockwise swing 'no'. For others a circular motion is 'yes', and so forth. To test the pendulum a question is asked to which the answer is known, for example, 'Am I a woman?' or 'Am I a man?'

Using the pendulum

It can take several attempts before a satisfactory movement is established and often the pendulum does not work if you are tired or under some stress. For this reason it is often better to have someone else do the dowsing if you want an objective answer. Once the 'yes'/'no' pattern has been decided, the actual question can then be asked. A neutral answer may sometimes be received if, for instance, the question is not answerable by a positive or negative, or the outcome is unclear. The best way to tackle this is to break the original question down into its component parts and ask for an answer for each of these.

It is also possible to dowse for health matters, though this should be done as an adjunct to conventional medicine, not as a replacement.

The pendulum can also be used to help a client decide on the use of correct medication, by questioning the pendulum, either over a sample of the medication, or even the words written on a piece of paper. This, however, requires an element of trust as much as intuition, but can help in having the patient feel they are still in charge of making decisions. Magically, the spell for enhancing the use of medication on page 275 might also be used at this point.

A pendulum can also give an indication of when to do things. So, in answer to the question 'When would it be best to carry out a certain spell?', think about each upcoming day of the week, or day in the month, and question the pendulum on each one in turn, until it reacts positively. Thus, if you were starting on a Sunday, using days of the week, and you received the following information: Monday – negative; Tuesday – negative; Wednesday – negative; Thursday – positive; Friday – positive; Saturday – negative/positive; Sunday – negative, the Thursday and Friday of that week would be best, while Saturday is less favourable. Or, you could use dates and begin with the day on which you were working (for example 1 March, positive, 2 March, positive, 3 March, negative and so on), 1 March and 2 March would give the most positive results. Other ways of using correspondences are shown later in the book.

As the practitioner becomes more proficient in the use of either the rods or the pendulum, they can both be used to ascertain the direction of a problematic area or source of difficulty or, as seen later, lost objects. Here the pendulum or rods are allowed to be at rest and the question asked 'From what direction is the problem coming?' Usually the pendulum or rods will swing towards the problem, and further readings can be taken to confirm this.

Opinions differ as to whether dowsing with a pendulum emanates from spirit or from spiritual energy. Mediums and channellers would claim the former, while other practitioners would prefer to think the latter. When you use spells, your own belief will enhance your working and it would probably be wise to consecrate your pendulum before you begin work, as on page 146.

Psychometry

STRICTLY DEFINED, PSYCHOMETRY is the ability to link into the vibrations of an object and to read its history. The easiest way to understand this is to accept that, like recording machines, most objects will pick up the emotions and feelings of their owners or wearers. Where there have been several owners of, for example, a piece of jewellery, the competent reader must be able to tell the difference between the experiences of the various owners.

Psychometry also makes it possible to divine a person's future actions, linking via the object to the Akashic records – all that is, was or shall be. In spell making – always with the owner's permission – it is often possible to judge if a spell will help the situation, whether matters are best left alone or sometimes what kind of adjustments need to be made and what support can be given to the sitter through the use of magic.

It is important that when you are reading for someone else you suspend your own belief and do not allow your judgement to become clouded by the emotions – and perhaps problems – presented in this way. As with clairvoyance, images that arise may be symbolic or belong to memory, and again a good reader will learn to differentiate between their own symbolism and a memory trace from the sitter.

There are strong similarities between psychometry and straightforward clairvoyance; many sitters, and indeed readers, prefer the former, partly because it tends to be the most showy demonstration of psychic powers. It also allows a degree of objectivity on the part of the reader, who can if necessary break the link simply by putting the object down. Almost any object can be used, from a flower that has been held for a short time by the sitter to a strand of their hair.

Using psychometry

This is a skill which takes time to develop, but is well worth the effort. There are several stages to the development and each one can be of use to the spell maker.

First, you must learn to put yourself in touch with an object. For the purposes of this exercise use a found stone, one that pleases you with its shape and feel. Remember that this initially is an entirely personal exercise. Ideally, the stone should fit comfortably and unobtrusively into your hand and your pocket so that you can work with it wherever you are. Strictly, you should not go searching for your stone, though there is a fine line between searching and recognizing a need.

When you find your stone, there are several things that you need to be aware of while you learn its story and learn how best to use it.

1. First you need to have some concept of how it became what it now is. Ask yourself was it once large and has now become weathered? Is it a piece of a larger stone that broke off somewhere? What has it experienced to get to you? Use your imagination to begin with, but as you develop a greater rapport with your stone, you may be quite surprised at some of the information you receive. Think now about how you can apply the concept of a journey to the way your life is at the moment.

2. Secondly, you need to have a concept of how you and it became connected. See it as energy and power, as it was in the beginning – a mass of gaseous material gradually becoming compact and manageable as an energetic force. Then see how the vibrations that it consists of reached out to you and made a connection, just as you did to it. Put yourself, through those connections, in touch with earth and all its power.

3. Begin to use the stone as an energizer. When you are tired, rub the stone; when you are sad, hold on to it and use it to gain a sense of permanence; when you feel out of touch, use your own sense of touch to re-establish links. Initially you may feel a little silly doing this sort of thing but gradually you will become more at home and will gain much benefit.

4. Next, the stone brings your head out of the clouds and makes you realize what is important to you. As life's journey starts in earnest, we all have grand ideas about where we will end up. Using the stone as a foundation, and always having it around you, gives the grounding necessary to successfully complete the journey. It makes you realize that no matter what, we are all of this earth and should be grateful simply for that. This gives the stone more power than is first realized, for it has the ability to attract us towards it again or to be magnetic. This is powerful indeed and should make us aware of our own magnetism and the ability to attract.

5. The stone can link you in to eternal wisdom. Just as it has come to you through aeons of time, so also you are composed of many different experiences – not just yours but also those of your forefathers. It can give you a sense of continuity, of belonging and of being nurtured – indeed of belonging to a much wider family. Your experiences have a validity all of their own, and you need never be totally alone when you have your stone to remind you of who you are.

6. There are times when you need to feel protected from harm, from the hard winds of reality which can buffet you in many ways. Your stone will remind you of your ability to weather those storms, to stand firm in the face of adversity and to come through unscathed. You are – and always have been – unique and can make use of those unique qualities as you journey through life.

7. You can also use your stone as a meditative aid. Just as a child uses a comforter, so your stone can help you to be at peace, to be contemplative and to get back to simplicity. In a place of silence, perhaps in front on your altar, by holding the stone and focusing your mind you can marshal your thoughts, plan for the future and let go of the past. Here you are using your stone as a 'worry stone'.

8. Your stone can remind you that you are part of a greater whole, that small as you are, there is much to understand and much to appreciate in this world of ours. Finally, if you wish, you can make your stone a repository for your dreams and desires and, as you sit quietly with it, remind yourself of all you can and want to be.

Do not try too hard with any of these steps, nor feel you have to attempt all of them at once. Just be content with each new realization or awareness as it comes to you.

When you begin to start reading other objects, perhaps a friend's engagement ring or a watch or brooch, you will largely use the same techniques though ultimately you will want to go on and from stage 4 onwards you will be reading for the wearer of the object rather than for yourself and will be describing their journey.

A little thought will show you that at stage 4 you may be able to help your friend by suggesting a spell such as Disperse Negative Emotion on page 273.

At stage 5 you might like to suggest a suitable crystal, rune or stave to help validate their experiences.

With stage 6, with your sitter's permission, particularly if you sense distress and difficulty, you might offer healing or a protection spell from the spells Compendium.

At stage 7 or 8 you might suggest that the owner of the object could use it as a point of power, and particularly to link with their higher self or guardian spirit at times of need. If of suitable material, the object could be left in the sunshine or held under running water to get rid of negativity or could become a symbol of hope as they move forward.

To move forward into seeing the future more clearly for your sitter, again you must always ask permission. While some people are quite happy for you to look into the future, others are simply comforted by the knowledge that they have been able to talk about themselves with someone who understands where they are coming from. Psychometry can give that comfort.

Palmistry

PALMISTRY WOULD NOT at first glance seem to have a place in a book about spells, were it not for the fact that any practitioner who works on behalf of other people, requires a deep understanding of human nature.

Palmistry is the marriage of two ancient disciplines – cheirognomy and cheiromancy.

The former studies what the shape, markings, texture and colour of the human hand tell us about the person's character, and the latter aims to use the information the hand holds to predict future events in life. (Hands can also indicate some diseases: excessively red palms can be a sign of serious liver disease, for instance.)

Like so much of divination, palmistry was first practised in China more than 3,000 years ago (where it was, and remains, part of a larger attempt to see the identity of the 'correct path' by scrutinizing not just the hand but the face and forehead) and in India, where it is closely linked to astrology.

In Victorian times, having previously fallen out of favour, palmistry came almost to be regarded as a science and was popular in upper-class salons, middle-class parlours and working-class kitchens alike. Carl Jung (1875–1961), the renowned psychologist, was fascinated by palmistry and his followers came to believe that the outward personality (how you relate to the world) is in the dominant hand and the inner (how you relate to your inner self) in the minor hand. The dominant hand (the more powerful, giving hand) reflects events that have happened and as they are unfolding now – achievements and disappointments, changes of opinion – with the three main lines (heart, head and life) representing the physical organs of the body. The minor hand (the one which allows us to take what others offer) can give an excellent insight into the subject's potential and what, deep down, they really want in life. In this hand, the heart, head and life lines signify the more subtle energies, spiritual, nervous and sexual, that drive the subject.

Palmistry, like so much of divination, depends on two things – instinct, or rather intuition, and a degree of trust between the palmist and the subject. The reading should take place in a relaxed atmosphere. A shaded room fragranced with essential oils is ideal.

An introductory chat can tell the palmist a great deal about the subject: which is the dominant hand; does the subject gesticulate as she talks; are the hands open and relaxed, or are the fingers clenched into a fist; are the fingers dressed with rings? During this time, the reader takes the opportunity of taking the subject's hand and looking at the texture, the colour, the condition of the fingernails, blemishes and, particularly, the shape of the hand.

Reading a Palm

The actual reading of a palm can be done by examining the hand physically (which many readers prefer) or by taking a palm print. Either way, the hands being studied must be washed and thoroughly dried and free of rings. Should you wish to take a palm print:

YOU WILL NEED

A tube of fingerprint ink (available from specialist shops)

A smooth metal or glass surface on which to roll out the ink

A hard rubber roller (available from specialist art shops or photographic supply shops)

Glossy paper

Tissues (to wipe the hands)

METHOD

❖ Squeeze some ink on to the smooth surface and push the roller back and forth until it is evenly coated.

❖ Roll the roller over the hand to be printed, before placing a piece of glossy paper on a soft or rubbery surface and carefully pressing the hand on to it gently.

❖ Roll the hand off the paper towards the edge, so that the edge of the hand as well as the palm is printed.

❖ Reassure your subject that any residual ink washes off easily.

Just as no two people, not even identical twins, have identical fingerprints, so no two people have exactly the same hands. That said, though, it is possible to identify six basic types of hand (as illustrated overleaf) that can, in themselves, tell a great deal about the subject of the reading.

Types of hands

1. The normal or practical hand

These tend to be on the clumsy side, with fingers that are short in comparison with the palm. People with this type of hand often lack patience and are quick to lose their temper. They also tend to be among the most passionate.

2. The square or elemental hand

People who have a tendency to being logical and perhaps, creatures of habit, often have square hands. They are also usually very helpful individuals who can be relied on in times of crisis. They are persistent to the point of doggedness, conventional, always above suspicion.

3. The spatulate hand

The hand and fingers of this type represent a fan, which indicates restlessness and excitability – the sort of person who can go from one extreme to another in the blink of an eye. Such people are often inventive risk-takers with an original view of the world that enables them to make discoveries. They are good company, but can be slapdash and have a tendency to bend the rules more than it is wise to do.

4. The philosophical hand

These long, bony hands often belong to teachers, philosophers and intellectuals, who are always seeking the truth. The minutiae of life are of little concern to people with philosophical hands, they are far too easily distracted. These are people who see the wider picture, often ignoring their immediate surroundings to the point that their untidiness borders on the eccentric.

5. The mixed hand

Neither one thing nor the other, these are probably the most difficult to interpret, often with a palm belonging to one type of hand, and fingers belonging to another. Sometimes such a hand is clawed, indicating long-term anxiety over financial matters, or that the person is over-timid and cautious in everything he or she does.

6. The psychic or pointed hand

Graceful and conic in shape with pointed, tapering fingers and a long palm, the psychic hand suggests an intuitive person who is happy to follow his own instincts and is usually quite right to do so. People with this type of hand often have a great deal of empathy with others.

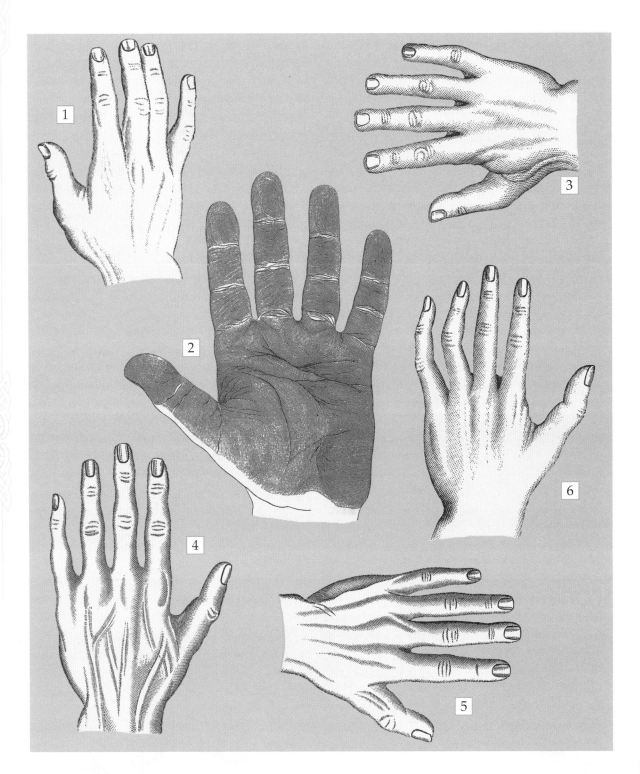

Fingers and thumbs

The next thing to look at is the thumb, which represents willpower, and see how it is held naturally. Insecure people tend to curl it up, defensively, within the palm, whereas the extrovert's thumb tends to curve outwards.

A 'normal' thumb is seen when the lower knuckle (nearest the palm) of the dominant hand's thumb is placed at the bottom of the little finger of the opposite hand; the thumb should be about the same length as that finger. Strong, thick thumbs say that the sitter has the capacity to deal with whatever life throws in their direction. Long ones indicate rational, clear thinking and leadership qualities. People with short thumbs tend to be subordinate to stronger characters, lacking the will to resist them, which often makes them unhappy. Aggressive tendencies are shown by short stubby thumbs.

More information can be gleaned from the thumb's phalanges (the sections between the joints), which are read from the top down, the first one representing will and the lower one logic. Ideally they should be about the same length. If the lower one is longer, then its owner is probably someone who thinks and talks a lot. If the upper phalange is longer, beware of a person who rushes head first into things and then cries for help as soon as trouble threatens. Sometimes a lower phalange with a slight 'waist' to it can indicate a tendency towards depression.

Low self-esteem is indicated by a flattened thumb pad and is something that often manifests itself in sexual promiscuity. A square tip indicates a practical nature, and a spatulate one shows that the owner is good with his hands.

The angle of the thumb to the index finger also yields significant information. If it is less than 45 degrees the owner has a tendency to be something of a control freak. An angle of 90 degrees between the two says that the person is a charming extrovert, outgoing and great company. Beware a thumb that curves significantly backwards: it often sits in the hand of a killer in every sense of the word – someone who has no respect for life in any form.

Generally, long fingers indicate that the person is something of a perfectionist, and extra-long ones say that he or she is prone to flights of fancy. Short fingers indicate an impatient nature.

Traditionally, each of the fingers is named as follows.

The first (index) finger, Jupiter, indicates ambition and expansion.

The second finger, Saturn, is connected with judgement and knowledge.

The third (ring) talks of exploits and achievements: it is the finger of Apollo.

The little finger, Mercury, is to do with observation and perception and with the ability to communicate.

The Jupiter finger

A long index finger points to self-confidence and awareness. Its owner is ambitious and more than able to achieve these ambitions. A leader, this is a person to whom one can turn during any type of crisis. A medium length shows that its owner is confident when confidence is called for, and modest when being such is the order of the day. Whoever has a short index finger is shy, perhaps scared of failure, can be insecure and full of self-doubt.

The Saturn finger

A long middle finger talks of ambition without humour. Those with long middle fingers work hard to get ahead, and will. A medium-length one indicates that the owner has the maturity to know when it is time to work and when it is time to play. A short middle finger is a sign of a careless person who dislikes routine so much that disorganization is a word often used about them.

The Apollo finger

The finger often associated with creativity, a long one points to an artistic nature that often leads its owner into considering design in any of its forms as a career. It can also warn of a

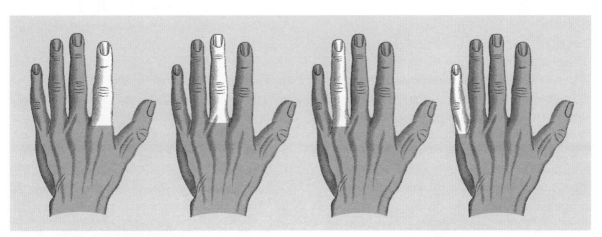

gambling streak. One of medium length still points to having a creative nature, but a more traditional, conservative one. A short ring finger can mean that there is little creativity in its owner's nature, though they may be good at implementing others' ideas.

The Mercury finger
Length here indicates intelligence and excellent communication skills that make their owners excellent writers and speakers. They might also have a stronger than average sex drive. A little finger that is medium in length says that the owner tends not to question accepted knowledge. A short one suggests a level of emotional immaturity and a tendency towards gullibility and naivety.

The comparative lengths of the fingers are also indicative of a person's nature. When the first finger is longer than the ring one, this is indicative of someone who is driven by their need to give a performance. Religious leaders and senior officers in the services often have such fingers.

Where the second finger is flanked by index and ring fingers of equal length, the owner has a serious, controlled nature with a well-developed sense of curiosity.

If the third finger is longer than the index finger, then an emotional, intuitive nature is indicated, someone who makes a good doctor or nurse, and to whom it is well worth listening.

If the little finger rises above the top joint of the ring finger, then this is a charismatic person with a quick wit and shrewd business abilities.

Shape
The shapes of the fingers are also significant. Square ones show a rational, methodical nature, someone who thinks a lot, perhaps at the expense of creativity. Fingers that are pointed indicate a sensitive nature, often fragile daydreamers who are artists or writers. Someone with conical fingers is usually a person with a flexible nature who has excellent negotiating skills and to whom emotional security is important, often over-important, to their wellbeing. People with spatulate fingers can be exhaustingly active not just physically but intellectually: they are innovators and inventors, explorers and extroverts.

Fingernails
Fingernails also play their part in hand-reading. Square ones indicate an easy-going temperament, while broad ones suggest a short fuse. Fan-shaped fingernails are a sign that the owner has been under some sort of stress for quite a long time. A gentle, kind nature is indicated by almond-shaped fingernails, but can say that the person is prone to daydreaming. A selfish, cold personality is shown by narrow nails. Wedge-shaped nails suggest that the person is oversensitive and can be somewhat touchy.

The nails can also indicate health problems. If they are dished, then the person's chemical balance is out of kilter. Dietary deficiencies may result in horizontal ridges forming in the nails, whereas rheumatism may cause vertical ones running down the nails.

The phalanges of the fingers
These, the sections between the finger joints, are read from the top down. The top one is concerned with introspection. The second corresponds to the subject's attitude to material concerns. The third deals with physical desires.

The major lines of the palm
The lines that criss-cross the palms of the hand are just some of the things at which professional palm-readers look. The professional interprets their meaning, taking into consideration what we have looked at already.

Plotting the chronology of the subject's life and assessing whether events have already happened or when they might do so, involves knowing where the lines begin. Horizontal lines should always be read from the thumb side of the hand, and vertical ones from the wrist. Broadly, you can take a normal lifeline as indicating the traditional idea of a life being three score years and ten, and measuring in ten units of seven years. This should give a fairly accurate estimate of timing. Flexibility is the keyword. Remember that in palmistry, as in all things concerned with divination, nothing is written in stone.

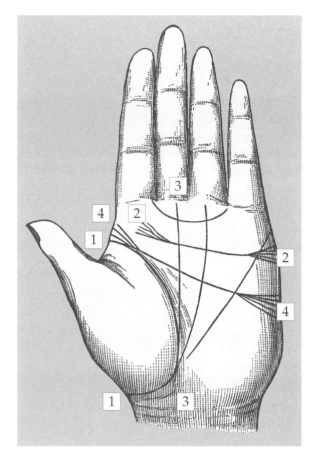

It is impossible to be precise as to where a line should start and stop. Lines differ from hand to hand. Some may be stronger in one subject than in another; some may be straight or straighter, while others have pronounced curves; some will start at the wrist, others above it. The line of one hand may stop at one particular mound while the same line on another subject's hand runs through it.

1. The life line
This is the line that curves downwards from close to the thumb towards the wrist. The closer to the thumb it starts the less vitality the subject is likely to have, whereas the wider the curve the greater the energy. A life line that is less well defined than the head line (see below) points to a person who is driven mentally rather than physically.

Chains in the life line are an indication of delicate health, and small lines rising from it denote versatility and physical activity. Lines that seem to swing out of the main one point to a desire to travel and see the world.

Upward hooks along the line after a possible problem has been indicated in the reading, suggest that the sitter has made a tremendous effort to get back on their feet after the setback; otherwise they indicate achievement.

Splits along the line mark huge changes and stressful times, perhaps conflict between domestic and professional life, a new job or relationship.

2. The heart line
This is the topmost major line, running horizontally from the side of the hand opposite the thumb. It's the line that reveals how we handle relationships, not just romantic ones. If it is almost straight, romance plays little part in the subject's life: he or she views other people in a chilly, somewhat rational way. A strongly curved heart line points to the subject who loves being in love and shows it, the sort person who takes the lead in any relationship.

A heart line that curves steeply below the index and middle digits indicates a lust for life: promiscuity can be shown by a short heart line close to the finger and points to the Mound of Saturn. Such a line also denotes practicality in matters of the heart. However, a line that ends under the middle finger suggests that the subject is the sort of person who is in constant need of love and reassurance.

If there are lots of branches off the heart line, the sitter enjoys meeting new people and will have a large circle of friends.

3. The fate line
The line that runs from the wrist upwards towards the Mound of Saturn represents career and those aspects of life that affect the way you think and feel – the practical, central supporting aspects of life. A strong fate line indicates that the subject has settled into life's routines and accepts them happily. If it is not there or is only very faint, then the sitter is unsettled and might have to change jobs several times before they make their way in life, and will have to do so with little or no help. A fate line that begins in the Mound of Venus suggests that the family will interfere, particularly in romantic matters and those relating to the sitter achieving his or her ambitions.

A fate line that almost reaches the middle finger says that the subject will enjoy an active old age. One that begins at the head line suggests that academic effort has played an important part in the subject achieving success in life. One that stops at the heart line is an indication of sexual indiscretion. An overly thick fate line means a period of anxiety at the time of life indicated by the chronology of the reading.

4. The head line

This is the line running between the life and heart lines. If it starts off tied to the life line, slavish obedience to, and dependence on, other people is indicated. If the two lines have distinct starting points (which is usual) a well-balanced, independent nature is indicated.

A long head line points to a person who thinks before he acts: a short one to someone who is quick-thinking and incisive. If the line doesn't slant at all, the subject is likely to be a person with a strong practical streak, sometimes lacking in imagination, but very focused. A slanting line indicates an imaginative and intuitive person – something of a dreamer or idealist. A line that curves rather than slants indicates lateral thinking.

Receptivity to new people is shown by the presence of lots of outward branches on the head line. If they point towards the Mound of Jupiter, leadership qualities are suggested. If they point to Saturn, a hardworking nature is indicated and success in a job that requires research. Artistic achievement is indicated by branches that point towards Apollo, and someone with branches pointing towards the Mound of Mercury should look to a career in the communications industry or business world. Downward branches suggest periods of depression, but one that runs to the Lunar Mound opposite to the thumb can expect success in the arts or humanities.

The fortune line

Often called the Line of Apollo, the line that runs vertically from the palm towards the middle finger is the line of fame, fortune and success in that which the subject finds important. If it is not there, the subject believes that success can only come through hard work. If there is a break in it, a period of some sort of struggle is indicated.

The Simian line

A strange anomaly which can occur is that of the Simian line where the head and heart lines are apparently fused together and reach right the way across the palm as one single line. People with Simian lines generally live their lives somewhat differently to most other people. They tend to live more intensely, but with an undercurrent of uneasiness, almost as though someone is looking over their shoulder. Many of the bearers of this line are supremely intelligent, ambitious, responsible and capable people with a strong will to help their fellow man.

The triangle

The triangle is a positive sign, though strong significance should be ascribed to it only when it stands as an independent mark. It shows mental acuity and success corresponding to the location of the mark. If found alongside a line, it will take on more significance depending on the line. The triangle possesses balance and enables the subject to work at consolidating success.

A wide triangle is an indication of an open person, always willing to take action and with passions that are easily aroused. Meanness of spirit is indicated by a small, cramped triangle.

The quadrant

A wide quadrant is an indication of an impulsive nature that cares little for what the world thinks. But a small quadrant, marked with many lines suggests timidity and fear, indicates someone who is constantly concerned about what people think of them.

The minor lines

Whereas most of us have the major lines engraved in the palms of our hands, many of us will not have all of the lines that follow – and their absence can be as significant as their presence.

The health line

The line that on many hands runs up the radial side of the hand towards the little finger and is sometimes called the Line of Mercury indicates an overdeveloped concern for health. Not as negative as this might sound, this line is often present in the hands of healers or those in the caring professions.

The Mars line

Running inside the life line, this is an indication of someone who has a great energy and vitality for life. It is often considered a protective line where problems are indicated on the lifeline.

The via lascivia

A horizontal line that runs across the Mound of the Moon at the heel of the hand can indicate that the subject suffers from allergies or that an addiction of some sort may cause problems. It indicates a love of the finer things of life.

The girdle of Venus

More often absent than not, it is seen as a semi-circle above the heart line beneath the Saturn and Apollo fingers. It suggests that the subject is a person of an unusually sensitive nature.

Travel lines

Running horizontally from the outer side of the hand, below the little finger and lying across the bottom and side of the hand in the lower left corner, these little lines indicate important journeys. The stronger and longer they are, the more personal significance the journey has in the subject's life.

The bow of intuition

A rather unusual line found opposite the thumb, starting at the heel of the hand and curving up towards the base of the little finger, this is an indication of intuition and prophetic ability.

The ring of Saturn

Another rare line, seen as a small arc below the middle finger, indicates a reclusive nature and an ability to be overly careful with material goods. It is sometimes found in the hands of hermits and monks.

The ring of Solomon

People who are well respected for their common sense often have this line, which runs round the base of the pad at the bottom of the index finger.

The mounds and minor marks

The raised pads on the hands are called 'mounds' or 'mounts' and vary in size and the degree to which they are pronounced. They speak of the subject's character. For the purposes of spell making, these mounds and minor marks will help to control the various energies used. Further study will give you the ability to be very specific in the directing of energy to the various Mounds of Saturn, Venus and Jupiter, where necessary.

Numerology

OUT OF NUMEROLOGY (the study of numbers), mankind developed the laws of mathematics that govern our lives. Many algebraic calculations, for example, were secret formulae used by alchemists and magicians. Numerology is concerned with the reduction of everything under consideration to the form of an arithmetical figure. The figure can then be interpreted by reference to the traditional meanings of numbers.

These interpretations date back to the time when man first visualized the interpretation of a number and associated it with spiritual meaningfulness. It was Pythagoras, the founder of geometry, who first asserted that numbers were the essence of all things, teaching his students at his school at Croton in Italy that each one had its own unique vibration and specific personality traits.

As it was believed that the planets had an effect on life on earth, there is also a beneficial connection between numbers and astrology, which has been with us for centuries. Each astrological sign is assigned a planet and a corresponding number, which, it can be assumed, have similar attributes. It should be understood however that figures themselves are merely signs that represent an idea of number, and are meaningless in themselves.

For historical reasons, the Sun and the Moon are allocated two numbers because, when the ancients devised the system, there were only seven known planets and nine numbers to be allocated.

Numerology is largely concerned only with the numbers one to nine, to which all other numbers are reduced. Zero is not strictly a number in numerology terms since it represents the Void (no-thingness), and is sometimes disregarded. Esoterically however it represents the feminine, the Great Mother, the unconscious, the absolute or hidden completeness. It does also help a number to change its vibration to a new subtler level of awareness.

The number ten, for instance, exists as a composite of the number one (1 + 0 = 1), and would be treated initially as the number one. Deeper research reveals that the person with this number is capable of effecting or leading change or advancement in others.

All subsequent numbers are treated in the same way (except for the master numbers), being reduced to a single digit for the purposes of interpretation. However, the numbers that make up the composite number will have an influence on the personality. For instance, while your main personality may be a number 5, you may have elements of 2+3 types within you.

The Birth Number

The most widely known calculation is that of the birth date. This is the number that reveals natural powers and abilities. It is often used as an indication of likely career choices. To calculate this number, the individual components of the subject's date of birth are written down and then reduced to a single number. Thus, 23 April 1966 would become (2+3) + (4) + (1+9+6+6) = 31 (3 + 1) = 4. This person can then research the meaning of the number 4. Other numerological calculations can be made from the name by assigning a number to each letter (see below).

Numbers explained

1 The associations of this number with the Sun and the Fire signs Leo, Sagittarius and Aries indicate the powers of leadership. Esoterically the number of resurrection, rising from the chaos of no-thing, it is linked with new beginnings, unity, breaks with the past and

Sun sign	Ruling planet	Number
Aries	Mars	9
Taurus	Venus	6
Gemini	Mercury	5
Cancer	Moon	2, 7
Leo	Sun	1, 4
Virgo	Mercury	5
Libra	Venus	6
Scorpio	Mars	9
Sagittarius	Jupiter	3
Capricorn	Saturn	8
Aquarius	Saturn	8
Pisces	Jupiter	3

limitless energy. While geared to assertiveness, masculinity and singleness of purpose, there can also be immaturity and a tendency to narrow-mindedness when thwarted.

People whose birth number is one are often striking to look at, with a mane of fair hair, a lean, athletic body and with beautiful skin that tans glowingly and quickly. The overall impression created by those with this number is one of action, fitness and good health.

2 Linked to the Moon, now a symbol of femininity, two brings strong intuition, the power of deep thought, attractive sensitivity and unselfishness. From an esoteric point of view, two symbolizes any duality such as balance, opposites or two ends of a spectrum. Men with two as their birth number are often closely in touch with their feminine side, and twos of both sexes are often fair-skinned, with pale, lustreless blonde hair and a dislike of bright sunshine. They may have a slight physique and show a tendency to underestimate themselves, something that leads to them having difficulties in standing their ground, though they may be quite gregarious.

They are often so quietly spoken that one has to strain to hear what they say. They also have a tendency to say one thing and do another, thus often causing difficulties in maintaining relationships, and can also be accused of a lack of responsibility.

3 Three is a mystical number in many cultures, as witnessed by the Holy Trinity of the Christian faith. Chinese philosophers believed that three was the number from which creatures that embraced the yin and the yang were created. People whose birth number is three are usually extremely intelligent and wise: they love life and have a strong sense of the sensual. They need freedom and fun in their lives, otherwise they may become listless and lackadaisical. The solid physique of youth can easily give way to fat in middle age.

Threes have outgoing personalities and prefer to be in company. They often have psychic abilities and love acquiring knowledge.

4 Another Sun number, albeit of the waning one, which in many cultures is symbolized by the serpent. Esoterically connected with the Elements and the square of stability, the number also reflects the four sides of human nature – sensation, feeling, thought and intuition.

Fours often have a tough, aggressive nature but keep it hidden under the well-balanced façade they present to the world. They enjoy hard work and appreciate the rewards this brings. They have tough bodies and quick, alert minds, though they can be quite diffident when it comes to starting relationships, because of a curious lack of confidence. Make friends with a four and they will remain loyal for life. They are however capable of lashing out when challenged, and can become very clumsy.

5 This is the number of the planet Mercury, messenger to the gods and son of Maia – the daughter of Atlas – after whom the fifth month, May, is named. Mystically, five represents the human body itself, human consciousness in the physical realm and the five senses.

Fives are mentally and physically always on the move. They are often slender of build and find it hard to put on weight, thanks to the effect their constant hurrying and scurrying has on their metabolism: actually getting things done is quite a different thing from just looking busy, however.

They have persuasive tongues, if a little devious, and can be utterly charming and sympathetic when they are attracted to someone. Normally cheerful, they can become anxious and impatient. Their agile minds make them inventive and their fertile imaginations make them good authors. Their behaviour may suggest genius – but it might just as easily say madness.

6 Venus's number, six is the symbol of partnership, love and marriage; in its higher form, of harmony and balance. Those whose birth number it is can be fairly certain that they will enjoy loving and fruitful relationships since their prime qualities are honesty, faithfulness and selflessness. Blessed with good figures, they enjoy looking good, if sometimes a little overdressed. Their love of the good things in life can lead to plumpness, however, and a degree of indolence. They do appreciate a beautiful home, sometimes being rather impractical.

With their attractive bright eyes, people with six as their number have pleasing manners and are outgoing and friendly. They can also be curiously introverted and enjoy the company of quiet, artistic people.

7 Seven is perhaps the most magical of the nine single-digit numbers with which numerology is concerned. There are seven days in the week, seven colours in the rainbow, seven pillars of wisdom, seven branches on the Jewish menorah, all commemorating the number of creativity and human wholeness.

Seven people have the ability to link the mysteries of the unknown to the practical explanations of life. They enjoy having 'alone' time to withdraw from society and think, since they are quite philosophical. They can often be quite sarcastic in situations where they feel insecure or threatened and can also be somewhat morbid. Money is not a priority for them, and neither are material items. Refined in the arts, they can also be expected to become scientists or inventors. Romantically, they are sensitive and understanding, and hate conflict, but can be hypercritical.

8

With Saturn its associated planet, eight is the number of secret, dark places. It is symbolic of the good aspects of old age – wisdom and patience – and the unfortunate ones – regret, disillusionment and failing health. It also signifies resurrection and infinity.

People whose birth number is eight are often lanky of build and are prone to having large, uneven teeth. Very rarely do they share their emotions and feelings, and they can have trouble expressing their thoughts in situations where they feel they need to be in control. They sometimes give their opinions in an overly forthright or dispassionate way. Power - and money - hungry number eight people often will stop at nothing to climb up the ladder of success, sometimes seeming completely ruthless. Failures and setbacks are easily overcome without the intervention from others, since they usually have exceptional business ability.

They mature earlier than their peers, and are often untrusting in relationships, constantly needing to be reminded of their partner's loyalty.

9

Mars, god of war, rules nine, the number of wisdom and virtue – and their opposites, ignorance and profligacy. Esoterically, nine symbolizes spiritual awareness and the beginning of a new cycle of existence, often that of a more subtle vibration.

Nine people often have powerful physiques, ruddy complexions and dark hair. Nines are intelligent and confident, with a strong sense of morals which can lead to impetuous and accident-prone behaviour.

Impulsive dreamers and romantics, they are prone to bursts of inspiration and instinctive answers to problems. While they can be full of vitality and enthusiasm, ambitious and energetic, they can also be insecure and quarrelsome, disliking intervention from others.

Master Numbers

Master numbers are 11, 22 and 33 and have to be treated slightly differently. These numbers contain a great deal of potential, which requires maturity and wisdom to appreciate. They can be reduced to 2, 4 and 6 and worked with in that way, the only problem being that usually there is a life task attached to the master numbers, which is for the betterment of mankind as a whole.

Eleven's life lesson is to achieve a balance between greatness and self-destruction. They need a great deal of faith in their search for stability, growth and personal power and their tools are intuition and sensitivity. The number represents illumination – the light of understanding both the physical the spiritual elements in life.

Twenty-two's lesson is that of the master builder, turning dreams into reality. Twenty-twos serve the world in a practical way, using idealism and inspirational insight to make things happen. Their goals must always be those that reach beyond themselves.

Thirty-three's life task – that of master teacher – gives guidance when required. Thirty-three is often self-effacing, not being willing to teach unless they themselves understand. They work towards the spiritual uplifting of mankind.

The three numbers may be thought of in ascending order as Vision, Action and Guidance.

The Destiny Number

This number shows life's purpose, the opportunities that will present themselves and how they should be used to achieve optimum potential. In calculating the destiny number, each letter of the full birth name is ascribed a number. These are then added together and treated as above, until a single number is reached. Letters are by tradition ascribed thus:

1	2	3	4	5	6	7	8	9
A	B	C	D	E	F	G	H	I
J	K	L	M	N	O	P	Q	R
S	T	U	V	W	X	Y	Z	

Thus, someone named at birth Pamela Jane Davey would be calculated as follows:

PAMELA JANE DAVEY
7 + 1 + 4 + 5 + 3 + 1 + 1 + 1 + 5 + 5 + 4 + 1 + 4 + 5 + 7
= 54 = 9

The name can, if desired, also be used for more refined readings, to give greater insight into one's personality. By reducing the numerical values of just the vowels of any name to a single numeral, we get a number (the name vowel number) that gives an indication that some say represents the Freudian ego, which is the exposed, conscious outer self – how we operate within the world. Correspondingly, the name consonant number, calculated using only the numerical values of the consonants, represents the Freudian id – the hidden, unconscious self.

I Ching

ONE CHINESE LEGEND has it that the I Ching came about in around 5,000 BC when Fu Hsi, the first Chinese emperor, was meditating by a river. Suddenly an animal that looked like some sort of tortoise, rose from the water. Fu Hsi, curious rather than scared, noticed that there were lines on its back in particular patterns. Intrigued, he pondered on the lines and on the pattern and after a while, felt that they helped him by making him a wiser man, with a greater understanding of his universe. A man of spirited generosity, he felt that if the animal had helped him it could help others, and set about drawing diagrams, a series of broken and unbroken lines, using the lines on the shell as his guide.

Another tale credits the same man, and dates the incident to around the same time and the same place, but has it that the animal in question was a dragon – dragons being held in particular reverence in China.

The lines that Fu Hsi noted were the eight trigrams – stacks of three lines, each of which in Chinese thought represent forces in Nature. These are:

Heaven
Earth
Thunder
Water
Mountain
Wind, wood
Fire
Lake, marsh

As with all things Chinese, the yin and the yang exerted their profound influence – the unbroken lines representing yang, the masculine or active principle that controls heaven, the day's activities, the Sun's heat, action and hardness. The broken lines are yin, the feminine, more passive aspect that controls the earth, the night's mystery, the cool Moon, softness and stillness.

The way that the trigrams are arranged is shown in the Pa Kua on page 16.

The trigrams became the basis of the I (pronounced 'ee') Ching, one of the most popular forms of divination in the East, and one that is increasing in popularity in the western world. It was 'King' Wen, who, when imprisoned by the tyrant emperor Chou Sin in around 1150 BC, refined the trigrams and combined them to form the six-line hexagrams or kua. He then wrote a commentary for each one.

While Wen was in prison, his eldest son Yu overthrew Chou Sin. Yu became emperor in his place and bestowed on his father the title 'King', by which sobriquet he has been known ever since, even though he never in fact ruled China. When Yu died, he was succeeded by his brother Tan, the Duke of Chou, who had been thoroughly instructed in the I Ching by their father. It was he who interpreted the meanings of each of the individual lines and it was at this point, around 1100 BCE, that the I Ching was considered complete.

It has long been known that the combination of any two trigrams gives us one of 64 hexagrams (six-line figures). It is said that within those 64 hexagrams lie the answer to every question that man can possibly have. Trigrams suggest the instinctual combination of separate principles into one complete whole, whereas the hexagrams allow for an analytical appreciation of the entire question. Individual lines give an explanation of the subtle energies at work.

For the western mind, without the innate understanding of Chinese philosophy, the I Ching can seem tremendously complex. Remembering that the Chinese treated the I Ching like a 'wise and profound friend', we must try to follow the Chinese way of thought. It is said that 'the sages set up the symbols in order to express fully their ideas; they devised hexagrams in order to show fully truth and falsehood; they appended judgements in order to give full expression to their words'. They worked on the principle of yin and yang – the passive and the active principles.

Casting the I Ching

One of the earliest methods of using the I Ching was to heat a tortoise until its shell cracked and to interpret the cracks that appeared! Fortunately things have moved on since then, and today there is more than one method.

Traditionalists use yarrow sticks to cast the I Ching. This is hugely complicated and involves fifty stalks of yarrow, one of which is set aside, and the manipulation of the remaining 49 stalks in four stages of operation. These four operations are repeated three times to form a line; as there are six lines, six operation sets are required for the whole process. For many people today this method is far too time-consuming.

Given the complexity of the yarrow method, it was inevitable that a simpler method of casting a hexagram would develop, and today the most common way is to use coins – 'the heavenly pennies'. Ordinary coins are perfectly adequate but it is helpful if you can find a set of Chinese coins, and dedicate them specifically for using the I Ching. Included here is a spell which is not Chinese in origin, but uses such a coin as a method of intensifying energy.

Reflections

Chinese coins often have a square hole in them which is symbolic of manifestation of prosperity. They can nowadays be obtained through the internet. The eight-sided mirror is a device used in feng shui to represent different aspects of life and, like the coin, to intensify or redirect energy. Here you can use both to bring you tangible gain. This is best done in the open air at the Full Moon.

YOU WILL NEED
Chinese gold-coloured coin
An eight-sided feng shui mirror

METHOD
❖ Ideally, the light of the Moon should pass through the central hole of the coin and reflect on to the mirror. You will need to use your own intuition to judge when you have the best reflection.
❖ Concentrate on the reflection and say:

> *Lady Moon, behold thy power*
> *I capture this and ask this hour*
> *Thy bounteousness on me you shower*
> *Bring me silver, bring me gold*
> *Long before the Moon grows old*
> *I ask a blessing*

Ch'ang O (Lady Moon) is the Chinese immortal who lives on the Moon. In one story, she is banished to the earth when her husband, Houyi the Archer, shot down the extra nine suns which were scorching the earth. She then ate the pill of immortality, and now lives on the Moon, betwixt and between two worlds. It is she who is petitioned here.

In using the I Ching for guidance, some people strike a balance between the ultra-traditionalism of the yarrow and the later method by using specially made I Ching stones, which are marked with either a yin or a yang symbol. The means may vary, although the interpretation remains the same, harking back across the millennia to Ancient China.

The method of divination is simple. Before you cast the coins the question to be answered should be carefully framed in the mind, and initially at least, you should get used to writing the question down. Only when the question has been thoroughly pondered upon should the coins be cast to create a hexagram, which is built from the bottom up.

The more particular the question, the more

detailed the answer that the I Ching will yield. A woolly question brings a woolly answer. Very often, the answer to one question leads to another, but again this should be thoroughly focused on before the later (and subsequent) hexagrams are created. Most practitioners create a relaxing atmosphere, perhaps with mellow lighting and burning fragrant incense.

Creating the hexagrams

Take three coins and, shaking them in the hand like dice, throw them down on a flat surface, each throw forming a hexagram line. Chinese coins were initially inscribed on one side only and had a hole in the middle so that they could be threaded together. The inscribed side was yin, the plain side was yang. Today, ordinary coins are inscribed on both sides. For the purpose of the I Ching, the 'tails' side is allied to the inscribed side and is therefore yin: the 'heads' side is assumed to be blank and therefore 'yang'.

Use three coins of the same denomination. If they have no obvious 'heads' or 'tails' decide which side is to be so ascribed. The head of each coin is given a value of three (yang is traditionally an odd number) and tails a value of two (likewise, yin is even). The totals will add up to either six, seven, eight or nine. The lines they create when cast are as follows:

Coins	Symbol	Value
3 tails	———O———	'Moving' yang
3 heads	———X———	'Moving' yin
2 tails/1 head	———————	Yang
2 heads/1 tail	——— ———	Yin

Lines that add up to seven (yang) and eight (yin) are accepted as being young energetic lines ___ and _ _ respectively. The numbers six and nine are mature yin and yang 'changing' or 'moving' lines and suggest that something must be adjusted before progress can be made.

The first throw of the coins gives the first line of the hexagram, the second the second one and so on, until a six-line hexagram has been created. As the hexagram is being built, mark each line on a piece of paper, from the bottom to the top,

in accordance with all Chinese writing. Initially, the 'moving lines' are read as if they were ordinary yin or yang ones. However, once the hexagram has been built, moving lines – or changing lines, as they are also known – are reversed in meaning: a 'moving' yin line thus becomes an unbroken yang line, and a 'moving' yang line becomes a broken yin one. Historically, moving lines have the following significance:

A moving first line points to a problem or a change that cannot find a solid foundation.

A moving second line indicates instability.

The third moving line suggests change due to shifts in time that cannot have been foreseen.

The fourth moving line can point to change brought about by another's involvement.

The fifth moving line points to beneficial changes brought about by an advancement of some kind.

The sixth moving line says that the situation regarding the question is unbalanced.

Interpreting the I Ching

The *I Ching (The Book of Changes)*, the Chinese manuscript in which the meanings of the 64 hexagrams are explained, is a work of intense beauty and predates even Lao Tsu's treatise on the Tao. Each hexagram is described and explained line by line in the words of the Duke of Chou. There are now many translations in existence and should you wish to undertake further study, it is suggested that you start with a simple translation, before attempting the more complex philosophical studies that are such an integral part of this system.

For the purposes of divination it is probably best that you find yourself a good translation of the original text, along with the original judgements and commentaries. If you wish to use the hexagrams in spell making or meditation only, because the ancient Chinese worked in ideagrams (little pictures), you need to be aware of the images conjured up by the trigrams which make up each hexagram. These are known by scholars of the I Ching as the Great Symbolism. Remember that the trigrams are the forces of nature which Fu Hsi first discovered. Also, for the Chinese, the family unit is extremely important and some of the names of the hexagrams reflect that importance. Here is one interpretation.

Lower Trigram \ Upper Trigram	Ch'ien	Chen	K'an	Ken	K'un	Sun	Li	Tui
Ch'ien	1	34	5	26	11	9	14	43
Chen	25	51	3	27	24	42	21	17
K'an	6	40	29	4	7	59	64	7
Ken	33	62	39	52	15	53	56	21
K'un	12	16	8	23	2	20	35	45
Sun	44	32	48	18	46	57	50	28
Li	13	55	63	22	36	37	30	49
Tui	10	54	60	41	19	61	38	58

1. Chi'en – The Creative

Judgement: Success is assured through the questioner's strength, power and persistence.
Great Symbolism: Heaven above Heaven which gives great power.

2. K'un 1 – The Receptive

Judgement: The enquirer should follow rather than lead, being responsive and receptive to advice.
Great Symbolism: The power of Earth doubled suggesting great support.

3. Chun – Initial Difficulty

Judgement: Initial difficulties can be overcome with perseverance. If help is needed, don't be afraid to ask for it.
Great Symbolism: Clouds and Thunder intermingled suggesting some danger.

4. Meng – Innocence

Judgement: Listen to the advice of other more experienced people and learn from it initially. Remain enthusiastic.
Great Symbolism: Mountain with a spring of Water beneath it. A need for resolute conduct.

5. Hsu – Waiting

Judgement: Help will be at hand when the time is right, so don't force the pace and worry. Wait and be ready.
Great Symbolism: Clouds above the sky, enjoyment at the present time.

6. Sung – Conflict

Judgement: Impulsive action, arguments and aggressive behaviour are to be avoided. If wisdom is available, accept it. Remain objective.
Great Symbolism: Heaven and Water moving away from one another, care should be taken initially.

7. Shih – The Army

Judgement: Perseverance will bring rewards, probably after receiving some good advice from a wise leader.
Great Symbolism: Earth above Water suggesting nourishment from wisdom.

8. Pi – Union

Judgement: Build up strong bonds by sharing experiences with others, and be sure you are confident in your own abilities. Help others and at the same time you will be helping yourself.
Great Symbolism: Water over Earth, correct relationship and partnerships.

9. Hsiao Ch'u – Taming Force

Judgement: Use your strength and power to clear small blockages from your path so that you are ready for the future. Restraint may be called for.

Great Symbolism: The Wind drives across the sky. Right movement within boundaries.

10. Lu – Treading Carefully

Judgement: Stick to the path you have chosen and press forward cautiously taking account of danger.

Great Symbolism: Heaven above with a marsh beneath, discriminating correctly.

11. T'ai - Peace

Judgement: Good fortune and harmony are all around, enjoy them and share them with others.

Great Symbolism: Heaven supporting Earth, communicating correctly.

12. P'i – Stagnation

Judgement: This is a period of stasis. Small irritations prevent progress.

Great Symbolism: Earth below Heaven but not properly communicating.

13. T'ung Jen – Companionship

Judgement: There are rewards to be had from working with others as long as everyone sticks to the tasks that have been allotted to them, and acts appropriately.

Great Symbolism: Heaven with Fire below, working in harmony.

14. Ta Yu – Great Possession

Judgement: Do the right thing in the given circumstances and success is yours for the taking.

Great Symbolism: Fire above Heaven, bringing out the best.

15. Ch'ien – Humility

Judgement: Be modest and carry things through to success.

Great Symbolism: Earth with a Mountain in the midst, achieving balance.

16. Yu – Joy

Judgement: Be prepared to delegate where necessary, planning carefully for the future. Act always with enthusiasm.

Great Symbolism: Earth with Thunder issuing from it, honouring the gods.

17. Sui – Following

Judgement: Take a back seat and let others take charge. Be flexible and avoid any conflict without letting your own goals slip from view.

Great Symbolism: Lake with Thunder within, suggesting letting things be.

18. Ku – Arresting Decay

Judgement: Think long and hard before taking action. After the decision, move forward with due consideration. If you have made mistakes in the past, now is the time to rectify them.

Great Symbolism: The Wind blows low on the Mountain, strengthening the situation.

19. Lin – Approach

Judgement: Think about the long-term effects of the situation. You can move forward provided you carry out right action.

Great Symbolism: The Earth above the Lake: tolerant approval.

20. Kuan – Contemplation

Judgement: Watch, listen and learn, being especially careful to carry out the right preparations for respect.

Great Symbolism: The Wind blows over the Earth: give instruction where appropriate.

21. Shih Ho – Biting Through

Judgement: Be positive about your own success. Legal or ethical constraints may achieve progress.

Great Symbolism: Thunder and Lightning needing firm laws and rules in place.

22. Pi – Grace

Judgement: Some action is useful, but the time is not right for sweeping changes.

Great Symbolism: Fire at the foot of the Mountain, proceeding in small steps to cultivate what is of use.

23. Po – Falling Apart

Judgement: It will not be helpful to make any movement whatsoever.

Great Symbolism: The Mountain rests upon the Earth with a need to strengthen one's position.

24. Fu – Returning

Judgement: Come and go as you please, but be ready to act appropriately and move in whichever direction is necessary after a short period.

Great Symbolism: Thunder within the Earth, going back when the time is right.

25. Wu Wang – Innocence

Judgement: Success is indicated, but only if there is right speech and right action. Anything else causes difficulty.

Great Symbolism: Under Heaven, Thunder rolls, simplicity is the keyword.

26. Ta Ch'u – The Great Taming Force

Judgement: Persevere in what you are doing, but make sure the focus is on matters away from home.

Great Symbolism: Heaven within the Mountain, learning from the past and ancient wisdom.

27. I – Nourishment

Judgement: Take care to nourish not only yourself, but others. Meditation or objectivity will help with your decisions.

Great Symbolism: At the foot of the Mountain, Thunder, keeping your own counsel.

28. Ta Kuo – Excess

Judgement: There is an inherent weakness in the situation, so this is a time for extraordinary action. Success is there, waiting for you.

Great Symbolism: Trees beneath the waters of the lake giving the ability to stand fearless.

29. K'an – The Deep Chasm

Judgement: Have faith in yourself, do what you know to be right and all will be well.

Great Symbolism: Water flowing without ceasing, continue with constancy.

30. Li – Clinging

Judgement: Be calm, firm and docile, knowing that the power of your conviction will lead to success.

Great Symbolism: Fire and brightness magnified, illuminating all things.

31. H'sein – Sensitivity

Judgement: Be sensitive to other's needs, recognizing what influence you can have on the situation.

Great Symbolism: A Lake on the Mountain, ready to be influenced and to influence others.

32. Heng – Perseverance

Judgement: Set your course and stay with it, having a goal in mind. Do whatever is necessary within reason to achieve success.

Great Symbolism: Thunder and Wind requiring one to stand firm.

33. Tun – Retreat

Judgement: If you judge the right time to withdraw from a difficult situation and are practical, you will weather the storm.

Great Symbolism: Mountain under Heaven requiring a dignified stance before a tactical withdrawal.

34. Ta Chuang – The Power of the Great

Judgement: This is a time of good fortune. If you act wisely and with forethought you will benefit from it.

Great Symbolism: Thunder in Heaven which requires that actions are correct.

35. Chin – Advancement

Judgement: Correct action brings its own reward in more ways than one.

Great Symbolism: The Sun rises over the Earth, suggesting that the wise man works to brighten his inner light.

36. Min I – Darkening of the Light

Judgement: Realize the difficulty of the situation and wait until things become clearer.

Great Symbolism: The light sinks into the Earth so things remain obscure for the time being.

37. Chia Jen – Family

Judgement: Let others adopt their rightful position, particularly in the balance of yin and yang, and only exercise authority when necessary.

Great Symbolism: Wind arises out of Fire and intuition and wisdom are used consistently.

38. K'uei – Opposition

Judgement: Try to stay in tune with the yin and

the yang by ironing out anything disruptive or inharmonious in your life.
Great Symbolism: Fire above and the Lake below. By admitting the tension between yin and yang, power is created.

39. Chien – Obstruction

Judgement: The only way to solve problems is to face them as they arise, having confidence in your own conscience.
Great Symbolism: Water on the Mountain, which suggests this is a time for the cultivation of right thought.

40. Chieh – Deliverance from Obstacles

Judgement: Solve the problem facing you, put it behind you and get on with things, paying due regard to what has happened in the past.
Great Symbolism: Thunder and rain set in. Problems can be handled properly.

41. Sun – Decrease

Judgement: Sincerity at this time is all important, even if it means making sacrifices for the greater good. If you do this willingly the gain will be yours in the end.
Great Symbolism: The Mountain with a marshy Lake below suggests control of passion and willing sacrifices.

42. I – Increase

Judgement: Fortune is on your side and you can make plans for expansion with confidence that they will be successful.
Great Symbolism: Wind above and Thunder below suggests that where circumstances are good there is increase but where they are bad avoiding action can be taken.

43. Kui – Breakthrough

Judgement: Wrongdoing can be exposed under the right conditions and, though there is some danger, friends and peers will support you.
Great Symbolism: The Lake arises above Heaven, and can therefore dispense its goodness without accumulating an excess.

44. Kou – Meeting

Judgement: Be resolute: inappropriate alliances can cause problems, both now and in the future. Make sure instructions are clear.
Great Symbolism: Wind beneath Heaven suggests making certain that information is properly given and in the right way.

45. Ts'ui – Gathering together

Judgement: Sincerity and openness will help you to make your relationships especially harmonious now. Finding a common cause will bring people together.
Great Symbolism: The Lake rests upon the Earth, preparing for all contingencies.

46. Sheng – Ascending

Judgement: Progress might be slow, but can be helped by the cultivation of best qualities. On the whole this is a satisfactory time.
Great Symbolism: Within the Earth, Wood grows, sometimes slowly but always receiving what is necessary.

47. K'un – Exhaustion

Judgement: Things are probably looking hard, but success is possible provided you keep your own counsel. Supreme sacrifice may be called for.
Great Symbolism: Water has drained from the Lake to a place below. Sacrifices will be called for and success requires willpower.

48. Ching – The Well

Judgement: Situations may change, but the central focus still remains unchanging. People may come and go and take what benefit they need. Only the method of approach can change and cause difficulties.
Great Symbolism: Water over Wood suggesting the pooling of resources for mutual benefit.

49. Ko – Revolution

Judgement: There is great progress and success, though you are only proved right after the event. Maintain your dignity and do not feel guilty.
Great Symbolism: Fire in the Lake. If they are not to extinguish one another, timings are important.

50. Ting – The Cauldron

Judgement: The cauldron suggests the idea of

cooking and plenty – hence nourishment. Flexible obedience and clear sightedness bring success.

Great Symbolism: Wood with Fire above, an image good for cooking, which gives the idea of stability.

51. Chen – Arousing Thunder

Judgement: Though there are certain things which are shocking, enough to make you apprehensive, you may continue to be content. Do not be frightened into making mistakes.

Great Symbolism: Thunder echoing loudly creating many shocks; put your house in order.

52. Ken – Mountain

Judgement: Maintaining your own integrity means that you are able to forget external difficulties and can preserve your equilibrium.

Great Symbolism: Two Mountains standing close together suggesting the need to keep focused on matters in hand.

53. Chien 2 – Growth

Judgement: Things develop as they should and there will be a successful outcome. A young lady marrying suggests the growth of maturity.

Great Symbolism: A tree upon a Mountain. Maintain dignity and good conduct so others may follow.

54. Kuei Mei – Marrying Maiden

Judgement: Nothing more needs to be done for the time being.

Great Symbolism: Thunder over the Lake, creating movement, not always appropriate.

55. Feng – Abundance

Judgement: Good fortune and good luck are yours for the asking. Worries will soon be a thing of the past: for a time at least.

Great Symbolism: Thunder and Lightning clear the Air and bring appropriate rules of conduct or punishments for past misdemeanours.

56. Lu – The Wanderer

Judgement: As the wanderer, it is possible to be in the right place at the right time for the right reasons. Small actions can begin great changes.

Great Symbolism: Fire on the Mountain suggests clarity and caution in bringing matters to fruition.

57. Sun – Gentle

Judgement: Go with the flow, keep moving towards your goals and be flexible, accepting help from those more knowledgeable than you.

Great Symbolism: Winds follow one another, gently penetrating where they are required. Ideas and customs spread through repetition.

58. Tui – The Joyous

Judgement: Good news and good fortune come your way. Your behaviour makes people realize you are in tune with your spiritual side.

Great Symbolism: Lakes resting with one another suggesting an increase of energy through common spiritual aims.

59. Huan – Dispersion

Judgement: Strong spiritual bonds result in firm and correct conduct for all. This leads to the dissemination of information over a wider area than previously.

Great Symbolism: Wind over Water, disseminating knowledge leading to temples and places of worship.

60. Chieh – Restraint

Judgement: You need to free yourself from needless restrictions as quickly as possible. You should be ready to take advantage of new opportunities.

Great Symbolism: A Lake with Water above, suggesting that it is time to consider one's talents and self awareness.

61. Chung Fu – Inmost Sincerity

Judgement: Plans made now for the future will flourish, particularly if they take you away from your comfort zone.

Great Symbolism: Water with Wind above; sincere appraisal allows the correct decisions.

62. Hsiao Kua – Great smallness

Judgement: Small matters are much better dealt with at this time so that everything falls into its rightful place, thus leading to overall success.

Great Symbolism: Thunder on the Mountain. Every small increase has a significant effect.

63. Chi Chi – Completion

Judgement: Though there is the potential for disorder, there is some progress and more success. Small matters need your attention if you are to reinforce the gains you have made.
Great Symbolism: Fire with Water above it suggests guarding against possible disaster.

64. Wei Chi — Before Completion

Judgement: Though there is progress and success, there is little advantage in getting involved in something new. Immaturity can lead to silly mistakes.
Great Symbolism: Water with Fire above; if matters are classified correctly, order is inherent.

Dice

THE USE OF DICE for all manner of games dates back to ancient times and is one of the oldest known methods of divination. The term for divination by casting dice or small objects as lots, is cleromancy; the Greek term for divining by dice is astragalomancy, from the Greek word for knucklebone.

In ancient Egypt, Greece and the Far East cubes of wood, metal or glass with their sides numbered from one to six were popular for gaming and also as a means of consultation. Thoth, the Egyptian god, is said to have been the first to have used dice and to have won his game. You could if you wish, dedicate your dice to this god. Today, Indian Hindus still use an ancient divining science called Ramala; the dice used are very similar to standard dice except they are spun on a rod. Tibetan monks practise a dice divination technique called Sho-Mo, using three ordinary standard spotted dice.

The opposite faces of a modern dice always add up to seven, a magical number of manifestation. There are in existence dice marked with mystic symbols specifically used for fortune telling and divining. For a spell worker, dice can be a quick method of answering a simple question.

Today, divination using dice is not as widespread as it once was, but Romanies are still thought to practise the art. Dice made of bone or ivory are said to be particularly receptive while wood, stone or a natural material are next best, but don't worry if yours are plastic, they will suffice.

This spell is a way of dedicating your dice for a specific purpose. If you propose to use your dice for divination, they should be kept separate from those you use for games and chance. The words of dedication should be appropriate for that purpose.

Dedication of Dice

This spell uses planetary correspondences and number symbolism (see pages 234-235 and 132). Properly charged – energized for games of chance – your dice should create the ability to have Venus, who is the Guardian of the Natural Order of things, on your side. Lady Luck – one of the other manifestations of the Goddess – also rules gambling.

YOU WILL NEED
Brass die (brass is sacred to Venus)
Wood die (perhaps sycamore, which is also sacred to Venus, or of another sacred wood – see pages 80-86). If you cannot find a wood die, an acrylic one will suffice
Money incense
Green candle

METHOD
✤ You will need to make a dedication of your die before you start. Use fairly flowery language in order to get the energy flowing.
✤ Say something like:

Oh Lady of the Morning Star
Come to me here from afar
This cube of chance
Its powers enhance
That it becomes my lodestar.

✤ Now it will depend on its material as to how you wish it to work for you.
✤ Brass is a material that traditionally heightens the intuitive powers so you could use words such as:

So show me now your bounty.

❖ Sycamore, which signifies love, receptivity and the ability to communicate, or one of the sacred trees such as holly, a symbol of luck, could be dedicated with the words:

Bring your knowledge to me.

❖ Your acrylic die, far from being inert, can be made magically powerful by intent.
Use words such as:

Awaken to the power of gain.

❖ Light the incense and candle.
❖ Pass each die through the incense smoke and through the candle flame, visualizing yourself winning with your lucky dice.
❖ When you win, put by a tenth of your winnings for charity or other good causes. This is known as tithing.

When playing games of chance it is thought that fingering the brass die will give the information needed to win. In divination, provided you have charged the dice for that purpose the same principle applies and information should come intuitively. You may also use the significance of number in numerology or from the list below.

Divining with dice

Traditionally, preparation for divination by dice is very simple. A circle is drawn in white on a board, about the size of a chess board, onto which throws are made, though a black cloth similarly prepared may be used.

Not everyone interprets dice that fall or roll outside this circle unless they fall on the floor, which suggests arguments or difficulties. Others believe that one die outside the circle indicates personal difficulties or an upset, two dice suggest arguments or disagreements with others, and three outside the circle mean good luck or the fulfilment of a wish.

There are certain rituals associated with dice throwing:
• Three dice must be used, held first in the cupped hands then shaken and thrown with the left.
• The best time for dice throwing is in the calm of the evening, preferably not on a Monday or Wednesday, since these are considered to be inauspicious days.
• To help concentration, silence must always be maintained during the shaking and throwing of the dice.
• If you wish, having finished your interpretation, the dice may be washed under running water or passed through the smoke of your favourite incense.

Add the numbers that appear on the upper surfaces of the dice, and interpret according to this list.

Three: The smallest number that can appear unless dice have fallen outside the circle as mentioned above. There will be pleasant surprises in the very near future.

Four: Unpleasantness of some kind may occur. Arguments or disagreement can be expected.

Five: Plans will come to fruition; a wish will be granted. You may receive unexpected information or assistance.

Six: A loss of some kind is forecast, probably of money but possibly of material goods.

Seven: You will be presented with a difficult matter to solve, possibly difficulties in business, money troubles, gossip and so on.

Eight: Expect criticism due to a lack of thought

Nine: Marriage, union or a relationship of value to you is forecast.

Ten: A birth, career change or new project are forecast.

Eleven: A parting, which may only be temporary, takes place.

Twelve: A message of importance for you or yours will arrive soon.

Thirteen: There will be disappointment or misery if you pursue a current situation.

Fourteen: There is a new friendship or unexpected help from an old friend.

Fifteen: Begin no new projects for a few days and take care when talking to others.

Sixteen: There is a pleasant journey forecast, which ultimately brings contentment.

Seventeen: A change in plan or viewpoint about a current situation may be necessary.

Eighteen: This is the very best number to appear and suggests a most fortunate outcome within a short time.

If the same number should turn up more than once, it signifies the coming of important news. To throw the dice so that one remains on top of the other can indicate the need for extreme caution in business, or in dealing with the opposite sex. If you wish to deepen the reading slightly, pay attention to the numbers on the individual dice and interpret accordingly. The results of the divination generally come to fruition within nine days.

Use your own insight to broaden the dice's divinatory ability. However, some words of warning. You should not cast and interpret the dice more than three times in a day. It is bad luck and could quite easily backfire on you. This was made the subject of a book written some time ago by Luke Rhinehart called *The Dice Man*. Given the climate of the time it proved thought-provoking and scary, yet indicated that divination has to be taken seriously.

Runes

THE WORD *'runa'* means 'mystery' or 'secret proceeding', and it seems likely that only the elders of a community and those who acted in a priestly capacity knew the true esoteric meaning of an inscription. To the ordinary person they were simply a means of divination.

The Origins of the Runes

No one knows exactly how old the runes are. Symbols similar to runes appear as cave markings as early as the late Bronze Age in 1300 BCE; they are mentioned in the Bible, but their use in ritual and as an oracle for consultation certainly pre-dates their use as a written language. Runic forms of inscription were evident – and seem to have been in use for some time – before the advent of written language inscriptions.

Runes were representations of matters that were important to the people and, like many of these systems, often had relevance in more than one way. An inscription could represent an animal, for instance, and could also stand for the qualities of that animal applied in certain situations. This animal power is echoed in shamanic totem animals. In this way, runes approach the concept of sympathetic magic and they can still be used in that way today.

The early runemasters and runemistresses developed a system of symbols composed of vertical and angled straight lines from their existing fund of mystic or religious symbols, which would endure when cut into wood or could be easily inscribed onto other natural materials. The 24 symbols became known as the Futhark or Futhork alphabet after the names of the first six runes (**F**ehu, **U**ruz, **Th**urisaz, **A**nsuz, **R**aido, **K**auno), and it is these 24 symbols – plus a blank rune representing Destiny – which now comprise the modern-day rune set. Ancient pagan or Anglo-Saxon runes are the same 24 basic runes with some variations in their form due to usage over the centuries.

As with the Ogham Staves, runes were no doubt initially cut in wood and probably later inscribed on stone. The straight lines could easily be cut across the grain in wood, and short upward or downward lines would survive when cut with the grain, which is why there are no curved lines in this system. The runes were a potent tool and source of learning which can still be applied today.

In interpreting the runes, we have used only the basic traditional meanings, although you may wish to follow other lines of enquiry and will obviously develop their use in divination, if you so wish.

Runes can also be worn as amulets, used as objects of power on your altar or as meditative aids. In earlier times, three types of amulets were recognized: there were objects for protection against trouble and adversity, those that drove away evil influences and those that contained substances such as herbs and oils used as medicine. The latter are not considered here.

Experiment and spend time with your runes until you find one or more that suit you in your workings. If you wish to bless them for personal use, follow the ritual below. Information on casting circles and the correct directions can be found on pages 231-233.

Consecration

This ritual for blessing the runes can equally be used to consecrate any personal jewellery, Ogham Staves and so on.

YOU WILL NEED

Consecration incense (see page 74)
White candle
Small bowl of water
Small bowl of salt or earth
Your chosen rune

METHOD

❖ Cast your circle.

❖ Ask for a blessing for the bowls, candle and incense, representing the quarters.

❖ Place the symbols in the appropriate directions.

❖ Pick up the object to be consecrated.

❖ Concentrate on the goals you want to achieve and the actions that you want to carry out then say:

Before you wandering spirits,
I bring this rune [name]
May its benefits be devoted to the work of the Lady and Lord.

❖ Light the incense and waft the rune through the incense smoke. Say:

By force of Air, be purified.
Be devoted to clarity.
May all aspirations be realized for the greater good of all.

❖ Then, having lit the candle, pass the rune through the flicker of the flame and say the following:

By the power of the dancing light, be purified.
Be devoted to longing.
May all aspirations be realized for the greater good of all.

❖ Sprinkle a few drops of water onto the chosen implement and say:

By the power of Njord's domain, be purified.
Be devoted to waves of ardour.
May all aspirations be realized for the greater good of all.

❖ Next, take the implement and bring it to the earth or salt and say:

By the power of earth and dust be purified.
Be devoted to resolute intent.
May all aspirations be realized for the greater good of all.

Here the four Elements – Air, Fire, Water and Earth – are honoured. If you wish, you may present the rune for further consecration to the God and Goddess.

Basic Meanings of the Runes
The Aett or Set of Freya, Goddess of Fertility and Love

Throughout the old Norse legends, the deities and heroes consistently paid the price of their actions. Odin, for instance, craved wisdom and went to the Spring of Mimir at the root of Yggdrasil, the World Tree. Mimir demanded one of Odin's eyes in exchange for a drink from the waters of memory. Odin accepted Mimir's price and never regretted it. This list gives the Nordic and English names for the runes.

Fehu (Cattle)

This is the rune of wealth and the price we have to pay for what we want – whether that is through action or inaction. The basic meaning of Fehu is wealth, which could be measured in the number of cattle owned - hence the image of cattle equates with wealth. The word 'fee' comes from this term.

As an amulet, this rune reminds us of our intrinsic wealth, but also of the price we must pay, whether that is through action or inaction.

Uruz (Aurochs)

This is the rune of strength, courage and overcoming obstacles. The Norse and Icelandic rune poems talk of privation for the herdsmen and tempering by ordeal. The aurochs was an enormous ox-like beast. Its horns were worn on Viking helmets, transferring by sympathetic magic the strength of the creature to the wearers.

The image of harsh reality and obstacles to be overcome by strength and endurance, live on in the poems of the north. Many of the runes use symbolism of the extreme conditions in which the Vikings lived. The aurochs was very much part of this environment. When we wear this as an amulet, we too become conscious of the aurochs' power.

Thurisaz (Thorn)

This is the rune of protection, challenges, secrecy and conflicts. The thorn tree, which can offer protection from intruders, is associated with this image. Frost giants or 'rime-thurses' who fought the gods, maintained the cosmic balance by representing the ancient rule before the Aesir (tribal gods) came into being. Thurisaz is also associated with Thor, who sought to protect the realm of the gods from the frost giants. Thurisaz is therefore a rune of challenge for those who want to make changes or go against long-held tradition. This becomes an amulet of protection and also of challenge.

Ansuz (A God)

This is the Father Rune, the rune of Odin, the All-Father. It is also the rune of inspiration. Odin wanted the gift of divine utterance (wisdom) for which he needed the mead of poetry, and again there was a harsh price to pay. The power of these runes is in the struggle to reconcile opposites, not in the battle between good and evil, when good always wins. This rune acknowledges man's own weaknesses and his journey towards a greater understanding. Wise words and the way we speak them can be of paramount importance. As an amulet, this rune represents wisdom and right speech.

Raidho (Riding)

This is the rune of travel and journeys. There is an impetus to change and a need for initiative. It uses the symbolism of the wheel – the Sun Wheel as it passes through the skies. Also suggested is the wheel on the wagon of the old fertility gods on their journey through the year. Raidho is also the rune of long and hazardous journeys. This rune suggests an impetus so powerful that change is inevitable. Action and uncertainty are sometimes necessary if we are to progress – preparation for any journey is always important. Symbolizing a journey, Raidho reminds us to be aware of our actions.

Kenaz (Torch)

This rune symbolizes the inner voice, inner strength, guidance and illumination. Kenaz is one of the Fire runes. A torch was made from pine dipped in resin, and lit both grand castle and hovel alike. All purpose, it was used to kindle the 'Need Fire' which was lit at times of celebration. The cleansing aspect of fire is important and this aspect of eradication is an important one when this rune is worn as an amulet. The fire within maintains clarity without.

Gebo (Gift)

Gebo is the rune of giving and of generosity. It is also the rune of mutuality. All issues relating to exchange – both giving and receiving – are signified in this rune. (In the Norse traditions a gift always required one in return, so giving must be done with thought.) Gebo can also indicate a gift or talent received from one in authority, so worn as an amulet it reminds us of the inherent knowledge available to us.

Wunjo (Joy)

This is the rune of success, recognition and personal happiness – success through determination rather than as a gift from others and happiness through one's own efforts. Traditionally, those who have been through hardship can sometimes appreciate life's gifts better and learn to take happiness as it comes. For the Vikings, happiness meant shelter, food and warmth; there is a practicality about this rune when worn as an amulet. Joy can be built from those three things.

The Aett or Set of Hagalaz or Heimdall, Watcher of the Gods

Hagalaz (Hail)

This is known as the Mother Rune and in the Futhark (rune alphabet) it occupies the position of the sacred number nine. Hagalaz had a geometric shape (the six-pointed star) found in the composition of many natural life forms, mirrored in fractals today. Hagalaz is regarded as the 'cosmic seed'; ice was involved in creation along with fire.

The Old Norse Rune Poem associates Hagalaz with the harvest and speaks of hail as the 'coldest of grains'. When hail melts it turns into water, but that metamorphosis can be painful. Therefore, Hagalaz has come to represent unwelcome external change. As an amulet it demonstrates that such change, if used positively, can transform sorrow into happiness.

Naudhiz (Need)

This is the rune of passion. The second Fire rune is one of the cosmic forces that shapes the fates of the world and mankind. It represents determination and signifies needs that are met by our own positive reactions to external hardship.

Need fires were lit from early times all over Northern Europe on the Wheel of the Year festivals such as Beltane and Samhain (see page 195). These fires represented the fire from within that has to be expressed externally – Naudhiz represents the fire sparked by friction. Such a fire is purging, and also one of new light and life, and it is this which is signified when the rune is worn as an amulet.

Isa (Ice)

This rune represents a blockage, or a period of inactivity that can be used for good by preparing for the right moment. Isa is the second ice rune and the fifth Element in the Norse world. The single vertical mark of the rune means that it is inherent within every other rune. Isa can be seen as the ice of winter, an enforced obstacle to movement. Nevertheless, the period can be used positively for deliberation and development.

For those who are fearful of going forward, Isa is a bridge between two ways of thinking. While change needs to be negotiated carefully, progress continues imperceptibly in the background. As an amulet, this rune reminds us of that continuing progress.

Jera (Year)

This is the rune of the harvest, of the results of earlier efforts. Jera represents a natural progression through the sequence of the seasons and various stages of life. It is invoked magically for fertility and achievement, a fruitful season or harvest and for the attainment of goals through hard work. When the cyclical nature of existence slows, it is important to recognize the principles of fertility and the generosity of the deities. As an amulet, it suggests the principle of fertilization.

Eiwaz (Yew)

This is the rune of natural endings, including death, but also promises new beginnings and rebirth. It was known that the bravest warriors would die to rise again and Eiwaz symbolized longevity and eternal life. The yew's resinous vapour is said to induce visions and it was also the tree of shamans and magic. Sacred to Ullr,

God of Winter and Archery, the yew tree gave a promise of better things to come; it is with this meaning that it is associated as an amulet. All things must pass, but all things must also return.

Perthro (Lot-Cup)

This is the rune of taking a chance, of confronting what is yet not known or revealed, and of the essential self. In some ways it is the rune of destiny. It is the casting of this rune that will decide the fate, whether one looks at the situation as a gamble or whether the decision is the will of the gods.

Gambling and divination went hand in hand in the Norse communities – decisions would be made by casting lots or sometimes runes. However, this was not a fixed fate. The gambler or diviner was expected to maximize his good fortune and take appropriate action to avoid any other potential pitfalls. It is this aspect that is used as an amulet.

Elhaz or Algiz (Elk-Sedge)

The rune of the higher self and one's spiritual nature, this can be the most difficult to understand. The image comes from that of eelgrass, which is similar to the reed. The symbolism is that of the double-edged sword, which can both protect and damage; it can therefore be used with a degree of duality. There is the need for care and understanding in making use of such a weapon, both spiritually and otherwise. As an amulet, this rune reminds us of our responsibilities.

Sowilo (Sun)

This is the rune of success. As always, the Sun is seen as the most positive and potent symbol, though this time as feminine rather than masculine. Experienced often as lightning, it is the third and most powerful Fire rune, melting the ice of winter and giving the crops a chance to grow.

The longest day celebrates the inherent power of the Sun and commemorates the ideas of giving supremacy to the representations of the Sun. Potential and victory are all intrinsic in this rune, and when you need reassurance this is a good rune to wear as an amulet.

The Aett of Tiwaz

Tiwaz (Star)

Standing for justice and altruism (and possibly self-sacrifice), this rune represents the pole or lode star. As a constant pointer, this rune helps us to keep faith in bad times. It remains visible at all times and symbolizes justice won through fair combat. This rune takes account of the natural imperfections we experience in life and as an amulet helps to keep us focused on matters in hand, but with an eye to the future.

Berkano (Birch)

This is the rune of spiritual regeneration, covering the arts of healing, fertility and mothering. The rune embraces the concepts of death, birth and rebirth. Celebrating the Earth Goddess and the Goddess of the Underworld, birch is used to invoke their protection. It promises new beginnings, perhaps on a different plane to the one experienced hitherto. An understanding of the principle of the feminine and the colonization of virgin territory is inherent in this rune. Looked at from an amuletic viewpoint, it promises growth and reintegration.

Ehwaz (Horse)

This is the rune of loyalty and harmony. Partnership between people or inner and outer worlds, friendships, moving house or career are all associated with this rune. Ehwaz is connected with the horse, the most sacred animal of the Vikings. It therefore represents harmonious relationships, illustrated best by that between horse and warrior. Mentioned only in the Anglo-Saxon Rune Poem, Ehwaz emphasizes the joy a horse brings to his rider, making him feel like a prince or minor god. As an amulet, Ehwaz represents the synergy man and beast can create.

Manaz (Man)

This rune stands for man as reflection of divinity. It is the power of human intelligence; the recognition that our lives are part of a greater whole and the ability to be compassionate and accepting of others. Celebrating the creation of the first man and woman who were given the breath of life, intelligence and a loving heart and their natural senses by Odin and his brothers, this rune commemorates the potential of the individual and the connection to the human race. As an amulet it reminds us of the power of the human being.

Laguz (Water)

This is the rune of initiation into life and unconscious wisdom and intuition. Laguz is the rune of water and the sea and signifies birth and new beginnings. Water is frightening yet life-giving and the Vikings used sea journeys as a symbol for a new start. The emotions will often take you into places you have never been before, provided you go with the flow. However, there is always an aspect of unpredictability about water. Wearing this rune as an amulet reminds us of just that.

Ingwaz (The God Ing)

This rune indicates a time of creative withdrawal in order to wait for new strength. There may be the promise of better times and a period of gestation, both human and symbolic. Ingwaz is a fertility rune that is powerfully associated with protection, especially of the home or hearth. Ingwaz or Ing was the God of the Hearth and consort of Nerthus, the Earth Mother. It was necessary for him to die in order to be reborn, and that period of withdrawal was just as important as the time of growth. Worn as an amulet, this rune teaches us to appreciate quiet times.

Othala (Homestead)

This is the rune of the home and of the sacred space. Domestic matters, family and finance are all important, for domestic tranquillity depends on material comfort. Stability depended on family and its continuance, so the homestead was of great importance to the Norse people. Being able to co-exist with others rather than living alone is an important learning experience, and belonging to a family allows us to experience such a thing. A sense of belonging and continuity comes across when this rune is worn as an amulet.

Dagaz (Day)

This is the rune of clear vision and awareness. It is an awakening and the coming together of two opposites. The mid-point of the day as experienced by the Norse world, was dawn and the rising of the Sun. In the Norse legends, Dag, son of Nott, the Goddess of Night, and Dellinger (Dawn), was given a white horse named Skin-Faxi. From his shining mane, beams of light chased away fears of the night. This rune holds all the promise of the dawning of a new day and the enlightenment that it brings.

Spells for Runes

It is possible to incorporate runes in your spells to represent an idea or principle that expresses succinctly what you wish to say. The first uses the synergy between partners – horse and man – to signify the energy needed to succeed, while the second uses the actual tracing of the symbol to draw in a protective power. The third spell uses the power of the image to enhance the purpose of the spell, while the fourth and fifth show particularly two different uses of the rune of clear vision and awareness, Dagaz.

Winning a Deal

This spell, in addition to the significance of the rune, also uses candle and colour magic. It is probably best done at the time of the Full Moon if the deal is a merger or acquisition, or at the time of the New Moon if it initiates new projects or implements new ideas. Thursday is also a good day, being one to maximize opportunities. Because you are using woods and plants in the incense, and so will create a fair amount of smoke, it is better to do the spell away from the office unless you can be undisturbed.

YOU WILL NEED

For success incense:
1 part each of basil, bay and oak
2 parts cedarwood
Bowl to mix incense
White candle
Your burin or a pin
Your copy of the papers necessary for the
successful deal

METHOD

❖ While you mix your incense, bear in mind the outcome you require. You might appeal to Thor (the strongest of the Norse gods) at the same time.

❖ Using the burin or pin, inscribe your candle with Ehwaz, the rune for success in partnership.

❖ Light your candle and the incense. Sit for a few moments then hold the legal papers in the smoke of the incense. Visualize the required outcome, such as signing the papers.

❖ While the candle is burning out, reinforce your vision of success.

Any outcome that occurs because of this spell is not time-specific, that is, you have not asked for a particular timeframe.

Boardroom Strength and Endurance

This spell is representative and uses the runic alphabet as a symbol for strength and endurance. The Norse people had a life of hardship and privation, and illustrated this in their runes. The idea that one gains strength from animals and their powers is shamanic in origin. Today we can draw on the same power in business. This spell should be performed in your boardroom.

YOU WILL NEED

The runic symbol Uruz (Aurochs) to represent strength, courage and overcoming obstacles

METHOD

❖ Choose a point level with halfway down the boardroom table. Mindful of the qualities you are calling on, 'walk' the shape of the symbol around the table, ensuring that that highest point is close to where the chairperson or principal speaker sits. If you feel you should include the whole table, 'walk' the rune again in the opposite direction.

❖ If you yourself anticipate a difficult meeting, draw the rune on a piece of paper and place it in your pocket for the duration of the meeting.

Calling upon the power of the aurochs, an enormous ox-like beast, is said to have given the Vikings the power for conquest. By the use of sympathetic magic in this spell, the boardroom, which today is so often the 'field of battle' and highly competitive, can become a more harmonious and fruitful environment.

Luck in Business

This spell uses a herbal charm bag which can be further enhanced by adding new coins, to represent money. By its use of comfrey, it protects the owner while travelling, and adds zing by dragon's blood. The runes intensify the energy for your own particular need. The spell is performed at the time of the Waxing Moon on a Wednesday or Thursday.

YOU WILL NEED

A drawstring bag about 5–10 cm (2-3 in) deep
Bayberry
Red clover
Comfrey
Dragon's blood
Mandrake root
5–6 tulip petals
3 new coins

METHOD

✤ Put equal measures of the herbs into the bag.

✤ Inscribe your full name on one side of the mandrake root, then the following runes on the other and put that into the bag along with the coins.

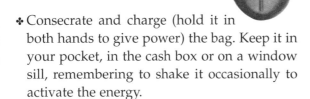

Dagaz (for clear vision and awareness)
Fehu (for wealth)
Tiwaz (for justice and altruism)

✤ Consecrate and charge (hold it in both hands to give power) the bag. Keep it in your pocket, in the cash box or on a window sill, remembering to shake it occasionally to activate the energy.

This works very well if you are in business for yourself. When inscribing the mandrake you can use the business name or logo if you wish. If you can make it a regular routine to reinforce its aims every week, you should not have any problems.

To Guard against Road Rage

Runes are often used along with other substances as protective devices. One aspect of these devices is to make them appropriate for the circumstances you are in. For protection against your own or others' road rage, you can use a sachet of herbs and the rune which represents travel, and fashion a charm bag, which is reactivated for its purpose on each journey. Each time you travel, remember that this particular device is specifically against road rage, so it needs to be held briefly beforehand to guard against unforeseen incidents. You should then set out on your journey calm and relaxed.

YOU WILL NEED

Piece of comfrey root
Two bay leaves
Rune of Elhaz inscribed on paper
A small piece of rose quartz
A rose pink or green sachet

METHOD

✤ As you fill your sachet or charm bag with the items, bear in mind the purpose of each object:

✤ Comfrey root for protection.

✤ Bay leaves to drive away negativity.

✤ The rune to remind you of your responsibilities.

✤ Rose quartz for healing and loving feelings.

✤ All the ingredients to represent your ability to be in harmony with the rest of the world.

✤ Place the sachet in the glove compartment or hang it from the rear view mirror where it cannot obscure the view.

When you find yourself becoming irritated or are faced by someone else's irritation simply look at, touch or hold the sachet.

Protecting your Home

This spell can be used when you have been burgled or your home has been violated in some way. It uses symbolism and representation and needs to be done as soon as possible after the event. There are several stages to the process and each one should make you feel progressively better. Tracing the rune without drawing it on paper means in this instance it has more power because it is visible to no one else but you.

YOU WILL NEED

Water for cleaning your home
Cleaning cloth
Essential oil (for a bath to rebalance your aura)
Candle (preferably white)
A large quantity of rock salt
A purification incense (such as frankincense or copal)

METHOD

✤ You will want to cleanse your house to get rid of undue influences, so use the occasion to get rid of anger at the same time.

✤ Put a few drops of essential oil in the water you use and as you do your cleaning, mentally clear the atmosphere in each room spiritually and emotionally, converting any anger into love for your home.

✤ When you have finished, throw away the cloth and water you used and as you do so mentally close off your association with the violator of your premises.

✤ Now make a ritual of your bath, lighting your candle for fresh energy then adding the essential oil and a teaspoon of salt.

✤ It is a good idea to keep the water trickling in and out of the bath to signify moving water, since you want to wash away any negativity, not stagnate in it.

✤ When your preparations are complete take the salt and, moving clockwise through the house, sprinkle a little in each corner of each room to remove all traces of the negative.

✤ Make the sign of the rune Dagaz at the windows and doors of your home, starting at the top left and using your most powerful hand.

✤ Each time you do this, repeat words such as:

Protect my home and keep it safe.

✤ Use your own words if you wish so that they have more meaning.

✤ Finally, at a point closest to the centre of your home, light the incense and let it waft throughout all the rooms to give a final cleansing and raise the vibration.

With this particular technique you have raised the vibration in your home, protected it and given yourself the opportunity to become slightly more aware of how precious your safe space really is. You will also have come to terms with fear. Skin-Faxi, Dag's white horse, is said to have chased away the fears of the night with beams from his shining mane so Dagaz is best used in a situation of unease such as this.

It is useful to remember that the difference between runes and Ogham Staves is that runes are Nordic and more associated with light, or the lack of it, and the effect it had on peoples' lives, whereas staves are Celtic and associated with trees or plants. You may find it interesting to compare and contrast the two and decide to which you more naturally relate.

You also might like to honour the respective Gods – Odin for the runes and Ogmios for the Ogham Staves. When working with any of the individual runes or staves, don't forget to pay due respect to the animals, trees and symbolism inherent in each one. By working in that way, when you wear them in amulets or use their representations in talismans, you will be linking into the intrinsic power in each rune or stave. When using the alphabetic equivalents in any way, also remember to allow for the energy that the letters contain.

Any ritual connected with either the runes or the Staves needs to reflect the simplicity of the images. A simple form of blessing which honours the four Elements might be, for instance:

Land, sun, lake and wind
Bless now the form of my working.

The Ogham Alphabet

BECAUSE THE CYCLE of their year was based on fertility and associated rites, the Celts divided their year into four segments.

Time of Harvest	Shadow Time
31 July – 31 October	31 October – 2 February

Time of Light	Dawning Time
30 April – 31 July	2 February – 30 April

As in so many cultures that were governed by the cycle of the year, the transition point of the Celtic day was at sunset, so the times when day and night met were seen as magical. The time of sunrise was thought to bring new energy and power. Therefore, sunrise and sunset are both considered good times to carry out any ritual or blessing that you may feel appropriate both for the Ogham Staves and the runes.

The Ogham alphabet originally had 20 letters in groups of five. Each of the 20 staves had a Sun (or marked) side and a Moon (or blank) side, giving 40 different meanings. These can be combined in many different ways for divination purposes, though today when used as objects of power for your altar or as amulets, they are often used singly. Five more complex letters were added later, but the original form consists of straight lines notched across a straight stave of wood. The Ogham Staves were also associated with colours, birds, animals and kings.

Making the Staves

You need to make a connection with the essential energy of each Ogham tree, so think carefully about the symbolism of each one and also about the wood from which the staves are made, usually oak (the sacred tree of the Druids), hazel (wisdom) or ash (the tree of the All Father). Each type of tree had particular significance and symbolism for the Celts. You could make individual staves from each of the wood types as appropriate or use wooden discs. Remember to mark the top clearly for easy identification.

You need 20 sticks or discs of similar size which can be marked at the top with a small cross. If you are using twigs, you should be able to carve a symbol at the top by scraping away some of the bark. You might also use the old method of rounding the twigs at one end and making a point at the bottom to differentiate between those which are thrown upright from those upside down. (You can of course use ordinary dowelling rods and shape them in the same way.) Keep the staves safe in a wooden box – preferably of one of the three principal woods – or a bag made of any natural fabric.

The Ogham Staves are a potent personal tool. You can use them either to seek support with a

difficulty or to gain a different perspective on life. To energize them, go for a walk where you can touch trees in their natural habitat or place your staves in sunlight. That way you form a truly deep connection. The symbolism of the Ogham Staves is as follows. In this list both the Celtic and English names are given.

Stave 1: Beith (Birch): *Beginnings/Regeneration*

The birch, linked with the Mother Goddess and the Moon, is the earliest of the forest trees except for the elder. Symbolizing the rebirth of spring, it is used extensively in cleansing rituals – hence the use of a birch broom still used in rituals to expel evil spirits. In New Year celebrations it expels the spirits of the old year. In ancient ceremonies of beating the bounds and marking out territories, it offers new opportunities for growth.

When used as an amulet, this signifies the innovator and the pioneer. It can give you the courage you need to begin afresh. When you choose to use Beith, which means 'shining', you are instigating new beginnings, opportunities based on experience and wisdom and the removal of the old destructive patterns. Remember that you can branch out into new ventures and find new stimuli and new happiness.

Stave 2: Luis (Rowan or Mountain Ash): *Protection*

This tree, sacred to the Moon, is known as quick-beam, the Tree of Life, the witch or witch wand. Traditionally, a rowan twig was pulled without a knife from a tree and fastened with red twine in the shape of a cross. It was – and is – used as a protective device for stables, cowsheds and outhouses and to protect the household and its enterprises from doubt or harm. It is the tree used most against lightning and psychic attack. The rowan is also an oracular tree, often found around ancient stone circles.

This stave signifies great intuitive abilities and inner resources. You would wear it as an amulet when you wanted to turn obstacles to advantage. When you are undertaking an important venture or delicate negotiations, or doubt your own abilities, the rowan stave might be used to remind you of the ability to overcome force by the use of intuition.

Stave 3: Fearn (Alder):
Firm Foundations/Security

The alder is the Tree of Fire, known as the Tree of Bran the Blessed (a hero god and god of the underworld). His severed head is said to be under the White Mount at Tower Hill in London, as protection, so that his beloved land would never be invaded. Whistles made of this wood were traditionally used to summon and control the four winds, so offering security against seemingly uncontainable elements.

This stave characterizes attention to detail and the ability to take small steady steps towards success; it symbolizes realistic targets. As an amulet it represents security, whether material, practical or emotional. There is reason for optimism, if matters are not left to chance – any venture or relationship endures only temporary problems.

Stave 4: Saille (Willow): *Intuition/Dreams*

The willow is the tree of enchantment, sacred to the Moon Goddess, who is the giver of moisture. It is often associated with rebirth, regeneration and the renewal of inspiration. Feelings and emotions that you experience can be a guide to right action as much as logic. As an amulet, it acts as a reminder of this.

More generally, this is the stave of the innovator and the pioneer and may indicate that this aspect of your personality is very strong. Saille indicates the use of imaginative faculties and suggests the need to trust intuitions and hunches, to follow your heart. Answers or directions are not clear – and yet you are aware of inner stirrings. You learn to use your dreams constructively, especially those that recur or seem especially vivid.

Stave 5: Nuinn (Ash):
Expansion

Ash is a Father Tree and very sacred to the Celts. It is the Tree of the World Axis (for example, Yggdrasil in the Norse tradition) and such Father Gods

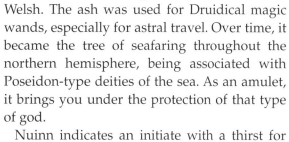

as Odin of the Vikings and Gwidion of the Welsh. The ash was used for Druidical magic wands, especially for astral travel. Over time, it became the tree of seafaring throughout the northern hemisphere, being associated with Poseidon-type deities of the sea. As an amulet, it brings you under the protection of that type of god.

Nuinn indicates an initiate with a thirst for knowledge and new experiences, the seeker of the truth, the explorer of new territories and opportunities. This stave can indicate an inner hunger or restlessness or, alternatively, powerful ambitions that evoke courage and confidence.

Stave 6: Huathe (Hawthorn/ Whitethorn):
Resilience/Courage

The whitethorn, the most common form of hawthorn, is the tree of the White Goddess (under the name Cardea), who used it to cast spells. It is believed to act as a shield against physical or psychic harm and is sacred to Mars and other northern thunder gods. It was set around sacred boundaries in order to deter evil. Hawthorn twigs gathered on Ascension Day are believed to have exceptional powers.

In general, the hawthorn symbol represents the power to fight for what is right and the determination to achieve goals. As an amulet, it offers the qualities of protection and tenacity. If you are feeling discouraged or need extra energy to forge ahead, Huathe is an assurance that it is possible to resist hardship and come through with courage.

Stave 7: Duir (Oak) *Strength/Power*

The oak is the tree of endurance and power, and was particularly special to the Druids. Equally spread between the three realms of heaven, Earth and the underworld, its roots extend as far underground as its branches reach up into the sky. Oak is always the wood used for the midsummer fire and to start the ceremonial fires lit at the great festivals, when the fire is lit inside the log, symbolically fuelling the Sun's power.

Duir represents leadership, knowledge, authority and a noble spirit, as well as pure masculine power, strength and assertiveness, although these qualities co-exist with nobility, idealism and altruism. When looking for qualities of determination, patience, strength of purpose and persistence, especially in matters of career and personal happiness, this is a good stave to use as an amulet.

Stave 8: Tinne (Holly): *Fire*

The original holly tree of the Celts was probably an evergreen version of the common oak tree (the evergreen scarlet oak, holm oak or holly oak). It was sacred to the Celtic god Taranis, who carried a club made of holly. It is a symbol of the promise of the renewal of life and is also protective of the household. Holly suggests that one is in tune with life's ups and downs and therefore signifies that there is a time for action and a time for withdrawal.

Holly marks a vital stage in the wider cycle of experience and suggests that however it presents itself – good, bad or indifferent – that stage is a building block for the future. As an amulet, it reminds you that better times will come if the faith is kept.

Stave 9: Coll (Hazel): *Wisdom*

The hazel is the Celtic Tree of Wisdom; the Druids carried a hazel rod as a symbol of authority. Hazel was also used to mark the boundaries of a court of justice and so it can be used to represent the overall concept of boundaries. A hazel rod is used for divining for water and buried treasure. It is also associated with the sacred number nine, because the hazel takes nine years to produce nuts.

Coll is the stave of the naturally wise person and represents intelligence, justice and recourse to traditional knowledge. When there are decisions to be made, the hazel stave indicates that an impartial response is required, using available expertise. As an amulet, it reminds the wearer of his own inherent sense of wisdom and justice.

Stave 10: Quert (Apple Tree):
Fertility/Abundance

This is the Celtic Tree of Life. Orchards

have always been considered to be sacred; to encourage a bountiful fruitful crop, not only of the orchard but also of the local land and community, apple trees were 'wassailed' (drenched in cider) and offerings were made to the gods. Traditionally, apple wood was used for wands to cast magic circles, especially for love and fertility magic.

Quert signifies an outgoing nature with much enthusiasm for life that attracts new ideas or interests. Positivity and many opportunities often lead to a generosity that is out of the ordinary. This stave allows the wearer to nurture projects that may be fulfilled over time. There is often a feeling of happiness and well-being associated with Quert, making it a powerful gift to give to someone as an amulet.

Stave 11: Muinn (Vine/Bramble): *Joy*

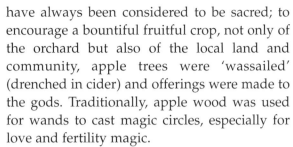

The vine, which was imported into Britain during the Bronze Age, has always been associated with spiritual as well as physical comfort. The native bramble or blackberry, which was the truly magical plant, was used more frequently for wine making because it grew wild. It is said that the bramble (or vine) was the only thing that Adam and Eve were allowed to take out of the Garden of Eden.

Muinn represents unbridled joy, embracing the whole continuum of happiness, physical and spiritual, and a natural exuberance. As an amulet, it suggests personal happiness rather than success. With personal contentment comes the ability to spread joy to others, just as the vine or bramble spreads itself.

Stave 12: Gort (Ivy)
Relationships/Loyalty

Ivy, traditionally regarded as the harbinger of death, was worn as a crown at the winter feast of Saturnalia. Though it was perceived to choke the tree around which it grew, it was also seen as being bound to that tree and remained evergreen, a symbol of hope. So it came to be traditionally associated primarily with fidelity, and a symbol of married love and loyalty. Houses with ivy growing on them are reputedly safe from psychic attack.

Gort suggests a loyal, loving person who is supportive and does not stifle lovers or friends.

When worn as an amulet, it reminds one to pay attention to love interests as well as work and other commitments.

Stave 13: Ngetal (Fern/Bracken/Reeds): *Riches/Prosperity*

Ngetal is an auspicious stave to use for all money-making endeavours and questions. The reed was originally an ancient Egyptian symbol of royalty and of learning. Its association with the height of the Sun's power at midsummer makes it a symbol of gold and riches. Ferns and bracken were reputed to produce their flowers on Midsummer Eve and become golden between eleven o'clock and midnight: the scattered seed indicated hidden gold that could be recovered by effort.

Ngetal suggests a shrewd business brain that makes use of ingenious ways of increasing profits. The stave is worth using as an amulet when you are initiating new business projects or need to consolidate business gains. Ngetal assures the success of any financial matters and money-making schemes.

Stave 14: Straif (Blackthorn):
Effort/Persistence

Often seen as a tree of hardship, the blackthorn produces white blossoms on an almost black branch and is said to bloom at midnight on Christmas Eve. Straif means 'to strive', and endeavour and perseverance are fundamental to the tree and its principles. It is incredibly hardy and forms a strong barrier linked with both physical and magical protection.

Blackthorn denotes the characteristics of the individual who has not had things easy but has developed willpower and determination because of this hardship. The blackthorn-braided crown is often kept in the home as a luck-bringer. Otherwise it is burned and scattered over the fields on New Year's Morning; blackthorn is said to ensure a good harvest in the coming year.

Straif stands for concentrated power and energy and therefore represents supreme will and determination in the face of adversity. As an amulet, it suggests that goodness of spirit will prevail.

Stave 15: Ruis (Elder):
Second Sight/The Unexpected

A waterside tree, the elder has white flowers that reach their peak in midsummer. This makes the elder another aspect of the White Goddess; it is truly the Fairy Tree. Ruis connects us to the hidden realms and our own spiritual and magical natures, giving us the art of clairvoyance.

The elder is the stave of the visionary, someone who is as secure in the divinatory arts and mystic perception as they are in the everyday world. The elder stave, worn as an amulet, will often give one a seemingly magical solution that comes in a dream or through insight. Where common sense and perception have not brought you an answer, watching the patterns in nature, such as in the growth of trees and flowers, can help you determine necessary changes.

Stave 16: Ailm (Pine/Silver Fir):
Clarity/Creation

The pine was worshipped by the Celts as a symbol of Fire and is one of the few trees that is both male and female. The silver fir is the tree of Druantia, the Gallic Fir-Goddess, a powerful representation of birth and creation. Symbolic of the eternal flame, Ailm stands for an inner creation becoming manifest and new ideas being put into practice. It involves illumination, insight and communication.

As an amulet, it signifies your own natural talents and that creative energies are all around you for you to use. Clarity of communication is of importance in ensuring that things happen as they should. Make use of the amulet to move away from uncertainty.

Stave 17: Onn (Furze/Gorse):
Transformation/Change

Gorse is a symbol of the early spring sun and was associated with the Gallic Goddess of Spring. Just as spring transforms the dead world of winter and gorse transforms the drab hillsides, the stave of Onn brings about a radical transformation in the energy available to you. In older times gorse was a complete crop, offering food for animals, flowers for the bees and, later in the year, bedding and fertilization for the next crop.

As a characteristic, Onn signifies a mind that is always open and adaptable, welcoming change. Wearing this stave as an amulet means that you can anticipate a change for the better, though there may be some upheaval and disruption along the way.

Stave 18: Ur (Heather):
Strong Emotional/Passionate Feelings
Heather is linked with the Gallic Heather Goddess called Uroica, shown sometimes as a queen bee. The heather originally bloomed scarlet at midsummer and so came to be associated with passion and the Mother Goddess. In Romany lore, white heather, being rare, is considered especially lucky. In Celtic legend it represents eternal love and the tears of the abandoned lover.

Ur is the stave of the person who feels deeply and is in tune with the emotions and strong feelings and desires of others, although these emotions are unacknowledged. Used as an amulet, it reminds the wearer to follow their heart and believe that what they long for can be theirs. They have only to ask for what they most desire.

Stave 19: Edhadh (White Poplar/Aspen): *Maturity/Healing*
The white poplar is the tree of the autumn equinox, of maturity and old age and a late harvest. It stands for the achievement of final ideas and also for letting go all that is no longer valid. The aspen is said to have been the tree used in the Crucifixion and now shakes at the resulting agony. Poplar leaves are said to have magical powers.

As an amulet, it offers hope for the future, based on experience of what is possible and not on romantic dreams. Edhadh personifies the natural healer and peacemaker, with a mature and balanced view. The stave represents the fruition of past efforts, when healing can be both physical and mental. It is time to balance the books and accept what is around you.

Stave 20: Ido (Yew):
Immortality/Rebirth
The yew is known as the Tree of Death throughout Europe and is a symbol of immortality because it lives so long. Associated with the Wheel of the Year and the aspect of the Triple Goddess dealing with death, Ido is the stave of endings, transformation and rebirth. However this is not pessimistic, but is merely an awareness of the cyclical nature of existence and the deeper meaning of life.

Ido is a stave that you may use as an amulet at the time of a natural change or ending of a phase. The yew always symbolizes rebirth and immortality, though there may be regrets. The coming to an end of a situation is, however, almost always a positive one, often leading to new opportunities.

Ogham Spells
Carried in your purse or about your person, the staves give a subtle vibration as a gentle reminder of what you know already. To use two or more staves, for instance as jewellery, not only means that you have the double reminder but you also have available to you power squared (that is, four times the power). To use three would give you nine times the power (three times three) and so on. Therefore, choose your staves wisely and well.

Risk-taking

This spell uses the Ogham Staves, supported by candles. The representation used here is Coll (Hazel) for wisdom – you could also use Fearn (Alder) for firm foundations. If you choose to use both, you might inscribe one on your candle and carry the other as you go about your business.

YOU WILL NEED
White candle
St John's Wort or sage oil
Your burin
The stave you will carry with you

METHOD
❖ Anoint your candle with the oil (for courage).
❖ Inscribe it with the Ogham Stave Coll which represents wisdom:
❖ Light the candle.
❖ Ask for help from the Irish god Ogma, who gave us the staves, in whatever task you are to undertake.

❖ As the candle burns out, think very carefully of what the risks might be in your venture and what you can do to minimize them.

❖ Before the candle burns completely through, pass the stave you will carry (in this case Fearn) quickly through the flame.

This spell is designed to give you the courage and wisdom to take risks in whatever way is appropriate for you. It need not be simply a business risk, but some way in which you must stretch your own boundaries. It does not ensure success but allows you the potential for achievement.

Second Sight

This spell draws together all the magical connotations of the elder (fairy) tree. In magic, the elder tree commands respect and there is a belief that you cannot cut down an elder tree, for in the words of the Wiccan Rede 'Elder is the Lady's Tree, burn it not or cursed ye be!' However, as can be seen, the tree is bountiful and shares with us clarity of vision.

YOU WILL NEED
Dried elderflowers
Goblet of elderberry wine or cordial
Scrying mirror
Infusion of elderflower petals and water
Clean cloth
Ogham Stave Ruis (Elder)

METHOD

❖ Scatter the dried elderflowers in your sacred space. Take a sip from the goblet of wine or cordial (the goblet itself is a representation of the Lady). Acknowledge her power in whatever way you feel is appropriate.

❖ Pick up your scrying mirror and wipe it with the infusion. Place it on a flat surface.

❖ Pick up the stave and sit quietly with it while looking into the mirror. State the difficulty you are experiencing or ask a question to which you require an answer. (You may find the solution comes to you either through the medium of the mirror or intuitively. It may come in a dream shortly afterwards.)

❖ When it feels right, thank the Lady and leave your sacred space.

❖ You can use the elderflower petals later as part of a potpourri or scatter them on open earth.

Using the elder stave in this way helps you to become a visionary, secure in your own clairvoyant abilities. Because you have acknowledged a powerful force of nature, you may find that you become much more readily intuitive.

Candles and Pennies

Fire and finance always seem to have a natural affinity, so a candle spell which incorporates pennies is a good way of drawing money and financial energy towards you. You do need to keep your demands within bounds so do not ask for more than you need. Colour is an important component and green is traditionally used in money spells. You could try this on a Friday.

YOU WILL NEED
A green candle
A glass
Enough small coins to half fill the glass
A safe space
Your burin

METHOD

❖ Place the green candle in the glass. Fill the glass halfway up the candle with the coins.

❖ With your burine, inscribe the candle with the Ogham Stave Ngetal for riches and prosperity.

❖ As you light the candle, state that you only want what is needed, not a penny more.

❖ Place the glass in a safe space and let the candle burn down to nothing so the wax is intermingled with the pennies. (There is a slight risk that as the glass gets hot it may shatter, though the pennies should absorb most of the heat.)

This is representative of the idea that money will 'stick' to you. Hopefully, having done the spell once you will not need to do it again. A variation on this, to manifest actual objects that are needed, is to inscribe the candle with a picture of what you require or to write the actual words on the candle.

Resolving a Quarrel

There are times when you must rely on your own maturity and experience to carry you through a difficult situation, perhaps a family quarrel or a work dispute. This spell reinforces your belief in yourself on a very subtle level.

YOU WILL NEED ————————————

A small piece of dowelling rod about 5 cm (2 in) long
A marker pen or burin

METHOD ————————————

✤ Inscribe or mark the round end of the rod with the symbol of Edhadh.
✤ Hold the stave in your power hand.
✤ As you do so allow yourself to feel the energy of its meaning – maturity and healing – flood through you, giving you the power to deal with the situation.
✤ Turn the stave, inscribed face outward, and see the energy from it flow towards the people concerned, surrounding them with its healing and reconciliation.
✤ Place the stave where you can see or feel it, perhaps on a shelf, in your desk or in your pocket. If the situation escalates, draw on the energy of the stave to calm it.
✤ When the problem is resolved, bury the stave or toss it into running water.

If you are unable to use wood for the stave the spell will work just as well by inscribing the symbol on a piece of paper or parchment and disposing of it appropriately. Do remember that this spell does not set a time limit on its resolution, so this may take some time.

REMEMBERING THAT DIVINATION is the art of discovering the will of the Divine, people would use anything that was available to them to try to interpret what needed to happen. The sigils of the runes and staves held a power of their own, as we have seen. The symbols in the art of tea-leaf reading do not have such power – they are simply interpretative devices.

Reading the tea leaves – tasseography – is often associated with the Romany way of life. However, it probably began not long after tea was first drunk, in China, as far back as 3000 BCE. Tea drinking spread throughout the Orient and India, whence the Romanies brought it, and the associated tea-leaf divination, to Europe.

Tea was an expensive luxury in Britain until late in the 19th century when large quantities were imported from India and Ceylon (present-day Sri Lanka), and so tasseography was a rare skill. It is perhaps unfortunate that reading the tea leaves became something of a parlour game to the Victorians – a notion which, for many, it still remains today.

Reading the tea leaves

The best tea to use is a good, traditional tea, the leaves of which are separate and firm, such as Earl Grey or Darjeeling. Allow one spoon per person and 'one for the pot'.

As the tea is brewing (three to four minutes is usually enough) ask whoever has questions to ask to concentrate on them. Pour the tea into plain white cups and enjoy drinking it – don't rush, just sip it as usual. If you want to continue concentrating, that's fine. If you want to enjoy a chat that's also fine – one of the secrets of successful tea-leaf reading is relaxation.

Rituals for reading the tea leaves vary from person to person. One trusted method is for the enquirer to take the cup – with only a little tea remaining – in their left hand and swirl it three times widdershins (anti-clockwise) for a woman or deosil (clockwise) for a man. The cup is then placed rim down on the saucer to drain away any tea that remains. The reader should then take the cup in their own left hand and interpret the patterns the leaves have made. Another method is to pour the tea into a cup through a strainer and either read those leaves only, or do so in association with the leaves left in the cup after it has been drunk.

Romany tradition states that a dry cup heralds good news, although if there is a trace of liquid remaining in the cup, there will a period of trouble in the near future.

Traditionally, leaves at the rim of the cup are equated with joy and happiness, whereas if they are at the bottom this means sorrow.

It is not just the leaves that are important – the positions within the cup, where the shapes form, also have an influence. For convenience, the cup is first divided into four quarters:

The quarter nearest the handle represents the enquirer. Leaves that stick to the cup in this area are concerned with them, their home and those closest to them. Depending on the images, masses of leaves that stick to the cup here could suggest that the questioner is being overwhelmed by responsibility for family and close friends, or it can mean that home and personal life is particularly rich.

The side opposite the handle is concerned with strangers, acquaintances rather than friends, the workplace, travel and other matters away from home. A large concentration here suggests that it is these issues that concern the enquirer at the moment, more than the family and the home.

To the left of the handle (from the seer's angle) is the area that stands for the past, with people moving out of the enquirer's surroundings. Unusually large areas here indicate that things unresolved in the past are having a bearing on the questioner's life. This is reinforced if there is an especially large concentration of leaves in this area, and if the leaves seem to be particularly dark.

The part of the cup to the reader's right is the area where leaves gathered represent upcoming events and people who are about to have an influence on the enquirer's life. An absence of leaves here should not be taken as a bad omen: rather that the questioner is more concerned with the present and the past than with what life holds in store.

As well as being divided into four quarters, the cup is also metaphorically cut in two horizontally. Images close to the rim indicate the present – days and weeks – while those clinging to the lower part of the cup indicate the more distant future – months and years. It is the reader's skill and intuition that decides whether the leaves in these positions are read from the perspective of timing or happiness, according to the belief mentioned above, or perhaps both.

Tea-leaf Images

Like dreams, the symbolism and imagery within tasseography is very individual. Indeed, because the images are representative of ideas, they share much of the same symbolism of dream interpretation, perhaps in a simplified form. We give a list below of some of the most widely accepted meanings.

What has a particular significance for one reader may mean something totally different to another, and anyone who wishes to use this form of divination in their magical work might prefer to build up their own library of meanings, using the list as a starting point. When you read the tea leaves for others, do remain consistent in your interpretations, otherwise you will end up by confusing not only yourself but also your questioners.

A

Abbey Sanctuary, future ease and freedom from worry.

Acorn At the top of the cup means success and gain: new beginnings. At the bottom means good health and an improvement in this generally.

Aeroplane An impending journey, either physical or emotional or a rise in position, if flying up; if broken or pointing down, a possible accident.

Anchor Stability and better business opportunities. Protection, love.

Angel Good news, clarity, business help.

Ant Industry and hard work. If more than one appears, joint projects and team work.

Apple Achievement. If more than one appears, long life, gain by commerce.

Apple tree Growth, fertility, change for the better.

Apes Secret enemies, copying of ideas.

Arch A journey abroad, new relationships.

Arrow Misfortune, a disagreeable letter from the arrow's direction.

Ass Mistake overcome by patience; or a legacy.

Axe Difficulties, job loss. At the top of the cup indicates the overcoming of difficulties.

B

Baby New ventures, interests or beginnings, small worries.

Badger Long life and prosperity, masculine concerns.

Bag A trap, though if open, escape from a difficulty.

Baggage Emotional or mental residue.

Ball If seeming to move away, variable fortunes, if moving towards you good things are coming.

Balloons May suggest celebration, but also temporary difficulties.

Basket Gifts to come, an addition to the family. If empty, too much effort has been expended.

Bat Confrontation of fears, fruitless journeys or tasks, idiosyncrasies in behaviour in the enquirer or those around him.

Bear A long period of travel, a protective influence or unwarranted aggression.

Beasts Other than those mentioned in this list, can foretell misfortune but may also suggest protection and wisdom.

Bell Unexpected news, good if near the top of the cup; if near the bottom, a warning.

Birds A lucky sign; good news if flying, a fortunate journey or freedom of spirit.

Boat A visit from a friend; protection; an important discovery which may be life-changing is on the horizon.

Book If open it's good news, the beginning of a new phase; if closed, an investigation is needed or a delay will occur

Boots Caution is needed before achievement is possible. If at the top of the cup, someone may be moving on.

Bouquet One of the luckiest of symbols, a happy marriage.

Bottle A celebration. A full bottle suggests a new challenge. However, more than one can show the potential for illness, or something carried too far.

Boxes When open, romantic problems vanish. When closed the questioner may be being narrow-minded or prudish.

Branch In leaf, a birth or fresh growth. If bare, disappointment in a project.

Bridge A favourable opportunity, a change of circumstance.

Broom A change in ideas, a good clear-out (physically and emotionally).

Building A removal or change of structure.

Bull Intransigence, slander by an enemy.

Bush An invitation into society; new friends or opportunities.

Butterfly Freedom, fickleness, hedonism, success and pleasure.

C

Cages Something is holding the questioner back, but shackles can be shrugged off and it is time to move ahead.

Candle Help from others, enlightenment, good ideas.

Car Approaching wealth, visits from friends.

Cart Fluctuations of fortune.

Castles Circumstances are about to improve; unexpected fortune or legacy.

Cats Deception or a false friend. If the back is arched, it indicates a nasty argument.

Chains New responsibilities, possibly an engagement or marriage. If broken, trouble in store.

Chair A guest or an addition to the family.

Cherries A victory or accolade of some sort.

Chessmen A short-term project may not come to fruition, so consider the long-term carefully. Manipulative people.

Circle Success, completion; can also mean the arrival of a baby.

Cliffs A dangerous situation. Risks can be taken.

Clouds Fears and doubts, possible difficulties.

Clover A lucky symbol, prosperity is in the offing.

Coffins A loss of some kind, the end of a project.

Coins Money and prosperity.

Comb An enemy, an irritation.

Comet Misfortune and trouble arriving suddenly.

Compass Journey to fresh horizons.

Cows Prosperity and tranquil times ahead.

Cross Suffering or a sacrifice.

Crowns Honour or a legacy along with the chances of a dream coming true.

Cup A reward or recognition, a gift.

D

Dagger Favours from friends or danger from self or others; beware.

Deer Quarrels, disputes; failure in trade.

Dish Domestic difficulties.

Dice A time to take a risk. Dots on dice may suggest timings.

Dog Loyalty, faithful friends; if at the bottom of the cup, a friend needs help.

Donkey A legacy long awaited.

Door An odd event; if open, a way forward; if closed, a temporary difficulty.

Dots Money-making opportunities; dots also underline the meaning of any other nearby symbol.

Dove A lucky symbol; progress in prosperity and affection.

Dragon A great and sudden, often spiritual, change – usually for the better.

Drums Quarrels and disagreements, scandal and gossip; a call to action.

Duck Increase of wealth or opportunity, often from abroad. Right action.

E

Eagle Honour and riches through a change of residence.

Ears Malicious rumours now or in the immediate future.

Egg A good omen. If more than one, an increase of some kind, a new project.

Eggtimer Time may be running out.

Elephants Wisdom and success.

Envelope Good news of some kind, although not always by letter.

Eye Be cautious.

F

Fan Flirtation or some sort of indiscretion.

Face A change, may be a setback. When smiling, a sign of happiness: but when frowning, opposition is around.

Falcon A persistent enemy, someone attacking a principle.

Feather Lack of concentration. More than one indicates indiscretion and instability.

Fence Limitations, minor setbacks though they are not permanent; someone is being overprotective.

Ferret Active enemies, sometimes working to undermine the enquirer.

Finger Emphasizes whatever image it points towards. With an exclamation mark, listen carefully, for the speaker is right.

Fire At the top of the cup, achievement; at the bottom, danger of haste.

Fish Good fortune, lucky speculation, good news from abroad.

Flag Danger from wounds inflicted by an enemy. Rally resources and act courageously, stick to your principles.

Flower Celebration, good fortune, success, happy marriage, reward. If a bud, be patient over a project. If drooping, the best time is past.

Fly Domestic annoyance, small irritations.

Foot A move forward, away from a known environment. If more than one, an important decision is to be made in the near future.

Fork False flattery, a parting of friends.

Forked line Decision, options of action.

Fountain Success, emotional freedom. Sometimes a sexually charged affair, or opportunity for misbehaviour.

Fox Treachery by a trusted friend. Also, subtlety in negotiations.

Frog Success in love and commerce.

Fruit Prosperity, possibly after hard work.

G

Gallows Sometimes a sign of good luck, but often a loss through imminent danger. A drastic end to a situation.

Gate When open, opportunity or future success; when closed, obstacles and loss. At the top of the cup, success through effort; at the bottom through change of circumstance.

Giant A person with a magnetic, dominant personality or a big ego. More than one indicates a large corporation.

Glass Integrity.

Glow A challenge, often mental.

Goat A sign of enemies. To a sailor it indicates misfortune.

Goose Happiness; a successful venture if warnings are heeded. Geese suggest a threat to a concept or principle.

Grapes Happiness, prosperity, self-indulgence, time to realize one's dreams.

Grass An inner restlessness, discontent, often with something that has to do with a long-term situation.

Grasshopper A great friend will become a soldier.

Greyhound Good fortune by strenuous exertion.

Gun Anger, aggression, a tricky situation where a cool head is needed.

H

Hammock An unconventional nature and perhaps a desire to opt out of responsibilities and take things easy. Relaxation while awaiting results.

Hammer Hard work is needed: triumph over adversity.

Hand If open it means friendship, often a new one; if closed, it means an argument or meanness in someone close.

Hare A sign of long journey or the return of absent friend.

Harp Love, harmony, marriage; success in love.

Hat Success in life, improvement, especially in a new job, change. May mean a formal occasion. An old rival.

Hawk A journey; an enemy; jealousy.

Head New opportunities; a promotion to a new position of authority.

Heart Pleasure, love, trust pleasures to come. Use tact when appropriate.

Heavenly bodies Happiness and success

Hen Increase of riches or addition to the family, a motherly person who may interfere.

Hills Obstacles to progress.

Horns There may be wrong intentions, stubbornness. A dilemma.

Horse Desires fulfilled through a prosperous journey. If galloping it means good news; if just the head is seen, it means a lover.

Horseshoe Good luck, a lucky journey or success in marriage.

Hourglass Imminent peril; there is the need to make a decision.

House Security, success in business or greater concentration on domestic matters.

Human figures Judged by what they appear to be doing

I

Iceberg Danger; someone has hidden depths.

Igloos Refuge from an emotional situation.

Initials Represent people in the enquirer's life.

Ink blot Doubts must be clarified; can mean an important document, probably legal.

Inkpots Important legal or official matters need to be communicated in writing.

Insect Problems are minor and easily overcome.

Islands A holiday, perhaps to an exotic location; increasing isolation, probably at work.

Ivy Honour and happiness through faithful friends.

J

Jewels Gifts.

Jackal A mischief-maker of no account.

Jug Good health, if full: if empty, money or resources are being frittered.

K

Kangaroo A rival in business or love; harmony at home.

Kettle Death, or – depending on position – minor illness.

Key Money, increasing trade, a good husband or wife; independence. Keys suggest enlightenment and new opportunities; two at the bottom of the cup warn of a burglary.

Kings A high-handed older person may or may not be an ally.

Kite Honour and dignity; wishes coming true.

Knife Disasters through quarrels and enmity, a broken friendship or divorce.

L

Ladder Promotion; a sign of business travel.

Leaf New life. Falling leaves indicate happiness in the autumn.

Leopard A sign of immigration and subsequent success.

Letter News.

Line Straight means progress and happiness; wavy means an uncertain path; forked means decisions; can also mean journeys.

Lily At the top of the cup, health and happiness, at the bottom, anger, strife.

Lion Greatness through powerful friends.

Lizard Trust your instincts; check all facts carefully.

Lock Obstacles.

Loop Avoid impulsive actions.

M

Magnet A new interest.

Man A visitor will be arriving

Mask Excitement; insecurity.

Mermaid Misfortune, especially to seafaring people.

Mirror The enquirer should question their motives.

Monkey Deception in love.

Moles Secrecy.

Moon As a crescent, prosperity and fortune. If obviously waning, luck is moving away.

Mountain Great goals but with many difficulties; powerful friends. Several mountains indicate powerful enemies.

Mouse Theft, danger of poverty through death or swindling.

Mushroom Sudden separation of lovers after a quarrel.

N

Nail Injustice, unfairness.

Necklace Unbroken means admirers; broken means danger of losing a lover.

Needle Recognition, admiration.

Nest Domestic matters, particularly those to do with comfort.

Nets Entrapment or security matters.

Numbers Very lucky, long life, good health, happy marriage.

Nuns Take notice of wise friends. Can also mean spiritual matters.

O

Oak Health, long life; wise ones will help you.

Oars Find your own solution, do not rely on others.

Oblong figures Family or business squabbles.

Octopus Overstretched resources; danger.

Ostrich Travel; obstinacy.

Owl Changes in life, gossip, scandal; sometimes an evil omen, indicative of sickness, poverty, disgrace.

Oysters Hidden depths and talents.

P

Padlock When closed, domestic or work-related issues are difficult; when open, freedom is in sight.

Palm tree Good luck, children to a wife, marriage to a maid; holiday coming your way; success and honour.

Parachute Help is at hand.

Parasol A new lover.

Parrot A journey, but it can also mean gossip.

Peacock Success and acquisition of property; a happy marriage; beware of friends' vanity.

Pear Great wealth and improved social position.

Pendulum Make efforts to restore harmony.

Pheasant A legacy.

Pig Good and bad luck mixed; greed.

Pigeons Important news if flying, if not, domestic bliss.

Pine tree Continued happiness.

Pipes A situation may be escalating.

Pistol Danger or disaster.

Purse At the top of the cup means profit; at the bottom means loss.

Pyramid Healing and psychic powers. The answer to a problem lies in the past.

Q

Question mark Need for caution.

R

Rabbit Fair success in a city or large town; need for bravery; multiple children.

Rainbow A need to be realistic.

Rake Take careful note of details.

Rat Treacherous acquaintances, losses through enemies.

Raven Bad news; divorce, failure in business; legacy.

Razor A lovers' quarrel and separation.

Reptile Quarrels and nastiness.

Rider Good news from overseas regarding finances.

Rifle A sign of discord and strife; possibly male aggression.

Ring Marriage; if near clouds, an interesting or possibly unhappy marriage.

Roads A new way forward.

Rocks Obstacles and difficulties which can be utilized.

Rose A lucky sign denoting good fortune and happiness; popularity.

S

Saw Interference, or troublesome strangers.

Scales Legal issues; if balanced it means a just result; if unbalanced it means an unjust result. Several scales indicate a lawsuit.
Scissors Quarrels, illness, possibly separation; better future to come; cutting of ties.
Serpent Spiteful enemies, bad luck, illness; sexual difficulties.
Shark Be careful when driving; danger of accident or death.
Sheep Good fortune; success and prosperity.
Shell Good news.
Shelter Sanctuary or danger of loss or ill health.
Ship A successful or worthwhile journey.
Shoe Change for the better.
Snake An enemy, but also wisdom; great caution should be exercised.
Spider A sign of money coming; reward for work.
Spinning wheels Variously, opportunities or deceit; the wheel of life, fate.
Spoon Generosity, brought about by someone elses's influence.
Squares Comfort and peace; news about money.
Star A lucky sign, health and happiness; hope; if surrounded by dots it foretells great fortune.
Sun Happiness, success, power.
Swallow A journey with a pleasant ending.
Swan Good luck and a happy marriage or partnership.
Sword Arguments; quarrels between lovers. If broken, victory over an enemy can be expected.

T
Table Social gatherings.
Tent Travel.
Thimble Changes at home.
Timber Business success.
Toad Deceit and unexpected enemies.
Tortoise Criticism, usually beneficial.
Tower Disappointment; the need for hard work.
Tree Improvements. Trees are a lucky sign; prosperity and happiness.
Triangle Something unexpected. Triangles are always a sign of good luck and unexpected legacies.

Tunnels Obstacles overcome by getting to the bottom of things.
Twisted figures Disturbances and vexation.

U
Umbrella Annoyance and trouble
Unicorn There is the need for a spiritual 'walk'; can also mean scandal; magical insights.
Urn Wealth and happiness.

V
Vase A friend needs help.
Violin Egotism.
Volcano Harmful emotions, particularly anger.
Vulture Bitter foes.

W
Wagon A sign of approaching poverty; can also mean a wedding.
Wasp Romantic problems.
Waterfall Prosperity.
Web Possible intrigue and deceit.
Whales Successful fulfilment of a big undertaking.
Wheel An inheritance about to come; if complete, it means good fortune; if broken, it means disappointment.
Windmill Success in enterprise.
Windows New insights or clarity.
Wings Messages.
Wolf Beware of jealous intrigues.
Woman Pleasure and happiness; several women indicates scandal.
Wood A speedy marriage.
Worms Secret foes.

Y
Yacht Pleasure and happiness.
Yew tree Death of an aged person, leaving his legacy to you.
Yoke Domination.

Z
Zebra Adventure, especially overseas.

The Oracles

THE READING OF tea leaves largely uses intuition for very basic interpretations. It is certainly an oracular art, in that it attempts to 'see' the future, but requires only basic knowledge and ability.

Those who today are called channels, clairvoyants, psychics and mediums were known as oracles in ancient Greece. The most famous oracle of all was undoubtedly the one at Apollo's shrine in Delphi. This Delphic Oracle was said to have originally belonged to Gaia, the Earth goddess. The site itself was called 'the navel of the earth' and was represented by a marble umbilicus-shaped object, which the temple was built to protect.

The gods were contacted through the oracles, who, by virtue of their special powers, were revered and cared for by the community. The most common way for the oracle to work was by what would nowadays be called trance-channelling, although there were other more indirect ways, such as by 'reading' the movement of oak trees.

It is more than probable that the 'communications' of the oracles did not always arise out of spiritual awareness. The heightened state of consciousness attained by these generally unsophisticated people, might be explained by the fact that most temples were situated near an earth fissure and permeated by fumes rising from the volcanic substrata. Shamans seeking the same state might well call on their knowledge of herbs and energy fields to achieve a similar change in consciousness. From a religious perspective, it was enough that the oracles and their people believed that they were in touch with the Divine.

'Anomalous cognition' is a wonderful term, describing a transfer of information to a subject in ways that are not at this stage properly understood. It is best described as knowing without quite knowing how you know, and is one of the intuitive senses. It fits descriptions of telepathy, extra-sensory perception, clairvoyance, the other 'clair' senses and other 'perceptive' paranormal abilities. The term 'anomalous cognition' is used by parapsychologists to describe the transfer of information and, in previous times, would have been thought of as being magical. Whether the transfer has a religious basis or a scientific, does not really concern us. We simply need to know that it works.

The spell below is a simple way of developing your own ability to use the divinatory tools already mentioned in this section.

Consulting the Oracle

For those who have developed intuition and learned to trust their clairvoyance, this spell offers a way of having information come to you when it is needed. Do this during the waxing of, or at, the Full Moon. The Greek goddess of justice Themis, on whom you will call in this spell, in her original form perceived all in the past, the present and the future.

YOU WILL NEED

Jasmine or lotus incense
Your particular divination tools (Tarot cards, runes, pendulum etc)
The contract or papers on which you need information
A chalice containing red wine or juice
Two purple candles in holders

METHOD

❖ Light the incense.
❖ Light the candles, placing them one on each side of the chalice.
❖ Place your divination tools and papers in between the candles with the chalice above them.
❖ Hold your hands over your divination tools or papers and say:

> *Goddess of Justice, Goddess of Law*
> *Bless my working here today*
> *Goddess of Honour, Goddess of Power*
> *Show me the answer that I seek,*
> *Through these tools I bid you speak.*

❖ Take three sips of the juice.
❖ Do whatever you have to do with your tools

– shuffle the cards and lay them out, lay out the runes, ask your questions of the pendulum.

❖ Sit quietly with the papers and if necessary reread them, knowing the answer will come to you.

❖ When you are finished, stand with your arms raised and say:

May the gods be thanked
May they aid me with their guidance.

❖ The candles do not have to burn out, but can be used for another divinatory spell.

You will not necessarily receive all the information you need immediately, but can expect to receive insights over a period. The spell can be reactivated very easily by holding your divinatory tools or the papers and repeating the last three lines of the first invocation.

The 'clair' senses

It is fair to say that the general consensus of opinion is that it is wiser not to set out deliberately just to develop the psychic senses such as clairvoyance (clear seeing) clairaudience (clear hearing of information) or clairsentience (clear feeling). If they develop naturally as part of your spiritual progression, then so be it.

Because there is such a fine line between our accepted everyday physical reality and the more spiritual – perhaps magical – realm, the medical world has difficulty in accepting that the development of altered perception is something which can be natural and desirable. It will therefore tend to see any evidence of the development of psychic ability, even when carefully managed, as a sickness and will attempt to 'treat' the problem. It requires a fair degree of discipline – if not courage – to continue on the path of development in the face of such disbelief.

Development of the siddhis

The yogis believe that there are three separate aspects to the development of the powers, or siddhis. They first arise from the 'warrior' aspect, which is principally connected with the physical realm in which we live. Five qualities are developed and are as follows:

• Knowing the past, present and future.
• Being able to be beyond duality and not needing to suffer pleasure/pain, cold/heat, soft/hard. All are equal.
• Knowing the way the mind works and being able to work with dreams.
• Being able to control the effect of fire, wind, water, poisons, weapons and the sun.
• Winning battles and being invincible.

The second aspect only becomes apparent in response to concerted efforts to develop the more subtle energies associated with the emotions. It can be seen that many of these powers are what might be called magical:

• Physical concerns have no effect on the body. The mind does not get confused and emotional conflicts, old age and death have little effect on the body.
• The individual is able to know what has been said, no matter how far away the speaker is. This is what is sometimes known as 'far viewing'.
• The novice learns to 'see' events and outcomes at all levels of existence. Thus they can assess the overall effect of an action.
• The body is capable of travelling at the speed of thought to any place. This is astral projection.
• The individual is able to shapeshift and thus to assume any form. There must be good intent behind this.
• There is an ability to have complete empathy with another person and eventually, spirit. This signals the beginning of trance mediumship, can be quite dangerous and should only be practised in the company of an adept.
• The initiate is able to die when he so desires and death has no meaning.
• There is an ability to see the 'sports of gods' and be able to participate in those games. For a warrior race, this would have similarities to being able to enter Valhalla and consort with the gods.
• The individual develops the ability to attain whatever is desired. (This gift has to be treated with respect, since often you can get more than you bargained for.)

• Obstacles, physical or otherwise, tend to melt into thin air and life is much easier to manage.

The third group of powers, while seemingly to do with control of the physical, are actually rather more spiritual gifts, where the physical has little relevance. They are considered to be the highest siddhi powers:

• The reduction of one's form to one atom gives invisibility.
• The body weight can be made to be very heavy.
• The body can be made light enough to levitate.
• Each respective organ is sensed in its entirety.
• To perceive other realms and those things not normally visible.
• To control the forces of nature and arouse specific energies in others.
• To have complete control over the physical senses, thereby arousing the subtle aspects.
• To achieve joy and tranquillity simply by willing it to be so. All misery and desires are meaningless. This last quality is the one that is most sought after and most difficult to obtain but is the highest state of bliss.

Highly sensitive people are often able to use their skills to 'read' for others in ways that seem quite strange to the ordinary layman. Healing and the laying on of hands is one such art that is today widely accepted. It is more than possible that phrenology and the need to understand the way the mind works, developed in this way.

Phrenology

DEVELOPED BY Franz Joseph Gall in the early 19th century, phrenology did contribute to medical science by first putting forward the theory that certain brain areas have localized specific functions, although it has today been largely discredited. Its basic premise is that the brain is an organ of the mind. The idea that since each individual develops their faculties differently, this will be reflected in the overall shape of the skull, and differences in bone structure in specific areas, is not now widely accepted. As with so many of the pseudosciences during the Victorian era, 'reading the bumps' was something of a recreational pastime.

Phrenology focuses on personality and character – as does astrology – and, in the study of cranial irregularities, has similarities to physiognomy. This was the study of facial features and the division of attributes into animal types, first used by the ancient Greeks.

A competent spiritual healer will often use the laying on of hands to channel energy to a specific problem, and a working knowledge of the various positions discovered through the study of phrenology can help with the accuracy of such activity.

Divination is an extremely complex subject, crossing the dividing lines as it does between magic, science and religion. In order to understand the latter, it is necessary to explore systems of belief as they have developed over the centuries – and this follows in the next chapter.

Mysticism and Magic

Human beings have sought spiritual knowledge and explanations for the meaning of life since time began. Magic was initially a way of explaining the unexplainable, but as time went on it became a way of making use of powers that are not always explicable or controllable. When the unexplainable happens, we devise rituals; these are ways of imposing order and seeking knowledge, either from those who have greater knowledge than ourselves or from within ourselves. As human beings, we have three basic drives that need satisfying: pleasure, knowledge, and survival. When we have combined these to our own satisfaction, we are able to develop mysticism – a sense of being connected with whatever we choose to call the Divine.

Exploring Mysticism

WHEN WE SEEK knowledge of deeper inner spiritual truths, we can only be certain of those we experience directly. This intuitive inner approach, to spiritual knowledge and experience of the Divine from within, is known as Gnosticism – the doctrine of salvation by knowledge of the Divine in its purest form.

Most practitioners of magic – whatever traditions they follow – will come across many of the following systems of belief at some point in their search for knowledge. They are the basis on which natural magic is founded. All of these traditions are part of the Western 'mystery' traditions, requiring primarily a philosophical contemplative approach before even attempting or needing to practise spell working. So, for many people in this day and age, their magical workings will contain elements from most of these systems of belief. In terms of knowledge of the Divine, whatever we perceive that to be, magic works when there is an understanding of the guiding principles behind it, and for all of these systems there is an awareness of the power of nature, of God and the interconnectedness of all things.

Neo-Alexandrian Hermeticism

THE SIGNIFICANCE OF the group of Greek writings that together are called the *Corpus Hermeticum* is that, in them, it is seen that man has an ability to achieve immortality through knowledge of the Divine. It is not possible to summarize the concepts in just a few words, but they were thought to be Egyptian in origin.

The writings are believed to take their name from the wisdom of their author, Hermes Trismegistus (Thrice Great), known as Thoth to the Egyptians as far back as 3,000 BCE. At that time, it was not unusual to ascribe such wisdom to one of the gods, though it has now been proved that the actual transcribers of the writings were a group of people writing in the second to third centuries CE, in Alexandria.

Until the Renaissance, the writings were not generally known in the west, but both before and since then, they have formed the basis of much religious and philosophical understanding, including that of Plato and others.

Gnosticism

BY THE TIME OF CHRIST, Gnosticism was simply another embodiment of a very old belief system, going back to at least the 6th century BCE and using what were perceived as various types of 'magic' as its tools. There were many sects within the religion itself, and this diversity of belief is an important facet of Gnosticism.

Gnosticism began to achieve some kind of unity in the early years of the first century CE, in response to the advent of Christianity. While often operating from hidden places, its adherents have ranged from magicians to theologians and alchemists – many of whom were branded over the years by the orthodox Christians, as non-believers and heretics.

The Greek word for knowing through observation or experience is *'gnosis'*. Gnostics used the word to mean 'knowledge gained', not through intellectual discovery, but through personal experience or association, particularly of the Divine. With that meaning, Gnosticism survives in one form or another in the present day.

This knowledge might be translated as 'insight', for gnosis involves an intuitive process of knowing oneself, and by extension knowing human nature and destiny. Such insight involves an understanding of spiritual truths, which can initiate the individual into the more esoteric mysteries, and alerts him to the awareness of the existence of the 'divine spark' within each of us.

A religion of mystery?

It is this 'special knowledge' of God and the Divine spark that allows Gnosticism to be categorized as a mystery religion, though to be fair, it probably did not properly achieve that status until after the birth of Christianity. When we explore the origins of Gnosticism, we find it has part of its roots in Zoroastrianism, a faith which believed in one God and which taught that the world was basically the battleground of two beings, Ahura Mazda, the god of light, creation, goodness and life, and Ahriman, the god of darkness, destruction, corruption, and death.

This duality and conflict between good and evil, or rather two polarities, is an integral part of Gnosticism in its later forms. A similar notion of duality and the balancing of two polarities is to be found somewhere in almost every major ancient religious movement, from both east and west, as we have seen in the section on the I Ching. Another major influence on early Gnosticism was the Dionysian cult and its later offshoot, Orpheanism, which were ecstatic cults.

In exploring Gnosticism, we also discover that Gnostics differed from their orthodox counterparts in their speculations about what occurred before Creation. If a creator god made this universe, then where did he live before that happened? Did he make our universe because he was forced to leave his old one for some reason? And who created God anyway?

The founders of Gnosticism believed in their own supreme transcendent being in one form or another, with a retinue of demigods and their representatives on earth. They had at least one 'exclusive' theory of creation and an account of the origin of good and evil. They later argued the need for an alternative to Judaism's 'jealous god' Jehovah (Jahweh), and at one point Gnosticism came very close to becoming the mainstream Christian church.

The Nag Hammadi Library

It was not until the discovery in 1945 of the lost documents of what has become known as the Nag Hammadi library – a collection of 13 ancient codices containing over 50 texts – that we in the modern day could understand better some of the questions above. The scriptures from Nag Hammadi reveal that Jesus seems to have taught his disciples in more depth than he did the masses, and this is in keeping with the idea that there were three levels of awareness for Gnostics: those who had an inherent knowledge of the mysteries; those who could be brought to an understanding of the mysteries; and those who would accept the teachings almost at face value.

Later Gnostics believed that Jesus had taught the apostles sacred knowledge, which was never put in writing, and which indeed should never have been committed to writing anyway. The disciples themselves were believed to be privy to these secret doctrines, which were open only to the initiated, and then only after the 'outer mysteries' or publicly acknowledged teachings had been mastered.

There are several categories of information within the Nag Hammadi writings, but perhaps two of the most important are the liturgical and initiatory texts and those writings dealing primarily with the feminine aspect of God and the spiritual principle, known as the Divine Sophia or Wisdom. In the Gnostic creation myths it is Sophia, as the last emanation of the transcendent God, who makes a mistake and creates the Demiurge – a vengeful, negative, egotistical, creator God. She must then set about putting right that mistake, ultimately achieving union with the Christ figure, in order to offer salvation and a way back to purity.

Gnosticism developed a unique understanding of the feminine aspects within divinity, something we see once again becoming increasingly apparent in the modern day, in a fresh appreciation of the Goddess and Mother Earth. The Gnostic images and myths of both the serpent and the labyrinth are as potent today as they were prior to the time of Christ. Indeed, the rich imagery of Gnostic beliefs and the iconography that evolved, has given rise to much symbolism, which has come down to us even today and thus has kept the spirit of Gnosticism alive.

Sophia herself, as the principle of feminine wisdom, is once again receiving the veneration she deserves as women worldwide continue to find their voices and understand their sexuality, and even androgyny takes on a new meaning when looked at from a spiritual perspective. Even in the modern-day world of pop music and media, there are instances of Gnostic belief surfacing and as time goes on, more and more people are beginning to appreciate the magical, spiritual and cosmic significance of this ancient system of thought.

Kabbalah

THE WORD 'KABBALAH', whether spelt with a K, C or Q, is derived from the Hebrew Qblh, the literal interpretation of which is 'an unwritten or oral tradition', from the Hebrew verb *qbl* – 'to receive'. There has been a resurgence of interest in the spiritual component of Kabbalah in the last ten years, it being particularly appreciated by people associated with the media – modern disseminators of information.

A Kabbalist may be described as a student of the hidden meaning of Scripture, which he interprets by the aid of what is known as the 'symbolical' Kabbalah. It is this symbolism that is studied at great length by sages from all religions. Nowadays, Christian Kabbalah refers mainly to the interpretation from a Christian perspective of what might be considered to be the occult – hidden – part of the Kabbalah. Much of its esoteric thought dates from the late 12th century and many rituals associated with Kabbalah form the basis for modern magic.

Broadly, the idea of emanation or manifestation (such a large part of spell working) is central to both Western Kabbalistic and alchemical belief. Kabbalah combines both philosophical and magical thought and in fact does not see them as being very different. Kabbalists believe that creation took place through the process of creation outlined below. Spell making mirrors this process.

When God created, he used what are known to Kabbalists as the three Mother Letters – 'Aleph', 'Mem' and 'Shin'. They are also associated with the first three Elements – Fire, Air and Water. Kabbalists are aware that there

must be movement of the energy within each Element or world, and also perceive that such movement or change in density occurs between each world. This means that the final emanation, or manifestation of energy, from these three into the fourth Element (Earth) has to be treated separately and is seen as the densest manifestation of all.

The world of Air would contain aspects of the world of Fire and in turn, a mixture of Air and Fire would be contained in the world of Water, while Earth would contain characteristics of all three. Therefore, Earth is a product – for want of a better word – from a pattern of unity (oneness), reflection (making two) then division or reharmonizing on a denser level. A little thought will show that, in many ways, this is something of a scientific truth, demonstrated particularly in the science of genetics and our modern-day understanding of DNA.

In Kabbalistic belief, successful creation into the denser worlds takes place in a zigzag pattern, by the movement of energy through the ten planes or levels of consciousness known as 'Sephiroth', or spheres of being. Each Sephira or sphere takes on its own unique characteristics and is only a partial, or slightly distorted, reflection of what precedes or follows it. This 'zigzag' of creation is called the 'Lightning Flash', and it is this that the practitioner versed in the Kabbalah uses in his magical practice. In effect, he moves what he wishes to manifest very quickly through the spheres of existence.

Even when we try to explain magic logically, this idea of a stepping down (or speeding up in the case of dematerialization) of energy levels still holds, and though nowadays magic is usefully thought of as making things happen, as a model the Kabbalah is a rich source of study for spell workers.

Platonic beliefs

Plato (427–347 BCE) and his student Aristotle gave a slightly different viewpoint from the Kabbalistic belief, introducing the idea of a *scala natura* – the scale of nature. Their belief was that the godhead was a source of abundance, which created successive life-forms in a hierarchical structure. However, the farther these forms are from the source, the less access there is to the very subtle life energy. The lowest in the hierarchical order is matter without structure, followed by rocks, plants, insects, animals, man, and finally spiritual and divine beings.

This whole idea of the 'Great Chain of Being', consisting of a vast number of links ranging from the most simple form of existence to the best possible and most perfect, continued right through the Middle Ages. Until the scientific thought of the 17th and 18th centuries turned the principle around, to recognize other models of creation out of which grew modern philosophical thought. Interestingly, Plato's concept is very close to the idea of refining the energy through successive incarnations seen in Hindu belief.

Philosophia Occulta

HEINRICH CORNELIUS AGRIPPA (1486–1535) was one of the most influential writers about magic at the time of the Renaissance. He called magic 'the most perfect and chief Science, that sacred and sublimer kind of philosophy and lastly the most absolute perfection of all most excellent philosophy'. His extensive writings form most of the basis of Western occultism, and still have relevance today.

He also divided philosophy into natural, mathematical and theological teachings, writing *Three Books of Occult Philosophy* to explain his theories. The first book deals with the world composed of the four Elements, Fire, Air, Water and Earth – the material world. The second deals with the celestial world – the Zodiac and the heavenly bodies . And the third deals with the spiritual world of angels, intelligences and ideas. Agrippa himself confessed that he was attempting to rescue ancient magic from charlatans and imposters. On a somewhat lighter note, Agrippa has recently appeared in the Harry Potter series of books.

Alchemy

ALCHEMY IS ALSO based on the belief that there are four basic Elements – Fire, Air, Earth and Water – and three essentials: salt, sulphur and mercury. It is said that ancient Chinese and Egyptian occult literature is the foundation upon which alchemy is based, not least that of the *Corpus Hermeticum.* Great symbolic and metaphysical systems have been built from these seven aspects (the Elements and essentials) of alchemy.

Alchemy is an occult art and called by some a pseudoscience – a set of ideas based on theories put forth as scientific, when they are not. The great alchemical work is to refine any chosen substance back to its original components, until its essence or life force is discovered and the alchemist learns the meaning of life, or rather how life manifests – how undifferentiated energy takes on its various forms.

Scientific fact or magical fiction?

As scientific methods came into being, there was a whole system built up, to discover how the four basic Elements combined and separated to form new substances. In fact, alchemy is the foundation on which the study of chemistry is based. Its main goals have been to learn how to transmute, to heal and to transcend the ordinary.

As time went on, it was realized that the search for the elixir of life had parallels with the search for the understanding of the human psyche – the essence of being – and that search still goes on today. Homeopathy and aromatherapy, which both use very subtle energies, in many ways owe their origin to the principles of alchemy. What was seen as magical in the early days has now become part of accepted thought, though the principles of life and manifestation (magic) are still not widely understood.

The acclaimed 17th-century seer Nostradamus, who is now thought by some to have been an alchemist, states quite clearly how he attempted to put himself in contact with greater powers or energies. In his first two quatrains (verses) he states:

1

Sitting alone at night in secret study;
It is placed on the brass tripod.
A slight flame comes out of the emptiness and
Makes successful that which should not be believed
in vain.

2

The wand in the hand is placed in the middle of the
tripod's legs.
With water he sprinkles both the hem of his
garment and his foot.
A voice, fear: he trembles in his robes.
Divine splendour; the God sits nearby.

Today we can appreciate this as a way of raising consciousness to achieve an energy which is usable in magical work. Below is a slightly more modern way of achieving the same purpose.

Raising the Power

This technique is similar to that used when you prepare your sacred space for magical working and employs the four Elements as a basis. Brass, was, and is, considered to be a conductor of subtle energies.

YOU WILL NEED

White candle
Brass candlestick
Bowl filled with water
Sea salt in suitable container
Wand

METHOD

❖ Place the candle in the candlestick and light it.
❖ Dip your hands in the water then, without drying them, in the salt. Rub your hands together lightly until they feel slightly warm.
❖ Pick up your wand in your most powerful hand and touch the tip lightly to the brass candlestick. Then place the tip of the wand in your other hand, thus completing a circuit.
❖ Sit quietly and contemplate the candle, allowing the energies to flow through you until such times as you either feel a change in energy within yourself or sense that you have no further need to continue.

You may then use the energy that you have generated to meditate, heal or care for others.

Over the years, the alchemist's search for the elixir of life has given rise to much misunderstanding because the original goals of alchemy became, in many people's eyes, the practical tasks of turning base metals (like lead or copper) into precious metals (like gold or silver) (transmutation); creating an elixir, potion or metal that could cure all ills (healing); and discovering an elixir that would lead to immortality (transcendence).

It was believed by the early alchemists that there was a magical substance that was capable of transmuting metals to be the universal panacea, and could also serve as the key to immortality. This was called the 'philosopher's stone' and is now considered to be much closer to the idea of the essence of life rather than immortality.

We can think of energy being divided into active and passive power, the active being the energies of life, and the passive the energy of matter. The energy of Life, called variously *Prima Materia* (literally 'first material'), Chaos or *Spiritus Mundi* (Spirit of the Earth), is a mixture of two principles – Fire and Air. Both are active in nature, but Fire is the more active, with Air being slightly more passive; matter, in potential, manifests its energy lower down the scale as Water and Earth.

To understand these ideas better, it is important to remember that these 'Elements' are not chemical or scientific compounds but are philosophical ideas or principles that can be made use of in magic. Extending the principle of emanation, we see that the lower realms of the mineral world, for example, have as their predominant energy Earth, some Water, and very little Air or Fire.

While Kabbalistic ideas of creation move from the more subtle emanation of energy to the denser, alchemical thought shows that we should be able to transmute material from the more dense emanations back to the more subtle, through several processes akin to those used by the early sciences – for instance, distilling gold from base metal. In many ways therefore the two concepts of Kabbalah and alchemy are reflections of each other and, when perceived in the magical context of having an effect on matter, are not dissimilar.

The first person to recognize that each substance had its own 'fingerprint' or signature that made it totally unique, was Paracelsus (1493–1541), whose original name was Theophrastus Bombastus von Hohenheim. A Swiss physician and alchemist, he travelled extensively and – settling nowhere – might be said to have been something of a hermit, trusting to providence; he acquired knowledge of alchemy, chemistry and metallurgy wherever he went. Paracelsus wrote a number of medical and occult works that contained a weird mixture of sound observation and mystical language.

Rosicrucianism

ACCORDING TO THE Rosicrucian legend, the order began with Christian Rosencreutz, who was born in 1378 in Germany. From 1393, he visited Damascus, Egypt and Morocco, where he studied at the feet of several masters of the occult arts. He began the Rosicrucian Order in 1407 when he returned to Germany, initially with three monks from the cloister in which he had been raised, then with eight. Christian Rosenkreutz died in 1484 and was entombed in the *Spiritus Sanctum* (House of the Holy Spirit) he had erected in 1409. Knowledge of his tomb was lost, but it was rediscovered in 1604, when its opening led to a resurgence of interest in the movement.

Rosicrucianism is a traditional and initiatory movement. An individual or small group of individuals who have been properly trained and initiated into the Rosicrucian system, will often work together for a common purpose. This is how some Rosicrucian organizations regained popularity at the beginning of the 20th century. Today there are several Rosicrucian orders.

Modern Rosicrucian groups have different beliefs about Christian Rosencreutz from the early ones. There are those who believe he actually existed as the early documents assert; others see the name as a pseudonym or magical title designed to preserve the anonymity of certain other historic people. Still others view the story as a parable and occult legend that points to a more profound truth.

Deep thinking and philosophy became a pastime for many Rosicrucians. People such as Jacob Boehme (1575–1624) and Louis Claude De Saint Martin (1743–1803) developed their own mystical belief systems. Boehme believed, for instance, that wisdom grew from personal revelation, while Saint Martin developed 'The Inner Way' of reintegration. This 'way' perpetuates a sacred system of initiation, in private, with great secrecy and specific ritual. He developed this 'way' after he had moved away from the technique used by his Rosicrucian peers to achieve their reintegration with the Divine – a technique that involved ceremonial magic.

The Cycles of Life

One aspect of interest, even today, to those who work magic, is the calculation of the Cycles of Life, a core Rosicrucian belief. Broadly, each seven-year period has a particular focus, and if the spell worker is able to attune themselves to these cycles successfully, their spiritual and magical workings can become more successful. This requires quite a feat of memory and there are many good sites on the internet which will give you this information.

Hermetic Order of the Golden Dawn

THE GOLDEN DAWN was a magical fraternity founded in London in 1888 by Dr William Wynn Westcott and Samuel Liddell MacGregor Mathers. It was designed by its founders specifically as a system of magic – not a religion, although religious imagery and spiritual concepts do play an important role in its work, and tolerance for all religious beliefs is stressed. The symbolism used within the Golden Dawn came from a variety of religious sources including Egyptian, Greek, Gnostic,

Judeo-Christian, Masonic and Rosicrucian. A requirement of the Hermetic Order is an ongoing study of the Kabbalah, astrology, the psychic arts or siddhis, alchemy and Egyptian magic among other things.

Although the society itself only lasted in its original form for a few years, today it is still an outstanding learning tool and people from many diverse religious paths would call themselves Golden Dawn magicians.

Shamanism

ALL OF THE ABOVE systems of belief are philosophical in origin, based on deep thinkers trying to make sense of the meaning of life. They resonate with the times in which they began. Pre-dating such philosophy was a perhaps more instinctive response by man to his surroundings – the practice of shamanism.

From archaeological and anthropological evidence, we know today that the practice of shamanism has existed for thousands of years, perhaps since the beginning of the human race. It has been around certainly since the Stone Age, and is still practised today. Shamanism attempts to bring in good fortune and drive out misfortune, to manage a duality that can cause distress. Yet, insofar as ritual is concerned, it shows a unique religious form in which the shaman contacts the deities spiritually, using singing and dancing in a largely spontaneous way. It is a practice that brings divination and healing together as its main components.

Evidence of shamanism has been found in all parts of the world. Particularly in isolated regions, it has survived almost unscathed and as a result the modern world is now coming to a better appreciation of the beliefs of the ancient tribes of the Americas, Asia, Africa and regions of Europe and Australia.

Shamanic Beliefs

Although there are differences of ritual found among the various peoples, there are some startling similarities. There is what has become known as the 'shamanic state of consciousness'

or 'ecstatic trance'. In the full shamanic state, the shaman (literally meaning 'he who knows') has various powers that he does not normally possess. He sees spirits and souls, and communicates with them; he makes magical flights to the heavens, where he serves as intermediary between the gods and his people; and he descends to the underworld, the land of the dead. He thus puts himself in touch with information not available to him in a non-trance state. Without this change of consciousness, the shaman will not be able to perform all the assignments and responsibilities he is called upon to carry out appropriate to his status.

This ability sets him apart from priests and adepts of non-shamanic persuasion, though some of the Christian sects, which rely on speaking in tongues, show a similar ability. In his altered states of consciousness the shaman remains in control, is capable of perceiving non-worldly realities, and is happy to act as a go-between among the various states of reality.

So that the shaman can access the shamanic state when required, he learns certain practices that help him to do so. He integrates singing and dancing into a standardized ritual, where he contacts his gods by dancing and placates them through singing. His practices include rhythmic activities such as drumming, rattling and chanting, purification rituals – isolation in darkness, sweat baths and sexual abstinence – and gaining greater mental control over his own 'inner' environment by, for instance, staring at a flame or concentrating on imagery. Some societies use psychedelic drugs for this purpose, though most claim drugs are not essential, perhaps even harmful.

The shaman accepts that he has access to three worlds – earth, sky and the underworld. They are connected by a central alignment represented by a World Pillar, World Tree or World Mountain. This same idea resurfaces in the tenets of the Kabbalah, with its Tree of Life.

Remaining lucid throughout all of his experiences, the shaman has various abilities that are not apparent in ordinary reality. He can ascend to the heavens, using mythical animals or by shape shifting (actually a type of change of consciousness similar to the ones seen in

Celtic practices), and he can descend to the underworld. In both places he can communicate with spirits and souls, and he can also act as intermediary between the gods and his tribe.

Central to the belief of the shaman is the idea that he (or she) has a guardian spirit, usually an animal or plant. In a 'vision quest', most often used by Native Americans, the initiate seeking his totem animal either deliberately goes into a 'trance' state or has a vivid dream in which his guardian spirit manifests. Sometimes he receives advice directly from the Great Spirit.

Traditionally, shamans are called to their profession in two ways: by heredity or by spontaneous and involuntary election by the supernatural beings, this often being the way in which women became shamans. In this day and age it is permitted to seek out shamanic training, but traditionalists are aware that these individuals may not be considered as powerful as those who have inherited the ability. This is believed to be because, for many, contact with other worlds is not considered normal within their culture and is therefore a learned response and perhaps therefore less powerful. Many such seekers will, however, undertake a vision quest assisted by an initiated shaman, thus gaining knowledge of the relevant world. The vision quest provides the average individual, not just the 'medicine man', with access to spiritual realms for help.

The Vision Quest

In more primitive societies vision quests are usually undertaken by males, often as part of the rites of passage during puberty. Such quests exert a huge influence on the individual on his way to maturity. They provide a focus, sense of purpose, personal strength and power. Initially, since for most tribes power was to be obtained for hunting and fighting, only the male could be a shaman, and his ability was measured by the larger number of his guardian spirits, by the intensity of his vision and by his greater power. Some tribes do have minor rites for girls to acquire guardian spirits, and as shamanism spreads it is now much more acceptable for women to be shamans, particularly within the healing traditions.

Most vision quests are solitary undertakings, but some are performed on a collective basis. Usually, sweat-bath purification rites precede the vision quest. Most Native Americans also believe that the vision seeker should abstain from sex for a period prior to his quest.

The individual goes either alone or with his mentor into the wilderness to a sacred place where he may fast, abstain from liquid, pray and 'meditate' for a vision – that is, he deliberately induces a change in consciousness. This vigil can continue for several days and nights. During this time he meets his guardian spirit, who empowers him with magical strength.

When seeking a guardian spirit, the individual most often asks to be given certain qualities or abilities, such as for hunting or healing. Vision quests are also undertaken in times of war, disease, death, and childbirth (to seek instructions for naming the child), in other words, occasions that affect the whole community.

In imparting powers, the guardian spirit may prescribe food taboos (for example in ancient Celtic lore it was forbidden for the hero Cuchullin to eat the flesh of a dog and for the bard Ossian to eat venison) and give instructions for adornment (such as shells, feathers, stones and robes) and for the assembly of the personal medicine bundle or talisman bag.

The medicine bundle might contain an unusual rock, strand of hair, feather, bird's beak, animal skin, sweetgrass, and so on. Each item in the bundle has a special meaning to the owner. It is a very precious possession, which represents a person's spiritual life and possesses powers for protection and healing. As the owner grows older more items might be added. By tradition, medicine bundles are buried with the owner when he dies or are passed on to a friend. In earlier times, a tribal medicine bundle was much larger; it was opened only on special occasions and contained special objects that could be handled only by certain members of the tribe.

On a personal level, the guardian spirit may teach a song or chant, which is used to reconnect the shaman with his guardian at any given time – almost like a self-hypnosis – and the spirit also serves as the shaman's alter ego, giving him animal power. This is very similar to the power of the magician in Celtic magic. The guardian spirit usually appears in animal form, though it may later change to human form, and becomes then similar to the spiritualistic concept of a guide.

All the instructions received by the individual must be followed to the letter or it is thought they will lose the power of the animal. The spirit will usually leave behind a physical token of the vision, such as a feather or claw, or will manifest some symbol that the new shaman may use. Sometimes the shaman cannot handle the magnitude of the energy, or feels it to be wrong or unsuitable, in which case a further attempt will be made later to contact the guardian.

Totem Animals

The belief in spirits in the form of animals comes from a strong conviction that animals and humans were once related. So within an altered state of consciousness, such as during ecstatic dancing, the shaman assumes the form and power of his favoured animal and then is able to perform his duties. He sees the animal, talks to it, and uses it to help him achieve his aims. The guardian's task is to escort the shaman through the underworld or to be with him in his ascent to the skies. The animal spirit is never harmful to the shaman, though he may stretch the individual's powers to the limit.

Guardian spirits may also protect an entire tribe or clan with the collective or individual power of the animal, when they are known as totem spirits. Totem guardian spirits are part of Native American culture, especially among the tribes along the northwest coast. Different totem animals are sacred to each particular tribe; no member of that tribe is permitted to kill a bear if that is the tribe's totem animal, but the tribe may use the flesh or skin of its totem if it is killed by another tribe.

Listed below are some significances according to shamanic traditions, for power and totem animals.

Ant Industrious and hardworking.
Badger Courageous.
Bear Guardian of the world, watcher, inner knowing, healing.

Buffalo Possesses great strength.
Crow Justice and fair dealings.
Deer Compassionate. Physical pacing, grace.
Dog Loyalty, guardian.
Dolphin Wise and happy, explores deep emotion, psychic abilities, initiator.
Dragon Rich. Qualities of fire, knowing the answer to many universal riddles.
Dragonfly Imagination, breaks through illusions thus gaining power through dreams. Teaches higher aspirations.
Eagle Expectation of power, high ideals, spiritual philosophy.
Fish Graceful, going with the flow.
Fox Elusiveness, agility, cleverness, sometimes deviousness.
Hawk All seeing, perception, observation, focus, protection.
Heron Intuition, organization.
Horse Freedom, stability. Courage.
Hummingbird Fierce warrior. Pleasure.
Jaguar Wisdom of the shaman, focused power.
Lion Nobility, symbol of the Sun. Protects through courage.
Lizard Vision.
Lynx Keeper of confidential information, perspicacity.
Mouse Innocence, faith, trust. An eye for detail.
Owl Symbolic wisdom, works with the Shadow, keeper of silence, riddler, beloved of Athena.
Panther A good, protective animal, suggesting the feminine.
Puma Shaman's companion on journeys to the other worlds, spirit of grace and silent power. Strength, elusiveness.
Rabbit Faith, fertility, nurturing.
Raven Inner journeys, dreams. Mystery, through sometimes the Trickster, messenger and watcher for the Gods.
Snake Transformation.
Spider Fate, weaver of destiny.
Stag Masculine power of regeneration, giver of spiritual gifts, beauty and mystical signs.
Swan Guide into dreamtime, dignity.
Turtle Shyness.
Wolf Earth wisdom, protection. Leader of the Way. Knowledge.

Meeting with your Totem Animals, Spirit and Spirit Guides

When you feel ready to meet your own totem animal, your concept of your Higher Self or your Spirit Guide, all of which operate on an internal level within your psyche, you might like to try a gentle technique such as the following:

1. Decide what will be the focus of this particular meeting and form a statement of intent such as 'I wish to meet my personal totem animal' or 'I wish to meet my Spirit Guide'.

2. Think very carefully about how your life might be changed by this meeting, but try not to have too many expectations.

3. Visualize a scenario where it would be possible for you to meet the entity you have chosen. Imagine how you would feel were you able to have such a meeting.

4. Allow yourself to drift into a meditative state, knowing that in due course the meeting will take place. Sometimes the animal will present itself in sleep after you have performed this exercise.

In shamanic societies it is the power of the animal which is more important than the actual animal itself. Totems are often representations of these mystical powers, which are very good at giving sensible advice. The ability to make links with your animals needs a good deal of practice, but the following is a spell that can be used to strengthen the contact you wish to have. It is deliberately called a spell rather than a technique because it contains many elements of candle, crystal and herb magic rather than pure shamanism.

Linking with your Totem Animal

Linking with your personal power animal initiates access to realms hitherto denied you. By consciously making a link with your personal animal, you open the way to a deeper understanding of the spiritual realms, aided by the sandalwood and backed up by the energy of the crystal.

YOU WILL NEED

White altar candle
Sandalwood anointing oil in a small bottle
Picture or ornament of your totem animal
Citrine or amber crystals
Blue taper candle
Your burin

METHOD

✤ Put the crystals on your altar to enhance the energy. Light the white candle.

✤ Charge the anointing oil with the energy you require in order to meet with your animal, whether that is knowledge, good fortune or, for instance, the gift of clairvoyance (clarity of perception).

✤ When you think the oil is fully charged, put the bottle on your altar and spend a minute or two breathing deeply in and out. As you inhale, see white light enter your body and surround all negative energy. (This may be physical pain, emotional trauma or spiritual distress.) When you exhale, see this negativity leave your body. When you feel it has all gone, be sure to breathe in positive white light to fill up the 'spaces' left.

✤ When you feel fully relaxed, focus on the candle flame and see yourself meeting your totem animal.

✤ Inscribe your birth number (see pages 132-134) at the top of the blue candle before putting the candle back in its holder.

✤ Rub some of the charged oil on the palms of your hands. Feel the energy with which you charged the oil warming your hands, then take the blue candle, hold it horizontally in front of you, and anoint it with the oil, drawing the oil from the centre to the tip towards you then turning it round and continuing in the same way. (This is to forge a link between the spiritual and physical realms, that of your totem animal and your own.)

✤ Focusing on achieving your desired result, hold the candle in the air above the image of the animal, rolling the candle backwards and forwards between the palms of your hands. As you do so, repeat:

Candle's power and animal mine
In this ritual now combine

Bring to me my heart's desire,
Powered by this magic fire.

❖ Light the blue candle and let it to burn down if you can, but watch the flame carefully and be aware of the changes in the flame. It may flare up or die down, and as you become more proficient you will be able to read the significance of this. (See Signs from Candle Burning on page 30.) You will probably feel more in touch with your totem animal as the candle flares up, but this is very individual.

❖ If you have to extinguish the candle, do so with a candle snuffer or between finger and thumb, and only use the candle again for the same purpose.

This animal acts as your guide when journeying in the spirit realms for yourself or others, so it pays to spend time developing trust not just in the animal itself but also in the links between you. You will find another spell on page 347 which deepens this contact and allows you to journey with the animal.

NATIVE AMERICAN TRIBES

The ceremonies and rituals of Native American tribes show a similar train of thought to other shamanic societies in the acceptance of animal representation, but have a development all of their own. Tribal belief does vary somewhat, although the basic elements are the same from tribe to tribe. For instance, the Arapaho, Arikara, Asbinboine, Cheyenne, Crow, Gros, Ventre, Hidutsa, Sioux, Plains Cree, Plains Ojibway, Sarasi, Omaha, Ponca, Ute, Shoshone, Kiowa, and Blackfoot Native American tribes all practised the Sun Dance.

The Sun Dance

The Sun Dance ceremony of these Plains Indians (containing three distinct groupings – northern, central and southern) celebrate slightly different beliefs. Some hold that the ceremony celebrates the creation story, but this is not part of the Shoshone belief. The Shoshone hold that the Sun Dance lodge, a sacred space formed in honour of the ceremony, is a representation of the cosmos. A Christian interpretation of the Sun Dance ritual was attempted in the 19th century, but it could only be interpreted as a ritual to restore health and could not easily be adapted to suit Christian thought.

Although the Sun Dance was outlawed in 1904, a number of tribes have relatively recently attempted to revive it in its original form and meaning, not just as a tourist attraction. As interest grows worldwide in natural magic, the true beauty and intrinsic significance of the ritual becomes more and more apparent. The Sun Dance originally safeguarded the coming year by re-creating the story of creation in much the same way as the Sabbat rituals do in Celtic belief (see pages 196-204).

As a sacred space, the Sun Dance lodge is a symbol of the world – a microcosm within a macrocosm – and is used to heal people in an environment where human interference cannot take place. The lodge is left to decay naturally after the four-day ceremony and must not be destroyed by any human agency. When the lodge is first constructed, the central pole is a cottonwood tree that has been particularly chosen and brought home with special ceremonies. It is the channel between people and God and can be seen as the World Tree or the Tree of Life. The Sun Dance facilitates a change of consciousness where visions and wisdom can be received. The tree, or rather a pole representing the central tree, is an integral part of shamanic belief being the connection between the spiritual and physical realms.

The Sun Dance symbolizes a resolution of the conflict between having to kill and eat buffalo to survive and viewing them as wise and powerful, even closer to the creator than humans. A buffalo head is attached at the top of the central pole to represent all game.

The natural course to the Plains Indians, since they believed that the buffaloes gave themselves to them for food, would be to make some sacrifice in return out of gratitude. Thus the sacrifice of the dancers through fasting, thirst and self-inflicted discomfort, also allows them to return something of themselves to nature.

Making the buffalo sacred, symbolically giving new life to it, means that treating it with respect and reverence is a kind of reconciliation. The Plains Indians believed that without the buffalo there would be death, and that the buffalo not only provided them with physical well-being, but kept their souls alive too.

The eagle also plays a large part in the Sun Dance and is a most sacred totem. The eagle flies high, being the creature closest to the Sun. Therefore it is the link between man and spirit, being the messenger that delivers prayers to the Wakan-Tanka (god). The eagle's nest, which is fixed just below the buffalo's head on the central pole, signifies the chief of the birds. Together the buffalo and eagle stand for the two levels of the universe: earth and sky.

Etiquette of the ceremony

There are various preparatory rituals which take place prior to the ceremony proper and after the last preliminary dance. Those taking part in the ceremony camp close to the lodge in a wide circle with the lodge at its centre.

On the first day of the actual ceremony the (male) dancers prepare by painting their faces and arms red with black spots. On the second day, yellow paint or clay is used. The hair is braided, sometimes with other decorations; the use of feathers usually indicates that the dancer has a guardian spirit. An eagle bone whistle is worn round the neck along with a tribal necklace containing eagle down. This down is also attached to the little finger of each hand, presumably to signify allegiance to the eagle as totem. The men are naked from the waist up but wear a richly decorated garment similar to an apron.

As the evening star rises on the first day of the ceremony, about 40 dancers march into the lodge and move to the back. Drummers then enter and sit at the front left (the south east). The ceremonial leader stands by the centre pole and asks Tam Apo – Our Father or Supreme Being – for his blessing. Songs are then sung, each repeated four times, the end of each signalled by the blowing of eagle bone whistles. The dancing is a monotonous kind of shuffle designed to induce a trancelike state. The dancers turn their faces towards the east, in the direction of the rising Sun.

The Shoshone name for the Sun Dance is 'dry-standing-dance'. Only short breaks are allowed during the three days of its duration and the dancers must fast and drink nothing for this period. As in the vision quest, this suffering is intended to make the supernatural forces show mercy and enable the dancers to heal their people. It is when the Shoshone are in the trance state towards the end of the Sun Dance that supernatural powers are most likely to be forthcoming.

On the second day, at dawn, single or pairs of dancers begin to dance. At sunrise all the dancers form five lines behind the centre pole. There is a great noise made with drumming and whistling; the dancers greet the Sun by stretching their hands towards it. With great attention, morning prayers are listened to before the dancers take care of their own physical needs. This ritual is repeated every day of the ceremony, as is the painting of the dancers which takes place each morning.

Now the healing rites begin. Intense drumming and dancing takes place about 10 o'clock and lasts about an hour, presumably to raise the vibration, before the people to be healed are brought into the lodge. They are treated by the medicine man at the centre pole. The injuries are brushed by the medicine man with an eagle wing to symbolize transference of the power from the World Tree – the centre pole. The healing of the sick and the blessing of the dancers both appear to be the same process, designed to offer support and supernatural power as necessary.

The third day is the hardest and most powerful. Medicine bags, which contain herbs and revered objects, are brought out and sacred pipes are passed around. Healing rites are generally performed when the Sun is in the ascendancy. The dancing, drumming and noise-making is more intense than ever and where the dancers feet have worn tracks, the pattern can be clearly seen. The third day is often when more vivid and sacred visions appear to the dancers; those that still have the energy to dance often have more intense visions, but by now many people lie on the ground, completely exhausted from the continuous dancing.

The dancers taking part are blessed on the fourth day at the centre pole, but the healings and blessings stop promptly at midday. Gifts, be they money, furs or blankets, are offered to the medicine man who, in the late afternoon, pours some water onto the ground while facing east, as an offering to Mother Earth. The resting dancers are then given some of the water, the first liquid to pass their lips since the dance started.

The gifts are then passed out to the women for distribution, though some are placed at the base of the pole as an offering. There is then a great feast with much energetic dancing in the evening or – as often happens – the participants are given time to refresh themselves and the feast may well take place on the following evening.

By looking at all the symbolism and ritual involved with the Sun Dance, we can see natural magic in operation. All parts of nature are linked together and are dependent on one another. Everything has a right to existence and can lend its energy to a greater whole. The changes of consciousness which occur in the dancers allow access to the power of animals, who reveal their physical and spiritual powers to the ordinary man as much as they do to the medicine man and initiated shaman.

The Sun Dance shows the continuity that there is in life. It suggests that there is no true end to life, but that there is a cycle of death and rebirth in which everything takes part. The Sun Dance carries the message that humans must give of themselves to help keep the cycles of regeneration going.

OTHER NATIVE AMERICAN RITUALS
Another example of Native American customs, which have been adopted by westerners searching for a different type of spirituality, is the sacred pipe ceremony.

There is a beautiful legend that the original sacred pipe was brought to two Lakota warriors by the White Buffalo Calf Woman, anything up to 2,000 years ago. It is said that she taught them how to pray and gave the Lakota people seven sacred ceremonies and a bountiful way of life involving the buffalo. When the woman left, she turned into a white buffalo calf. She also promised to return.

The first of the ceremonies was the purification ceremony known as the sweat lodge; the second was the child-naming ceremony; the third was the healing ritual; the fourth was the acceptance of relatives or the adoption ceremony; the fifth was the marriage ceremony; the sixth was the vision quest, and the seventh was the Sun Dance. Today, people working in a shamanic way have chosen to adopt some of these ceremonies.

Lately there has been conflict over whether non-Native Americans should be allowed access to the sacred ceremonies. Many feel that it is time for Native Americans to reclaim their right to the sacred pipe. Abuse of its ceremonies by those who refuse to follow stringent ceremonial protocols, has reached the dangerous point where some feel the spirit world may abandon the pipe. Should westerners choose to adopt such customs in their magical workings, they must ensure that they give due deference to centuries-old beliefs and do nothing that can cause distress, or any other form of difficulty, to those whose beliefs have been handed down generation to generation through oral tradition.

However, many practitioners will find, in common with Native Americans, that suitable rituals, information and knowledge are received in dreams. As you become more immersed in the culture and customs, you too may well receive this intuitive information. Treat this as a gift, not a right.

All rituals suggested here that are adapted from older cultures approximate as closely as possible to the original intent of the ceremonies. Below are suggestions for two incenses which may help to re-create an atmosphere that is conducive to working in a shamanic way.

Mexican Magic Incense

2 parts copal resin
1 part frankincense resin
1 part rosemary

This incense is particularly suitable for use in Mexican and American-based folk magic rituals and spells.

❋ Nine Woods Incense ❋

1 part rowan wood (or sandalwood)
1 part dogwood
1 part poplar
1 part juniper
1 part cedar
1 part pine
1 part holly branches
1 part elder (or oak)

METHOD

✤ Take the sawdust of each of the above, mix together and burn indoors on charcoal when a ritual fire is necessary or desired but not practical.

The incense emits the aroma of an open campfire and is particularly good when working shamanically or with the Spirit of Nature.

Shamans in the East

In Northern Siberia and the Far East, shamanism developed slightly differently; it was based on a more dualistic conception of the universe, and showed a number of mythological and cult forms. The natural world had its parallels in the spiritual world, each level of which was inhabited by spiritual beings. Again the shaman, a pivotal figure, acted as an intermediary between them. His clothing and paraphernalia were particularly important as part of his ritualized entry into the other worlds. His clothing symbolized animals and birds found in the spirit world, which helped him to communicate with them, his tambourine summoned his ancestor spirit upon whom he rode, and his head-dress and warder, a symbol of authority, characterized the centre of the universe.

Other figures of birds, beasts, reptiles, fantastic creatures and anthropomorphic figures of wood, fur and metal called *ongons,* which are dwelling places for shamans' helper spirits, are used to form a circular structure that symbolizes the universe and the cycle of birth, death and rebirth. The *ongons* are an essential tool of Siberian shamans and are most often taken with the shaman when he or she goes to the location of a ritual. Another tool of the Siberian shamans

are *shagai,* which are sheep anklebones used for divination as well as for traditional games. Roughly cubical in shape, each side of the bone has a specific name and meaning.

The shamanism of the Siberian peoples has preserved many otherwise archaic forms of worldviews, rituals and artefacts. The Garuda bird, for instance, is the king of the birds, similar to the thunderbird of Native American legend. There is a spirit called Mongoldai Nagts (Mongol Uncle) who guards the entrance to the lower world so that spirits cannot travel back and forth to the upper world without permission. This has distinct similarities to the Doorkeeper in Spiritualist belief, who performs the same function on an individual level.

Celtic Religions

NOWADAYS THERE ARE many magical practices that claim to have their origin in Celtic religions and thought. Many people will wish to carry out research in order to work as closely as possible with the old traditions. It is unfortunate that our modern-day knowledge of Celtic mythology and religion is hampered by misrepresentation, both unintentional and otherwise, by other belief systems. Above all, the Celtic religions were rich in oral tradition and story, only recorded later by Christian monks and others.

By and large, though, the belief systems of the Welsh andthe Irish show remarkable similarities, which are echoed by the Gauls. Their gods and goddesses and the stories about them are similar, their names only varying according to the local dialect – Lugh in Ireland matches Llyr in Wales, for instance. Celtic religion featured many female deities such as mother goddesses and war goddesses. The Mother Goddess of the Celts was often conceived as a warrior, instructing the hero in supernormal secrets of warfare and the arts of transformation. This close cooperation with the Divine arose principally from the observance of the Wheel of the Year (see page 195) and its seasons in nature.

According to the tenets of the Celtic magician, there was – and still is – a unity in nature that allowed for a degree of transmutation between species. The Celtic magician, in attempting to transform him or herself, used willpower in a very focused way and actually tried to assume the form and nature of the person, animal or thing he wished to become – in other words to shape-shift.

So far as other people were concerned, when he wished to transform them he would transfer the characteristics of the animal or being by the use of his will-power, resulting in the target having to adopt the shape of the animal or being. This power could obviously be used for good or evil and has overtones of totemism. The incantations (obaidh) used at this time were recited in verse.

Charms and Enchantments

Among the more potent and important enchantments of the Celts was that known as 'fith fath' or 'fath fith', which was employed to bring about invisibility. Invisibility by the aid of fith fath (pronounced 'fee far') was well known in Ireland. It was said to have been given first to the Tuatha De Danann (the original inhabitants of Ireland) by the god Manannan, whose lordship of the sea gave him power over shifting fogs and the creation of illusion. One of the more recent uses was to fool the excise men on smuggling expeditions. The enchantment went thus:

> *A magic cloud I put on thee,*
> *From dog, from cat,*
> *From cow, from horse,*
> *From man, from woman,*
> *From young man, from maiden,*
> *And from little child.*
> *Till I again return.*

The Celts believed that the witch, fairy, or indeed any woman with supernatural powers, had a bunch of cords made up of nine cow fetters. This burrach, cow fetter or spancel was a cord or thin rope made from horsehair with a loop at one end and a knob at the other for fastening it. These fetters probably later evolved into the nine-knotted 'witch's ladder' – a modern version of which is given below.

The old-style charm associated with this implement especially ensured that a person who was struck, adjured 'by the nine cow-fetters', would carry through any task imposed upon him. The 'wyrd woman', who travelled around the countryside seeking victims, in much the same way as Hecate is said to have done in Greek mythology, would strike him with her deadly cow-fetters which she used when milking deer. Such a blow made the victim so fey that anyone could beat him in combat.

The charm used was as follows:

> *To lay thee under spells and crosses under [pain of being struck by] the nine*
> *Cow-fetters of the wildly roaming, traveller-deluding fairy woman,*
> *So that some sorry little wight [stooge] more feeble and misguided than thyself*
> *Take thy heart, thine ear and thy life's career from thee.*

Wyrd, which of course gives us the word 'weird', was a mysterious force that acted as a kind of fate or fury – a destructive force. This force or power could not be destroyed completely, only avoided on a temporary basis. Any woman having this power was obviously much feared.

In this can be seen the struggle against female authority and power, particularly when that power is used in a malign way. This struggle is epitomized over and over again in the heroes' tales in both Celtic and Anglo-Saxon myth, and through these it is but a short step to a belief in the power of evil in women. Ordinary everyday tasks thus often assumed magical significance. Plaiting and knotting, such traditionally female occupations, developed into a specific kind of magic.

Witch's Ladder Charm

This modern-day charm using plaiting and knotting can be of two types. One is a general-purpose charm for protection and good luck, while the other can be dedicated for a particular intent. Nowadays such an implement incorporates ideas from other cultures as well, such as the feathers or coloured objects. Plaiting, because it makes three strands into one, represents the three aspects of the Triple Goddess – Maid, Mother, Crone – becoming one, suggesting the power of the feminine.

For a General Purpose Charm

If possible, this ladder should be made on the night of a Full Moon for maximum effect.

YOU WILL NEED

White candles

Incense of your choice

Consecrated water (see Consecrating your tools on page 233)

White cord

Red cord

Black cord

Nine feathers or coloured objects to incorporate the following meanings:

Red for physical energy

Blue for knowledge, peace and protection

Yellow for happiness, prosperity and emotions

Green for self-awareness and matters of health

Brown for steadiness and respect for others

Black for mystical insight and wisdom

Grey or white for spiritual harmony and balance

Peacock feathers – or those with specific markings – for protection and clairvoyant abilities

METHOD

❖ Consecrate your sacred space.

❖ Light your candle and incense.

❖ Using about 1 metre (3 ft) of each coloured cord, tie the ends together, plait them and say:

> *Cord of red,*
> *Cord of black,*
> *Cord of white,*
> *Work enchantment here tonight.*

❖ About every 10 cm, knot in the feathers or objects. You can usually tie a secure knot around the feather or object for this purpose.

❖ While doing this, say suitable words, such as, when using yellow:

> *With this feather and this string,*
> *Prosperity this charm will bring.*

❖ Repeat this until the plait is finished and tie a knot at the end.

❖ Tie both ends of the plait together to form a circle.

❖ Pass the finished ladder above the candle flame then through the incense smoke.

❖ Sprinkle the ladder with the consecrated water and say:

> *In the names of the God and the Goddess*
> *By Air, Earth, Fire and Water*
> *I do thee bless.*
> *Of objects nine and cord of three*
> *As I will, so shall it be.*

Hang the ladder in an unobtrusive place, but where you yourself will see it every day.

To make a charm for a specific purpose, the method is the same as that for a general purpose one. The difference comes in ensuring that your cord, objects and/or feathers are geared to your specific purpose. You will probably find that you need only three objects or feathers (representing body, mind and spirit). Let the words flow naturally and do not be too surprised if you find yourself inspired.

Not all spells and charms were as negative as the original nine cow fetters, however. Various stories abound of receiving knowledge through supernatural means, conversations with elves, fairies, leprechauns and other strange occurances, such as finding helpful information unexpectedly at the appropriate times.

The Salmon of Knowledge

The Irish believed in the Salmon of Knowledge, which had acquired its powers through eating the nuts of the sacred hazelnut tree that fell into the well in which it lived. Druids and magicians alike sought this magical fish in the hope of partaking of its flesh. Indeed, Finn McColl, an Irish hero, is said to have caught and cooked the salmon. On burning his thumb, he sucked it and developed the ability to perceive events before they happened – today known as clairvoyance. This story bears a strong resemblance to the Welsh story in which Gwion is burnt by the magical potion he is preparing, much to the displeasure of Ceridwen who intended the potion for her son.

Celtic Art

Prior to the arrival of the Christians, Celtic spiral designs were already in use, commemorating both the Goddess as Mother Earth in her journey from the underworld and also the path that we must take towards enlightenment. Much Celtic art shows this in the form of fantastic animal illustrations. Simple spiral designs developed into more sophisticated ones and then evolved into intricate knotwork that was more labyrinthine than spiral. Sophisticated spirals exist in the same early works where the knotwork and animal designs are still somewhat rudimentary.

Later, the astonishing degree of ornamentation and detail in *The Book of Kells*, a set of illuminations that decorate a translation of the four Gospels in Latin, demonstrates the way that monks of the period (around CE 800) used such artwork as a working meditation – not to the Goddess but for Christian purposes. This labour of love was a true offering to the Divine, yet remained within the traditions of the culture. Art forms often have the ability to link different ways of thinking and belief systems.

Celtic religion and Druidism are often inextricably linked in the minds of many people. They are not necessarily one and the same thing, Celtic religion being based much more in folklore while Druidism was a totally different set of beliefs, with a philosophical background based on an appreciation of natural forces.

Druidism

IT HAS LONG BEEN thought that the word 'Druid' probably came from the Greek *drous*, which means 'oak', therefore suggesting that the Druids would be the priests of the god or gods identified with the oak tree. However, it may also be derived from the word *vid*, meaning 'to know', which would lead one to believe that the Druids were considered to be the wise ones of the community.

The History of the Druids

While Druids are mentioned frequently in ancient scripts, little is truly known of their way of life because their traditions were principally oral and yet secret. In their society they were accepted as the teachers of moral philosophy and science; public and private disputes were referred to them for arbitration. Their authority was as much social as religious and they enjoyed many privileges, including in Gaul – though not in Ireland – exemption from military service and the payment of taxes. Many received great honours.

There were three principal classes of Druids: bards, prophets and priests, although religious teachers, judges and civil administrators would often also be Druids. They were adept at understanding the movement of the planets, the mysterious powers of plants and animals and the art of natural magic. It is for this last reason that they could be considered the wise ones – that is, having knowledge of nature herself. They regarded the oak tree and the mistletoe, especially when the latter grew on oak trees, with great awe, and usually held their rituals in oak forests. These rituals seem also to have been associated with stone circles and other natural groves. The Druids were often assisted by female prophets or sorcerers who did not always enjoy the same powers and privileges.

From evidence unearthed in modern times, it is thought that Celtic Druids may have been the linear descendants of the megalithic builders of the late Neolithic and Bronze Age period in Europe. The Druids were also educators, particularly of the nobility, and it is almost certain that Merlin in the story of King Arthur, rather than being just a magician, was also a Druid. Their instruction was very wide-ranging and far-reaching. One component was the learning by heart of a large quantity of verse, which presumably meant that their memories were honed at the same time as they learned the traditions of their calling and their community. When the Druidic tradition died out in approximately the 1st to 3rd centuries CE, largely as a result of ferocious Roman oppression, their store of bardic sacred songs, prayers, rules of divination and magic was lost. Much of the information we have today comes from translations made at a much later date, often as late as the 13th century.

Julius Caesar noted that the Gauls held a tradition that Druids were of British origin. He had made as extensive a study as he could of the latters' doctrine and concluded that the principal point was that the soul did not die, and that after death it passed from one body into another. Some Greek writers are said to have believed that the Druids had borrowed this idea from the philosopher Pythagoras or one of his disciples.

Certainly, the Druids had a philosophy, but it is more than likely that the belief in the continuation of life arose as much from observation of the cyclical pattern of nature as from anything else. They do not appear to have feared death, regarding it simply as a transition stage in the immortality of the soul. Indeed, they sometimes seemed to have welcomed death – particularly if it was a courageous one – to the puzzlement of those who struggled to understand them.

Druidic Customs

The practice of human sacrifice, apparently carried out by the Druids, is now known to have been a survival of pre-Druidic custom and more than probably was regarded as an efficient way of disposing of unpleasant elements in their society. Druids would have presided dispassionately at such ceremonies – in the sense of being guardians of the correct balance within the community rather than being wanton murdering high priests. Indeed, the Druids seem also to have presided over traditional religious ceremonies, such as the placing of deliberately broken objects in the water of streams and wells as offerings to the gods.

Accounts are given also of the ritual harvesting of mistletoe. This had to be cut with a golden knife or sickle and gathered without it being contaminated by touching the ground, the plant being caught in a white cloth by attendants waiting below. Two white bulls were then sacrificed, after which the priest divided the branches into many parts and distributed them to the people, who hung them over doorways as protection against thunder, lightning and other evils.

The folklore, along with the magical powers of this plant, blossomed over the centuries. It was understood, for instance, that mistletoe took on the character of its host tree in some ways. Mistletoe grown on oak was in very subtle ways different from mistletoe grown on apple trees. A sprig placed in a baby's cradle would protect the child from fairies. An entire herd would be protected from harm if a sprig were given to the first cow calving after New Year.

In both Gaul and Ireland, Druids were not just representatives of a religion but an integral part of the community. Written records seem to prove that Druids had withdrawn from Gaul in the face of the Roman army by the end of the 1st century CE, but there continues to be evidence of their existence in Ireland much later. The similarities between the Irish and Gallic Druids are quite pronounced. In Ireland particularly they were most often found in the service of kings, in the role of advisers as a result of their skills in the use of magic and the voice as a vehicle.

Magical Training

The voice in Druidic magic is truly an instrument or tool, and it was through the voice that magical change could be brought about. A change of consciousness could be self-induced in the Druidic bard and this would then allow for the spontaneous transmission of wisdom – a kind of channelling – which often took the form of poetry. This poetic tradition was known as Roscanna (vision poetry) and was used in magical incantation. The poetry itself was intended to be ambiguous to the uninitiated and was full of arcane and archaic references. Ultimately they were spells in the true sense of the word, that is, magical words designed to have a particular effect. Unfortunately, in some later magical traditions, the purity of true Druidic poetry descends into mere doggerel verse.

The concept of the triad is central to Druidic culture and has become a rule in much of their later recorded poetry, which gives form to a basic belief that everything has a threefold nature. Knowledge, Nature and Truth lead to wisdom and the bardic tradition allows this to be taught to the masses. The Druidic moral code is based on the premise that each person, not fate or the will of gods, is responsible for his or her own conduct. It is characterized by a sense of fair play, honour and justice. The myths and tales of the heroes of old gave a strong sense of this, to a people who often needed extreme courage just to survive.

As with all belief systems based on a closeness to nature, there were certain times of the year when the people were closer to the Otherworld and they were inevitably aware of the power, majesty and implacability of Nature herself. Fire worship was an integral part of the Celtic Druidic tradition, both as a life-giving force and also as a potential destroyer or cleansing agent. The ritual 'Need Fire' lit at the important festivals expressed the high esteem the Celts held for fire, as a source of inspiration as well as light. (It is interesting that on 2 February at Imbolc [see page 199], the feast of Brighid – who was also the Celtic goddess of poetry – is based on the maintaining of the eternal flame.)

Druidism demonstrates the management of both low and high magic, for it is within the differing states of consciousness that a particular type of magic becomes possible. We have seen that a central teaching in Druidism is a personal responsibility for one's own actions. The use of offerings, prayers, sacrifices, ritual, taboos and other physical means in order to communicate with – and influence – divine powers is a carefully thought out act of responsibility.

The deliberate nurturing of the powers such as clairvoyance and the calling of Elemental powers to help others, the ability to bring unjust war to an end, and the knowledge of natural patterns and influences, suggests that the Druid's powers were actually a function of his place in his community. It was a chosen path of service. In other words, he chose to become a Druid and to work through the various initiations of bard, prophet and ovate.

Modern Druidism

The modern practice of Druidism does seem to straddle all aspects of magical practice but is principally a path to personal development and spiritual integrity. To understand the Druid way of thought in the modern day is to recognize a sense of responsibility within the flow of natural forces. By making use of the inspiration given to us by Mother Nature and understanding the ebb and flow of the energies around us, we are able to utilize the power within ourselves and the world around us. We can communicate with the spirits of plants, rocks, the earth itself. Even given the frenetic pace of urban living, it is still possible to live our lives successfully; though many of the old ways of worship may have gone by the board, we can still adapt and modify our own rituals to enable us to change our lives for the better.

In days gone by, it would take as long as 19 years to become a fully-fledged Druid. This followed the premise that it is better to travel slowly on any path of spiritual development, but also symbolized the return to a starting point – a full circle – since this was the time between two similar eclipses of the Sun and Moon, suggesting an understanding of both the overt and occult forces within the aspirant's being. The novitiate would come to an understanding of body, mind and spirit and their own place in the universe and would then be ready to pass on the knowledge to others.

Nowadays bardic training introduces all the basic concepts of Druidism and shows you how it is a vibrant journey following the cycle of the year, which you can practise in the modern world. The aim of the training is to help you express yourself fully in the world. Through it you discover the source of your own creative power and learn how to express it in ways that are appropriate for you. You also learn how to use ritual correctly, how to create a sacred space and to use the directions and the Elements. These rituals help to attune you to the world around you and to the rhythms of the earth, the Sun and Moon and the stars. In this way you gain access to your own inner space, that part of you which connects with life itself.

As with all systems of spiritual advancement, there are some people who prefer to work alone and others who need to work as part of a group. There are advantages to both ways and part of the sense of community, working in groups, is that almost inevitably you will find someone who has had similar experiences to your own. Even if you do work alone, much information can be shared using the world-wide community of the internet and cyberspace.

The process of initiation can be completed much more quickly nowadays than previously; the training for each area of understanding takes more or less a year, although full initiation into the various levels of awareness takes place only when the pupil is ready, whether that initiation happens in private or within a 'grove' or group.

In common with all belief systems, the beginning of the Druidic ritual is indicated in an appropriate way. The opening phrase 'We are here to honour the gods', focuses the minds of the participants on the matter in hand. In a group used to working together, the Gaelic phrases might be used, but not if there are beginners because this might cause confusion. Sound might also be used to capture attention; perhaps the sounding of a horn or a roll of drums.

Druids do not consider it necessary to mark the four quarters of a sacred space (temple or grove) as do most Wiccans or Kabbalists. The sacred grove is already sanctified and protected, so there is little need to call for additional power. It is activated by simple processing around it. It is the space itself that is important and it is an open, welcoming one rather than closed, unless a particular ritual demands it.

For the Druid, the Element of Fire is the motivating force, with the other three – Earth, Water, Air – forming a trinity or triangle of power rather than a square. Druidic 'circles' actually work much more on the spiral shape, which expands to take account of additional energy available. If the energy pattern becomes visible psychically it will manifest as a cone of power or vortex.

Druidic thought recognizes the symbolism of the tree – the triad of the roots that drop down into the earth, the branches that spread out towards the sky and towards others and the trunk, all of which give stability. The information on Group Working given on pages 248-249 will help with further clarification.

African Religions

PERHAPS THE BEST-KNOWN African-based religion today is voodoo, which is, at its core, shamanic. As many as 60 million people worldwide are thought to practise voodoo. Generally it seems that it flourished wherever the slave trade was particularly widespread.

Voodoo

Voodoo, which came into prominence in Haiti, is probably the best example of the assimilation of African belief into other cultures. The structure of voodoo was actually the result of the enforced intermingling of African slaves from different tribes. Little attention was paid to their spiritual needs, so in despair, a common thread had to be found by the slaves themselves. They began to invoke not only their own tribal gods, but also to practise rites other than their own. This tribal mixture can be seen in the names of different rites and in the gods, such as Damballa, Obatala, Oshun and Shango, who are still worshipped and who were originally deities from all parts of Africa. The slaves mixed practices and rituals from numbers of tribes and in the process developed a completely new religion that very quickly gained popularity.

The French rulers of Haiti realized that this new religion was a danger to their colonial system and so they denied all Africans the right to their own religious practices, severely punishing anyone found practising voodoo. The French decreed that all slaves be baptized as Catholics, and so Catholicism became superimposed on the African rites and beliefs (which the slaves still practised, either in secret or concealed as harmless dances and parties). This religious struggle continued for more than three centuries, but none of the terrible punishments inflicted could totally obliterate the faith of the Africans.

Followers of this new religion of voodoo actually considered the addition of the Catholic saints to be an enhancement of their faith and set about incorporating Catholic hymns, prayers, statues, candles and holy relics into their rituals. Tribal deities were often given the aspects of Catholic saints; they did not become the Catholic saints, but retained their original characteristics and personalities while adopting the symbolic trappings of Catholicism and the saints whom they seemed to resemble most.

The whole structure of voodoo reflects its history. The cross as a symbol, for instance, was easy to accept because it was already a powerful representation in the tribal religions, as the crossroads where the spiritual and material worlds meet. It was adopted as the symbol of the powerful god Legba, who is the guardian of the gates, the messenger of the gods and has multiple faces. As the Trickster, he is the child who wants things he cannot have. The saint most closely associated with Legba is St Peter, who holds the keys to the kingdom of heaven.

The practice of Voodoo

Voodoo priests and priestesses are first of all healers, diviners and protectors from evil spirits, thus again showing their shamanic background. In many ways they are more dispassionate in their judgements than perhaps the Judeo-Christian religions, and much misunderstanding has grown up over their use of poppets and image magic. Ritual killings and deliberate harm have as little to do with voodoo as Satanism does with Christianity. The idea of the wholesale sticking of pins into dolls is an unfortunate misapprehension derived from the media; the art of sympathetic magic used in an apparently negative fashion makes good copy.

The three main elements of traditional healing in African-based religions are the prevention of, and protection from, difficulties; the discovery of the causes of these difficulties; and their eradication.

Part of any healer's work is the management of the process of dying. A healer will know when no more can be done through his own art, will advise the family accordingly and will hold himself available to aid in the transition process. The ancestors and recently departed family members play a large part in the rest of the work of traditional healers, which relates to protecting clients from possible harm.

Healers consult the spiritual realm by invoking and conferring with the ancestors. Most afflictions are believed to come from external forces, so protection against them involves warding off the negative aspects of witchcraft and maintaining an equilibrium with other people, and with the spirits.

Thus, protection includes paying penance and seeking forgiveness for real or imagined offences. The healers may use herbs and other substances that are ingested, sniffed or smoked in a ceremonial pipe. It can be seen that this has similarities with both the Sun Dance and the sacred pipe ceremonies practised by Native Americans. They will also use their dreams, through which the ancestors give them the ability to diagnose a problem. Many traditional healers drum, dance or follow specific rituals, after which they perform ceremonial acts; they then provide medicines against imbalance or charms and totems to protect.

Many customs, such as the ritual use of whips, dancing and sacred designs, have been misunderstood for lack of understanding the cultures on which such practices were based. They were seen as aberrations and evil practices but a little thought will reveal that they have a basis in shamanism.

Like other shamanic cultures, healers in the voodoo religion dress in special robes, beaded necklaces and head-dresses. The necklaces they wear consist of beads, objects that have spiritual significance, and plant or animal parts that are thought to have medicinal uses. These objects also signify the healer's status.

Hoodoo

Hoodoo is strictly neither a religion nor a denomination of a religion, although it does blend elements from several African and European religions. It consists of a great deal of African folklore magic along with a considerable amount of Native American herbal knowledge and a smattering of European folklore (much of which pre-dates Christianity). Modern-day practitioners of hoodoo also often have an extensive knowledge of medieval manipulation of energy, Jewish Kabbalism and some Hindu mysticism.

Voodoo, as we have seen, is a set of beliefs, a religion, whereas hoodoo developed and survived because its techniques and magic are known to work. The ability of an individual to change their circumstances and those of others through ritual and spells, is seen as personal power. Practitioners do believe in supernatural powers but they are free to believe in any god or gods of their choosing.

The only god in hoodoo that seems to have survived from the African pantheon is Legba, the teacher god. It is he who meets the traveller at the crossroads. It is said that if you wish to learn a skill, such as how to play an instrument, you should wait with it at a crossroads on either three or nine specified nights or mornings. On your first visits you will probably see a series of animals. On your last visit, a large black man or a devil will appear. Provided you are not afraid and do not run away, he will request to borrow the item you have. He will then show you the proper way to use it by using it himself. When he returns it to you, you will suddenly have the power to excel with it.

The practice of Hoodoo

The lack of the need for overt consecration means that the practice of hoodoo is a mystical art. Some of its practices may be incorporated and used by priests and priestesses, but the art can also be used as a separate worldly skill by anyone, without initiation. Again it is a demonstration of a system of belief, which has grown up using material that is readily available to the practitioner. Perhaps it is also for this reason that many of its rituals and techniques are based on the magical properties of herbs, roots, minerals, animal parts and the personal possessions and bodily secretions of people.

Foot track magic, for instance, was often used to compel someone to do something they perhaps did not wish to do. Hoodoo gives magical power to a person's footprint, and when this particular ritual is used various powders and herbs are placed in the path of the recipient – sometimes in a buried container or bottle. Initially these 'witch's bottles', as they became known, would be filled with nail clippings, hair or any bodily fluid or excreta known to belong to the original magician. Later they became objects of protection and would be buried near a home or placed within the walls for this purpose. Such bottles were made until the early 19th century, and indeed the charm bottles in this book are a modern-day, somewhat sanitized version of the art.

'Crossing' is a variation of foot track magic where a cross or mark is placed where it is known the victim is going to walk. The antidote to this magic is black pepper which is said to keep your footprints from making any sort of impression, so that even if anyone does get hold of them, their magic will have achieved absolutely nothing. You wear it inside your socks or shoes. Magicians and sorcerers will also cast spells to improve one's luck or ward off evil spirits.

Macumba

This is the Brazilian form of voodoo. Macumba is an umbrella term that embraces two principal forms of African spirit worship – Candomble and Umbanda. Candomble ceremonies start with invocations to the gods, prayers, offerings and possession of the faithful by the gods. Umbanda incorporates the worship of the Catholic saints along with the beliefs of the Brazilian Indians.

Macumba is often referred to as black magic, but this aspect is really more the system known as quimbanda, whose practitioners simply draw their power from unruly spirits. The work is more mischievous, and therefore their practices are often considered tainted.

One Macumban celebration held on 1 January, is where more than a million celebrants wade into the ocean at dusk and a priestess known as *mao de santo* (mother of the saint, therefore drawing parallels with the Virgin Mary) lights candles and then purifies and ordains other young priestesses. As the Sun goes down, celebrants decorate a tiny wooden boat with candles, flowers and figures of the saints. At midnight the boat is set sail from the shore; if the boat sinks, Yemanji, a Water spirit, has heard their prayers and accepted their offering, promising her support and guidance for another year.

La Santeria

La Santeria, or the Way of the Saints, came about when the Yoruba people were taken to Cuba and forced to worship the saints of the Catholic church, as mentioned above. This religion is famous for its 'magic', which is based on knowledge of the mysteries or spirits, which are the servants of God and rule over every force of nature and every aspect of human life. The spirits can be counted on to come to the aid of their followers. It is said that they will guide the practitioners to a better life in all ways, and will show them how to interact with the spirits to improve not just their own life, but also the lives of others. This means that practitioners of La Santeria live their lives in an altered state of awareness.

Obeah

Although related to the voodoo of Haiti, Obeah, which originates in Jamaica, has always been strictly opposed to Christianity. Obeah can be viewed as a 'tower of power', a huge source of energy that can be communicated with by the obeah priest in special ways. Obeah pre-dates Christianity and is an occult tradition that includes healing and divination. The obi stick used by the Obeah man of Jamaica is thought to be a representation of the rod of Moses, which he used to part the Red Sea. The Obi-man and his stick were often used as a threat to young children if they were being naughty. Obeah still has the connotations of evil and black magic, attributed to it by many of the white missionaries of years gone by.

Obeah includes many elements easily recognizable as shamanism. These arise out of a simple search for knowledge, which later develops further into practices seen within voodoo. Obeah looks for power over the world and environment in which its practitioners live, and can be seen as one of those aspects of awareness that feeds perhaps on fear.

Rather than rigidly adhering to some carefully laid down formula, the African-based religions have grown, changed and expanded to take account of the needs of the people they serve, while maintaining the beliefs that are at their core.

Witchcraft and Wicca

THE ROOTS OF WITCHCRAFT are just as ancient as the roots of voodoo. Like voodoo, 'The Craft' or witchcraft should never be confused with Satanism, the outright worship of Satan. The true witch has nothing to do with such worship, even though there are some Satanists who will, wrongfully, call themselves 'witch'.

Wicca is the practice of the religion of witchcraft, with its own set of beliefs, while The Craft is more properly the practicalities of the art of witchcraft, such as spell making and healing. It is the misunderstanding of this differentiation that has led to persecution in the past. Neither is witchcraft the old lady with a warty, crooked nose and pointed hat so beloved of myths and fairytales, nor is it the beautiful women or evil wizard so hyped of the modern media.

Witchcraft old and new

At rock bottom, modern witchcraft owes its roots to both Gnosticism and shamanism, although in many ways, in being brought forward into the modern day by people such as Gerald Gardner and Alexander Sanders, some of that shamanic integrity has been radically changed. In becoming almost an urban religion, it has become very diverse in its practices and beliefs and, on the surface, it is sometimes difficult to perceive the basic core convictions.

Witchcraft develops through the large number of groups that exist with intrinsic bonds to one another. On the whole, these are looser than those that you will find between the various Christian churches. Each group or coven has its own traditions and beliefs, develops its own rituals and can exist – if necessary – in isolation, much as Gnostic groups did in the pre-Christian era. It is perhaps this latter quality that has given rise to the huge upsurge in the existence of solitary witches but has also resulted in the survival of The Craft despite persecution and danger.

The basic principles of The Craft are as follows:

1. The first principle is that of love and is expressed in the ethic 'do as you will, so long as you harm none'. This love is not emotional but is seen as an outpouring and sharing of a basic energy or force as communicated in relation to other beings, whether they are human or otherwise. Harm, which is seen as unethical, is unjustified action with no cause; harming others can be done by word, thought, or deed. Doing something that ultimately harms oneself is obviously not acceptable.

2. The witch should act within the structure of the Law of Cause and Effect. Every action has its reaction, and every effect has its cause. This is a principle that holds within the human realm. It is believed that all things happen according to this law. From a human perspective – though not from a divine – nothing in the universe can occur outside this law, though we may not always enjoy the relationship between a given effect and its cause.

3. Supplementary to this is the Law of Three, which states that whatever goes forth must return threefold, whether good or ill. Our actions affect others more than people realize, and the resulting reactions are also part of the package. It is a very basic application of the tenet 'As ye sow, so also shall ye reap'. This is why magical spells and rituals must be very carefully considered and full responsibility accepted before action is taken.

4. For this reason, anyone practising witchcraft needs to recognize and harmonize with universal forces in agreement with the Law of Polarity. Everything is dual; everything has two poles; everything has its opposite; for every action there is a reaction; everything can be categorized as either active or reactive in relation to other things.

5. Recognizing this polarity means that, while the Wiccan religion acknowledges that fundamentally there is one Ultimate Being, members worship and relate to the Divine as the archetypal polarity of God and Goddess, the Male and Female principle, the All-Father and the Great Mother. As has been said:

Godhead is one unique and transcendent wholeness, beyond any limitations or expressions; thus, it is beyond our human capacity to understand and identify with this principle of Cosmic Oneness, except as It is revealed to us in terms of Its attributes and operation.

These five concepts are supposedly as close as humans can get to the Godhead, given the constraints of the human limits of understanding and expression. The practice of the 'Mystery Religions', however, allows mankind to live within the principle of cosmic oneness.

'As above, so below' is another principle that can be accepted. That which exists in the macrocosm (the heavens) exists, on a smaller scale and to a lesser degree, in the microcosm (the physical world). The powers of the universe are present also in the human being, though on the whole they are not properly utilized. The abilities and qualities of 'being' can be activated and used if the proper techniques and initiations are practised. The secrets of the hidden knowledge must be concealed from the unworthy, however, because much harm can be done by those who have power without responsibility.

The Craft is a natural religion, seeing in nature the expression and revelation of divinity. It is possible for humanity to exert the power of the gods; to be a channel for the Godhead to manifest in a multitude of ways.

Wicca in its many forms

The main traditions and beliefs in the craft include Gardnerian Wicca, Alexandrian Wicca, Dianic Wicca, the Faery tradition, many branches of Celtic-based Wicca and other forms, which are often called Eclectic Wicca. Wiccans draw their practices and information from many different sources. They may call themselves witches.

Wiccans accept that everything emanates from the 'One World' – the universe – and is in perpetual motion. All things rise and fall in a tidal movement that reflects the motion inherent in the universe. Therefore the Wiccan practitioner celebrates, harmonizes with, and makes use of, the natural flow expressed through the sequence of the seasons and the motion of the solar system. These ritual observances are the eight great festivals of the year, known as Sabbats, referred to as the Wheel of the Year. Operating the Laws of Polarity, the Wiccan is also conscious of the forces and tides of the Moon. Examples of spells and rituals using these forces are given shortly.

There are numerous ways of honouring the Moon and one of the simplest is to honour the sanctity of your own life. This you do by paying special attention to Diana, Goddess of the Moon and the Woodlands, for a short time every day, and recognizing the life connection between you and every living creature.

You might hang apple slices, nuts and seeds in your garden for her creatures. At the same time, honour Diana by saying:

Diana, Goddess of the Woodlands, I make this offering in recognition of your power to care for your creatures.

You may find that you are then drawn to one animal in particular. If this happens, try to keep a representation of that animal close beside you so that you are constantly reminded that you and your body are the medium between much earth energy and other creatures. This is linking with the idea of totem or soul animals.

Having a representation of Diana and her creatures in your home or sacred space is a reminder that you honour her each time you do something to give assistance to the earth and its creatures. Whenever you think of this, you might repeat these words:

Goddess of the Silver Moon,
Lady of the Forests,
Hear my praises to you
As you protect your creatures,
Protect now me and mine.

Use of symbolic representations of the natural and divine forces of the universe is an effective way of contacting and utilizing the forces they denote. The Wheel of the Year personalizes the relationship between the Lord or Sun God and his Lady, the Goddess. The natural progression of the seasons is seen as a reflection of that relationship.

The Wheel of the Year

The cycle of the Wheel of the Year, based on the idea of growth and decay, is in terms of ritual even more pertinent to magical working than, for instance, astrology with all its complexities. It enables us to give a structured approach to our ordinary, everyday lives.

The Wheel of the Year for pagans consists of eight Sabbats (celebrations of belief). All of them are solar in nature, commemorate the stages of the relationship between the Sun God and Mother Earth and mark the passing of the year with natural milestones, such as planting and harvest.

Some pagans would define the Sabbats as major and minor. The major – and best-loved – ones are Samhain, Imbolc, Beltane and Lughnasadh. The minor ones are Yule (winter solstice), Ostara (spring equinox), Litha (summer solstice) and Mabon (autumn equinox). This subdivision is by no means made by all pagans, many of whom feel that the Sabbats are of equal significance. It should be remembered that these seasonal celebrations will be celebrated in reverse in the southern hemisphere.

All eight celebrations have particular rituals associated with them and can be celebrated in as simple or complex a manner as you please. It is a time to honour the life force, however one perceives it, and to give thanks both for – and to – it. At these times, the Goddess (the feminine principle) may be perceived as the Lady, the Moon Goddess or any of the forms of the Triple Goddess – Maid, Mother and Crone – that are appropriate. The God (the masculine principle) is worshipped as the Lord, the Sun God or as the consort of the Goddess.

In any of the rituals given as examples, you are free to respect and address both God and Goddess as you please. It is the intention that is important, and any self-respecting magical practitioner will eventually get to the point where the rhythm and power of their own words will enhance the ritual. This is, after all, the naming and sounding of Sacred Words of Power, but with your own emphasis.

Many of these seasonal celebrations have been appropriated by the Christian religion; we see this particularly at Candlemas, which was

THE WHEEL OF THE YEAR

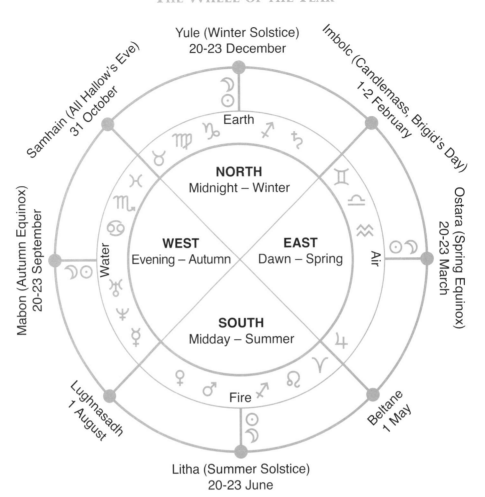

originally Imbolc, Easter which was the celebration of Ostara, and Christmas which, of course, is the Yule festival. Many of the customs that survive today have their origins in the seasonal festivals. Those around Yule have survived almost intact.

Traditionally, 23 December is the only day not ruled by a tree or its corresponding Ogham letter in the Celtic tree calendar. The Celtic tree month of Ruis (Elder) runs until 22 December and the month of Beth (Birch) begins on 24 December, leaving a one-day intercalary period known as 'the Secret of the Unshewn Stone'. This was designed to bring the calendar back into line with the solar year. In Britain on this day there was elected the Lord of Misrule, Fool and King of the Bean (who was chosen by getting the bean in the celebratory pudding). The Christmas tree fairy is said to represent the White Goddess – she can be seen as Isis or any

of the Great Mother Goddesses who give birth to the Sun Gods at midwinter.

Greenery associated with this time also has its own traditions. At his celebration of joy, Saturnalia, Dionysus wore a crown made from ivy – an evergreen and therefore symbolic of everlasting life and light. Holly has also always been sacred to Saturn and as such, played a part in the Saturnalia carnival. It features in Celtic folk myth, in the battle between the Holly King and the Oak King for supremacy of half of each year.

Sabbats

The need for correctness of conduct is epitomized in the concept of the Wheel of the Year, as the God and Goddess come together in innocence and later part in the cycle of birth, death and regeneration. The natural order was believed to have depended not solely on the regular and precise performance of rituals, but also on the conduct of the people, particularly of its leaders, outside the sacred precincts. This meant that certain freedoms and restrictions were imposed at the times of the Sabbats (festivals).

The Celtic year started with Samhain to encompass the period of rest before the God and Goddess became active. This concept is still honoured today in the modern-day rituals performed at the times of the Sabbats. Some examples of the rituals are given below. They are all designed for group working, although it is perfectly acceptable to perform them alone.

Samhain – 31 October

Although the Celtic year starts with Samhain, it is also the third and final Harvest Sabbat. The dark winter half of the year commences on this Sabbat. Traditionally, the door between the physical realm and that of spirit is now open. At this time, the Dark Mother and the Dark Father – the Crone and her aged Consort – are paid due respect.

Food offerings are left on altars and doorsteps for the wandering spirits and a candle is often placed in the window to help the spirits and ancestors to come home. The coming darkness signifies a time of chaos and mayhem when often nothing is what it seems. For this reason, any ritual should always be performed within a consecrated and circle for your own protection.

YOU WILL NEED

*Black candle to represent the dying God or a yellow one inscribed with the symbol of the Sun
Grains, fruits and dried flowers as offerings to the Goddess
Runes, tarot cards and other divination tools
Corn or other suitable bread for the spirits of the dead
Samhain incense as shown below*

METHOD

✤ Cast your circle and build up your cone of protection.

✤ Invoke the God and Goddess by saying:

*I ask for your blessing Dark Mother
and Father of Darkness,
As the veil between two worlds thins,*

*I greet my ancestors and loved ones
who have gone before me.
May only those who wish me well enter
within this circle.
We greet all those gone before us and
who are free of Earth's ties.*

✤ Spend a few moments thinking of your loved ones, then say:

We thank you for your presence here tonight.

✤ Next, light the God candle and say:

*Tonight, as all you dead souls walk
amongst the living,
As we pass through into the shadow of
darkness, we do so gratefully.
We know it is the wheel of the year turning.
We thank the Gods and Goddess for the glittering
prizes of the summertime.
Tonight, the Lord of the Hunt, the Lord of the Sun,
quietly moves from us.
It is the wheel-a-turning and it will turn
again till the Sun rises from the Moon.
Here, this candle symbolizes the
Lord of the Sun – its quenching, his passing.*

✤ Blow out the God candle, do not light it again until Yule.

✤ You must now acknowledge the Crone aspect of the Goddess by saying:

*The decreasing Moon and stars are the
gifts you gave.
Oh Goddess of wisdom and magic speak to us of
your wisdom and power.
Understand it will be used wisely.
Pass on your energy and force so that our spells
rituals and divinations will be enthused.
Understand again, oh Goddess, they shall bring no
harm to your creatures.*

✤ Now dismiss the spirits of the ancestors by saying:

*Aid us as we look beyond the long
dark days of winter.
Go in peace.*

Afterwards, use your divination tools to gain a perspective on the coming months, hold a simple feast, close the sacred circle then bury the offerings. Also, leave a plate of food for the spirits still at large.

✳ Samhain Incense ✳

1 part dittany
¹/₂ part pine
1 part sandalwood
¹/₄ part patchouli
¹/₄ part benzoin resin
Few drops of pine oil

Yule – 23 December

Yule is a celebration of rebirth and the renewing of the old. It is the start of longer, lighter days as the Lord of the Sun arises from his sojourn with the Goddess. Here, light becomes important as we use sympathetic magic to ensure the return of the Sun. The ancient Egyptians also watched and waited for the star Sirius to announce yet another birth, that of Horus as the son of Osiris from the womb of Isis at this time.

The Yule log symbolizes the continuation of light and this ritual honours that tradition. Before performing this ritual, you might want to decorate your home with evergreens, although mistletoe, which is sacred to both Druids and the Scandinavians, is still banned from Christian churches as being unholy. For the purposes of this celebration, consider that the Yule log is your altar. The celebration is designed for a group, so there is some preparation necessary beforehand in order to get the full effect from it.

Wish Branch

You will need a wish branch to indicate your desires and wishes for the coming year. Prepare this before you attend the celebration. You can spray the branch with silver or gold paint, but do not forget to ask permission of the nature spirits before you do so.

YOU WILL NEED
Yule incense as shown below
Ribbons and cords in various colours
Small representations such as cake or Christmas tree decorations or children's toys, of your most important aims and desires (you might use one item for each month: be as creative as you like)
Small wrapped sweets tied with coloured thread
Branch of your chosen sacred wood

METHOD
❖ Light the incense.
❖ Meditate on the coming year and what you would most like to see happen.
❖ You might also include your wishes for your family and friends, or for your larger world.
❖ When you have decided on your intentions, choose decorations or toys appropriate to your wishes. Decorate the branch according to your own creativity. (This is an intensely personal object and will be used later in the celebration.)
❖ Take the branch to the celebration.

Preparation of Yule Log

So often nowadays there is nowhere to burn the Yule log properly but it is quite in order to substitute this method. This prepared log can then be used year after year and, of course, becomes increasingly powerful the more it is used. The log can be of any of the sacred woods. The first time it is prepared, it should be done by the leaders of the group and strictly should be consecrated afresh each year with a simple prayer to the God and Goddess.

YOU WILL NEED
Red and green candles (one candle for each member of the group, plus an extra green one for the leader)
Suitable log large enough to accommodate the candles
Silver foil

METHOD
❖ In the log bore a hole large enough to hold each candle, plus two extra.
❖ Line each hole with silver foil or a metal cake cup for safety so that the Yule log does not catch fire. (Alternatively, you could wrap the end of the candle in silver foil.)
❖ As you do so, ask for a blessing from the God and Goddess for the work you do.

Yule Celebration

YOU WILL NEED ——————————
Prepared Yule log
2 white candles
Black candle from Samhain (to represent the God)
Prepared red and green candles as above
Group's wish branches
A wreath (symbolic of the Wheel of the Year and of the Goddess)
Yule incense as shown below

METHOD ——————————
❖ Cast your circle and light the incense.
❖ Place the Yule log in a prominent position.
❖ Light the white candles at either end of the Yule log.
❖ Place the God candle in front of the log and say:

Here this candle symbolizes the Sun God,
Its final flicker, His passing and here its flame once
again lights His return.

❖ Light the God candle from one of the altar candles.
❖ The leader should then light their green candle and say:

Blessed be the Maiden Goddess.
May this world be forever young in her presence.

❖ From that candle a second candle is then lit. The words now used are:

Blessed be the Mother Goddess,
fresh and rosy with babe.
And so shall all that springs from her be strong,
adventurous and bountiful.

❖ Then light a third candle from the second and say:

Blessed be the deep-rooted Goddess,
Wise, powerful and temperate,
The keeper of wisdom and the
ever-turning wheel.

❖ Each member then steps up, lights their candle from the last and places it securely in the Yule log.
❖ Finally the leader lights a last candle to complete the ritual and while facing towards the East says:

Tonight, the Lord of the Sun is born again.
The Goddess and the God are together in harmony.
The Sun reaffirms as the wheel is
a turning once again,
We praise the Goddess and the newly born God,
our Father and Mother.

❖ Now, if liked, each participant may talk about their wishes for the next year whilst placing their wish branches around the Yule log, or in a large vase nearby.

⚜ Yule Incense ⚜

1 part clove
1 part juniper
1 part cinnamon
½ part dried orange peel

Imbolc – 2 February

Imbolc, the festival of the Maiden, marks the centre point of the dark half of the year. It is the time of blessing of the seeds and consecration of agricultural tools, and the time when the ewes are brought down for lambing. As the world prepares for growth and renewal, all maiden Goddesses, but particularly Brighid, are honoured; the Crone of winter transmutes into the young Maiden of spring.
This particular working is designed to be a group activity.

YOU WILL NEED ——————————
Two white candles for the altar
White candle and holder for each person present
Brighid's incense as shown below
Reed cross
Corn dolly, if wished
White linen cloth (to represent Brighid's mantle)
Creative writings such as poetry or songs
Sheep's milk or fruit juice
Plain biscuits or shortbread

METHOD

✤ Light the altar candles and the incense.
✤ Invoke Brighid using words such as:

Lady of Light,
Maiden and Goddess,
Bless us with your presence here tonight

✤ Wrap the corn dolly in the white cloth and say:

As you offered your mantle for
sanctuary for the babe,
So we signify this tonight.
As bride we honour you also.

✤ Place the dolly on your altar.
✤ Now each person should take a candle and, in a clockwise direction starting with the leader, light them and place them safely at your feet so the lights form a circle.
✤ Share the creative writings with the group.
✤ Afterwards, spend a few moments thinking of Brighid's power and say as a group:

As this flame burns,
So let it signify the eternal flame sacred to Brighid.

✤ The leader should lift up the reed cross and say:

Protect us now as the light brightens.
We honour your symbol.

✤ The cross may be placed either on the altar or at the front door of the meeting place.
✤ Afterwards, share the sheep's milk or juice and biscuits to reaffirm community.
✤ Your personal candles should be extinguished and may be taken home and relit in the main window of your home.

❈ Brighid's Incense ❈

3 parts frankincense resin
2 parts dragon's bood powder or resin
½ part red sandalwood
1 part cinnamon

Since Brighid is the guardian of the sacred flame as well as the Goddess of poetry, candles are lit. On Imbolc in Ireland they make Brighid's Cross. Also known as Bride's cross, it is sometimes three-legged, a triskele, signifying the fact that she is in fact a Triple Goddess. Often it is an equal armed cross woven from reeds, according to ancient patterns.

Ostara – 21 March

The ancient goddess Eostre – a Saxon deity who marked not only the passage of time but also symbolized new life and fertility – was supposedly the key symbol of this celebration, which we now know as Ostara. Legend has it that the goddess was saved by a bird whose wings had become frozen by the cold of winter. This process turned the bird into a hare, which could also lay eggs.

However recent research has revealed that this is legend is not genuine, since it was the Venerable Bede who first wrote of Eostre in CE 730. The connection between the Moon and the hare is in fact much older, in that the hare is a symbol of the Moon and fertility in many cultures, particularly Chinese. It is fertility and the Moon's cycle that is of importance in this spring festival. Nowadays the Hare has degenerated into the Easter bunny.

Remembering that in essence this is a fertility spell, if you do not wish to contemplate the possibility of pregnancy, decorate your eggs in colours other than red. You would then dedicate the celebration to the fertility of the land and a nice touch might be to think specifically of a land which is suffering drought or other difficulties.

YOU WILL NEED

Spring blossom and flowers to decorate the altar
Small statue or soft toy to represent the hare – or the bunny

*Representations of the phases of the Moon, cut
from silver paper (you should have at least
representations of the waxing crescent Moon, the
first quarter, the Full Moon, the last quarter and
the waning crescent)*
Hardboiled eggs
Thread or string
Red paint and decorations
Marker pen
Glue
A branch of spring blossom in a vase
One raw egg
Bowl
Cinnamon stick

METHOD

❖ Decorate the altar with the spring blossom
and flowers and place the statue or toy on the
right of the altar.

❖ Decorate your hardboiled eggs, using one for
each phase of the Moon. Be as creative as you
like and complete the decoration by marking
the eggs with an appropriate symbol of your
desire.

❖ Glue the thread or string to the eggs and
decorate your branch with them.

❖ Spread the Moon symbols in front of the
branch. Pick up each one and contemplate the
significances of them.

❖ Think of the journey that the Moon makes
and the significance of the Goddess in her
three aspects of Maid, Mother and Crone (it is
as Mother that you honour her here).

❖ Break the raw egg into the bowl and stir it
with the cinnamon stick.

❖ Hold the bowl up and ask a blessing from
Ostara.

❖ When you have finished take the bowl
outside and pour its contents upon the earth
– otherwise a houseplant will do – as a
blessing and to encourage fertility.

❖ Keep the branch as fresh as you can for as
long as you can. One Moon cycle is good.

*This ritual is more difficult to describe than it is to
do. The significance of the raw egg is obvious, and
the cinnamon represents love, fire and passion. The
representation of the hare or rabbit signifies the
presence of the masculine at this ritual, which is
essentially feminine.*

Beltane – 1 May

Belenus or Bel was a Celtic Sun God whose
coronation feast Beltane (meaning 'Fire of Bel') is
celebrated on 1 May. Beltane has long been
celebrated with feasts and rituals – as summer
began, the weather became warmer and young
people would spend the entire night in the
woods. It was a time when married couples
were given permission to be unrestricted in their
behaviour without censure, and when marriages
of a year and a day could be undertaken.

The maypole was a symbol of the sexuality
that abounded at the time. The weaving of the
ribbons symbolized the sacred marriage of the
God and Goddess. For this reason any ritual
performed at the beginning of May takes on the
symbolism of a marriage feast. This is the time
for youth and vitality.

This fertility ritual celebrates the union of the
God and the Goddess. By now the Goddess is
moving into her Mother aspect and her life
energies are becoming more abundant. For this
ritual each participant will need to bring a
white flower, preferably with five petals to
represent the Elements plus Spirit. The
cauldron represents the fertile mother.

YOU WILL NEED

Beltane incense as shown below
White ribbon
*Red ribbon (about 1 metre [3 ft] of each per
participant)*
White flowers as mentioned above
Cauldron filled with flowers

METHOD

❖ Light the incense.

❖ Wearing a flower garland if you wish, face
East.

❖ Hold the ribbons with the end of the white
ribbon covering the end of the red one (this
represents the Goddess being supported by
the vitality of the God) and begin to plait
them together and say:

*Father and Mother Goddess,
it is the time of your union.
Through your happy joining, so shall
happiness spread*

*Through your abundance,
so shall nature be abundant.*

❖ As you finish your plait, lay it in front of you.
❖ While each individual is waiting, contemplate your flower, re-dedicating yourself through its perfection at this time to the service of the God and Goddess.
❖ When everyone has finished, the leader should gather the plaits together and bind them into one simple maypole symbol.
❖ As this is done everyone should say:

*Praise to you ancient God and Goddess.
You are our creators and from your union shall all beings rise and awaken.
Sacred art thou.*

❖ The flower petals can be strewn on the ground to signify abandonment.

Afterwards, the ribbon symbol might be hung in the sacred space or placed on the ground. Follow up the ritual with a spring blessing or activity – a simple feast of breads, cereals and dairy foods perhaps.

❋ Beltane Incense ❋

*1 part rose
¹/₂ part frankincense resin
¹/₂ part musk root*

Litha – 21 June (Summer Solstice)

Midsummer Night's Eve is of importance for many people because of the folk customs still associated with it. This is the longest day of the year – a day on which both light and life are plentiful. This day is also known as Alban Heruin by the Druids.

Known at this time as the Green Man with a face surrounded by foliage, or the Lord of the Forests, the Sun God is at his strongest on this day. His day was celebrated by the burning of Sun Wheels, which were very large, to ensure fertility and prosperity in the coming year. This ritual is also a celebration for the Goddess. She is now with child and nature reflects this with abundant growth. Now is a fine time for magical and purifying rites.

This ritual commemorates those ancient Sun Wheels and purification by fire.

Prior to attendance at this ritual, each individual should make a Sun Wheel in a similar way to the charm ball (see page 83). If you wish, you can use the charm ball you have already made.

Ideally this ritual is one that is performed outdoors. Whether you are inside or out, you should always make sure that you have plenty of water on hand to douse any exuberant flames.

YOU WILL NEED

*Red candle (to represent the Sun God)
Green candle (to represent the Goddess)
Sun Wheel for each individual
Cauldron or safe place in which to burn the wheels
Water
Midsummer incense (as below)*

METHOD

❖ Cast your circle.
❖ Face south and say:

*On this day the Sun is high,
the light is bright and the Earth is warm.
As the Sun God blazes above,
may the flames of our ritual blaze below.*

❖ Light the Goddess candle on the left of your sacred space and say:

*Mother of Nature, Lady of the firmament,
Bless thy fruitful womb, Which I honour.*

❖ Light the Sun God candle on the right of your sacred space and say:

*God of fertility and fruitfulness,
Blessed Lord of the blazing Sun,
Seed and nurturer of life,
May you be blessed.*

❖ Hold a Sun Wheel above your head and say:

May the Lord of the Sun burn away all that troubles, pains and distresses us.

❖ The leader should light the Sun Wheel and when it is burning properly, drop it into the cauldron or prepared space and say:

By the powers of all that is,
Two who are one,
We banish all negativity from our lives.

❖ Each individual should then consign their own Sun Wheel to the fire, repeating the same words. If the group is a very large one, obviously more than one cauldron or burning space can be used.

❖ When all are burnt, add water to the ashes then each individual may, if they wish, touch their third eye with the forefinger of their right hand, which has been dipped in the ash, and say:

Let my mind, my heart and my hands
Be dedicated to the service of the
God and the Goddess.

❖ When you have finished bury the ashes out of doors.

Midsummer Incense

2 parts sandalwood
1 part mugwort
1 part camomile
1 part gardenia petals
Few drops of rose oil
Few drops of lavender oil
Few drops of yarrow oil

Midsummer workings usually include those for prosperity, fertility and plentiful harvest. Your feast at this time might be of cakes and mead.

Lughnasadh – 2 August

Lughnasadh is the first of the three harvest Sabbats and is also known as Lammas in Scotland, where it is celebrated on 1 August. The word 'Lughnasadh' means 'the funeral games of Lugh'. Lugh was the Irish Sun God and he hosted the games in honour of Tailte, his foster-mother – hence the presence of the corn dolly. This day originally coincided with the first reapings of the harvest, giving the first seeds and fruit for storage in order to ensure future crops. At this time autumn begins; the Sun God is not yet dead, but allegorically loses some of his strength as the nights grow longer and the Sun rises farther towards the south.

For the feast afterwards, it is usual to have cider and bread. The colours for dressing your altar, if you choose to use one, are red and orange.

After you have finished this ritual, join in with a communal activity such as a walk in a forest or, when in an urban situation, through parks or alongside water.

YOU WILL NEED

Lugnasadh incense as shown below
Orange candles
Basket of grain heads
Basket of ripe fruit, berries and seeds
A corn dolly placed in a prominent position
Red altar cloth if used

METHOD

❖ Cast the protective circle.
❖ Light the incense and candles.
❖ Pass the basket of grain around the group so that everyone has a handful.
❖ Face east and say:

Now let us honour the Goddess in her fullness,
Her nurturing allows us to conserve her
fruitfulness as the energy of the God wanes.
We love and honour her as the mother of all nature
and share the power of her beneficence.

❖ Everyone should rub the grain heads together in their hands and allow the grains to fall on the ground. (This is ritual grain threshing.)
❖ Take a piece of fruit.
❖ Taste it and appreciate its flavour then say:

We are one with the fruits of the harvest.
Their energies are our energies.
Hail Goddess of the Moon,
Hail worldly Mother, Hail Sun Lord.
Show us the path to goodness and light.
May all your harvests be bountiful.

❖ Finish off the fruit, berries and seeds.

❖ Spend some time meditating on the sense of community brought about in the sharing of the fruit.

❋ Lughnasadh Incense ❋

2 parts frankincense resin
1 part heather
1 part dried apple blossoms or peel
1 part blackberry leaves

Mabon – 21 September

This is the second harvest Sabbat of the pagan year and is known by the Druids as Mea'n Fo'mhair. It is the time of the Crone – the God prepares for death and rebirth at this time of the autumn equinox when the dark days of the year are looming. It is also a time that is connected with mystery and the balance of light and dark.

When working with a group, everyone can follow the actions of the leader in this simple ceremony. It can be performed in the open without an altar if preferred.

YOU WILL NEED

Red candles
Mabon incense as shown below
Willow staff to cast your circle
A basket of autumn leaves
Fruits, berries, pine cones and oak sprigs
Brown altar cloth

METHOD

❖ Dress your altar if using one.
❖ Cast your circle using your stave or enter your sacred space.
❖ Light the candles and incense.
❖ The leader or High Priestess lifts the basket of leaves in both hands and says:

The bitter fevered days move in, watching the trees
and the leaves as they fall.
Our Lord of the Sun rides the wild
wind horses westerly
As the ghostly night wraps its arms
around the world.
Fruits flourish and the seeds fall
into waiting earth.

I know this to be a time of equals,
where nature's scales come into balance.
Through the deathly veil I know life finds a way.
Life's glory needs death's silence.
The dark winter shadows reveal
the wheel a-turning.

❖ Then the basket is passed around the circle and everyone takes a handful of leaves.
❖ Each person lets their leaves fall gently within the circle.
❖ Place the offerings on the altar or in the circle. Place the basket of leaves within the circle and say:

O cauldron protector, great Goddess of the
decreasing Moon,
Watcher of secret magic and long gone myths,
Show me the way to greater wisdom.
Show me the way O Goddess!
Show me the way to peace in all things.
I will bear thy knowledge well.

The fruits, berries and pine cones may be left in place as offerings to the Goddess and Nature Spirits (if doing the ritual in the open).

❋ Mabon Incense ❋

1 part sandalwood
1 part cypress
1 part juniper
1 part pine
1/2 part oakmoss
1/4 part oak

Magical pastimes, such as the collection of seeds to ensure next year's harvest, can be carried out at this point (do not forget to ask permission as you do so). Have a simple feast and close the circle.

There does comes a point when the personalization of just the God and Goddess as Lord and Lady alone can become somewhat restrictive. The next section, while bearing the relationship between male and female in mind, also celebrates the cultural influences and the natural energies which support us here on Earth.

Deities and their Worship

THE MORE ACCUSTOMED you become to making spells, the more you will begin to appreciate the power of the various deities and how that power was used by our forebears. While many of us probably subscribe to the belief that there is one God, we cannot help but marvel at the complexity of the energies and powers that go into making up that entity. For this reason it is sometimes more comforting to be able to approach that complexity in the way our forefathers did – with reverence for a particular aspect. We do this when we call upon the various deities.

In a book such as this, where the perspective is as wide as possible, it would be remiss not to give some information on the deities associated with the major religions, particularly when those religions are of such antiquity. Unfortunately it is possible only to give information on a basic level, but it will enable you to begin exploring for yourself the myriad energies available to you.

Most religions pay due attention to the masculine and feminine polarities and energies, as we have already seen in the celebrations of the Sabbats. When you choose to personalize those energies, you find yourself in a new relationship with them. In many ways the personalization of energy is one of the most important aspects of working with the deities. It allows us to feel close to something that is otherwise intangible; to feel that we are in touch with another dimension of being that is considerably wiser and more powerful than we are.

For many people, perceiving the masculine as Lord and the feminine as Lady is enough. Others need something more mundane and down to earth, and will attribute the masculine to the Sun and the feminine to the Moon, and thus allow themselves access to the rich symbolism there is in doing so. Many others will want to break down aspects of the masculine and feminine into various qualities and find it easier to work with representations of those qualities. Universal power in its entirety is often difficult for the beginner to understand or work with, yet ultimately we have to recognize its potency.

By placing representations of the deities on your altar or in calling on them to assist in your spells, you are accessing an energy which perhaps would not be otherwise be available to you. At all times you must be comfortable with this and will therefore use the entities that most appeal to you. Only use a deity from a belief system other than your own if you feel it is right.

Included here is a comprehensive selection from a number of belief systems, mostly major deities, but also some rather intriguing minor ones. There are some spells, rituals and incenses to give you some idea of how to call upon the gods or to use their energies. You may like to research further, both to find gods and goddesses appropriate for your own workings and also for spells which satisfy your creativity.

Celtic (Gaul, Irish and Welsh) Gods and Goddesses

Gaulish Gods

Belenus (also Bel) is the God of light and the Sun, also known as the Shining One. The most extensively worshipped Celtic god, he has particular authority for the welfare of sheep and cattle. The Feast of Beltane (see pages 201-202) means 'Fire of Bel'; he was later connected with the Greek God Apollo.

Cernunnos is a god of fertility, life, animals, wealth and the underworld. Usually shown with a stag's antlers, he carries a purse filled with coins. The horned god, he is born at the winter solstice, marries the Goddess of the Moon at Beltane and dies at the summer solstice. Worshipped all over Gaul, he is identified as Herne the Hunter in Britain. With the Goddess of the Moon, he jointly rules over the cycle of life, death and reincarnation.

Petition to the Horned God

Cernunnos means 'the Horned One' and at times of change he is invoked in his guise of ruler over the cycle of life. Because of his virility he has a lust for life that we all need. This spell does not use incense, but should you wish to use one for any other celebration of the god, two are given below. This spell is probably best done at sunrise and in the open air.

YOU WILL NEED

A clear space in woods
Stone markers for the four compass directions
Some green branches (preferably of oak but otherwise your favoured sacred tree)

METHOD

❖ Place your stones according to the four directions and while you do this listen to the sounds around you.

❖ You may become aware of a change in energy, in which case acknowledge the presence of the Nature Spirits (see page 88).

❖ Place the branches (sacred to Cernunnos) close to the centre where you are working, which has now become your sacred space.

❖ Stand in the centre of your sacred space.

❖ Put your hands in the God position (arms outstretched).

❖ Say:

> *Great Horned Leader of the Hounds*
> *Lord Cernunnos hear my call*
> *You, who move with the rhythm of the forests*
> *Upon your knowledge let me draw*
>
> *Potent Huntsman who dances with the serpent*
> *Of knowledge, forever virile and gracious*
> *Grant me the power of potent movement*
> *Let me move too within the mysterious*
>
> *Speaker with the ancient shamans*
> *Who bridge this world and the next*
> *Unstoppable as force of nature*
> *Aid my footsteps forward free from the past.*

❖ Now stand quietly drawing on the power of Cernunnos as you contemplate your next life move.

❖ Deliberately put the past behind you and resolve to move forward with all courage and speed.

❖ When your ceremony is complete, scatter the stones and the branches so that you leave no trace behind.

This is not a spell to help you make a decision, more one to increase your energy levels. It is more to help you to move forward swiftly, to allow matters to drop into place so that your path forward can be unimpeded. The assumption is that you have already decided what you want to do.

There are two incenses which are ideal for use when appealing either to Cernunnos or any of the rulers of the cycle of life.

❋ Cernunnos Incense ❋

1 part pine
1 part sandalwood
Pinch of valerian
½ part cinnamon
Few drops of musk oil

❋ Horned God Incense ❋

2 parts benzoin resin
1 part cedar
1 part pine
1 part juniper
Few drops of patchouli oil

Ogmios is the God of scholars and eloquence. Known in Ireland as Ogma, he is a hero god who invented the runic language of the Druids, the Ogham Staves. Sometimes associated with the Greek Heracles, he is shown as a bald old man, dressed in a lion's skin.

Sucellus is the guardian of forests and the God of agriculture; he also ferries the dead to the afterlife. He is often portrayed with a huge hammer and a dog by his side. In this aspect he links with the Norse Thor and the Egyptian Anubis.

Taranis, whose name means 'the thunderer', has as his symbols the wheel, representing the Wheel of Life and the lightning flash. He is sometimes identified with the Roman God Jupiter and the Norse God Thor.

Teutates is a god of war, fertility and wealth; his name means 'the god of the tribe'. He was greatly worshipped at a time when human sacrifices were made. He was the counterpart of the Roman god Mars and was also known as Alborix, King of the World.

Gaulish Goddesses

Belisama is goddess of light and fire, forging and craft; she is the wife of Belenus. She relates to the Roman goddess Minerva, and to the Greek goddess Athena. Her name means 'most brilliant'.

Epona is the goddess of horses, mules and cavalrymen. She is usually shown lying on a horse, sitting sidesaddle or standing surrounded by many horses. Her other symbol is that of the cornucopia – the horn of plenty – which suggests that she may also have been a fertility or corn Goddess.

Rosmerta is a goddess of fertility and wealth. Her stick with two snakes links her to Mercury, messenger of the Roman gods. The cornucopia – another of her symbols – identifies her as a fertility goddess and thus connects her with Epona.

Irish Gods

Bres is the god of fertility and agriculture. He is the son of Elatha, a prince of the Fomorians, and Eriu, a queen of the Tuatha De Danann.

Bile corresponds with the Gaulish God Belenus and shares his attributes.

Dagda (also Dagde, DaGodevas) is God of the Earth and Father-God, that is, the masculine principle. A formidable warrior and skilled craftsman, he has a club that can restore life as well as kill. His symbols are a bottomless cauldron of plenty and a harp with which he rules the seasons.

Dian Cecht (also Dianchcht) is a god of healing. He rules the waters that restore life to the old and dying gods. When Nuada (king of the Tuatha De Danann) lost his hand in battle, Dian Cecht made him a silver one.

Lugh was worshipped during the thirty-day midsummer feast in Ireland. Magical sexual rites undertaken in his name ensured ripening of the crops and a prosperous harvest. He is linked with Rosmerta in Gaul and also corresponds to the Roman god Mercury. His animal totems are the raven and the lynx, representing deviousness. He is known as Lleu in Wales.

Nodens was a god of healing. His magic hounds were also believed to be able to cure the sick.

Irish Goddesses

Airmid is a healing goddess and has responsibility for medicinal plants. She is the keeper of the spring that brings the dead back to life.

Boann is a goddess of bounty and fertility, whose totem is the sacred white cow. She was the wife of Nechtan, a water deity. One story is that the father of her son was Dagda.

Brighid (also Bridget, Brigit, Brighid, Brigindo) is the goddess of healing and fertility, patroness of smiths, poets and doctors. Often symbolized by a white swan or a cow with red horns, she was thought to be the daughter of Dagda. Her festival is that of Imbolc, observed on 2 February. She shares attributes with the ancient Greek Triple Goddess Hecate.

Brighid's Celebration

Imbolc is a celebration of light and the returning spring. It also corresponds to Candlemass in the Christian church, which appropriated existing festivals for its own use. Candles were made at this time from the remaining animal fat, so you may like to attempt to make your own candles by following the instructions on page 28. It was at this time that the sheep were brought down from the hills to lamb in safety, hence the presence in this spell of the lambswool, which is also thought to have been used at birthings.

YOU WILL NEED

A bound bunch of greenery
Enough green branches to mark out your circle
As many white candles as you like
A small wicker basket lined with lambswool to signify Brighid's bed
White flowers to fill the basket
Your cauldron or a safe container holding seeds and a white taper candle

METHOD

❖ Sweep your sacred space deosil (clockwise) with the bound greenery.

❖ Mark out your circle with the branches, working clockwise again. (This represents the fence that was erected to protect the sacred flame of which Brighid is keeper.)

❖ Place the candles clockwise within the perimeter of the circle and light them, saying as you do:

Brighid of the Sacred Flame,
bless our workings here tonight

❖ Place the flowers in the basket, the basket on the left of your altar and the cauldron on the right.

❖ Light the taper candle, then pick up some of the seeds and allow them to trickle through your fingers onto the ground and say:

Deep in the earth, the Maiden stirs
We welcome her, as she returns to our realm

❖ Take flowers from the basket and scatter them within the circle.

❖ Say:

Here on the earth the Maiden blossoms
We welcome her as she returns

❖ Replace the basket on the altar, step back and raise your arms as though you were embracing the world and say:

Here in this place the Goddess manifests
We welcome her as she returns

❖ Remain for a few moments in this position as you feel the energy building up around you.

❖ When you feel ready pick up the cauldron with its lit taper candle and place it in the main window of your home, allowing it to burn out.

❖ Leave the basket on the altar overnight.

❖ Remember to thank the Goddess for her presence, secure your sacred space and blow out the remaining candles if it is not safe to leave them.

This ritual commemorates the return to life of the Maiden in the cycle of the year. Placing the candle in the window is an old custom to welcome home the traveller and reassure him that all is well within. It also signifies the sacred flame, for Brighid is a fire goddess, patron of blacksmiths: her fire is kept alight at a shrine in Kildare in Ireland, commemorating her Christian counterpart St Bridget.

Danu (also Don in Welsh) probably existed earlier as Anu, the Universal Mother. She is said to be to be the mother of Dagda, God of the Tuatha De Danaan.

Morrigan is the goddess of war and death. Married to Dagda, she is linked with negative femininity and the more fearsome characteristics of the Triple Goddess. She could transform into a crow or raven.

Tuatha De Danann ('People of the Goddess Danu') are the members of an ancient race who inhabited Ireland before Danu made Dagda, her son, their God. They perfected the use of magic and are credited with the possession of magical powers and great wisdom. The plough, the hazel and the Sun were sacred to them.

Welsh Gods

Amaethon is the Welsh god of agriculture.

Bran is a hero god and also the god of poetry and the underworld. His name means 'raven'.

Belatu-Cadros is a god of war and of the destruction of enemies. His name means 'fair shining one'. The Romans linked him with Mars.

Dewi is a dragon god, represented by the Great Red Serpent. The official emblem of Wales is derived from this representation.

Dylan is a sea god, brother of Lleu. He is said to have slipped into the sea at birth, possibly in order to avoid the curses their mother Arianrhod placed upon them.

Gwydion is a warrior and a magician god. He was brother to Arianrhod. There are various stories about him – the most well-known suggesting that he fathered Lleu and Dylan or that he raised and passed on his knowledge to Lleu.

Lleu (also Lleu Llaw Gyffes) is god of arts and crafts, also a solar and hero god. His name translates as 'the fair one has a skilful hand'. Brother of Dylan, he was denied a name by his mother Arianrhod (see below). Overcoming the problems thus given, he became one of the most revered of Welsh gods.

Lleu's Spell

This spell honours the Celtic culture-bringer and solar god (Lleu to the Welsh, Lugh to the

Irish, Lugus to the Gauls). As Lleu, he was cursed by his mother Arianrhod that he would have no name unless she named him herself; that he would bear no weapons unless she armed him herself; and that he would not have a wife from any race that now lived on this earth. He duly overcame these difficulties to become all powerful.

YOU WILL NEED

Two orange candles
Lleu incense (see below)
A corn doll decorated with flowers (to represent Lleu's wife)
Picture or representation of a bow and arrow, your boline or a ceremonial dagger (to represent a weapon)
Barley, oats and wheat ears to scatter
A loaf of bread (to commemorate the Saxon Feast of Bread)
Beer or cider

METHOD

❖ Light the candles and the incense.
❖ Wait a few moments for the incense to permeate the atmosphere.
❖ Take the doll in your left hand and the arrow or dagger in your right.
❖ Present these in order to the God as you say the words:

> *Lleu, named Little One by your mother,*
> *Armed in her defence and*
> *wed to the Flower Maiden*
> *Join now in my/our rite as we/I honour you*

❖ Replace both the doll and the arrow or weapon on the altar.
❖ Taking a seed head, rub it between your fingers and scatter it over the altar to represent threshing the grain.
❖ Say:

> *May these seeds signify the*
> *harvests still to come.*

❖ Pick up the loaf and break off a large piece, placing it to one side (this is distributed to the animals later).
❖ Say:

> *Here we offer you the fruits of our labour which we*
> *share with your creatures.*

❖ Break off a small piece of the loaf and say:

> *Now I partake of your goodness,*
> *May I be at one with you.*

❖ Eat the bread.
❖ Take a sip of beer or cider and say:

> *As my thirst is quenched,*
> *so shall be that of the rest of the world.*

❖ If you are in a group then the bread and cider is shared among you and if the ritual is performed out of doors, the remains are given to the birds and animals at that time.

The partaking of the bread and cider also celebrates Lammas, at which the first of the grain harvest is consumed in ritual loaves. If this spell is performed indoors, you might like to use the beer or cider as a form of wassailing (libation) of a local tree. Even the popular pastime of feeding the ducks with your bread honours the tradition. The athame or ritual knife is not used since it cannot be so for aggressive purposes. This time is also sacred to the Greek Goddess of the Moon and the Hunt, Artemis, hence an arrow – her symbol can be substituted.

Lleu Incense

1 part cedar
1 part juniper
¹/₂ part sandalwood

Math is an eminent magician and lord of North Wales, brother of Don, the Welsh mother-Goddess. Returning from battle he discovered that his foot-holder, who had to be a virgin, had been raped by his nephews (see Arianrhod). Furious, he turned them first of all into a stag and a hind, then a boar and a sow, and then a wolf and a she-wolf.

Welsh Goddesses

Arianrhod is a Moon goddess. Her name means 'silver wheel'. She is the daughter of Don, sister of Gwydion. Given the position of foot-holder to

Math, and therefore supposedly a virgin, she nevertheless gave birth to Dylan and Lleu, cursing the latter, thus taking her revenge on all men. She is an aspect of the Triple Goddess.

❊ Moon Goddess Incense ❊

2 parts benzoin resin
1 part white onion skins
1½ parts allspice
1½ parts camphor
½ part poppy

Branwen is the goddess of love and beauty. She is linked with the Greek goddess Aphrodite and the Roman goddess Venus.

Ceridwen is best known in her aspect of the 'Dark Goddess'. She was the keeper of the Cauldron of Inspiration and Knowledge. She causes things to be reborn (changed, by having been given her protection) and at the same time is in charge of the actual process of generation. She has the power of knowing what is needed, whatever the circumstances. Ceridwen corresponds to Brighid.

Rhiannon is believed to be the Welsh counterpart of the Gaulish horse goddess Epona and the Irish goddess Macha.

Egyptian Gods

Amun (also Ammon, Amon Ra) was a supreme god of the ancient Egyptians. His worship spread to Greece, where he was identified with Zeus, and to Rome where he was known as Jupiter Ammon.

Anubis is the god of mummification and protector of tombs and is often represented as having a jackal's head. He is said to have weighed the souls of the dead against a feather.

Atum was known as 'the complete one'. He is a great creator-god thought to have been the oldest worshipped at Heliopolis. He is usually shown as a man wearing a double crown.

Apis, a God depicted as a bull, symbolized fertility and strength in war. Apis was worshipped especially at Memphis.

Bes is a protector of women during pregnancy and childbirth. Fond of parties and sensual music, he is also credited with being able to dispel evil spirits.

Geb (also Kebu, Seb, Sibu, Sivu) is a God of the earth, earthquakes and fertility. His sister Nut was his counterpart as the Sky Goddess.

Horus, a sky god whose symbol is the hawk, is usually depicted as a falcon-headed man. He was regarded as the protector of the monarchy and his name was often added to royal titles. He assumed various aspects and was known to the Greeks as Harpocrates (Horus the Child).

Khephra (also Khephera, Khopri) is said to have been self-created and God of the Dawn Sun. His symbol is the scarab beetle, which stands for health, strength and virility. Wear a scarab amulet to invoke Khephra's protection.

Khonsu, whose name means 'he who crosses', was a Moon god worshipped especially at Thebes and was the divine son of Amun and Mut.

Osiris, a god originally associated with fertility, was the husband of Isis and father of Horus. He is known chiefly through the story of his death at the hand of his brother Seth and his subsequent restoration by his wife Isis to a new life as ruler of the Afterlife.

Ptah was an ancient deity of Memphis, creator of the universe, god of artisans and husband of Sekhmet. He became one of the chief deities of Egypt and was identified by the Greeks with Hephaestus.

Ra, the supreme Egyptian Sun God, was worshipped as the creator of all life and often portrayed with a falcon's head bearing the solar disc. He appears travelling in his ship with other gods, crossing the sky by day and journeying through the underworld at the dead of night.

❊ Sun God Incense ❊

1 part frankincense resin
1 part benzoin resin
1 part cinnamon
½ part coriander

Seth, as one of the oldest of the Egyptian deities, is the god of chaos and evil. He is shown as a man with the head of a monster.

Thoth is the God of knowledge, law, wisdom, writing and the Moon. He is also the measurer of time and depicted either as an ibis, a man with the head of an ibis, or as a baboon.

Egyptian Goddesses

Bast (also Bastet) is a goddess who is usually shown as a woman with the head of a cat and wearing one gold earring and carrying a sistrum in her right hand. She is the goddess of pleasure, dancing, music and joy. Cats were considered to be her sacred animal and were therefore protected from harm.

Bast's Spell

In Egypt cats were under the protection of Bast, hence they were once seen as witches' familiars. This spell and its invocation link you with that goddess and seek her protection for you and your pet. Cats, worn in the form of an amulet, mean the wearer seeks her protection. They are often worn as small charms on bracelets.

YOU WILL NEED

Lunar incense (equal measures of juniper, orris root and camphor)
2 white candles
An image of a cat (perhaps a charm, figurine or brooch)
If you can find one, an image of Bast

METHOD

❖ Light your incense and your candles.
❖ When ready invoke the power of the goddess by saying:

Goddess Bast Goddess Bast
Mother of Mahes from centuries past
Feline keeper of the Royal flame
Hear me now, as I call your name

Wise bestower of feminine scents and charm
Let me and mine never come to harm.

❖ Now offer the amulet to her.
❖ Pass it through the smoke of the incense and through the flame of the candles.
❖ Hold it up and say:

With this token that I carry
Of your wisdom and your knowledge
Never doubt I will acknowledge
Those who take this path beside me
As we safeguard your sacred memory.

❖ Wear your amulet to remind you of loyalty to Bast and all she represents.

Often, when you have made a dedication to Bast, you become far more aware of cats and their habits. Frequently you find you have been given a gift of some sort, which acknowledges the link. This might be something you need or perhaps an opportunity to do something you have always wanted to do.

Hathor is a sky goddess, the patron of love and joy, represented variously as a cow, with a cow's head or ears or with a solar disk between the cow's horns. Her name means 'House of Horus'.

Isis is first a nature Goddess, wife of Osiris and mother of Horus. Her worship spread to Western Asia, Greece and Rome, where she was identified with various local goddesses. When Seth killed Osiris she sought his scattered body in order that she could give birth to Horus, a sky god.

☀ Isis Incense ☀

1 part myrrh resin
1 part frankincense resin
½ part orange peel
¼ part gum arabic
½ part vetivert

Maat is the goddess of truth, justice and cosmic order and was the daughter of Ra. She is depicted as a young and beautiful woman, seated or standing, with a feather on her head.

Mut is the queen of all the gods and regarded as the wife of all living things. She was also the wife of Amon and mother of Khonsu. She is usually depicted with the head of a vulture. Her name means 'the mother'.

Nut, the Sky Goddess, was thought to swallow the Sun at night and give birth to it in the morning. She is usually shown as a naked woman with her body arched above the earth, which she touches with her feet and hands.

Sekhmet is a fierce lion goddess, counterpart of the gentler cat goddess Bast and wife of Ptah at Memphis. Her messengers were abominable creatures who could bring about diseases and other curses on mankind.

Classical Gods

Greek Gods

Apollo, son of Zeus and Leto, and brother of Artemis, is presented as the ideal type of manly beauty. He is associated with the Sun and linked especially with music, poetic inspiration, archery, prophecy, medicine and pastoral life.

❋ Apollo Incense ❋

2 parts frankincense resin
1 part myrrh resin
1 part cinnamon
½ part bay

Asclepius, as god of healing and the son of Apollo, is often represented wearing a staff with a serpent coiled round it. He sometimes bears a scroll or tablet thought to represent medical learning.

Chaos is the first created being, from which came the primeval deities Gaia, Tartarus, Erebus and Nyx.

Cronus (also Kronos) is the leader of the Titans and the ruler of time. He married his sister Rhea, who bore him several children who became Gods, including Zeus, who eventually overthrew him.

Dionysus was called Bacchus by the Romans and was originally a god of the fertility of nature. Associated with wild and ecstatic religious rites, in later traditions he is a god of wine who loosens inhibitions and inspires creativity in music and poetry.

Erebus is the primeval god of darkness, son of Chaos.

Hades is the God of the Underworld who received as his weapon the helmet of invisibility. He captured Persephone as his consort, causing chaos in the upper world when Demeter went searching for Persephone.

Helios is the Sun personified as a god. He is generally represented as a charioteer driving daily from east to west across the sky.

Hephaestus is the god of fire (especially the smithy fire) and was identified with Vulcan by Romans. He is also the god of craftsmen of all kinds – metalworkers, blacksmiths, leatherworkers, weavers, potters, and painters.

A Spell for Artists and Craftsmen

This spell appeals to the Hephaestus in his capacity as patron god of artists and craftsmen. He was himself a divine craftsman who was lame as a result of having interfered in a quarrel between his parents Zeus and Hera. It was he who taught humankind the value of work and to excel at one's craft.

YOU WILL NEED

Red candle to represent energy not passion
Blue candle for wisdom
Smoky incense to represent the God's forge
The tools you use in your craft (paint brushes, pens, hammer, cloth etc.)

METHOD

❖ Place the red candle on the right of your sacred space, the blue on the left and your tools in between.

❖ Put the incense in the middle above your tools.

❖ Light your incense and build up a smoky atmosphere.

❖ Light the candles, red first then blue.

❖ Pick up the tool you use most, hold it up and say:

> *Hephaestus, God of the forge,*
> *Who despite your disability,*
> *Fashioned articles of beauty*
> *Fit for the Gods*
>
> *Come to my aid*
> *Help me to create things of beauty*
> *Fit for human use.*
> *Help my inability to create those articles*
> *I see with the inner eye*
> *And cannot make manifest*
>
> *Help me now I pray*

❖ Now pass your preferred tool through the smoke of the incense.

❖ Hold it for a few moments, until you can feel its energy and sense it becoming alive in your hands, then say:

> *Hephaestus, I give you my thanks*

❖ When you are next working, make a small offering to the god in thanks – perhaps a coin, a small painting or article you have made.

Hephaestus' Roman counterpart was Vulcan, so it is quite acceptable for you to change the incantation somewhat if you wish. Both gods were lame, so are thought to appreciate the difficulties that mere humans have. Often a concept does not become tangible in the way we wish and this spell is designed to help in that manifestation.

Hermes is the messenger of the gods and the god of merchants, thieves and public speaking. Usually pictured as a herald equipped for travelling with broad-brimmed hat, winged shoes and a winged rod, he was identified by the Romans with Mercury.

❋ Hermes Incense ❋

1 part lavender
¹⁄₂ part gum mastic
¹⁄₂ part cinnamon

Hypnos, the god of sleep, was the son of Nyx (night).

Pan, as a god of flocks and herds, is usually represented with the horns, ears and legs of a goat on a man's body. He was thought of as loving mountains, caves and lonely places as well as playing on the pan-pipes. He is also a god of Nature.

Poseidon is the god of the sea, water, earthquakes and horses. When angered, he was perceived as needing to be pacified. He is often portrayed with a trident in his hand and is identified with the Roman god Neptune.

Proteus is a minor sea god with the power of prophecy but who would assume different shapes to avoid answering questions.

Silenus, an ancient woodland deity, was entrusted with the education of Dionysus. He is shown either as stately, inspired and tuneful or as a drunken old man.

Uranus is a personification of heaven or the sky, the most ancient of the Greek gods and the first ruler of the universe.

Zeus is the supreme god. He was the protector and ruler of humankind, the dispenser of good and evil and the god of weather. He was identified with Jupiter by the Romans.

Greek Goddesses

Achlys is the Greek Mother – the first being to exist, according to myth. She gave birth to Chaos.

Amphitrite is a sea goddess, wife of Poseidon and mother of Triton.

Aphrodite is the goddess of beauty, fertility and sexual love, identified by the Romans with Venus. She is portrayed both as the daughter of Zeus and Dione, or as being born of the sea foam.

❋ Aphrodite Incense ❋

1 part cinnamon
1 part cedar
Few drops of cypress oil

Arachne is a spider Goddess. Originally a mortal, she was a talented weaver who challenged Athene to compete with her. Athene was greatly displeased by Arachne's subject matter and in retribution turned her into a spider.

Artemis, a huntress goddess, is often depicted with a bow and arrows and is associated with birth, fertility and abundance. She was identified with the Roman goddess Diana and with Selene.

Athene is identified with the Roman Minerva and often symbolized as an epitome of wisdom and strategy; she is also called Pallas. Statues show her as female but fully armed; the owl is regularly associated with her.

Cybele is a goddess of caverns and of the primitive earth. Also known as a bee goddess, she ruled over wild beasts.

Demeter is a corn and barley goddess, and also goddess of the earth in its productive state. She is mother of Persephone. She is identified with Ceres and also Cybele; her symbol is often an ear of corn.

Hecate is the goddess of dark places, often associated with ghosts and sorcery and worshipped with offerings at crossroads. Identified as Queen of the Witches in the modern day, she is frequently identified with Artemis and Selene; her name means 'the distant one'.

Hecate's Spell

This is a spell which uses an incantation to Hecate in her capacity as the goddess of the crossroads. She therefore can assist in the making of important decisions, which is why she is approached in this instance. Her sacred day is Friday, so that would be the best day to perform this spell.

YOU WILL NEED ──────────────
Hecate incense
Small bowl containing honey

METHOD ──────────────────
❖ Light your incense.
❖ Contemplate your decision. If necessary write down all the options.
❖ Stand with your arms in the Goddess position (arms crossed) to acknowledge the presence.
❖ Read the incantation below aloud and let the energy of it flow through you for a few minutes.

All powerful Hecate, goddess of victory
Bestower of good fortune and infinite wealth
Hear my prayer, that I send through this
sweet-smelling smoke

Wise Watcher of the crossroads and
the forking alleyways
Of sailors, and travellers and all journeying folk
Hear me now as I too humbly make my approach.

❖ Raise the bowl of honey and say:

Accept this offering of fresh clear honey
As sweet and as pure as your fine beauty
Bestow divine light
Bring me clarity
Hear my prayer now
As I choose which road.

❖ Put the honey bowl down.
❖ Raise your arms again in acknowledgement of Hecate.
❖ Lower your arms.
❖ Sit down quietly, knowing that the answer will come to you and that you will know which decision to make.

You may not receive an answer immediately, but rest assured that one will come. Hecate is known as one of the goddesses who works at night, so you may find you receive an answer through dreams.

❋ Hecate Incense ❋

3 parts sandalwood
2 parts cypress
1 part spearmint

Hera was worshipped as the queen of heaven and a marriage goddess. The Romans identified her with Juno.

Hestia is a goddess of hearth and fire, much like Brigid. She was believed to preside at all sacrificial altar fires and prayers were offered to her before and after meals. In Rome, Hestia was worshipped as Vesta.

Nemesis is a goddess usually portrayed as the agent of divine punishment for wrongdoing or presumption. She is often little more than the personification of retribution.

Nike is the goddess of victory, who challenged her suitors to outrun her.

Persephone was called Proserpina by the Romans. From a magical perspective her story symbolizes the return of fertility to the earth. Hades, king of the underworld, wanted her as his wife, carrying her off and making her queen of the underworld. Demeter, her mother, unable to find her, began to pine and famine began to spread around the world. Eventually it was agreed that she would spend six months on earth and six months in the underworld.

Selene, the Goddess of the Moon, is identified with Artemis.

Themis is the daughter of Uranus (Heaven) and Gaia (Earth). She is the personification of order and justice, who convenes the assembly of the gods.

Roman Gods

Cupid is the god of love and was identified by the Romans with Eros. He is often pictured as a beautiful naked boy with wings, carrying a bow and arrow, with which he pierces his victims.

Janus is an ancient Italian deity. He is guardian of doorways, gates and beginnings and protector of the state in times of war. He is usually represented with two faces, so that he looks both forwards and backwards.

Jupiter is the chief god of the Roman state, giver of victory, and is identified with Zeus. Also called Jove, he was originally a sky god associated with lightning and the thunderbolt. His wife was Juno.

Mars is the god of war and the most important god after Jupiter. He is identified by the Greek with Ares and was probably originally an agricultural god. The month of March is named after him.

Mercury is the god of eloquence, skill, trading and thieving. He was a herald and messenger of the gods, who was identified with Hermes.

❊ Mercury Incense 1 ❊

2 parts benzoin resin
1 part frankincense resin
1 part mace

❊ Mercury Incense 2 ❊

2 parts sandalwood
1 part gum mastic
½ part lavender
Few drops of lavender oil

Neptune is the god of water, originally fresh water and latterly of the sea. He is also the god of horse-racing, and is also identified with the Greek Poseidon.

Horse Racing

This spell calls on the power of Neptune in his lesser-known aspect as the god of horse-racing. It utilizes the modern-day tools of that pastime, as well as some correspondences from ancient times.

YOU WILL NEED —————————
Green candle (for money)
Neptune incense
Betting slip
Bowl of fresh water
Salt
Seaweed or oakmoss
Pen

METHOD —————————
✤ Light your candle and the incense.
✤ Pass the betting slip through the incense smoke.
✤ Place it under the bowl of fresh water.
✤ Add the salt to the water to represent Neptune's transformation from freshwater god to god of the sea.
✤ Add the seaweed to the water.
✤ Stir the water clockwise with your right index finger.
✤ Say the following words:

> *Neptune, keeper of intuition,*
> *Carer of horses, steeds of men,*
> *Work wonders now at my behest*
> *With a winner may I be blessed.*

✤ Let the candle burn for at least an hour.
✤ Take the betting slip and sit quietly for ten minutes.
✤ Write out your betting slip, watch your race and await results.

One of Neptune's qualities is his capriciousness, so unfortunately it is not possible to guarantee winners every time. Having appealed to Neptune in the right spirit though, overall you should gain by his beneficence.

❊ Neptune Incense ❊

½ part myrrh gum
1½ parts copal resin
2 parts sandalwood chips
1 part dried Irish moss
3 drops oakmoss oil

Pluto is the God of the Underworld and of transformation. He has responsibility for precious metals and was sometimes known as the Rich One.

Saturn is an ancient god identified with the Greek Cronus, often regarded as a god of agriculture. His festival in December, Saturnalia, eventually became one of the elements in the traditional celebrations of Christmas.

Silvanus is an Italian woodland deity identified with Pan. He is also worshipped in the Celtic religion.

Roman Goddesses

Angerona is the goddess of secrecy and is portrayed with her mouth bound and sealed, her finger raised to her mouth in a gesture of warning.

Bona Dea is an earth goddess of fertility who was worshipped by women only – no men were allowed present during her rites. The Romans would even cover up statues of the male gods when her rite was performed.

Ceres, the corn goddess, is commonly identified by the Romans with Demeter.

Diana is an early goddess identified with Artemis and associated with hunting, virginity and the Moon.

Juno is an ancient mother goddess and became the most important goddess of the Roman state. She was the wife of Jupiter.

Minerva is the goddess of handicrafts, commonly worshipped and associated with Athene. Because of this association, she came to be regarded as the goddess of war.

Muses (Roman and Greek) are the goddesses who presided over the arts and sciences. Customarily nine in number (Calliope, Clio, Eurterpe, Terpsichore, Erato, Melpomene, Thalia, Polyhymnia and Urania), their functions and even their names differ widely between the various sources.

Venus, the supreme goddess of beauty, is identified with Aphrodite and was honoured as the mother of the Roman people. In earlier times, she was a spirit of kitchen gardens.

Vesta, the goddess of the hearth and household, was considered important enough to have her own handmaidens, the vestal virgins.

Norse Gods and Goddesses

Deities in Scandinavia were originally of two sorts – Aesir and Vanir. These latter were largely nature deities rather than fertility gods and goddesses, and were incorporated into the former after warring with them.

The Scandinavian creation myth is that the gods Odin, Vili and Ve, three brothers, were walking by the sea when they found two trees out of which they fashioned the parents of the human race, giving them spirit, life, wit, feeling, form and the five senses. They then retired to Asgard where they dwelt in a great house or hall called Gladsheim. Valhall in Gladsheim was Odin's place of the warriors, while Yggdrasil, the 'World Tree' – a universal column sustaining everything – was one version of the Tree of Life. It is sometimes thought to be the sacred ash tree.

Gods

There are many Scandinavian deities. Some of the most important ones to appeal to in spell making are:

Balder, whose name means bright, was the son of Odin and Frigg. The wisest of the gods, his judgements were final. He was killed by Loki, who gave him mistletoe, the only plant that had not agreed to protect him.

Frey is the God of Yule, traditionally born on the winter solstice, usually 21 December. He is a god of peace and plenty who brings fertility and prosperity. His effigy was paraded by the people on a wagon throughout the land, in the dead of winter.

Loki is the personification of malicious mischief. Probably initially a fire god, he is supposed to bring the gods great hardship but also to be able to relieve this. He is somewhat capricious and not to be trusted. He is known as The Trickster.

Njord rules the winds and quietens both the sea and fire. He is appealed to when undertaking a journey, and when hunting. He is worshipped by seafarers. Also the god of wealth, he is often coupled in toasts with his son, Frey.

Odin (also Woden) is a magician and wise one. He learned the secrets of the runes by hanging himself from the ash tree Yggdrasil for nine nights. He was a shape-shifter and was known as Father of the Gods. Wednesday (Odin's Day) was named after him.

Thor is the Thunderer, who wields his divine hammer – he was the strongest of the Gods. His chariot racing across the sky is said to generate thunder, though other stories suggest this is done when he blows into his beard. He is also a fertility god. Thursday (Thor's Day) was named after him.

Tyr is the god of battle, identified with Mars, after whom Tuesday is named.

Goddesses

Freya, the daughter of Njord, is the goddess of love, beauty and sexuality. She is said to choose the souls of those who have fallen in battle to take them to Valhalla (Odin's heaven). She is particularly skilled in magic.

Freya's Spell

Freya's specialities are the runes, shape shifting, clairvoyance, divination and prophecy. The best day to carry out this spell is on a Friday which, of course, is special to Freya, but you can also perform it when you need to be particularly clear in your psychic skills.

YOU WILL NEED

Altar table
Pieces of amber
Shiny metal (clean tin foil will suffice)
White candles
Burin
Images of swans and cats (Freya's animals)

METHOD

❖ Decorate your altar with the images, amber and metal.
❖ Inscribe runes from the Set of Freya (see pages 146-148) appropriate to your wish, on the candles.
❖ Light the candles and allow them to burn down, bearing in mind as you do so, your request.

Frigg is Odin's wife and the foremost of the Asyngur (Goddesses). She is the patroness of the household and of married women. She was, and is, invoked by the childless. Also the mother of the Aesir, she gives her name to Friday. She was inadvertently instrumental in Balder's death – all things took oaths not to hurt him, except mistletoe, which was considered by Frigg to be too young.

Idunn possessed the apples of immortality, which rejuvenated the gods when they grew old. Because Scandinavian gods were not immortal, they therefore depended upon her and her good will for the continuation of life.

Norns are the three virgin goddesses of destiny (Urd or Urder, Verdandi and Skuld). They sit by the Well of Fate at the base of the ash tree Yggdrasil and spin the Web of Fate.

Ostara's symbols are the egg and the hare. While not strictly Nordic, she is a Germanic goddess of fertility who is celebrated at the time of the spring equinox. She was allegedly known by the Saxons as Eostre, the goddess of spring, from whom we have derived the word Easter, though modern-day research tends to disprove this.

Ostara's Spell

This ritual acknowledges spring's beginning, and celebrates the Goddess in her Maiden form. It is a time for fertility rites and pruning spring blossom. The ritual celebrates the glory of the coming of springtime and the banishing of darkness. A group working such as this, makes use of the old customs.

YOU WILL NEED

Fresh flowers
Green and yellow candles
Cauldron
Hard-boiled eggs (one for each member of the group)
Ostara incense (see below)

METHOD

❖ Light the candles and incense and cast your circle, placing the flowers around the perimeter of the circle.
❖ Fill the cauldron with the eggs (any remaining eggs should be placed in the circle). The filled cauldron represents the womb of the Goddess.
❖ If the cauldron is small enough, raise it in both hands or, if not, place both hands on it and say:

Hallowed be the Great Goddess,
our Mother and our provider.
The bleak winter storms subside leaving
life to flourish outward.
It peeps out quietly, refreshed by the
God and Goddess's power.
We feel you. We thank you for all your gifts.

❖ Now concentrate on the flowers and say:

217

May we carry within us a total understanding of all living creatures, both great and small. Mother Goddess, Father God, show us how to worship the earth and all it holds.

❖ Now is the time to decorate your eggs and perhaps hold a simple feast.

Traditionally, now is when life quickens within the Goddess and she manifests her beauty in the pastel colours of springtime. Decorated eggs have been used to celebrate spring since the time of the Ancients.

❋ Ostara Incense ❋

1 part jasmine
1 part rose
1 part violet

Skadi was the consort of Njord and is said to have preferred to live in the mountains rather than by the sea. She is the Goddess of death, independence and hunting.

South American Gods and Goddesses
Gods

Bacabs (Mayan) are the gods of the four points of the compass, who hold up the sky. They are also lords of the seasons.

Chac (Aztec and Mayan) is a rain and vegetation god. He is also the lord of thunder, lightning, wind and fertility and revered particularly by farmers.

Cupara (Jivaro) and his wife are the parents of the Sun, for whom they created the Moon from mud to be his mate. The children of the Sun and Moon are the animals.

Hunab Ku (also known as Kinebahan) is the chief god of the Mayan pantheon, the Great God without Form, existing only in spirit.

Huehueteotl (Aztec), a fire god, is also patron of warriors and kings. Associated with creation, he is often depicted as a crouched old man with a bowl of burning incense on his head.

Hurakan (Mayan) is god of thunderstorms and the whirlwind. His name gave us the word 'hurricane'. At the behest of his friend Gucumatz, son of the Sun and the Moon, Hurakan created the world, the animals, men and fire.

Imaymana Viracocha and **Tocapo Viracocha** (Inca) are the sons of the creator god Viracocha. They gave names to all the trees, flowers, fruits and herbs and supervised the people, telling them which of these could be eaten, which could cure, and which could kill.

Inti (Inca) is a Sun god. His image is a golden disk with a human face surrounded by bright rays. Every day Inti soars across the sky to the western horizon, plunges into the sea and swims under the earth back to the east. His sons, Viracocha, Manco Capac and Pachamac, are all creator gods.

Itzamna (Maya) is a sky god and healer and son of Hunab Ku. God of drawing and letters, patron of learning and the sciences, Itzamna is said to be able to bring the dead back to life.

Kinich Ahau (also Ah Xoc Kin) (Mayan), the Sun god, is usually shown with jaguar features, wearing the symbol of Kin (the Mayan day). As Ah Xoc Kin, he was associated with music and poetry.

Kukulcan (Mayan) is a serpent god and has similarities to Quetzalcoatl of the Aztecs.

Ngurvilu (Araucanian, Chile) is god of lakes and seas.

Pillan (Araucanian, Chile) is god of fire, thunder, and war, chief of all the gods. Aided by brigades of evil spirits, he causes earthquakes and volcanic eruptions, blights crops, creates storms and sends war.

Quetzalcoatl (Aztec) is an ancient deity and greatly revered; he is also believed to have been the creator god and is identified with the planet Venus. He is also identified with breath, wind, rain and sea breezes. The incense below is a powerful one, that is suitable for use in spells and rituals which appeal to Quetzalcoatl or any of the major Aztec gods and goddesses.

❋ Sahumeria Azteca Incense ❋

2 parts copal resin
2 parts frankincense resin
1 part rosemary
1 part sage
1 part lemongrass
1 part bay
½ part marigold
½ part yerba santa

Tezcatlipoca (Aztec) is an all-powerful god who can see everything that happens in the world as it is reflected in his mirror. He is associated with night, the jaguar, sorcery, natural forces, human strength, weakness, wealth, happiness and sorrow.

Tupan (Tupinamba, Brazil) is god of thunder and lightening. When Tupan visits his mother, the passage of his boat causes storms. The Tupinamba respect, but do not worship, Tupan.

Viracocha (Inca) means, literally, sea foam. The creator and teacher of the world, Virococha made new people out of clay after the Great Flood. On each figure he painted the features, clothes and hairstyles of the many nations, and gave to them their languages, songs and the seeds they were to plant. Bringing them to life, Viracocha ordered them to travel underground and emerge at different places on the earth. Then Viracocha made the Sun, Moon and stars, and assigned them to their places in the sky.

Goddesses

Auchimalgen (Araucanian, Chile) as Moon goddess and wife of the Sun wards off evil.

Evaki (Bakairi) is goddess of night. She is said to place the Sun in a pot every night and move it back to its starting point in the east every day.

Ix Chel (Maya) is consort of Itzamna and goddess of the Moon, weaving and medicine. Except for Hunab Ku, all the other gods are the progeny of Ix Chel and Itzamna.

Mama Quilla (Inca) is goddess of the Moon and protector of married women. Her image is a silver disc with a human face.

Tonantzin (Aztec) is a goddess of fertility.

Xochiquetzal (Aztec), originally a Moon goddess of the earth, flowers, plants, games and dance, is principally a goddess of love. Also beloved of artisans, prostitutes, pregnant women and birth, she is the most charming of the Aztec pantheon. She is responsible for butterflies, symbolic of love, death and rebirth, transformation, hope, freedom, and spiritual awakening, and birds.

Freedom of Spirit

Butterfly goddesses have reigned in cultures as diverse as Minoan Cretan and Toltec Mexican.

This spell calls on Xochiquetzal and Itzpapálotl, the Mother Goddess of the Chichimec people. It acknowledges the idea that the butterfly represents the soul.

YOU WILL NEED

One white candle
Representation of a butterfly – a picture, a brooch or something similar
Copal oil
Mexican Magic incense containing copal, frankincense and rosemary
Flowers and vegetation

METHOD

✦ Anoint the candle with the oil from base to tip to signify freedom from the mundane and ordinary.

✦ Light the incense and the candle.

✦ Take the representation of the butterfly in both hands and contemplate for a short time what freedom represents to you. This may be, for instance, the freedom to be creative, to travel, or simply the freedom to be yourself.

✦ Bearing in mind the two Mexican goddesses, say:

Xochiquetzal, Itzpapálotl,
protectress and Mother
I ask you both to set me free from
wordly concerns
That my soul may fly as does the butterfly
Pursuing glory and freedom's Holy Flame.

✦ Tuck the representation of the butterfly into the flowers and place them above shoulder height in a safe place, to represent spiritual freedom.

✦ Allow the candle to burn out safely.

✦ Do not be too surprised if you notice more butterflies around you, or see them in places or at times you would least expect.

The butterfly has inspired a wide range of sacred and secular objects, from ritual masks, shaman's rattles, stone carvings, temple murals, and Tarot cards, to jewelled combs, haute couture, furniture design and fabulous fabrics. Their appearance in your life is simply acknowledgement of your new-found freedom.

Sumerian, Assyrian and Babylonian Gods and Goddesses

Many of the gods and goddesses shown below are well-known through myth and other stories handed down through time. Only true scholars of the period are able to differentiate between the cultures. The creation stories however give us access to some very primeval, raw energies. These entities release a great deal of energy for use in magic and spell making, so only use them if you feel confident that you have learnt to understand them.

Gods

Anshar is father of all the gods. Anshar is the male principle, Kishu, his sister, the female. Anshar is the sky, Kishu the earth. He led the gods in the war against Tiamat.

Anu is the god of the sky and one of four Sumerian creator gods. Lord of all, the fountainhead of order in both the natural and supernatural worlds, Anu dwells exclusively in the celestial heaven.

Apsu is the Abyss, the waters upon which the earth floats. When the gods were first created, their noise disturbed Apsu, who complained to the great dragon Tiamat (see below).

Ea (also Enki) is the god of water, particularly fresh. He is the supreme god of magic and wisdom, patron of the arts and consulted as an oracle. Mating with Ninhursag, he created plants and gave men agriculture. In Sumerian belief he is the son of Nintu.

Enlil is the god of earth and wind and the master of men's fates. One of four Sumerian creating gods, he is the god who dries up the flood waters, yet who brings rain, fills the sails of ships and boats; and fertilizes the palm blossoms. He is the god who struggles against the suffering of the world and is the active principle which drives the earth.

Gilgamesh was, like Hercules, a hero-god, two parts divine and one part human. Gilgamesh, having fought and tamed the wild man Enkiddu, set out with him on a quest. Enkiddu's death drove Gilgamesh to seek immortality, and eventually with his wife, he was granted eternal life by the gods.

Kingu is consort of Tiamat and keeper of the tablets of destiny, which hold the divine plan for all the cosmos. Ninhursag used Kingu's blood to make the first man, and from this comes the rebellious aspect of human nature.

Marduk is the counterpart of the Sumerian Anu and Enlil. Chief god of Babylon, he became the lord of the gods of heaven and earth after conquering Tiamat, the monster of primeval chaos, thus bringing order and life to the world.

Nebo (also Nabu) is god of writing and speech, speaker for the gods. Nebo maintains records of men's deeds and produces them for judgment after death. His symbol is the stylus.

Nergal is god of the underworld, consort of Ereshkigal.

Shamash (also Babbar) is the son of Sin, brother and husband to Ishtar. The enemy of darkness and all the evil darkness brings, in Sumeria he is a god of divination. He requires justice of earthly kings and champions their subjects, especially the poor.

Sin is the Moon god who flies through the sky in his sailing boat every night. Wise and secretive, the enemy of all evil spirits, he is the counterpart of the Sumerian Nanna.

Tammuz (also Dumuzi) is an agricultural god. The god who dies and rises again, he became the personification of the seasonal death and rebirth of crops. He corresponds to the Greek Adonis and to the Green Man.

Goddesses

Astarte (Phoenician) is a goddess of fertility and sexual love; she later became identified with the Egyptian goddess Isis and the Greek Aphrodite, among others.

※ Astarte Incense ※

1 part sandalwood
1 part rose
Few drops of orange oil
Few drops of jasmine oil

Damkina is the Earth Mother goddess, wife of Ea and mother of Marduk.

Ereshkigal is goddess of the underworld, consort of Nergal. Some consider her a dark side, aspect or sister of Ishtar. When Ishtar descended into the underworld, Ereshkigal tricked her into leaving part of her clothing or insignias at each of the underworld's seven gates as she passed through them. Standing naked at the seventh gate, Ishtar threw herself on Ereshkigal's mercy. Ereshkigal confined Ishtar in the underworld until Ea contrived her release with a trick.

Reflection of Evil

Erishkegal ruled over the seven hells (states of illusion). In her best-known aspect she is destructive and vengeful yet – as with many of the Crone aspects of the Goddess – she is often a necessary part of the lessons we need to learn.

YOU WILL NEED ───────────
Banishing incense
Two black or dark purple candles
Mirror
Wand
Tarot cards or other divination method
Moon symbol (perhaps a circle of dark paper)
Herbs in a bowl (a mixture of blessed thistle, rosemary and bay laurel)
Incense burner

METHOD ───────────
❖ Light the candles.
❖ If you use incense charcoal, the herbs can be slowly dropped on the lighted charcoal at the appropriate time in the ritual.
❖ Burn the banishing incense first of all, in order to clear a space for your working.
❖ Cast your circle or dedicate your sacred space as usual. Call upon the four winds or Elements to guard the circle.
❖ When finished, stand facing the east.
❖ Raise your arms in greeting and say:

Between the worlds I consecrate this space
Beyond time, this rite leads to the ancient way,
Come now, you gods of greatest strength
Deepest, Darkest, most omnipotent I greet you.

❖ Take your wand into your power hand (the one you project power with most easily). Holding your arms outstretched, say:

The cycle of the Moon reaches her darkest place
Yet the wisdom of the Dark Mother is here within.

Only the uninitiated would use
that power for wrong
At this darkest time is also power for good.

❖ Tap the altar three times with the wand and say:

Hear me, Wise One
As I call upon you now.
Show me the paths that I must tread
Thus may we clear this sense of dread.

❖ Mix the herbs lightly so that the perfume is released, then hold the bowl up over the altar, and say:

I offer these herbs to cleanse and purify,
Accept them as both offering and token.

❖ Regularly add small amounts of herbs to the burner. (Often the amount of smoke produced will show you from which direction the negativity is coming.) Continue to add small amounts of herbs throughout the rest of the ritual.
❖ Take the Moon symbol in your power hand and the mirror in the other, the reflective side away from you. (With the mirror you will send the negativity back to the source that it has come from. It is wisest if you think of it going back to the source of evil rather than rebounding on the perpetrator of your difficulty.)
❖ Go to the east, hold up the mirror and symbol then say:

I command you, all evil and
unbalanced powers that come from the east,
Return from whence you came.

❖ Go to the south and say:

I command you, all evil and
unbalanced powers that come from the south,
Return from whence you came.

❖ Go to the west and say:

I command you, all evil and
unbalanced powers that come from the west,
Return from whence you came.

❖ Go to the north and say:

> I command you, all evil and
> unbalanced powers that come from the north,
> Return from whence you came.

❖ Stand in the centre of your sacred space and put the mirror down.
❖ Raise the Moon symbol skyward, saying:

> By the symbol of the Moon Goddess, I ask for
> protection from all negative influences.
> Lady of the Moon, I ask for new ideas and
> beginnings and the wisdom and
> guidance to act upon them.
> I believe that strengthened by your perception and
> skills I shall be free.

❖ Ask the Dark Moon Goddess for guidance.
❖ State as clearly as you can what is going wrong in your life and what changes you would like to see happening - whether to yourself or others.
❖ Take up the wand, draw a circle in the air clockwise and say:

> Goddess of dark and unlit places
> I acknowledge you.
> Within your secret realms
> You change your form.
> So seven times within each little hell
> I beg for change
> As complete as is this circle.

❖ Sit quietly to receive inspiration and insight.
❖ Follow this with divination with tarot or your chosen method to give you a clearer insight. You might do a spell for binding or removing of problems. If you do carry out any other magical working, before you begin do not forget to thank Erishkegal for her presence.
❖ When everything is completed, hold your wand over the altar and say:

> Spirits of Fire, Earth, air and sea.
> Circle of power now work for me.

❖ Sense the energy of the circle being used to bind the negativity.
❖ Close the circle in your normal fashion.

This spell is somewhat involved and needs to be carried out with a sense of commitment. Erishkegal ruled over dark magic, revenge, retribution, the waning and dark Moon, death, destruction and regeneration and therefore helps us to discover our own personal 'darknesses'. Erishkegal's sister Ishtar had to overcome the former's jealousy and terrible power in order to come to terms with her own task.

Ishtar (also Inanna) is a goddess whose name and functions correspond to those of Astarte. A great goddess, the goddess of love and war, Ishtar's worship involved phallic symbols, sacred whores and painted priests in women's clothing.

Ninhursag is an Earth Mother, corresponding to Egyptian Ma'at.

Nintu (also Ki) is a great Sumerian goddess, wife of Anu and mother of all gods. She created humans from clay.

Tiamat is the representation of primeval chaos. Angered by the gods, she fought against them and was slain by Marduk. Being split in two, one half became the Heavens and the other the Earth. She is sometimes known as the Great Serpent and gave rise to the concept of the original Leviathan – the primeval monster of the deep.

African Gods and Goddesses

In African religions, many beliefs go back some 6,000 years and there are numerous deities and traditions associated with them. Only a few are included here and, as always, your own personal research will give you much satisfaction, should you choose to appeal to these gods and goddesses.

Anansi (various tribes) is a creator god. He is also a trickster and corresponds to Loki. Viewed as something of a scoundrel, he is well liked and many amusing and fanciful stories are told of him. He is often used to frighten children.

Anyiewo (Ewe) is the Great Serpent who comes out to graze after the rain. The rainbow is his reflection.

Buku (various West African peoples) is a sky god sometimes worshipped as a goddess. Buku created everything, even the other gods.

Danh (also Dan Ayido Hwedo) (Dahomey) is a snake god; the Haitians know him as Dan Petro. Danh is often portrayed with his tail in his mouth as a symbol of unity and wholeness, similar to the ouroboros. As the rainbow, he is a spiral around the earth and holds it together. He is known in voodoo as Damballa.

Dxui (Bushman; to the Hottentots, Tsui; to the Xhosa and Ponda, Thixo) is a creator god. He took the form of a different flower or plant every day, becoming himself at night, until he had created all the plants and flowers that exist.

Eshu (Yoruba) is a trickster and shape-shifter who can change his form at will. He also knows all human tongues, and acts as a go-between for mortals and the gods.

Gunab (Hottentot) is the enemy of Tsui-Goab (see below). He kept overpowering him but the latter grew stronger after each battle. He is considered responsible for all misfortune, disease and death.

Gua (Ga tribe of West Africa) is the god of thunder, blacksmiths and farmers. He corresponds to Thor. Gua's temples are often found at blacksmith's forges.

Leza (Central Africa) is known to a number of peoples. He is the supreme god who rules the sky and sends wind and rain.

Mawu-Lisa (Ewe) are the great god and goddess of the Sun and Moon. Lisa is the Sun and Mawu is the Moon.

Mulungu (East Africa) is God, the Supreme Being. The concept of a supreme being and creator is nearly universal in Africa and is known by many names. Mulungu is said to speak through thunder, but is considered to be somewhat remote.

Ngai (Masai) is a creator god. Ngai gives each man at birth a guardian spirit to ward off danger and carry him away at the moment of death. The evil are carried off to a desert, while the good go to a land of rich pastures and many cattle.

Nyame (Ashanti) is the Supreme God of Heaven, both the sun god and the Moon goddess. Nyame created the three realms: the sky, the earth and the underworld. Before being born, souls are taken to Nyame and washed in a golden bath. He gives the soul its destiny and places some of the water of life in the soul's mouth. The soul is then fit to be born.

Nyasaye (Maragoli, Kenya) is the chief god of the Maragoli. Spirits aid the Maragolis' work, and they are represented by round stones circling a pole, which represents the god, thus echoing the concept of the World Tree.

Tsui Goab (Hottentot) is a rain god who lives in the clouds, a great chief and magician. Tsui Goab made the first man and woman from rocks. He fought consistently with Gunab.

Unkulunkulu (Zulu) is both the first man and the creator. He showed men how to live together and gave them knowledge of the world in which they lived.

Yo (Dahomey) is a trickster, neither god nor human, Yo's greed constantly gets him in trouble.

Oceanic Gods and Goddesses

There are many gods and goddesses indigenous to the Oceanic region, and the few discussed here show the similarities between creation myths. It has proved difficult to narrow down the Australian gods and goddesses into their Aboriginal tribes.

Agunua (Solomon Islands) is a serpent god. All other gods are only an aspect of him. The first coconut from each tree is sacred to Agunua.

Bunjil (Australian) is a sky god. He made men out of clay while his brother, Bat, made women out of water. To mankind Bunjil gave tools, weapons and religious ceremony.

Daramulun (Australian) is a sky god, a hero. There are many tales of his adventures. Daramulun is usually portrayed with a mouth full of quartz and a huge phallus, carrying a stone axe.

Dream Time (Australian) is the period of creation when the gods brought the world and all living creatures into being.

Gidja (Australian) is a Moon god. In the Dream Time, Gidja created women by castrating Yalungur, for which he was punished by Kallin Kallin. Gidja floated out to sea and ended up in the sky, where he became the Moon.

Great Rainbow Snake (Australian) is also known by many other names. The great giver of life, he lives in a deep pool. He stretches across the sky and shines with water drops, quartz and mother of pearl, whose iridescence holds his life force. In the Dream Time, the Great Rainbow Snake created all waterways – which must not be contaminated with blood – and all living creatures.

Io (New Zealand) is the Supreme Being of the Maori, master of all the other gods, known only to the priesthood.

Kallin Kallin (Australia) punished Gidja for castrating his brother Yalungur, the Eaglehawk. Kallin Kallin then took Yalungur as his wife and so established the custom among Australian aborigines of taking wives from different communities.

Marruni (Melanesia) is the god of earthquakes. Marruni's tail terrified his wives, so he cut it into pieces and made animals and human beings from them.

Maui (Polynesia) is a trickster and a hero god. He lived when the world was still being created, and fought on the side of humankind, constantly struggling to get them a better deal. Maui raised the sky and snared the sun. His death at the hands of Hina brought death into the world.

Nareau (Micronesia) as Old Spider created the world from a seashell, but the heavens and the earth were not properly separated, so Young Spider enlisted the aid of Riiki, the eel, to fix the problem. They then created the sun, Moon and stars, and a great tree from which came the race of men.

Pele (Polynesia) is goddess of volcanic fire and sorcery. She lives on Mount Kilauea in Hawaii. Altars to her are built beside lava streams, though strictly only her descendants worship her.

✳ Pele Incense ✳

2 parts frankincense resin
1 part Dragon's blood powder or resin
1 part red sandalwood
1 part orange peel
1 part cinnamon
Few drops of clove oil

Qat (Polynesia) is a creator god. Qat was born when his mother, a stone, suddenly exploded. He made the first three pairs of men and women by carving them from wood and playing drums to make them dance. He stopped night from going on forever by cutting it with a hard red stone, which is the dawn. Qat sailed away in a canoe filled with all manner of wonderful things, leaving behind the legend that he would one day return. When the Europeans first arrived in Polynesia, many believed that he had finally returned.

Tawhaki (Polynesia) is the god of thunder and lightning. He is said to be noble and handsome.

Tu (Polynesia) is a god of war.

Wondjina (Australia) are the primordial beings of the Dream Time, who created the world. They give both rain and children, and the paintings depicting them are refreshed every year so that they will continue to bring rain at the end of the dry season.

Yalungur (Australia) defeated the terrible ogress Kunapipi, was castrated by Gunja and thus became the first woman.

It is possible to see from this list that every culture had, or has, its own pantheon of gods and goddesses, many of whom shared similar attributes. Misunderstandings between cultures often gave rise to persecution and the need for assimilation of the deities, as we have already seen, for example, in African-based religions.

Paganism

THE TERM 'PAGANISM' was often used in a derogatory way by the early Christians. It is this that gives a clue to the real beliefs held by the original pagan people, for in the early days they would believe implicitly in the power of the earth and the blessings of the sun. Their lives were ruled by the vagaries of the seasons and they developed their own ways of placating and supplicating the powers, which they perceived as much mightier than themselves.

Whether they called these powers gods or spirits did not matter; it was important that they developed a relationship with them. Sometimes the powers could be tamed, sometimes they were made angry and would not co-operate. There were times when one power could be called upon to intercede on a person's behalf, and other times when one must accept the fate meted out.

There are many forms of paganism, although the most relevant form of paganism to practitioners of magic today is probably neo-paganism. In their attempts to reconnect with nature, neo-pagans often use the ancient forms of imagery and ritual in order to get the best from their spell working but adjust them so that they are more relevant to the needs of modern people.

The next section is a rather eclectic mix of information drawn from many sources, which will allow you to form your own opinion as to your most efficient and advantageous way of working. Whether having done so you wish to call yourself pagan is, naturally, up to you.

Spells Preparation

Once you have a clear idea of what magic and spells entail, you will want to perform them under the best possible conditions. There are many ways of doing this, and this section gives you clear instructions on which you can base your own individual practice.

Getting The Best From Your Spells

PERSONAL PREPARATION IS very important and this section tells you about ritual baths and how to tailor them to your needs. Then comes consecrating your sacred space, which consists of (usually) setting aside a part of your home where you feel safe and unthreatened. For many, this means setting up an altar that can be left in position permanently, but for others the sacred space cannot be a permanent one. Those objects that you normally need to include in your working – such as your candlesticks, altar furnishings and so on – will also need to be consecrated (dedicated to the purpose) as indeed will any tools that you use, such as your athame and wand. Before that, you must learn how to cast your circle and this is also discussed.

Following this, is the information you need to make use of astrological correspondences and planetary influences. Each star sign has a particular influence, which it exerts on us and what we do, and learning how to use these influences to the best of your ability will maximize your spell making and gives a good deal of extra power when it is needed.

Each day and each hour is 'ruled by' – receives a particular influence from – the planets. If you are looking for expansion, for instance, you would use the influence of the planet Jupiter. Many spell workers prefer to use the night hours to work in, not necessarily because it is dark, but because it is quiet and the 'hours' – divisions of time – are often longer than our normal 60 minutes.

While colour magic was briefly discussed on page 23, by learning a little more about the use of colour correspondences you can again enhance your work. A short list is included to help you. Words of Power are used in many traditions and some examples are given. There is a tremendous amount to learn and to remember, but gradually you will find that you

settle down into an accepted way of working, and will begin to use any or all of the above knowledge almost instinctively. The trick is to take things slowly and add one new bit of knowledge as you become more proficient.

PREPARATIONS FOR SPELL WORKING

Several processes become automatic when preparing for spell work. If you choose to wear special clothing, for instance, then this has to be prepared before you actually start your personal preparations. Overleaf there are some suggestions for personal robes, which can be laid out with some ceremony before you begin.

Ritual Bathing

Important magical workings require you to take a ritual bath which cleanses, purifies and clarifies your energy so that you are able to get the best results possible. Many practitioners prefer to take a ritual bath before performing any magical workings. For what you may consider 'lesser' magic you do not need to bathe, but may prefer to cleanse yourself by running your hands over your body before you embark on any working.

Ritual Bath

Ritual bathing arose in times gone by from a perceived need to be in as 'virgin' – that is, unsullied – a state as possible. This is what gave rise to working skyclad, that is, without clothes, so that there were no encumbrances between the practitioner and his or her gods or deities.

The candles used in this ritual can be in the colours of the Elements or those most appropriate to your purpose, for example; pink (tranquillity), blue (wisdom), green (self-awareness) and red (passion). For spiritual matters, use purple. There are some suggestions on page 77 for oil blends you might like to use in your bath.

YOU WILL NEED ─────────────

Large white candle
Votive candles according to your need
Essential oil to remove negativity (e.g. rosemary)
Homemade bath salts
Ritual bath oil blend
Large glass of mineral water or juice

METHOD

* Anoint the large white candle with the essential oil and ask for positivity, health and happiness as you do so.
* Do the same with the votive candles according to your need. You may, if you wish, inscribe a symbol to represent your purpose on each candle. You could use runes, Ogham Staves or numbers and symbols appropriate to your belief.
* Run your bath and mix in the bath salts. As you mix in your salts, bless the water and charge it with your intent – be that a particular magical working, a relaxing evening or a successful meeting.
* Light the candles, first the white one followed by the votives. Place the latter safely around the bath. The white candle should be placed wherever you feel is safest.
* You have now created a sacred space for yourself.
* Lie back and enjoy your bath and at some point drink your water or juice, visualizing your whole system being cleansed inside as well as out.
* Before you get out of the bath, thank the water deities for this opportunity to prepare thoroughly for the new energies available to you.
* If you are to perform a magical working, then keep your mind focused on that intent.
* On this occasion, for safety's sake, when you have finished your bath, snuff out the candles.

Making your Bath Salts

Commercial bath salts will do absolutely nothing on an esoteric level – they have too many chemical additives and artificial perfumes – so it is a nice touch to make your own, using single essential oils, blends and/or herbs. The fact that you have mixed them yourself means they are infused with your own vibration and therefore will work on a very subtle level. If you are using a blend of essential oils it is wise to mix them first, to allow the synergy between the oils to develop. Matching your bath salt perfume to your incense perfume does wonders for your inner self.

YOU WILL NEED

3 parts Epsom salts
2 parts baking soda
1 part rock salt (or borax)
Bowl for mixing
Natural food colouring
Ritual bath oil blend
Handful of herbs (optional)

METHOD

* Mix the first three ingredients thoroughly in the mixing bowl.
* Use your hands, as this will enable you to imbue the salts with your own energy.
* This is your basic mixture and can be perfumed or coloured in any way that you please.
* Add your colouring first and mix to your satisfaction.
* Follow with your oil blend, a drop at a time. Be generous with the oils, since the salts will absorb a surprising amount without you realizing. As with all oils and perfumes, however, your nose is the best judge – there is no right or wrong amount.
* Add the herbs to the mixture and combine thoroughly.

When you wish to use your salts, add approximately 2 tablespoons to a full bathtub and mix well.

Clothing and Jewellery

Inevitably there are certain things you will need to remember before you begin your magical working. While you are preparing and putting on your robes or ritual gowns following your ritual bath you might spend time in reflection, silent meditation or prayer. Prior to the beginning of any spell and while dressing, concentrate on the matter in hand. Alternatively, simply focus on the Supreme Being, Cosmic Responsibility and/or a successful outcome, and ask that the event to follow helps you in your learning.

There is no limit to what can be worn. Some recommend white robes with black cords or vice versa, while others simply suggest that you are comfortable in what you wear. Many people will spend a great deal of time, energy and effort on fashioning suitable robes; if you would like to make your own, any fabric is acceptable, although you might like to use one of the fabrics that corresponds to the planets. You may find some of them more comfortable than others! The fabrics are:

Planet	Fabric
Sun	Brocade
Moon	Silk
Mercury	Linen
Venus	Satin
Mars	Tweed
Jupiter	Velvet
Saturn	Hessian

Having chosen the fabric, you can then decide if you wish to decorate your robe or not. You might, for example, like to use some basic symbols which have a universal meaning – the circle which symbolizes infinity, totality and eternity as well as the abyss, or 'no-thing'; the dot which signifies unity and a beginning; the vertical line which suggests the vibrant, energetic principle, or the horizontal line which is the passive, more fixed principle. All of these basic symbols can be joined together in many different ways to enhance their meaning and to indicate broader, equally important, concepts. Another form of decoration you may wish to consider are the astrological symbols.

The idea is that when working magically, you leave behind the ordinary mundane world, so also remember to turn off mobile phones, put away keys and name tags, remove money and other objects from pockets and so on.

It will be a matter of choice as to whether you wear jewellery or not. Magical jewellery such as the pentagram, ankh or rings with magical symbols or significance are often worn, although they are by no

means essential. Many prefer not to wear watches, since time is considered irrelevant. It is often better not to use perfume or cologne unless it is based on essential oils that are suitable for the work in hand, or complement any incense being used.

Poppets

A poppet is a small doll or figurine made from wood, paper, material or clay. It is shaped roughly in human form and is used primarily for magic spells. Originating from West African belief systems, poppets can be used to represent and help either you or someone else.

Only make a poppet of someone else if they have given permission, such as when you wish to help or heal someone. To make one without permission, or for inappropriate reasons, creates the wrong energy vibration and introduces a negativity into your magical workings.

Making a Poppet

When you are making a poppet, it is good to have either taken a ritual bath or to have meditated – both on whether the use of a poppet is appropriate at this time and how best to make use of the poppet. This is to ensure that insofar as is possible, you have removed any subjective feelings and emotions about the subject, and are acting only as the creator of the object. You know then that you are acting only as the channel for the energy that is being used.

YOU WILL NEED

Paper or card (to act as a template)
Soft material such as felt or cotton
Needle and thread
Straw, paper or cotton wool
Herbs, appropriate to the spell you are
performing, may be used

METHOD

✤ Draw the outline of a simple human figure on the card or paper, then cut it out. It should ideally be at least 10 cm (3 in) high.

✤ Fold the material in two and place the template on it.

❖ Cut around the template.

❖ Sew the figures together, leaving a small area open.

❖ Turn the figure inside out so the stitches are on the inside.

❖ Stuff the figure with the straw, paper, cotton wool or herbs. You can personalize the poppet by adding a lock of hair to the filling.

❖ You can also use buttons for eyes, or draw on facial features if you wish.

❖ Finish sewing the material together.

Your poppet is now ready for use. Do not destroy it when you have finished with it – either give it to the person whom it represents or bury it safely in the earth.

Consecrating your sacred space

If you are going to be carrying out a fair number of rituals or spells, you will really need a sacred space or altar along with various other altar furnishings. Whether your altar is inside or outside does not matter. To set it up indoors, your altar and/or sacred space should preferably be in a quiet place in the home, where it will not be disturbed and where candles can be burned safely.

The space first needs to be dedicated to the purpose of magical working. You can do this by first brushing the area clean with an ordinary brush, concentrating your thoughts on cleansing the space as you work physically to bring this about. Mentally cleanse the space three times, imagining doing it once for the physical world, once for the emotional space and once spiritually.

If you wish, you may sprinkle the whole area with water and with salt (which represents the earth). You might perhaps also burn incense such as benzoin, jasmine or frankincense to clear the atmosphere. Think of the space as somewhere you would entertain an honoured guest in your home – you would wish the room you use to be as welcoming as possible. You will later use your besom to keep the sacred space clear.

If you travel a lot or are pushed for space, you might dedicate a tray or special piece of wood or china for ceremonial working. This, along with your candles and incense, can then be kept together in a small box or suitcase. Otherwise, you could dedicate a table especially for the purpose. Ideally, you should not need to pack up each time.

You will also need a 'fine cloth' – the best you can afford – to cover the surface. Place your cloth on your chosen surface and spend some quiet time just thinking about its purpose. You may, if you wish, have different cloths for different purposes or perhaps have one basic cloth, which is then 'dressed' with the appropriate colour for each ritual.

Setting up your altar

To turn your dressed table into a proper altar, you will need as basics the following objects:

1. Two candles with candle holders – you might like to think of one representing the female principle and one the male. In addition, you may also choose candles of a colour suitable for the ritual or spell you are working.
2. An incense holder, and incense suitable for the particular working.
3. A representation of the deity or deities you prefer to work with. An image of the Goddess, for instance, could be anything from a statue of the Chinese Goddess of Compassion, Kuan Yin, to seashells, chalices, bowls, or certain stones that symbolize the womb or motherhood.
4. A small vase for flowers or fresh herbs.

As already mentioned in the Principles and Components section, there are other objects that you are likely to need for your ceremonial working. Briefly, these are:

1. An athame, which is a sacred knife for ceremonial use; it should never be used for anything else.
2. A white-handled knife (called a boline) for cutting branches, herbs, and so on.
3. A burin, which is a sharp-pointed instrument for inscribing magical objects such as candles.
4. A small earthenware or ceramic bowl, or a small cauldron, for mixing ingredients.
5. A bowl of water.
6. A bowl of salt or sand, representing Earth.
7. A consecrated cloth, or a pentacle, on which to place dedicated objects.

Some people additionally use bells to summon the powers of the Elements, while others have additional candles with the colours representing both themselves and the work they wish to do. You can also have other items on your altar, such as crystals, amulets and talismans.

You can do what you wish with your own altar. You should have thought through very carefully the logical or emotional reasons for including whatever you have there. You might, for instance, choose to have differing representations of the Earth Mother from diverse religions, or include a pretty gift to establish a psychic link with the person who gave it to you.

Dedicating your altar

Now you have turned your space into an altar, dedicate it in such a way that it will support any workings you may choose to do. One good way is to dedicate it to the principle of the Greater Good – that none may be harmed by anything that you may do. (Remember that traditionally any harm you instigate deliberately will return to you threefold, particularly when it comes from such a sacred space.) It will depend on your basic belief just how you choose to dedicate the altar further, perhaps to the Moon deity and all her manifestations, perhaps to the gods of power.

Try to put as much passion and energy into the dedication as you can, and remember to include a prayer for protection of your sacred space. Some people will need to cast a circle each time they do a working, while others will feel that just by setting the altar up in the way suggested, the space is consecrated henceforth. If you wish to follow the principles of feng shui rather than Wicca within your work, your placings will be slightly different, as they will also be if you choose to follow the tenets of other religions.

However, whatever you do, you should take care to dedicate all of your tools and altar furnishings to the purpose in hand. You are empowering them and making them usable only in ritual and magical work. If you try to use them for any other purpose, you will negate that magical power.

Consecrating altar objects

If you are not using completely new objects as the basic furnishings (such as candle holders) on your altar, you should cleanse them before you dedicate them to your purpose. Treat them in the same way as you would any crystals you use, by soaking them overnight in salt water to remove anyone else's vibrations and then standing them in sunshine (or moonshine) for at least twelve hours, to charge them with the appropriate energy.

When you are ready, hold each object and allow your own energy to flow into it, followed by the energy of your idea of Ultimate Power. (That way you make a very powerful link between yourself, the object and the Ultimate.) Ask this Power to bless the object and any working you may do with it, and perceive yourself as truly a medium or channel for the energy.

Hopefully, each time you use any of the objects, you will immediately be able to reinforce that link rather than having to re-establish it. It is like a refrain continually running in the background. Now place the objects on your altar in whatever way feels right for you.

Finally, if you wish, create and cast your circle (see below) so that it includes yourself and your altar. The magic circle defines the ritual area, holds in personal power and shuts out all distractions and negative energies. You now have a sacred space set up, which is your link to the powers that be. Again it is a matter of personal choice as to whether you choose to rededicate your altar and what it contains on a regular basis.

Casting a circle

Purify yourself first. You can do this by meditating, or taking a ritual bath. One way is to try to keep the water flowing, possibly by leaving the bath plug half in, or by having a shower. This reinforces the idea of washing away any impurities so you are not sitting in your own psychic rubbish. Ideally, your towel – if you choose to use one – should be clean and used only for the purpose of your ritual bath.

Wear something special if you can, something that you only wear during a ritual or working –

perhaps your robes. You can always add a pretty scarf or a throw in the correct colour for your working. This sets apart spell working from everyday confusion.

Decide on the extent of your circle, which should be formed in front of your altar. Purify this space by sprinkling the area with water followed by salt – both of these should have been blessed or consecrated with simple words.

Sit quietly for as long as you can inside the area that will become your circle. Imagine a circle of light surrounding you. This light could be white, blue or purple. If you are in a hurry and cannot purify and cleanse fully, reinforce the circle of light by visualizing it suffused with the appropriate colour for your working.

Circle the light around, above and below you in a clockwise direction, like the representation of an atom. Feel it as a sphere or as a cone of power. Sense the power. Remember that you can create a 'doorway' through which your magical energy may exit. You should always feel warm and peaceful within your circle. As time goes on, you will be able to differentiate between the various energies.

Use your own personal chant or form of words, according to your own belief system, to consecrate your circle and banish all evil and negative energy, forbidding anything harmful to enter your space. Remember, you are always safe within your circle if you command it to be so.

If you wish, invite the gods and goddesses to attend your circle and magical working. Relax and be happy.

You can use objects on the ground to show the boundaries of the circle, such as candles, crystals, cord, stones, flowers or incense. The circle is formed from personal power. This may be felt and visualized as streaming from the body to form a bubble made of mist, or a circle of light. You can use the athame or your hands to direct this power.

The cardinal points of the compass may be denoted with lit candles, often white or purple. Alternatively, place a green candle at the north point of the circle, yellow candle at the east, red candle at the south and blue candle at the west. The altar stands in the centre of the circle, facing north in the direction of power.

An Alternative Method of Circle Casting

This method probably owes more to the practices of Wicca than any other way, though you do not have to be Wiccan to use it.

YOU WILL NEED

Besom
Ritual tools (athame, etc.)
Candle to represent your working
Altar candles to represent the Goddess and God
Any of the ceremonial or consecrational incenses on pages 73 and 74
Heatproof dish for the incense
Compass (to work out directions)
Candle snuffer

METHOD

✤ Cleanse the sacred space symbolically with the besom.
✤ Place the altar in the centre of the circle facing north.
✤ Set up the altar as described above.
✤ Light the candles on the altar.
✤ Start with the candle representing the Goddess on the left, then the God on the right. In the middle, follow with the candle which represents your magical working. Light the incense.
✤ Move towards the northern edge of the area you are enclosing.
✤ Hold your left hand out, palm down, at waist level. Point your fingers toward the edge of the circle you are creating. (You can, of course, use your athame if you have consecrated it.)
✤ See and feel the energy flowing out from your fingertips (or the athame), and slowly walk the circle, clockwise. Think of the energy that your body is generating.
✤ Continue to move clockwise, gradually increasing your pace as you do so.
✤ Move faster until you feel the energy flowing within you.
✤ The energy will move with you as you release it.
✤ Sense your personal power creating a sphere of energy around the altar. When this is firmly established, call on the Elements which rule the four directions.

❖ Your circle is now consecrated and ready for you to use for whatever magical purpose you need. You will require the candle snuffer when you close your circle after your magical working.

Consecrating your tools

Most magical traditions make use of the familiar magical Elements of Earth, Air, Fire and Water. Some traditions have specific tools which are important to them. As mentioned previously, there is also a fifth magical Element – that of Spirit. There is a consecration ritual in the Runes and Ogham Staves section on page 146 that is suitable for your tools, but perhaps the simplest consecration that can be made is to offer each of the objects to Spirit that they may be used for the best purpose possible. You can specifically dedicate any tool using a short invocation such as:

I dedicate this magical tool to the purpose for which it is intended.

You can, of course, be as creative with your speech as you desire. Anything else that is done will be according to the traditions of your own belief.

With all your tools, when you first purchase them or have them made, cleanse them before use, then dedicate them by filling them with your own energy as you did with your altar objects. You might also offer them to your favourite deity (see pages 205-224), or indeed the most appropriate ones for the particular tools - perhaps Mars for an athame.

Ending your magical working

As well as all the preparations necessary for successful magical working, it is equally important to finish off correctly. When you have finished your ritual or working, remind yourself that you are as pure a channel for the energies that you have called upon as possible. These energies *must* be returned whence they came, so visualize them passing through you and being returned to where they belong. At the same time, remember that you are blessed by these energies and by the fact that you have used them with good intent.

Closing a Circle

❖ Thank the Elements' rulers, if you have called upon them, for attending the ritual.
❖ If you used ritual tools, holding your athame, stand at the north. Pierce the circle's wall with the blade at waist level. If you wish, simply use your index finger to achieve the same end.
❖ Move clockwise around the circle. Visualize its power being sucked back into the knife or your finger. Sense the sphere of energy withdrawing and dissipating.
❖ Let the outside world slowly make itself felt in your consciousness. As you come back to the north again, the energy of the circle should have disappeared. If it has not, simply repeat the actions.
❖ If you have laid items to mark out the circle, remove them. If you have used salt and water, you may save the excess salt for future uses, but pour the water onto the bare earth. Bury any incense ashes.
❖ Put out the candles. Start with those that have marked the cardinal compass points, followed by any others used.
❖ Next put out the one representing the God energy and finally the Goddess candle. Never blow them out (some say this dissipates the energy). Either snuff or pinch them out.
❖ You may can leave the candles to burn out on their own if you wish.
❖ Put away your tools if you are not able to leave your altar in place.

BEST TIMES AND CORRESPONDENCES FOR SPELL WORKING

Truly efficient spell working requires a knowledge of the correspondences that were set up many eons ago when life was a good deal simpler. These correspondences meant that actions carried out at a certain time created very specific results. Through continual usage, it became clear that the position of the planets ruled various areas of life, creating the principle of the rulership of the planets and symbolism – an integral part of magical working today.

The table given here lists some of those correspondences, including those of the angels and archangels. More detailed information on the archangels can be found on pages 249-251.

CORRESPONDENCE TABLE

Sun Sign	Planet	Element	Day	Magical Use
Aries (21 March – 19 April)	Mars	Fire	Tuesday	Passion and sexuality, energy, willpower, vigour, courage and strength. Determination
Taurus (20 April – 21 May)	Venus	Earth	Friday	Romantic love, friendships, beauty, courtship, artistic abilities, harmony
Gemini (22 May – 20 June)	Mercury	Air	Wednesday	Wisdom, healing, communication, intelligence, memory, education
Cancer (21 June – 22 July)	Moon	Water	Monday	Psychic pursuits, psychology, dreams/astral travel, imagination, intuition, reincarnation
Leo (23 July – 22 August)	Sun	Fire	Sunday	Power, magic, health, success, career, goals, ambition, drama, fun, authority figures, law
Virgo (23 August – 22 Sept)	Mercury	Earth	Wednesday	wisdom, healing, communication, intelligence, memory, attention to detail, correspondence
Libra (23 Sept – 22 Oct)	Venus	Air	Friday	Love, partnership marriage, friendship, beauty, courtship
Scorpio (23 Oct – 21 Nov)	Mars, Pluto	Water	Tuesday	Courage, energy, breaking negativity, physical strength, passion, sex, aggression, energy
Sagittarius (22 Nov – 21 Dec)	Jupiter	Fire	Thursday	Publishing, long-distance travel, foreign interests, religion, happiness, wealth, healing, male fertility, legal matters
Capricorn (22 Dec – 19 Jan)	Saturn	Earth	Saturday	Binding, protection, neutralization, karma, death, manifestation, structure, reality, the laws of society, limits, obstacles
Aquarius (20 Jan – 18 Feb)	Saturn, Uranus	Air	Saturday	Psychic ability, meditation, defence, communicating with spirits
Pisces (19Feb – 20 Mar)	Jupiter, Neptune	Water	Thursday	Music, rhythm, dancing, spiritual matters, healing and religion, medication

Colours	Crystal	Flowers/Herbs	Angel
Reds, burgundy	Ruby, garnet, bloodstone, diamond	Gorse, thistle, wild rose	Samael
Blues, greens	Sapphire, emerald, jade	Violet, wild rose, red rose, coltsfoot	Anael
White, spring green, silver, yellow	Diamond, jade, topaz, aquamarine	Iris, parsley, dill, snapdragons	Raphael
Pale blue, silver, pearl, white	Emerald, cat's eye, pearl, moonstone	Poppy, water lily, white rose, moonwort	Gabriel
Gold, red, yellow, orange	Amber, topaz, ruby, diamond	Marigold, sunflower, hops	Michael
Pastel blue, gold, peach	Diamond, jade, jasper, aquamarine	Rosemary, cornflower, valerian	Raphael
Cerulean blue, royal blue, amethyst	Opal, lapis lazuli, emerald, jade	Violet, white rose, love-in-a-mist	Anael
Dark red, brown, black, grey	Ruby, garnet, bloodstone, topaz	Basil, heather, chrysanthemum	Samael, Azrael
Lilac, mauve, purple, amethyst	Sapphire, amethyst, diamond	Carnation, wallflower, clovepink, sage	Sachiel
Grey, violet, dark brown	Onyx, obsidian, jet, garnet	Deadly nightshade, snowdrop, rue	Cassiel
All colours	Zircon, amber, amethyst, garnet	Snowdrop, foxglove, valerian	Uriel, Cassiel
Purple, violet, sea green	Sapphire, amethyst, coral	Heliotrope, carnation, opium poppy	Sachiel, Asariel

MOON PHASES

Moon Correspondences

The Moon represents the feminine principle and is a symbol for the natural cycle of birth, life and regeneration. Her best personification is that of the Triple Goddess (Maiden, Mother, Crone) which is an image found in many early religions. The lunar phases (Waxing, Waning or Full Moon) can be made use of when planning your magical work. You will soon find that you become instinctively aware of these phases and can use them effectively.

It is always useful to have your rituals and spells coincide with the appropriate astrological influences. For example, spells and rituals calling on the Moon and involving the Element of Earth, should be performed during a time when the Moon is positioned in one of the three astrological Earth signs of Taurus, Virgo or Capricorn. Spells involving the Element of Fire should be done when the Moon is in Aries, Leo or Sagittarius; spells involving the Element of Air when the Moon is in Gemini, Libra or Aquarius; and spells involving the Element of Water should be performed when the Moon is in Cancer, Scorpio or Pisces.

You could also use the appropriate incenses for your rituals and there are other correspondences in the application of magic that might be utilized at·these times:

Moon in Aries

Magic involving anything to do with authority, leadership, rebirth, moving on or spiritual conversion should achieve success. Healing rituals for ailments of the face, head or brain are also best performed at this time.

Moon in Taurus

You can work magic for love, security, possessions and money. Healing rituals for illnesses of the throat, neck and ears are also undertaken during at this time.

Moon in Gemini

Magic for anything to do with communication, including writing, e-mails, public relations, moving house or office and travel is favoured. Ailments of the shoulders, arms, hands or lungs also respond well to healing rituals done now.

Moon in Cancer

This is the best time to work magic for home and domestic life, and also any nurturing activities. Healing rituals for ailments of the chest or stomach are best carried out now.

Moon in Leo

Courage, fertility and childbirth are all ruled by Leo, as is the power over others, so this is the best time to work such magic. Healing rituals for problems of the upper back, spine or heart all seem to have some success now.

Moon in Virgo

At this time magic worked for questions involving employment, intellectual matters, health and dietary concerns is much enhanced. Healing rituals for ailments of the intestines or nervous system are also best performed now.

Moon in Libra

Magic involving artistic work, justice, court cases, partnerships and unions, mental stimulation, and karmic, spiritual, or emotional balance receive a boost when worked at this time. Healing rituals for ailments of the lower back or kidneys have additional energy now.

Moon in Scorpio

This is the best time to work magic involving sexual matters, power, psychic growth, secrets and fundamental transformations. Healing rituals for difficulties with the reproductive organs are also most effective during this period.

Moon in Sagittarius

This is the opportune time to work magic for publications, legal matters, travel and revealing truth. Healing rituals for ailments of the liver, thighs or hips are also done at this time.

Moon in Capricorn

This is an ideal time to work magic for ambition, career, organization, political matters and recognition. Healing rituals for the knees, bones, teeth and skin are best performed at this time.

Moon in Aquarius

This is the best time to work magic involving scientific matters, freedom of expression, problem-solving, extra-sensory abilities and the breaking of bad habits or unhealthy addictions. Ailments of the calves, ankles or blood receive benefit from healing rituals.

Moon in Pisces

Magic worked on the psychic arts involving dreamwork, clairvoyance, telepathy and music is enhanced at this time. Healing rituals for problems with the feet or lymph glands benefit from the flow of energy.

Magical Days

The days of the week, because they are ruled by the various gods, create an energy which is best for certain types of magical working. Following is a list that, while not completely comprehensive, will give you some idea of when to perform your spells. Each day's planetary ruler and optimum colours are also given.

Sunday (*Sun – yellow, gold, orange):* ambition, authority figures, career, children, crops, drama, fun, goals, health, law, personal finances, promotion, selling, speculating, success, volunteers and civic services.

Monday (*Moon – white, silver, grey, pearl):* antiques, astrology, children, dreams/astral travel, emotions, fluids, household activities, imagination, initiation, magic, New Age pursuits, psychology, reincarnation, religion, short trips, spirituality, the public, totem animals, trip planning.

Tuesday (*Mars – red, pink, orange):* aggression, business, beginnings, combat, confrontation, courage, dynamism, gardening, guns, hunting, movement, muscular activity, passion, partnerships, physical energy, police, repair, sex, soldiers, surgery, tools, woodworking.

Wednesday (*Mercury – purple, magenta, silver):* accounting, astrology, communication, computers, correspondence, editing, editors, education, healing, hiring, journalists, learning, languages, legal appointments, messages, music, phone calls, siblings, signing contracts, students, visiting friends, visual arts, wisdom, writing.

Thursday (*Jupiter – blue, metallic colours):* business, charity, college, doctors, education, expansion, forecasting, foreign interests, gambling, growth, horses, luck, material wealth, merchants, philosophy, psychologists, publishing, reading, religion, researching, self-improvement, sports, studying the law, travel.

Friday (*Venus – green, pink, white):* affection, alliances, architects, artists, beauty, chiropractors, courtship, dancers, dating, designers, engineers, entertainers, friendships, gardening, gifts, harmony, luxury, marriage, music, painting, partners, poetry, relationships, romantic love, shopping, social activity.

Saturday (*Saturn – black, grey, red, white):* binding, bones, criminals, death, debts, dentists, discovery, endurance, farm workers, financing, hard work, housing, justice, karma, limits, manifestation, maths, murderers, neutralization, obstacles, plumbing, protection, reality, sacrifice, separation, structure, teeth, tests, transformation, wills.

Planetary days and hours

Each hour of the day and night is also matched to a planetary influence. Planetary hours can be very useful, especially if you can't wait until the right Moon phase or even the right day to perform your magical working. You can, of course, wait for both the appropriate day and planetary hour, if you wish. Planetary hours are divided into two parts: sunrise to sunset and sunset to sunrise.

Once the principle is understood, calculating the planetary 'hours' is relatively easy. The calculation goes back to when there were no clocks to measure time. The periods of light and dark were each divided into 12 equal portions, which were called 'hours'.

Therefore, if the number of minutes of daylight is divided by 12, it is possible to discover exactly how long a planetary hour is. For example, if the Sun rises at 7am and sets at 4pm you would have 9 normal hours of daylight. This would then have to be divided by 12 to calculate when each new planetary hour begins. Thus:

9 hours multiplied by 60 minutes
gives 540 minutes
540 minutes divided by 12 gives 45 minutes.

Therefore each daytime magical hour would be equivalent to 45 minutes normal time and you would measure accordingly.

From sunset, things would be slightly different – a little thought will show why so many magical practitioners work at night!

Using the example above, there are 15 hours out of 24 left. Thus:

15 hours multiplied by 60 minutes
gives 900 minutes
900 minutes divided by 12 gives 75 minutes
Each night-time hour would be therefore be
equivalent to 75 normal minutes.

Because only the Sun and six planets – not all ten planets – are used as correspondences, you have a chance to use those influences either during the day or during the hours of darkness. Planetary hours are always calculated with reference to the rising sun, so each time you wish to use a planetary hour, you must first know precisely when the sun rises where you are living. The influence can either help or hinder your magical efforts.

How to discover the best planetary hour

- Decide on which influence you would like most for your magical working.
- Consult the Magical Days list on page 237 to decide which planet is most appropriate.
- Find out at what time the sun rises in your area – it changes slightly from day to day. You can usually find this information in a daily newspaper, on television or the internet.

HOURS OF THE DAY

Hour	Sunday	Monday	Tuesday	Wednesday	Thursday	Friday	Saturday
1	Sun	Moon	Mars	Mercury	Jupiter	Venus	Saturn
2	Venus	Saturn	Sun	Moon	Mars	Mercury	Jupiter
3	Mercury	Jupiter	Venus	Saturn	Sun	Moon	Mars
4	Moon	Mars	Mercury	Jupiter	Venus	Saturn	Sun
5	Saturn	Sun	Moon	Mars	Mercury	Jupiter	Venus
6	Jupiter	Venus	Saturn	Sun	Moon	Mars	Mercury
7	Mars	Mercury	Jupiter	Venus	Saturn	Sun	Moon
8	Sun	Moon	Mars	Mercury	Jupiter	Venus	Saturn
9	Venus	Saturn	Sun	Moon	Mars	Mercury	Jupiter
10	Mercury	Jupiter	Venus	Saturn	Sun	Moon	Mars
11	Moon	Mars	Mercury	Jupiter	Venus	Saturn	Sun
12	Saturn	Sun	Moon	Mars	Mercury	Jupiter	Venus

- Look at the two planetary hours charts and choose one of them. Your choice will depend on whether you prefer working in the day or after sunset. On the relevant chart, find the day and hour you wish to use. If the matter is urgent, you would have to choose today.
- You have hopefully already noted the planetary influence you need for your particular working. Find that planet under the day you chose. You might decide you needed Jupiter's influence on a Monday – that would be hour 3. Using the example above, the best time to do your working during the day would be hour 3 or hour 10 of that day (between 8.30 and 9.15am or between 2.30 and 3.15pm).

THE SIGNIFICANCE OF COLOUR AND ITS SYMBOLISM

Colour is something that, over time, you will use as a natural adjunct in your magical workings. It can be used in your robes, to dress your altar, or in your candles as representative of the vibration you wish to introduce. By and large, the colours you choose for your workings will be those appropriate for your intention (the purpose of your spell).

There are other uses of colour in magic as well. Some simple colour symbolism is listed below.

Silver is almost always associated with the lunar goddesses and workings with the Moon, whereas **white** symbolizes purity, chastity, spirituality, transformation and transmutation. It is said to contain within it all the other colours, so always use white if you have nothing else available. Use it also when you want focus and a protective influence.

Purple, indigo and **violet** are the royal colours and are therefore associated with wisdom and vision, dignity and fame. They are often used when honouring the Goddess in her aspect of Crone and the God as King, according to some traditions of magic. These colours command respect and promote psychic and mental healing. Purple connects with true creativity, with the mystic and with spirituality and is also to do with one's proper place within the overall scheme of things.

Sky blue signifies communication, not just between people, but also between the realms so is good for meditative practices and also for

HOURS OF THE NIGHT

Hour	Sunday	Monday	Tuesday	Wednesday	Thursday	Friday	Saturday
1	Jupiter	Venus	Saturn	Sun	Moon	Mars	Mercury
2	Mars	Mercury	Jupiter	Venus	Saturn	Sun	Moon
3	Sun	Moon	Mars	Mercury	Jupiter	Venus	Saturn
4	Venus	Saturn	Sun	Moon	Mars	Mercury	Jupiter
5	Mercury	Jupiter	Venus	Saturn	Sun	Moon	Mars
6	Moon	Mars	Mercury	Jupiter	Venus	Saturn	Sun
7	Saturn	Sun	Moon	Mars	Mercury	Jupiter	Venus
8	Jupiter	Venus	Saturn	Sun	Moon	Mars	Mercury
9	Mars	Mercury	Jupiter	Venus	Saturn	Sun	Moon
10	Sun	Moon	Mars	Mercury	Jupiter	Venus	Saturn
11	Venus	Saturn	Sun	Moon	Mars	Mercury	Jupiter
12	Mercury	Jupiter	Venus	Saturn	Sun	Moon	Mars

help with study and learning. It is also used to symbolize Water. Other shades of blue signify peace; strength; calm; recognition of the real self and the ability to express wisdom.

Green, which belongs to Venus, promotes love, fertility, beauty, wealth, prosperity and harmony – symbolizing balance and self-knowledge, that is, knowing our capabilities. Associated with the Earth in its guise of the Green Man and with the Great Mother in her nurturing form, it suggests emotional healing and growth.

Gold and **yellow** represent vitality, strength and rejuvenation. They are used to promote physical healing, hope and happiness. Yellow inspires rational thought and strong will. It is also an emotional colour in the sense that it represents your relationship with the outer self and the world in which you live. Related to the Sun gods and the Element of Air, both gold and yellow may also be used for protection.

Orange has a healing vibration, particularly of relationships. It is also associated with material success and legal matters. A highly creative vibration, it often relates to childhood and emotional stability as well as imagination.

Red is recognized as being symbolic of passion and sexual potency and intensity. It is usually associated with Fire, with the quality of courage and with healing of the blood and heart.

Pink signifies friendship, love, fidelity and the healing of emotions. It also symbolizes creativity and innocence and is associated with the Goddess in her aspect of Maiden.

Brown promotes the healing of the Earth, symbolizes the hearth and home, and is also connected with the animal kingdom. It can also be used for the blending of several intentions.

Black is not a colour but is the absence of both light and colour. It can therefore be used to banish negativity. It is often seen as the colour of the Goddess in her Wise Woman form.

Words of Power

Signs and symbols are an important part of magic and are very easily universally recognized. In other words, any competent magician or alchemist would easily be able to read the information that was being passed on. Much of the magical language that we use today has come down to us from the Kabbalah, which was primarily an oral tradition (learned through the spoken word).

There were certain ideas that the ordinary layman was capable of understanding and others that only the priesthood were capable of assimilating. Knowledge was power and that knowledge must be jealously guarded lest it fall into the wrong hands. The writings were therefore in code, and had a tremendous power and energy invested in them. The sense of awe and wonder they generated was phenomenal. Now, as these messages become open to interpretation, they still are able to generate that same sense of awe and wonder.

While the writings of Kabbalah were obviously in ancient Hebrew, it was believed that the letters and numbers had very powerful vibrations. To keep the writers' intentions hidden, it was possible to substitute other phrases and letters or numbers for what was originally noted down, and it all became very confusing. It is this that has generated so much interest recently in the Bible Code and other so-called 'secret' messages.

There are many different 'codes' that can be used to signify various aspects of magic and here the Hebrew and English equivalent are shown. The following is an example of how English letters can be transferred into numbers using Kabbalistic beliefs:

Kabbalah Table

1	2	3	4	5	6	7	8	9
A	B	G	D	E	O	Z	F	T
C	K	Gh	Dh	H	U		P	Tz
I	Kh	M	M	N	V		Ch	
J	R	S	Th		W		Ph	
Q		Sh			X			
Y								

Below are some other alphabets and their equivalents. In theory there is nothing to prevent you from mixing up your alphabets in magical writings, though purists would cringe at such an idea.

Words of Power are those which create a very specific vibration linking us with the divine. Practitioners of yoga, for instance, will use the very powerful Om or Aum accepted as the vibration of creation. Followers of Islam chant the 99 'Beautiful Names' of Allah. Hebrew mystics and magicians use the secret names of God, such as Yahweh, Adonai and Elohim. Native Americans observe chanting in preparation for many activities and ceremonies. Chants, or mantras, are also greatly venerated in other shamanic societies.

It is the use of Words of Power that can enchant something or someone – to enchant initially meant to surround someone with a vibration, which brought about transformation. In ancient Greece, female sorcerers and seers are said to have howled their chants, believing that this created the powerful vibrations to augment the power of their chants. Early and medieval sorcerers and magicians sang their chants in very forceful voices in order to raise power.

This practice predated the raising of highly focused energy developed by modern day magicians and spell workers. These latter use as their mantras (mind-makers) the names of the Goddess and of the Horned God as well as the names of other deities. Chants also are done for magical purposes to achieve an altered state of consciousness and create psychic energy. Below is one such chant, which should be repeated at least nine times.

Eko, Eko Azarak

Eko, Eko Zomelak

Eko, Eko Cernunnos

Eko, Eko Aradia

Words of Power may also consist of rhymes, alliterative phrases – including nonsensical ones – and charms that are created or taken from other sources such as books or poetry. In some magical traditions it is believed that a

Royal Arch Cipher

A	B	C	D	E	F	G	H	I	J	K	L	M

N	O	P	Q	R	S	T	U	V	W	X	Y	Z

Hebrew Alphabet

A	B	G	D	H	V	Z	Ch	T	I	K
א	ב	ג	ד	ה	ו	ז	ח	ט	י	כ

L	M	N	S	O	P	Tz	Q	R	Sh	Th
ל	מ	נ	ס	ע	פ	צ	ק	ר	ש	ת

Greek Alphabet

A	B	G	D	E	Z	E	Th	I	K	L	M
Αα	Ββ	Γγ	Δδ	Εε	Ζζ	Ηη	Θθ	Ιι	Κκ	Λλ	Μμ

Νν	Ξξ	Οο	Ππ	Ρρ	Σσ	Ττ	Υυ	Φφ	Χχ	Ψψ	Ωω
N	X	O	P	R	S	T	U	Ph	Ch	Ph	O

Runic or Futhark Alphabet

A	B	C	D	E	F	G	H	I	J	K

L	M	N	Ng	O	P	R	S	T	Th	U

241

chant used as a tool for healing should not be used more than three times, lest the chanter becomes infected by the very condition he or she is attempting to cure.

CONSTRUCTING SPELLS AND RITUALS

Traditionally, spells, formulas and rituals were recorded in the Grimoire which, of late, has become known as the Book of Shadows. There is often controversy over whether one's magical books should be called a Grimoire or a Book of Shadows. Really it depends on which traditions of magic you have been taught.

The word Grimoire simply means 'a book of learning'. It came to mean the records kept by true practitioners of magic, as they wrote down the secret keys they discovered as they progressed along the path of initiation. The best-known Grimoire was the translation of one made widely available at the beginning of the 20th century – that of King Solomon. This book was of great antiquity and traditionally is seen as the magical key to the Kabbalah. In truth, it was the key to the mysteries and has since formed the basis of other magical systems.

The first Book of Shadows is said to have been written by Gerald Gardner as he developed modern Wicca in the 1920s. The Book of Shadows does not serve as a diary, but reflects religious rituals, their modifications and any other workings that need to be recorded.

Both books were traditionally secret writings, often written in coded language. The Book of Shadows follows the same principle, although obviously with modern communication, much of what used to be hidden is more readily available.

Most solitary practitioners will treasure the records of their workings, whether they choose to call it a Book of Shadows or a Grimoire. Either book becomes part of a rich tradition. Any self-respecting practitioner will both want and need to keep a record of all of these aspects of magic for future reference. You will need to find an easy way of remembering what you have done. Utilizing the worksheets and the respective headings below will help you to do this.

These can also be used, should you wish, with modern technology. Computer and software programs can be tremendously helpful in keeping records in a fashion that is suitable for passing on to other people.

Spells and Formulas Record Sheet

Type of Spell or Formula: This should state very clearly what the type of spell is, for example blessing, binding, and so on. When developing formulas for lotions and potions, for instance, you need to be clear as to the exact purpose.

Date and Time Made: This gives a cross-reference should you wish to use the correct planetary hours or magical days.

Reference: You should develop your own system of reference; this might be, for instance, according to the time of year or alphabetically. Do also remember to keep safely somewhere a record of how you have developed your reference system, so that others may benefit from your experience.

Astrological Phase: If you have an interest in astrology you will probably want to record where the planets are when you prepare the spell or formula. A decent ephemeris (list of planetary positions) can be of great help here, though there are also many sources of information on the internet.

Specific Purpose: You should always state the specific purpose of the spell or formula very clearly. This is partly because it helps to focus your own mind, but also because it leaves no one in any doubt as to your intentions. Should you have more than one main purpose, you should also record these.

List of Ingredients and/or Supplies Needed: Having all your ingredients to hand ensures that you are working with maximum efficiency and are not misusing or needing to adjust the energy by leaving the sacred space. Also, when you repeat a working you will need to replicate what you did the first time; even one small change in ingredients can make a tremendous difference to the outcome.

Specific Location Required: You may well need to perform some spells within a certain area or setting. Also you may discover that your own energy responds to some locations better than others.

Date, Time and Astrological Phase when Used: In all probability you, will not want all your spells to take effect at the time you cast them. Let us suppose you have applied for a job and wish your spell to work at the time of interview. You would need to carefully calculate the date, time and astrological phase of the interview as well as the time you are actually casting your spell, and incorporate both sets of information into your working.

Results: Record carefully all aspects of results you feel are associated with your working. This record should include how successful you consider the spell to be and how it might be improved. There will be some unexpected results, some that appear not to give a tangible result and others which come into play some time after they were expected.

Deities Invoked during Preparation and/or Use: Often a particular god can be helpful in bringing about a needed result for a spell. You will chose the most appropriate for your purpose and can always petition a different one at another time.

Step-by-Step Instructions for Preparations and/or Use: Often when spell working, movements and words are intuitive and instinctive; the more you are able to remember what you did the more likely you are to achieve similar results. Also, should you require them for someone to work on your behalf or to undertake someone else's magical training, you will have an exact record.

Additional Notes: Here you should record for each occasion anything that seems strange, bizarre or noteworthy, so that you know what to expect next time.

In each of the spells throughout this book there is a list of ingredients and special articles which may be required to achieve a result for that particular spell. Because each individual brings their own energy into the process, you may find that you intuitively want to change something, whether that is an ingredient, a container or the words used. This is absolutely fine, and means that your spell has a very personal feel to it.

Many rituals are particularly beautiful because they show an inherent appreciation of the world in which we live. Particularly in the pagan and neo-pagan belief systems, they have achieved a new lease of life. Creativity of all sorts is, however, an important part of spell making and magic; and other magical systems, which rely on an awareness of a more cosmic spiritual philosophy, retain also their own magical power and energy. Rituals may be thought of as offerings to Ultimate Power. The Ritual Record Sheet differs slightly from the Spells and Formulas Record Sheet.

Ritual Record Sheet

Type of Ritual: There are many types of ritual and here you will record whether it is one of invocation, honouring, supplication (asking a favour) or thanks.

Date and Time Made: It will help if you are consistent in how you record this, for example time (am or pm)/date/month/year.

Moon Phase and Astrological Correspondences: As you become more proficient, you will wish to become more accurate and will want to be sure that you have drawn in all the power that you can. In the more advanced forms of magic particularly, creating the best conditions for success means knowing the Moon phases and astrological correspondences.

Weather: The weather conditions can have a profound effect both on your mood and on the way in which your ritual is carried out. A ritual honouring Thor or Mars (both gods of war) would have more energy done during a thunderstorm for instance.

Physical Health: Your health is important in any magical working. You owe it to yourself to make sure you are as well as you can be. You must always remember that you are as much an instrument or tool as articles such as your incense holder or athame. You would not, after all, wish to use a contaminated incense holder during your workings.

Purpose of Ritual: This should always be stated very clearly, along with any secondary purpose or agenda. You might, for instance, wish to honour Bridget on her day of 2 February but also wish to gain her help for a pet project. Both intents should be stated and a suitable form of words chosen.

Tools and Other Items Required: You should list carefully how you laid out your sacred space and what you used for a particular ritual. You might well find yourself motivated to use a particular herb or object, for instance, and unless you record it you may not remember why in future.

Deities or Energies Invoked: You should start off any ritual with a clear idea of the specific energies you require for success. According to your own beliefs, that may require the presence of a particular god or gods. If you find yourself invoking or calling on a specific energy, then acknowledge that by keeping a record of it. Even a simple candle lit to help someone, uses energy and requires dedication.

Approximate Length of Ritual: This is recorded so that you know, should you wish to repeat the ritual, that you have enough time in which to carry out your allotted task. If a ritual takes half an hour and you only have 20 minutes you are not treating yourself, the ritual, or the powers you are calling upon, fairly if you hurry the process.

Results of Ritual: Record carefully the results of your ritual, how you felt, how the energy has changed and so on.

Ritual Composition: Again, record in your own words exactly what you did and how.

Most rituals have a basic form, but your input is important, and what you do intuitively is just as important as the basic form. During your rituals do not be surprised if you find yourself performing an action you would not expect. Just go with the flow, but remember that you are in charge.

Additional Notes: Note down anything else you need to remember; for example, how you might improve the ritual the next time, peculiar feelings, strange or bizarre occurrences and specific thoughts and ideas that might come to you.

A Ritual of Gestures

This very simple ritual acknowledges the four 'directions' and the Elements they rule. It is used to help raise the energy in any particular spot, in preparation for spells and magical workings. It needs little special knowledge, and all you need to remember is that the Goddess represents the feminine principle and the Horned God the masculine.

METHOD

❖ Stand in your sacred space.
❖ Quieten your mind as far as you can.
❖ Breathe deeply for a short while, trying to breathe out a little longer than you breathe in.
❖ Turn your attention to the deities you are going to ask for assistance.

Face north:
❖ Put your hands out in front of you, palms facing the earth.
❖ Use your hands to sense the solidity and fertility of the earth.
❖ Invoke (call on) the powers of the earth as you do so.

Turn towards the east:
❖ Raise your hands slightly higher with elbows bent, your hands with palms facing away from you.
❖ Spread your fingers fairly wide and hold this position.
❖ Invoke the forces of Air and sense movement and communication.

Now face south:

* Keeping the elbows straight, make your hands into tight fists.
* Raise your hands above your head and feel the energy flow through you.
* Invoke the forces of Fire – power, creativity and necessary destruction.

Turn to the west:

* Extend your cupped hands in front of you as though you were carrying water in them.
* Sense all the qualities of Water and invoke the forces of Water through the gesture.

Face north again:

* Raise both hands to the sky, with the palms upwards and the fingers spread wide as though you were throwing your whole self at the sky.

* Pull towards you the energy of the universe with all its mystery.
* Acknowledge Ultimate Power.
* With your receptive hand (the one that pulls in power) held high, make the shape of the crescent Moon with your thumb and forefinger. (Tuck the other fingers into the palm of your hand.)
* With this action, acknowledge the reality of the Goddess, and her presence with you.
* Sense all her qualities and power and make an act of reverence.
* With your projective hand (the one that gives out power) held high, create an image of the Horned God by bending down the middle and fourth fingers toward the palm, holding them with the thumb. Lift the forefinger and little finger up to the sky.
* Acknowledge the energy and power of the Sun.
* Sense the presence of the God with you.
* Make an act of reverence.
* Now if you can, lie down flat on the ground.
* Stretch your legs and arms in the shape of Perfect Man, arms out sideways and legs outstretched. In this way you create the pattern of a pentagram.
* Sense the energies and powers of all the Elements coursing through your body, becoming part of you, and you part of them.

* Recognize them as coming from the One, the Goddess and God combined.
* Now do whatever you have to do from a mental standpoint – meditate, ask for help or make a dedication.
* Your ritual is finished when you feel complete. Now stand up.

Various cultures have theories about how magic works. Many modern magicians give some very deep hypotheses, ranging from philosophical argument to material reasons. Most are searching for a basis for understanding what works well, and what does not. Over many, many years the ceremonial magical ritual in its basic form is known to work. Its form has been handed down in various cultures, with regional variations, over the centuries. The basic form is that the magician works within a cast circle, uses consecrated tools and the magical names of various entities to evoke or invoke powers.

THE PROCEDURES AND PROTOCOL OF RITUALS

The trainee magician finds it hard to admit that their rituals do not always work out, often because there is too much personal or emotional investment or because the ritual has not been properly understood. Sometimes nothing appears to happen, or does not happen at the expected time; sometimes there are unexpected side effects; and sometimes it is only with hindsight that we realize that events have occurred that lead to the right resolution. The question then that most people ask is 'does it work?' By and large it seems to, at least for some people some of the time. There can, of course, be no judgements about what is good and bad in ritual – what works for one may not work for others.

The way we invoke (bring towards) and evoke (send away) powers and the traditional use and naming of angels, spirits, gods and goddesses, ancestral spirits and so on, are useful mental constructs, or rather, creative visualizations. These are a comfort to those who need to be conscious of personalities with whom to work. There are times when difficulty or stress within our personal lives makes it too difficult to gain access to the highest forms of energy without the feeling that we have an intimate relationship with these 'beings' and therefore the need to give them personalities.

Ritual gives an accepted formula for such access but that is not the end of the story. Here we think of the individual approaching a being or beings in whom he stands in awe and therefore requiring intermediaries to make his pleas for him. As soon as he or she moves beyond these 'mediators', the magician has to confront the nature of consciousness itself. He therefore becomes something of a mystic – someone who believes in the existence of realities beyond his own perception or intellectual appreciation and in the transcendence of God. Just as the magician has had to use mediators to gain access to the Supreme Power, so also there is the belief that the Supreme Power must 'step down' its energy from its very high level in order to effect changes on a physical level.

This raising and lowering of consciousness is a first principle of Eastern esoteric philosophy, and is at the root of the Kabbalistic doctrine of emanation and the Sephiroth, the ten creative forces that intervene between the infinite, unknowable God and our created world. This doctrine has been adopted by many 20th-century magicians as a useful complement and tool in whatever traditional model of magic they were weaned on. There is a belief among most magical practitioners that while gods, goddesses and so on may well be simply creations of consciousness or archetypal images they can, and indeed should, be treated as if they were real. Whether one believes that magic is the manipulation of one's own or a higher being's consciousness, it is useful to address these higher beings with respect and to accord them the dignity long-held belief requires. This respect is a necessary part of all ritual and spell making, whether one works individually or as part of a group.

Individual Working

There are certain procedures that most practitioners are prepared to acquire nowadays, on an individual level which can also be used in group working. Whether you work in a Kabbalistic manner, are Wiccan/Pagan or are simply interested in enhancing your own magical working, certain techniques will be fundamental to your practice and will soon become second nature.

This is because the magicians of old recognized that they – in their own way – were intermediaries between the higher beings or gods and the physical material world. Right from the beginning, they needed some way of feeling different while working magically, defining those differences and marking a space in which they could work safely without interference from either malign powers or interfering humans.

It was often safer to work alone in those days, for there was little understanding by the ordinary person of either what the energies were or even how they worked. If a malign energy did manifest, then it could be contained within the designated space; the magician was at his most powerful within that space and yet at the same time, he had done all that was necessary to ensure that he was a fit vehicle for whatever he needed to do.

The rituals that were developed then have stood the test of time and can be used today in much the same way. Indeed, because the rituals have been performed so often for specific magical purposes, they have developed an energy of their own and become powerful in their own right.

For example, the Lesser Banishing Ritual of the Pentagram can be performed on your own, to purify a room for further magical work or meditation and also can be used for protection. It has a much higher vibration than simply casting a circle, however, and in addressing the archangels appeals to the highest authority for protection and assistance. Rather than appealing to the Elements, we now go to those beings or energies who are in charge of the Elements and make a direct appeal to them.

When we use the old names, we link into a stream of consciousness that quite literally has a resonance that causes a reaction within the universe. From that reaction there is a shift or response in everything in existence. Not only do we dignify the archangels, we dignify ourselves.

The Lesser Banishing Ritual of the Pentagram

The first part of this ritual, that of the Kabbalistic cross, is used by the practitioner to open themselves to the powers of the universe and to state that they are present and ready for work. By calling the energy of the universe into the practitioner through the centre of his being, the mind, body, and soul are energized and aligned with cosmic forces. The practitioner is then able to direct these energies with wisdom and at will. It is suggested that if you can do so, perform at least the first part of the ritual – which deals with the personal self – every day.

METHOD
❖ Stand facing east.
❖ Perform the Kabbalistic cross as follows.
❖ Touch your forehead with the first two fingers of your right hand and visualize a sphere of white light at that point.
❖ Chant:

Atah (this translates roughly as Thou Art)

❖ Lower your hand to your solar plexus and visualize a line of light extending down to your feet and chant:

Malkuth (the Kingdom)

❖ Raise your hand and touch your right shoulder, visualizing a sphere of light there and chant:

Ve Geburah (and the power)

❖ Extend the hand across the chest tracing a line of light and touch your left shoulder where another sphere of light forms and chant:

Ve Gedulah (and the glory)

❖ Clasp your hands in the centre of your chest at the crossing point of the horizontal and vertical lines of light.
❖ Bow your head and chant:

Le Olam, Amen (for ever, amen)

This first part in particular, brings about a quiet mind free of 'chatter' from the everyday world. This is useful in meditation and also in spell working when concentration is needed. This quiet mind is of extreme importance so that the correct energies can be focused properly into the work in hand. While English words are largely used in rituals, here there are words which, through tradition and long usage, have become Words of Power. The ritual acknowledges the archangels in their proper place and creates a very positive space in which to work.

The effects of the complete ritual, which is in two parts, are first and foremost on the astral (more subtle) energies, though it uses the pentagram (five-pointed star traced on the body, see Essential Ritual, below) as a sign that the practitioner recognizes his place on earth as man. There is, in effect, a stepping down of the energies to make them usable, although the practitioner's own power is raised or enhanced.

The protection that the pentagrams give is to banish any negative energy that may be present on any level whatsoever. In previous times it was thought that the magister or practitioner had mastery over the power he or she was using. Today it is regarded in terms of a collaborative effort between spiritual or magical energies and the practitioner. This does not mean there is any less respect.

The Essential Ritual

METHOD
❖ Facing east, using the extended fingers, trace a large pentagram with the point up, starting at your left hip, up to just above your forehead, centred on your body, then down to your right hip, up and to your left shoulder, across to the right shoulder and down to the starting point in front of your left hip.
❖ Visualize this pentagram in blue flaming light.
❖ Thrust your fingers or athame into the centre.
❖ Chant:

YHVH (Yod-heh-vahv-heh)
(This is the tetragrammaton, a four-letter word of power – translated into Latin as Jehovah)

Turn to the south.

❖ Visualize the blue flame following your fingers, tracing a blue line from the pentagram in the east to the south.

❖ Repeat the formation of the pentagram while facing south.

❖ This time, chant:

Adonai [another name for God translated as Lord]

Turn to the west, tracing the blue flame from south to west.

❖ Form a pentagram again, but this time chant:

Eheieh [Eh-hay-yeah – another name of God translated as I Am or I Am That I A]

Turn to the north, again tracing the blue flame from west to north.

❖ Repeat the tracing of the pentagram and chant:

Agla (Ah-gah-lah – a composite of Atah Gibor le olam Amen)

Return again to the east, tracing the blue flame from north to east.

❖ Push your fingers back into the same spot from which you started.

❖ You should now visualize that you are surrounded by four flaming pentagrams connected by a line of blue fire.

❖ Visualizing each archangel standing guard at each direction, extend your arms out to your sides, forming a cross.

❖ Chant:

Before me RAPHAEL (rah-fah-ell)
Behind me GABRIEL (gah-bree-ell)
On my right hand, MICHAEL (mee-khah-ell)
On my left hand, AURIEL (sometimes URIEL, aw-ree-ell or ooh-ree-ell)
Before me flames the pentagram, behind me shines the six-rayed star

❖ Repeat the Kabbalistic cross as you did at the beginning and chant:

Atah
Malkuth

Ve Geburah
Ve Gedulah
Le Olam

As can be seen, Raphael is in the east, Gabriel in the west, Michael in the south and Uriel in the north. Sometimes Michael and Uriel are transposed by some practitioners. These archangels are the four guardians of the cardinal directions and you will find references to these cardinal directions in many of the spells and rituals.

This ritual sometimes seems to be too complicated for most people, so let us try to simplify the process of ritual so you can understand the thinking behind it. As time goes on and you become more proficient, you may wish to return to these individual rituals and familiarize yourself with them.

Group Working

Rather than working as a solitary practitioner, many people will seek a community of like-minded individuals on the basis that their own individual powers are thus enhanced. A method of group working is given here, although it is very easy to adjust this for work on an individual basis. The rituals used for a group represent a cooperative act of worship, which widens the scope of the ceremony to encompass larger objectives than just the personal; we can then consider our joint responsibility for the world in which we live, and a more universal perspective.

At the same time, through working in a group, a more focused atmosphere can be created – a raising of consciousness so that each participant receives wisdom and energy commensurate with their needs and understanding. True initiation into the mysteries of magic, for instance, is a private silent process, but an initiation ceremony accompanied by ritual can be seen as a more formal process for marking unmistakable long-term changes in the consciousness of the practitioner.

The purpose of rituals used in this way, is to create an inspiring and expressive atmosphere in which to give life and meaning to the connection between the ordinary and the sublime. Symbolism takes on a meaningful existence and through colour, sound, movement and imagination, becomes a vibrant language of the soul. Rituals help us to do several things:

1. To learn the proper application of a basic structure for personal use and to understand the relevance of ritual.
2. To increase an understanding of the flow of energy that we experience and to develop confidence in the use of symbols.
3. To contribute to the group awareness of members thus helping them make the best use of their individual and group powers.
4. To create spiritual and emotional conditions where initiation on an inner level is accepted and experienced, and where we can accept heightened states of awareness as the norm.
5. To use knowledge of ritual and power as a way of achieving personal spiritual health, so that the rituals themselves eventually become unnecessary and are recognized simply as a way of gaining access to the ultimate. They may then be replaced by direct experience.

By using the same rituals for both individual and group work, these are seen as complementary and members of the group are able to enhance their experience on both a personal and shared level. Practitioners can take the insights gained from group work into the personal sacred space and come into contact with an awareness of a new level of activity and vice versa. A magical ritual is far superior if it succeeds without side effects and therefore can be shocking if there are untoward results. Traditional forms of magical ritual – often first taught in a group situation – tap a basic and, if misunderstood, possibly dangerous force, which has to be channelled and directed properly. Group work can form a training arena that is also protected, to enable the fledgling magician to learn the craft.

THE ARCHANGELS

The four archangels can be found in a variety of protective incantations and invocations. Their purpose is to guard the four quarters or cardinal points. They are an almost universal symbol that can turn up in many different aspects, from nursery rhymes to the guardians of the dead.

For our purposes, they might be thought of as extra help in living our lives successfully. Think of yourself making a connection to Michael for love, so that you can love more fully; Gabriel for strength, to fill you with power for the next day; Uriel for suffusing you with the light of the mind or understanding; and Raphael for healing all your ills. When you are having a hard time, you can send a brief prayer or request to whichever one is appropriate.

Generally there are, in fact, considered to be seven archangels and it will depend on your own teaching as to which school of thought you choose to follow in naming them. Because the teachings were initially by word of mouth, there are many different lists of archangels deputed to help the world upon its way. The four archangels considered here are the ones that appear consistently in most lists and are therefore the best known universally. They are the ones most often called upon in magical workings. The only problem is that sometimes Michael and Uriel appear to swap places in some traditions, which can be confusing. If the attributions given here do not feel right, try the ritual the other way about and change the words accordingly. Do ensure that you still call upon all four archangels, however.

Michael, which means 'Who is as God' in Hebrew, is one of the seven archangels and also chief of the four closest to God. The Roman Catholic Church regards Michael in much the same light as does the Catholic Church, his festival, Michaelmas, being held on 29 September. He is known in mythology as the one who attempted to bring Lucifer back to God. In Ezekiel's vision of the cherubim, or the four sacred animals, he is the angel with the face of the lion. Michael is often visualized as a masculine archangel dressed in robes or armour of red and green. He stands in the attitude of a warrior amid flames. Bearing either a sword or a spear, Michael is the guardian against evil and the protector of humanity. He is stationed in the south.

Raphael is one of four archangels stationed about the throne of God; his task is to heal the earth. Initially he was pictured with the face of a dragon, but this was changed in later imagery to the face of a man. He is often visualized as a tall, fair figure standing upon the clouds in robes of yellow and violet, sometimes holding the Caduceus of Hermes as a symbol of his healing powers. He is God's builder or composer and has the task of building or rebuilding the earth, which the fallen angels have defiled. Raphael's name in Hebrew means 'Healer of God' or 'God has Healed'. Raphael Ruachel ('Raphael of Air') is stationed in the east.

In Hebrew, **Gabriel** means 'Strong One of God'. He is one of the four archangels who stand in the presence of God, and was sent to announce to Mary the birth of Jesus. In Ezekiel's vision of the four sacred animals, he has the face of the eagle. Gabriel is often visualized as a feminine archangel holding a cup, standing upon the waters of the sea, and wearing robes of blue and orange. Gabriel is also at one with the higher ego or inner divinity. Gabriel Maimel ('Gabriel of Water') is stationed in the west.

Uriel (or Auriel's) name in Hebrew means 'Light of God'. Specifically, he is the angel or divinity of light – not simply of physical light, but of spiritual illumination. Also referred to as 'The Angel of Repentance', he is the angel of terror, prophecy and mystery. He was sometimes ranked as an archangel with Michael, Gabriel, and Raphael and believed to be the angel who holds the keys to the gates of Hell. He is also often identified as the angel who drove Adam and Eve from the Garden of Eden and was thought to be the messenger sent to warn Noah of the forthcoming floods. As 'Uriel Aretziel' ('Uriel of Earth') he is stationed in the north. He is often seen rising up from the vegetation of the earth holding stems of ripened wheat and wearing robes of citrine, russet, olive and black.

Archangels and the Elementals

Each archangel of the Elements has as his servant one of the kings of the Elemental kingdoms. By tradition, each of the Elements ties in with certain nature spirits, of which the dryads are only one sort. They are:

Air

Raphael has as his servant Paralda, King of the Sylphs, who appears to clairvoyant vision as a tenuous form made of blue mist always moving and changing shape.

Fire

Michael is accompanied by Djinn, King of the Salamanders, who appears as a Fire giant composed of twisting living flame surrounded by sparks which crackle and glow.

Water

Gabriel's servant is Nixa, King of the Undines, who is seen as an ever-changing shape, fluid with a greenish blue aura splashed with silver and grey.

Earth

Uriel is served by Ghob, King of the Gnomes, seen traditionally as a gnome or goblin who is squat, heavy and dense.

You do not necessarily have to call on these Elementals specifically in your rituals, but you should be aware of their energies in that they are the servants of the archangels and not yours.

Petitioning the Archangels

This spell uses the higher aspects of the guardians of the directions and petitions the four archangels according to their qualities – Michael for love, Gabriel for strength, Raphael for healing and Uriel for clarity. Uriel, the 'light of God', is represented by the candles. When you perceive a lack of something in your life, petitioning the archangels helps to fulfil it.

YOU WILL NEED
Three white candles
Plate on which you have scattered sugar

METHOD
✤ Stand the candles on the plate with the sugar all around the candles.
✤ Light the candles.
✤ Put the plate and candles in the highest place

you can safely reach at home. This signifies the status we give the archangels

❖ You may now ask for three wishes from your guardian angels St Raphael, St Michael and St Gabriel.

❖ You might for instance ask one wish for business, one wish for love, and one wish which seems unlikely to happen.

❖ Bear in mind that you may only petition the archangels if it is really important.

❖ If you like, address each of the archangels by name, or use the same invocation you used in the Essential Ritual. This is protective and protects you from inadvertently making silly mistakes. To remind you, the words are:

Before me Raphael
Behind me Gabriel
On my right hand Michael
On my left hand Uriel

God be thanked.

❖ Let the candles burn right out.

Share this spell with others on the third day (after you requested the wishes) and help to pass on the benefit of your gain. You should use this spell wisely and not make ridiculous requests with it. If what you wish does not happen, accept that it is not right for you to make that wish, and do not repeat the request.

Throughout the preceeding sections there are various spells which have eased you into the world of magic. The information given touches on many subjects and aspects of spell working. You now have enough knowledge to permit you to develop your magical self. The Compendium which follows is only a small selection of the wealth of opportunities available to you.

Compendium

This part of this book is in effect a Grimoire - a collection of spells divided into sections. The sections are Friendship, Love and Relationships; Health, Healing and Wellbeing; Money, Luck and Career, and Protection. At the end is a pot-pourri of miscellaneous spells.

Each spell has an introductory paragraph with information as to what type of spell it is, the best time to carry it out if possible and which discipline it comes from if known. We then tell you what you will need: candles, incense, special tools or objects, then give you the method to use. Some spells require incantations, some invocations and others simple actions to make them work, and this is laid out for you.

Lastly there is a short paragraph which tells you what you might expect, though as always we would remind you that results can sometimes be unexpected, or indeed not take place at all!.

Friendship, Love and Relationships

THE MAJORITY OF PEOPLE probably first become aware of spell making in an effort to influence someone else's feelings in their favour. While strictly this is apparently a misuse of energy there is a place for such spells in that they help to make us feel better about ourselves and more confident in dealing with other people. They perhaps influence us as much as other people.

Attracting a New Friend

Working magically can sometimes be a lonely business. However, we do have the means at our disposal to draw people towards us in friendship and love. This spell draws to you a friend rather than a lover – someone of like mind who enjoys the same things that you do. It is best performed during the waxing phase of the Moon.

YOU WILL NEED

Three brown candles
Sheet of paper
Pen

METHOD

❖ Light the candles.
❖ On the sheet of paper, write down the attributes you would like your friend to have.
❖ Say each one out loud.
❖ Fold the paper in half twice.
❖ Light the edge of the folded paper from one of the candles and repeat the words below :

With heart and mind I do now speak
Bring to me the one I seek
Let this paper be the guide
And bring this friend to my side.

Pain and loneliness be no more
Draw a companion to my door.

With pleasures many and sorrows few
Let us build a friendship new.

Let not this simple spell coerce
Or make my situation worse.
As I will, it shall be.

❖ Let the paper burn out then snuff out the candles.
❖ Use these candles only for the same type of spell.

Within the next few weeks, you should meet someone with some or all of the qualities you seek. Remember that you have called this person to you, so you can have the confidence and the time to explore the relationship properly. Never ever be judgemental about qualities in your new friend that are not ones that you have requested.

Freeze Out

There are many ways of 'freezing people out', and this one which uses ice is good since it will only last as long as the ice remains frozen. The spell should only be used to prevent harm to yourself and others, not to bring harm to anyone else. It is only used if you know the name of the person involved. A good time to do the spell would be with the waning Moon.

YOU WILL NEED

Magically charged paper and pen
Water in a bowl

METHOD

❖ Write the name of the person concerned in the middle of the paper.
❖ Fold the paper away from you at least four times all the while sensing the person's influence waning.
❖ Dunk the paper in the water until it is well soaked. Leave it overnight if necessary.
❖ Put the wet paper into your ice compartment or freezer.
❖ Leave it there until you feel the danger is over.
❖ You then release the spell, by taking the paper out of the freezer and using words such as:

All danger passed
I set you free

❖ Dispose of the paper in any way you wish.

You must never forget to set the other person free, lest you find yourself bound to them for longer than is healthy for either of you. By the laws of cause and effect you must ensure that your actions do not rebound on you.

To Clarify Relationships

The art of braiding is one which can be used in spell making to represent many things. In this particular spell it is used to signify the coming together of three people and in the unbraiding an amicable resolution. In the use of colour the spell is focused either on the outcome or on the people concerned.

YOU WILL NEED

3 lengths of ribbon of suitable colour
You can use astrological colours to represent each person or you can use one colour to represent the situation
For example:
- *Red for a relationship soured by anger*
- *Blue for a business relationship*
- *Green for a relationship in which finance is importance*
- *Yellow where communication is difficult*

METHOD

❖ Decide before you begin what it is you are trying to achieve.
❖ If it is important to bring people together, then as you are braiding you will concentrate on this.
❖ If it is seen as necessary for them to go their separate ways, while you are braiding you will concentrate on the intricacies of the situation and perhaps the ability to bring about open and frank discussion.
❖ Once you have finished braiding, you have a completely new object which is a representation of the relationship between the various parties.

❖ You should now dedicate the braid to the best outcome for that relationship.
❖ Put the braid somewhere safe for at least 72 hours, preferably in constant moonlight and sunlight.
❖ Only when the reason for the spell is fulfilled (e.g. reconciliation between people, full honest communication, a successful business partnership) can you think of dismantling the braid.
❖ As you undo it ask that the people involved can go forward in life in whatever way is appropriate for them, gaining what they have needed from their association.
❖ You may of course wish to keep the braid without undoing it.
❖ Do not use the ribbons for other magical purposes.

A braiding spell comes under the heading of a knot spell and is a gentle way of affecting the outcome of a situation. It is, of course, not necessarily a quick way of resolving anything but is often surprising in its outcome.

To Win the Heart of the One you Love

This is a very old folklore spell. Using a bulb is symbolic of love growing unseen and unrecognized for a time, finally flowering at the right time. You cannot simply leave it alone, but must tend it carefully if it is to grow successfully.

YOU WILL NEED

Onion bulb
Your burin
New flower pot
Earth or compost

METHOD

❖ Scratch the name of the one you love on the base of the bulb with your burine.
❖ Plant it in earth in the pot.
❖ Place the pot on a windowsill, if possible facing the direction in which your sweetheart lives.
❖ Over the bulb, repeat the name of the one you

desire morning and night until the bulb takes root, begins to shoot and finally blooms.

❖ Say the following incantation whenever you think of the other person:

> *May its roots grow,*
> *May its leaves grow,*
> *May its flowers grow,*
> *And as it does so,*
> *[Name of person]'s love grow.*

You do need patience for this spell and you may well find that you lose the impetus for the relationship before the spell is complete. This would suggest the relationship may not be right for you.

Chocolate and Strawberry Delight

Chocolate is said to be an aphrodisiac, a mild euphoric, and helps to heal depression. It is therefore extremely effective in love potions and spells. In this spell two ingredients are brought together to help you to enchant your loved one. Strawberries are well known as lovers' fruits.

YOU WILL NEED

Strawberry incense
Pink candles
A plate of strawberries
Melted chocolate

METHOD

❖ Be very clear in your own mind what you want to happen before you start.

❖ Be aware that it is not right to influence the other person against their will or their natural inclinations. You should use this spell to prepare the ground for true relationship.

❖ Light the candles and the incense.

❖ Dip each strawberry in the chocolate.

❖ As you do so, visualize you and the other person together enjoying one another's company, becoming closer and so on.

❖ Say the words below (or something similar) as you prepare the fruit:

> *Lover, lover, come to me*
> *And even then you shall be free*

> *To come, to go just as you please*
> *Until to stay your heart decrees.*

❖ Do be aware that you have not put a time limit on this so if you cannot handle such an open relationship choose different words.

❖ As you enjoy the fruit together be prepared to take responsibility for what occurs.

This spell can be quite powerful, particularly if you use the same pink candles when your lover arrives. Strawberries and chocolate both come under the rulership of Venus the Goddess of Love, though there is a belief that Jupiter also has a connection with strawberries.

To Obtain Love from a Specific Person

This spell uses fire as its vehicle, not as candle magic but in your cauldron. You use an incantation and can also use magical ink and parchment if you so wish. The spell is best done at night-time and in using the power of the number three is not just for lust but also for love.

YOU WILL NEED

Your cauldron or a fireproof container
A piece of paper
Pen and red ink
Fragrant wood or herbs to burn (you could use apple, birch and cedar)

METHOD

❖ Light a small fire in your cauldron or container.

❖ Cut out a piece of paper that is 10 cm x 10 cm (3 x 3 inches).

❖ With the pen and red ink draw a heart on the paper and colour it in.

❖ Write the name of the person that you desire on the heart three times.

❖ If you wish do this from the edge to the middle in a spiral, to signify how deep your love goes.

❖ While doing this be thinking of his or her heart burning with desire for you just like the flames of the fire.

❖ Kiss the names on the heart three times.

❖ Place the paper in the fire while saying these words three times:

Soon my love will come to me
This I know that it must be
Fire come from this wood
Bring love and caring that it would
Make our hearts glow and shine,
bringing love that shall be mine!

❖ Sit quietly as the paper burns, visualizing your lover coming towards you.

❖ After you are finished concentrating for a few minutes, extinguish the fire.

❖ Say quietly three times:

So, let it be

Do not get impatient if nothing happens for a while. Simply have confidence that you will be given an opportunity to have a relationship with this particular person. How you handle the relationship thereafter is entirely up to you.

To Focus your Lover's Interest

If you find that your partner's attention seems to be wandering, try this spell. It is best performed on a Friday, the day sacred to Venus the Goddess of Love.

YOU WILL NEED
A clean piece of paper
A pen you like (you can use your magical implements if you like)

METHOD
❖ Taking your pen, write your first name and your lover's surname on the paper.

❖ Draw either a square or circle around them. Use the square if you decide all you want with this person is a physical relationship, and the circle if you are utterly convinced this person is right for you.

❖ With your eyes closed say:

If it be right, come back to me.

❖ Cut the square or circle out and place it inside your pillowcase for at least three nights.

❖ Your lover should show renewed interest.

This is one spell that occasionally does not work. It is said that Venus will not assist if there is any intrinsic reason for the relationship not to work out – for instance, if your partner no longer loves you, you may be unsuccessful in your aim. This you must accept, knowing you have done the best you can.

To bring Romantic Love to You

This spell is one that uses herbs, crystals, candle and colour. The herb rosemary traditionally signifies long memory, the rose quartz crystal signifies love and the colours signify love and passion. It is designed to concentrate the mind and to attract love to you as opposed to a specific lover.

YOU WILL NEED
Small box
Red marker/pen
Rose or vanilla incense
A sprig of rosemary (for remembrance)
A piece of rose quartz crystal
Pink or red votive candle

METHOD
❖ Sit in your own most powerful place. That might be inside, outside, near your favourite tree or by running water.

❖ Write in red on the box

Love is mine.

❖ Light the incense – this clears the atmosphere and puts you in the right mood.

❖ Put the rosemary and rose quartz in the box.

❖ Put anything else that represents love to you in the box (drawings of hearts, poems, or whatever – be creative).

❖ Remember, this spell is to attract love to you, not a specific lover so don't use a representation of a particular person.

❖ Be in a very positive state of mind.

❖ Imagine yourself very happy and in love.
❖ Light the candle and say:

I am love
love I will find
true love preferably
will soon be mine

Love is me
Love I seek
my true love
I will soon meet.

❖ Now sit for a little while and concentrate again on being happy.
❖ Pinch out the candle and add it to the box.
❖ Let the incense burn out.
❖ Seal the box shut and don't open it until you have found your true love.
❖ When you have found your lover, take the rose quartz out of the box and keep it as a reminder.
❖ Bury the entire box in the earth.

Because in this spell you reproduce a positive state of mind and you are imagining what it is like to be in love, you set up a current of energy which attracts like feeling. In sealing the box you are 'capturing' the vibration of love and all things then become possible.

To Clear the Air between Lovers

When communication between you and your partner seems difficult, you can forge a new link using this spell, which is representational. You will need to have confidence in your own power though.

YOU WILL NEED

A crystal ball or magnifying glass
Your partner's photograph

METHOD

❖ Place the crystal or magnifying glass over the image of your partner's face.
❖ Because the features are magnified, the eyes and mouth will appear to move and come to life.

❖ Simply state your wishes or difficulties and what you feel your lover can do about them.
❖ He/she will get the message.

This way of working is very simple, but you do have to trust that you yourself are an able transmitter. Often we do not realize how difficult communication can be and here we are trying to make your partner understand how you feel, not to change them.

Confidence in Social Situations

Charm bags are a very efficient way of carrying reminders which can add extra zest to life. This one is used to help you overcome shyness, perhaps when you are meeting new people or doing something you have never done before. It is done during the Waxing Moon.

YOU WILL NEED

A small drawstring bag about 2.5-5 cm
(1-2 inches) deep - you could use a colour such as yellow to enhance communication
Ground nutmeg
Pine needles
Dried lavender
Piece of mandrake root

METHOD

❖ Put a pinch or two of the nutmeg, pine needles, dried lavender and mandrake root in the bag and tie it closed.
❖ Consecrate and charge the bag during the waxing phase of the Moon so that you can use positive energy.
❖ Wear the bag around your neck or keep it in your pocket. You should feel a surge of energy whenever you are in a social situation which you find difficult to handle.
❖ When you feel you no longer have need of the support your bag gives you, you can scatter the herbs to the four winds or burn them.

It is the consecrating of the bag which turns it into a tool for use in everyday situations, so choose your words carefully to express your particular need. Try to approach one new person everyday or go into one new situation, until you lose your fear.

To Create Opportunities for Love

This is not a spell to draw a person to you, but more to 'open the way' - to alert the other person to the possibility of a relationship with you. The spell should be performed on a Friday. The use of your mother's ring is symbolic of continuity.

YOU WILL NEED

A wine glass
A ring (traditionally your mother's wedding ring would be used)
Red silk ribbon about 80cm (30 inches) long

METHOD

❖ Put a wine glass right way up on a table.
❖ Make a pendulum by suspending the ring from the red silk ribbon.
❖ Hold the pendulum steady by resting your elbow on the table, with the ribbon between your thumb and forefinger. Let the ring hang in the mouth of the wine glass.
❖ Clearly say your name followed by that of the other person. Repeat their name twice i.e. three times in all. Then, thinking of them, spell their name out loud.
❖ Allow the ring to swing and tap against the wine glass once for each letter of their name.
❖ Tie the ribbon around your neck, allowing the ring to hang down over your neck, close to your heart.
❖ Wear it for three weeks, and repeat the spell every Friday for three weeks.
❖ By the end of the third week, the person you have in your sights will show an interest, unless it is not meant to be.

Let's assume there is someone in whom you are interested, but the interest does not seem to be reciprocated. This spell ensures there are no hindrances, but there has to be at least some feeling for it to stand a chance of working.

Friendship

This spell calls on several disciplines; candle, representational and incantation. It is best performed at the New Moon, since you are trying to bring about new ways of relating to people and also hoping to meet new friends.

YOU WILL NEED

Several sheets of paper
Pen
Jasmine, lavender or patchouli essential oil in a carrier oil such as almond
A white candle

METHOD

❖ Anoint the candle with a few drops of the oil.
❖ Inscribe it with the Ogham Stave for friendship, Ur: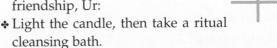
❖ Light the candle, then take a ritual cleansing bath.
❖ Anoint yourself with more of the oil paying particular attention to the pulse spots.
❖ Take one sheet of paper and draw a figure to represent yourself - it does not have to be good art.
❖ Make sure your gender is recognisable.
❖ Write underneath the figure all those attributes which make you a good companion e.g. funny, bubbly, curious etc.
❖ On the other pieces of paper draw representations of both men and women and the interests you would like them to have which are similar to yours.
❖ Briefly hold between your hands the paper which represents you, together with each of the other papers making sure that the drawings face one another.
❖ Say each time:

Let us meet each other
Let us greet each other
Let us become friends
Let us become companions
And if we grow to love one another
Then so be it.

❖ Put a drop of oil on one corner of each of the papers.
❖ Now spread the papers out in front of you and visualize a link from you to each of the others, almost like a spider's web and say:

Spider Woman, Spider Woman,
weave me a charm
Make me good enough,
clever enough them all to disarm.

❖ Now let the candle burn out.

❖ You should find that new friends appear before the next New Moon.

All life can be seen as a network, and each individual is a strand within that network. Spider Woman is a North American goddess who weaves charms and reveals the power and the purpose of each strand. She keeps you aware of the importance of these connections in your life.

To Beckon a Person

This is a very simple method of putting out a vibration which, if a relationship has a chance of succeeding, will make the other person aware of you. It does not force the other person to do anything, but simply paves the way.

METHOD
❖ Say the following:

> *Know I move to you*
> *as you move to me.*
>
> *As I think of you,*
> *Think also of me.*
>
> *As I call your name,*
> *Call me to you.*
> *Come to me in love.*

❖ Say the person's name three times (if known).

You may need to recite the whole spell several times in order to feel the proper effect. You may also need to remember that a loving friend is just as important as a friendly lover.

To Draw a New Love to You

Charm bags, talisman bags or mojos, whatever tradition they come from, are useful in bringing about a certain result. Friday is the day of Venus and her specific hours are the eighth hour of the day and the third and tenth hour of the night, as per the Planetary Hours chart on pages 238-239, so are ideal times to perform this spell.

YOU WILL NEED
A small drawstring bag
5 rose petals
A couple of pinches of catnip
Heather
Vervain
1 inch (2.5cm) piece of jasper or rose quartz

METHOD
❖ Your bag could be pink for love, or red for passion with your drawstring a different colour to add other qualities.

❖ During the waxing phase of the Moon at your chosen time, put all the ingredients in the bag, then consecrate and charge the bag.

❖ Wear it around your neck or keep it in your pocket.

For a Lover to Come to You

This spell is reputed to work very quickly, so do not be too rash. Red candles represent passion, so you must take responsibility for whatever happens when you call your lover to you.

YOU WILL NEED
Two silver pins
A red candle

METHOD
❖ Stick two silver pins through the middle of a red candle at midnight.

❖ Concentrate on your lover and repeat his or her name several times.

❖ After the candle burns down to the pins, your lover will arrive. It is also said that if you give your lover one of the pins they will remain bound to you.

❖ If you wish companionship rather than passion, use a candle of a colour appropriate to the other person's astrological sign.

This spell is one used to influence someone else, so be very careful how you use it. Pins were often used in magical work in times gone by, because they were readily available. One old custom was to ask a bride for the pins from her wedding dress, for which you must give her a penny.

To Achieve your Heart's Desire

This is quite an effective spell and does give you something to do while you are waiting for true love. It makes use of candles and of plant magic. Timing is important since it uses the rising of the sun, as also is colour (red to represent passion).

YOU WILL NEED
A fresh rose (preferably red and perfumed)
Two red candles

METHOD
❖ Find out the time of the next sunrise.
❖ Just before going to sleep, place a red candle on either side of the rose.
❖ The next morning at sunrise take the rose outside.
❖ Hold the rose in front of you and say:

This red rose is for true love.
True love come to me.

❖ Now go back inside and put the rose between the candles again.
❖ Light the candles and visualize love burning in the heart of the one you want.
❖ Keep the candles burning day and night until the rose fades.
❖ When the rose is dead, pinch out the candles and then bury the rose.

There are many spells for love and this one is extremely simple, except that it requires some effort to get up early in the morning. The concentration that you put into it as you burn your candles focuses your mind on the matter in hand.

To Forget about an Ex-lover

This spell is done best at the time of the Waning Moon or New Moon. It is not done to get rid of a former partner, but to exorcize your bad feelings about them. It is sensible to finish the spell by sending loving thoughts to them. Woody nightshade is poisonous and you may not care to use it, in which case you can use a bulb of garlic.

YOU WILL NEED
Photograph of your ex-partner
Suitable container for burning the photograph (one in which the ashes can be saved)
Root of bittersweet (woody nightshade, which is poisonous) or a bulb of garlic
Red cloth or bag

METHOD
❖ Place the picture of your ex-partner in the container. Set it alight.
❖ Gather up all your hurt and pain as the picture burns down. Feel them flowing away from you as you say these words or similar:

Leave my heart and leave me free
Leave my life, no pain for me.
As this picture burns to dust,
Help me now, move on I must.

❖ Repeat the words until the picture is burnt out.
❖ Taking the herb root or garlic, hold it first to your solar plexus.
❖ Allow the bad feelings to flow into the root or garlic. Touch the root or garlic to your forehead, indicating that you have converted the bad feelings to good.
❖ Wrap everything, including the container of ashes, in your red bag or cloth.
❖ As soon as convenient, bury it as far away from your home as possible.

If you have had a relationship which is argumentative and turned nasty it is often better to end it and move on. This must always be your choice but if you wish to try again you may like to try the To Stop an Argument spell on page 262.

To Have a Person Think about You

This spell works over time. A relationship that grows slowly generally has more chance of success than a whirlwind romance and that is what is represented here. Small seeds represent the many facets of a relationship. The spell is done as the Moon is growing in power.

YOU WILL NEED

Packet of seeds of your choice
Pot of soil (to grow them)
A small copper object such as a penny
(Copper is sacred to Venus, the Goddess of Love)

METHOD

❖ On a night when the Moon is waxing, go outside and hold the penny in the moonlight.

❖ Bury the penny in the soil in the pot.

❖ Sprinkle the seeds on top to form the initial of the other person's name.

❖ As the seeds germinate, love should also grow.

❖ Remember that just as plants need nurturing so does love, so you will need to look after the growing seeds.

It is said that the plants will grow and flourish if the love is meant to be, but will wither and die if there is no real energy in the relationship. For those who are not very good at plant-care, you might choose to put a reminder to nurture somewhere prominent.

To Have Your Love Returned

This spell is candle magic and also representational. It is a little more complicated than most because it requires an understanding of symbolism. It is best done on a Friday. The objects you use need not be the real things, but they can be miniaturizations such as cake decorations.

YOU WILL NEED

Pink candle
Blue candle
Gold candle (to represent the relationship)
Horseshoe (to represent luck in love)
Key (to represent the key to your heart)
Two roses
An article of your love interest's clothing (failing that, use something of your own)

METHOD

❖ Light the pink and blue candles (pink first if you are female, blue if male), followed by the gold.

❖ Place the horseshoe and key on either side of the candles, with the roses between them.

❖ When the candles have burnt down, wrap the flowers, the key and the horseshoe in the clothing.

❖ Place the items in a bedroom drawer and leave them alone for fourteen days. If after this time the flowers are still fresh, this is a good sign.

❖ You should then bury them or put them (along with the horseshoe and key) in a pot pourri.

You might use this spell when you think a relationship with someone would be worthwhile. If you cannot find an article of the other person's clothing, a handkerchief or some other small article will do as well. If that is not possible then use a square of pink material.

To Heal a Rift

This spell is a Romany one which works on the principle of making two things one. The apple always has been a symbol for love, and pins are a symbol of industriousness denoting the effort which must be put into the relationship.

YOU WILL NEED

A fresh apple
Knife
Clean sheet of white paper
Pen
2 pins, cocktail sticks or twigs

METHOD

❖ Cut the apple in half.

❖ Tradition says it is helpful, but not vital, if the seeds stay whole. If they don't, reconciliation may simply be a little bit more difficult to bring about.

❖ Write the woman's full name on the paper. Next to it, write the man's. Ensure that the space taken up by the names doesn't exceed the width of the halved apple.

❖ Cut out the names. Place the paper with the names between the two halves of the apple.

❖ Visualize the marriage or relationship being healed.

✤ Skewer the apple halves together, inserting the pins or twigs diagonally from right to left and then vice versa.

✤ If you are healing your own relationship, send your love to the person concerned and ask to receive their love in return

✤ If it is for someone else then visualize the couple surrounded by a pink cloud or aura in a loving embrace

Divorce is disliked among the Romanies even today. When action is required to heal a seemingly irreparable rift, this spell can begin a process of reconciliation. To finish off the spell, Romanies use their campfire to bake the apple until it appears whole.

To Strengthen Attraction

If you love someone but feel that they are not reciprocating, try this spell. Be aware though, that by using this spell you are trying to have a direct effect upon the other person. You are using representational magic because the hair stands for the person you are hoping to influence.

YOU WILL NEED

A few strands of the person's hair
A rose scented incense stick

METHOD

✤ Light the incense.
✤ Repeat the name of the one you long for several times, saying each time:

[Name] love me now.

✤ Hold the hair on the burning incense until it frizzles away.
✤ As the hair burns, think of their indifference dissipating and being replaced by passion.
✤ Leave the incense to burn out.

Before you perform this you should have tried to work out why the other person feels indifferent and consider whether what you are proposing is appropriate. If, for instance, the person you want to attract has not learnt how to commit to a relationship, it would be unfair to try and influence them.

To Stop an Argument

This is a spell to stop an argument between you and another or to change their feelings of aggravation. You are using colour and representational magic here. So that you do not let your own feelings intrude, you might take a ritual bath first. The plate is used for two reasons in this spell. Firstly being glass it reflects back to the person, and secondly through its colour it raises the whole question to its highest vibration.

YOU WILL NEED

Glass plate
(Deep purple if possible, but if not, clear will work just as well)
Picture of the person with whom you have argued

METHOD

✤ Place the picture face down on the plate for no more than 15 minutes. You do not want to over-influence the recipient, so spend a few moments remembering the good times you have had.

✤ For this reason, if using an ordinary photograph you should also be aware of where the negative to the picture is so that you are only using positive energy.

✤ The person should either drop in or communicate in some other way within 24 hours so you can resolve your difficulties.

✤ If they do not, repeat the procedure for no more than 15 minutes.

✤ If after a third time you still haven't heard from them, do try to give them a call or visit them because their feelings should have changed.

✤ You will then know that you have done all you can to be on good terms with them.

It is often difficult to get back onto a normal footing with people after an argument, so do be prepared to apologize for any part that you have had in the difficulty. Remember that you are only dealing with that particular argument, not deeper issues within the friendship.

Garment Spell for Fidelity

This spell uses the combination of nutmeg and intimate garments in a form of sympathetic magic, combined with herbal magic. It is said to keep a partner faithful. It obviously can be done at any time, particularly when you suspect that your partner may be open to temptation.

YOU WILL NEED

2 whole nutmegs
A pin or your burin
Wide red ribbon
A pair of your and your partner's clean underwear
Large white envelope

METHOD

❖ Carefully scratch with your burin or the pin your partner's initial on one nutmeg and your own on the other.
❖ Tie them together with the ribbon.
❖ Wrap them in the underwear and then place in the envelope.
❖ Sleep with the envelope under your pillow if your partner is away or you are separated from them.

Nutmeg was at one time the most expensive spice available so one would have to be fairly serious about the relationship to be willing to lock away such an expensive commodity. This spell is probably not to be entered into lightly, nor is it designed to keep someone with you against their will.

To Rid Yourself of an Unwanted Admirer

Occasionally people get into a situation where they are being pursued by someone whose attention is a nuisance. Rather than reacting in anger, it is often easier to open the way for the unwanted suitor to leave. This spell, done on a Waning Moon - often does the trick.

YOU WILL NEED

Vervain leaves
A fierce fire

METHOD

❖ Light a fire.
❖ Pick up the vervain and as you do so call out the name of the offending person.
❖ Fling the leaves on the fire and say:

Withdraw from me now I need you not.

❖ There is a requirement to declaim passionately, and to use some force, in any spell that is designed to drive someone from you. Therefore, be very sure that you do not wish this person to be in your life in any way.
❖ Ensure the fire is properly and safely extinguished.
❖ Repeat the action three nights in a row.

Preferably this spell should be performed outside, but it can be also be performed indoors if you have a suitable fireplace and provided you are careful. Strictly, one is supposed to gather the vervain leaves, though with urban living this is a bit of a tall order. Make sure you have at least a couple of handfuls of the dried herb.

To Find a New Lover

This spell works best if performed at the time of the New Moon. You use everything new so that you change the vibration and can look forward with hope. It is representational and is carried out at the time of the New Moon for the same reason.

YOU WILL NEED

Heart shaped rose petal or a red heart cut out of paper
Clean sheet of white paper
New pen
New candle (preferably pink)
New envelope

METHOD

❖ On the day of a New Moon, cut a red heart out of paper or card.
❖ Take the paper and with the pen write on it:

As this heart shines in candlelight,
I draw you to me tonight.

- ❖ Bathe and change into nightclothes.
- ❖ When you feel ready, light the candle and read the invocation out loud.
- ❖ Hold the heart in front of the flame and let the candlelight shine on it.
- ❖ Place the heart and spell in the envelope.
- ❖ Seal it with wax from the candle.
- ❖ Conceal the envelope and leave it untouched for one cycle of the Moon (28 days).
- ❖ By the time the Moon is New again, there should be new love in your life.

So many need companionship and partnership to boost their feeling of self-worth that to do a spell like this means, as always, that one must be willing to take on everything that a partnership brings.

A Lover's Token

This bottle is quite a nice one to give to your lover as a token of your love and to intensify the link between you. The herbs are all well known for their association with love, and because of the link between the bottles should help you to communicate.

YOU WILL NEED

For each token:
A glass bottle with cork, any size will do
A handful of dried rose petals (preferably from flowers given to you by your lover)
Dried/fresh rosemary (for love and strength)
Dried/fresh lavender
Rose oil or water
Wax (pink or red is good for love)
Pink ribbon

METHOD

- ❖ Crush the rose petals and place in the bottle.
- ❖ Put in the rosemary and/or lavender, then add the oil or rose water almost to the top, leaving some room for air to circulate.
- ❖ Cork the bottle and drip wax over the cork to sea lit. Lay the ribbon on a flat surface.
- ❖ Place the bottles one at either end of the ribbon.
- ❖ Gradually move them towards one another along the ribbon to signify you meeting with your lover.

- ❖ When they meet, tie the ribbon round your partner's bottle and give it to them.
- ❖ Place yours on a shelf, dresser or anywhere where it will not be disturbed.

These bottles are tangible evidence of the link between you and your lover. You may use them to remind you of the good times or soothe you in the bad. The ribbon signifies the link between you, so when you think of it you have immediately connected.

Herbal Charm to Attract Love

This is a charm that uses both colour, herbs and knots in its fashioning. Love is always of interest, but do remember that you need to be clear in your aspirations. Numbers are also used, seven being a particularly potent one.

YOU WILL NEED

Acacia, rose, myrtle, jasmine or lavender petals, in any combination or singly
A red heart cut from paper or felt
Copper coin or ring
A circle of rose or red coloured cloth
Blue thread or ribbon

METHOD

- ❖ Place the petals, heart and coin or ring on the cloth and visualize the type of lover you are looking for.
- ❖ Tie the cloth into a pouch with the blue thread or ribbon, using seven knots.
- ❖ As you tie the knots you may chant an incantation, such as:

Seven knots I tie above,
Seven knots for me and love.

- ❖ Hang the pouch close to your pillow and await results.

This charm is designed to draw someone towards you and does not guarantee that you will necessarily fall madly in love with the person who comes along - you have simply made yourself attractive to them. If this is so then be prepared to let the other person down gently.

Fidelity Charm

This spell uses the Elements combined with herbal magic. It is an old spell and comes from a time when every spell-maker would use what was easily available to them. The best time for performing this spell is around the time of the New Moon.

YOU WILL NEED

6 large ivy leaves (gathered at the time of the New Moon)
Burin
Granular rose or jasmine love incense
Container suitable for burning the ivy leaves

METHOD

✤ Using the burin inscribe one word of the following phrase on each leaf:

Keep my true love with me

✤ Light the incense and in the container burn the inscribed leaves with the correct order of speech.
✤ Whilst you are doing this, say

Goddess of love, God of desire,
Bring to me fidelity.

✤ The above uses the Element of Fire. To use Water cast the leaves into a stream or other flowing water and say:

Message of love, I set you free
To capture a love and return to me.

Ivy highlights the quality of fidelity. You should not use this spell if you are not prepared to offer fidelity in return.

To Bring Someone into your Life

This spell can be used to attract love towards you or to draw a companion closer. It should be started on the night of a New Moon. It is representational in that the cruet set suggests a pairing, and also uses colour.

YOU WILL NEED

Salt shaker
Pepper shaker
(or two objects which obviously make a pair)
A length of pink ribbon about one metre long

METHOD

✤ Assign one article as the feminine person and one as masculine.
✤ Take the piece of pink ribbon, and tie the female object to one end and the male to the other, leaving a good length of ribbon between them.
✤ Every morning untie the ribbon, move the objects a little closer together, and retie the knots.
✤ Eventually the objects will touch.
✤ Leave them bound together for seven days before untying them.
✤ By this time, love should have entered your life.

There are several spells which make use of the idea that two people must travel along a set path. This one is used to signify the path of love. It also suggests in the tying and untying of the ribbon the freedoms there are in the relationship.

To Rekindle your Lover's Interest

This technique is worth trying when your lover is not paying you enough attention. You are using the laurel leaves to back up the energy that you are putting into making the relationship work. This spell uses herbal and elemental magic.

YOU WILL NEED

A large quantity of laurel leaves
A fire

METHOD

✤ Sit in front of the embers of a fire and gaze into them, concentrating on your lover.
✤ Keep your gaze fixed into the fire.
✤ With your left hand, throw some laurel leaves onto the embers.
✤ As they burn say:

Laurel leaves burn into the fire.
Bring to me my heart's desire.

❖ Wait until the flames die down, then do the same again.
❖ Repeat the actions once more.
❖ It is said that within 24 hours your lover will come back to you.

Again this is a spell which must allow the person who you are targeting choices. To keep your partner by your side if they are unhappy would not be right. This spell does allow you to give careful consideration as to what fidelity and security you require within a relationship. This spell is similar to To Rid Yourself of an Unwanted Admirer on page 263 and demonstrates how different herbs used in similar ways can bring about different results.

Resolving a Love Triangle

Sometimes it is possible to get caught up in a situation where three people are in a love triangle. It would be wrong to influence anyone one way or another, so here is a way of resolving the situation that should not harm anyone. It is best done at the time of the Full Moon.

YOU WILL NEED
Three lengths of string each about a metre long
An open space where you will not be disturbed

METHOD
❖ Form a triangle on the ground with the three pieces of string so that the ends are just touching.
❖ Step into the middle of the triangle.
❖ Appeal to the Triple Goddess in her guise of Maid, Mother and Crone. Use words such as:

Triple Goddess hear my plea
I ask you now to set us free
It's not a problem I can alter
So help me now lest I falter.

❖ These words put you in touch with your own inner self which means that you make the decision which is right for you.

❖ Wait for a few moments to allow the energy to build up then raise your arms in a 'V' shape (the Goddess position) and say:

So let it be.

❖ Allow yourself time to consider the problem from all perspectives before making a decision as to how you should act.
❖ Each time you consider the position, remember to repeat the first two lines of the verse above.

It usually takes a little time for a situation like this to reach some kind of resolution, but this spell allows you to feel supported and cared for. Gradually it will become apparent as to the action you must take and you can accept that it is the ultimately the best outcome for everyone.

To Ease a Broken Heart

This spell contains many of the types of magic normally used in spells. There is candle, herbal and plant magic as well as representational. It is designed to make you feel better rather than have an effect on anyone else.

YOU WILL NEED
1 strawberry tea bag
Small wand or stick from a willow tree
Sea salt
2 pink candles
Mirror
Pink drawstring bag
Quartz crystal
Copper penny
Bowl made of china or crystal that is special to you
1 teaspoon dried jasmine
1 teaspoon orris-root powder
1 teaspoon strawberry leaves
1 teaspoon yarrow
10 drops (at least) of apple-blossom oil or peach oil
10 drops (at least) of strawberry oil

METHOD
❖ Charge all the ingredients before you begin.

- On a Friday morning or evening (the day sacred to the Goddess Venus) take a bath in sea salt in the light of a pink candle.
- As you dry off and dress, sip the strawberry tea.
- Use a dab of strawberry oil as perfume or cologne.
- Apply makeup or groom yourself to look your best.
- Cast a circle with the willow wand around a table on which the other ingredients have been placed.
- Light the second pink candle.
- Mix all oils and herbs in the bowl.
- While you stir, look at yourself in the mirror and say:

> *Oh, Great Mother Earth,*
> *Nurture and protect me now.*
> *Let me use the strengths*
> *I know I have.*

- Look into the mirror after you have finished mixing the ingredients and say:

> *Mother of all things,*
> *All that is great is mine,*
> *Help me now to be the person I can be*
> *and let me overcome my difficulty.*

- Put half the mixture in the pink bag and add the penny and crystal.
- Carry the bag with you until you feel you no longer need it.
- Leave the other half of the potion in the bowl in a room where you will smell the fragrance. Repeat this ritual every Friday, if you so wish.

Unfortunately, the break up of a relationship can truly knock our confidence. This spell is designed to restore yours as quickly as possible. It does not matter who is right or wrong, simply that you are able to go forward with dignity.

Health, Healing and Wellbeing

THE SUBTLE ENERGIES which come together to give each person their unique makeup are very precious and can be conserved and enhanced. We as spell workers have a responsibility to make ourselves as healthy and whole as possible and in so doing can also help others to overcome problems and difficulties. We learn to appeal to a universal energy and its various parts to help the world go round a little more easily.

To get Rid of Warts

Warts have been said to be the mark of magic so you may wear yours with pride! If you find them unsightly then try this simple, safe spell from folklore. Ideally done at the time of the Waning Moon, this spell involves no pain and should not leave any trace of the wart.

YOU WILL NEED

Higher vibration incense such as sandalwood
Coin for each wart (ideally it should be a copper coin that you have had for a while)
Spade or trowel

METHOD

- Light the incense.
- Prepare your coin by holding it in the incense smoke for no more than half a minute.
- Charge the coin with your personal energy.
- Rub the coin on the wart saying these words in your head for as long as you feel is needed:

> *Blemish begone, do not return*
> *Leave no scar nor mark nor burn.*

- Visualize the wart transferring to the coin.
- When this is done bury the coin in the earth, this time saying the above words out loud.

❖ Forget about the coin and within a calendar month the wart should be gone.

This spell can be done on others. Modern day medicines can be harsh and wart remedies which burn them off usually burn the skin as well. Children especially may find the burning of warts uncomfortable and this is a safe alternative that can be fun to try.

A Light Spell

This spell enables us to practice in the safety of our sacred space, before venturing out into the everyday world. It is not so much a healing technique as an energising one. The closer we come to an understanding of the powers that we use, the less we need protection and the more we can become a source of spiritual energy for others.

YOU WILL NEED
As many white candles as feels right
(An odd number works well)
Equivalent number of holders
Anointing oil of frankincense

METHOD
❖ Anoint the candles from middle to bottom then from middle to top. This is so you achieve a balance of physical and spiritual energy.
❖ Place the candles in the holders on the floor in a circle about six feet in diameter.
❖ Standing in the circle, light the candles in a clockwise direction.
❖ Stand in the centre of the circle and 'draw' the energy of the light towards you.
❖ Feel the energy as it seeps throughout the whole of your body, from your feet to your head.
❖ Allow the energy to spill over from the crown of your head to fill the space around you.
❖ It should feel like this around your body:

❖ Now, visualize this cocoon of light around you gently radiating outwards to the edge of your circle of candles.
❖ When you feel ready, sit on the floor and allow the energy of the light to settle back within you.
❖ Ground yourself by sweeping your body with your hands in the shape of the above figure, but do not lose the sense of increased energy.
❖ Snuff out the candles in a clockwise direction, and use them only to repeat this technique until they are used up.

Gradually, as you become used to the sense of increased energy, you should find that you are more able to cope with difficulties and to become more dynamic in the everyday world. It will become easier to carry the light within you not just within the circle of candles, and you may find that you perceive more ways in which you can 'help the world go round'.

A Medication Spell

As you begin to understand colour correspondences, you can begin to use them in spells to keep you well. Many people have to take medication of one sort or another and this spell helps to enhance the action of your particular one. It does mean that you must take your medication at the times given by your health practitioner but you can add additional potency.

YOU WILL NEED
Your given medication
Healing incense (mixture of rosemary and juniper)
Anointing oil
Square of purple cloth
White candle

METHOD
❖ Anoint your candle with the oil.
❖ Light your candle.
❖ Light the incense and allow the smoke to surround you.
❖ Sit quietly and imagine that you are well.

❖ Really feel what it is like to be functioning fully.

❖ Sense how the medication will help you.

❖ Pick up your medication and allow the healing energy to flow through you to the medication.

❖ When you feel it is charged sufficiently put it on the purple cloth and leave it there until the incense and the candle have burnt out.

❖ As you take your medication in future visualize the link between it and you as it helps to alleviate whatever your problems are.

❖ You can further help yourself if, before you take your prescription to the pharmacist, you place it under a white candle and ask for it to be blessed.

Do please remember that this technique is not a substitute for medication. You are asking for help in healing yourself and using everything that is available to you. The spell is designed to enhance the healing energy so that you can make maximum use of it. In working in this way you will also be enabled to do all you can to make adjustments in lifestyle and diet.

Enhancing Confidence

In the old days many people thought that noise was a way of getting rid of demons so it was customary to shout when banishing such nasty things. Today we also recognize that psychologically we can be encouraged by passion, so this is a way of self-encouragement, and an appeal to our own 'inner demons'.

YOU WILL NEED ────────────────
A bell or rattle
Rousing music
Your voice

METHOD ──────────────────
❖ Preferably choose a time when you will not disturb others and when you will not be disturbed. Choose a short affirmation that expresses your best hopes for yourself.

❖ This might be:

I will survive

❖ or

I can overcome any problem

❖ or

I have the confidence to do anything

❖ or

I am my own best friend

❖ Play your music until you feel uplifted by its mood.

❖ Take up your bell or rattle and dance around the room.

❖ Proclaim your affirmation at the top of your voice at least three times and preferably nine.

❖ When the music finishes resolve to do three different things in the next week which demonstrate your new-found confidence

❖ Each week reaffirm your confidence in the same way, changing the words as necessary

This spell does seem to have an almost immediate effect. Even if you feel silly at first, having confidence is often about losing your inhibitions, and this is one way which can help. As a support for this, have fun drawing your own particular 'demon' even if it is only as a stick figure.

Ceridwen's Spell

This spell pays homage to Ceridwen, a Welsh Goddess and nurturer of Taliesin, a Druidic Bard. She is invoked here, and asked for the gift of inspiration, called Awen by the Druids. This brings poetic inspiration, prophecy, and the ability to shape-shift (become something else). In bringing about change, this becomes a spell for creativity in all its forms. One of Ceridwen's symbols is the cauldron.

YOU WILL NEED ────────────────
cauldron
Seeds (preferably of wheat)

White candle
Incense made up of:
1 part rosebuds
1 part cedarwood chips
1 part sweet myrrh

METHOD

❖ Blend your incense the night before you plan to use it.

❖ Light your incense and the candle.

❖ Place the cauldron in front of you and half fill with wheat seeds.

❖ Stir the cauldron clockwise three times and let the seeds trickle through your fingers as you say:

Ceridwen, Ceridwen,
I seek your favour
Just as you searched for the boy Gwion
So I search for the power of Awen
Inspiration to be what I must,
to discover the known,
And to flow with change.
Grant, I pray, this power.

❖ Since Awen is a threefold gift you should repeat the stirring of the cauldron twice more or alternatively once on each of the following two days.

❖ When you have finished, tip the remains of the incense into the cauldron and bury the contents.

❖ The candle may be snuffed out, but do not use it for anything else.

Ceridwen is said to have brewed herbs together to bring the gift of inspiration to her ugly son Agfaddu. Gwion was set to mind the potion but, in being splashed by the potion, absorbed its powers. In escaping the wrath of Ceridwen he became a seed of corn and was swallowed by her in the guise of a black hen. The Welsh bard Taliesin born nine months later was thus an initiated form of the boy. Artists, writers and poets can all seek this kind of inspiration.

Cleansing the Aura

This spell is a cleansing one which uses nothing but sound and can be done anywhere though the open air is better. It will depend on your own sense of yourself what sound you use but the one given is known to be successful.

YOU WILL NEED

An open space
Your voice

METHOD

❖ Find a spot in which you feel comfortable within your open space.

❖ It will depend on what you are attempting to get rid of which spot is better. Be sure to take plenty of time over choosing this until it feels absolutely right.

❖ Settle yourself comfortably on the ground.

❖ Take a big deep breath and then breathe out.

❖ Your breath out should be slightly longer than the in breath.

❖ Do this three times to clear your lungs

❖ Now take a further deep breath and this time as you exhale say as loudly as you can:

Ahh… Ee… Oo…

❖ Repeat the sounds at least twice more increasing in intensity each time until you are actually screaming

❖ If you can, continue for two more sets of three (nine times in all, though six is fine.)

❖ Finally sit quietly, place your hands on the earth or the floor, re-orientate yourself in your surroundings and absorb fresh energy as you do so.

❖ Become aware of the sounds around you.

❖ Leave the area.

This is quite a powerful technique and you do need to be quiet for the rest of the day, so that you can allow the energy to settle. The technique is a good way to deal with the frustrations of your everyday world and often results in being able to look at things from a different perspective.

Drawing Out a Latent Talent

This charm is to bring out an existing talent and develop a potential, not give you one you don't already have. If you have a secret ambition you might try this spell. It uses herbs as its vehicle and could be done at the time of the Crescent Moon.

YOU WILL NEED

A small drawstring bag about 10 cms (3 inches) deep
Liquorice root powder
Rose hips
Fennel
Catnip
Elderflower

METHOD

❖ Put a pinch or two of the liquorice root, rose hips, fennel, catnip and elderflower in the bag.
❖ Once assembled, hang the bag outdoors at dusk.
❖ At midnight, remove the bag and place it around your neck. If you like you can make an affirmation before you sleep.
❖ Say these words or similar:

As I sleep, I shall learn of my best potential.

❖ You must then wear the charm bag for a full twenty-four hours to allow the spell to work.
❖ After that time you can place the charm bag under your pillow the night before anything important is to happen when you feel you need some extra help in reaching your goals.

Sleeping and dreaming are often the best way we have of self-development. Most of us have secret ambitions but are prevented by doubts from succeeding. This spell helps to make those fears irrelevant.

Fertility Spell

This spell uses symbolism in the use of the fig and egg, but also ancient methods of acknowledgement in the offering to the Earth Mother for fertility. Crops were often offered to the goddess in the hope of a good harvest and in this spell that hope is for new life. The spell is best done at the time of the New Moon or in spring time when the Goddess of Fertility is commemorated.

YOU WILL NEED

Frankincense and sandalwood incense
White candle
A fig (fresh if possible)
A fresh egg
A clear glass bowl
A marker pen
Your boline
A trowel

METHOD

❖ Light your incense and the candle.
❖ Put the egg on the left and the fig on the right, the bowl in the middle.
❖ Draw a symbol of your child on the egg.
❖ Very carefully break the egg into the bowl and place the empty shell on the left side again.
❖ Make a small cut in the fig with your boline and carefully scrape the seeds into the bowl.
❖ Place the remains of the fig into the egg shell to represent the physical baby within the womb and again replace it on the left side.
❖ With your finger, stir the contents of the bowl clockwise three times and say:

As these two become one
May the Goddess and the God
Bless our union with child

❖ Leave the bowl in the middle and allow the candle to burn out.
❖ Take the bowl and the eggshell with its contents to a place where you can safely bury them.
❖ (Your own garden is good if you have one otherwise a quiet secluded spot.)
❖ Place the eggshell in the ground and pour over it the contents of the bowl.
❖ As you cover it with earth say:

I offer to Mother Earth
A symbol of fertility
In love and gratitude for her bounty

271

❖ Now await developments without anxiety.

This spell is full of symbolism. The fig represents not only fertility, but also is thought to feed the psyche – that part of us that some call the soul. The egg is an ancient symbol of fertility and indeed of the beginning of life. Bringing the two together acknowledges your sense of responsibility for the continuation of life

Healing the Body

This spell works on a simple principle, that of identifying within the body whether the pain it is suffering is physical, emotional or, as is often the case, has a more deep-rooted spiritual component. It uses visualization and colour as its vehicles and calls on Raphael the Archangel of Healing for help.

YOU WILL NEED ────────────

Large piece of paper
Red, yellow and purple felt tip pens
Black marker pen

METHOD ────────────

❖ Draw three concentric circles.
❖ The inner one should be purple, the middle yellow and the outer red.
❖ Add a circle for the head and lines for the legs, so you have drawn a representation of yourself.
❖ Now, thinking of any health difficulties you have, with the black marker put a small mark on the drawn 'body' to represent that pain.
❖ Keep your pen in contact with the paper and ask Raphael for help.
❖ You might say:

Raphael, Raphael, Angel of ease
Help me to understand this pain please

❖ You should find that your mark is closer to one circle than the other.
❖ Remembering that this method is not a self-diagnostic tool at all - it is simply designed to help you to come to terms with the pain or difficulty - note which colour this is:

❖ Red represents pain which is purely physical
❖ Yellow usually signifies an emotional cause
❖ Purple tends to have a more spiritual basis
❖ Sit quietly and draw that colour into yourself as though you were marking within your body where the pain is.
❖ Next mentally flood that part of your body with white light.
❖ For the next two days sit quietly and make the invocation to Raphael again.
❖ Repeat the drawing in of colour and the flooding with white light.
❖ At the end of that time you should begin to have an understanding of the causes of your pain and how your body is reacting to trauma.

It must be stressed that this method is not designed as a substitute for medical diagnosis. It is a method of pain management which links with subtle energies to bring about healing on different levels. You may need to explore further some of the insights this gives you.

Good Health Wishing Spell

This spell is worked at the time of the New Moon and is incredibly simple to do. Bay leaves possess a great deal of magical power and are used for granting wishes. This spell can be used to fulfil a range of desires, and here is used to bring about health and happiness.

YOU WILL NEED ────────────

3 bay leaves
Piece of paper
Pencil or pen

METHOD ────────────

❖ During a New Moon, write your wish on a piece of paper and visualize it coming true.
❖ Fold the paper into thirds, placing the three bay leaves inside.
❖ Fold the paper towards you.
❖ Again visualize your wish coming true.
❖ Fold the paper into thirds a second time, thus forming an envelope.
❖ Keep it hidden in a dark place.

+ Reinforce your wish by repeatedly visualizing it coming true.
+ When the wish comes true, burn the paper as a mark of thanks.

This little envelope of power can also be included in a mojo or talisman bag to add more power to it. In that case try to be as specific as you can in your wish. You can, using it this way, impose a time limit on the spell coming to fruition, though it is often better not to do so.

Self Image Spell

In many ways this spell is one which is about loving yourself, hence the use of pink candles and love oil. In the use of incantation you are making a link with the principle of beauty and with the Goddess of Beauty in one of her many forms.

YOU WILL NEED

*At least one pink candle, more if you prefer
A handheld mirror
Love oil*

METHOD

+ Dress the candle(s) with the love oil, working towards you since you want to feel differently about yourself.
+ Have in mind your ideal qualities of beauty as you do so.
+ Light the candles and stare deeply into the mirror.
+ See first the person you are now.
+ Visualize the change you want.
+ Then 'see' the person you would like to be.
+ Recite this incantation out loud:

*Sacred flame as you dance
Call upon my sacred glance.
Call upon my better self,
Give me [your request]*

*Blessed flame shining brightly,
Bring about the changes nightly
Give me now my second chance
My beauty and glamour please enhance*

*Power of three, let them see, let them see,
let them see.*

+ You can now snuff out the candle and relight it the next night, burning it for at least an hour.
+ Repeat the incantation at least three times.

The power of visualization is a very strong tool. Each of us has an inner beauty which if we work with it is a tremendous help in daily life. Once we are prepared to recognize it, it becomes evident to others. This spell accomplishes that recognition.

Disperse Negative Emotion

Here is a simple technique for dealing with negative energies such as anger and resentment. It uses the Elements and their qualities in a very positive way. The circle of light links with spirit, the dark stone represents Earth and the water acts in its cleansing capacity.

YOU WILL NEED

A dark stone

METHOD

+ Visualize a circle of light around yourself.
+ Hold the dark stone in your hands.
+ Place it over your solar plexus.
+ Allow the negative emotion, perhaps anger and resentment, to flow into the stone.
+ Try to decide what colour the emotion is, and how it arose in the first place. It sometimes helps to counteract such an emotion by changing its colour.
+ Raise the stone first to your forehead to signify clarity. Next, place it over your heart (this helps to raise the healing vibration to the correct level).
+ If it seems right, use words such as:

*With this stone
Negative be gone,
Let water cleanse it
Back where it belongs.*

+ This reinforces the idea of the stone holding your anger.

* Concentrate and project all your negative emotion (anger, resentment etc) into the stone.
* Visualize the emotion being sealed inside the stone.
* ake the stone to a source of running water in the open air and with all your energy throw it as far as you can.
* It also helps if you can get up to a high place to throw your stone away, since this way you are using Air as well.

This is a similar technique to A Wish Afloat except that here you are deliberately using the Elements to clear away negative emotion. This leaves space for positivity and good new things to come into your life. Under no circumstances should you allow the anger and resentment to build up again as this will negate the positivity created.

Overcoming your Shadows

This spell, which signifies letting go the hurts of the past in a way that allows you to move forward with fresh energy into the future, can be performed at the time of the New Moon. By carrying it out every New Moon you are gradually able to cleanse yourself of the detritus of the past, often as far back as childhood.

YOU WILL NEED
Cedar or sage smudging stick or cleansing incense
Bell
Athame or ritual knife
White candle
Cakes and wine or juice

METHOD
* Cast your circle using the smudge stick or incense to 'sweep' the space as you move around the circle clockwise.
* Think of your space as being dome-shaped over your head and cleanse that space too.
* Ring the bell.
* With your arms raised and your palms facing upwards, acknowledge the Goddess and say:

Great Goddess,
Queen of the Underworld,
Protector of all believers in you,
It is my will on this night of the new moon
To overcome my shadows and bring about change.
I invite you to this my circle to assist and protect
me in my rite.

* Hold your athame or knife in your hands in acknowledgement of the God and say:

Great God,
Lord of the Upper realms,
Friend of all who work with you,
It is my will on this night of the new moon
To overcome my shadows to bring about change.
I invite you to my circle to assist me and protect
me in my rite.

* Light the candle and say:

Behind me the darkness, in front of me the light
As the wheel turns,
I know that every end is a beginning.
I see birth, death and regeneration.

* Spend a little time in quiet thought. If you can remember a time either in the last month or previously when times have not been good for you, concentrate on that.
* While the candle begins to burn properly remember what that time felt like.
* Now concentrate on the candle flame and allow yourself to feel the positivity of the light. Pick up the candle and hold it high above your head.
* Feel the energy of the light shower down around you, the negativity drain away.
* Now draw the power of the light into you and feel the energy flowing through you.
* Pass the candle around you and visualize the energy building up.
* If you wish, say:

Let the light cast out darkness.

* Now ground yourself by partaking of the food and drink. Thank the God and Goddess for their presence.
* Withdraw the circle.

This is a very personal way for you to acknowledge the God and Goddess in your everyday life. While on first acquaintance it appears to be a protection technique, it is actually one to enhance your energies and to allow you to be healthy and happy in all levels of existence.

Healing a Depression

Depression is not an easy illness to handle and you should not regard spells such as this as a substitute for medical care. However a mojo or talisman bag can be of tremendous support in the process of getting better and has the effect of continually 'topping up' the energy needed to overcome difficulty.

YOU WILL NEED

Your burin or a pin
Piece of angelica root for a woman
Pine cone for a man
Clary sage oil to dress the objects and to use as incense
Sprig of rosemary
Small dog tag, lucky coin or token
White candle
Red flannel pouch or talisman bag

METHOD

✤ If the person you are helping is a woman, then inscribe her initial on the angelica root and dress it with some of the clary sage oil.
✤ If a man then do the same with the pine cone.
✤ When using a lucky token, charm or sprig of rosemary take care to dedicate it specifically to the person concerned.
✤ Say something like:

May this token of good luck bring healing to
[name of person].

✤ With the dog tag inscribe it either with the person's initials, their astrological sign or the rune symbol Kenaz for inner strength:
✤ Repeat the words above as you do this.
✤ Place the objects in the pouch.

✤ Light your candle and the incense.
✤ Dress the bag by dropping a little oil on it.
✤ Pass the bag and its contents over the candle three times whilst visualizing the person well and happy and also asking your favourite deity to help you in your task.
✤ Give the bag to the person concerned asking them to keep it with them at all times for at least a week.

Your subject should sense an improvement in mood within the week. You can reinforce the bag's efficiency every now and then by burning a candle for a short while and directing the energy at the bag. If you are not able to give the bag to the person concerned then hang it somewhere prominent so you are reminded of them occasionally and can send loving energy their way.

Healing Image Spell

This spell uses the very old technique of representing a person as a poppet or small doll. It is similar to To Know the Child Within except that the poppet represents another person. Remember that healing takes place in the way that the recipient needs, not necessarily in the way we think it should happen.

YOU WILL NEED

Poppet
Blue candle
Salt water

METHOD

✤ Following the instructions on page 229 create your poppet to represent the person you wish to help already completely healed and whole.
✤ Take the doll into your sacred space.
✤ Light the blue candle (to represent healing).
✤ Sprinkle your poppet with the salt water and say:

This figure I hold made by my art
Here represents [name person],
By my art made, by my art changed,
Now may he/she be healed,
By art divine.

❖ Pass the poppet quickly through the flame of the candle and visualize the person being cleansed of their problem.

❖ Hold the poppet in both hands, breathe gently on it and visualize first the poppet and then the person being filled with Divine healing energy.

❖ Pay particular attention to the areas in the physical body of your friend with which you know they are having difficulty.

❖ Imbue the poppet with the idea of being healed from a mental perspective.

❖ Think of spiritual energy infusing the doll, and therefore your friend, with the spiritual help that they need.

❖ Visualize the person concerned being completely filled with white light, well, happy and filled with energy.

❖ Keep the poppet in your sacred space until it is no longer needed.

❖ At this time, enter your sacred space, take the poppet, sprinkle it with water and say:

By Divine art changed,
By my art made,
Free this poppet from the connection with [name].
Let it now be unmade.

❖ If the poppet contains direct links with the person - such as hair - burn it in an open fire. If it does not, dispose of it in any way you wish.❖ If you have used a crystal at any point in this spell, this should be cleansed by holding it under running water and perhaps then given to the person as a keepsake or for protection.

We are not just asking for alleviation of the symptoms, we are asking for help from a holistic perspective. You do have a responsibility if you are working on someone else's behalf to do nothing which will make matters worse for them, therefore think very seriously about using this method.

Healing Others

This is a spell using crystals, candles and incense. It is also representational in that you use the paper to represent the person you are healing. If you use an altar then work with that, but the spell can also be completed by recognizing that the space between the candles is sacred.

YOU WILL NEED

3 candles:
Blue for healing
White for power
Pink for love
Healing incense (1 part allspice, 1 part rosemary)
Paper with name of the person you wish to be healed
Clear quartz crystal

METHOD

❖ Place the candles on the altar or in your sacred space in a semi-circle, with the white candle in the middle.

❖ Place the incense on the left if the recipient is a woman, on the right if male. Light the incense.

❖ Place the paper with the person's name in the centre.

❖ Put the quartz crystal on top of the paper.

❖ Be aware of your own energy linking with whatever you consider to be the Divine.

❖ Breathe in the incense and feel your energy increasing.

❖ When you feel ready, release the energy.

❖ Imagine it passing through the crystal - which enhances it - to the recipient.

❖ As you are doing this, say:

[Name] be healed by the gift of this Power

Remember that healing energy is used by the recipient in whatever way is appropriate to them. A physical condition may not necessarily be healed, but you may have started an overall healing process. Often the person is given the emotional strength to withstand their trials and tribulations so that an inner healing occurs.

Physical Body Change

In this spell you use the power of the crystal to make changes. By bringing the problem into the open you are creating a way to a change on an inner level which brings healing with it. This can be done at the time of the New Moon.

YOU WILL NEED ──────────
Small piece of paper
Pen
Quartz crystal
String

METHOD ──────────

❖ Take the piece of paper and write your name on it.

❖ Draw on it what part of the body you want changed and what you want to look like.

❖ If you want to change more than one area, draw the whole body and mark what you would like to change.

❖ Hold the paper in your hands and imagine the body-part changing from what it looks like now to what you want it to look like.

❖ Fold the paper up any way you like and tie it to the crystal.

❖ Once more visualize the body part changing again.

❖ When you feel that changes are taking place, untie the string, tear the paper up and scatter it to the wind.

❖ If you wish, you can bury the crystal to signify the fact that you have internalized the changes you have made.

This spell is very good for changing aspects you don't like. It may take a few days or even longer to see results, so please be patient. The spell should not be used to try to heal conditions of a medical nature.

Purifying Emotions

This spell is one that helps you to release negativity and distress that may build up when you do not feel that you are in control of your life. It uses the four Elements to do this and may be performed on any evening during a Waning Moon. It has been kept deliberately simple so that you can spend more time in learning how to make your emotions work for you rather than letting them overwhelm you.

YOU WILL NEED ──────────
White candle
Bowl of water
Bowl of salt
Dried herbs (such as sage for wisdom)
Vessel in which the herbs can be burned

METHOD ──────────

❖ Stand in your sacred space, light the candle and say:

I call upon the Elements in this simple ceremony that I may be cleansed from the contamination of negativity.

❖ Wave your hand quickly over or through the flame and say:

I willingly release negative action in my fire.

❖ Rub the salt on your hands and say:

I release stumbling blocks and obstacles in my earth.

❖ Put the herbs in the container and light them. Wave the smoke in front of you, inhale the perfume as it burns and say:

I clear my air of unwise thoughts.

❖ Dip your hands in the water and say:

*I purify this water.
Let this relinquishing be gentle.
Purified, cleansed and released in all ways,
I now acknowledge my trust and faith
in my own clarity.*

❖ Spend a little time thinking about the next few weeks to come.

❖ Recognize that there may be times when you need the clarity you have just requested.

❖ Now dispose of the ingredients immediately in the following way.

❖ Put the salt in with the ashes then pour the water on the ground so that it mingles with the ashes and salt.

It is often helpful to find some sort of ceremonial way of releasing energy which enables you to let go of an old situation which is still troubling you. A good time to do this is just before a New Moon, so that you can begin a fresh cycle with renewed vigour.

To Cure Sickness

Knot magic is good for getting rid of illnesses; this spell is one that will help to do this. It works on the principle of binding the illness into the cord, so is a form of sympathetic magic combined with positive thought.

YOU WILL NEED

20 cm (8 inch) length of cord
Pen and paper
Container of salt

METHOD

- Mark the cord six times so that you have seven equal lengths.
- Take a few deep breaths and feel your energy connecting with the earth.
- Repeat the following words six times and tie a knot in the cord each time:

Sickness, no one bids you stay.
It's time for you to fade away.
Through these knots I bid you leave,
By these words which I do weave.

- Put the cord in the container of salt (this represents burying in the earth).
- Create a seal for the container with the above incantation written on the paper.
- Dispose of the container, perhaps in running water.

The number six has particular relevance here: it is widely accepted as the number of the Sun, which is restorative and regenerative.

The Spell of the Shell

This is a lunar spell which calls on the power of the Moon and the waves. It is also representational because the shell is a long accepted symbol for the Goddess and signifies her ability to take all things to her and effect changes. In this example, we use an Ogham Stave to represent healing, though the spell can be used for other purposes as well. It is performed at the seaside.

YOU WILL NEED

Shell
A symbol of your desire
Fine nibbed marker pen

METHOD

- To perform this spell, you must find a suitable shell in shallow water.
- Take the shell and dry it thoroughly.
- Draw your chosen symbol upon the surface of the shell.
- For healing, we suggest the Edhadh Ogham Stave:
- Place the shell upon the shore so that the tide will bring the waves across the shell.
- When the shell is in place, draw a triangle in the sand, enclosing the shell completely.
- The symbol upon the shell must be facing upwards (towards the Moon).
- Meaningful words, or phrases, may be placed upon the shell also, or simply written in the sand (inside the triangle).
- Finally, face the Moon and say the following words of enchantment:

Goddess of Moon, Earth and Sea,
Each wish in thy name must come to be.
Powers and forces which tides do make,
Now summon thy waves, my spell to take.

- Leave the area now and the spell is set.
- Once the waves come, then your wish will be taken out to the spirits of the sea.
- It will usually take about seven days for a lunar spell to begin to manifest, but it can take as long as 28 days.

This type of magic is what we called 'little works' and belongs to the folk-magic level of spell making. Take care to note the phase of the Moon (waxing for the gain of something, waning for the dissolving of something). You are using natural objects which to the uninitiated mean nothing.

To Clear Evil Intent

This spell can be used if you suspect that somebody is directing unhelpful energy towards you which is making you sick. Words have particular force, so in expressing your feelings forcibly as in line 2 of the incantation, you are turning the energy back on the perpetrator.

YOU WILL NEED

Length of string
Bottle

METHOD

❖ Tie a knot in the string.
❖ Place it in the bottle and bury it in earth.
❖ After three days dig it up.
❖ Put the bottle on the floor or ground and say:

A curse on me you buried deep
To make me sick, you nasty creep.
I placed a knot into this twine
And so your work was worked in vain.

❖ Shatter the bottle, carefully pick up the string and undo the knot; the original curse is now invalid.
❖ Dispose of the bottle remains in any way that you feel is appropriate.
❖ Burn the cord and blow the ashes to the wind.

In some ways this could be called a protection spell, but since the 'curse' could cause you to be ill this spell guards your wellbeing. The curse is transferred by the power of your spell to the cord, which is then disposed of by burning. The assumption is that your magic is stronger than the person who has wished you ill.

To Know the Child Within

This spell is a variation on a technique which appreciates that we all have aspects of ourselves which can go unrecognized and therefore undeveloped. By using your sacred space in which to work, you are enhancing the connection you make to that part which remains childlike. The main tool is visualization.

YOU WILL NEED

Green or blue candle to signify healing
An incense or essential oil which reminds you of your childhood
Doll or poppet to signify the child you once were
Salt water
White cloth
Your altar, which could just be a table which you dedicate to this purpose

METHOD

❖ Light your candle and the incense.
❖ Choose a particularly good childhood memory.
❖ Hold the poppet in your arms and think about the child you once were.
❖ Now treat the poppet as though it were a child.
❖ Say:

I name you [use your own childhood name or nickname]

❖ Hold the poppet in your arms, croon to it, rock it, and talk to it.
❖ Tell it everything you would have liked to hear as a child.
❖ Imagine that it talks to you and tells you how it feels and what it wants.
❖ You may even hear your own childish voice.
❖ Let your own voice change in response. Play with the poppet.
❖ Now become aware of your adult self again.
❖ Sprinkle the doll with a little salt water to cleanse away the negative past.
❖ Raise your own energy by whatever method you prefer - breathing, colour, a brief meditation or an appeal to the gods.
❖ Visualize yourself pouring that positive energy into the doll, which represents your own inner self.
❖ Imagine the child you would have liked to have been, and project that image into your doll.
❖ Continue until you can feel a change in the energy and you feel at peace.
❖ During that time you may find that you are crying or laughing just like a child. This is simply a release of energy and is perfectly acceptable.

+ You may find that the poppet or doll begins to feel vibrant and alive, glowing with white light and love.
+ Kiss the poppet or doll.
+ Wrap it in white cloth as you would a baby and lay it to rest on your altar.
+ Leave the candle to burn out.
+ Leave your sacred space secure.

It is important that you give yourself time now to return to normal, so you will need to spend a little time just appreciating the person you have become. Ground yourself by whatever method you choose, touching the ground, taking a walk, having a bath or whatever you prefer. A nurturing activity such as cooking is also good. You will probably find after this technique that you tend to dream somewhat vividly, as you uncover some of the joys and hurts of childhood.

Radiant Health

This spell uses invocation to enable a person to attain and maintain radiant and perpetual health. You can enhance the energy by finding an open space, free of pollution. and using sunlight, moonlight, wind or rain as part of the process. Sunday is an ideal day to perform this spell as this is the day that health matters are highlighted.

YOU WILL NEED ───────────────
An open space or your sacred space
Coriander seeds tied in a small muslin bag

METHOD ───────────────
+ In your sacred space or the open space, first sense your own aura - your subtle energies which make you unique.
+ Hold your hands over your heart area and then move them down to just below your solar plexus. You should sense a change in energy in your hands.
+ This is the point in your body sometimes called the 'point of power', the place where your life energy resides.
+ Now, facing the east with your arms spread wide and the palms of your hands upwards, say the following:

Great God of the Heavens, and Lord of All Power,
Grant me the right to feel and perceive
the true life force that is mine,
So that I may have everlasting well being.
Grant me, O Great God, this favour.

+ Now run your hands around your body from top to toe in a sweeping motion, not quite touching your body.
+ Raise your arms again and visualize the Universal healing energy sweeping towards you as you repeat the incantation above.
+ Take a deep breath, visualizing and feeling the energy being drawn in and down to the solar plexus.
+ As you slowly exhale, see the energy travelling to your extremities and filling you with power and healing.
+ Do this at least three times or for up to fifteen minutes at a time.
+ Place your hands on your point of power and repeat the incantation a third time, this time sensing the energy settling into your point of power.
+ If you are in an open space become aware of the power of sunlight, moonlight, wind or rain.
+ Finally take a ritual bath into which you have put the coriander seeds.

The purpose of this spell is not to cure you of any ailment but, by enhancing your energy, to help your health overall. Please always seek the services of a qualified doctor or health practitioner if you know, or suspect, your health is compromised in any way.

Balancing your Energies

This spell principally uses the energy of the earth and of candles. The spell can be performed either during the day if you particularly appreciate the light, or at night when you honour the Moon. Often it is good to perform it outside as an appreciation of energy returning to the earth.

YOU WILL NEED ───────────────
Fresh flowers for your sacred space
Single white flower

Bowl of water large enough to hold the flower
Green and yellow candles
Jasmine or rose incense

METHOD

❧ Prepare your sacred space as usual, making sure you use plenty of fresh flowers to decorate.

❧ Float the single white flower in the bowl of water, thinking all the time of its beauty.

❧ Light the candles, thinking all the while of the freshness of Mother Nature's energies.

❧ Light the incense and become aware of the differing perfumes created.

❧ Quietly consider the cycle and power of Nature.

❧ Stand with your feet about 18 inches apart.

❧ Become aware of your connection with the earth, mentally reaching towards the centre through the soles of your feet.

❧ Feel the energy rising through you towards the light.

❧ Reach towards the light and feel its energy moving downwards through you.

❧ Let those energies mingle with those of the earth.

❧ Allow the new energies to swirl around and through you, cleansing, healing and balancing.

❧ Say:

Lady of flowers and strong new life
Be born anew in me tonight.

❧ When you feel refreshed ground yourself by running your hands over your body from head to toe.

❧ Sit quietly for a short while and contemplate how you will use your new energy.

❧ Finally, allow your energy to settle in your solar plexus.

This spell is designed to replace old stale energy with new vital force. You should come away feeling refreshed and invigorated. While this spell has similarities to rituals to Ostara, the single white flower also represents the Moon and therefore feminine energy.

Isis Girdle

This spell is one based on knot magic and is used to ensure that your energy is at the right level for your magical work. Buckles, belts or girdles were often associated with Isis or Venus and therefore aspects of femininity. They represent physical well-being and moral strength. It can be performed on a Wednesday.

YOU WILL NEED

3 lengths of cord about 3 metres (9 feet) each

METHOD

❧ Decide before you begin the purpose of your girdle.

❧ To specifically use one for health issues you might choose the colour blue, or to work from a spiritual perspective choose purple or white.

❧ Begin braiding the cord and as you do so bear in mind that you are fashioning three aspects of self, body mind and spirit to become one source of power in all that you do.

❧ In this way the braid becomes an extension of you and also a protector of your being.

❧ Call on the power of Isis as you do so to give you strength and determination

❧ Tie a knot in both ends to tie in the power

❧ Now consecrate the girdle by holding it in your left hand and circling it three times anticlockwise with your most powerful hand, while saying words such as:

Isis, Mistress of the words of power
Cleanse this girdle for my use

❧ See it surrounded by bright light and glowing brightly.

❧ Let the image fade.

❧ Next circle the girdle clockwise three times with your power hand and say:

Isis, Goddess of the Throne
Protect me from all ill

❧ Again perceive the girdle surrounded by light.

❧ Next put the girdle round your waist and say:

Isis, Goddess of Perceived Truth
Thy wisdom is reality

❖ This time feel the energy in the girdle and say:

I stand ready to do thy work

❖ In future, each time you put on the girdle you should be able to sense the energy, giving you the power to carry out your chosen task.

This is quite a powerful spell to do. Not only does it protect you from illness, it also prepares you to be able to help others as they require it. Since Isis rules intuition, you find that you are in a better position to understand others pain and distress.

Knot Spell

To rid yourself of problems or a troublesome situation, you can use a representation of the problem in a tangled and knotted length of yarn. There are then differing ways of getting rid of the problem. This spell is best done at the time of the Full Moon and is in two parts.

YOU WILL NEED

Biodegradable string or cotton yarn
Ingredients for a ritual bath (including candles and a purification oil)
Three candles - one in your astrological colour, one dark or black (to represent negativity) and one white (to signify a life without problems)

METHOD - PART ONE

❖ Your string needs to be biodegradable because it reinforces the idea that your problems will dissolve.
❖ The string or yarn can be in the appropriate colour for the problem to be solved (green for money, red for love, etc).
❖ Sit quietly and think of all your fears and problems.
❖ Let them pass into the yarn.
❖ Tie this in knots to symbolize how mixed up your problems makes you feel.
❖ One way of dealing with your difficulties is to take the knotted yarn to a high place and let the wind blow it away, along with your negativity.
❖ A second way is to bury the yarn in soft ground, though this method will mean that

the resolution of your problems may come slowly.
❖ A third way is to begin to untie the knots and as you do so ask for help in seeing and understanding solutions.
❖ This last method does not have to be done all at once but can be done over time.

METHOD - PART TWO

❖ Whichever method you use make sure you take a ritual bath or shower cleansing after working with the string.
❖ Anoint the candles with a purification or blessing oil.
❖ Anoint the dark candle from the end to the wick to remove bad luck.
❖ The others are done from the wick to the end to bring you what you desire.
❖ Have your ritual bath as usual.

This spell has two parts, first getting rid of the problems then cleansing yourself of the effects. Only then can you decide how you are going to make changes in your life so that you do not attract yet more problems.

Mars Water

Water charged with iron was at one time considered to be a healing potion, creating a way of treating anaemia. Today it is considered to be more of a protective device and, when under attack, to enable you to send a curse or hex back where it belongs.

YOU WILL NEED

Iron nails or filings
Large jar with lid
Enough water to cover the nails

METHOD

❖ Put the nails or filings in the jar and cover them with water.
❖ Close the jar and leave undisturbed until rust begins to form.
❖ The jar can be opened occasionally to check on its condition, which helps the formation of rust. This should take about seven to ten days.

✤ After this time the jar may be shaken and the water then strained and used as appropriate.

✤ Keep adding water as necessary to the jar thereafter to maintain its potency.

✤ You should not need to renew the nails unless the concoction begins to develop mould, in which case throw everything out and start again.

✤ When using the water you may like to give acknowledgement to Mars by using a form of words such as:

Mars, God of War protect me now as I
[state task]

You can use some of the water in your ritual bath or to cleanse and empower your hands before an important event. A business situation which required you to be more than usually aggressive might need a crystal charged in Mars water to make it especially powerful.

Midsummer Fire Spell

Ancient rites dictated that domesticated animals were driven through fire both to cleanse and protect them on Midsummer Day. On a practical level this would get rid of any infestation of bugs and fleas, but on a magical level such action would ensure fertility and good harvest. It does humans no harm to partake in this ritual either.

YOU WILL NEED
Enough sacred wood (hazel and rowan perhaps) to build two small fires

METHOD
✤ Build two fires with only a small walkway between them.

✤ When the fires are going well lead your animals between them making sure that the animals and you yourself are wreathed in smoke.

✤ If possible you might do this twice more.

✤ Make sure the fires are properly extinguished before leaving the area, lest you do any damage to surrounding vegetation.

✤ A different way of achieving the same purpose is to take a lit branch of sacred wood and pass it over around and underneath the animal.

✤ This is a form of 'smudging' (see p000) but you will probably need help to keep the animal still.

Remembering that in an agricultural society the health of the animals was just as - if not more important than - their owners, there are many protective rituals which can be adopted for today's society. Water with the appropriate essential oils could be used instead of the fire branch to protect pets.

Moon Wishes

This spell uses candles and meditation. It can be done at both New and Full Moon, and uses the Moon's energy. By meditating before you sleep you are opening yourself up to allowing the influences from your Higher Self – the part which knows what is right for you – to come through.

YOU WILL NEED
Five white candles
A coloured candle of your choice (perhaps representing the wish or perhaps in the colour of your astrological sign)

METHOD
✤ Clear your mind of all clutter or meditate for a short time to be sure you have clarified your wishes.

✤ Place the white candles in the shape of a pentagram where they can burn safely.

✤ Light the five white candles starting from the top first and working clockwise.

❖ Alternatively, if you prefer, light them according to the connecting lines of the pentagram - again starting at the top.

❖ As you do so say:

> *Moon above which glows so bright*
> *Guard my sleep so deep tonight*
> *I pray to you with this request*
> *My life works out at my behest.*

❖ Allow the candles to burn for at least half an hour before putting them out and composing yourself for sleep.

❖ The next morning light the other candle and meditate or contemplate your wishes for another thirty minutes.

❖ Spend some time visualizing what life will be like when your wishes are granted.

❖ Repeat this whole procedure for the next three nights.

❖ Finally, on the fourth morning, relight all of the candles and allow them to burn out while you play some rousing music that means something to you.

❖ In the last hour while the candles are still burning reconsider your wishes and make any adjustments to them which seem realistic.

This spell does take some time to complete and also requires that you spend a fair length of time in contemplation. This does mean however that you can be realistic in your expectations and there should be few blocks to achieving what you want. There is little need to be frivolous.

Self Esteem

This spell uses visualisation, candles, cord and colour, and requires very little effort, though it takes a week to finish. It is a spell that men can do very easily and can see and feel the tangible results. It works on the self esteem and on virility.

YOU WILL NEED

> *Seven short lengths of cord, about six inches long*
> *Seven tea lights*
> *Seven small squares of red paper or cloth*

METHOD

❖ On returning from work, place a tea light on one red square.

❖ Surround the tea light by the cord, laying it on the red square.

❖ As you do so say:

> *This represents me and all I feel myself to be*
> *I wish to be [strong, virile, at ease with myself –*
> *your choice of words]*

❖ Let the tealight burn out.

❖ Next morning knot both ends of the cord saying as you do:

> *This cord carries my intent to be*
> *[your choice of words]*

❖ Carry the cord with you and when you need to, remind yourself during the day of your intent.

❖ Repeat the procedure for seven nights using the same words and either the same intent or another which feels more appropriate.

❖ Repeat the same procedure as the first morning also.

❖ At the end of the seven days either tie the cords together in one loop (end to end) or tie them so they form a tassel.

❖ Either way hang them by your mirror where you cannot fail to see them.

❖ Each morning for about six weeks choose which affirmation you wish to use that day and make sure you have acted accordingly.

This spell has a long term effect on your personality. Each time you make the morning affirmation you are calling on the power of the whole to assist you in being the sort of person you want to be. Any behaviour which does not fit that image, soon drops away.

Sleep Well

Smoky quartz is sometimes known as the 'Dream Stone'. It is an able tool for meditation, and helps you to explore your inner self by penetrating the darker areas with light and love. Because of this, it is effective in releasing negativities like grief, anger and despair by removing depression. It is mildly sedative and relaxing and a good balancer of sexual energy. The cairngorm stone beloved of the Scots, which we have seen in the section on the Evil Eye, is a form of smoky quartz.

YOU WILL NEED

Piece of smoky quartz
Piece of paper
Pen
Your bed

METHOD

✤ When you have prepared your sleep environment, sit quietly holding the smoky quartz and bring to mind any old hurts, anger, depression and difficulties you may have.
✤ Do not be afraid that doing this will bring on depression, because with this technique you are aiming to rid yourself of the depression these things bring.
✤ Put aside the quartz for the moment and write down on the paper all that you have considered and thought about.
✤ Now pass the quartz three times over the bed to absorb any negativity.
✤ You might use the sign of infinity from top to bottom.

✤ Wrap the paper round the quartz and place it under your pillow with the intent that it will help you to overcome your pain and hurt.
✤ Go to sleep, and in the morning, remove the paper and dispose of it by tearing it up and flushing it away or burning it.
✤ If you wish you can repeat the process for the next two nights, by which time you should find you feel much relieved.
✤ Finally cleanse the stone under running water and keep until you need it again or dispose of it as you do in Disperse Negative Emotion on p273.

Another use for smoky quartz is to reflect an intrusive energy back to the person concerned. If you are receiving unwanted attention from someone, place a piece of smoky quartz or cairngorm in your window and know that you can sleep protected.

To Find the Truth

Without the truth one cannot make sensible decisions. As one's intuition grows it becomes easier to tell when people are not telling you the truth. Until that time a simple spell like this ensures that the truth is revealed in the right way. It uses herbs and candles.

YOU WILL NEED

Handful of thyme
Red candle
Flat dish or pentacle on which to put the herbs

METHOD

✤ Place the thyme into the dish and say:

> *Clarification I now require*
> *So that truth is spoken*
> *Let what is hidden now*
> *Be brought into the open.*

✤ Light the candle and say:

> *Speak truth with passion*
> *And goodbye to caution*
> *As the truth is said*
> *May I not be misled.*

✤ Allow the candle to burn down until the wax drips into the herbs.
✤ Bury the cooled wax and herbs, preferably at a crossroads, having first blown any loose herbs to the wind.

The herb thyme is said to bring courage, which is often needed to bypass our inhibitions. The colour red often represents sexual passion, but here is much more the passion for truth. Do remember therefore that sometimes the truth can hurt, and you may have been being protected.

To Remove Obstacles

In this spell Ganesha, the Hindu elephant-headed god, is invoked to ensure the success of any difficult task and to grant wishes. Because he represents a combination of strength and shrewdness, he is able to get rid of the most intimidating of barriers. The spell can be adjusted to encompass all sorts of life decisions

YOU WILL NEED

Yellow candle
Red candle
Your favourite flowers
Sandalwood incense
Figure of Ganesha or of an elephant
Cooked rice
Pen and paper

METHOD

❖ Light the incense and place the flowers and the rice in front of the figure.
❖ With your hands together and fingertips pointing to your forehead, bow to the statue and say:

> *Greetings, Ganesha.*
> *Welcome to my sacred space*
> *With your help, all success shall be mine.*
> *I come to you, knowing you will grant my wishes*
> *All impediments are removed.*
> *I honour your presence,*
> *Good fortune be with you and with me and mine.*
> *I praise you Ganesha!*

❖ Light the candles and tell Ganesha what you most desire.
❖ Now commit your wishes to paper and place the paper under the statue. Say:

> *God of wisdom, God of strength*
> *Loving bringer of success*
> *Take now these wishes of mine.*
> *Mould them, shape them, work them*
> *Till together we can bring them to fruition.*

❖ Bow as before and put the candles out.
❖ Repeat for the two following days, finally letting the candles burn themselves out.
❖ Afterwards, do not disturb the statue for three days and never ask for the same thing twice.

Before long, a new way will be shown to enable you to achieve your objective. Give thanks by sharing your good fortune with others and making a further offering to Ganesha who appreciates effort made.

To Slow Down a Situation

When things are happening too fast and we feel that life is running away with us it is possible to slow things down. For this we use the power of Saturn and his control of time coupled with the idea that if something is frozen it allows us time to think and consider our actions. We simply make use of everyday articles which are easily available.

YOU WILL NEED

Paper
Black pen and ink
Your freezer

METHOD

❖ On the front of the paper either write a few words about, or draw a representation of, the situation you feel is moving too fast.
❖ On the back of the paper draw the symbol for Saturn.
❖ Pop the paper into your freezer or ice-making compartment and leave it until you feel you can handle your problem again.
❖ Tear the paper into small pieces and flush away or burn it safely.

This spell is similar to 'Freeze Out' except that we use the power of Saturn, the Roman god of Time and agriculture. By using the freezer we are bringing this spell up to date and utilizing the idea of solidifying something rather than allowing it to flow.

❧

A Healing Technique for Someone Else

There is a whole art in knot tying which actually arose among the Celtic people and later became an illustrative art. If you are able to do it the reef knot - beloved of scouts and woodcrafters - is the ideal knot for this spell, since it will not come undone. Tying a knot can also be used as healing for someone else.

YOU WILL NEED

A length of grass, string or ribbon

METHOD

✤ This requires you to tie a double knot in your chosen material. In using material which will return to the earth and rot away you must also think of the pain or difficulty as dissolving.

✤ Tie one knot going first from left to right and saying words such as:

Pain begone
Tis now withdrawn

✤ Now tie a knot in the opposite direction and use words such as:

This pain is held
Its effects dispelled

✤ Now bury the knot, preferably well away from the person concerned.

✤ As you bury it, give a blessing such as:

Bless this place and make it pure
Ill gone for good we now ensure

✤ Now you can leave nature to do its work.

In this spell you tie your knot with the idea of binding the pain and then getting rid of it. This may be a slow process if the condition is a long-standing one and sometimes we have to remember that there are spiritual lessons to be learned through sickness. Obviously the person concerned should also have medical help, so part of your responsibility is to ensure that this happens. Do not feel that the spell has failed if changes are not seen; they may be taking place at a much deeper level. Follow this with the witches ladder

Money, Luck and Career

IT MIGHT BE EASIER to think of this section under the title of Resources. Most of us need - or at least imagine that we need - more money or the wherewithal to do more with our lives and the spells in this section are designed to help you do just that. Mainly they will help you to move away from the so-called 'poverty mentality' and perhaps help you to realize that you deserve to be rewarded for living according to your principles.

Attracting Extra Money

This is a representational spell since the money in your pocket is representative of a greater fortune. Use this only at the time of a New Moon and make sure you are in the open air. It is said that the spell is negated if the Moon is seen through glass.

YOU WILL NEED
Loose change

METHOD

✤ Gaze at the Moon.

✤ Turn your money over in your pocket.

✤ As you do so, repeat the following three times:

Goddess of Light and Love, I pray
Bring fortune unto me this day.

✤ You will know that it has worked when you find extra money in your pocket or your purse or come across money unexpectedly.

In previous times the Moon was recognized as much as the Sun as being the bringer of good luck. This spell acknowledges that and allows you to make use of her power. It is said to ensure that you have at least enough for bed and board until the next New Moon.

Footwash for Money

This is a folklore recipe and would strictly only become a spell if an incantation or invocation were added. Black Cohosh is better known as a herb to be used at the time of the menopause, but here is used as a footwash which will lead you to money.

YOU WILL NEED

Black Cohosh root
Cup of boiling water
Small bottle

METHOD

❖ Soak the root in the cup of boiling water for fifteen minutes.
❖ Strain the water and throw away the root.
❖ Put the liquid in the bottle for seven days and leave it alone.
❖ On the eighth day, rub the liquid all over the bottom of your shoes.
❖ Be alert to your own intuition until money comes your way.

It is said that you will either find money, win it, or gain it in some legal manner. This, by its method, cannot really be used to gain a specific amount, but you can bear in mind what your needs are.

Money Doubling Spell

This spell is representational and helps double any denomination of paper money that you have. You are asking that the money be increased so you may also use a herb which has this effect. You are also appealing to the highest authority in asking the Angels to help you.

YOU WILL NEED

Paper money (preferably new and as much as you can spare)
White envelope
Cinnamon powder
Wax to seal the envelope

METHOD

❖ Place the money in the envelope, along with the cinnamon powder, and seal it with the wax.
❖ Fold the envelope, leave it in your sacred space and say once, every day, for seven days:

Hear me, angels in your glory,
Hear me now Zacharael.
I see the need for the common good
And ask for this to be increased.

❖ Hold the envelope up, and perceive that it feels heavier than it was.
❖ Keep the envelope in your bedroom for safety.
❖ After you receive more money, open the envelope, and share what was in the envelope with others.

Zacharael means 'remembrance of God' and is the angel who reminds us not to be bound by material concerns. For this reason, when we have truly shown that we understand both the value and the illusions associated with money we should never go short.

How to Speed Up a Happening

Sometimes we find ourselves in a situation that is not happening quickly enough for us, such as a business deal or house purchase. We can then use our knowledge of colour and herbs and spices to speed things up. We may not always know what other circumstances surround the problem, so it is wise to bear in mind the words 'if it be right' or 'An it harm no-one'.

YOU WILL NEED

Red candle
Fast luck incense
Cinnamon powder
Papers associated with, or representative of, the problem

METHOD

❖ Sprinkle each of the papers with cinnamon powder.
❖ Arrange in a pile.
❖ Place the candle on top of the papers.

❖ As you do this repeat the following words three times:

Time passed, time fast
Let this [event] happen

❖ Light the incense and the candle and allow them to burn out.

A Case for Court

This spell should help you to obtain the verdict you wish for in a court case. It is simple to do and can also give you the confidence to face your ordeal with courage.

YOU WILL NEED

Several pieces of paper
Pen (all magically charged if possible)
Orange candle (for legal matters)
Fireproof dish
Scissors

METHOD

❖ Sit in a quiet space and light the candle.
❖ Breathe deeply several times to help clear your mind.Look at the issue from the perspectives of the other people involved (your opponents, the judge, jury and so on).
❖ Try to think of all possible scenarios which might occur, being realistic in your assessments.
❖ Write down each one on a single piece of paper.
❖ See yourself handling each scenario calmly and factually.
❖ Concentrating on the candle flame, call on your own favourite pantheon of gods and ask for right action. You might for example petition the Egyptian goddess Ma'at, Themis the Greek goddess, or Forseti the Norse god.
❖ Ask that there will be clarity, honesty and justice in the situation.
❖ Take a brief look at each of the scenarios again and write down any new ones which then come to mind.
❖ Now choose the outcome you most desire and put that piece of paper under the candle while it burns out.

❖ Take the rest of the papers and cut them up into small pieces.
❖ Set light to them in the fireproof dish by first lighting one piece from the candle.
❖ When these have burnt out, flush them away under the tap or blow them to the four winds.
❖ When you go to court, take the paper with your desired result, put it in your pocket, and when you find yourself in difficulties hold the paper unobtrusively in your hand to give you courage.

This spell does not automatically ensure that you will win your case, particularly if there is dishonesty involved. Remember that you are asking for justice, which may involve some kind of penance or penalty on your part.

A Magical Pomander

As our knowledge of herbs and magic increases, we are able to use old-fashioned ideas and charming customs and perhaps return them to their original use. Pomanders, aromatic spheres that are prepared by studding oranges with cloves, have been used since medieval times in a practical way to keep bad smells at bay. Magically they can be used to attract money and for protection and - when they have lost their fragrance - as an offering through fire to the gods.

YOU WILL NEED

An orange with an oily skin
A nail or knitting needle
A good quantity of whole cloves
Cinnamon powder
Plastic bag
Ribbon
Pins

METHOD

❖ Stud the orange with whole cloves complete with stems, bud side out.
❖ It is easier to insert the cloves if you poke a small hole first with the nail or knitting needle.
❖ Space the cloves evenly in a pattern that pleases you, leaving room to tie the ribbon.

The cloves will move closer together as the orange dries out.

✤ As you work keep your intent for the pomander in mind.

✤ Place the powdered cinnamon in the plastic bag, and shake the pomander inside the bag until it is well coated with the powder.

✤ Leave in a warm place to dry out, which may take up to six weeks.

✤ Check frequently that the orange is not going mouldy, but try not to open the bag.

✤ Lastly, tie the ribbon around the pomander, fixing it securely with the pins.

✤ Hang the pomander where you can both see it and enjoy the fragrance.

✤ When you come to dispose of the pomander, throw it into a fire.

✤ Say:

As I return this to its Element
Sun, Jupiter, Venus
I thank you for your help.

✤ Made in this way the pomander can last up to a year before its fragrance completely fades.

This pomander is multi purpose. All the components are ruled by the element of Fire and the relevant deities and planetary influences are Sun for the orange, Jupiter for the cloves and Venus for the cinnamon.

Achieving a Dream Job

Candles always work well when dealing with aims and aspirations. This spell introduces some of the techniques beloved of those who believe in using the Element of Fire, which represents drive. This particular spell is best begun on the night of a New Moon.

YOU WILL NEED

2 brown candles (to represent the job)
Green candle (for prosperity)
A candle to represent yourself (perhaps your astrological colour)
Prosperity incense such as cinnamon
Prosperity oil such as bergamot, or blended patchouli and basil

METHOD

✤ Light your prosperity incense.

✤ Anoint the candles with the prosperity oil from wick to end, since you want the good things to come towards you.

✤ Place one of the brown candles in the centre of your chosen space. Place the green one on the right, with your personal candle on the left. (These candles should be in a safe place; they have to burn out entirely.)

✤ As you light your personal candle, say:

Open the way, clear my sight.
Bring me chance, that is my right.

✤ Light the green candle and say:

Good luck is mine and true victory,
Help me Great Ones, come to me.

✤ Light the brown candle and say:

Openings, work, rewards I see,
And as I will, So Must it Be.

✤ Leave the candles to burn out completely.

✤ Each night for a week - or until the candle is used up - light the second brown candle for 9 minutes while contemplating the job and the good to come out of it.

You need to identify exactly what you mean by 'a dream job'. It is of little use aiming for something which is beyond your capabilities, though you might go for one initially which will begin to take you to where you want to be.

Activating a Wish

It is easy to categorize the granting of wishes as a separate area of spell-making, but, depending on the offering you make, it could be classified as crystal, candle, herbal or symbolic. Timings and other correspondences can be according to your wish or need.

YOU WILL NEED

Your chosen gift to the Elements, spirits or

deities (this might be an appropriate crystal, plant, rune or piece of metal)

A suitable place to make that offering (perhaps a quiet woodland, a running stream, a high place, or in urban areas a park, waterway or high building)

METHOD

- Before you begin you will need to have given some thought to your wish.
- Be very specific in stating what you want otherwise you may get more than you bargained for.
- State your wish clearly and as briefly as possibly, addressing your deity or spirit by name or title if you can, for instance:

Pan and spirits of the woodland
Hear now my request
I wish for health, love and happiness
For [name]

- When you make your offering, be appropriate. For example:
- If your wish is for material goods or finance you could use a crystal or coin and bury it to signify the tangibility of your desire.
- If your wish has an emotional content then you might throw your offering into running water.
- If your wish is for knowledge or information then signify this by getting up to a high place and using the currents of air.
- You might for instance choose to scatter some plant seeds to help restore the ecological balance.
- If choosing to use the Element of Fire outside then be responsible, use only dead wood and never place your fire close to plants or buildings.
- Repeat your wish three times.
- This is so that any negative attached to your desire should have dropped away by the third request and by then you will also be more aware of your own feelings and whether you really want what you are asking for.

Making wishes is a quick way of making things happen within your everyday world, often without having to carry out a full-blown ceremony. As you get to know your own capabilities you will be able to take advantage of the moments which are presented to you.

For Study and Concentration

It is sometimes important to go right back to basics to gain the help we need. This is a herbal and colour formula spell which also calls on the powers of Bridget, the goddess of poetry, or on Sarasvati, the Hindu goddess of Knowledge. Your sachet will be purple for the former and white for the latter.

YOU WILL NEED

2 parts rosemary
2 parts basil
1 part caraway seeds
1 part dried rind of citrus fruit
(a part equals one quantity)
Small bowl to mix the herbs
Small cloth bag about 15cms in size
Silver thread or cord

METHOD

- Combine the herbs thoroughly while chanting either:

Bridget, Brighde fashioner of words,
Help me now as I seek your aid
Let me now bring you honour
In what I have to say today.

- Or, for Sarasvati:

Sarasvati, divine consort of Brahma
Mistress of knowledge
Teach me to use words wisely and well
My doubts and fears I pray you dispel.

- Now put the herbs in the bag, tying it securely with the silver cord.
- Place the sachet somewhere within your work area where you can see it.

You should find that simply by focusing on the sachet you are able to free your mind from distractions and find inspiration as you study for exams or write your articles and masterpieces. If you become really stuck then pick up the sachet and allow some of the fragrance to escape, remembering to tie it back up when you are finished.

Legal Success

This spell is based on ancient herb and folk magic. To influence the outcome of legal procedures, the associated papers are 'dressed' to give added power to any decisions that have to be made. The technique is very simple and, of course, can also be used in business proceedings, but in this case should probably be carried out away from the office.

YOU WILL NEED

Your documents
Dressing powder, consisting of:
unscented talcum or powdered chalk
Deer's Tongue leaves
calendula flowers
ginger or cinnamon powder

METHOD

❖ Combine the leaves, flowers and ginger or cinnamon powder in equal measures with the talcum or chalk.
❖ Place your documents on a flat surface and sprinkle them thoroughly with the mixture.
❖ Draw your finger nails through the powder in wavy lines from top to bottom.
❖ Concentrate as you do so on the desired outcome.
❖ Leave the papers overnight then in the morning shake off the powder.

This spell does not seem to work if there is any dishonesty or deliberate nefarious dealings on your part. However if you are completely above board it is possible to turn things in your favour. 'Dressing' papers can also be carried out if you have important exams or studying to do. This spell and Success in Finding a Job are by definition very similar. You simply need to know and understand your herbal correspondences.

Eliminating Personal Poverty

A modern-day adaptation of an ancient formula, this spell ensures that you always have the necessities of life, such as somewhere to stay and enough to eat. Because it becomes part of your everyday environment, you simply need to refresh the ingredients when you feel the time right.

YOU WILL NEED

Small glass container containing equal quantities of:
Salt, sugar and rice
Safety pin

METHOD

❖ Fill the container with a mixture of the salt, sugar and rice.
❖ Place the open safety pin in the centre of the mixture.
❖ Put the container in the open air where you can easily see it.
❖ Occasionally give the bowl a shake to reinvigorate the energies.

Though this spell has no particular timeframe, the more confident you become in your own abilities the quicker it will work. Rather than using salt, sugar and rice you can use a pot-pourri of your choice. Shaking the container also keeps the energies fresh and you must use your intuition as to when they need changing.

Fast Luck Oil

This oil contains herbal essences, all of which have the effect of quickening up a spell. However, there is need for a word of warning, since many people nowadays have sensitivities to so many substances. Wintergreen if ingested internally is highly toxic so you should be extremely careful when dealing with it and cinnamon oil can irritate the skin. When it is used to dress a candle however the combined oils are an efficent and speedy way of making things happen.

YOU WILL NEED

A small bottle
10 drops wintergreen oil
10 drops vanilla oil
10 drops cinnamon oil
Carrier such as almond oil

(If you wish you can suspend a small piece of alkanet root [Bloodroot] in the bottle for a deep red colour and extra power)
You can also, for money spells, add gold or silver glitter

METHOD

❖ Carefully combine the essential and carrier oils in the bottle.
❖ Shake well and repeat as you do so at least three times:

> *Fast Luck, Fast Luck*
> *Bring to me my desire.*

❖ Now add the other ingredients if you are using them and leave the bottle in a cool dark place for at least twenty four hours for the oils to blend.
❖ After this time you can use the oil to dress your candles.
❖ Remember that, as you are drawing luck towards you, you should dress the candle from the top down.
❖ If you are using Fast Luck Oil for a money spell concentrate on money coming towards you, use a green candle and repeat the words above.
❖ Use a brown candle if you have a business deal you need to accelerate, but this time it is wise to add a few flakes of silver or gold glitter.
❖ To bring love into your life use a pink candle, visualize your ideal person coming into your life and repeat the words above, adding:

> *If it be right for all concerned.*

❖ Let the candles burn out safely.

You should have some indication that this routine is working within about thirty-six hours. If there is none, then you must consider what obstacles there are to progress. These may have come to light since you began the spell and you can attempt to remove them before carrying out the procedure again.

Gambling Spell

This spell activates a good luck charm which can be used whenever you gamble. The acorn is a symbol of fertility and good luck and takes on the quality of its parent tree, the oak, which is considered to signify strength and power.

YOU WILL NEED
Acorn
Gold paint
Narrow paintbrush

METHOD

❖ Sit quietly for a few moments, holding the acorn in the hand you consider to be your most powerful and visualize yourself receiving your winnings.
❖ Now carefully paint the acorn with the gold paint.
❖ Make sure that you completely cover it.
❖ Repeat the following at least three times while doing this:

> *When chance's dice I choose to throw*
> *Little seed of acorn grow*
> *As I gild thee here and now*
> *Bring me gold and silver*

❖ When the paint has dried keep the acorn in your pocket or wallet.
❖ Remember that you have used a living plant and should therefore return an offering to the earth in some way - perhaps plant another acorn in a wild place.

Do not expect to win large amounts of money using this spell. It is much more likely to be a steady trickle, through whatever way you choose to gamble. Occasionally for best results you should share some of your winnings with others, so that your good luck is passed on.

Money Bottle

Spell bottles were originally created to destroy the power of an evil magician or witch thought to have cast a spell against the bottle's creator.

The bottles consist of a container, usually glass, filled with various objects of magical potency. All are concentrations of energy, created and empowered for specific magical purposes.

YOU WILL NEED

Tall, thin glass bottle
5 cloves
5 cinnamon sticks
5 kernels of dried corn
5 kernels of dried wheat (or 5 teaspoons of wheat flour)
5 pennies
5 10p pieces
5 20p pieces
5 sesame seeds
5 pecans
5 whole allspice

METHOD

- Put the ingredients into the bottle, making sure the top is secured tightly.
- Shake the bottle for five minutes while chanting words such as:

> *Money gain, silver and herbs*
> *Copper and grain hear my words.*

- Place the money bottle on a table somewhere in your house.
- Leave your purse or wallet near the bottle when at home so that the power is transferred.
- You should find that money will come to you, perhaps in unexpected ways.
- The number five is used to effect change. In financial matters it suggests movement into another phase of material gain.

You can if you wish bury this bottle close to your home rather than actually keeping it indoors. If you do this however it is a good idea to acknowledge it in some way every time you pass it. You can do this by leaving a small gift such as a pretty pebble or some wildflower seeds.

Money Charm

This is more properly a charm rather than a spell because you have formed a different object (the bag) and given it power through incantation. As always, a money charm like this relies on the energy set up between you and the money. If you recognize that money is a resource, you can adjust the spell to ask for resources rather than money itself.

YOU WILL NEED

A square of green cloth
Allspice, borage, lavender and saffron
Crystals (such as garnet, ruby and emerald or rock salt)
Three silver coins
Gold and silver-coloured thread

METHOD

- Hold the three silver coins in your hands.
- Breathe on them four times and say:

> *To the spirits of Air I say*
> *bring some money my way.*

- Put the herbs, crystals and coins on the cloth.
- Tie the cloth into a bag using eight knots in the thread. (It is probably easiest to fold the thread into two and tie knots round the neck of the bag.)
- Hide the bag in a safe, cool, dark place, away from prying eyes for eight days.
- After eight days money should be coming in.

Be as realistic as possible, imagining what you will do with the money and how best it will be used. Once you have made the bag, meditate daily on what you want. By using the three silver coins and four breaths you create the vibration of the number seven which is considered to be both a lucky, and spiritual, number.

Money Spell

This is a spell to help you come to terms with money and your attitude to it and should be performed around the time of the Full Moon. Most of us at some time or another have financial problems. We may not have enough, we may not manage it very well, there may be demands on us that we can't or don't feel we can meet.

There are two versions of this spell and you should choose the one you are most comfortable with. If you are really hard up you will find it simpler to use play money, however if you are very brave you may choose real money. Choose the largest denomination of money – either pretend or otherwise – that you are comfortable with.

YOU WILL NEED

Green taper candle
Mint or honeysuckle oil
Play money of various denominations or a single note of the largest denomination of real money you can afford

METHOD

❖ Two days before the Full Moon, take the green candle to your sacred space.
❖ Carve several pound signs on the candle, thinking of a more prosperous life as you do so.
❖ Anoint the candle with the essential oil.
❖ Place it in the holder and set it in the middle of your sacred space.
❖ Light the candle.

If using play money:

❖ Spread out your 'money' in front of the burning candle.
❖ Handle it, sort it, play with it.
❖ Spend at least 5 to 10 minutes thinking about your attitude to money, how you would use it if it were real.
❖ Extinguish the candle.
❖ The next night, light the candle again.
❖ Play with the money again, thinking about how you might make it grow.
❖ After 10 to 15 minutes, extinguish the candle.
❖ The third night, the night of the Full Moon, do the same again; think about how you would help others.
❖ Before the candle burns out completely burn a large denomination note of your play money after you have finished sorting it.
❖ This is your offering to the Gods but it also represents your acknowledgement that money is simply an energy to be used.

If using real money:

❖ The ritual is the same except that during your meditation on the first day you should think about how you wish to spend the money you are going to accrue.
❖ During the second ritual visualize it growing and becoming more. See yourself going to the bank to put money into your account or some such action.
❖ On the third night you have a choice:
❖ You can either burn the money, place it somewhere safe, perhaps on your altar as a reminder of your good fortune, or give it to charity. It is important that you do not use it for your own purposes.

This spell does require a certain amount of courage, but having the confidence to take a risk and burn money- play or real - really can open up your mind to the opportunities for prosperity.

Removing Misfortune

This spell uses plant magic combined with folk magic and the meaning of numbers. Burying an object binds the energy of what it represents and reciting prayers raises the vibration to the point where any negativity is nullified. The instruction 'Within sight of a church' suggests that the bad luck then is overseen by the Angels.

YOU WILL NEED

Three small jars (small jars such as honey or baby food jars work well)
Nine cloves of garlic
Nine thorns from a white rose or nine pins

METHOD

❖ Pierce the garlic cloves with the pins or thorns saying forcefully while doing so:

Misfortune begone from me.

❖ Put three of the cloves and pins in each jar.
❖ Bury each jar within sight of a church.
❖ Say the Lord's prayer each time you do this.
❖ Walk away and don't look back at what you have done.

This spell can give impressively fast results. As soon as you become aware of the misfortune you are suffering, look for a common theme – i.e. are the problems financial, love etc – and actually name them in the words you use. Because you have addressed it three times it cannot remain.

Silver Spell

This spell relies on the use of candles and takes about a week to perform. Before you begin, believe you have prosperity and that you have no money worries. Consider your attitude to money. You will probably find that the spell is best begun on a Friday.

YOU WILL NEED

A small bowl
Seven silver coins
A green candle and holder

METHOD

❖ Place the bowl, the candle and its holder on a flat surface in your home, where it will be passed every day.
❖ For the next seven days put a coin in the bowl.
❖ After seven days, take the candle in your hands and imagine prosperity coming to you.
❖ Sense the opportunities that you will have with money.
❖ Be aware of the energy that has been given to money.
❖ Place the candle in the holder.
❖ Pour the seven coins into your left hand.
❖ Draw a circle with your hand around the coins.
❖ Put the first coin right in front of the candle.
❖ As you place it, say these or similar words:

Money grow, make it mine
Money flow, Money's mine.

❖ Place the other coins around the candle one by one and repeat the incantation.
❖ Finally light the candle and allow it to burn out.
❖ Leave the money in position for at least three days.
❖ It is better you do not spend this money if at all possible.

This spell is another one which is designed for long term security. Just as you built the energy very slowly, so the gains will build slowly too. A variation of this spell is to take a scallop shell which represents the Great Mother and place the coins in that, leaving them as an offering.

To Banish your Debts

This particular spell uses candle and incense magic and, if you wish, the art of magical writing. You could choose incense or oil for purification or protection, whichever seems right for you. It is suggested that you perform this at the time of the Waning Moon as this can be used to help take away the difficulty.

YOU WILL NEED

Incense of your choice
Purple candle
Oil of your choice
Rolled parchment or paper, 6cms wide and as long as you like
Black pen or pen with magical black ink
A pin or your burin
Unbreakable candle holder

METHOD

❖ Light the incense and dress the candle with the oil.
❖ List all your debts on the parchment.
❖ Draw a banishing pentagram on the back of the parchment. This is drawn lower left point to top to lower right to top left to top right and back to lower left.
❖ Carve another banishing pentagram with the pin or burin on the candle.
❖ Place the rolled parchment in the candle holder then tighten the candle on top.
❖ Do this carefully since your candle will eventually set the paper alight.
❖ Concentrate on banishing your debts.
❖ Visualize your happiness and relief when the debts are banished.
❖ Light the candle.
❖ Take the candle to the East and ask that the Spirit of Air acknowledges your intention to be debt free.

* Replace the candle in the holder, making sure it is safe to burn out where it stands.
* In your own words, ask for the debts to be banished and replaced with prosperity.
* Allow the candle to burn out completely, but as it comes to the end make sure that you are present.
* The paper will catch fire and flare up, so it must be properly attended to.
* As you do this, be aware of the lifting of the burden of debt.

You should not expect your debts to simply disappear, but the wherewithal to clear them should come your way quite quickly. This might be, for instance, in the form of an unexpected gift or the opportunity for some extra work. Once your debts are cleared you are honour-bound not to create the same problems again.

To Attract a Wealthy Male Partner

This spell uses symbolism, herbalism, candles and colour to achieve a purpose. The dragon is a symbol of wealth, wisdom, power and nobility, while ginseng is said to enhance virility. The supposition is that by putting all of them together you create the right vibration for attraction. If performing this the first time, then do it at the time of the New Moon.

YOU WILL NEED ———————————
Red candle
A representation of a dragon (a picture, statue etc)
A piece of ginseng root about 3cms long or powdered ginseng

METHOD ———————————
* Light your candle.
* Pick up the ginseng root or powder and say:

By the power of this Man root
I pray for one to come to me
Strong and brave, wise and astute
Funny and loving to look after me.

* Then pick up the dragon symbol and say:

Power of the dragon, strong and true
Hear me now as I call to you
Bring me a man that I can love
And one that I can be proud of.

* Place the two objects in front of the candle and allow it to burn out.
* When it is done place the representation of the dragon on a high shelf to represent status.
* Either keep the ginseng root beside your bed or use the powder as an incense additive until it is used up.
* By that time your new man should have arrived.

You can use your own form of words to bring the kind of man you want. Be careful though as you may get more than you bargained for. To attract a woman would require more feminine symbols such as a fish or a ladybird, and angelica root instead of ginseng.

Want Spell

Since Mother Nature supplies our most basic needs, this spell uses the cycle of her existence to help fulfil your wants. The leaf is representative of her power and you are using natural objects to signify that all things must come to pass.

YOU WILL NEED ———————————
A marker pen
A fully grown leaf

METHOD ———————————
* Write or draw on the leaf a word, picture or letter that represents the thing that you want.
* Lay the leaf on the ground.
* As the leaf withers, it takes your desire to the Earth.
* In thanks, Mother Nature will grant your wish.
* You may also throw the leaf into running water or place it under a stone if you wish.

This is a spell which owes a great deal to folk magic and an appreciation of the cycle of growth and decay. In such spells, it is usual to use a leaf that has fallen rather than pick one from a tree. If you do the latter you should thank the tree for its bounty.

String Spell

This spell is another representational one and is very simple to do. It pays homage to the art of knotting and makes use of your sacred space if you are able to leave your altar in place. Otherwise simply use a windowsill in broad sunlight or moonlight.

YOU WILL NEED

A length of string long enough to outline your material desire

METHOD

❖ Sit quietly with the piece of string and pour your wish into it. Try to have a clear picture in your mind of what you want.

❖ Tie a knot in one end of the string and say:

With this knot the gods I implore
Bring this [your desire] my way, for sure.

❖ Tie a knot in the other end and say:

With this knot I lock it in
With thanks for the gift that it will bring.

❖ Lay the string on a flat surface and fashion it into as close a picture of your material desire as you can.

❖ Leave it in place for at least three days.

❖ When your wish has manifested, thank the gods either by giving something to charity or offering your skills to your local community.

This spell seems to work best if you actually need the object you are representing. The gods do not grant their favours without some effort on your part so use your gift wisely and well. Your relationship with the gods is always a two-way street.

Open Sesame

Sesame seeds are said to have the power to open locks, reveal hidden passages and to find hidden treasures. They also are used in magic to induce lust. However here they are used in a much more mundane way, to attract money.

YOU WILL NEED

A pretty glass or ceramic bowl
Handful of sesame seeds

METHOD

❖ Place the sesame seeds in the bowl.

❖ Put the bowl somewhere near the door of your home in a safe space.

❖ Each time you pass the bowl on the way out, give it a stir with your Apollo finger (the ring finger) of your right hand.

❖ Change the seeds every month, and dispose of the seeds by burying them or throwing them into running water.

When going for a job interview try to ensure that you have some sesame oil. Decide what salary you want, then touch a little of the oil on the pulse spots on your wrists. Be confident in asking for the required sum.

Success in Finding a Job

When you submit a job application, manuscript for publication, or anything that requires paper there are several things that you can do, using herbs and crystals as well as some techniques based on ancient beliefs. One or all of the parts of the techniques can be used, but first you must make your combined incense and dressing powder base. This spell is similar to Legal Success on page 292, but uses different herbs for a slightly different result.

YOU WILL NEED

1 tsp ground cinnamon
1 tsp ground ginger
1 tsp ground lemon balm
Few drops of bergamot oil
Bowl

METHOD

❖ Mix all the ingredients together in the bowl.

❖ For a dressing powder add a carrier such as powdered chalk or talcum powder which should be unscented.

❖ To use as incense leave it as it is, and burn it on a charcoal disc in a heatproof burner

FOR THE SPELL PROPER

YOU WILL NEED

Your papers (application form etc)
Any supporting documents (e.g. your CV, covering letter)

METHOD

❖ Light your incense

❖ Before you begin writing or filling in your forms 'smoke' the paper on which you will write. This consists of wafting the required amount of paper or the application form in the incense smoke and asking a blessing for the process you are about to start.

❖ You may wish to place a crystal on your desk to help in the writing or you could place it on or near your printer.

❖ You might use tiger's eye for clearer thinking or tourmaline to attract goodwill. Be guided by your own intuition.

❖ Once you have completed the forms or the writing you can 'dress' each page individually.

❖ On the back of each page sprinkle the dressing powder.

❖ Draw your four fingers through the powder in wavy lines from top to bottom so they leave very clear tracks.

❖ Leave for a few moments, then shake off the powder, all the while visualizing the success of your project.

❖ Finally, you can leave the papers in front of the image of your chosen deity if you have one, or offer them for a blessing overnight

When you have done this, you know that you have done as much as you can to ensure success as is humanly possible. It is literally now in the hands of the gods. Obviously, you will already have done or will be doing any necessary research into your project on a physical level.

To Create Opportunity

This spell appeals to the Roman goddess Ops who used to be petitioned by sitting down and touching the Earth with one hand, since she was a deity of prosperity, crops and fertility.

During the Full Moon, using sympathetic magic, a wish doll (poppet) representing health and happiness is made to draw opportunities towards you.

YOU WILL NEED

A bowl of sand (to represent the earth)
Green cloth
Needle and thread
Pen
Cinnamon or cedar incense
Dried camomile, vervain or squill
Mint and honeysuckle oil

METHOD

❖ Make a poppet out of the cloth as on page 229.

❖ While concentrating on the opportunities available to you, write your name on the poppet and stuff it with the dried herbs that have had a few drops of the oils added. Sew the figure shut.

❖ Light the incense.

❖ Hold the poppet in the incense smoke.

❖ Say:

Goddess of opportunity,
Bring good fortune now to me
Guide me by your gentle hand
For I am as worthy as these grains of sand.

❖ Let the sand trickle through your fingers to signify touching the earth.

❖ Repeat this an odd number of times (seven works very well).

❖ Keep your poppet safe, you do not have to have it with you at all times, just with your possessions or papers.

❖ For the spell to continue to work, renew it every Full Moon.

This is a good spell to use for business opportunities, since the poppet can be kept unobtrusively in a drawer or cupboard and hopefully will become imbued with the excitement of your day-to-day work. It can also be used when you wish to enhance your career prospects.

To Help Make a Decision

This spell uses colour and candles to allow you to make a decision over two opposing outcomes. You are in a sense taking the dilemma to the highest authority in order for the best outcome to become apparent. Do the spell at the time of the New Moon if there is a new beginning involved.

YOU WILL NEED

Two yellow candles
White candle or your astrological candle
Length of purple ribbon just over half a metre long
Two pieces of paper
Pen

METHOD

❖ This spell takes three days to do in total.
❖ Place the white candle on the exact middle of the ribbon.
❖ This ribbon signifies the highest possible spiritually-correct energy.
❖ Place the two yellow candles either end of the ribbon.
❖ Write the two possible outcomes on the pieces of paper and fold them separately.
❖ Place these two papers under the yellow candles on top of the ribbon.
❖ Light the middle (white) candle first and then the two outer (yellow) ones.
❖ Acknowledge the fact that you will be extinguishing them as part of the spell.
❖ Burn the candles for at least an hour, so that a link is properly made.
❖ Consider both decisions carefully.
❖ Snuff the candles out and next day move the papers and the outer candles closer to the middle candle.
❖ Roll the ribbon in towards the centre against the candle bases.
❖ Relight the candles and again burn for at least an hour, considering your options carefully.
❖ Each day repeat until all the candles are grouped together.
❖ (This should take at least three days, and, if time allows, longer.)
❖ Ensure that you have at least an hour's burning time left for the final day.

❖ Allow the candles to burn out and within three days you should find it easy to make a decision.

This process allows due consideration of all the pros and cons of the various options. It provides the energy for the correct decision and allows you to be rational and objective while still taking account of the emotional aspect. It keeps your mind focused on the matter in hand. You do not then 'stand in your own light' – get in the way of your own success.

To Improve Work Relationships

This is a combination of a candle and mirror spell and is designed to improve the work environment. It works equally well for all levels of work relationship. Often spells to do with work are best done at home and a reminder taken in to reinforce it. The spell is carried out for seven days and then reinforced once a week. Tuesday or Thursday are good days.

YOU WILL NEED

Small mirror that will fit unobtrusively in your drawer
White candle
Oil such as jasmine for spiritual love or ylang ylang for balance

METHOD

❖ Anoint the candle.
❖ Light the candle and burn it for at least an hour.
❖ Concentrate for a few minutes on the image of your boss or colleague as they are when they annoy you.
❖ Look in the mirror and visualize them being pleasant and calm.
❖ See yourself working with them as an efficient team.
❖ Carry on doing this each evening for a week then do it once a week thereafter for at least six weeks.
❖ In between times keep the mirror in your work desk drawer and reinforce the positive visualization of your colleague or boss being calm every day.

You should see an improvement after a week – others may also notice a change as time goes on. As you become less stressed you may find you become more creative and can deal with other petty annoyances.

Weaving Success

The use of ribbons is an extension of knot magic and is often used in binding or protection spells. However, this one is an unobtrusive way of enhancing the energy of your business as well as ensuring its security. Braiding three strands links us with the triple-aspected Great Mother – Maid, Mother, Crone.

YOU WILL NEED

Three equal lengths of ribbon:
dark blue for success in long-term plans, and clarity
yellow for mental power, wealth, communication and travel
brown for grounding, stability, and endurance
A large safety pin

METHOD

❖ Pin the three ribbons together at the top to make braiding easier.

❖ Braid the ribbons neatly together.

❖ As you do so, repeat the following words as often as you feel is right remembering the significances of the colours:

Great Mother Great Mother
Come to me now
As these strands weave and become one
May this business grow.

❖ Now loop the braid around the front door handle so that anyone who comes into the business must pass it.

You should find that the qualities you have woven into the business begin to bring results very quickly. Combinations of different colours will have different results; red will bring vitality and willpower, orange success and prosperity through creativity and yellow communication, mental power and wealth.

Protection

ALMOST INEVITABLY protection spells form an integral part of any spell-worker's armoury. When you are working with powers which are not well understood you can open yourself up to all sorts of negativity, and sometimes sheer goodwill is not enough to protect your own personal space – you need a little extra help. Equally as you develop your own abilities it becomes possible to protect those around you from harm.

Animal Protection Spell

When we work with Nature we are often called upon to protect her creatures. These would range from our own pets to animals in the wild and also those animals which have become our totem animals. This spell uses photographs to represent these animals or you could use small figurines. The candles are used to focus your energy and the oil to create a safe environment.

YOU WILL NEED

Two green candles
One white candle
Picture or figurine of the animal
Protection oil
Consecrated salt and water
If protecting your pet, include its favourite treat

METHOD

❖ Light the two green candles being conscious of the conservation issues in regard to your animal. Light the white candle to represent the animal concerned.

❖ Put the photograph under the white candle or the figurine next to it and say:

Spirit of fire burning bright,
Give your protection here this night.
The moon above for this animal dear
Gives shelter and so freedom from fear,
Draw close all spirits of the same
Come hither! Come hither!
Power of the wild and strength so great!
Defend and safeguard this one's fate.

✤ To complete the spell, either give your pet its treat or scatter the crumbs outside for other animals to enjoy.

The animals you are drawn to are believed to be the ones who in return for your care will also protect and teach you. By being aware of their needs you become part of the cycle of Nature and of life.

Animal Stones

The ancients were very good at perceiving shapes in stones and wood and believed that such shapes could be made to hold the spirit of the animal 'trapped' in such a way. Many artists today are still able to do this, and we too as magic makers can make use of this art. When on your wanderings you find an interesting stone or piece of driftwood, look at it with fresh eyes and turn it into a fetish – the correct meaning of which is an object that is believed to have magical or spiritual powers.

YOU WILL NEED

A pleasantly shaped stone or piece of wood
Paints and brushes
Decorations such as beads and ribbons
Glue or fixative
Incense such as benzoin or frankincense
A small box

METHOD

✤ Light the incense
✤ Sit quietly with your object and let it 'speak' to you.
✤ Allow the ideas to flow as to what it might become – your totem animal, a bear, a horse or perhaps a dog or cat.
✤ Decorate the object appropriately, taking care to enhance the natural shaping rather than to change it.
✤ You can now consecrate it in one of two ways.
✤ Pass the object quickly through the smoke of the incense three times to empower it with the spirit of the animal.

Or

✤ Place it in the box with an appropriate image or herbs and bury it for three days or place it on your altar for the same period. This allows the metamorphosis to take place and the spirit of the animal to enter your now magical object.

It is now ready for use, perhaps to help you access the wisdom of the animals, as a healing device or for protection.

Ancients believed that the fetish must be fed appropriately so that it retained its magical powers. Today, corn is an appropriate 'food', as is pollen, although you can use your imagination, since it is your creation. Should you not feed (energize) it for a period you may need to consecrate it again for it to work properly.

Banishing Powder

Most herbs can be pulverized either in a pestle and mortar, a coffee grinder or in a blender to make various powders for specific purposes. In an emergency you can also use commercially dried spices and blend them yourself. The following powder is designed to get rid of pests, both human and otherwise. It has a slightly oriental feel to it.

YOU WILL NEED

Equal quantities of peppercorns
(black, white, cubeb, paprika etc)
Similar quantity of ginger
Wasabi (Japanese horseradish) powder

METHOD

✤ Grind all the ingredients together.
✤ As you do so visualize the pest walking away from you into the sunset.
✤ Sprinkle the resulting powder sparingly around the edge of the area you wish to protect.
✤ You can also sprinkle the powder where you know it is where the pest will walk.

There is no need to make it obvious that you have sprinkled this powder. Indeed the more unobtrusive it is the better. You should be aware however that since the spell uses the idea of heat, all the ingredients are 'hot' the powder should not be used when you are angry, and you must be very sure you do not wish to have any contact with your 'pest'.

Animal Protection Collar

A simple way to protect an animal and to have them behave well is to plait your own collar for it to which you can attach various objects. Try to use natural materials wherever possible. Using the same principle as Mesopotamian cylinder seals you may like to make your own protective device, or you could use an inscribed pet tag, or a small charm bag. Choose the colours of the cords carefully according to the animal's temperament or to signify the quality you wish the animal to develop; e.g red for a hunting dog, silver for a nocturnal cat or a mix of colours.

YOU WILL NEED

Three pieces of cord slightly longer than the circumference of your pet's neck, to allow for braiding and tying.
A small cylinder name tag or a disc inscribed with the animals name and address.
A small charm bag about 10cm (3 inches) square with cord or ribbon tie
Small quantity of child's clay
Small piece of flint
Small piece of coral
Small crystal of rose quartz
Your burin
Pen

METHOD

✤ Carefully braid the cord, while calling on your chosen deity for protection for your animal, and weaving in the intention for good behaviour.
✤ Form a rough cylinder from the child's clay and before it dries out completely, inscribe it with a protective rune, Ogham stave or the name of your preferred deity.
✤ Attach it to the collar you have woven, or place it in the charm bag.
✤ If you are using the cylinder type of dog tag, write the symbol on the back of the paper in the cylinder; if using a circular disc inscribe it on the back.
✤ Place the flint, the coral and the rose quartz in the charm bag and attach it to the collar.
✤ Put the collar round the animal's neck again calling for protection.

Obviously if your animal is fully grown you cannot expect a total change of behaviour all of a sudden without additional training. Sometimes an animal needs protection as much from its own behaviour as anything else. This spell gives you a starting point and a foundation from which to work.

Blessing for the Heart of the Home

This is a candle, crystal and representational spell which calls upon Hestia, goddess of the hearth and home, to bring her qualities of constancy, calmness and gentleness to bear on your home. Hestia is supportive of the family and home and was praised by the poet Homer in ancient Greece.

YOU WILL NEED

Lavender candle
Small silver or brass bowl in which to stand the candle
Lavender flowers
Small piece of amethyst

METHOD

✤ Before placing the candle in the bowl raise the latter above your head in both hands and say:

Hestia, you who tends the holy house
of the lord Apollo,
draw near, and bestow grace upon my home.

✤ Place the candle in the bowl, making certain the candle will stand firmly.
✤ Light the candle and when it is properly alight pass the amethyst three times through the flame and say:

Hestia, glorious is your portion and your right.

❖ Place the amethyst in your hearth or close to your fireplace.
❖ (If you have no fireplace then as close to the centre of your home as possible.)
❖ Sprinkle some of the lavender flowers across your doorway to keep your home safe. Say:

Hail Hestia, I will remember you.

❖ Allow the candle to burn down and then place some of the lavender flowers in the bowl, leaving it in a safe space.

At times when the atmosphere in the home becomes somewhat fraught, this spell can bring a period of peace and tranquillity. The bowl, lavender flowers and amethyst are all sacred to Hestia and remind you of her presence.

To Summon Help from the Elements

This is only one way to summon help from the Elements. You use representations of each Element and address the spirits of each element in turn to seek their assistance. When you have finished your task each element is then honoured by returning it to the earth.

YOU WILL NEED
White candle (to represent Fire)
Small bowl of salt or sand (to represent Earth)
Small bowl of water
Incense such as bergamot (to represent Air)

METHOD
❖ Light the incense and the candle.
❖ Bear in mind as you do so at this stage that you are making use of the Elements of Fire and Air.
❖ Call upon the power of these Elements.
❖ Ask for their help in the work you are about to do.
❖ Use your own words preferably but do keep it simple.
❖ You might say for Fire something like:

I request your presence, Oh Spirit of Fire
I ask for your help, your power I require.

❖ For Air your words might be:

Come to me now, Oh Spirit of Air
I pray above all for a mind that is clear.

❖ Lift the bowl of salt and likewise invoke the powers of the Earth Element. Say perhaps:

Approach now I pray, spirit of Earth
Help I do need, and prove now my worth.

❖ Do the same with the water and say:

Come to me now, Oh, Spirit of Water
My feelings are clear your strength is now sought for.

❖ When you have finished, sprinkle the salt or sand on the earth, pour the water onto the earth, bury the ashes of the incense and snuff out the candle.

This is not a spell as such, but more preparation for magical working. Whereas you can cast a circle within which to carry out your more important workings this allows you to set up a sacred space very quickly.

Cleansing the Body of Negative Energies

This spell uses candle magic and an appeal to the Elements. One aspect needs to be noted. Black candles were once associated with Black Magic and malevolence but today are much more used to represent loss, sadness, discord and negativity.

YOU WILL NEED
White candle (for positive energy)
Black or dark blue candle (for negative energy)
Green candle (for healing)

METHOD
❖ In your sacred space, place the candles in a triangle with the green candle closest to you. Clear your mind of everything except what you are doing.

✤ Light the white candle, being aware of its symbolism and say the following:

Earth, Fire, Wind, Water and Spirit;
I ask thee to cleanse my body of all negative energies.

✤ Light the black or blue candle, being aware also of its symbolism.
✤ Repeat the words above and pause to let the energies come to a natural balance.
✤ Light the green candle and again repeat the above words.
✤ Sit back, keep your mind clear and be peaceful for at least 10 minutes.
✤ When the time feels right either snuff out the candles or allow the green one to burn right down so that you are filled with healing energy.

You should feel rested and relaxed and more ready to tackle problems as they arise. Make this part of your weekly routine till you feel it no longer to be necessary.

To Reverse Negativity or Hexes

Try this candle spell using the element of Fire to reverse any negativity or hexes you become aware of being sent in your direction. Anger from others can often be dealt with in this way, but deliberate maliciousness may require more force. You need to be as dispassionate as you can when dealing with a hex, which is defined as 'an evil spell'.

YOU WILL NEED

Purple candle
Rosemary oil
White paper
Black ink
Fire-proof dish such as your cauldron or an ashtray

METHOD

✤ Visualize all blocks in your life-path being removed.
✤ Anoint your candle with the oil.

✤ On the piece of paper write in black ink:
✤ All blocks are now removed.
✤ Fold the paper three times away from you.
✤ Light the candle and burn the paper in your dish.
✤ Invoke the power of Fire and its Elemental spirits by repeating three times:

Firedrakes and salamanders,
Aid me in my quest,
Protect me from all evil thoughts
Turn away and send back this hex.

✤ After the third repetition close the spell in whatever way is appropriate for you.
✤ A simple statement is enough:

Let it be so.

No-one has the right to curse or malign another person and all you are doing with this spell is turning the negativity back where it belongs. When you use the power of Fire you are harnessing one of the most potent forces of the universe, so be sure you use it wisely and well.

Household Gods

Household gods are found in most folk religions. In Rome, the penates were household gods, primarily guardians of the storeroom. They were worshipped in connection with the lares, beneficent spirits of ancestors, and, as guardians of the hearth, with Vesta or Hestia. This spell is representational and pays due deference to them for protection from harm.

YOU WILL NEED

A representation of your household gods
(a statue, a picture or something significant for you)
Representations of your ancestors
(perhaps a gift from a grandparent, an heirloom, a photograph)
Fresh flowers or taper candles
Incense sticks of your choice
A bowl of uncooked rice
A bowl of water

+ This technique offers food to the gods and the ancestors and blends pagan and Western thought.
+ Place your representational objects either close to your kitchen door or near the cooker, today often considered the heart of the home.
+ Light your incense and place the bowls in position in front.
+ Light the candles or place the flowers so that you have created a shrine.
+ Spend a little time communing with the penates and the lares.
+ Welcome them into your home and give thanks for their help and protection. (In Thailand a sometimes quite intricate 'spirit house' is provided away from the shadow of the house for the ancestors.)
+ Their presence is acknowledged each day in order that they do not become restless.
+ Replace the water and rice weekly.

Remembering to honour the household gods and the ancestors means that their spirits will look favourably upon us. Often if there is a problem, taking it to the household gods for consideration is enough to have the resolution become apparent.

Invoking the Household Gods

This ritual is best performed during the Waxing Moon. It could be considered a kind of birthday party, so feel free to include food and drink as part of it, if you so wish.

YOU WILL NEED

Pine cones, ivy, holly, or something similar
Symbol appropriate to your guardian (e.g. a crescent moon for the Moon Goddess)
Small statues of deer or other forest animals
An incense that reminds you of herbs, forests and green growing things
Green candle in a holder
Your wand

METHOD

+ Decorate the area around your guardian symbol with the greenery and small statues.

+ Clean the guardian symbol so that there is no dust or dirt on it.
+ If the symbol is small enough put it on the altar, otherwise leave it nearby.
+ Light the incense and candle. Stand before your altar and say:

Guardian spirits,
I invite you to join me at this altar.
You are my friends and I wish to thank you.

+ Take the incense and circle the guardian symbol three times, moving clockwise and say:

Thank you for the help you give to keep this home clean and pleasant.

+ Move the candle clockwise around the symbol three times and say:

Thank you for the light you send to purify this space and dispel the darkness.

+ With the wand in the hand you consider most powerful, encircle the symbol again three times clockwise and say:

I now ask for your help and protection for me, my family and all who live herein.
I ask that you remove trouble makers of all sorts, incarnate and discarnate.
I thank you for your love and understanding.

+ Stand with your arms upraised. Call upon your own deity and say:

[Name of deity] I now invoke the guardian of this household whom I have invited into my home.
I honour it in this symbol of its being.
I ask a blessing and I add my thanks for its protection and friendship.

+ If you have more than one guardian, change the 'its' to 'their' and so on. Spend a few moments caressing the symbol, sending out the thought that the guardian is important to you.
+ Be aware of the subtle changes in atmosphere which occur as the protective spirits become part of your environment.
+ Finally, thank the unseen participants.

To Protect a Child

By the time a child is about seven he or she is beginning to venture out into the world away from home often without either of the parents being present. Teaching your child a simple protection technique is helpful for both you and them. This is based on Eastern ideas.

YOU WILL NEED

Your child's imagination

METHOD

❖ Discuss with your child the best image they can have of protection. This might be a shield, a cloak, a wall or more effectively being surrounded by a cocoon of light.

❖ Working with their own visualization image, have them experience what it is like to feel safe and protected.

❖ Agree that whenever they are frightened or under pressure they can use this visualization.

❖ Now whenever you have to be separated from them, repeat these words or similar to yourself three times:

Forces of light, image of power
Protect [name of child] till we meet again.

❖ Now perceive them surrounded by light and know that they are as safe as you can make them.

You may need to reinforce for the child the idea of them feeling protected by their own image, but coincidentally you are teaching them to have courage and to experience their own aura and circle of power. You may well find that your parental antennae tend to be alerted quite quickly when your child is having a problem.

To Prevent Intrusion into a Building

In this spell you use visualization and power to create a barrier to protect your home or a place of business. This means that only those who you want to enter do so and anyone else will be driven away. The spell can be reinforced at any time.

YOU WILL NEED

The power of your own mind

METHOD

❖ Sit in your sacred space and gather your energy until you feel extremely powerful.

❖ In the main doorway to the building, face outwards and visualize a huge wheel in front of you.

❖ Put your hands out in front of you as though grasping the wheel at the positions of twelve o'clock and six o'clock with your left hand on top.

❖ Visualize the energy building up in your hands and forming a 'light rod' or laser beam between them.

❖ Bring your hands through 180 degrees so they change position (right hand now on top).

❖ Pause with your hands at nine o'clock and three o'clock and again build up a light rod between them.

❖ As you do so say something like:

Let none with evil intent enter here.

❖ Again feel the energy build up between your hands and say:

May those who would harm us, stay away.

❖ Bring your hands together level with your left hip and 'throw' the energy from your hands to create a barrier in front of the door.

This powerful spell should be sufficient to prevent all intrusion, but you could reinforce it by treating all other entrances in the same way and could also visualize small wheels at the windows. You might vary the technique by tracing a banishing pentagram on the door itself.

Fire Protection Spell

This spell uses the Element of Fire to protect you and create a visual image which you carry with you throughout your daily life. It requires a clear space outside of about twenty feet in diameter initially and you must be careful not to set any vegetation alight through the heat of your fires. You can also perform this spell on a beach.

YOU WILL NEED

Enough fallen wood to feed four fires
Dry brushwood or paper to start the fires
Matches
Water to douse the fire

METHOD

❖ You should make sure that you only gather fallen wood or driftwood.
❖ Make sure you have enough to keep each of the fires burning for about half an hour.
❖ Taking up one of the sticks of wood, draw a rough circle about eleven feet in diameter.
❖ Determine the four directions North, East, South, and West (use a compass, the sun, moon, or stars).
❖ Lay a small pile at each point just inside the circle but do not light them.
❖ Reserve any spare wood safely beside each pile to keep the fires burning for at least half an hour.
❖ Walking to the South first, light the fire proclaiming as you do:

Nothing from the South can harm me
Welcome Spirits of the South.

❖ Wait until one of the pieces of wood is burning, pick it up and move to the West. Light the fire and say:

Nothing from the West can harm me
Welcome Spirits of the West.

❖ Again take up a burning branch and move to the North.
❖ Light the fire while saying:

Nothing from the North can harm me
Welcome spirits of the North.

❖ Again take up a burning piece of wood and take it to the East.
❖ Light that fire and say:

Nothing from the East can harm me
Welcome spirits from the East.

❖ Take up a burning branch and carry it to the South.
❖ Thrust it into the southern fire and choose a new branch.
❖ Trace an arc with it above your head from South to North, saying:

Nothing from above can harm me
Welcome spirits from above.

❖ Finally, throw the wood down in the centre of the circle and say:

Nothing from below can harm me
Let spirits come who wish me well.

❖ This last stick represents Aether or spirit and this technique has created a sphere of energy which you can call on whenever you need it.
❖ You can replace that piece of wood into the southern fire if you wish, or contemplate it as it burns out.
❖ Replenish the fires from the reserved wood pile as necessary.
❖ Sit in the centre of the circle and recognize that the fires are purifying and cleansing your personal environment on every level of existence.
❖ Watch each fire carefully to see if you can perceive the spirits of the Elements:
Salamanders for Fire
Gnomes, Dryads or Brownies for Earth
Sylphs for Air
Undines for Water
❖ Revel in the warmth of the fires, appreciate their light and sense their protection.
❖ Remember these feelings for they are what protects you as you leave this space.
❖ When the fires begin to die down, douse them with the water and bury the embers to prevent them flaring again.
❖ Erase the markings of the circle and leave the space.

This spell or ritual (depending how ornate you wish to make it) as it is done in the open air creates a barrier of protection for you, but may also make you more conscious of how fire works. In this case it consumes that which is dead and finished with, leaving only its power in its wake.

Protection Bottle

The idea behind this protection bottle is that it is made very uncomfortable for negativity and evil to stay around. As you progress and become more aware you become very conscious of negativity, while at the same time needing protection from it.

YOU WILL NEED

Rosemary
Needles
Pins
Red wine
Glass jar with metal lid (a jam jar is ideal)
Red or black candle

METHOD

✣ Gather together rosemary, needles, pins and red wine.
✣ Fill the jar with the first three, saying while you work:

> *Pins, needles, rosemary, wine;*
> *In this witches bottle of mine.*
> *Guard against harm and enmity;*
> *This is my will, so mote it be!*

✣ You can visualize the protection growing around you by sensing a spiral beginning from you as its central point.
✣ When the jar is as full as you can get it, pour in the red wine.
✣ Then cap or cork the jar and drip wax from the candle to seal.
✣ Bury it at the farthest corner of your property or put it in an inconspicuous place in your house.
✣ Walk away from the bottle.

The bottle destroys negativity and evil; the pins and

needles impale evil, the wine drowns it, and the rosemary sends it away from your property. It works unobtrusively like a little powerhouse and no one need know that it is there.

TO TRAVEL SAFELY

In travel spells you use more than one correspondence to achieve a safe journey. In this day and age you can use all sorts of representations to help with this, from protecting your luggage to making the journey pleasant to protecting your person. The nest three spells can be used as appropriate whenever you are travelling.

Protecting your Vehicle

If you are a passenger, the first method given below is a simple unobtrusive way to protect you and your driver. If you yourself are driving, the second enhanced method may give you more peace of mind.

YOU WILL NEED

The power of visualization

METHOD

✣ Visualize a sphere or bubble of light around the vehicle and mentally seal it with the sign of the equal armed cross above the bonnet.

Enhanced technique
YOU WILL NEED

Few drops of frankincense oil
Stick of frankincense or other protection incense
If desired a small charm such as a dolphin or eagle

METHOD

✣ Before any long journey, put a few drops of frankincense in water and wipe over the wheel arches with a sponge dipped in this water.
✣ Burn the stick incense inside the vehicle and pass the charm through the smoke to bless it.
✣ Hang the charm in a prominent place or put it in the glove compartment.
✣ Finally protect the vehicle as in the simple technique.

❖ You can expect to feel happier and to feel safer through having carried out the protection spell, but this does not mean that you can afford to take risks with your driving and you should observe all other safety precautions as well.

For some people travelling can be a real ordeal. These three techniques can protect the traveller and give considerable peace of mind during what is, after all, a period of transition. When you arrive safely at your destination it is always worthwhile making a small offering to the powers that be that have helped you in thanks.

To Protect your Luggage

YOU WILL NEED

A sprig of rosemary
A purple ribbon

METHOD

❖ Place the rosemary inside your case.
❖ Trace the sign of the pentagram over each lock.
❖ Weave the ribbon securely round the handle.
❖ Say three times:

> Protected is this case of mine
> Return now safely in good time.

Practically, you should recognize your luggage anywhere, and if you do have to lose sight of it, for instance when flying, it has been made safe, and will come back to you quickly. Thieves are unlikely to think that it is worth stealing and it is not likely to get lost.

Protecting Yourself Prior to the Journey

YOU WILL NEED

Four tealights
Few drops of protective oil such as sandalwood or vetivert

METHOD

❖ Take a leisurely bath placing the tealights securely at each of the four corners of the bath.
❖ Add the essential oil to the bathwater.
❖ Visualize all your cares being washed away and at some point begin concentrating on the journey to come.
❖ Do this without anxiety just savouring the enjoyment of the journey.
❖ To this end you might light a yellow candle for communication and ask that you be open to opportunities to enjoy new experiences, get to know new people and understand the world in which you live.
❖ You can blow the tealights out when you have finished your bath and relight them when you return home as a thank-you for a safe journey.

Now prepare a charm bag with:

1 part basil
1 part fennel
1 part rosemary
1 part mustard seed
1 pinch of sea salt
1 clear quartz crystal
A coin or bean for luck
A square of indigo cloth
One white cord
If liked, add a representation of a wheel and/or a piece of paper with the name of your destination

❖ Spread the cloth so that you can mix the herbs quickly.
❖ Hold your hands over the herbs and ask for a blessing from Njord the Norse god of travel or Epona the Horse goddess who accompanied the soul on its last journey.
❖ Gather up the herbs and the representative objects in the cloth and tie it into a bag making sure it is bound securely with the white cord.
❖ Keep the bag secure about your person.

You should find that your journey is accomplished without too much trouble and that people are eager to assist you when you need help. You may well find that you are observing more than is usual or are being asked to participate in experiences which might otherwise pass you by.

To Make Bad Luck Go Away

This spell can be adapted to use any of the Elements you choose to help the energy to work. Remember that Fire consumes, Air dissipates, Water washes away and Earth eliminates. You might do this spell at the New Moon to signify new beginnings or on a Saturday to change blockages into valuable experiences from which you can learn.

YOU WILL NEED

Square piece of paper at least 10 cm x 10 cm (3 x 3 inches)
A black marker or magical black ink and pen
Your cauldron or a fire- proof dish if using fire
Material to start your fire (such as pine chippings)

METHOD

❖ At night time light a small fire in your cauldron or dish.
❖ If not using fire then decide where and how you wish to dispose of the paper.
❖ Write on your paper the words:

BAD LUCK

❖ Think hard about when circumstances have not gone well for you and write them all down.
❖ Draw a big X across the paper with the black marker.
❖ Put the paper into the fire and say three times:

Fire, fire brightly burning
Let me see my luck now turning
Change all that's bad now into good
My life to be then all that it could.

❖ Sit for a few minutes, concentrate on the bad luck being gone and the good luck coming your way.
❖ Extinguish the fire and dispose of the ashes appropriately.
❖ You can use any of the methods shown below to dispose of the ashes. Just substitute the ashes for the paper.

❖ If you decide to use the Element of Earth then tear the paper into small pieces. knowing that the bad luck can no longer trouble you and make a similar incantation such as:

Earth dark, cool and strong
I ask you now to right this wrong
All bad luck eliminate
In joy let me participate.

❖ Bury the paper, walk away and don't look back.

❖ If using the Element of Water, find a rushing stream or a source of fast flowing water - at a pinch a flushing toilet can be used.
❖ Again tear the paper into small pieces.
❖ As you dispose of the pieces say:

Water, water, rushing pure
Take away bad luck for sure
Charge my senses as you flow
These negatives I will outgrow.

❖ Take time to think about how full your life can be without the bad luck.
❖ You no longer need to keep thinking 'Poor me'.

❖ If using the Element of Air, either get up to a place as high as you can - the top of a tall hill or building perhaps - or walk to a crossroads. At a pinch, a forked road will do.
❖ Tear the paper up into pieces.
❖ Throw or blow the pieces to the four winds.
❖ Say:

Winds of change, set me free
Take bad luck away from me
Dispel its power within the air
I beg you now grant me my prayer.

❖ Take a deep breath and this time as you breathe in be conscious of the fresh energy you are taking in.

Any of the parts of this technique is enough to dispel the bad luck so a combination of them will be more than enough to change your life. You do however have a responsibility after this to understand yourself and how you draw negative influences towards you.

Breaking the Hold Someone has Over You

This spell owes a lot to visualisation and the use of colour and in many ways is a learning experience in trusting your own abilities. It can be used in emotional situations, where you feel someone is taking advantage of you, or when you are bound to someone by perhaps a false sense of duty. This technique can be done in more than one sitting, particularly if you do not want any changes to be too dramatic.

YOU WILL NEED

A strong visual image of the link between you and the other person
A cleansing incense (such as frankincense, copal or rosemary)

METHOD

* Your image must be one that you feel you can relate to fully. Perhaps the easiest to see is in the form of a rope joining the two of you together.
* If you are good at seeing colour then the best to use is something similar to iridescent mother of pearl, because that contains all colours.
* You might see the image as a rigid bar, which would suggest that there is an inflexibility in the relationship between you which may require you to deal with the expectations of others.
* The incense is used to create an environment which is free from other influences; this is just between you and your perception of the link you have with the other person.
* Light your incense and sit quietly, considering carefully the link between you.
* Become aware of the flow of energy between you and gently withdraw your own energy, seeing it returning to you and being used for your own purposes rather than the other person's.

(This may be enough to bring about a change in your relationship which has a satisfactory outcome for you.)

* Next think carefully about how the other person makes calls on your time and energy - whether these are physical, emotional or spiritual.
* Resolve that you will either not allow this to happen or will be more careful and sparing in your responses.
* You might develop a symbol for yourself which you can use when you feel you are being 'sucked in'.
* Preferably use one which amuses you, since laughter is a potent tool. You could use the image of a knot being tied, a cork or a stopcock.
* If you decide that you no longer wish to be associated with the person, use a technique which signifies breaking the link. It will depend upon your own personality and that of the other person as to how you do this.
* Visualizing the link simply being cut may bring about a more powerful ending with tears and recriminations, whereas a gentle teasing out of the link may be slower but less painful.
* It is here that you must trust your own judgement with the thought that it must be done for the Greater Good. If therefore you feel that at least some links must be left in place you can do this, for instance if you would wish to know when the other person is in trouble.
* Finally see yourself walking away from the person, free of any bonds between you.
* Always ensure that you leave them with a blessing for their continuing health, wealth and happiness.
* Now you will only become involved with them at your own wish.

You can see from the above that at all points you have a choice for your course of action. This is because each stage must be considered very carefully, and not done in anger. You must remain as dispassionate as you can and always remain true to your own principles.

Pet Protection Spell Bottle

Pets can be particularly sensitive to atmosphere so it is wise, if you do a lot of spell work which deals with negativity, to protect them against being inadvertently contaminated. The herbs and candle work do this very efficiently.

YOU WILL NEED

Wine bottle
Small jar of soil
Small jar of salt
Bay leaf
Tablespoon of dill seeds
Tablespoon of fennel seeds
White taper candle
Your burin or a pin
Carnelian stone

METHOD

✤ Put half the soil into the bottle.
✤ Add half the salt on top of that (to make layers).
✤ Next add the bay leaf and the dill and fennel seeds.
✤ Put the rest of the salt on top of this and the rest of the soil on top of the salt. Drop the carnelian stone on top of everything.
✤ On the taper candle Use the burin or pin to carve the word:

Protect [pets name]

✤ Fit the candle into the top of the bottle. If it is too big, wedge it in or warm the bottom slightly until it stays securely by itself.
✤ Burn the candle when convenient. You don't have to burn it all down at once, but eventually the candle will burn itself out.
✤ When the candle will not stay lit any longer but forms a plug for the top of the bottle, put the spell bottle near the place your pet spends most of his or her time.

If you are fearful that your pet may be stolen, add a sprig of rosemary to the herbs in the bottle. You can expect to become very aware of your pet's wellbeing in the light of this spell. Conditions you have not previously noticed may become apparent.

Moon Protection for the Amulets

This technique can be used to protect an object that you use as an amulet. Obviously you are also taking in the power from the Moon as well. This is best done at the time of the Full Moon.

YOU WILL NEED

Your chosen amulet
A glass of spring water

METHOD

✤ Place a crystal or amulet that you regularly carry in the glass of spring water a day before the Full Moon.
✤ The following day, on the evening of the Full Moon, stir the water three times with your right hand in a clockwise motion.
✤ Then take the glass in your hands and swirl the water in it around, moving the glass in a clockwise, circular, stirring motion three times.
✤ Then repeat these words aloud:

Oh Light of the Moon
Wrap me
Protect me
Keep me from harm.

✤ Remove your amulet from the glass.
✤ Raise the glass towards the sky, acknowledging the Moon.
✤ Lower the glass, bring it to your lips and drink the water.
✤ Carry the amulet with you till the next Full Moon in order to ensure full protection.
✤ Repeat this process every month to benefit from the amulet's influence.

When an object has been blessed by the Moon, you enter under her protection. You symbolically take in her power by drinking the water. Amulets are seemingly inanimate objects which have been given power by the incantation.

To Break a Curse

There are various ways to break a curse or a malicious spell. Here you use an object to represent the curse, incense to clear it and an incantation to deflect it. You then allow natural forces to do their work.

YOU WILL NEED

Cleansing incense such as benzoin or Dragons Blood

Black candle (to represent the negativity)
White candle (for positivity)
A sachet containing equal parts of:
St. John's Wort
Lavender
Rose
Bay
Verbena
Lemon
Your athame
Bowl of water
Bowl of salt
Glass or china plate

METHOD

❖ Light the incense and candles and place them on your altar (black on left, white on right).
❖ Pass the sachet through the incense smoke and put it on one side.
❖ Hold the lemon in both hands and allow the lemon to signify the negativity. Think of all the negative things that have happened to or around you and push them into the lemon, particularly if you suspect they are associated with the curse.
❖ Put the lemon on the plate.
❖ Dip your knife or athame in the water then slice the lemon into three pieces.
❖ Touch each piece of lemon with the tip of the athame.
❖ As you do this, repeat the following:

Three times three, Now set me free

❖ Visualize the lemon drawing the negativity away from you and into itself.
❖ As you do this, repeat:

As sour as this lemon be
Charged and cut in pieces three
With salt and water I am free
Uncross me now, I will it be.

Lemon sour, lemon sour
Charged now with power

Let this lemon do its task
It's cleansing power I do ask
As this lemon dries in air.
Free me from my dark despair.

Uncross! Uncross! I break this curse
But let not my simple spell reverse
I wish no ill, nor wish him pain
I wish only to be free again.

❖ Take each lemon slice and dip it in the salt, making sure it is well coated.
❖ Set the slices back on the altar and say:

As it is my will, so mote it be.

❖ Leave the lemon pieces on the altar where they can dry. Once dry the spell is complete and the lemon can be thrown away or buried.
❖ If however the fruit rots instead, you must repeat the spell.

While waiting for the fruit to dry, keep the sachet with you at all times. It will help to protect you from the effects of the spells and turn away any negativity sent in your direction.

To Break a Spell you've Cast

There are times when we have cast a spell that we should not have done, either because we have not thought it through or because we have reacted in anger and later realize that it was inappropriate. Then we are honour bound to undo it. This spell is representational and the best time to do this is after midnight at the time of the Waning Moon.

YOU WILL NEED

As many white candles as you feel is appropriate
Purifying incense (such as benzoin or rosemary)
Rosemary oil
Angelica or rosemary herbs
A bead from a necklace you own - clear if possible (you could use a much loved piece of jewellery or crystal if you don't own a necklace)
Small square of black cloth
Cord or thread

METHOD

❖ Anoint your candles with the rosemary oil, working from bottom to top, since you are sending the spell away.

✤ Light the incense and let it burn for a few moments to raise the atmosphere.

✤ Light your candles and as you do so think very carefully as to why you cast the first spell, what it has caused and why you wish it removed.

✤ Then say:

Great Mother, I ask a favour of you
On [date] I cast a spell to [insert type of spell]
I now ask for it to be removed and rendered harmless
May it have no further power or gain.

✤ Place the bead or jewellery and the herbs on the black cloth and say:

Here I make sacrifice to you knowing that I must relinquish this object as token of my good intentions.

✤ Knot the cord around the cloth, saying as you do:

I transfer the power of the spell to this object
And enclose it within its own darkness
So be it.

✤ Use three knots for finality.

✤ Seal the knots by dripping wax from one of the candles on them.

✤ Then take the bag to a source of running water or a clear space and throw it away as far from you as you can

✤ If your first spell was done in anger or fear, then say:

Begone anger, begone fear
It is done.

You should find that you have got rid of any negativity you may have felt. Insofar as you have given up something which belongs to you, you have cleared yourself of the law of cause and effect and of any spiritual difficulty as a result of your initial action.

To Protect your Teenage Daughter

This spell arises out of the ceremonies to honour the Maize Goddess in Mexico. Today it deals effectively with teenage fears and difficulties, particularly as it honours the maiden aspect of the triple goddess. It is in many ways a rite of passage and is both a protection and an initiation. It should not be performed unless the girl herself feels that she is ready for such a ceremony, or in need of it.

YOU WILL NEED

A white nightgown or simple dress
Maize broom corn tops (silks)
Two or four white candles (optional)
Water which has been blessed

METHOD

✤ Traditionally this ceremony was carried out to cleanse and protect a young girl who had been frightened by inopportune advances, whether human or otherwise.

✤ It is inevitable that the teenagers of today will find difficulty in talking about their fears and doubts, but if they can be encouraged to think about them prior to this spell it is helpful.

✤ The girl should be dressed in the white gown and then lie face downwards with her arms spread outwards in the shape of a cross.

✤ If using candles place them either at her hands, her feet and head or in all four positions.

✤ Do whatever you intuitively feel is right.

✤ 'Sweep' her back and legs with the silks, using the blessed water at the same time.

✤ Sprinkle her from head to foot with the water.

✤ Petition the goddess using words such as:

Goddess of fertility, power and love
Bless this child here tonight
Protect, guard and guide her as
she grows to womanhood
Let her not be troubled by childish fears
But grow to be the woman that
she knows she can be.

✤ Ask the girl now to think about her own future to take time to dream and imagine the sort of person she would like to be.

- As you sit quietly with her visualize a white light surrounding her and ask that she be protected from harm.
- You might at this point wish to make use of the opportunity to encourage her to talk about her dreams and fears, but try not to put pressure on her.
- If you have used candles then you can snuff them out but do not use for other magic.

Hopefully this will give your teenager a deeper appreciation of who she is and what she may become. Obviously she must give her consent to what you do together, and it is a time which must be treated sensitively. Knowing that she is protected does not give licence to take risks, simply to act responsibly.

When You Feel Threatened

We all go through times when we feel that we are under threat, perhaps at work when schedules are tight and tempers are about to snap; or maybe in the home when tensions are making themselves felt, creating a chill in the air. This spell, which calls for excellent visualization skills, protects you by forming a crystal shell around you, protecting you from the bad vibrations of ill temper.

YOU WILL NEED

A clear crystal of quartz or any favourite one that is full of clear light.

METHOD

- Place the crystal where it will catch the sunshine.
- Sit near it and breathe in deeply through your nose.
- Hold your breath for a moment or two before exhaling through your mouth.
- Repeat this several times, absorbing the light cast by the crystal as you inhale and exhaling any negative feelings, doubts and darkness.
- After a minute or two, stand up and begin visualizing a crystal-like ring rising around you, from your feet upwards, getting higher and higher with each breath you take.
- When the crystal ring is above head height,

see it close over you, forming any shape in which you feel comfortable to be enclosed - a pyramid perhaps, or maybe a dome.
- Still breathing deeply, feel the 'crystal' form a floor beneath your feet.
- Conversely, sense a link between you and the centre of the earth.
- Stretch your arms and feel your fingers touch the sides of your 'crystal'.
- Look upwards and see the top of the dome or pyramid point.
- If you can, also try to view yourself from outside the protective crystal in which you have surrounded yourself.
- Now say:

Within this crystal, I am safe from negative thought,
And am so wherever I might be.

- When you feel it is right to do so, return to normal breathing and see the crystal open to allow you to step outside it or perceive it dissolving.
- This visualisation can then be used wherever you are, perhaps in crowds, a sticky situation or simply under pressure, safe in the knowledge that you can return to it whenever you need to.

Those who have used this spell find that keeping a crystal in the house, office, or wherever else they think they may need protection from negativity strengthens the spell's potency. The spell to Protect a Child on page 307 is a similar sort of spell, and if the idea of being inside a crystal seems strange you could start off with that method instead.

A Pot-Pourri of Spells

THERE ARE MANY SPELLS which do not easily fall into the categories we have chosen. We have included a number of these here so that you may get a flavour of how to widen your perspective and thus further enhance your magical working. Always be prepared to adapt any given spell for your own purposes, but remember to keep the correspondences correct.

Get Rid of a Bad Feeling

To rid yourself of a bad feeling, someone who is bothering you, or a situation that is difficult to handle, you can use the power of air to shift it away from you. In this spell you can use colour to reinforce the magic. Choose a balloon in the more spiritual colours of purple or blue to work at the highest vibration.

YOU WILL NEED
Coloured balloon
Pieces of paper
String
Pen

METHOD
* Write on single pieces of paper each thing you wish to be free from.
* Tie them onto the string at regular intervals like a kite tail.
* Take everything up to a high place if possible, a crossroads if not.
* Blow the balloon up and tie it securely with the string.
* As you do so say:

> *As I bind these things together*
> *May I be free of them forever.*

* Release the balloon into the air and watch it be blown away.
* As this happens send it on its way with these words:

> *Spirits of Air and all things good*
> *Take these problems, lift my mood*
> *Give me freedom, Give me rest*
> *And let me be what is my best.*

* Now turn round, walk away and don't look back.

When you perform this spell you are allowing the difficulty to be taken away from you. It can however be quite a gentle process with usually little conflict or confrontation.

A Statement of Intent

This is perhaps not so much a spell, but a statement of intent which is probably best kept very private. It should encapsulate a promise to yourself to maximise your potential in every way. You may feel that telling someone about your personal undertaking actually lessens its value and makes it somehow less attainable. Similar to an affirmation, the statement needs to be short and succinct so that every time you think about it it has impact for you.

YOU WILL NEED
At least 2 pieces of paper
2 postcards
Pen and ink (magical if possible)

METHOD
* First take a piece of paper and write down as many things as you can think of that you:
want to do,
would like to do,
feel you ought to do.
(These need not be in the form of an organized list but can be scribbled down at random.)

* Look carefully at each of your statements and eliminate any that seem to repeat themselves.
* On another clean sheet of paper formulate a sentence which, for you, is powerful, meaningful and expresses the repeated sentiment properly.
* Do this for each of your core thoughts that become apparent.

+ With your second sheet of paper, try to reduce the sentences to one very powerful and relevant description of your mission or task in life.
+ Keep it as short but also as forceful as you can.
+ Keep these two pieces of paper in a safe place for future reference.
+ The second stage of this exercise is to write out your mission on two postcards.
+ Place one of these by your mirror or on your bedside table where you will see it when you first wake up.
+ Repeat the statement at least three times as soon as you are awake and also just before you settle for sleep. This is so that it is almost the first and last thing that you think about during the day.
+ Repeat the statement as often as you can during the day, preferably at least three times a day.
+ Place the other postcard where you can see it in your work area. With this postcard remember to move it around so that it does not become 'just part of the scenery.'
+ Your main personal undertaking contains within it many sub-statements so that you can if you wish concentrate as well on these sub-statements or can change the focus of your main statement in order to include another aspect. Because this statement is so personal it is yours to do with as you will; the only thing you must do is to make it work for you.

Moving the postcard once a week and thinking about the statement reinforces the intent behind it and gives you the opportunity to change the statement should you so wish. It helps to focus your mind but also allows the subconscious to 'hear' the intent and to internalize it.

Four Winds Spell

This is a herbal spell which also honours the four directions. It is easy to do and simply requires that you know what you want. You can either use a single herb or a number, whichever your intuition tells you. The lists of herbs in the Principles and Components section should give you enough information to make an informed choice. This spell actually seems to work more effectively using dried herbs since they scatter to the four winds better.

YOU WILL NEED

Dried or fresh herbs appropriate for your purpose
Small bowl or bag to carry the herbs

METHOD

+ Over about a week gather the herbs you need together.
+ Mix the herbs together. Quantities and proportions do not matter so long as you have, after mixing, a large quantity.
+ While mixing them together bear your intent in mind.
+ Put the mix into your bag or bowl and carry it up to a high place.
+ Start with the direction which suits your purpose.
+ Throw a handful of herbs in that direction saying:

[Direction] wind, accept now my offering,
Hear my request.

+ Do the same with the other directions in the same way.
+ Now spin round at least three times either throwing handfuls of herbs or allowing them to fall from the bag, as you do.
+ Chant:

Winds of power, winds so fine
Bring to me what is rightly mine

+ Stand still and allow the world to settle around you.
+ Give thanks to the Elements and walk away.

Here you are using the Elements of Earth, Fire, Air and Water, and also in the wind more specifically Air. The herbs act both as a vehicle for your request and as a gift to the Elements.

Moon Power

This spell can be performed indoors as well as outside. It is representational since you use a paper moon or flower. In the incantation the Moon is represented as a white swan. This should be done at the time of the Full Moon and is designed to bring the energy of the Moon within your grasp until the next Full Moon.

YOU WILL NEED
A bowl of water
White paper moon or flower

METHOD
❖ Float the paper moon or flower in the bowl.
❖ Raise the bowl towards the Moon in the sky and say:

Hail to thee white swan on the river.
Present life, tide turner,
Moving through the streams of life, all hail.
Mother of old and new days,
To you, through you,
this night we cling to your aura.
Pure reflection, total in belief,
touched by your presence,
I am in your power and wisdom.
Praise your power, your peace,
my power, my peace.
I am strong. I praise. I bless.

❖ Replace the bowl on your altar. Stand for a few moments appreciating the power of the Moon.

This spell is purely an incantation to the Moon and is therefore very simple. It needs no other tools or techniques except a physical representation of the Moon. Water is sacred to the Moon and therefore we offer her that which belongs to her.

Magical Writing

This spell magically charges the paper and ink you will use in some of your spells. If the request in your spell is to increase something, it is done between New Moon and Full. To minimize or get rid of something then it should be done during the Dark of the Moon or when the Moon is on the wane.

YOU WILL NEED
Paper (either real parchment or parchment type)
quill pen, or if you can find one a feather
sharpened to a point
Ink in the correct colour for your request (see pages 239-240)
Candle, again in the correct colour for your request
Appropriate incense

METHOD
❖ Light the candle and the incense (for instance, use green for fertility or money and perhaps blue for healing).
❖ Write out your request carefully.
❖ Some people will write it three times, others nine.
❖ Simply do what feels right for you.
❖ Hold the paper in the smoke from the incense for as long as feels right.
❖ Fold the paper into three and place it under the candle.
❖ Let the candle burn out, but just before it does burn the paper in the flame.
❖ Alternatively, you might bury the paper in fresh earth and allow time to work slowly. As you become more proficient your intuition to guide you.

This spell relies on a principle similar to that of sending a letter to Santa Claus. The magically charged paper can also be used to address the gods by name and can be used for yourself and on behalf of others. If you petition for others, however, do not tell them what you are doing, as it nullifies the good. Using magically charged paper and ink can become an integral part of your spell making.

You may like to have some ready prepared and charged paper and ink so that as your knowledge of symbolism increases, rather than writing out your request in longhand, you can use symbols to signify your desires. You might, for instance, use a key to symbolize your need for a house, the picture of an anvil to suggest partnership and a sheaf of corn to suggest abundance. You could also use symbolic languages such as the runes.

TO FIND LOST OBJECTS

It is highly irritating to lose something and, as always, there are different methods available of having them returned to you. Below are two different methods which have been used for many years.

Appealing to St. Anthony

This prayer or formula is often used to have a lost object returned. In it you seek the help of St Anthony of Padua, a Catholic saint of the twelfth century. The incantation is now considered to be a folk remedy. In this spell at the same time you 'pull' your object back towards you.

YOU WILL NEED —————————————

A length of thread or string

METHOD ————————————————

+ First try to remember when you last saw the object.
+ See it quite clearly in your mind's eye.
+ Imagine tying your thread or string to the object
+ Go through the motions of pulling it towards you.
+ Repeat these words three times:

> *Something's lost and can't be found*
> *Please, St. Anthony, look around.*

+ You will often get a sense of where the object is.
+ Conversely you may come across it unexpectedly.
+ Don't forget to thank St. Anthony for interceding on your behalf

The words used are found in similar forms all over the world demonstrating clearly the link between folk customs and the church. You should not need to use this spell too often if you learn to keep important articles in safe places; then when you do need St Anthony's help it is easily available.

Pendulum

This is a different method of finding something you have lost, particularly if it is in the immediate vicinity. It utilizes the pendulum and is a quick way, before you have fully developed your psychic abilities, of checking your intuition.

YOU WILL NEED —————————————

Your pendulum which may be a crystal on a short chain, a ring suspended on a thread or a similar object

METHOD ————————————————

+ Normally, a pendulum is used to answer yes/no questions, but here you take note of the direction in which it swings
+ When you have made a link with the lost object either by visualizing it or deciding why you need it, hold the pendulum in your most powerful hand and support your elbow on a flat surface.
+ Allow the pendulum to begin to move and sense which direction it seems to pull more strongly.
+ If you are a beginner, repeat the procedure three times.
+ More often than not it will find your object through indicating more than once the direction in which it may be found.
+ Follow the direction shown and unearth your object.

Occasionally an object will disappear completely and not be returned by one of the above methods. It is pointless becoming stressed since it will then reappear in its own good time if you still have need of it. If this does not happen, simply consider that it is subject ti spiritual law which means that you no longer require it.

Willow Spells

You can use knots to 'fix' a spell – that is to hold energy to prevent something from happening or to release energy so that it happens at a chosen time. You may use string, ribbon or perhaps, more effectively, living natural grasses. Willow withies such as those used for basket weaving, are good to use for this type of spell since willow enhances intuition. Knots enable you to make sure the energy you have directed goes where you want it to go.

YOU WILL NEED ──────────────
A short length of string, ribbon, grass or withy

METHOD ──────────────
❖ As always you should be conscious of the fact that it is wrong to try to force someone to do something against their will. Therefore carefully consider your actions and be very clear as to why you are trying to influence a particular situation.
❖ You might, in spells where the timing is important, prepare the groundwork for success but tie a knot to keep some control over when the circumstances dictate a proper release.
❖ Let us assume that you have a court case which needs some careful management and you need to make an impact.
❖ Take your chosen length of material and as you tie a simple knot, chant words such as:

As this knot is tied in thee
The power is held until set free
'Tis bound, until on my command
The knowledge needed comes as planned.

❖ Put the tied object in your pocket, then – perhaps on the morning of the case – at your chosen moment release the knot. This will enable you to have all the information and energy you need for a successful outcome.
❖ You can also use this same knot tying to enhance your dream content though the procedure is slightly different.
❖ If you wish to find the answer to a problem in your dreams, having carefully thought things through as much as you can, hold the withy in your hand and allow your energy to flow into it.
❖ Tie a simple knot whilst saying :

Catch now my dreams and hold them still
That I may know what is thy will
Create a space that I may see
What answer will be best for me

❖ Sleep with the tied knot under your pillow and wait for inspiration
❖ You may not receive the answer on the first night, so be prepared sleep with the knot in place for at least three nights.

While the answer may not always come in a dream, usually you will find that shortly afterwards the resolution comes about in a flash of inspiration, a certainty of the right action or through information from an outside source. The method ensures that you have received help from both your own inner self and the powers that be.

To Engender Friendship

When we meet new people we do not always know quite how they will perceive us, so this is a good spell to help us be open to new experiences but also to protect ourselves from unwarranted intrusion. You need good powers of visualisation, and little else.

YOU WILL NEED ──────────────
A new experience

METHOD ──────────────
❖ Before you are in a situation where you may be meeting new people or experiencing something new find a quiet place.
❖ Stand with your feet about 18 inches apart so you are well grounded.
❖ Visualize a bright light rising like a mist from around your feet and flowing up round you till it reaches above your head.
❖ Think of this as your protective cloak and be aware that only you can give permission for it to be penetrated in any way - emotionally or psychically.
❖ Say:

I protect myself from harm

❖ Now bring a similar light down round you from above being aware that this light will bring out the best qualities in you and say:

I now shine and so charm

❖ Lastly see the two lights and mists intermingling so that you sense your own energy field around you and know you are presenting a true picture to the outside world.

❖ You can now go forward confidently into your new situation, telling yourself that you are the most noticeable/vibrant/happy person there.

This spell does not mean that you are arrogant or pushy, it is simply a technique to create a persona that is warm and welcoming to other people. It means that they see you as you really are, but also means you are in control of any situation which may arise.

Resolving Unfair Treatment

A binding spell is performed by grasping the negative energy that is propelling a person or object, and stopping it. If you desire justice, which often we do, then call upon Egyptian goddess Maat, she who balances the scales. This spell might be used if you feel you are being unfairly treated by a colleague or a family member.

YOU WILL NEED

Black ribbon about 30 cm (12 inches) long
White feather (to represent Maat)
Frankincense incense

METHOD

❖ Light the incense at least half an hour before you take action so that your sacred space is as clear as you can make it.

❖ Contemplate your difficulty and acknowledge any part you may play in it.

❖ Tie three knots in the ribbon - one in the middle and one at each end.

❖ As you tie the first, say:

Negativity here be bound.

❖ As you tie the second:

Nastiness I do confound.

❖ As you tie the third:

By power of three, I you impound.

❖ Put the ribbon and the feather together on your altar or sacred space.

❖ Leave it alone for three days for justice to be done.

❖ After this time take the ribbon and bury it, if possible in open ground.

❖ Keep the feather in your drawer or purse as a reminder of your willingness to be free.

You must remember to control your own emotions of hatred or fear, for you must be above reproach. When you feel that the problem has dissipated, be tolerant and try to remain on good terms with the person concerned, but never tell them what you have done.

A Chocolate Spell

Chocolate was the Aztec's Food of the Gods. In Mexico it is a required offering during the Days of the Dead which are November 1st – also known as All Souls day – and November 2nd and can be used to attract those who have passed over. Here it is used as an offering to calm the sacred space and remove the influence of restless spirits.

YOU WILL NEED

Your altar
A bar of the best chocolate you can afford
Metal dish
Four Element candles
Copal incense
Tea lights for those you wish to remember
One extra for the restless spirits
Your cauldron filled with marigolds

METHOD

❖ Cast your circle since this is a time when the spirits are abroad.

❖ Light your four Element candles.

❖ Light the incense to cleanse and sanctify the area and to draw the spirits home.

❖ Light your tea lights, except for the extra one, remembering each person briefly.

❖ Say:

*I greet my ancestors and loved ones who
have gone before me*

❖ Light the extra tealight and say:

I welcome those who wish me well

❖ Break up the chocolate and put it on the metal plate, keeping one small piece in reserve.
❖ Hold the plate carefully over the tea lights until the chocolate begins to soften and perfume the air.
❖ Contemplate what death means to you as you do so. (You may become aware of the presence of the spirits.) Say:

*Welcome those who share my feast
May those not at rest now be at peace*

❖ Eat your own small piece of chocolate.
❖ Place the plate with the chocolate outside your front door for the spirits to enjoy. Sit quietly as the candles and tea lights burn down and enjoy the sanctuary of your sacred space.
❖ Close the circle when you are done.

Since the Day of the Dead occurs at the same time as Samhain this is a suitable way of celebrating and making space within your life for the good things to come. As you contemplate change and the death of the old also spare a thought for the life you wish to lead in the year to come.

Reinforcing of a Personal Space

In using the Goddess image as a focus this spell is representational. It uses a mirror to represent light and power and also uses numerology (the power of numbers) in the nine white candles. Nine signifies pure spirituality and therefore the highest energy available.

YOU WILL NEED ———————————
*Protection incense
9 white candles*

*An easily held round mirror
A representation of the Goddess*

METHOD ————————————————
❖ Light the incense.
❖ Place the candles in a ring around the Goddess image.
❖ Light the candles, beginning with the candle most directly before the Goddess image and each time repeat these or similar words:

*Light of Luna,
Protect me now.*

❖ When all are lit, hold the mirror so that it reflects the light of the candles.
❖ Turn slowly in each direction, ensuring that you throw the light as far as you can in each direction.
❖ Then spin round as many times as you have candles, continuing to project the light and say:

*Goddess of love, goddess of light,
Protect this space.*

❖ Pinch out the candles and put them away safely until you need to use them again.

This technique is slightly unusual in that you pinch out the candles rather than allowing them to burn down. This is because it is the intensity of light which is required not the length of time it burns. This is a good way of rededicating your sacred space whenever you feel it necessary.

A Wish Afloat

This spell uses plant or rather tree magic and running water to convey the energy. It also uses the art of visualization and can be very effective in manifestation spells, particularly if you get to know your tree correspondences. Ideally it should be done at the time of the New Moon.

YOU WILL NEED ———————————
*A twig or small branch of your choice
A bridge across a stream or river or a high rock
where you can see the tide of the sea*

METHOD

* In order not to disturb the Nature Spirits or harm the tree, strictly you should use a twig that has already fallen off the tree.
* Remember that Mother Nature appreciates a gift as much as you do, so wherever possible be prepared to share with the spirit of the tree.
* Shape the twig as much as you need to according to the wish you intend to make.
* When you feel the time is right stand on the bridge or rock and link with the spirit of water.
* Say why you have come, using words such as:

Tonight I come to you with a small request
Carry for me now my desire out into the open sea
That I may [state request].

* Concentrate on what you want to wish for and see it in your mind's eye.
* Repeat the words above aloud.
* Now throw the twig as far upstream or into the tide as you can.
* As the twig floats past you repeat the request again and ask for a blessing from the appropriate tree spirit.

This way of working combines the spirit of the tree with the spirit of water and means that you have some pretty powerful energy available to you.

Stop Gossip

This spell utilizes representational magic and is a way to stop malicious gossip. It is useful in a workplace environment where almost inevitably factions arise and people become embroiled. All that is necessary is to identify the ring leader.

YOU WILL NEED

A sample of the person's handwriting (failing that, a piece of paper which has been handled by them)
A jar with a screw top lid
Wax to seal it

METHOD

* Place the sample of handwriting or paper in the jar and screw it tightly shut.
* Carry this away from the offending person.
* If the badmouthing does not stop immediately, take the jar and seal it with the wax saying:

Gossip and ill-feeling begone
Trouble us no more.

* This should have the desired effect.
* When the difficulty is clearly past remove the paper from the jar and burn it.
* Do not use the jar again for magical purposes.

Remember with this spell that you are not binding the person, you are stopping their specific action, so releasing the paper means you are indicating that you are no longer involved with, or troubled by, them. They must be free to go their own way. Also try to make sure that you do not get involved in other gossip.

Sanctifying of the Moon

There is a ceremony or ritual which belongs to the Jewish heritage and which honours the New Moon in a very specific way. It is said that the Moon was unhappy with her apparently secondary position in relation to the Sun, and that God placated her with her own special ceremony. While the ritual is addressed to the Moon, it also honours the renewal of the cycle of femininity and therefore it is an appropriate one with which to acknowledge the power of the matriarch. We give it here in the form of the old words since they are so meaningful.

METHOD

* After the third day of the New Moon every Jew should, either alone or along with their whole congregation, salute the Moon with a prayer. They should go together to a place where they can see the Moon best and from there look up at the Moon.

* The words to be repeated are:

Blessed art thou. O Lord our God, King of the World,
Who with his Words created the heavens and with the breath of his Mouth the heavenly Hosts:
A Statute and a Time he gave unto them, that they should not vary from their Orders,
They were glad and they rejoiced to obey the Will of their Maker,
The Maker is true and his Works are true:

And unto the Moon, he said that she shall monthly renew her crown and her Beauty toward the Fruit of the Womb
For they hereafter shall be renewed unto her,
To beautify unto their Creator for the Glory of his Name and of his Kingdom
Blessed art thou, O Lord, the Renewer of the Months.

❖ Then say three times:

Blessed is thy Former, blessed is thy Maker, blessed is thy Purchaser, blessed is thy Creator.

❖ Next, rise up onto the toes and say three times:

As well I jump towards thee and cannot reach to touch thee, so shall none of mine enemies be able to touch me for harm.

❖ Then say three times:

Fear and Dread shall fall upon them,
By the Greatness of thine arm they shall be as still as a stone.
As a stone they shall be still by thy Arm's Greatness;
Dread and fear on them shall fall.

❖ Then following words should then be said three times to each other:

Peace unto ye, unto ye peace, David, King of Israel liveth and subsisteth.

This acknowledgement of the Moon's validity was an important part of ancient Jewish thought. The words are not a spell in the true sense of the word, but they are still truly potent.

To Rid Yourself of a Problem

This spell is so simple to do that it has to work. It is best done at the time of the Waning Moon, and makes use of the Elements to symbolize completion.

YOU WILL NEED

An old shoe (usually the right one)
Pen
A fire, natural running water or the sea

METHOD

❖ Write your problem on the sole of the shoe
❖ Put the shoe on and stamp three times
❖ As you do so, say:

Begone, troublesome times

❖ Either, throw the shoe into the fire and ensure that it burns properly.

Or
❖ Throw the shoe into the stream of water and watch it disappear.

Or
❖ Throw the shoe into the sea and walk away.

❖ As any of these happen, visualize the problem getting less and less until it disappears.
❖ Often during this time inspiration may come to you as to how you can deal with the difficulty.

The reason that you use the right shoe is because this is considered the more positive and assertive side of the body, which is normally the one needed. However, if it feels more natural to use the left shoe the result will usually be more passive and non-confrontational.

Feast of Divine Life

All agrarian societies celebrate harvest time – the time of abundance. The Egyptian Feast of Divine Life celebrated the moon and the belief that it provided the Waters of Life. Nowadays we recognize the cycle of life the wheel of the cosmos as it turns. We can still honour the Triple Goddess in all her forms – Maid, Mother and Crone – as was done of old. At the time of the harvest she is honoured more as the fertile mother.

YOU WILL NEED

Green candle
Yellow candle
Cauldron
Wand
Three symbols of a fruitful harvest (e.g. bread, apples etc.)

METHOD

❖ Prepare your sacred space as usual, including your altar and say:

> *The harvest is now done.*
> *A peaceful winter lies before us.*
> *Dark and light strike a balance.*
> *Thanks be to the Triple Goddess.*

❖ Light the coloured candles.
❖ Carrying the candles, move clockwise around the ritual area, commencing and completing in the East.
❖ At each cardinal point, pause and say:

> *Triple Goddess, bless the year's harvest that I bring.*

❖ Place the candles safely and alight on the altar. Tap the cauldron three times with your wand and place the symbols in the cauldron then say:

> *Life brings death, brings life.*
> *The wheel of the cosmos turns never-ending.*
> *The negative is replaced by the positive.*
> *I honour the Triple Goddess,*
> *Harvesting my thoughts*
> *I honour the Triple Goddess.*

❖ Meditate for as long as feels comfortable then close the circle.

When you have finished, be sure to share the harvest with others of the Goddesses creatures. You might like to bury the apple near an apple or fruit tree as an offering, to scatter the bread for the birds and to scatter herbs if you have used them on waste ground.

Cherokee Prayer Blessing

This is a blessing which is a lovely gift to give to someone as they move into a new home. It is not a spell as such but adds a special vibration all its own.

YOU WILL NEED

Paper or parchment
Pen
Incense such as Nine Woods Incense

METHOD

❖ Light the incense.
❖ On the paper write (or have inscribed if you do not have a steady hand) the following words:

> *May the Warm Winds of Heaven*
> *Blow softly upon your house.*
> *May the Great Spirit*
> *Bless all who enter there.*
> *May your Mocassins*
> *Make happy tracks in many snows,*
> *and may the Rainbow*
> *Always touch your shoulder.*

❖ Pass the parchment through the smoke three times and present the gift neatly rolled.

The Cherokee philosophy is that even the smallest drop of Cherokee blood makes one a Cherokee. While few people can lay claim to such ancestry we can share the awareness that we are all inter-related .

A Spell for the Garden

If you have a garden it is a nice idea to acknowledge the four directions and to make it as much a sacred space as you can. We do this by using the correspondences of the four

Elements. Once the garden is blessed it can be used for any of the Sun, Moon and Nature rituals you find appropriate.

YOU WILL NEED

A compass
Garden flares or citronella candles to represent fire
Solar fountain or birdbath to represent Water
Wind chimes or child's windmill to represent Air
Small collection of stones and pebbles to signify Earth

METHOD

✦ Consecrate the objects according to the method on page 231 for Consecrating Altar Objects.
✦ Place the objects in the correct positions asking for a blessing as you place each one
✦ You might call on the Spirits of the Elements, the Nature Spirits or on your best loved deity.
✦ Finally, stand in the middle of your garden, raise your arms and say:

Gaia, Gaia, Mother of all'
Bless this ground on thee I call
Make it safe for all within
Peace and tranquillity may it bring.

✦ Obviously you may use your own words if you wish.
✦ Spin round three times to seal the energy, then sit on the ground and appreciate the newfound energy.

If you have very little space, we suggest that you combine all of the elements in a terracotta solar fountain and place it in the East. Terracotta represents Earth, the solar aspects suggests Fire, the fountain Water and the East the Element of Air.

To Give Encouragement

This is a spell which enables you to work with someone without them necessarily knowing what you are doing. This is used only for positive encouragement or to let someone know that you care about them and what they

do. Anything else will rebound on you threefold

YOU WILL NEED

A jade, rose quartz or amethyst crystal
Frankincense or one of the blends suitable for the purpose
Oil burner

METHOD

✦ Light the burner.
✦ Pour a little additional oil into your hand and rub your hands together to raise power.
✦ Hold the crystal in your most powerful hand and pass it through the fumes from the oil burner three times.
✦ Face the direction you know the recipient to be.
Say

Goddess of Love, Goddess of Power,
Hear me now as I thee implore
Help [name] to do what they must
Create the conditions for their success.

✦ Build up a ball of energy around the crystal until it is as powerful as you can make it.
✦ Place the crystal by the side of your bed, directing the energy of the ball towards the recipient and know that it will be transmitted to the recipient as self-confidence for the task in hand.
✦ Visualize the person concerned standing tall and confident in a shaft of light stretching from the crystal to them.
✦ Next morning, wash the crystal under running water and store until it is needed or give it to the person concerned.

This spell works because you have no expectations. Your gift of encouragement is freely given without thought of reward. The payoff comes when you see the recipient succeed in their own way.

Magical Dreaming

The knowledge that can be acquired through dreams opens up a whole library of creativity which is ours to use if only we have the courage. Our biggest problem is that unless we have undergone some kind of training to remember and/or categorize our dreams, or unless we are creative types, with the ability to think laterally, it is all too easy to forget the content of our dreams on waking. Even when we do remember a dream, if our thought processes tend towards the logical, there is every chance we won't believe what the dream is telling us without receiving some proof of its validity.

Inspired Dreaming

Most of us aren't in the position of the 19th-century scientist Friedrich Kekule, who was able to prove the validity of one of his dreams with a piece of groundbreaking science. While trying to solve the structure of the benzene molecule, Kekule dreamt of a snake eating its own tail. This gave him the vital information he had been searching for, that the molecules formed a complete ring. This particular symbol echoes the ouroboros (the symbol of the cycle of existence), which is often used in magical workings as a protective device.

Dreams can give us a much wider perspective and newer appreciation of magical and spiritual skills. One definition of spirituality is the awareness of dimensions of existence beyond that of the purely physical. It is thought that babies in the womb 'dream' themselves into physical existence. Dreams also give us access to another dimension of being – spirituality and the use of power. In fact, many Eastern cultures see sleep as a preparation for death and a learning experience.

Today, many people will admit to having creative flashes of inspiration following dreams. It is as though a missing piece of jigsaw suddenly fits into place, allowing them to see the whole picture and therefore to make sense of a creative problem. Often a fragment of music, poetry or apparent doggerel will linger in the mind, which on consideration is not as beautiful or pertinent as it has seemed in the dream, but does contain the seeds of an idea or project. The mind has opened up to possibilities and potentials far beyond the waking consciousness. Meditation can often aid in this process of creative dreaming, whether we use it to open up before sleep to the creative self or after dreaming to gain a greater understanding. Examples of such techniques are given on pages 331–333.

As adults, with the realization that we are very much part of a greater whole, we can begin to take responsibility for the creation of a better, fuller existence for ourselves and finally accept that out of that creation we can build a better and more stable future. Whatever stage of understanding we may have reached, dreams can help and encourage us or indicate that we are going down a particular route that may not be worthwhile.

Dreams can be taken as events in their own right and can be interpreted as such. Whether they make sense, or whether we choose to act on the information given, is decided by the dreamer. We can also accept dreams as an expression of the unconscious creative self, which can contain a message given either in an easy-to-understand form or in the language of symbolism, where initially the meanings are not easily discernible.

It is when we begin to recognize the creativity behind the process of dreaming that we open ourselves up to different ways of approaching our own talents and abilities in a novel way. One of these is in the use of magic and the power to influence events.

The Hypnagogic and Hypnopompic States

With practice, the states between waking and sleeping (or indeed sleeping and waking) can be a time when wishes and desires can be given substance and brought into reality in a particularly magical way.

Briefly, the hypnagogic state is one which occurs between waking and sleeping, while the hypnopompic occurs between sleeping and waking. The best explanation of these two states comes from the realms of spiritualism. The astral planes are those levels of awareness wherein are stored the various thought-forms that have occurred, and in the hypnagogic and hypnopompic states the mind has some access to those realms, without actually seeing spirit form.

While dream interpretation itself does not necessarily require an understanding of the 'hypno' states or vice versa, we can often use dream images and the hypno states to enhance our magical workings. The half-and-half awareness of consciousness and the semi-dream state that we have within the hypnagogic state gives us an opportunity to follow a line of thought which can clear away problems in an almost magical way. Learning to use incantations, colour and symbolism in this state can be highly productive. One such incantation might be:

May the good I have done remain,
May the wrongs I have done be washed away.

At this time the mind is in idling mode, when a review of the day can lead to insights about our behaviour or beliefs in surprising ways. By using this pre-sleep state to 'download' each day's material, the mind can then bring forward deeper and more meaningful images in dreams, the understanding of which eventually allow us to take more control of our lives. The Daily Audit Plan on page 338 helps with this process. We learn to dream magically and creatively rather than simply using dreaming as a dumping ground. We then start the next day with a clean slate, and can use the hypnopompic state to bring order to the coming day.

This can be an exciting time, and can open up all sorts of possibilities, such as the exploration of telepathy, ESP (extra-sensory perception), healing and so on. It is our choice as to which route of exploration we wish to undertake.

By their very nature, flashes of ESP are symbolic and indistinct. When they occur spontaneously in the 'hypno' states they are more readily accepted as valid, and capable of interpretation in the same way as dream images. By becoming more practised at working in that state, we become more able to use the magical and psychic senses if we so wish. We are able to make use of a far more creative input than our 'normal' awareness.

RELAXATION, MEDITATION AND VISUALIZATION

As aids to dreaming, the techniques of relaxation, meditation and visualization are all excellent tools. The more proficient you become in these techniques the easier it is to attain creative dreaming. Some suggestions are included below:

Relaxation Technique

An easy relaxation technique, which can be performed whether or not you choose to use meditation, is as follows:

* Beginning with the toes, first tighten and relax all the muscles in your body, so that you are able to identify the difference between tight and relaxed.
* Tighten each part of your body in turn.
* First tighten the toes and let go. Do this three times.
* Then tighten the ankles and release them. Again repeat three times.
* Tighten the calves and let go. Again repeat three times.
* Tighten the thighs and let go. Repeat twice more.
* Finally for this part, tighten the full length of your legs completely and release, again repeating three times. (This exercise is good for restless leg syndrome.)
* Now move on to the rest of your body.
* Repeating three times for each part, tighten in turn your buttocks, your stomach, your spine, your neck, your hands, your arms and your neck (again), your face and your scalp.
* Finally, tighten every single muscle you have used, and let go completely. Repeat three times. By now you should recognize the difference between the state of relaxation at the beginning of the exercise and the one at the end.

In time, with practice you should be able to relax completely just by doing the last part of the exercise, but for now be content with taking yourself slowly through the process.

Meditation

One of the best ways of helping both dreaming and working magically is meditation. When you train yourself to recall material that you need and use personal symbolism you improve your ability to concentrate and be aware. Practising regularly brings many benefits. The aim in meditation is to keep the mind alert yet relaxed, and focused upon a single subject, rather than to listen to the 'chatterbox' in your head. A short period of meditation or creative visualization last thing at night gives you access to the full creative world of dreams, while a similar period in the morning allows you to work with and understand the dreams you have had.

Meditation Techniques

First, choose a place where you will not be disturbed, remembering to disconnect telephones, pagers and computers. To begin with, five minutes' meditation is enough.

❖ Sit in an upright chair or cross-legged on the floor with your back supported if necessary; it is important to be as comfortable as possible, although probably not to lie down, since you may fall asleep before the process of meditation is completed.

❖ Partially close your eyes to shut out the everyday world, or close your eyes completely. If you are an experienced meditator, you may find it easier to focus your eyes on the bridge of your nose or the middle of your forehead.

❖ Begin to breathe evenly and deeply; initially breathe in for a count of four and out for a count of four. Once this rhythm is established, breathe out slightly longer than you breathe in but at a rate that is still comfortable for you.

❖ Rather than being conscious of your breathing, become more aware of the breath itself. As you inhale, breathe in peace and tranquillity; as you exhale, breathe out negativity. It should be possible to achieve a deep state of awareness. Any stray thoughts can be noted and dealt with later.

❖ At night you may instruct yourself to remember any dreams that may follow, or consider any problem you may wish to solve. You may also use this period to visualize creatively something that you desire, so that this may be carried over into your dreams.

Sometimes the best structure of a spell can present itself for consideration at this time. Obviously in the morning your concentration may be focused on the solution to your problem, the realization of your desires or a magical technique, which can help achieve the result you need.

As you practise more you may find that your period of meditation will last anything up to 20 minutes. When you finish the meditation, try to keep your mind as clear as possible. Keep your physical movements unhurried, flowing in harmony with your tranquil state in preparation for magical working.

Dream Incubation

When we learn how to ask for guidance and help through dreams, or choose to make life-changing decisions using magical means, we are truly becoming creative. This ties in with the belief that somewhere within there is a part of us that knows what is the best, or ideal, course of action. This aspect is called, by some, the Higher Self. Often we are not consciously aware of it, but giving ourselves permission to access it through dreams can have a profound effect on the way we manage our lives.

Obviously the Higher Self can be effectively used for problem-solving, and for clarifying feelings we cannot otherwise handle. However, more importantly, working with dreams can give us ways of dealing with our own fears and doubts. This leads to the positive use of power to enhance our natural abilities and talents. There is then the potential to obtain results in what often seems to be a magical way. To drive away bad dreams you may like to hang a dream catcher by your bed as the Native Americans do, or to carry out the following spell to achieve the same purpose.

To Drive Away Bad Dreams

This spell uses herbal magic and correspondences to clear the bedroom of negative influence. It is often a good idea to use material that is easily available, so you might use sprigs of rosemary, sage, Lady's bedstraw, maize silks or broom-corn. Since you want something taken away you should perform this magical working as the Moon wanes.

YOU WILL NEED ──────────────
Bowl of warm water
Salt
Your chosen sprigs of herbs
String

METHOD

✤ Dissolve the salt in the warm water.

✤ Tie the herbs together.

✤ Dip the sprigs in the water and sprinkle the corners of the room with the water.

✤ Use the sprigs to sprinkle the salt water on your bedclothes, and particularly round the head and foot of the bed.

✤ When you have done this, place the herbs under your pillow, or if you prefer, under the middle of the bed.

✤ The next morning, discard the herbs at a crossroads if you can, either by burying them or allowing them to disperse to the four winds. Otherwise ensure that you have carried them well away from your home.

✤ This carries all negativity away from your bedroom and bed.

This spell uses rosemary which brings clarity, sage for wisdom, ladies bedstraw which is said to have lined the manger at Christ's birth, and broom corn, which is used in worship of the Mexican goddess Chicomecohuatl. All these herbs bring cleansing, not just of the room but also of the occupant's aura or subtle energy. On the basis that one should always replace negative with positive, you may like to use the following technique to bring about positive dreams.

Having prepared your environment, this next technique is of most use when there is a strong, deeply felt association with the issue or request being considered – in magical terms, ideal conditions for spell working. It is like being able to consult an encyclopedia that contains a wealth of information – in fact, the Higher Self.

Asking for the Dreams you Want

This works perhaps most effectively for those who have already learnt how to recall and record their dreams as shown below. These methods have already established the lines of communication, but it also works well for those who have learnt to meditate, or for those who use other kinds of self-management tools such as creative visualization or chanting. The technique is a very easy one, particularly if you have learned through work or other experience to remain focused on issues at hand.

✤ Use as a memory jogger the word 'CARDS', which stands for the following points:
  • Clarify the issue
  • Ask the question
  • Repeat it
  • Dream and document it
  • Study the dream

'**C**' means that you spend some time in clarifying exactly what the issue really is. When you identify the basic aspects of what seems to be blocking your progress or where you are stuck, you can gain some insight into your own mental processes. You have thus prepared the groundwork.

Try to state the issue as positively as you can; for example 'Promotion passes me by' rather than 'I am not getting promoted'. The subconscious tends to latch on to negative statements rather than positive, so if you state the problem negatively you are allowing negative energy to gain a foothold. Don't try to resolve the situation at that point.

'**A**' suggests that you ask the appropriate question using an old journalistic technique: 'Who? What? Where? When? Why?' Then sort out in your own mind exactly what the relevant question is. For instance, in our example, you might ask:

Who can best help in my search for promotion?
What must I do to be in line for promotion?
Where do the best opportunities lie for me?
When will I be able to use my greater experience?
Why is my expertise not being recognized?

You can see that all these questions are open questions, and are not necessarily tied to any time frame. They do allow you to decide where your knowledge of magical influence or spell making is best applied. If you ask a confused question you may well get a confusing answer, so try to get as close to the heart of the matter as you can. Conversely, by asking inappropriate questions you may notch up answers you do not wish to have.

Repeat the question. Just as restating an incantation builds up power, by repeating the question over and over you are fixing it in the subconscious. Blocks of three repetitions often work very well, so repeating three sets of three (nine times in all) means that it should have reached deep into your unconscious.

As you compose yourself for sleep and use your relaxation techniques, tell yourself that you will have a dream that will give you an answer to your question or problem. Dream command means informing your inner self that you will have a dream that will help. If you wish, as you repeat the question tap lightly on your third eye in the centre of your forehead.

One word of warning. The dreaming self is quite wayward, so to begin with you may not receive an answer on the night you request it. You may only receive part of an answer, or nothing for several nights, and then a series of dreams that tell you what you need to know. It is a highly individual process, and no one can tell you how it should be. With time you will recognize your own pattern, but be prepared to be patient with yourself.

Dream it. When you do dream, document it briefly as soon as you can, noting down the main theme, and anything else you consider might help you in your magical practice.

Study the dream in more detail when you have time enough to do so. Look carefully at the imagery within the dream, which will probably be fairly clear-cut and straightforward. Look for details, clues and hidden meanings, see whether you can apply any of them to situations in your normal everyday life, and use your knowledge of symbolism to help you decide whether developing a spell or ritual will make your life more fulfilling or easier to handle. Sometimes the suggestion for a new way of acting or the answer to a question can come from applying the information to a different part of your life, before you even get down to tackling the question you have asked.

As you become more proficient at dealing with the information that becomes available to you, you may find the nature of your questions changes and becomes much more pro-active. For instance, you may find yourself asking, 'How can I make so and so happen?' or 'What if I did . . ?' This is true creativity and gives you the opportunity to practise your spell making and your magic in a number of different ways.

It is the exciting process of the appearance of the magical 'you' appearing in your external life.

A Dream Journal

Keeping a dream journal – that is, recording each and every one of the dreams you can recall – can be a fascinating but a somewhat difficult task. Over a period of time, while it can give you information from all sorts of angles, it is an extremely efficient tool in magical working.

You may find that you go through a period when most or all of your dreams seem to be around a particular theme, for instance that of the Gods and Goddesses. Thinking that you have understood that series of dreams, you can explore the theme in waking life and enhance your knowledge.

It can be interesting to discover months, or perhaps years, later that the same pattern and theme recurs, with additional information and clarity. By keeping a dream journal at the same time as recording the methods and results of your magical spells, you are able to follow and to chart your own progress in becoming adept at magic.

The dreaming self is highly efficient in that it will present information in different ways until you have got the message. Equally, that same dreaming self can be very inefficient in that the information can be shrouded in extraneous material and symbolism, that will need teasing out of the rubbish. It is up to you to decide which explanation is more relevant, so if you are using your dreams as a magical tool you will interpret them in that light.

Keeping a Dream Journal

A dream journal allows you to assess not just the content of your dreams, but also the pattern of your dreaming. Many people seem to be highly prolific dreamers, others less so, and many more have what could be called 'big' dreams very rarely. In fact, we all dream at some point every night, often without remembering, though it does appear that the more we learn to remember our dreams the more proficient we become at dreaming. It is as though the more we use the 'muscle' the better it responds.

* Any paper and writing implements can be used – whatever is most pleasing to you, though it can add extra power if you have prepared your journal and implements specially. You could prepare them according to the technique for magical writing.
* Always keep your recording implements at hand. You can if you wish use a tape recorder to record your dream. 'Speaking' the dream fixes it in your mind in a particular way, enabling you to be in touch with the feelings and emotions of the dream. It is sometimes easier to explain the dream in the present tense. For instance, 'I am standing on a hill' rather than, 'I was standing on a hill'.
* Write the account of the dream as soon as possible after waking. Not everyone is interested in analysing their dreams, but keeping an account of the more inexplicable or 'way-out' kind is helpful.
* Use as much detail as possible. A hastily scribbled dream is much less easy to decipher than one which goes into more detail.
* Be consistent in the way that you record your dreams. One simple scheme is given below.
* If attempting to learn how to use your dreams magically, note at which point you become aware that you are dreaming.

Recording your Dreams

This technique is an easy way for you to record your dreams. Obviously the first three parts only need to be recorded if you intend to submit your dream to an outside source. If you intend to keep your dream journal private, this method gives you the opportunity to look carefully at each of your dreams and return to them at a later date if necessary, perhaps to compare content, scenarios or other aspects. It can also allow you to quantify your own progress in the art of self-development.

* Name
* Age
* Gender
* Date of dream
* Where were you when you recalled the dream?
* State the content of dream

* Write down anything odd about the dream (e.g. animals, bizarre situations etc.)
* What were your feelings in/about the dream?

DREAM MANAGEMENT

If you are just beginning to record your dreams the important thing is not to try too hard. Being relaxed about the whole thing will give far more potential for success than getting worked up because you cannot remember your dream or because you do not appear to have dreamed at all. The more you practise the easier it becomes.

If you do decide to keep a dream journal it is worthwhile incorporating it in the preparation for your night's sleep. By making these preparations into something of a ritual it can help to concentrate your mind on the activity of dreaming, and thinking over a situation before you go to sleep, or meditating on it, can help to open the doors of the unconscious to some of the answers you are seeking.

Carefully laying out your tools, rereading some of your old dreams, using deep relaxation methods, assisted by relaxing oils or herb teas, and even asking the superconscious for usable material, can all assist in the creative dreaming process.

Sleep

In myth, Hypnos, the god of sleep, was usually personified in winged form as one of the inevitable forces of nature. He is always pictured as young and fair though some say he was the father of Morpheus, the god of dreams. A sip from Hypnos' cup or a touch from his staff is said by some to send you into blissful sleep until his mother, Nyx (Night), has fled the sky.

YOU WILL NEED
Cup of herbal tea such as chamomile
Dream journal
Pen
Crystal to help with dreams such as diaspor or jade

METHOD
* Hold the cup in both hands and say:

Hypnos, Lord of Sleep, son of Night
Bless this cup and give me rest
That I may benefit from all your might
And know forever what is best

❖ Drink from the cup.
❖ Put the journal and the pen together, close to your bed, with the crystal on top.
❖ Say:

Morpheus Morpheus, shaper of dreams
Crafter of light not all that it seems
Send me now, images fit only for kings
Those that fulfil my deepest yearnings
Let me remember all that I learn
True to myself, to you I now turn

❖ Now compose yourself for sleep and await developments.

Morpheus had special responsibility for the dreams of kings and heroes, and gave shape to those beings who inhabit dreams. He is petitioned here in the knowledge that you are a monarchs of all you survey and that your journal will help you to understand.

On waking

In the morning, try to wake up naturally, without the shrill call of an alarm clock. There are various devices on the market such as daylight simulators that come on gradually, dimmer switches, and clocks that have a soft alarm, graduating in intensity. Even a radio or tape recorder programmed to play soft relaxing music can be used. Using such waking aids can help you eventually to hold on to the hypnagogic state and use it creatively. It is worth noting that some dreamers have reported that the spoken word seems to chase away a dream.

On waking, lie as still as possible for a moment, and try to recall what you have dreamt. Often it is the most startling thing or feeling which you will remember first, followed by lesser elements. Transcribe these elements into your journal, and write the 'story' of the dream. This may well give you an initial perception that is sufficient for your needs, both in the everyday and from a magical perspective.

Sometimes much can be gained from taking the dream action forward using the questions, 'What happens next?' or sometimes 'What if?'. Let us assume that your dream has been of an argument with someone who is close to you in waking life. You wake with the situation unresolved, but are aware that this suggests some inner conflict. Try then to imagine what would happen if the argument continued. Would you or your opponent 'win'? What if your opponent won? How would you feel? What if you won?

Working creatively with dreams

When you have been recording your dreams for some time you may find it useful to turn one of them into a creative project. This could be a painting, sculpture or other artistic process; it could also be a short story perhaps taking the dream further forward, a play, or even using nature creatively – it needs to be something that takes one beyond normal everyday activities. Look particularly for magical and fantasy aspects, for you are trying to access the world of magic in a slightly different way from that of ordinary spell making and ritual.

By acknowledging the creative processes in dreams and making them tangible within the normal sphere of reality, you are opening yourself up to all sorts of possibilities and changes of consciousness. In the Dream Spells and Techniques section overleaf there are suggestions for setting up such creative projects.

One of the benefits of deliberately dreaming creatively is a different perception of events in the world around you. Colours may appear more vibrant, shapes sharper, and sounds clearer. These changes can be quite subtle, but usually bring more focus to your awareness and allow you to use creativity to its best advantage in small things as well as more important ones. Life begins to take on new meaning.

Dream symbols, because they are archetypal and tap into a wider consciousness than your own, give fertile ground for meditation which can allow unconscious insights to come to the surface, giving rise to even greater creativity. You may wish to meditate on the overall feeling or one particular aspect of the dream. When you find yourself dreaming about your chosen project you have come almost full circle – from an acorn to an oak tree and back to an acorn – a situation akin to rebirth.

It does not matter whether the project is good or bad; what is important is the enjoyment that you achieve from doing it. One of the most fulfilling aspects of such a process is the realization that you have entered a stream of consciousness that belongs to all of us, but which so few manage to tap into. This 'locking on' can give a strong physical sensation as much as an emotional or spiritual one. The counter-balance to this is the number of times that you will get stuck or come up against a brick wall in this part of the process, but perseverance does brings about a greater understanding of your inner more magical self.

For the purposes of self-development you may like to keep a separate journal or record of the processes and stages of awareness experienced during this strenuous activity – it is worthwhile spending a short while each day working with your project, and a journal allows you to see how far you have travelled in this journey of discovery. It can be fascinating to see, for instance, in looking back over your daybook how you have found it easier as time goes on to recognize when the fears and doubts arise, and how you have dealt with them.

It may be that your creative journal takes precedence over the dream one or vice versa. It is possible that with time you will recognize that your dreams change when you are in a more overtly creative phase. You may be able to unblock a creative block by asking your dreams for an answer or by using the in-between states. You will gradually find that you will be able to intertwine the various states of awareness when necessary without losing the reality of each one. This is the true use of dream creativity and is truly living magically.

DREAM SPELLS AND TECHNIQUES

To have the courage to transcend any fears, doubts and barriers that we all have in becoming creative and working magically, we need to be in touch with our own 'inner being' and the creative urge that is ours by right. We must move from feeling that we are prevented by circumstances from being the person we know we can be, to taking control of our lives and being able to link to that stream of knowledge and awareness that enables us to create our future.

To do this we have to be intensely practical. To that end, this section contains the exercises, tips and techniques that will help you to develop creative dreaming. You do not necessarily need to follow the order given below, though this is the one that is probably the simplest, because it takes you from when you first remember and record your dreams to using them with full awareness.

Dreaming with intent is such an integral part of magical working and spell making that it is worthwhile taking the time to develop the art to help you to enhance conscious spell making and also to enable you to use dreaming itself as a magical tool.

Work Plan

Dreamwork can be defined as any activity that you choose to carry out once you have had a dream. It entails working initially only with the content of that particular dream. Later it can be investigated along with other dreams, to see whether it is part of a series or perhaps clarifies other previous dreams.

The dream can be looked at in several different ways. You should be able to:

❖ List all the various components.
❖ Explore the symbols with all their shades of meanings.
❖ Widen the perspectives and components.
❖ Work with the dream in as many different ways as possible to complete unfinished business.
❖ Work with the spiritual significances.
❖ Bring the message through to everyday life to make necessary choices and changes.

The components

The components of a dream are the various parts: the scenario, the people, the action, the feelings and emotions. Each has its role to play in your interpretation and it is only when you consider the dream really carefully that you will be able to appreciate some of the more subtle meanings. In lucid or creative dreaming, it is feasible to make changes to any or all of these things, though not necessarily all at once.

The more adept you become at recognizing your own individual way of creating your dreams, the easier your own interpretation will be. Making a simple list will help you to do this.

Psychologists Calvin Hall and Robert van de Castle, in an effort to be scientific, developed the method of quantitative coding which is still used nowadays in dream research. This led to the cognitive theory of dreams, which meant that dream content was divided into several categories. There were characters, emotions, interactions, misfortunes, objects and settings. By dividing dreams up in this way, they recognized that these expressed the way we see our family members, friends, social environment and the self. Dreams reflect waking concerns, interests and emotional focus. When carrying out their research they discovered that there were strong similarities in dreams from people all over the world.

The symbols

When the mind has a message to impart, it will often present the information in symbolic form. It is important, therefore, for you to understand the symbolism of your dreams. Over time, you will develop your own symbolism: certain things in dreams, which have relevant meaning for you. The conventional symbolism of dreams is very rich in imagery.

Particularly in magical work, it is worth while taking a thorough look at your dreams, so that any symbols within them can be properly interpreted. Any good dream interpretation book will act as a starting point. With any of your dreams, it is useful to make an alphabetical list of your dream content and then decide whether it can be interpreted symbolically rather than literally.

The perspectives

Perhaps the most satisfactory dreamwork is deliberately to widen the perspective within the dream and consciously to push it further. Thus, you might like to see what would happen next to one of the characters. For example, what would happen if the action that was being carried out were continued? How would the other characters react? How would this change the dream? If a particular character acted in a different manner, would the whole dream change, or only parts of it? How much would you want characters to support you or leave you alone?

You can see that these considerations mark the beginning of you taking control within your dream, and you are therefore moving more authoritatively into dreaming magically. Another way in which you can change perspective is to look at your dream as if you were one of the characters. If this were so, would you 'direct' the dream differently? Would there be a different outcome? Working with your dream in this way enables you to become more aware of the effect on various parts of your personality (the characters in your dream).

Working with your dreams

You can use any approach you are comfortable with to look at issues connected with your dreams. You might like to use either the Jungian method of working, or those shown on pages 341–343. The Jungian method recognizes the archetypes (basic constructs) as important elements of everyone's personality. It is these that give us myths and fairy tales.

Working with the spiritual significances

From the idea that God, as seen in primitive societies, gives dreams, we would speak nowadays more of a recognition of spiritual influences. This is when your truly altruistic and selfless side recognizes that you must make adjustments to your everyday behaviour if you are to live your life as fully as possible. Magical working takes on new meaning when your intuition informs your everyday spell making.

By and large, the spiritual significance of a dream has much to do with your sense of responsibility to the rest of your community or the world in which you live. If a dream does not allow itself to be interpreted in any other way, you may wish to interpret it from the perspective of the Greater Good – that which benefits mankind rather than just the individual. The three things to look for here are right thought, right speech and right action. The questions you might ask yourself are: How does this dream help me to be a better person? What information does it give me to help others? What fresh understanding does this dream bring me?

Bringing the message through

Once you have learnt to explore dreams in several different ways, you will be able to practise new patterns of behaviour, think in new ways, change some attitudes and create a new way of being. As time goes on, you will find that you can, in the dream state, practise your new mode of behaviour carefully before actually making radical changes in your everyday life. You should also be able to get a fair idea of what effect your behaviour will have on other people in your life.

You will find various techniques and spells throughout this section for expanding your dreams and learning how to work magically through them. If you are to use your dreams to help you to deal effectively with your everyday life, there are certain techniques that you must practise first, in order to clear your mind successfully so that you can work perceptively and honestly with magical energies.

Daily Audit Plan

As part of your nightly routine to clear your mind initially for dreaming, and later for magical working, it is wise to do what might be called a daily audit. This consists of doing a review of your day and balancing the good with the bad. You might like to concentrate on your behaviour and decide whether you have acted appropriately or not, or simply to decide which parts and actions of the day have been productive and which not. Your audit will be of the issues that concern you most at that particular time. Your starting point should be the hour immediately preceding bedtime – you should then work backwards throughout the day until you reach your time of awakening.

✤ Take a sheet of paper and divide it into two columns. On one side list actions and types of behaviour you consider 'good' and on the other those you consider 'bad' or 'indifferent'.
✤ Looking at the bad side first, review where your behaviour or action could be improved

and resolve to do better in the future. You may like to develop a technique for yourself that represents your rejection of the disliked patterns of behaviour. This can be as simple as writing down the behaviour and discarding the paper on which it is written; you may choose to use the Bay Leaves spell shown below.

✤ Now look at the good side and give yourself approval and encouragement for having done well. Resolve to have more of the good behaviour and, if you wish, form an affirmation which indicates this.
✤ Where your behaviour has been indifferent, resolve to do better and to give yourself more positive feedback for having made the effort.
✤ Forgive yourself for not having achieved a best result and praise yourself for doing your best. This is the aspect of 'balancing your books'. Now let your day go, do not dwell on the negatives and go peacefully to sleep.

This exercise helps in the process of keeping you spiritually strong and clear in your purpose.

Bay Leaves Spell

This spell uses plant magic and fire to achieve its purpose. The bay leaf possesses powerful magical properties. The first part is best done at the time of the New Moon, and the result will often have come to pass by the time of the Full Moon.

YOU WILL NEED
3 bay leaves
Paper or parchment
Pen
Candle

METHOD
✤ Write down your intent to change your behaviour three times on the paper, repeating the wish aloud.
✤ Place the bay leaves on the paper.
✤ Fold the paper into thirds and visualize your wish coming true. Now fold the paper into thirds once again and hide it away in a dark place. Keep visualizing your behaviour changing as you do this.

❖ Once you are satisfied with your new behaviour, light the candle and burn the paper in the flame as a thank you. Allow the candle to burn out.

Bay promotes wisdom, so protects you from making mistakes. This is obviously a spell best done in private. You should never reveal your intent to others, so be very clear that the intent is for the Greater Good.

Remembering your Dreams

To be able to remember your dreams, and to use them as magical tools, you need to train yourself to remember most of the content of your dreams. Good-quality sleep is the first prerequisite for this since, while you are training yourself, you may find you wake up fairly frequently. Later you will be able to remember both small and important dreams, but first of all you must get into the habit of a particular routine.

❖ If you have an illness or are taking medication, please check with your doctor or medical practitioner before undertaking this exercise.
❖ Decide which sleep periods you are going to monitor. A good idea is to give yourself an approximate four-hour period to have a proper sleep, then to monitor everything after that.
❖ Set your alarm or wake-up device – preferably soft light or soothing music – for the time you wish to wake. Under no circumstances allow yourself to be 'shocked' into wakefulness, for example, by very loud music. It is counter-productive because it is most likely to chase away the dream.
❖ When you have woken up, lie perfectly still. Do not move until you have recalled your dream with as much detail as you can remember.
❖ Write down your dream, including as much information as you can, and work with it – for instance, noting symbols or ideas for magical working – when you are ready to do so.
❖ It is here that your dream journal will come in useful, because in it you will also be able to record fragments of dreams, which at the time may not seem to have relevance but, later on, may do so.
❖ Dreams are thought to be remembered best from periods of Rapid Eye Movement sleep, so with practice you should begin to discover when these periods are. Don't be too worried if at first your dream recall seems to be deficient. You will get better each time with practice.
❖ Try not to let the affairs of the day get in the way when you first wake up. You can begin to consider them when you have paid attention to, and taken notice of, your mind's night-time activity.

How to have a 'Magical' Dream

This technique is extremely simple and is a potent tool in dealing with our own internal gremlins. More importantly, it is a way of raising our consciousness and of developing our ability to access our creative, magical minds. However, unless you hit upon it involuntarily, this is a technique that needs some training. Try not to be disappointed in the results you achieve at first, since it can be guaranteed that you improve with practice if you have the patience.

1. Prepare yourself for sleep
As you prepare yourself for sleep, give yourself the instruction that tonight you will have a creative or magical dream. Form an affirmation of intent along the lines of a very simple statement such as, 'Tonight my dream will be magical.' Keep the statement that simple because you are simply learning to open your mind to possibilities. The content of the dream does not actually matter at this point.

2. Repeat your affirmation
Repeat your affirmation, either out loud or to yourself, as many times as you need to in order to fix it in your own mind. This in itself is helpful, since it is teaching you how to focus your mind on one thing at a time. An affirmation is a simple, positive statement encapsulating as succinctly as possible what you intend to happen.

3. Hold your intent in mind

Keep your mind on your intention, and then allow yourself to drift off into sleep.

4. Note your degree of awareness

When you wake up, note the time and whether you remember having been an observer or a participant in your dream. Also note how long you think you were in that state of awareness. Your estimation will probably not be very accurate to begin with, but this does not matter, since you will become more proficient as time goes on.

Incubating a Specific Magical Dream

When you have had some success with incubating (creating or growing) the type of dream that you want using the CARDS method shown on page 332, you can then progress to developing a specifically magical dream. Do be patient with yourself, because you may not at first find that you have created the exact environment or content you want. Gradually, however you will find you are 'hitting target' more and more often.

Practise this technique at times when you know you will be able to make use of the information, record it, or carry out research to resolve any doubts that may need further explanation.

1. Prepare the focus of your dream

This might be to understand a particular ritual, discover the correct incense or herb to use for best results or even to develop a new spell. Before you go to bed, take the time to narrow your thoughts down to a single idea or query which states clearly the subject of your concern. Do remember that although you are focusing on this single idea, you are also seeking the widest – or perhaps most important – information you can access, so this may manifest in more than one dream.

Write your idea or query down and use a visual image, such as a picture or appropriate symbol, to fix the idea in your mind. Memorize the idea or query and visual image. Try to incorporate a trigger word, sound or symbol

which alerts you to a deeper state of awareness. Remind yourself that when you dream of that particular trigger you will know that you are dreaming. Repeat to yourself at least three times 'When I dream of [whatever you have decided], I will remember that I am dreaming.'

2. Go to bed

It is important not to let anything else intrude on your concentration. So, without further ado, go to bed and make yourself comfortable.

3. Keep the phrase or image in your mind

Concentrate on your phrase and image and deepen your awareness. Imagine yourself already dreaming about your query. As you become more proficient at controlling your dreams, if there is something you want to experiment with in the dream, such as flying, concentrate on the idea of being in full control.

4. Meditate on the phrase

Keep your objective in focus until you fall asleep. If at all possible, don't let any other thoughts come between thinking about your issue and falling asleep. If your thoughts wander, just revert to thinking about your phrase and its magical significance.

5. Follow your focus

When you have begun dreaming, try to be extra-aware of matters pertaining to the issue in hand. Do not try to take control of your dream, since you are allowing your own unconscious self – that part that is in contact with all magical and other knowledge – to 'speak' to you through the dream. Accept that symbols and information will appear which can be sorted out afterwards and allow the dream to reach its own fulfilment. Note your impressions and be aware of as much of the content of the dream as you can.

6. Keep the dream active and sustain it if you can

Remember that magical information has a language all of its own and often needs interpreting in more than one way. While you do not need to take control of the dream, you do need to trust your own intuition to be aware of how much information it can assimilate. For this reason, you should learn that it is possible to go back into a dream in order to highlight issues that have not been fully understood.

7. Returning to the everyday

As you wake up, try to remain for a time in the hypnopompic (half-awake) state and learn to check whether you feel you have received adequate information in order to proceed. Finally, rouse yourself to full consciousness, and be ready to record everything that you have learnt.

8. Record the dream

Record the dream as shown previously, deciding exactly how it has answered your question or intent.

Analysing your Dream

You will want to get into the habit of analysing the content of your dreams more fully for magical significances. A simple way to do this is to divide it into segments so that you can consider each part of the dream and whether it had any relevance to your magical workings or not. For instance, dreaming of one of the gods or goddesses might alert you to the whole realm of their rulership of herbs, crystals and other magical necessities. The main theme of the dream may open up a number of other possibilities which you have not previously considered.

Make the following headings under which to analyse your dream:

+ The dream.
+ The dream segments.
+ The differences/similarities in the segments.
+ The main theme of the dream.

ADVANCED TECHNIQUES

Now, having practised all of the basic techniques for magical dreaming, you are ready to move on to the more advanced methods. Before you do that, however, take time to consolidate what you have learnt. Think carefully about what you have been doing and consider whether you are satisfied with the results.

+ Is there anything that you could do to improve your methods?
+ Do you want to try anything else?
+ What do you now want to happen?
+ How do you want to use magical dreaming in the future?
+ Do you need to do further research?
+ Do you want to put yourself in touch with other people who are practising magical dreaming?

The more advanced techniques help you to focus on your objectives, and to decide whether you are more interested in researching the actual technique or whether you want to be creative and help to make things happen.

It often helps to alter the way you express yourself to accommodate the creativity of dreams. If your day-to-day way of self-expression is through words, then experiment with colour or with form. If you enjoy music, try to find a particular piece that expresses the mood of your dream. If you are a sedentary sort of person, express elements of the dream through movement such as dance or Eastern disciplines of t'ai chi or qi gung. The basic idea is that you can use your dreams to enhance your creativity in everyday life. They can act as starting points for projects or they can be used to explore other modes of self-expression.

Directing your Dreams

This technique is a way of achieving changes of a mystical kind. Learning the technique helps to consolidate the idea of being able to create magical changes in your own environment. At this stage it is more a matter of actually changing the environment in which your dream takes place. Remember that you can do anything you please in the dream state, and later may be able to effect changes in your everyday life. This is an extension of creative visualization. You can either use the idea of the 'big screen' or of a stage production.

+ Begin with a remembered dream. Start by changing something small in it and gradually work up to bigger changes.

341

+ Replay the dream and do everything at different speeds. Play with what you are creating, using your imagination to manipulate the dream reality. It is important to have fun with this since you are deliberately operating your creative ability.

+ You might then like to think of yourself as the director and producer of your own play. You can use any props you like and experiment to achieve the right atmosphere.

+ Follow this up by creating a stage set for your next learning experience.

+ Recognize that you are creating a reality that has many possibilities but you have the power to chose your own.

The IFE Technique

Life teaches us that we have to have restrictions. From an early age we learn what is acceptable behaviour and what is not. On the whole we are taught that to be spontaneous is dangerous, and we must be 'sensible'. Within the framework of creativity and magical dreams, however, we have the freedom to be totally eccentric and to use patterns of behaviour which re-educate us in the art of personal freedom.

Most creative people have a very highly developed ability to create fantasies. If you dare to take spell making to its limits you will find that you are capable of doing and being things that are not possible except in an altered state of consciousness, just as the magicians of old used to do. Shape shifting is one example of this.

One yoga exercise that is designed to give a sense of the meaning of life is to try to discover what it is like to be a tree or flower or an otherwise sentient (aware) being. This exercise consists of three stages, which we call here the IFE Technique.

+ Imagine what it would be like to be your chosen object.
+ Feel how the object feels.
+ Experience being that object.

Because the rational aspects of everyday life are suspended during creative dreams and magical working, you should be able very quickly to reach a state of awareness where it is easy to do all of these things. You could practise being the opposite sex, being an animal – domestic or otherwise – or, if you are feeling brave, being something like a rock or the sea.

Initially you will probably not be able to hold this state for very long, but with practice you will find that it becomes easier, and that you can widen your perception to encompass other states of being as well. You might, for instance, try to experience what it would be like to be suspended in space or time, to belong to other worlds or even to sense what you will be like in 20 years' time.

When you are suitably relaxed, it is also possible to use other techniques to help you in the art of magical working.

+ A simple way of preparing for creative dreaming and magical working is to use contemplation. In this, as a precursor to meditation, you give yourself a visual image of the subject in hand.

+ You might, for instance, think of the words 'spell making' as being carved out of a block of wood. Holding this image in your mind, let it develop in its own way and just watch what happens.

+ You might wish to consider the idea of a visit to Egypt or some other far-flung country to enhance your magical workings, so again you hold the idea in your mind and contemplate it. This might lead to the opportunity for an actual visit or a dream which clarifies an issue for you.

+ When you have become proficient at contemplation, you can then attempt meditation, which is a further stage of allowing the image or thought to develop spontaneously of its own accord. You may then wish to take the results of your meditation back into creative dreaming and magical working.

Crystals

Many people believe that working with crystals can enhance dreaming and help us to access the wisdom that is available for each of us through these natural objects. It is as though the subtle energies act as both receivers and transmitters and give the ability to tune into those aspects of knowledge both of ourselves and of the world in which we live.

Most good crystal or New Age shops will have a good selection of stones and their meanings. It is a simple matter to programme your crystals in a similar way to the method shown in Consecrating Altar Objects on page 231 in order to help you in your dream work.

Understanding Archetypal Images

Archetypal images are basic concepts, patterns and symbols that we all have hidden in the collective unconscious until we choose to activate them. They appear in dreams, mythology and fairy tales and are a rich source of imagery in magical working. On page 110 there is a meditation using Tarot. The basics are repeated here since the same method can be used for myths, planets, numbers and so on.

Tarot

In the case of the Tarot, you use the cards as a mental and visual starting point to help you to make sense of them and the feelings they evoke in you. There are eight steps to this process:

1. Sit quietly where you will not be interrupted.
2. Holding the card you have chosen from your own pack, look at it in detail. What comes to mind as you do so?
3. Think about your own life at this moment and how the card you have chosen applies to you. How can you apply your knowledge of the meanings of the card in the situations in which you find yourself?
4. Contemplate the card and allow yourself to feel how powerful the energy of the image is.
5. Now close your eyes and try to visualize yourself as part of the action of the card. How does it feel to be the main character? How do you interact with the other aspects of the card?
6. Determine that the energies of the card will become part of your magical vocabulary and that its power can be accessed through dreams.
7. Note in your journal which card you have chosen and go to sleep with it in mind.
8. When you wake up, note down your dream as usual with particular relevance to the card

you studied the night before. It may be that one of the apparently minor aspects of the card comes to prominence and has specific relevance to you and your lifestyle.

Myths, Astrological Planets and Numbers

These can be treated in a similar way to the Tarot:

1. Choose a particular trigger – a myth, planet or number – and think about how the story, or the qualities, might apply to your life at this moment.
2. Contemplate the story or qualities and feel how powerful they are. Here you are preparing to use both imagination and visualization.
3. Put yourself in the position you wish to be in, that is, as a character in the myth, on a planet or expressing its qualities. Imagine what it would be like to be part of that scenario. If working with numbers, think of the qualities of the number you have chosen and sense them within you (see pages 132–134).
4. You might like to use your sense of shape – a square, a pentagram and so on – to explore its qualities. A pentagram will feel different from a square and this is truly exploring the meaning of numbers and shape. This is the beginning of an understanding of sacred geometry (see page 17). Gradually you should be able to become aware of the qualities of each shape and can progress to a more solid shape.
5. Try testing the boundaries of that shape and move the figure to be larger or smaller. Play with the shape in any way you like. Make it into a solid object and try to find out what it would be like to be inside such an object.
6. Allow yourself to go to sleep and remember that with enhanced awareness you can do anything you choose. Dreams triggered by myths, planets, archetypal images and so forth will have a far deeper content than 'ordinary' dreams. They are a rich library of magical knowledge.

CREATIVE PROJECTS

Dreaming is fertile ground for the development of creative projects. Such projects help to ground the energy developed in dreaming and mean that you have a tangible manifestation of the energy available to you. Your starting point can be a dream which triggers off ideas or ideas which you develop through dreams – or both. Remember that the process of creativity has its roots in magic and manifestation, since in effect you are creating something out of nothing.

1. Choose a dream that is best suited to the project in hand. This could perhaps be a story, play or dance. Make a note of the original idea in your creative journal.
2. Write down the titles of pieces of music, paintings, poems and so on which appeal and fit your theme. Be alert to words you might use or shapes that interest you. Spend some time thinking about your project and enjoy the research entailed, perhaps at the same time asking for suitable dream content.
3. Make as many notes as you like and if you have been in the habit of recording your dreams, look to see whether some of the images can be used in this project. You can also use the technique given above in Understanding Archetypal Images.
4. You will often find that you go through a particularly productive period, though sometimes you may feel very stuck. Make a note of any problems and negativities that arise in creating the project. These can be resolved through directed dreaming.
5. It is worthwhile carrying a notebook or tape recorder with you at all times, so that you can note down any inspirations that occur. This may also give you further material for other creative work.
6. You may find you run out of enough energy to complete the project. Meditation, contemplation and even working a spell to clear the blockages or give you extra energy may all help to give you the impetus to finish off what you have started.

You will note that there are several instances where dreaming is used to help in the process of creativity. This is perhaps one of the best outcomes of the art of creative dreaming: to realize that you have within you a huge store of previously untapped energy which is now accessible.

Focused Reverie

By the time you have begun to make your dreams work for you, you are in a position to manipulate your dreams even further. Almost inevitably we come up against the question of whether the technique about to be described is lucid dreaming or not. While it is described here as focused reverie, it really does not matter what name you choose to give it. The technique is to remember the dream up to the time you woke up, then consciously choose to take the dream as a whole forward.

It has already been suggested that you might work with characters and objects in your dream. This method can be extended to include the whole dream and simply allows the dream to continue in its own way. The steps to achieve this are quite simple:

1. Remembering the dream as it was, make contact with each part of the dream as though it were still happening to you.
2. Now put yourself in the position of observer and allow the dream to unfold around you.
3. Do not attempt to influence the dream at all. Just allow it to happen.
4. If the action or characters get stuck, then assume that that is the point at which you would have woken up.
5. Think about why the dream will not go any further. Resolve to deal with any issues that might arise.
6. You might choose to influence your future dreams in the light of what you discover.

This technique is in effect a kind of meditation or waking dream and unites the dream state with the ordinary everyday world.

SLEEPING AND DREAMING SPELLS AND TECHNIQUES

Anyone who decides to become a spell worker, magician or adept will very quickly appreciate the tool that sleep is. It rejuvenates, revitalizes and indeed with practice becomes a carrier for the magic that one instigates. Included below are several techniques and spells designed to make use of the tool par excellence.

To Make a Dream Pillow

Dream pillows may be used for several purposes. You can use them to enhance sleep, in which case any of the following six herbs may be used: catnip, hops, lavender, thyme, valerian, vervain (to prevent nightmares). Should you wish to affect your dreams, you can also consult the incense section and use the herbs listed for Psychic Powers, Divination and Prophetic Dreams.

YOU WILL NEED

1 part each of at least five dried herbs from those shown above
Bowl
Dried orange and lemon peel
¹/₂ part mugwort
1 part myrrh or frankincense resin
2 pieces of lightweight cloth such as muslin
Needle and thread
Your personal choice of decoration, e.g. ribbon, buttons

METHOD

✤ Burn a little of the frankincense or myrrh resin to cleanse your working area.
✤ Mix the five dried herbs in the bowl in whatever proportion feels right. While doing this, think carefully about the purpose of your dream pillow; for example hops will give a sound sleep, mugwort induces psychic dreaming and camomile promotes a feeling of wellbeing.
✤ Crumble the dried peels into small pieces and add the rest of the finely ground resin to this mixture.
✤ Sew together three sides of the material, leaving one side open so you can easily fill the pillow with the herbs. Make a mental link with Hypnos, the Greek God of sleep or Demeter, Earth Mother.
✤ Decorate the bags with magical symbols, Moons or your own personal preferences. Fill the pillow (not too full) with the herb and resin mixture and sew up the final side. Your dream pillow is now ready for use.
✤ You may now use your dream pillow whenever you require. Slip it into your pillow case and inhale deeply.

Dream pillows are very useful if, for instance, you are away from home and need to create a certain ambience, or if you need continuity while working on a particular dream project. A typical use of a dream pillow in shown in the spell Dream Power overleaf.

A Spell for While you Sleep

Knot magic has a particular effect in 'binding' or fixing a spell in place and with the addition of colour it is possible to use ribbons to bring about a desired outcome. Various colour correspondences are shown on pages 239–240. By using your own bed as a focus, your magical work can be done while you sleep. This is a very personal way of working and one which can bring particularly positive results.

YOU WILL NEED

Four lengths of appropriately coloured ribbon which can be easily tied
Four pins
Your bed

METHOD

✤ If your bed has bedposts, simply knot a length of the correct colour ribbon for your purpose around each post.
✤ Each time you do this, say:

> *With this knot of coloured ribbon*
> *Bring to me the power hidden.*
> *Grant me that right*
> *Throughout this night.*

✤ If your bed has no posts then carefully pin the knotted ribbon to each corner using the same words.
✤ Each night for two further nights touch each ribbon knot in turn and repeat the words above.
✤ Leave the ribbons in place until you no longer feel the need for them.

You can expect to have some fairly vivid dreams over the following three nights, which may help you to develop the qualities you seek. This spell allows your unconscious self to work in a protected space without the chatter of day to day matters.

Keep your Child Safe

This simple technique is based on an old nursery rhyme which began life as a prayer. It protects a child as they sleep and introduces them to the idea of being able to make use of their dreams. Many children go through periods of having bad dreams and this technique teaches them that they need not be afraid while in the safety of their own bed.

YOU WILL NEED

Glass of water
A clear quartz crystal
Few drops of lavender oil
Pine cone

METHOD

+ The articles above represent – in order – water, earth, air and fire and have several significances in protection spells
+ When first activating the spell, hold the crystal in your hands for a few moments to activate its protective powers. Do the same with the glass of water.
+ Drop the crystal into the water and add a few drops of lavender oil.
+ Visualize your child shielded from all harm.
+ Hold the pine cone in your hands and ask for its powers of regeneration to be activated. Place the charged glass and the pine cone together on the bedside table.
+ Repeat the words:

Matthew, Mark, Luke and John,
Bless the bed he lies upon
Four corners to his bed,
Four angels round his head:
One to watch, one to pray,
And two to bear his troubles away!

+ Obviously if you have a little girl you will use the words 'she' and 'her' instead of 'he' and 'his'.
+ Each morning throw away the water in the glass – this is not for drinking – either down the toilet or outside your door since it is by now 'contaminated'.
+ Renew the water each night, repeating the rhyme as you do so, and refresh the other objects as you feel it necessary.

This way of working is unobtrusive and does not frighten the child. If you make the last part of this spell an aspect of the nightly routine, as your child grows up he or she might like to participate in the actions and words and should develop a sense of security because of them. If your child has nightmares, use the pine cone as part of your soothing technique by giving it to him or her to hold.

Dream Power

When you need to make someone aware of something, perhaps a healing energy or information that they need to make a decision, it is possible to influence their dreams, without them being aware that you have had anything to do with the matter. You actually make a link for them to higher authority.

YOU WILL NEED

A square of fabric
Needle and thread
Cotton wool or other stuffing
Handful of herbs or a few drops of essential oil
(preferably lavender and rosemary)
Paper and pen

METHOD

+ Sit quietly in your sacred space, gather your thoughts and decide precisely what it is you want the person to hear, or perhaps feel. Write down your wish on the piece of paper in as few words as possible.
+ Make a dream pillow using the square of fabric and stuffing. Add a quantity of lavender and rosemary or a few drops of oil. Put in the piece of paper last, then sew up the end.
+ Put the dream pillow on your altar.
+ Because this is on behalf of someone else you might wish to reinforce your sacred space for your petition. Gather your energy into your solar plexus then hold your hands over the dream pillow. As you do this, say the following:

Goddess Divine Holy Mother,
I petition you herein for another.
[Name] does not understand
Creating trouble quite unplanned
Holy Mother, Goddess Divine,

Send a dream, awaken the mind.
Show the way through, the way that's right
Give them the truth by clear starlight
Holy Mother, Goddess Divine,
Open the way for a clear sign
Bring them clarity while they sleep
So much from experience that they can reap.

✤ Change the incantation to suit your purpose if you wish.
✤ You might give the dream pillow to the person concerned as a gift or hang it in a prominent place in your own sacred space.

Remember that this does not force a person into any particular course of action. This spell allows them to make decisions that are right for them, and you know you have done all you can to help. You have acted as wisely as you know how.

Totem Animal Dream

This technique is similar to Linking With Your Totem Animal on page 180, but carries the process one stage further in that you have a special request in mind. The representation of a bear is used here, but you may choose to use your own totem animal. The more tactile this image is the better, though you would not use for instance a teddy bear, since this has become more of a fantasy animal. You need to be able to hold whatever you choose in your hand.

YOU WILL NEED

Psychic Dream incense as below
Small representation of a bear (such as a charm or toy)
Your dream journal
Pen

METHOD

✤ Burn the incense before you go to bed.
✤ Using the representation of the bear as a starting point, hold it in your hand.
✤ Visualize your bear or animal to be as lifelike as possible (only use a picture or photograph if nothing else is available). You may find that the image you finish up with is nothing like the one with which you first started – this does not matter.

✤ Ask the animal for the assistance you need. Wait quietly until you sense the animal's co-operation.
✤ Visualize the bear allowing you to climb onto its back and the two of you starting out on your journey.
✤ By now you will have achieved a slightly altered state of consciousness and can allow the bear to take control.
✤ Allow yourself to drift gently off into sleep, knowing that you are perfectly safe. Alternatively, remain in a state of waking awareness until you feel satisfied that you have received the information you need, then compose yourself for sleep.
✤ In the morning, record your dreams and impressions and correlate them to the request you made.

Often in using this method you do not receive the answer immediately, but you will find that the answer will present itself, usually within 72 hours of initiating the process. If no such answer is apparent, repeat the technique at intervals until you are confident in the result.

Sleeping and Dreaming Incenses

Finally, here are some incenses specifically geared towards sleep and dream time. Throughout the book you will find others you may deem more suitable for your own purposes. You might, for instance, burn the planetary incenses when working with planets, as in the Archetypal Image techniques above. Just a short warning; burn the incenses before you go to sleep so that you do not put yourself or other members of your household at risk.

※ Rest and Sleep Incense ※

½ part catnip
½ part dill
¼ part poppy
1 part lemon verbena
½ part motherwort
Few drops of lemon verbena oil

Note: The following two incenses can be used when you wish to enhance either aspects or the power of your dreams

※ Sleepytime Incense ※

1 part poppy seeds
1½ parts camomile
1¼ parts willow

※ Psychic Dream Incense ※

2 parts sandalwood
1 part rose
1 part camphor
Few drops of tuberose oil
Few drops of jasmine oil

※ Prophetic Dream Incense ※

2 parts frankincense resin
1 part buchu
1 part mugwort

Burn this incense before you go to bed to stimulate the psychic mind and to ensure that your conscious mind remembers your dreams in the morning.

※ End Nightmares Incense ※

1 part thyme
1 part willow
1 part camomile

Working with dreams, either creatively or magically, is, of course, a foundation for making things happen or, if you like, creating an alternative reality. The purists would perhaps say that this is not possible and it is not for us to change what is preordained. It is worth remembering that the word 'present' can also be written as pre-sent and that in effect is what you are achieving in magical dreaming. You are creating a reality which can become the one that maximizes both your potential and that of those around you. You are creating a magical world.

Conclusion

So be it

Holding fast to no particular discipline but believing that if it works then do it, we offer this encyclopaedia of spells, techniques and information as a way for you to explore your own magical creativity. Finding the magical self is a journey of exploration, which can become a lifelong task. As always, it is only possible to give guidelines – signposts along the way- as to what has worked for others and what should therefore work for you. For this reason, if a spell doesn't work for you in the way that it has been given in this book, do try it again on another occasion and use your intuition to decide what might be changed or adjusted to suit your own personality.

There are so many spells available across many disciplines that it is only possible to take a few steps along the road of exploration with you. The actions taken during the process of spell making become so individual that only you yourself know what you actually did to make a particular technique work.

For this reason, spell making is at one and the same time a hidden art and one which needs to be shared - an occupation that is truly creative in its output. You do actually have the ability to make things happen or rather to help in their manifestation You are, however never quite sure what the end result is going to be, but must trust that it will always be for the Greater Good. Someone else may well do exactly the same thing and end up with a totally different result, but one which is right for them.

As you search for knowledge, both esoteric and otherwise, do bear in mind that there are, from our perspective, certain constraints on the use of spells. In our view, spells should never used to ill-wish or harm someone – it will only rebound on you at some stage. You yourself must take full responsibility for what you do, and indeed of the effect your thoughts can have on your universe, so always think very carefully and be very aware that as you progress and become more proficient, spells are literally Words of Power.

Finally, this book is in reality no more than a reference book. Over the years, spells have come to us from many sources and we share them with you in a spirit of openness and freedom. If we offend anyone then we apologize. If we help someone then we are grateful and if others find tranquillity then 'May the Gods be praised'.

Spells and Techniques